Praise for Book 1 in
"The Muskoka Novels" series:
The Summer Before The Storm

"*The Summer Before The Storm* - a very good read:
One shouldn't judge a book by its cover, but the glossy photograph of the prow of an antique boat and the line "The First of the Muskoka Novels" invited me in....

It is impossible not to be drawn into the lives and emotions of the eminently believable characters...

Wills melds historical fact and fiction with aplomb, giving the reader insight into Muskoka's gracious bygone era and the horrors that faced so many young Canadian men and women in World War I." - *Gillian Brunette, Hunstville Forester*

The following are excerpts from readers' comments.
You can read more at *theMuskokaNovels.com*

"It was an absolutely wonderful read. I haven't been that emotionally invested in a story in many years."

"I knew this novel was far above average when I found myself neglecting important business matters to sneak in another hour or two of reading. If you like grand scale novels, this is the one. I anxiously await book two."

"This is another fabulous read. You have a way of drawing the reader into the lives and emotions of your characters. Your characters are so very real, I felt I was right there with them."

"You have just become my new favourite author."

"You have created a masterpiece. I loved every moment I shared with [your characters]... I am very appreciative for your depiction of the First World War. My grandmother lost two brothers in that war and I've always felt that I had no real understanding of it... This novel gave me a glimpse of the horror of war; it felt like a first hand account."

"I couldn't put it down!! Just loved it and can't wait for the next one!"

Elusive Dawn

Book 2 of "The Muskoka Novels"
by

Gabriele Wills

MIND *SHADOWS*

Cover photo by Melanie Wills (DoubleHelixCreations.com)
Cover design by dubs & dash (d2-group.com)

Library and Archives Canada Cataloguing in Publication

Wills, Gabriele, 1951-
    Elusive dawn / Gabriele Wills.

(The Muskoka novels ; bk. 2)
ISBN 978-0-9732780-3-3

    1. World War, 1914-1918--Canada--Fiction. I. Title. II. Series: Wills,
Gabriele, 1951- . Muskoka novels ; bk. 2.

PS8595.I576E48 2008   C813'.6   C2008-907034-8

For information about the music quoted in the book, visit
TheMuskokaNovels.com

Comments are always appreciated at books@mindshadows.com

First edition
Published by Mindshadows
Mindshadows.com
Printed and bound in Canada

Foreword

In order to fully appreciate Book 2, it is recommended – but not essential – that Book 1 in the series, *The Summer Before The Storm*, be read first.

Many thanks to the following people for help with research, marketing, or sales: Bill Edwards, Amitav Dash, Bill Dubs, The Rev. Fay Patterson Willsie, Laurie McLean, Katherine McCracken and Guelph Museums, Trudy Davis, Dr. Geoffrey and Shirley Seagram, Kathleen James, Amy Weitzel, Jeannette Gropp, Anne Vinet, Kay and Michael Wills, numerous members of The Great War Forum and the Canadian Expeditionary Force Study Group, Barbara J. Johnson and the IODE, Mary Storey and the Muskoka Boat & Heritage Centre, the staff of the Canadian War Museum's Military History Research Centre, Rony Robinson and Ravinder Sanghera of BBC Radio Sheffield, Dr. Ian Rotherham, Jim Curran, and Andrew McCarthy.

I would like once again to express my deepest love and gratitude to my family for their unflagging support. My husband, John, as well as helping to edit, has taken on the challenging and critical task of finding innovative ways to promote and distribute the books. My daughter, Melanie, is my constant sounding board for ideas. Her thoughtful input has immeasurably enriched the stories. I also appreciate her editorial and photographic skills, since a book's cover does indeed add to its appeal. She is still engaged in the monumental task of filming and editing a documentary about my journey as a writer. See *DoubleHelixCreations.com* for more info.

In memoriam: Thanks to my feline family, Cally and Gingy, for over 18 years of companionship, for sharing my desk, ruminating on life from the office windowsill, supervising and criticizing from the comfortable sidelines. Both appeared in *The Summer Before The Storm*, and are still with us in spirit.

This book is dedicated to my brother, Vic Tavaszi, and his family, Laurie, Alex, and Alyssa, who are also enthralled with island summers on the lake.

The Islands

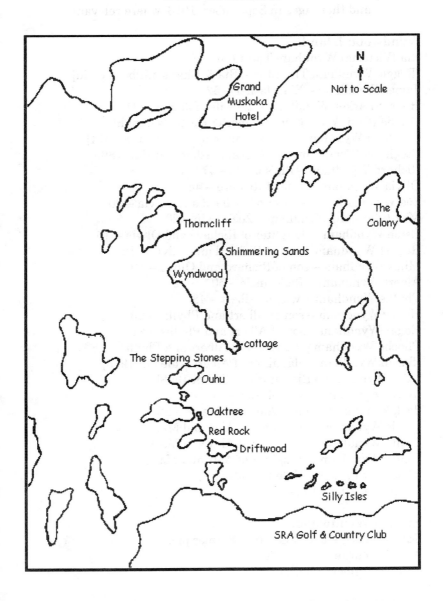

N

Not to Scale

Grand Muskoka Hotel

The Colony

Thorncliff

Shimmering Sands

Wyndwood

cottage

The Stepping Stones

Ouhu

Oaktree

Red Rock

Driftwood

Silly Isles

SRA Golf & Country Club

Cast of Characters

and their ages in September, 1916, where relevant

Wyndwood Island:
Ria (Victoria) Wyndham Thornton – 20
[Reggie Wyndham Thornton – Ria & Chas's stillborn child]
James Wyndham – Ria's father – 52
Helena Parker Wyndham – 2nd wife of James – 31
Cecilia (Ceci) Wyndham – James & Helena's daughter – 1
[Augusta Wyndham – Ria's grandmother – died in 1914]
[Reginald Wyndham – Ria's grandfather – died in 1896]
Richard Wyndham – Ria's uncle – 47
Olivia Wyndham – wife of Richard – 44
Zoë Wyndham – daughter of Richard and Olivia – 20
Max (Maxwell) Wyndham – Zoë's twin – 20
Esme Wyndham – daughter of Richard and Olivia – 15
Rupert Wyndham – son of Richard and Olivia – 12
Miles Wyndham – son of Richard and Olivia – 10
Albert Wyndham – Ria's uncle – 50
Phyllis Wyndham – wife of Albert – 48
Henry Wyndham – son of Albert and Phyllis – 23
Edgar Wyndham – son of Albert and Phyllis – 21
Phoebe Wyndham – daughter of Albert and Phyllis – 18
[Sarah Wyndham – daughter of Albert – died in 1905]
[Alex Wyndham – Ria's uncle – died in 1908]
Marie Wyndham – wife of Alex – 43
Jack Wyndham – son of Alex and Marie – 22
Lizzie Wyndham – daughter of Alex and Marie – 19
Emily Wyndham – daughter of Alex and Marie – 17
Claire Wyndham – daughter of Alex and Marie – 15
Thaddeus Parker – Helena's father
Carter Jenkins – Helena's divorced husband

Staff at Wyndwood:
Toby (Tobias) – caretaker and steamer pilot
Mrs. O'Rourke – Richard's cook
Pringle – Albert's butler

Thorncliff Island:
J. D. Thornton – financier
Marjorie Thornton – his wife
Chas (Charles) Thornton – son – 24 – married to Ria Wyndham

Rafe (Ralph) Thornton – son – 21
Fliss (Felicity) Thornton – daughter – 16

Ouhu Island:
Professor Thomas Carlyle – physics professor
Hannah Carlyle – his wife – pharmacist
Dr. Blake Carlyle – son – 24
Dr. Ellie (Eleanor) Carlyle – daughter – 22
Daphne Carlyle – daughter – 18
Derek Carlyle – son – 15

Red Rock Island:
Edward Carrington – mill owner
Rena (Rowena) Carrington – his wife
Justin Carrington – son – 23
Lydia Carrington – daughter – 20
[Vivian Carrington – daughter – died 1915]
Simon Carrington – son – 27
Grace Carrington – Simon's wife
Keir & Megan Shaughnessy – Rena's parents

Driftwood Island:
Ernest Spencer – Senator, lawyer
Kathleen Spencer – his wife
Freddie Spencer – son – 22
Emma Spencer – daughter – 19
Arthur – son – 16
Maud & Hazel Spencer – younger children
[Archie Spencer – son – died 1915]

Ravenshill Island:
Howard Roland – Pittsburgh industrialist
Erika Roland – his wife
Troy Roland – son – 22
Felix Roland – son – 21
Kurt Roland – son – 19
Stuart (Stu) Roland – son – 17
Eugene Roland – son – 15

Oaktree Island:
Oswald Oakley – Pittsburgh steel magnate
Letitia Oakley – his wife
Louise Oakley – daughter – 17

Martin, Roger, & George Oakley – younger sons

The Colony:
Edelina Fuerstenberger – artist
(Father) Paul – former Catholic priest

Others in Canada and the U.S.A.:
Hugo Garrick – famous New York songwriter
Josiah Miller – foundry owner
Bobby Miller – son – 20
Rosie Miller – daughter – 18
Anders Vandeburgh – New York photographer – Lizzie's boss
Dr. Lorna Partridge – Ellie's colleague at medical school
Irene Partridge – her widowed mother, a nurse
Montgomery (Monty) Seaton – American author of *The Doomed*

England:
Lady Beatrice Kirkland – 67 – Augusta Wyndham's cousin
Alice Lambton – 14 – friend of Ria
Grayson – Ria's butler
Theadora (Thea) Prescott – American journalist
Lady Meredith Powell – publisher of *Homefires*
Lady Sidonie (Sid) Dunston – 22 – socialite widow of Percy
Quentin, Viscount Grenville – Sidonie's eldest brother
Martha Randall – VAD friend of Zoë
Johanna Verbruggen – Sophie's nanny
Enid Robertson – helps run Maple Leaf Club
The Earl and Countess of Netherton – Antonia Upton's parents
Lady Georgina (Georgie) – Antonia's sister – 21
Lady Veronica (Ronni) – Antonia's sister – 19
Lady Alexandra (Alex) – Antonia's sister – 17
Bernard (Bunny) – Antonia's brother

WATS:
Major Pat Bosley-Smythe (Boss) – Commanding Officer
Captain Fanny Radstone (ComRad) – Commandant of Calais unit
Carly Stratton – 22 – one of Ria's roommates
Sybil Fox (Foxy) – 23 – one of Ria's roommates
Lucinda Ashby-Grey (Cinders) – one of Ria's roommates
Lady Antonia Upton (Tuppy) – 22
Henrietta Maltby (Hennie)
Winifred Turville (Baby)
Betty Haydon-Wicks (Hayrick)

Dora Pettigrew (Petty)
The Honourable Cordelia Hazlett (Hazy)

France:
Major Lance (Lawrence) Chadwick – 32 – Cavalry
Lieutenant Eddie Stratton – RFC pilot – Carly's brother
Lieutenant Jonathan Telford – RFC pilot
Captain Adam Bentley – Cavalry
Billy Farthington –Intelligence Officer at Calais
The Duchess of Axminster – runs hospital for convalescent officers
Zachary – artist – orderly at Duchess's hospital
Sophie Dumont – 6 – daughter of flower shop owner
Monsieur Lemieux – lawyer in Calais
Madame Fortin – chocolate shop proprietor
Major Hal Goodwin – CO at Marquise aerodrome
Tom – Ria's former footman in Canada
Bruce McPherson – one of Chas's pilots in the Flying Dragons
Madeline – mother of Chas's illegitimate son, Charles

Priory Manor:
Mrs. Prendergast – owner of Priory Manor
Mrs. Skitch – cook-housekeeper
Beryl – maid
Enoch – gardener
Tilda – maid
Patrick – footman
Branwyn – scullery maid
Gareth – her son – apprentice gardener
Clive – stable boy

Real People Mentioned or Appearing (Alphabetically):
Raymond Asquith – eldest son of Prime Minister Herbert Asquith
Nancy Astor – wife of Waldorf Astor – owned Cliveden
Sir Max Aitken – became Lord Beaverbrook in Dec. 1916
Albert Ball – RFC ace with 44 victories
Louis Blériot – French aviator and airplane designer
Billy Bishop, VC – Canadian in RFC – highest scoring British Ace
    with 72 victories
Oswald Boelcke – top German Ace in latter part of 1916
Sir Robert Borden – Prime Minister of Canada, 1911-1920
Rupert Brooke – poet, died en route to Gallipoli, April 1915
Margaret Burden – granddaughter of Timothy Eaton
Lord Hugh Cecil – in charge of recruitment for the RFC

Winston Churchill – British politician, Minister of Munitions 1917
George Cohan – American entertainer, composer, producer
Duke of Connaught – former Governor General of Canada
Duchess of Connaught – his wife
Dr. Cox – eye specialist In Nova Scotia
General Sir Arthur Currie – became Commander of the Canadian
    Expeditionary Force in 1917
Sir John Craig Eaton – owner of Eaton's department stores
Lady Flora Eaton – his wife
Escoffier – famous London chef
Sir Joseph Flavelle – Chairman of the Imperial Munitions Board
General Haig – Commander of the British Expeditionary Force
Al Jolson – renowned American entertainer
Rudyard Kipling – author – along with his wife, was on executive
    committee of the Maple Leaf Clubs – friend of Sir Max Aitken
Dr. Ladd – Boston surgeon
Rosa Lewis – owned Cavendish Hotel in London
Lady Diana Manners – aristocratic socialite
Lieutenant Colonel John McCrae – Canadian doctor and poet who
    wrote "In Flanders Fields"
Earl of Minto – former Governor General of Canada
Lady Minto – his wife
Hauptmann Karl Niemeyer – commandant of Holzminden prison
    camp in Germany
Sir Henry Pellatt – financier – built Casa Loma in Toronto
Princess Patricia – daughter of Duke & Duchess of Connaught
Manfred von Richthofen – Germany's top Ace with 80 victories
Oswald Robertson, MD – credited with establishing the first blood
    bank during the last year of the war
Theodore (Teddy) Roosevelt – former U.S. President
Stinson sisters – trained pilots in San Antonio, Texas
Major Jack Scott – CO of RFC 60th Squadron in the spring of 1917
Robert (Bob) Smith-Barry – RFC pilot renowned for his highly
    effective training program
Tom Thomson – one of the Canadian Algonquin Group of painters,
    later known as The Group of Seven
Major-General Hugh "Boom" Trenchard – in charge of the RFC in
    France
Woodrow Wilson – President of the United States, 1913-1921 –
    owned an island in Muskoka

The Anxious Dead.

by John McCrae
1872 - 1918

O guns, fall silent till the dead men hear
   Above their heads the legions pressing on:
(These fought their fight in time of bitter fear,
   And died not knowing how the day had gone.)

O flashing muzzles, pause, and let them see
   The coming dawn that streaks the sky afar;
Then let your mighty chorus witness be
   To them, and Caesar, that we still make war.

Tell them, O guns, that we have heard their call,
   That we have sworn, and will not turn aside,
That we will onward till we win or fall,
   That we will keep the faith for which they died.

Bid them be patient, and some day, anon,
   They shall feel earth enwrapt in silence deep;
Shall greet, in wonderment, the quiet dawn,
   And in content may turn them to their sleep.

Prologue

My Darling Child,

Mummy is going off to war. I need to do this for you and for myself.

Perhaps by seeing his world, I can begin to understand how your father could have betrayed us.

Cousin Jack thinks that Chas's affair with the French girl saved his life. But why didn't he turn to me for help if he was in a funk?

I'm not sure I can believe Jack anyway. Grandmother said he wasn't to be trusted, that he would do anything and use everyone to get ahead. She thought he might be ruthless because he grew up so poor. Is he such a staunch friend to your father because he wants to work for your grandfather, or in some other way take advantage of the Thorntons' wealth? I would never have thought that of Jack before, but if he were truly my friend and devoted cousin, he should have prevented Chas's liaison in the first place. Max or Edgar or Henry wouldn't have tolerated that kind of behaviour from him.

Was Jack perhaps hoping that Chas would change his mind about marrying me so that he could attempt to seduce me again? Grandmother tried to ensure that Jack couldn't easily marry me, not without losing his inheritance. And anyway, he's supposed to be in love with my dear friend, Ellie. I know that she is with him. Has he just been using her as well? I think that Ellie is more realistic than I, because she doesn't seem to expect Jack to be faithful to her. And I'm convinced he's having an affair with Lady Sidonie, who I suspect is Chas's former lover from his Oxford days.

I had always thought Justin a steadfast friend, but he has failed me as well. He says it wasn't his place to tell me about Chas's affair. I know he only found out at Christmas, but he should have persuaded Chas to confess, and not leave me to find out in that cruel and shocking way that your father has a son with that woman.

That's the hardest to bear.

Cousin Bea thinks that I'm not being very mature about all this. She says she's never seen a man as devoted as Chas is to me. She believes he realizes that he's made a terrible mistake, and that if I love him, I should forgive him.

Your father claims that he can't live without me, that he will do anything to redeem himself.

Words, words, words! They evade, they deceive. They excuse, prevaricate, lie. What they can't do is erase deeds or change facts.

And they can't ease my pain. My heart is shattered. I don't know if I can ever find all the pieces again.

I hardly care now if I survive this war. I would be happy being with you again, my darling child.

Your loving mother.

Ria looked out at the Irish Sea and shivered as she recalled its icy embrace. She tucked the letter into the bouquet of white roses, and laid them on the grave. Tenderly she stroked the polished red granite headstone that read "Reggie Wyndham Thornton, Beloved infant son of Victoria and Chas. Innocent victim of the *Lusitania.*"

By the sea, by the sea, by the beautiful sea,
You and I, you and I, oh how happy we'll be....

Chapter 1

A late summer breeze skittered across the broad veranda, jostling the rattan rocker. Zoë Wyndham wasn't easily spooked, but for a moment it seemed as though her grandmother had reclaimed her favourite chair.

She had been dead for two years, and her cottage had stood empty for most of this summer of 1916.

Odd that Toby, their ancient caretaker, hadn't put the veranda chairs and tables back into storage after the Dominion Day Ball that Uncle James and his ambitious young wife, Helena, had given here. It was as if Toby expected the family to return at any moment, even though Zoë's cousin Ria now owned the place, and she was in England for the duration of the war. Toby opened the French windows every fine day to keep the house aired, and must have swept away the cobwebs from the rafters.

Sheets covered the furniture in the expansive sitting room that stretched across the front of the cottage. The playful wind squeezed through the screen doors and chased dust motes around the tarnished silver trophies on the mantelpieces. Although the ghosts of a lifetime of memories crowded the room, Zoë felt it was too large and empty.

Built almost forty years ago, the "Big house", as it was now called, had been her home for at least three months every summer of the first eighteen years of her life, along with all her Wyndham relatives – at least those she had known about. For the past two summers, Zoë and her family had lived in their own new and smaller cottage along the west shore of the island, at Silver Bay.

It was the summer of 1914, when Jack had joined the family and the war had been declared, that their idyllic lives had begun to unravel.

Zoë couldn't help associating Jack's coming with the dramatic events of that summer, although, of course, he wasn't responsible for Grandmother's death, or Ria's estrangement from her father, or Edgar's lameness, or their friends going off to war – some, like Vivian and Archie, never to return. But the sudden appearance of an unknown, destitute cousin had surely been an omen.

Zoë skin prickled as she heard the faint creak of floorboards above. In an empty house where people had stepped out but were expected to return at any moment, the spaces were wrapped in comfortable solitude. But in a place that stood vacant, abandoned, there was an eerie, almost menacing feeling to the emptiness, the warmth of vibrant bodies and the echoes of chatter long dissipated.

She was startled as an airy, disembodied voice sang:

The King was in his counting house counting out his money,
The Queen was in the parlour eating bread and honey,
The maid was in the garden hanging out the clothes,
When down came a blackbird and nipped off her nose.

Zoë relaxed as her cousin drifted down the steps. "What are you doing here, Phoebe?"

"Maryanne and I were visiting our old room."

When they had all lived here, Zoë and her sister, Esme, had shared a room with Ria and Phoebe. Although now eighteen, Phoebe seemed much less mature than fifteen-year-old Esme. Phoebe still carried her sinister, two-faced doll, Maryanne, tucked into her arm.

"Do you miss living here?" Zoë asked, for Phoebe's family had also built their own cottage, not far along the east shore.

"This *is* where I live," Phoebe stated. "The new cottage doesn't have any of *me* in it. It just smells of wounded trees." Maryanne turned her sad but subtly malevolent face towards Zoë. "Bits of me are everywhere here." Phoebe went over to the fireplace and said, "This is where I stood when Jack and I put our trophies on the mantle and he kissed me."

"That wasn't you, Phoebe. Ria and Jack won the Stepping Stone trophies that summer. And Jack never kissed you."

"Of course he did!" Phoebe said smugly. "You just didn't see it."

Zoë recalled all too vividly that night of the Dominion Day Ball in 1914 when Phoebe nearly caused a scandal by accusing Jack of something even worse than kissing her. That was when they had begun to realize that Phoebe truly was mad. Their friend, Blake, who had been studying psychiatry, had already suspected that Phoebe was suffering the torments of schizophrenia.

"Maryanne says you always think you know better just because you're at university. But Mama says that you'll be a lonely old maid because no man wants to marry an opinionated bluestocking who enjoys spending time with lower class wastrels. Does she mean the work you did at the Settlement House?" Without waiting for an answer, she added brightly, "I think I will marry so that I can be someone else, like Victoria. She became Ria

Thornton and lives in England, and Victoria Wyndham is gone. Maybe she drowned on the *Lusitania* with Vivian."

"You know that Ria survived the *Lusitania*, Phoebe. When you see her again, you'll realize that she's just the same as always, only a little older. As we all are."

But Phoebe seemed oblivious to Zoë's words. She sat down at the piano. "I played this for Jack the first night he was here. Remember?"

"Yes, Grandmother asked you to play some Chopin."

"Don't look at her and she can't tell you what to do now," Phoebe whispered conspiratorially.

"What are you talking about, Phoebe?"

"Grandmother. She's watching us." Phoebe sighed with exasperation. Other people were so blind and saw only what they wanted or expected to. Just because Grandmother was dead, didn't mean she was gone.

Although she suspected that Phoebe was hallucinating, Zoë instinctively looked over at the chair where her grandmother had usually held court. She and Blake, who was now with the Canadian Army Medical Corps in France, had had quite a lengthy correspondence about the soul. If it existed after death, was it an amorphous entity that was visible to certain sensitive people? If so, Zoë wondered if Phoebe was not so much mad as bedevilled by spirits.

"But I just ignore her and she can't scare me anymore," Phoebe confided. "Only when the storms come, because she gets angry when I'm upset. Then her eyes burn like coals and her face melts into an evil, horrid skull. I always know when she's here because she smells all mouldy."

Of course, there was a musty, dusty smell to the place because it hadn't been properly cleaned since the Ball two months ago. Much as she might want to believe in the scientific and rational, as Blake did, Zoë still felt disquieted.

She was glad when Edgar hobbled in. "Mama's been looking for you, Phoebe," he said to his sister. "You know she doesn't like you to come here."

Phoebe crashed her hands onto the keys in violent discord. "Mama wants to suck the life out of me! I don't like our new cottage! I want to be here, and Victoria wouldn't mind. I'll keep all the memories alive for her until she returns. She'll be so pleased! Mama thinks that Victoria's essence is drifting about here and will contaminate me and turn me into an undisciplined hoyden like her, but that's just nonsense!"

Edgar and Zoë looked at one another with helpless resignation. "Come and I'll take you for an ice cream at The Grand," Edgar said to Phoebe. The Grand Muskoka Hotel was an opulent resort nearby, where the family often dined and danced.

"Just you and me?"

"Yes."

She clapped her hands in glee and picked up Maryanne from the piano bench. "You'll have to stay in the boat, because you know that Edgar thinks you're too little to be taken out in public," she said to the doll. "Can we go really really fast in the boat?" she asked her brother enthusiastically.

"OK. As long as you don't tell Mama. You go and get ready and I'll be along in a minute."

When Phoebe had gone, Zoë said, "You're very good with her, Edgar."

"Papa either ignores her 'giddiness' as he calls it or gets stern, and Mama seems unable to cope. And no, they still won't get any professional help for her. They maintain that she's merely immature, not insane. I worry about her, Zoë. She's been going to the Dragon's Claw a lot this summer."

The Dragon's Claw was a section of the path encircling the island that narrowed dangerously for a few feet along a cliff face. It was where their grandmother had fallen to her death. Phoebe had never been allowed to go along there, although the others had been used to it.

"I hope she doesn't think she can fly, or dive off there," Zoë said with concern.

"So do I! I think it was silly to build our cottage nearby, but Mama wanted to be close to the back bay, because she says its the best beach where she's not exposed to the afternoon sun. Papa is talking about dynamiting the cliff to get rid of the path, and use the debris to create a new one along the shore."

"Good Lord!"

"Things have certainly changed since the others left. And now you're heading overseas as well. Bloody hell, Zoë, I wish I were going with you! It's so unfair that I have to stay behind when most of my friends are abroad. Even Ellie says she's going over next year when she finishes medical school. Perhaps I should join Henry at Oxford, since this blasted ankle is keeping me out of the war." Henry was Edgar's older brother, who had lost an arm at

Ploegsteert in the Ypres Salient. His injury had allowed him to retire honourably from the war and realize his dream of studying medieval history. "But I worry about what would happen to Phoebe if I left. Not that Papa would let me go anyway."

"You're twenty-one. Your father can't stop you."

"He can stop my salary or any sort of allowance."

"He's not becoming like Grandmother, threatening to disinherit you every time you defy him, is he?"

"God, I hope not! Henry says he's content with his inheritance from Grandmother and the pittance he'll earn as a scholar. But he does have some of his own investments that are paying handsome dividends. I have more extravagant interests than he does, so I'm not willing to give up my salary. I'd best go and see to Phoebe," he said with a sigh. "I'll see you tonight at the Thorntons'."

Zoë felt sorry for Edgar as she watched him trudge painfully away. It seemed absurd to *want* to go war when so many were dying or returning home maimed, both in body and mind. But she could understand Edgar's frustration at being left out of the world where his friends were risking their lives for what had seemed a noble cause.

She wandered back out to the generous veranda, which enveloped the cottage. She loved this view of the lake – framed by stately pines – across the sparkling, lichen-encrusted granite slab that sloped down to the large dock. The rocky and ragged islands afloat on the cobalt blue water already glowed with the tinge of autumn. Soon the trees would drip with bloody reds, burnished oranges, and luminous golds. As if they had spent the summer absorbing the colours of the sunsets to slowly reveal these horded treasures.

This southern point of the roughly triangular sixty-acre island was shaggy with ferns, blueberry bushes, and saplings sprouting among the rocks, in the pockets of rusty pine needles. When they had all lived in the Big house and had roamed and played here, the undergrowth had been constantly trampled, and Toby and his helper had culled the saplings. But Toby, who was in his seventies, had to maintain the house and grounds alone now, since so many of the young servants had gone to war or to more lucrative jobs in factories. The tanbark paths, too, were being invaded by grasses. Nature was constantly trying to reclaim her dominion, and Zoë fancifully imagined the house itself being encroached upon, besieged, and finally reabsorbed into the landscape if Ria didn't come home soon.

Half a dozen iridescent blue dragonflies settled on the veranda railing, fanning their wings, and Zoë wondered if that was a message from Ria, who had an affinity with these insects. They seemed to flock to her, especially at emotional moments.

She had not yet heard how devastatingly Ria's life had just changed.

Eleanor Carlyle came around from the dance pavilion, which lay to the east of the cottage. "Your mother said I might find you here."

"I'm just trying to capture all this before I have to say goodbye," Zoë explained. She was heading to Britain in a few weeks with the first contingent of VAD – Voluntary Aid Detachment – nurses going abroad. "I always hate leaving here at the end of summer, but this time I don't know when I'll be back. Ria says she really misses Wyndwood, that her soul hungers for it. So I've taken lots of photographs to give her." Zoë smiled. "I am so looking forward to seeing her! And Blake." She couldn't help blushing, although Ellie had known for years that Zoë was in love with Blake. "And the others, of course."

Eleanor offered her a cigarette, and they lit up as they perched on the veranda railing and leaned against posts, facing each other. She said, "You know what you should do with that brother of mine? Seduce him."

"Ellie!"

"I'm serious. If he hasn't yet come to his senses then he needs to be shaken out of his melancholia." Their friend Vivian Carrington had never realized that Blake had been infatuated with her. She had been aboard the *Lusitania*, planning to meet up with her secret and forbidden fiancé, who was in the Veterinary Corps. Her body was never recovered.

When Zoë had last seen Blake at Wyndwood on the Dominion Day weekend the previous summer, he had gently advised her to abandon her infatuation for him and find happiness elsewhere. She had convinced him not to close any doors between them, because she loved him no matter what he thought. So she had written to him three or four times a week, and he had written back more and more frequently, especially since he had gone to France, his letters becoming increasingly intimate. "Only you and Blake could spark a romance intellectually," Ellie had once observed with a laugh.

Ellie blew out a satisfying stream of smoke and watched it drift away on the breeze as she said, "You two were meant for each other. I just hope he's not too blind to see that. Granted Vivian was beautiful and vivacious and all that twaddle. But I'll wager Blake never had a deep and meaningful conversation with her, like he did so often with you over the years, especially when you were at the university. The rest of us sometimes felt rather superfluous when you and Blake started talking." The others she referred to included Zoë's twin, Max, Vivian's brother, Justin, now a lawyer and a Captain in the Canadian infantry, and Freddie Spencer, who had just graduated as an architect, and was going overseas imminently with the Corps of Engineers. His older brother, Archie, had been killed in the Second Battle of Ypres.

"By the bye, you know that Freddie has a pash for you," Ellie said offhandedly.

"So you keep telling me. He's as much a beloved friend as Justin and Simon and Chas and...."

"But Blake has stolen your heart and gone away," Ellie quipped, paraphrasing a popular song. "And you're going after him. Don't deny it! And don't hold back. I expect he'll be ready for some serious canoodling."

Zoë laughed despite her disquiet at this too intimate conversation with her friend. "You're outrageous!"

"Just realistic. Men have *needs*, you know, especially when they think they might be blasted to pieces at any moment. Or when they've seen others who have. Even the army knows that and turns a blind eye to all those lads going off to visit French mademoiselles in licensed brothels. Blue lights for officers. Red for the men. At least they're somewhat regulated. But Blake tells me that they have special venereal disease hospitals in Britain for all the cases. Anyway, you can't be too prissy about things like that, being a nurse."

"I'm not, and I won't become self-righteous. But I am a bit scared, Ellie. We've seen some terrible injuries to the fellows who've survived – missing limbs, smashed faces, brutalized flesh. I can only imagine how horrible it must be to see them before they're patched up. And to see the ones who don't make it. I'm not sure I have the stomach to watch all that suffering and the indignities to the body, or the strength to help them."

"You have enormous reserves, Zoë. Just try not to let your compassion overwhelm you. It takes quite a bit of detachment to deal with severe injuries and death. I expect that if you actually make it to France, you *will* be doing and seeing things you could never have imagined."

Zoë realized that Ellie's suddenly serious look meant that she had probably heard some horrendous things from Blake. During the past year when Zoë had taken her VAD training while still attending the university, she had borrowed medical texts from Ellie, who had laughingly said, "You never do anything by half measures, do you? Are you planning to become a doctor now?"

Although Zoë had enjoyed learning about anatomy and diseases, she had replied, "Never! But I do want to understand something about what I'll be doing as a nurse."

"And when you've learned more medicine than the trained nurses, you'll be even more unpopular with the Sisters than VADs already are."

Zoë had been disappointed and annoyed to discover that her first stint as a volunteer nurse this summer had involved little more than scrubbing floors, emptying and scalding bedpans, making beds, serving meals, and washing dishes. Even the fact that her mother was running the convalescent hospital in the Rosedale mansion that Ria had inherited from their grandmother held no sway with Matron. If Zoë wanted to be a VAD then she had no more rights than the other volunteers. It was why Zoë was so anxious to go overseas and have a chance to do some real nursing.

Because she knew Sir Henry Pellatt, who was the head of St. John Ambulance in Canada, Zoë managed to go with this first overseas VAD contingent. And because she had the support of Canada's Governor General, the Duke of Connaught, her request to work at the Duchess of Connaught's Canadian Red Cross Hospital, near Cousin Beatrice's country manor, had been approved. But she would try to get posted to France after the mandatory three-month probationary period.

Now Ellie, with her usual cheekiness, said, "In my opinion, everybody should have sex at least once before they die. Although once is never enough. Vivian never did, so she said. I hope that Archie managed to. I think the motto for our generation is going to become 'Sin today, because tomorrow you could be minced meat'."

Zoë laughed as she said, "I'm going to miss you, Ellie!"

"Don't worry, I'll be there next year when I've finished my internship. Nobody's going to keep me out of all the action!"

They watched one of the lake steamers approaching the front dock, which had been built specifically to accommodate the large ships. Even cottagers with their own yachts or motorboats relied on the big steamers to transport their households, as well as guests and family, to and from their summer residences. They were as much a part of the landscape as the islands.

Gracefully the *Medora* glided towards them. Tall and white with black and red trim, she had two full-length decks housing a dining room, lounge, smoking room, and promenade areas. She could carry three hundred or more passengers along with their crates, trunks, pianos, and even cows.

"I wonder who's coming. Mama didn't say we were expecting anyone," Zoë said.

The ship slid with practiced ease against the dock, a couple of crew jumping off to secure her to the bollards while two uniformed men disembarked.

"Max!" Zoë cried with delight. And Freddie. She ran down the path, with Ellie sauntering along behind. "You look so smart in your uniform!" she said to her twin brother, embracing him joyfully. "As do you, Freddie." Both had done the Officer Training Corps courses while at university, so they had been commissioned as Lieutenants. She could see that Freddie hoped for a hug as well, and couldn't disappoint him, although she didn't want to encourage his infatuation with her.

"Gosh, but it's good to be here," Freddie said. He was tall and lean with a cheerful demeanor that was reflected in his pleasant features.

"We weren't expecting you," Zoë said to Max.

"We decided to surprise you. We're on embarkation leave. Freddie wanted to come to the lake for a few days, but his parents have already closed up the cottage, so I told him to come along with me. He'll go to Ottawa after the long weekend." Freddie's father, a lawyer, was also a Senator. He had taken on several important war-related projects that kept him in the capital more than usual.

"We couldn't miss the Labour Day Ball," Freddie said.

"It's at Thorncliff this year," Ellie told them. "I hear that Fliss organized it all, so it should be interesting." Felicity Thornton – Fliss to her friends – was the only daughter of the immensely wealthy J.D. – banker, stockbroker, financier. Her eldest brother, Chas, was married to Ria.

"What I want more than anything right now is a swim," Freddie said. "Anyone game?"

"Always," Max said.

"I take my bathing suit with me wherever I go," Ellie said. "It's in my canoe."

"Oh, I'm going to miss this," Zoë said, wrapping her arm about Max's as they ambled towards their cottage. The twins were close, and hadn't seen each other all summer. Zoë fervently hoped and prayed that this would not be the last time she and Max would be here together. She pushed away terrifying thoughts and said brightly, "But isn't it odd to think that we'll be in England soon?"

"Swimming in the Thames at Cousin Bea's?" Max joked.

"Probably not by the time we arrive. October can't be that much warmer in England."

"I've already told Freddie that he'll have to stop calling Cousin Bea 'Lady Kirkland', because Justin says she's virtually adopted all of us, and how lucky we are to have her to go home to for leaves and convalescence," Max said. "Of course, you have to get wounded for the latter, which isn't something I want to think about at the moment."

Zoë knew that Max, although not a pacifist and certainly not a coward, went reluctantly to war, unlike so many of the men who sought excitement or glory or just felt it was their unquestionable patriotic duty. Max wondered whether all this sacrifice of young lives was justified. "A brutal war orchestrated by inept old men, callously destroying a generation of young men in what is essentially an Imperialist struggle," he'd once said.

"It's time to strip off the uniform and forget about war for a while," Ellie said.

Silver Bay was a glorious crescent of pale sand partway up the west side of Wyndwood Island. At the north end of the bay was a small point, which the cottage straddled. About half the size of Ria's Big cottage, it had ample room for Zoë's family of seven as well as guests.

The granite foundation seemed to have been sculpted out of the rock on which it perched. A deep, L-shaped veranda, partly screened, wrapped around the south and west sides. The spacious sitting room with its ten foot high ceiling dominated the south side with the vista of Silver Bay spread before it, as well as views to the west, including the majestic sheer cliff face of Old Baldy half a mile away. A wide arch opened directly into the dining room, expanding the aspect to the north. On the ground floor there was also an office, bathroom, box room, and the best guest room. It was where the grandparents stayed so they wouldn't have to manage the stairs. The kitchen and servants' wing stretched eastward from there.

Upstairs were two large dormitories – one for the girls and the other for the boys – with extra beds in both for cousins and friends, as well as the master bedroom, two guest rooms, and a bathroom. At the west end was the screened "sleeping porch". Here, hammocks and camp beds could be set up for those torrid nights when even the air was too enervated to move. With screens around the three sides, it was the coolest place in the house, and popular with the kids at any time.

Sheltered from the main thrust of the winds at the edge of the point was a matching two-slip boathouse with a two-room change house on one side and a canoe house bumped out on the other. Above was a generous reception room and large deck where parties could be held. Both the cottage and the boathouse had electric lighting, powered by a generator, which Toby looked after.

Freddie had designed and supervised the construction of it all two years ago, while he had still been an architecture student at the University of Toronto. Zoë and Max had commissioned him as a present to their parents. They had all given Freddie their input, but Zoë was impressed with the skill and artistic flair that had gone into the design. It was sometimes hard to associate that with easygoing Freddie. But also a reminder that there was a depth to him that she had never explored, and something he was not inclined to flaunt.

Richard and Olivia, the twins' parents, were overwhelmed by Max's sudden appearance on the veranda where they were having tea and lemonade with the children and Jack's youngest sister, Claire, who was staying with them. After refreshments, everyone changed into their swimsuits and splashed about in the bay. It had been a blisteringly hot summer, and the lake still retained the warmth of those scorching days, although it was early September.

"This is smashing," Freddie said gratefully.

"Heavenly," Ellie agreed. "Zoë and I haven't spent much time up here either." Trying to qualify as many doctors as quickly as possible to help with the war, the university had instituted summer courses, so Ellie had just finished exams.

"I've been dreaming about this all summer," Max said. They were lounging in the shallow water after a vigorous swim. "This must have been the hottest summer ever, and to spend it training and marching in full uniform carrying sixty pound packs of gear was cruel. A lot of chaps fainted with heat stroke. I think I'll just stay right here all weekend."

His brother Rupert, who was twelve, was building sandcastles nearby with ten-year-old Miles. He said, "Good, then may I wear your uniform?"

"If you do, the Regimental Police will come and cart you off to the war," Max kidded.

"May I go to war, Mama?" Rupert asked. "Max and Zoë will look after me."

"I'm afraid we'll be much too busy, Rupert," Zoë said, trying not to laugh.

"You know, Rupert," Freddie said with some gravity, "it's much preferable to be an officer when you go to war, so you should do your OTC training. Of course that means that you should also attend university, and if you study engineering, they'll let you build bridges and roads."

"I think I should like that," Rupert said, staring at his sandcastle. "Much more than having to kill people." He grinned at Freddie, and Zoë felt grateful to him for his thoughtful intervention.

"I want to paddle around the island. Come along, Sis," Max said to Zoë.

"I thought you were staying in the water all weekend?" Rupert remarked.

"Hyperbole, that's called, Rupert," Zoë explained.

"Meaning I can't believe anything Max says?"

"Meaning you have to decide if he's being silly or not."

"Hyperbully, I like that word," Rupert stated.

Everyone laughed, and Olivia gently corrected him as she told him the precise meaning of the word.

"I'm off home to help with dinner," Ellie said. "I'll see you later." The Carlyle's island, Ouhu, was the closest to Wyndwood, and one of the Stepping Stone Islands, which stretched over to the mainland. The Spencer's island, Driftwood, was also among them.

"I think I shall stay put," Freddie said as Max and Zoë headed off to the boathouse for a canoe. "Actually, may I help you design another castle?" he asked the boys, much to their delight. "I have a compulsion to build things."

When Max and Zoë had rounded the north end of the island, he stopped paddling, allowing the canoe to drift as he said, "Do you think it's fair to Lydia if I ask her to become engaged to me?"

Zoë wasn't completely surprised. She knew that he and Lydia Carrington were crazy about each other.

Max went on before Zoë could respond. "I think it may be asking a bit much for her to wait for me, if... well... if I didn't return."

"She loves you, Max. If something happened to you, she'd be distraught whether or not you're officially betrothed, or even married." Thinking about what she and Ellie had spoken of earlier, Zoë felt that Max and Lydia should delight in each other while they were able to. Why not get married tomorrow and have a week of bliss before God-knows-what happened to them?

"Oh no, I couldn't do that to Lydia. Tie her down in marriage. If I came back horribly crippled or grotesquely maimed I wouldn't want her to feel she had to honour our engagement. I've heard of men surviving with no limbs or without a face." He shuddered. "I wouldn't expect her to live with something like that. It's much harder to back out of a marriage. I just thought that if we were betrothed, I could feel that she was waiting for me, and I'd have something to look forward to instead of wondering if she had a new beau."

"I think that you should give her the choice, Max. I expect she'd marry you tomorrow and follow you to England."

He shook his head. "I couldn't ask that of her after what happened to Vivian." Vivian had been Lydia's older sister. "But I *will* propose to her, and we'll plan a wedding for the summer after the war." He grinned broadly at Zoë. "You should see the ring I bought her!" He was suddenly serious. "Hell's bells, do you think her parents will *allow* her to marry me?"

Zoë laughed. "I don't see why they should allow anyone who speaks in hyperbully to marry their daughter. Of course they will!"

"Then start paddling because I'm going over right away to ask them. Lydia wrote to say that they'd be here this week."

"You're not going dressed like that, I hope?" Zoë joshed.

"My uniform, I think. Don't you?"

When they returned to the cottage, Max told his parents.

"Lydia's a lovely girl, and we'll be delighted to have her as a daughter-in-law," Richard said.

Olivia added, "But I do think it's a good idea to have a long engagement. You're both still very young." Max was twenty and Lydia, nineteen. "Your father was twenty-five when we married."

Zoë was rarely angry with her mother, but she felt the urge to point out that life was different now than it had been for them. The young generation didn't have time to wait. If they were old enough to bear the burdens of the Empire upon their shoulders, perhaps forfeit their lives, then they should be old enough to enjoy love. She said merely, "I expect Max will be much older than his years by the time he returns."

Olivia looked at her and could see the unspoken "if" in Zoë's eyes. "Perhaps you're right. We must certainly have a celebration! That is, you'd best go and talk it over with Lydia first, hadn't you?"

Max showed Zoë the ring before he left. It was an exquisite pearl surrounded by diamonds. "Fit for a princess," Zoë declared.

"Yes. She is."

Zoë returned to the beach, where Freddie and the boys had built an entire medieval castle. Freddie must have explained the architectural terms, since Miles proudly showed her the buttresses and crenellations and curtain walls.

"It's unfortunate you can't build castles for our soldiers," Rupert said. "They'd be ever so much better than trenches."

"More comfortable, but too easy to knock down with bombs. See?" Freddie said as he threw a stone at their creation, crumbling a section of wall.

"Hmm. I expect warfare has changed since the days of knights and castles."

"Indeed it has," Freddie said.

"Are you scared?" Rupert asked.

"A bit."

"Then why are you going?"

"To help all the soldiers who are already fighting. So we can win the war."

"Like that poem, *In Flanders Fields*. We learned that in school." With a dramatic, sonorous voice Rupert quoted:
Take up our quarrel with the foe:
To you from failing hands we throw
The torch; be yours to hold it high.
If ye break faith with us who die
We shall not sleep, though poppies grow
In Flanders fields.

"I thought it crackerjack to have dead guys talking! *We are the Dead...* I guess it's like your brother Archie talking to you, asking you to come and help. Did you know that Lydia's family knows Colonel John McCrae's family – he's the poet – because they all live in Guelph?"

"Yes, I'd heard."

"Let's plan a cottage for Max," Zoë said to divert the conversation from the war. "We'd put it over there, in the curve of the bay."

"Why does Max need his own cottage?" Rupert wanted to know.

"For when he gets married." To preempt more questions, Zoë said, "And where would you like your cottage when you're much much older?"

"On top of the boathouse, like our games room. Remember when Jack lived up in Ria's boathouse? I thought that was crackerjack!"

"So what do you think Max's cottage should be like?" Freddie asked.

They all gave their input as he scratched a floor plan in the sand with a twig.

"And now one for Zoë," Miles insisted.

"What would you like, Zoë?' Freddie asked her.

"I love the one you've already built for us."

"A matching one at the other end of the bay, then?" he said with a grin.

They heard Max even before they spotted him coming around Ouhu. He let out a whoop and raised his paddle.

"I think she said 'yes'," Zoë remarked.

"Lucky fellow," Freddie said, meeting Zoë's eyes. She quickly looked away.

. . .

From the glowing horizon, the sky faded upwards to peach, pink, mauve, with a deepening purple to the east, all the colours mirrored in the still water as the Wyndhams arrived at Thorncliff Island, just north of Wyndwood. Music drifted down from the luxurious summer home, across the clipped lawns embellished with granite outcroppings, and through the artistic scattering of pines.

Because of the war, there were no longer liveried footmen to greet them at the dock, but some local boys had been hired to tie up the boats. Lanterns lined the paths and the southern shoreline of the twenty-acre island.

An orchestra played in the enormous ballroom, and many people were already dancing. Although sixteen – and three-quarters she was quick to remind people – Fliss looked quite grown-up, Zoë thought, as she greeted her guests with admirable poise and practiced ease.

"I'm delighted that you could come!" she said to Max and Freddie. "This is an unexpected treat. I can hardly believe that you're going to see Chas soon. And you too, Zoë. Oh, how I wish I could come as well! I must find some time to talk to you. Do go and say hello to Mummy. She'll be so glad to see you."

Marjorie Thornton suffered from an undetermined ailment that left her a semi-invalid. They had known her all their lives and spent a few minutes catching her up on their recent activities. She said, "It's so valiant of you all. But I do despair for you young people, having to endure all this. And I miss darling Chas terribly! And now Rafe is planning to join the RFC. I'm not sure I can bear it. Yes, I know that Chas is a wonderful hero – a decorated flying Ace – what a silly term, but there you have it. You must all be very careful. I'm devastated that we'll never again see Vivian and Archie. You're all so dear to me."

"You mustn't distress yourself, Mrs. Thornton," Freddie said. "And we'll give Chas and Ria all the news when we see them."

They were joined by a group of women, including James Wyndham's young wife, Helena – Ria's stepmother. Although she was now their aunt, Zoë and Max didn't address her as such, nor would she have wished it.

The young people excused themselves as Helena said to Marjorie, "I was just telling the ladies that Chas has won a Military Cross and a bar to his Distinguished Service Order. You must be so proud!"

"We saw his photograph in the paper again," Ada Vandemeer said. "How handsome and heroic he looks."

Marjorie smiled half-heartedly. "I just wish he were home again."

Ignoring her remark, Helena said, "It's quite the social life our Canadians lead in England. James's cousin, Lady Beatrice Kirkland – some of you met her in 1914, of course... Well, she wrote to say that Victoria is rather a favourite of Nancy Astor, who owns Cliveden, which is quite the hub of *the* social set. Her husband, Waldorf, will succeed to the title of Viscount one day. But, of course, they are Astors." By which she meant fabulously wealthy, as everyone knew. "Imagine, Victoria took Mrs. Astor up for a flight in an aeroplane!" Although she didn't like her stepdaughter, Helena was careful never to criticize her publicly. Some prudently worded remarks sometimes left no doubt that

Victoria was a bit of a loose canon. But she was the daughter-in-law of one of the richest men in Canada, and cherished by her Thornton in-laws, even if her own father had little time or affection for her.

"I can't imagine how Chas could have allowed Ria to take up flying," Marjorie said. "It scares me to think of it. But young people these days are so bold."

"And accomplished. Just look at what Victoria has done, setting up the Maple Leaf Club, working with Rudyard Kipling and Lady Meredith Powell, and others." Helena loved to mention important people as if they were her acquaintances as well as Ria's. Her stepdaughter was useful after all. Even more so if she would just stay in England and keep mingling with the aristocracy.

Helena had been thrilled to discover that James had notable aristocratic relatives in England. Baby Cecilia would capitalize on that somehow. In the meantime it was enough that she was Daddy's little princess.

. . .

Daphne Carlyle was convinced that she was a changeling. She might look like a pale and watery reflection of her dynamic sister, Eleanor, but that's where the resemblance ended. She couldn't understand why her family thought that poverty was a virtue, or not having and wanting nice things, somehow ennobling.

Of course it was good of them to help people who had less than they did, but her parents didn't approve of the opulence and extravagance of the homes and lifestyles of people like the Thorntons.

Daphne had spent every summer at the cottage since she was three years old. Her grandfather, a doctor, had bought Ouhu Island back in the eighties when he had been on a restorative fishing holiday. But he had never had the time to do more than camp on the island for a week or two every summer. Daphne's mother, Hannah, had inherited Ouhu and enough money to build a tiny cottage, which would easily fit into the Thorntons' ballroom. Because Daphne's father suffered from hay fever, summers spent in ragweed-free Muskoka were most beneficial for him.

This summer, while Hannah and Ellie had worked in the city for much of the time, Daphne had been in charge of looking after her younger brother and father at the cottage. They had no maid now, but she didn't mind the cooking and cleaning, so long as she could be here. There was plenty of time left to canoe and play tennis and otherwise amuse herself with her friends.

But all too soon they would return to the city, to their comfortable, middle-class house in the Annex where they wouldn't see most of their island friends, other than Zoë's family, until next summer. And she would be expected to attend university, even though she had no interest or particular aptitude in anything. She didn't have Ellie's passion to become a doctor and save the world. Daphne wanted only to have a safe and easy life, creating a comfortable home where family and friends would feel welcome and happy and far removed from all the nastiness of the world.

Why should anyone work, just for the sake of working, if they didn't have to? Her parents seemed quietly disdainful of anyone who didn't have a career, while some of the wealthy tended to think professionals and other working people beneath them. Running multi-million dollar enterprises as they did, or being a financial titan, like J.D. Thornton, was, of course, completely different.

Mingling with the super-rich all these summers of her childhood had given Daphne an appreciation for what wealth could do, how you could surround yourself with beautiful things and influential people. And surely having so much money that you could give generously to charities and fund museums, hospitals, and universities was a good thing.

So now that she was eighteen, she had begun to ponder how she could forever be part of that secure and complaisant world. Unfortunately, there were very few eligible and currently available men who interested her. Chas Thornton had been the dreamiest of them all, but Victoria Wyndham had snatched him up. His brother, Rafe, she found somewhat alarming and unpredictable. Dangerous even. Freddie Spencer was stuck on Zoë, even though she was in love with Blake. Max was nice and funny, but he was betrothed to Lydia Carrington now, and also going off to war.

Daphne had decided that she didn't want to marry a soldier. Blake had written that so many people were psychologically damaged by their wartime experiences – even Victoria because of her ordeal on the *Lusitania*. This war was a curse on her generation, and Daphne didn't want to be constantly reminded of it, or live with someone who could never forget. If only life could be as simple and fun as it had been those idyllic summers of her youth!

Edgar Wyndham was the only one of their closest friends left, and he couldn't go to war because his broken ankle hadn't healed properly. Daphne liked him well enough, and he knew how to enjoy his wealth. But he was besotted by Ellie, who was in love with Jack Wyndham.

Although Jack was by far the most handsome of the Wyndham men, Daphne had gleaned from his sisters that they had had an impoverished childhood. Jack might be clever and ambitious, but even with his recent inheritance from his grandmother, he was not in the same league as his cousins. Not that that mattered to Ellie. But Daphne suspected that Jack was looking for a lucrative alliance, and felt sorry for her idealistic sister. Jack would never marry her.

If only Edgar would realize that she, Daphne, was better suited to him than her sister.

Daphne joined him on the sweeping veranda. She had seen him leave the ballroom after a dance with Ellie, undoubtedly once more rejected. She could tell by Ellie's dismissive laugh.

"May I have a cigarette?"

Edgar was leaning against the railing, looking out at the lake, and turned around in surprise. "Oh, Daphne. Would your parents approve?"

"Perhaps not. But I'm old enough to make my own decisions," she pointed out.

"I suppose you are," Edgar replied, eyeing her assessingly. As though it had just occurred to him that she was no longer one of the younger children relegated to other activities.

That was her mother's fault, she thought, since even that summer before the war started, when she was already sixteen, her mother had made her look after her younger brother, Derek, instead of allowing her to participate in the older crowd's activities.

When Edgar had lit her cigarette, she said, "I hate it when summer ends, and especially this year, since I have to start university. How did you manage to get out of attending?"

Edgar laughed. "You don't want to go?"

"I know what you're thinking. How could a Carlyle *not* go to university?" Daphne's father was a physics professor at the university and her mother was a pharmacist, once more practicing her vocation now that the war had opened up new opportunities, and her children were pretty well grown up. Daphne's parents prized intellectual and artistic pursuits, and thought that their daughters as well as their sons should have sound, professional careers. Marriage with a like-minded partner would be a bonus.

"What do you want to do?"

"Just what other girls want — to devote myself to raising a family and having fun."

"I wish your sister felt that way," he said ruefully.

"Mum and Dad think I'm terribly unambitious, so I've been told I have to study something. I do enjoy cooking, but they don't think that would lead to any sort of *proper* career. That's what servants do. So I'm stuck with Domestic Science. It's better than pharmacy or law, and I could *never* be a doctor. Ugh! Having to deal with sick people all the time!"

Edgar laughed again, and realized that Daphne had managed to cheer him up. He knew he didn't have a chance with Ellie, but never gave up trying. She was the only girl around here who excited him. But perhaps Daphne, a more gentle and unassuming soul, had possibilities. Edgar was feeling the needs of any virile young man. Whores weren't an attractive option. Marriage was what he desired, with sex available whenever he craved it. Ellie had been right to tell him once that he wanted a wife who would cosset him, not a career woman like her.

"Shall we go and shake a leg?" he asked her when he had stubbed out his cigarette.

"If you're up to it," she replied, referring to his stiff and often painful ankle.

"Of course I am," he replied, giving her a suggestive look that made her blush.

How innocent and sweet she seemed. The kind of girl who probably appreciated being pampered, and would in turn be an adoring wife. And if she wasn't as dramatically beautiful as her sister, she had a translucent, alabaster complexion and startling green eyes. Edgar felt himself melting a little. And quite suddenly jovial.

.   .   .

At eleven o'clock, earlier than they had expected, Olivia asked Max to drive her and the boys back to the cottage. "Rupert says he has a stomach ache."

"Has he eaten all the chocolates and licorice all-sorts?" Esme asked. She and Claire were allowed to stay up for the entire party and to sleep over with Fliss. Which meant that they'd be chattering away until the birds took over at dawn.

"He says not," Olivia replied. "Perhaps he had too much sun today."

"I'll come with you, darling," Richard said. "All I really want is my bed."

"I'll come along for the ride," Lydia offered. She and Max had barely been apart all evening. They were so obviously and happily besotted with one another that it seemed cruel to expect them to do anything without the other. Even though it was only a few minutes by boat to Silver Bay.

Olivia felt a sharp pang of sorrow. How unfair that they would soon be separated by this war. And for how long? She didn't dare think the worst. Max would come back to them. She needed to cling to that belief.

But how young Max seemed! Zoë was definitely more mature, and Olivia felt confident that Zoë could look after herself. It would be good for Max to have Zoë nearby in England. The twins had always relied upon one another.

But it was absurd for these children to be going off to war! Couldn't she somehow stop them? She had given birth to them; surely she had some control over their destinies. Surely she could refuse to allow them to venture into danger. Wasn't that what parents were supposed to do?

You protect your children from getting burnt or drowning or being run down by a motorcar. You take them to church and instill Christian ethics, tell them that murder is a sin. But when they're eighteen, you're expected to hand them rifles, send them into an unthinkable hell, and tell them that they'd better shoot to kill if they want to come back alive.

Olivia tried to clear her mind of these distressing thoughts as they sped home. There was a sliver of moon amid a scintillating, star-speckled canopy. Usually the lake worked its magic upon her, but at the hospital she had seen too many young lives shattered, and couldn't stop thinking that Max might be another. He was too gentle and kind to survive this war. Olivia wanted to scream. And she wanted God to hear. If he was there.

·   ·   ·

"Do you want to fuck me?" Phoebe asked Bobby Miller.

They had sneaked away from the dance, and Bobby had held her hand on the way down to the tennis pavilion beside the lake. It felt so nice, her hand in his firm grip.

"Christ Almighty, Phoebe!" he said with an astonished, embarrassed laugh.

"Don't blaspheme, Bobby. God will punish you, and Mama would be so angry she wouldn't let me talk to you any more."

"But Christ, Phoebe, do you know what you're saying?"

"Of course. I had this discussion once before, at the Dominion Day ball the summer before the storm."

"What storm? What are you talking about?"

"The war. It's like a storm that's not going away. Anyway, people seemed surprised that I knew what fucking is. And embarrassed the way adults are when they don't want children to know something. But I'm not a child anymore, and I'd like to be cuddled and kissed."

They had reached the relative darkness of the pavilion, and Bobby pulled her close. "It means more than that, Phoebe. And I can show you if you like. It starts like this."

His kiss was surprising. She hadn't expected his mouth to be so soft, and when his tongue touched hers, it was like a shock that tingled through her whole body. His hands running along her back were playing strange, quivery notes deep inside her. She moaned when he squeezed her breast.

"Don't stop," she said breathlessly. She had never felt such intense pleasure, and never wanted it to end. How greedy adults were to keep this secret of fucking from the young. This was better than ice cream or candy.

"Oh, I won't. But we have to go somewhere safer, where no one can find us."

"The eastern change house. I don't expect anyone will go there." Thorncliff had three of them scattered around the island so that people could change into their swimsuits.

Bobby grabbed her hand eagerly. "You're a special girl, Phoebe. A real peach!"

•　　　•　　　•

Ellie wandered down to the tennis pavilion, recalling when she and Jack had discovered their overpowering attraction to one another here that blissful summer of 1914. She ached for those kisses now. And the steamy sex. He had been her first and only lover. It had been almost two years since Jack and Chas had left to join the Royal Flying Corps in England.

She and Jack had made no commitment to each other, and she suspected that he was enjoying the companionship of other women. But judging from his letters, she knew that he loved her at least a little.

It was too much to hope for marriage. She knew that Jack was determined to become as rich and powerful as this elite and privileged society to which she belonged only by default. And only in the summers.

The pavilion was empty, with no would-be lovers necking in the shadows cast by the lamplight. And Ellie lamented that most of her dearest friends were at the war.

There was an enclave of Americans whom she had come to know better during the few weeks she had spent here these past two summers. Their cottages were mostly clustered at the southern end of the lake, so except for parties and events, they had tended to keep to themselves, as the Stepping Stone and Wyndwood crowd had. But since the SRA – Summer Residents' Association – Golf and Country Club had opened on the mainland just at the end of the Stepping Stones, she had met the Americans more frequently on the tennis courts and in the clubhouse, where there were also weekly dances.

One of them approached her now. "Hi, Eleanor. I wonder if I could have a word?"

Ellie liked Troy Roland. His family had summered on the lake for seven years. They weren't as enormously wealthy as most of the others in their social set, although they owned a paint manufactory in Pittsburgh. Troy had just completed a chemistry degree at Harvard.

"Of course."

"I heard that Blake is at a base hospital in France now. Did you know that Harvard has a General Hospital set up along the coast there as part of the British contingent?"

"No, I didn't."

"I know we're supposed to be neutral, but a lot of us can't help taking sides. My mother is actually German, so it makes it more difficult for us. Although even Mum thinks that her countrymen have gone mad." Troy smiled. He was handsome, Ellie thought, with sharply intelligent blue-grey eyes, and a surprisingly beautiful mouth.

"As kids we spent many wonderful summers roaming about the Bavarian hills with our cousins. But Felix gets terrible hay fever, and so when the Fremonts told us about Muskoka not having ragweed, Dad decided that we should spend summers here instead. In any case, he was falling out with his brothers-in-law.

He wasn't happy with Germany's increasing militarism. My one uncle is a General, and his sons are also professional soldiers. Two of them became pilots. We recently heard that one was shot down." Troy watched her as he said, "By the famous Ace, Chas Thornton."

"Good God!" Ellie searched his face to see if he was teasing her. "Bloody hell!"

"It does rather bring it home, doesn't it?" Troy said, offering her a cigarette. "How close we really are to one another."

"And here you are consorting with the enemy."

He laughed. "Hardly that. The Thorntons are friends. Chas was only doing his job. As was Hartwig."

"It must be uncomfortable being stuck in the middle like this."

"A bit awkward, certainly. But I've decided that I'd like to help the Allies somehow. Not by fighting. So I was considering driving an ambulance or enlisting as an orderly. There are always ads for volunteers. I wondered what you, being a doctor, thought would be the most helpful."

Ellie was flattered that he wanted her opinion. And it was sincere, she thought, not just flirtation. "Both are important, so you couldn't go wrong with either. I'd say it's a matter of what appeals to you. Driving an ambulance is more dangerous."

"And probably more exciting," he said with a grin.

"That's very generous of you. Wanting to help in a war that your country's not even involved in, especially when you have relatives on the other side."

"I've looked at the issues carefully, trying to be fair-minded. And I've decided that the Allies are fighting for survival and for the same democratic values that we believe in. I'm behind Teddy Roosevelt on this one. He's been lambasting Wilson for keeping us out of the war, especially after the *Lusitania*. And he thinks that the German- and Irish-Americans who are lobbying to maintain our neutrality are unpatriotic. Teddy says there's no such thing as a hyphenated American who is a good American."

"You don't feel any sort of loyalty to Germany?"

"Not a bit of it. Some nostalgia perhaps for those summers in the mountains. But I'm simply an American and ready to fight for that privilege. Our law states that anyone who enlists in a foreign army automatically relinquishes American citizenship. But that wouldn't be the case if I joined the Harvard Medical Unit or the American Ambulance Service. My parents aren't pleased that I want to do this. Think I'm playing at soldiers or something rather juvenile. And maybe I *am* trying to escape from the life they have prescribed for me. Sorry. You don't want to hear all that. I just wanted another opinion."

"I think it's very noble of you. So you'll be leaving soon?"

"As soon as possible. We're going home to Pittsburgh early next week. I'll have to decide by then."

"I might see you in France next year."

Troy was surprised. "I can't imagine that the army will send women doctors to the Front."

"I don't see why not. There are plenty of nurses there, and volunteers, like Zoë. Anyway, I may circumvent them completely and just join one of the Scottish Women's Hospitals. Blake said there are a few other private hospitals run by British women in France as well. The Duchess of Something-or-other."

Troy shook his head. "What's wrong with working in the hospitals here or even in Britain?"

"London will be good for a while. But I've always wanted to see Paris, and I'll never get there otherwise," Ellie said with a grin.

Troy laughed. "I can see there's no dissuading you."

"Absolutely not."

"Then before we both end up in uniform, Eleanor, how about a dance?" He offered her his arm.

"Absolutely." She wrapped her arm about his as they sauntered back towards the house. "And my friends call me Ellie."

"Thank you, Ellie."

"Oh, hello, Phoebe," Ellie said as the girl suddenly appeared on the path, heading for the house.

Phoebe looked at Ellie and Troy rather vacantly. Why were these people impinging on her bubble of euphoria? Her body still tingled with awakened desire. Deep inside her, in a secret place where Bobby had seemed to fit perfectly, there was an intense glow of warmth that she could see emanating from her. She wasn't worried about this because she knew that everyone else was too blind to see it.

There had been a sharp pain for only an instant, and Bobby had said, "This is how God made us, Phoebe. To be together, like this. Doesn't that feel good now?" And he had moved inside her so that she had felt an explosion of ecstasy that had surely come from God. Fabulous, brilliant colours had danced in celebration around them. She had never felt such pure joy.

When Bobby had tidied her up, she had said, "Why did no one ever show me this before? This is what heaven must be like."

He had laughed. "I expect you're right. But here on earth, only married people are supposed to enjoy sex. That's what the adults say, anyway. I think that if you like something, you should just do it."

"They don't want us to have fun, do they? Parents."

"I figure we're old enough to do what we like, don't you, Phoebe?" He'd kissed her again and she had let his tongue explore her mouth. "You're really something, Phoebe! Who would have thought...? But we'd better get back now or your parents will wonder what happened to you. You mustn't tell them about this, Phoebe. They would be very angry, and not let me see you again."

"I won't tell them or let them interfere. And I do want to see you again, Bobby. Will we get married now and go away so that they can't tell us what to do?"

He'd laughed somewhat nervously. "Maybe we will one day, Phoebe. But there's a war on. You go back first so that they won't think we've been together. And remember, this is our secret. Shall we do it again sometime?"

"Oh yes."

Sex, he'd called it. That was that secret thing that her mother alluded to as unclean and sinful. "Your dirty place," was what her mother called that part of her, and had told her that women suffered for the sins of Eve by bleeding from their dirty place every month. It was a punishment from God, and in the old days, women hadn't even been allowed to go into the church when God's disfavour was upon them.

But her mother could surely never have had sex or she wouldn't think that way. Poor Mama, missing out on something so intense and exquisite that Phoebe couldn't even describe it. Except that she had felt God and his goodness.

And it had changed her. She was infused with Bobby's spirit. She had felt it leave him in a warm rush that had washed her clean of the devils of her mother's repressive philosophy. She felt languid yet powerful. She wanted to take off all her clothes and lie with Bobby, letting his tongue lick her everywhere, and once again enter her like a key into a lock. He had freed her. Now she could soar with angels and frolic among the colours.

Ellie noticed Phoebe's dreamy vagueness and wondered momentarily what was up with her now. In Phoebe's precarious mental state, one was never quite sure whether she was competent or hallucinating. But as she seemed happy, Ellie wasn't concerned.

Later Ellie noticed a joyful Phoebe dancing with Bobby Miller, and overheard his younger sister, Rosie, say to her sisters and friends, "Bobby seems to be spending a lot of time with Phoebe tonight. I know that she's a Wyndham, which makes her very hoity-toity, but she's queer in the head, don't you think? I wonder what he's up to."

The Millers were new on the lake this summer, and Ellie didn't have much time for them. Rosie's father had been a small foundry owner until he'd secured a government contract for armaments. Suddenly they had money, and had bought the Farley's island after the Farleys' only son had been killed at Ypres. The Miller parents were decent enough, but their five offspring, except for the eldest, Joey, were too full of themselves.

Ellie and Troy danced often, and managed to escape to the veranda to talk.

"Can I conjecture that you don't want to play with paints?" she asked him astutely.

Troy laughed. "I did when I was a kid. I'm the eldest so Dad expects me to take over the business when he's ready to retire, and my brothers are supposed to join me. Part of my job is to find better paint formulations, new colours, that sort of thing. Nothing wrong with that, of course. Someone should. But I've discovered that I'm more interested in other aspects of chemistry as well as biology. Perhaps geared to medical research."

"Even more worthwhile."

"Not according to Dad. He says he built this business for us, so that his sons would have good, solid futures. He thinks me ungrateful and foolish to want to do anything but carry on his work."

"Odd how people who forge their own careers and lives tend *not* to allow their children to do the same. I will make a pact with myself not to force my children to become doctors. God knows, I might well discourage them."

"I expect you'll just inspire them."

Ellie looked away from his intense gaze. "So tell me about wandering the hills of Bavaria. Did you meet Hansel and Gretel in the dark forests?"

Troy laughed. "I feel I could have. My mother's eldest brother is Baron Aldrich von Ravensberg. They grew up in a castle in the Allgäu region of the Alps, which he inherited."

"Hell's bells! Another bloody aristocrat!"

"They're not well off, but would uphold their dignity and obligations no matter how impoverished. The castle is a dark, cold, spooky old place, always crumbling, part of it dating back to the eleventh century, not particularly large but never cozy or comfortable. Positively medieval. But the scenery around it is spectacular. Icy lakes and streams tucked between snow-capped mountains, deep, towering forests, wildflower-sprinkled meadows."

"I see why your island is called Ravenshill. But Muskoka must pale by comparison."

"Not at all. I love it here, and feel much more at home among the warm, vast, friendly lakes. Mountains can be intimidating, oppressive even. You're right that it doesn't take much to imagine witches and trolls lurking there. Here, there's more of a feeling of tranquility and harmony with nature. Maybe a sense that the land hasn't been subjugated for centuries and infused with vengeful spirits, just gently used by nomadic peoples."

"That's very poetic," Ellie said, impressed. "And now here we are, the first to impose ourselves and our ambitions upon the rocks and lakes. Clear-cutting the forests to make the Wyndhams wealthy," Ellie stated sardonically. "Polluting the air and water with smelly boats and unsanitary 'sanitary' arrangements so that we and the tourists can enjoy the 'unspoiled wilderness'."

Troy laughed.

"So I expect you speak German fluently," Ellie said.

"Yes. And my cousins were brought up with English, since my Baron uncle, at any rate, thinks that all culture springs from England, and that his children should revere Shakespeare and Chaucer. Both his sons went to Cambridge. Ernst, the heir, is quite a naturalist. Unlike our other cousins, he prefers to observe and document the wildlife rather than kill it. He's in the army now, of course, but a rather gentle soul, so I do worry about him. Rainer was working for the German Consulate in London when the war broke out. He'll make a good diplomat. If he survives."

Ellie could see that he was concerned about them, and probably torn about taking sides. "My father insisted we learn German, since so many scientific and medical papers are written in it. But I struggle with those."

"I can well imagine!"

"How did your parents meet?"

"Dad was recovering from pneumonia, and decided, on the advice of his doctor, to take some sea air and a month at a spa. So he embarked on his first ocean voyage, and went to Baden Baden in the Black Forest, where my mother was also taking the waters. He maintains he fell in love with her at first sight." Troy's gaze was disconcerting.

Ellie was feeling quite guilty about Jack when she let Troy kiss her chastely on the lips. But hell, why shouldn't she enjoy herself when Jack undoubtedly was?

The lyrics of a song she and Troy had just danced to kept playing in her head.

I had pictured in my mind, some day I would surely find,
Someone handsome, someone true, but I never thought of you.
Now my dream of love is o'er, I want you and nothing more,
Come on, enfold me, come on and hold me just like you never did before,
You made me love you, I didn't want to do it, I didn't want to do it.
You made me want you, and all the time you knew it, I guess you always knew it...

Which was silly really, since she wasn't falling for Troy. Perhaps it was for Jack.

They were interrupted as Zoë rushed over saying, "There's something terribly wrong with Rupert. Toby went to fetch Dr. Rumbold from Port Carling, but he's gone to Gravenhurst for a wedding and won't be back until tomorrow." Richard had sent Toby to find her and Ellie. "Can you come?"

"Of course! I'll have to fetch my medical bag."

"I'll take you over," Troy offered. "Perhaps there's something I can do to help."

Max and Freddie bid hasty farewells to the Thorntons. Lydia insisted she wanted to come along as well.

Toby, who fortunately had the use of Ria's motorboat, had already gone back. Max drove the short distance home at top speed.

As soon as they pulled into their boathouse, Zoë jumped out and ran up to the house. Rupert was lying on the sofa in the sitting room groaning. He seemed to have just vomited, as Olivia was removing a bowl from his side. She looked anxiously at Zoë and said, "He says there's a terrible pain in his stomach."

Zoë knelt beside her brother and laid her hand on his brow. He was hot, but pale. "Show me where it hurts, Rupert."

He pointed to his lower abdomen.

"Ellie will be here in a few minutes to look after you," Zoë said, stroking his head soothingly. "You're being a very brave boy."

"I don't want to be brave. I want it to stop!" He curled up in pain.

"Is Rupert wounded? Like the soldiers in the hospital?" Miles asked. He looked frightened.

Freddie went up to him and said, "No. He has a tummy ache. Why don't you and I go up to bed? I'm sure Rupert will be much better by morning."

Zoë threw Freddie a grateful look as he extended his hand to Miles, who took it, saying, "Are you sure it's OK if I go up without Rupert?"

Olivia gave him a kiss on the top of the head, saying, "Yes, of course it is. You get some sleep, my chick."

Miles was already in his pajamas, so Freddie tucked him into bed. "Will Rupert get a medal for being brave? Like Chas and Jack and Justin?"

"I expect we can make one for him. Why don't you think about what it should look like and we'll design it in the morning."

Freddie turned off the lights, but Miles said, "I don't like the dark. Not without Rupert."

"But it isn't completely dark. There's this magic that happens when you scrunch your eyes closed for a few minutes. Ready?" Miles squeezed his eyes shut. "Keep them closed," Freddie warned. "OK, now open them and look at the window. What can you see?"

"Stars."

"Lots and lots of them. See how much light they give you?"

"I've seen them in the professor's telescope," Miles declared importantly. Ellie's father had a telescope mounted on the second storey balcony of their cottage. "Should I make a wish?"

"Absolutely. Why don't I sit here while you close your eyes again – a bit longer this time. Then you can tell me if you see even more stars." It didn't take Miles long to fall asleep.

Ellie and Troy arrived just a few minutes behind the others. She hadn't even taken time to change out of her evening gown.

Zoë said softly to her, "I think it could be appendicitis."

"OK, young man, let's see what you've done to yourself," Ellie said to Rupert.

"I didn't eat all the licorice all-sorts," Rupert mumbled between groans.

"I'm sure you didn't. Now let me just touch you here."

He didn't protest until she suddenly released the pressure. "Owww! You made it worse!"

"Sorry, chum. But now that we know what's wrong, we're going to fix you." Ellie rose from his side and asked to speak to Olivia and Richard in the office. Zoë and Max went as well.

"You're right, Zoë. It's acute appendicitis. He needs emergency surgery. There's no time to get him to a hospital. I don't even know where the closest one is. Probably Toronto."

"What will happen...?" Olivia began.

"If the appendix bursts, then there's nothing we can do for him."

"Oh, dear God!" Olivia said, clasping a hand across her mouth and turning away. Richard put his arm about her and held her tightly.

Zoë stated emphatically, "You'll have to operate, Ellie."

She nodded reluctantly. "So it seems. But you must know that I've never done one of these before. I've only assisted. I don't have proper equipment, but fortunately I do have some ether in my bag."

"We have confidence in you, Ellie. Do what you can," Richard said. "Now tell me what you need."

"The dining room table. Clean blankets and towels laid on top. Rubbing alcohol. As much gauze as you've got. One of your fresh shirts, Mr. Wyndham, and an apron. A kerchief to cover my hair. Zoë to help me."

The friends looked at one another in a panic. "We're going off to war, remember?" Ellie said. "This *should* be a cakewalk."

"Can I help?" Troy asked when they returned to the sitting room where he and Lydia had been comforting Rupert.

"Would you like to try your hand at being an anaesthetist? I have ether."

"I've seen it used..." Troy started to say. Ellie looked at him knowingly. Although she had never done it, it was considered a lark for medical students to inhale enough ether to feel intoxicated. She was certain that chemists did it as well. "Sure I can do it."

They all helped to prepare the dining room for surgery. Rupert looked scared when Richard carried him in and laid him on the table. Movement was obviously very painful for him. Olivia forced back tears as she kissed him. He clung to her saying, "Mama, what's happening?"

Richard pulled Olivia out of the room as Ellie explained, "You're going to have a little nap, chum, and when you wake up, you'll start to feel better. Troy is going to put this towel over your face so you can smell this sweet ether. Just breathe normally."

As soon as Rupert lost consciousness, Troy removed the ether-infused towel. He stayed at the head of the table, watching Rupert for signs that he might be recovering his senses, in which case he would apply more ether.

Ellie thought it was lucky that Troy had come along. It was comforting to have a chemist looking after the administration of the ether, with it being so highly volatile and extremely flammable. She was also grateful for the electric lighting which was brighter and safer than acetylene gas or, God-forbid, paraffin lamps.

She was surprised that her hands weren't shaking when she made the incision. But she knew exactly what to do. "Bingo!" she said when she located the inflamed appendix. "It hasn't burst."

With Zoë's help, the operation was over quickly. "Nice tidy stitches, Dr. Carlyle," Zoë said with a grin.

"Mum did insist upon my learning needlework when I was young, although I hated it. She always said it would come in handy."

"You did a super job, Ellie," Troy said, obviously impressed.

"We just have to hope that everything was sterile enough and that there's no infection. But thank you, team, for your excellent work. Nurse Wyndham, you've been blooded, and have graduated from bedpans."

A delighted Zoë went to the sitting room to tell the others. Olivia burst into tears of relief. "Thank God," Richard said. "*We'll* tidy up and you all come and rest. Mrs. O'Rourke has made a pot of tea and sandwiches. She insisted she couldn't sleep anyway, and that it was best to keep busy." Mrs. O'Rourke had been their cook for twenty years, and had always indulged the children in the kitchen, even allowing them to help her bake cookies. She had obviously been as anxious as everyone else, since she dabbed her eyes with her apron when she heard the good news.

Richard, Max, Freddie, and Troy carried the still-unconscious Rupert in the blankets, like a makeshift stretcher, from the "operating table" to the downstairs guest room, where Olivia would watch him. Ellie offered to stay over in case there were any complications.

Max laced the tea with brandy and the young people munched sandwiches as they watched the lake start to emerge from the fading darkness. Lydia was curled up against Max with her head on his shoulder. Her parents had stopped by on their way home from the ball, and she had persuaded them to let her stay for the night, or what was left of it.

Ellie and Zoë had doffed the aprons and Richard's shirts. Ellie shivered in her sleeveless gown. Before she could fetch her shawl, Troy took his jacket, which he had discarded earlier, and draped it around her shoulders as he said, "That might have been a medical first. An operation performed in evening dress."

"A tale to tell your grandchildren," Ellie said.

"Hell, I'll dine out on this! Intrepid, beautiful young women performing surgery in ball gowns in the Canadian wilderness – who can beat a story like that?"

They all laughed.

"You've also inspired me," Troy added. "I've decided that I'm going to join the Harvard Medical Unit in France as an orderly. To see if I want to become a doctor. I expect there's all kinds of research to be done into anaesthetics."

The warm smile that he gave her made Ellie fall for him just a bit. As did the comfort of his jacket with its pleasantly masculine smell.

"Besides, I'll get to wear a British uniform, which I think will be jolly good fun," he said in an attempt at a British accent.

"I'd leave off the accent, though," Max chaffed.

"How's your French?" Ellie asked.

"Very rusty. *Mademoiselle from Armentieres, Parlay-voo?*" Troy began to sing the popular wartime tune amid much laughter.

"Let's finish the ball in the boathouse," Max suddenly suggested. "We'll dance to the sunrise. It's not often we can do this."

Zoë could sense his desperation. Although weary, she wasn't ready to go to bed either.

Ellie thought she would be exhausted, but actually felt invigorated by the challenge and exhilaration of a successful operation.

Max grabbed a couple of bottles of champagne, and they trooped down to the spacious room above the boathouse that was set up with tables for playing cards and games, sofas for lounging, and a gramophone, with lots of room for dancing, particularly with the French windows open onto the balcony.

Ouhu was materializing out of the mist. The nights were noticeably cooler now, and the warm lake seemed to be steaming.

From the outset, it was obvious they were going to be in couples. Max and Lydia, of course, trying discreetly to spoon. Ellie and Troy discovering their interest in one another. Leaving Zoë and Freddie.

She tried to keep things lighthearted, because she really liked Freddie and didn't want to hurt him, or give him a false sense that he meant any more to her than before. It was easier when Max put on lively tunes and they all whirled about energetically. But with the rising of the sun, the music became mellower and they, tired now, clung to one another as they swayed back and forth.

It was immensely arousing, Ellie thought, as Troy pulled her closer to the slow music. His subtle caresses were melting her reserve. She said to him, "I feel like dipping my feet into the lake. Want to come?"

He placed his jacket about her shoulders once again as they went to sit on one of the docks that flanked the boathouse. Unceremoniously, she hitched up her gown, pulled off her stockings, and dangled her feet in the water. "Ah, that's exquisite."

Troy laughed as he shed his shoes and socks, and rolled up his trousers. "You're an extraordinary woman, Ellie! Completely refreshing." He leaned over and kissed her, but not so chastely this time. Then she was in his arms, and Jack was momentarily forgotten.

When he released her – reluctantly – she said, "It's been an eventful night."

"Life changing, I'd say."

"You really are thinking of becoming a doctor?"

"Most definitely. Watching you save Rupert's life – because you did, you know – made me realize that I want to make a difference, too. Not just running a factory and finding ways of making more money, which is my father's definition of success."

"I'm glad." Ellie leaned against him, suddenly very tired, but contented. He gently massaged the nape of her neck, and she nestled closer to him.

"Hey, you must be exhausted. And I should get back. Want to come sailing with me this afternoon?"

"Oh yes," Ellie murmured, practically asleep on his shoulder.

"Come along, Dr. Carlyle. Let's get you into bed."

"Mmm. Yes, let's."

Troy laughed.

·   ·   ·

It was nearly noon when Zoë, Ellie, and Lydia woke. The girls had merely stripped off their gowns and fallen into bed.

Ellie was delighted that Rupert didn't have a fever, and was sipping some beef broth. He glowered at her as he said, "It still hurts."

"But differently, right? And it will feel better soon. You have a battle scar now, chum."

He grinned. "And a medal! Look what Miles made for me." It was fashioned from a maple leaf that had been waxed and was attached to a bright red ribbon.

"And look at the cottage that Freddie designed for me. Isn't it crackerjack?"

It was a fanciful boathouse with the upper story shaped like the prow of a ship reaching out over the bottom floor like the peak of a cap, a diving board sticking out from its end. A slide curved down to the water from one of the sides, and a rope bridge led from the back to a platform on a fortuitously placed tree. There was a smaller upper deck, like a captain's wheelhouse, with windows all around and a telescope fixed to the tiny balcony off it.

"That's my bedroom up there, see?"

"I do indeed. What a fabulous place! Are you going to have Freddie build it for you when you're older?"

"I want it right now. When I'm older like you, I may not want to have a slide and a tree house."

Ellie laughed. "Don't count on it, chum. I'd love a place like this. And I'd be going down the slide every morning for my swim."

"Could I, Mama? Could you ask Freddie to build this for me?"

"I'm afraid not, my chick. Freddie's going off to France, and we have to do our bit by not wanting too much," Olivia said.

Rupert looked crestfallen. "Yes, I suppose so. I can imagine it though, can't I? It is crackerjack, isn't it?"

"It certainly is," Zoë said. "And so is the fact that you're looking so much better today. I'll bet you forgot that the stitches hurt."

"It's not *so* bad," he agreed. "Mama said that Ellie saved my life, and that I mustn't complain. I guess you're a pretty good doctor, Ellie. Thank you. And you, too, Zoë."

Ellie ruffled his hair. "My pleasure, Rupert. I hope you'll invite me to tea when you have your boathouse cottage one day."

"I will!"

"I really need to go home and change out of this dress," Ellie said to Zoë, who offered to drive her to Ouhu.

Richard waylaid them and said to Ellie, "We're honoured to be your first official patients, so I'd like to pay you for your services."

"That's not necessary, Mr. Wyndham. I'm delighted that I could help, and that Rupert seems to be recovering well..."

Richard interrupted her protestations. "You can't make a living if you treat your friends for free."

She demurred and said, "The usual charge for a visit is $5, which I think is excessive since it's the best part of working people's weekly wage..."

"I'd like you to take $100, Ellie, so that you can equip yourself properly."

"Good God, I could equip a clinic with that!"

"We can't put a monetary value on what you've done for us, Ellie, but I'd gladly give you $10,000 if you'd take it."

"I'm grateful for your most generous hundred. I'll be the best-equipped physician in the city. And a couple of new frocks will come in handy."

"You might consider doing what our doctor in Toronto does. Charge your moneyed patients double or quadruple, and a pittance from the needy."

She grinned. "A man after my own heart."

•   •   •

Lydia was allowed to move in with Zoë until Max left, while Esme and Claire went to stay with Fliss for the week.

The friends played tennis at Thorncliff and golf at the SRA Country Club. On the holiday Monday they took a picnic lunch and canoed to Old Baldy. They climbed up the gentle backside to the top of the bare cliff, and admired the vast expanse of island-dotted lake while they nibbled sandwiches and drank champagne. Edgar and Daphne joined them, and Troy had become a part of their crowd.

Afterwards they decided to visit Edelina, whom they had hardly seen this summer.

Edelina Fuerstenberger, in her early thirties, was a talented and successful artist who had a log cabin on Mortimer's Island. Because she attracted other artists, as well as poets and freethinkers, her place had become known locally as "The Colony", and was shunned by many.

Edelina, always ahead of the current fashion, was wearing a straight dress that just covered her knees, and she was barefoot. Two years previously, she had been thought daring, even wanton for her shorter hemlines, which were now commonplace. She greeted her visitors warmly. Ellie was a particularly good friend. She said, "You've met Troy Roland before, haven't you, Edelina?"

"Indeed I have," Edelina replied, giving him a meaningful smile.

Troy reddened as he looked away from Edelina's forthright gaze.

Ellie noticed and was somewhat confused. She knew that Edelina was uninhibited about sex, and had had several affairs, even, she suspected, with Chas that summer of 1914, before he'd become engaged to Ria.

And why should it bother her if Troy and Edelina had had a fling? Ellie believed that people needed to be liberated from the damaging Victorian ideas about sex – something unmentionable that was dirty and disgusting and conducted with more duty than pleasure in matrimonial secrecy. Sex wasn't and shouldn't be shameful or guilt-provoking. She felt weak-kneed whenever she recalled her own intimacy with Jack.

"I see that you have friends staying," Zoë said. There were several tents set up around the large fire pit. When the war had first been declared, Edelina, being of German heritage, had discovered that some of her "friends" had preferred not to be associated with her.

"Yes. And a couple of confused young men who are pacifists, hiding out since they can't always face the censure of overly zealous women handing them white feathers. They're not cowards. In fact, it takes a great deal of courage to stand up for your beliefs when they go against the mainstream."

"And if the government brings in conscription, then the poor chaps will have an even harder time of it," Max said.

"Yes, indeed," Edelina agreed. "I think that's why many are joining up voluntarily now, so that they won't be seen as doing it merely under the dictates of the law." She gave Max a knowing look. "Well, my dear friends, I suspect that you've come to say more goodbyes."

Over glasses of wine on the veranda, they caught her up on their latest news. "I feel infinitely sad to see you leaving. Paul is going as well," Edelina said as he joined them. He had once been a

Catholic priest, but had been part of The Colony for the past four years. "He's going to be a stretcher-bearer."

"I need to see if I can still believe in God," Paul said. "I've heard some terrible stories from returned soldiers." He regularly visited the convalescents at the Wyndham Hospital. "I'm beginning to suspect that I may well have to subscribe to Edelina's philosophy of the sanctity of nature. Perhaps that *is* all there is." He walked away dejectedly, and Ellie thought that she had never seen him happy.

"I'm not sure that Paul can survive without God," Edelina said sadly.

"I can't imagine that he'll find Him on the battlefields," Ellie said. "Quite the contrary."

"Perhaps he'll find Him in the spirit and valour of the men," Troy pointed out.

"Perhaps he will," Edelina said with a grateful smile. "I won't give up hope just yet."

When they left, she handed Zoë, Max, and Freddie each an unframed watercolour she had done. "To remind you of Muskoka, and small enough to take with you. And here are some to give to Ria and the others."

"Edelina, they're fabulous!" Zoë enthused. They were relevant autumn scenes – Silver Bay for Zoë and Max, Driftwood Island for Freddie, the point of Wyndwood for Ria, Ouhu for Blake, and so forth. They were, of course, softer than the usual bold strokes and vibrant colours of her oils, but so evocative of the lake.

"I'll expect one next year, Edelina," Ellie said. "But Troy's also going over now."

"Then you must have one as well," Edelina insisted, giving him one of a canoe on the Shadow River, caught between sky and water, perfectly reflected. "I think of this as how we are, drifting between two realities. It's a study I did for a large painting."

"It's beautiful and profound, but I can't accept this, Edelina," Troy demurred. "You hardly know me."

"I think perhaps our souls have met before, Troy. There are some things you must just accept in life. One is how you feel, not what convention or others tell you that you should. So we *are* friends." She smiled warmly at him.

"Thank you. I shall treasure this."

They had come in two boats, Edgar driving his and taking the others home, leaving Ellie to go with Troy. She motioned him to pull into Pirate's Cove at the north end of Mortimer's Island.

"Tell me why you seemed rather uncomfortable seeing Edelina," Ellie asked him when he stopped the boat.

"It's actually quite embarrassing. Do you remember the Dominion Day Ball at Wyndwood, the summer of 1914?"

"Of course. Edelina and Paul were there."

"It's where I first met her. Unfortunately, my mother was with me at that moment." Troy hesitated. "You must understand that my mother is a very religious and moral person. A good person, really. She has extremely high standards and expects others to live up to them as well. I'm afraid she'd heard stories about nudity and free love at The Colony, and so when she was introduced to Edelina, she completed snubbed her. In fact, she turned to me and said in German, just loud enough so that Edelina wouldn't fail to hear, that immoral women with dirty priests in tow should not be tolerated in polite society."

"Oh dear."

"I was mortified. Mom isn't usually rude, but she does have a strong dislike, even fear, of Catholics. She's Lutheran and believes that the Catholic Church is a 'religious whore'."

"And what does she think of us atheists?" Ellie watched him carefully, and noticed that he was slightly shocked by her admission.

"That you are lost souls, and need to find God and redemption. And that it would be her duty to bring you back into the fold."

"I'm a confirmed lost sheep, I'm afraid. So I don't think she'd approve of me at all."

"She wouldn't approve of this either," Troy said, taking her into his arms and kissing her deeply. When he released her he said, "I think I rather like Edelina's philosophy. I've been struggling for years to escape the stultifying quicksand of my mother's religious fervour. Being away at Harvard saved me. My father is much more reasonable, but for the sake of harmony, allows my mother to rule the roost and is able to ignore what he doesn't agree with. She doesn't approve of drink, for example. She thinks it's a sign of a weak character succumbing to the devil's influence. But she does allow Dad to have a glass of wine with dinner. When he wants more, he goes to his club. She knows it, of course, but pretends she doesn't. We boys aren't allowed anything except a small glass of wine when we have guests to dinner. If she sees us indulging at parties, we're for it when we get home."

"So you've been terribly corrupted today," Ellie said. "Champagne, intelligent conversation with Edelina and a priest..."

"...A few kisses," he added with a grin.

When he kissed her this time with barely controlled passion, Ellie wondered if he had ever had sex, and thought it perhaps unlikely. She had seen what damage fanatically religious people could do, terrorizing their children and making them instinctively afraid and ashamed of perfectly normal, healthy desires. She was tempted to seduce him, to not let him go off to war a virgin, as she had so flippantly said to Zoë only a few days ago. But he would undoubtedly feel obliged to marry her afterwards. And there was Jack.

"Do I sense a romance blossoming?" Zoë asked Ellie later as they were preparing for a small engagement party for Max and Lydia.

"Oh, hell! I don't know! I really like him, Zoë. A lot. But..."

"You're sweet on Jack."

"Yes. I'm just not sure where I stand with him."

"Why not see what happens with Troy? Perhaps the two of you are better suited."

Only Ria and Chas knew that Ellie and Jack had had an intensely passionate affair before he left, and so had a deeper commitment than just a summer flirtation. And Ellie was not about to enlighten Zoë. "I won't close any doors just yet."

• • •

"Are you sure no one will come along here?" Bobby Miller asked Phoebe. They were at the east gazebo on Wyndwood, about halfway up that side of the island.

"Edgar and Daphne are picnicking with Zoë and Max and the others over at Old Baldy. Mama is afraid to walk along the Dragon's claw – that's the cliff between here and the cottage. So we're all by ourselves," Phoebe said with a trilling laugh as she began to undress.

"Here, let me help," Bobby said, excited by her lasciviousness. When she stood proudly naked before him he said, "You're deliciously voluptuous, Phoebe."

Others called her chubby. She much preferred Bobby's sensual word, "voluptuous", and felt intensely powerful. "Make me see God again, Bobby," she said.

"Oh, I will."

• • •

Zoë, Max, and Lydia took Freddie to the Lake Joseph train station early on Tuesday morning. He bid them farewell reluctantly.

Zoë was ashamed at feeling relieved when he had gone, but she hated to think that he had any hopes of being more than a friend. And yet, she found his absence curiously depressing since the others all had someone with whom they preferred to spend time alone. So she played games in the boathouse with the boys, Rupert having rebounded remarkably quickly.

As did the weather, the days becoming unusually hot again. Ellie stayed over one night and the girls went skinny-dipping.

"I really wanted to do this once more before I left," Zoë said as they swam in the darkness, lit by a swelling moon and crisp stars. The night was chilly but the water was delightfully warm, almost soporific. "It will be difficult to get out of this soup," Zoë said. "Oh, did you see that shooting star? And another!"

"If it's true that shooting stars are the souls of the dead departing for heaven, then the sky should be ablaze with them," Ellie said wryly. "I can't believe you'll soon be gone! This winter will be hell without all of you nearby."

Lydia started to cry, and mumbled, "I'm sorry. I'm trying to be brave, but..."

"Life is difficult and we're entitled to admit it," Ellie assured her. "But for now, let's just enjoy this moment. The water feels positively sensual as it caresses your naked body. Like a lover."

"You brazen woman," Zoë jested.

"We modern women need to be. Remember what I told you, Zoë. *Carpe Diem*. Or in your case, *Carpe Blake*."

Zoë laughed. *Seize Blake*. If only she could.

.   .   .

Phoebe didn't bother to wear her bloomers when she knew she would see Bobby, so that he could easily hitch up her skirt and enter her.

It had been tricky getting together, since her mother never let her go anywhere without Edgar. But he took Daphne to the Country Club to play golf or tennis every day, and Phoebe had pestered long enough so that Edgar had given in and taken her along. Bobby had already told her that he and his siblings spent so much time at the club that they claimed it as their own.

Phoebe would play tennis with whoever needed a partner – sometimes Bobby – and then wander off along the shore with an ice cream cone while Edgar and Daphne had a drink in the bar.

Bobby had discovered a convenient copse of cedars that screened them from view on all sides. They giggled over their daring and defiance. And Phoebe grew stronger with every communion with God.

.   .   .

On the day before they were planning to close the cottage, Ellie went to the Country Club with Troy to play tennis. It was a close match but Ellie won.

"You really are good," Troy said as they walked off the court. The two of them had played together a few times this week at Thorncliff, beating the others.

"Chas taught me."

"That explains it. But maybe you and I can beat him in the next tennis tournament. I think he's had the cup long enough." He was referring to the annual event held at Thorncliff.

"*If* we ever have it again," Ellie said disconsolately. Marjorie Thornton did not intend to hold the tournament until Chas was home. And if he didn't return?

The SRA's four clay courts lay between the clubhouse and the golf course, and were usually busy, since most cottagers didn't have terrain flat enough to accommodate a court. And now that servants were hard to find, few had enough staff to maintain them anyway.

The clubhouse was a sprawling U-shaped building that embraced a flagstone patio and a small harbour with rows of docks. The long bottom of the U was the ballroom where events were held on special occasions, and dances on Wednesday and Saturday evenings. It could also be rented for private functions. One short wing housed the billiard and ping-pong tables; the other was a lounge with cozy leather chairs nestled around small tables. The bar served alcoholic beverages as well as tea and cakes, ice cream and sodas. Dozens of French windows opened onto the patio from all three wings, and people wandered in and out with drinks and ice cream cones.

There was a piano in one corner of the lounge, inviting impromptu performances. Which is what Troy did when a few of his friends, just in from golfing, insisted he give them a tune.

He played with such élan and exuberance, his fingers flying across the keys with complete command of the instrument, that Ellie was astonished. And also by the pieces he played. *Pretty Baby* and *You Made Me Love You.* He winked at her, and she felt her cheeks grow hot.

"You're fabulous," she said in awe when he rejoined her at their table. "Even better than Chas and Max."

He laughed. "Finally I've beaten Chas at something! Of course Max's mother is better than any of us. She could have been a concert pianist."

"But you really are talented. My family, on the other hand, is supremely untalented. Daphne is the only one of us who kept up her lessons, and she can just about manage to coax some recognizable sounds out of our old piano."

"My parents were a bit worried that I would decide to go into show business instead of Harvard." He grinned. "I saw this amazing performer on Broadway – Al Jolson – and he made me realize that I wasn't up to those standards."

"But you can entertain the troops when you're overseas," Ellie said with a smile. "I expect that will be good medicine for them."

"And if I don't make it as a doctor, I can always play in cinemas," he joked, referring to the pianists who accompanied the silent films.

Troy's brothers walked into the room and came up to their table. "Was that you showing off at the piano?" Stuart asked as he pulled out a chair and plunked himself down. "Hi, Eleanor."

The other three grabbed chairs from nearby tables and joined them. She thought once again what a handsome family they were. Troy at twenty-two was the eldest, and the youngest was fifteen.

"I just won the golf game," seventeen-year-old Stuart told them. "So you owe me a drink, Kurt."

"A lemonade or ice cream soda. You're too young to drink liquor," Kurt told him.

"I don't see why. When we join the war, I'm going to enlist, so if I can be a soldier, why can't I drink?"

"We haven't joined the war yet, and you're too young to enlist anyway," Troy pointed out. "And Mom would be unhappy to hear you talk about drinking, as you well know."

Stuart slouched down in his chair, sticking his legs out comfortably and crossing them at the ankles. "Hey, did Kurt tell you that he's going to join the Lafayette Escadrille?" That was a squadron of American pilots who worked for the French. "Mom is going to have kittens, with you both going to France."

"Are you?" Troy asked Kurt.

"You know I've been keen on flying," Kurt replied. "And I keep reading in the papers about the Aces, like Chas. It's darned exciting! So why shouldn't I go? The French train you."

"How do feel about shooting down your cousins?" Troy asked him rather brutally.

"Only Guntram is in the air force now. I never liked him much anyway. He really enjoys killing things."

"They all went hunting. It was how they were raised," Troy pointed out.

"But Guntram was particularly sadistic. Always picked on me." Kurt looked away as if there were some unpleasant memories he was trying to suppress.

"I think it's kind of stupid that you'll be in a French uniform and Troy in a British one, when you're Americans," Eugene, the youngest, said.

"I expect that if the war drags on much longer, we *will* be putting on American uniforms," Troy said.

"Spending three months here in the summers, I feel as if we already *are* at war," Kurt said. "It involves friends. We know fellows who've been killed. Even Vivian Carrington. I want to help the Allies win. I'm not prepared to wait until Wilson finally gives in to popular pressure or loses the election. Besides, I hate Chemistry," he added with a grin.

"You've only had a year of it. Give it a chance," Troy said.

"Or switch to Economics, like me," Felix suggested. At twenty-one, he was going into his last year at Harvard.

"That's even more vile," Kurt said.

"What *do* you want to do?" Eugene asked him.

"Fly aeroplanes, of course, sonny."

Eugene kicked at him, saying, "Don't call me that!"

"Kiddo!"

"Skunk!"

"Tyke!"

"Fink!"

"Boys!" Troy admonished. "Enough already. And to think that anyone in his right mind would let Kurt be responsible for an aeroplane," he teased.

"Just for that, I won't give you a ride."

"Thank goodness!"

"Hey, if Victoria Wyndham, I mean Thornton can fly a bus, why shouldn't I be able to?"

"Because you're not as mature as she is. And unless you want to get a kick up the backside from Eleanor, you'd better watch the 'if a *mere* woman can do it so can I' attitude."

Ellie laughed. "If you need mending, just remember that we women can also stitch you up," she said to Kurt.

"OK. Sorry," he replied with an endearing grin. "Troy said that you were planning to go over next year, to work in a hospital in France. That's darned brave of you. And Zoë's going over now."

"We can all meet up there," Ellie said. "Won't that be strange?" She exchanged a warm glance with Troy.

"Hey, I'm not going to be left out," Stuart said. "I'll be eighteen by then. So just try to stop me!"

"I think you should join that new Professional Golfer's Association and win tournaments," Eugene said.

"He's not *that* good," Felix observed.

"I whupped your ass," Stuart said.

"Children, if you're going to be rude, you can eat your ice cream elsewhere," Troy remarked. "Ellie and I were trying to have a civilized conversation."

"Oooo. Interrupting the lovey-dovey stuff, are we?" Stuart said. "Come on you guys. I'll whup you in tennis, too."

"Sorry," Troy said when they went off, razzing each other.

"Don't be. I'm not easily shocked or offended. And I like your brothers." Suddenly serious, she said, "I have a terrible feeling that we may recall this moment, wishing that we could have it back."

He reached across the table and put his hand on hers. "Oh, I think we always wish that for special moments." His smile promised there would be many more. "But Stu still needs his ass kicked."

Ellie laughed.

On their way back to the boat, they were waylaid by a group of older teenaged girls.

"Oh, Troy! You must come to my party on Saturday," Rosie Miller said.

"Hello, Rosie. I'm sure you know Eleanor Carlyle," he said pointedly.

"Do I? Let me think... Do you have that cabin on Oohoo?"

"*Oh-you-who*," Ellie corrected. She knew full well that Rosie knew who she was. "Yes."

"Is it true that your mother works?" Rosie asked incredulously.

"It is indeed. She's a pharmacist."

"Fancy that," Rosie said, turning to her coterie of companions and rolling her eyes behind Ellie's back.

Ellie was aware and prepared to ignore the slight. But Troy also noticed, and she could feel him tense. "Eleanor is a doctor. She saved a boy's life last weekend," he told them.

"Golly! Then I expect she won't have time to come to our party." Rosie and her entourage flounced away giggling.

"Neither will I," Troy called after them, barely controlling his anger.

Ellie put her hand on his arm and said, "It doesn't matter. I wouldn't go anyway. I'm not fond of the *nouveau riche*. They're so pretentious."

"But that sort of attitude really galls me."

"I expect we'll see more of that here over the next years. I know that Augusta Wyndham – that's Zoë's grandmother – never really cared for our company. But while we were a relatively small community, the attitude generally was that we were all neighbours, no matter our social status. Certainly the rest of the Wyndhams and the others never treated us differently. The new cottagers may be trying to draw more distinct lines, but they don't have the status that we old-timers enjoy. They're all upstarts, no matter their wealth."

He grinned. "How many years does it take to become an old-timer?"

"At least fifteen," she said with mock seriousness. "But we'll make an exception in your case." Ellie took his proffered hand and said, "You're really sweet, but you should know that I'm rather snobbish myself. I feel quite contemptuous of frivolous girls who haven't anything more substantial in their heads than fashions and boyfriends."

Troy laughed. "I think I'm falling in love with you, Dr. Carlyle."

"Oh dear."

When they left in Troy's motorboat, he didn't head toward Ouhu, but around the Silly Isles and behind one of the larger, uninhabited islands. He stopped the boat in a secluded cove and said, "That was rather ominous, what you said earlier."

Ellie knew right away. "*Oh dear.*"

"Precisely. Is there someone else?"

She hesitated, and looked at him regretfully as she admitted, "Yes."

"Are you betrothed?"

"I would have told you if I were! Look, Troy, I'm sorry if I've given you the wrong impression. I like you and we've had fun, but..."

He stopped her with a kiss. "Will you write to me, Ellie?"

She was flustered, which was a novel experience. "Yes... Of course. But..."

He pulled her into his arms and gave her a lingering, seductive kiss, and then murmured against her cheek, "You know what they say... *All's fair in love and war.*"

Chapter 2

"So, Miss Wyndham, you're Canadian."

"Yes."

"What brought you to England?" Commanding Officer Pat Bosley-Smythe asked. In charge of the Women's Ambulance and Transport Service – WATS – she was a tall, large-boned woman in her late twenties with a determined expression, but a twinkle in her eye. She exuded tremendous energy, like someone who had happy control of her life. Ria thought that those who volunteered their services to an unconventional and dangerous occupation had to be committed and enthusiastic.

"My husband joined the RFC in 1914," Ria said rather proudly, and wondered that it mattered to her. She wanted to add that Chas was a highly decorated Ace, having won the DSO and a bar, as well as the MC. But one of the reasons she had reverted to her maiden name was so that she wasn't just the wife of the famous aviator, Chas Thornton. It was also because, at the moment, she no longer felt like Ria Thornton. That naïve and besotted young wife had existed in a fantasy world. "I came over when it appeared that the war was not about to end by Christmas."

"I trust you don't think that going to France will allow you to see your husband more frequently?" Major Bosley-Smythe eyed her intently.

"Not at all. He has his war to fight. I have mine," Ria assured her, staring back steadily without revealing anything.

"Home leave is two weeks every six months."

"I understand." Ria was still holding her gaze, as if engaged in subtle battle.

"The Women's Ambulance and Transport Service is a rather elite group, Mrs. Wyndham. We pride ourselves on our skills, courage, getting on with the job under severe and sometimes impossible conditions, all the while maintaining a sense of humour and decorum. We expect you to change a tyre and serve tea with equal élan."

"Are you concerned that we wild Colonials aren't up to the task?" Ria challenged.

"Why don't you tell me about yourself, Mrs. Wyndham?" the Major said patiently.

Ria knew what the Major was looking for. She'd been in England long enough to understand that class held more sway here than in Canada, and that the upper crust had a sense of entitlement, whether they had money to back them or not. But it was an easy game for her to play. "Je parle le français assez aisément. Ich spreche auch ein wenig Deutsch. And my Italian is passable. I've won swimming and canoe races, and tennis tournaments." With Chas. And with a stab of pain, memories of that last summer they had been at the lake flooded back.

"I ride, sail, drive cars and motorboats, and fly aeroplanes. I can also fix both automobile and aeroplane engines. I've hosted dinner parties and balls, and I play the piano." With wonderful expression, Chas had teased her that magical summer night at Wyndwood when she had been in disgrace and he had come to keep her company. And their relationship had grown beyond their usual flirtation.

"Before I left Canada, I turned my estate in Toronto into a convalescent hospital for soldiers. Since I've been in England, I've organized and run the Maple Leaf Club for Canadian soldiers at Thameshill, which is a manor house near Marlow." But Major Bosley-Smythe would not have approved of both officers and men being welcome there, even though the war was already blurring the lines between them. Her "well-bred" cousin Henry had been merely a private in the infantry, while her disinherited cousin, Jack, who had grown up desperately poor and had had to quit school at fourteen to support his family, was already a Captain in the RFC. "But since the processes and personnel are in place and everything is running efficiently, I'm no longer needed there. If you'd like references, you may contact my cousin, Beatrice, the Countess of Kirkland, my friends, Lady Meredith Powell and Lady Sidonie Dunston, Major and Mrs. Astor, the Board of Directors of the Maple Leaf Clubs, which includes Rudyard Kipling, Earl Grey, and Lord Milner. I'm also related to the Marquess of Abbotsford and the Earl of Leamington."

Ria was silently amused to note that the Major tried not to be impressed. And felt suddenly resentful that it was so important to have British connections, or otherwise be dismissed as a rough Colonial. One who was, nonetheless, prepared to fight and die for the great British Empire. So much unappreciated fodder. Although they were British subjects and carried British passports, Canadians were often snubbed. Ria thought that perhaps it was time for Canadians to have a distinct identity and voice.

"Jolly good! I must warn you, Mrs. Wyndham, that life in the WATS is harsh. Some of our recruits don't last more than a few weeks. Young women seem to think that just because they can drive the family motor, they can drive ambulances at the Front. It's gruelling, horrific, and often dangerous work. Not for the faint-hearted, or those unwilling to give up their creature comforts."

"Major Bosley-Smythe, I survived – barely – the sinking of the *Lusitania*. I lost my baby and several friends in that disaster. I need to take an active role. Sitting safely on the sidelines is not an option."

The Major softened toward her. "It seems you've done admirable work already. Do you really want to undergo more hardship?"

"I'm trying to make sense of this war. I have skills that can help."

"Are you really twenty-three? You look so young." Ria was only twenty, but knowing she'd be rejected because of her age, she had lied on her application.

Ria shrugged and said nonchalantly, "It must be the Canadian climate. I'm prepared to lend my Rolls-Royce Silver Ghost and to donate an ambulance." She had already investigated the cost, and decided she could easily afford the £500. Her father-in-law had given her $50,000 to set up a household in England, which amounted to £10,000. But as they lived with Cousin Bea, she hadn't used much of it, and had barely touched her own considerable wealth, since Chas had his generous allowance as well. His military income was negligible, although Chas was proud of actually having earned it. So he contributed that to the Maple Leaf Club.

"That's extremely generous of you, Mrs. Wyndham! Would your husband approve?"

"The car is mine." A wedding present from Chas. "With the current petrol restrictions here, it will be put to much better use at the Front."

"Jolly good! I expect you know that this Corps is run along military lines. We've certainly had no lack of press. Partly because we're in the public eye and have already been criticized for doing things that women are not supposed to, we have certain standards to maintain. Anyone who doesn't abide by the rules is sent back.

"We have several convoys, most of them with the Belgian army. They have embraced our help, but unfortunately the British and the Red Cross haven't, until recently. They think that women, other than nurses, have no place in the arena of war. You may find there is some hostility towards us. It's why we have to be more efficient, dedicated, and fearless than the men who feel threatened by our presence.

"Don't bother bringing civilian clothes as you'll be in uniform at all times, and we don't allow jewellery. Much too dangerous to wear rings while working."

Ria wondered why she was still wearing hers. "Of course."

"And we don't tolerate smoking in public. You may, of course, smoke in private. WATS may interact with officers during their time off, but always with a companion in the evenings. There's to be no suggestion that we are lacking in morals. We don't encourage fraternization with regular soldiers."

"My husband is a Captain."

"Well then, Trooper Wyndham, allow me to welcome you to the WATS. Now let's talk about practicalities. We have a training program. You say you have mechanical experience. Can you vulcanize tyres and rebuild an engine?"

"Yes. And I've done the St. John Ambulance First Aid training."

"You'll need some signalling and stretcher-bearing instruction, but I expect you'll be ready to go in a few weeks. I think I'll send you to the 3rd Unit in Calais, with the British. I expect that you can impress them with your Colonial charm. You have an extraordinary smile, Wyndham. Don't be afraid to use it." The Major flashed her own. "Here's where you order your uniform," She handed Ria a note. "Our billets can be bitterly cold, so bring warm things for yourself. We also enjoy ourselves, so you might care to bring tennis equipment and a bathing costume. In addition to our membership fee, we have a weekly charge of 10 shillings towards communal supplies. I trust that won't be a problem?"

"Not at all."

"Good. Then I shall see you in France, Wyndham. By the way, the girls call me 'Boss'."

.   .   .

The WATS uniform was a khaki tunic, with a red cross badge on each sleeve, over a split skirt, the hem exactly ten inches from the ground, white shirt and red tie, high leather boots or puttees with ankle boots, and a soft beret-like cap. For mechanical work there were also breeches, smocks, and overalls.

Ria ordered three uniforms. Although some could be bought off the rack, she had hers tailor-made. They would be ready in a week.

When she arrived back at Cousin Bea's London townhouse laden with a dozen shirts, short and tall leather boots, and warm woolen undergarments, she was surprised and annoyed to see Jack there.

Cousin Bea, who had come to London to provide moral support and advice, had returned the previous day to her country estate, Bovington Abbey, when Ria had asked her if she could be alone. Either Cousin Bea hadn't passed the message along to Jack, or he had chosen to ignore it.

"I thought you'd be staying at Bovington for a while," she said pointedly to Jack.

"It's a bit dull without you. I came to London for some nightlife."

"Then I shall go elsewhere until your leave is up."

"Ria..." He tried to pull her into his arms for a comforting embrace, but she was reminded of how intimate they had become before she had fallen in love with Chas. She was suddenly back in the summer of 1914 when Jack had aroused her with kisses and caresses.

"*Don't* touch me, Jack!" She drew away from him sharply, as if his hands had singed her.

"I just don't like to see you so hurt...."

"You came up to see Sid, didn't you? You're having an affair with her. Don't deny it! What about Ellie?" She practically spat at him as she said, "How can I believe anything you say? You're all liars and cheats. That's why you men stick together!"

She swept up the stairs and into her bedroom, where she pulled out one of the suitcases that Bea had brought her. She had more than a week before her training was to start, and knew exactly where she would go first. To Ireland to visit her baby's grave.

.   .   .

Jack felt his arm growing numb, and he could really use a smoke, but he didn't want to disturb Sid, who had nodded off in his arms. She would awaken soon in any case, and he would be obliged to leave. For the sake of propriety, she never allowed him to stay overnight, although the servants undoubtedly knew what was going on. And would gossip.

He had been disconcerted that Ria had guessed.

Lady Sidonie was the widow of Chas Thornton's friend, Percy, eldest son of Montreal shipping magnate Sir Montague and his censorious wife, Lady Margaret Dunston. Sid and Percy had been married only a year before he had been killed at the Front. She was beautiful and spirited, but was herself looking for someone wealthy, so Jack's relationship with her would never be more than a few snatched hours of pleasure.

He briefly entertained the thought that Ria might become available again. There had definitely been a spark between them, as even their grandmother had noticed, thereby arranging her will to discourage their marriage. But Ria had tumbled for Chas, so Jack had changed his strategy.

And now Ria had left Chas. Divorce might be growing in popularity, especially among the upper classes, but it was still scandalous. Not that that would stop Ria at all. If she never forgave Chas, she might yet be seduced by her charming cousin. With her respectable fortune, Jack could build his empire.

Except that Ria was as angry with him as with Chas. Hell, did she expect that he should have prevented Chas from having the affair with the French girl? It had happened before Jack had even realized she existed. And would it have made a difference then if he'd kept Chas from seeing her? Once Chas had fucked her, he'd jeopardized his relationship with Ria. So did it really matter that the affair had lasted until Chas had found out that Ria was very pregnant, and had urged her to come to England? He'd been a changed man since losing their child and almost losing her in the *Lusitania* disaster. But Ria felt betrayed.

So it was back to Jack's plan to marry Chas's sister, Felicity, once she was old enough. She wrote to him regularly, earnestly but with a hint of flirtatiousness. She sent him photos, too, of herself and his youngest sister, Claire, not quite brazen enough to send one of just herself. As if she were his sweetheart. It was unfortunate that Fliss didn't have the surprising and stunning beauty of her brothers. She looked very much like her mother, the kind of girl one might generously call handsome. Of course the fortune that she would come with made her infinitely more appealing.

Although Jack did consider Chas his best friend, he had no qualms about regarding Fliss as an asset. He liked her well enough, but could never love her. He would be kind to her and see that she was happily settled into a social life that would help him get ahead and promote his interests. He was sure that her father, J.D., had not married for love either, but for money and connections. J.D. recognized Jack's potential, and was willing to take him into the business when the war was over.

Jack had a sudden and sharp longing for Ellie. She had invaded his being so that she was never far from his thoughts, much as he might try to deny his enchantment with her. He wouldn't admit that it was love. That had no place in his schemes, unless it came attached to wealth. And Ellie, the doctor, would never have that, or even aspire to it.

So he couldn't really understand his obsession with her. He was amused to think of these three very different, very beautiful women who attracted him. Ria, with her blonde fragility that belied a steely will and adorable audacity. Clever, crusading Ellie, with her pre-Raphaelite sensuality. And Sid, the dark-haired seductress who was uninhibited and fun-loving. And so well connected.

Sid stirred and smiled sleepily at him. "If you were rich, I could wake up in your arms every morning. What a delectable thought."

"You mean you wouldn't insist upon having your own bedroom?" he asked with a chuckle, for he knew that she had with Percy.

"Not at first. Only when you became tedious or neglectful. But money is such a bore, or at least the lack of it."

Sid's aristocratic family was barely hanging onto an immense Elizabethan estate, Blackthorn, which she had a passion to restore and preserve. Percy had left her very comfortably off, but the trust fund would end with her death or remarriage. The only thing she owned outright was this substantial London townhouse.

"Which I intend to remedy," Jack assured her.

"Max thinks that if you don't get blown to bits, you'll be a force to be reckoned with one day." She was referring to Sir Max Aitken.

Jack was flattered that Sir Max had taken notice of him. They had met at one of Sid's parties and had discussed the effects of tariffs on business and imperialism. "I'd like to take some lessons from him."

"I expect he recognizes a kindred, ruthless spirit," she said, looking askance at him. "And when you're as fabulously wealthy as he is, you may rescue me from the tedium of widowhood."

"You wouldn't mind being married to someone ruthless?" he quipped.

"You know I like dangerous men," she said, rolling on top of him.

The thunder of distant explosions seemed to punctuate her statement.

"An air raid!" Sid cried with glee. She turned out the lights and went to the window, drawing back the blackout curtains, which were now mandatory. "Oh look, there's a Zepp to the north, heading our way."

The graceful, silvery behemoth was pinned in the beams of dozens of searchlights. Anti-aircraft fire burst around it like holiday fireworks. As if in celebratory greeting. Even though it appeared to be on the outskirts of London, they could hear the whine of shells and the cacophony of explosions.

"Oooh, there are a few more in the distance. They've just been spotted by the lights." And began dropping their bombs.

"We should go to a shelter, or at least your cellar," Jack suggested half-heartedly.

"Don't be absurd, darling. The basement is the servants' domain. This is the only excitement I get. I really can understand why you men *want* to go to the Front. There's something deliciously stimulating, almost erotic, about danger. It makes you realize that you're alive."

"Aren't you worried about your reputation – if we should be killed and they find our naked bodies?" Jack teased as he draped her silk peignoir around her shoulders.

"I don't give a damn! Let the sanctimonious prudes realize that I lived and loved and had more fun than they did." She kissed him passionately.

More seriously, she said, "I do worry about you, Jack. And Chas. Aren't you afraid your luck will run out?"

Jack and Chas were both Flight Commanders, each with five other pilots under his command. "I expect that Chas is going to be made Commanding Officer of his own squadron soon. And COs are not supposed to fly over enemy lines except on special missions."

"Do you get scared?"

"Oh I get the wind up, of course. A man who doesn't is a fool. A bit of fear helps to keep you focused and alert."

"I've just had a brilliant idea! Do you have your sketchbook with you?"

"Always."

"Then let me show it to Max. You've done some remarkable drawings and watercolours of life at the Front, and you know he's head of Canadian War Records. Part of what he's doing is recording the events at the Front. I'm sure I could talk him into taking you on as an artist or in some other capacity. You'd still be doing war work, but essentially away from the front lines."

Jack was concerned that his luck would run out. He'd seen too many of his colleagues die. New pilots, still inadequately trained, were lucky to last three weeks at the Front. The fighting was becoming fiercer all the time, and the Germans were constantly finding new ways of outdoing them. Right now the Allies had the upper hand in the air, but Jack knew that the Germans would soon come up with something – a more powerful new aeroplane or aggressive tactics – to reverse the advantage again.

He had every intention of surviving this war intact, and Sid's plan was perfect. There was a feeling of contempt among the men at the front lines for those doing safe desk jobs. But like Chas, he had already demonstrated his courage and skill, having been injured in a crash, downed six enemy aircraft – which made him an Ace – and won a Military Cross. So he'd paid his dues in the past two years. If he worked for Sir Max Aitken and proved himself worthy, then who knew what possibilities lay ahead for his career. He was sure he could impress Aitken with his financial acumen.

Jack had joined the RFC in large part to be seen as a loyal friend to Chas, in the hope that when they returned from the war, he would be accepted by the Thorntons, not only into the business, but as an equal. And as a husband for Fliss. But their shared experiences had bound them as nothing else could have. Chas had saved Jack's life, for which Chas had received his DSO. Jack had never had a closer or truer friend. So there was no need to feel they had to stick together for the duration. Their lives were irrevocably entwined.

"You're as brilliant as you are beautiful," Jack said, nuzzling Sid's neck as he stood behind her with his arms about her waist.

"What idle flattery," she retorted with a laugh. "But I adore it. Oh, look! It's been hit!"

The Zeppelin had been twisting in different directions, as if it were impaled on the beams of light and writhing to free itself. Suddenly it burst into flames, its nose drooping down, fire scrambling up the sides until it was completely ablaze and plummeting toward the ground.

"Poor bloody buggers," Jack couldn't help saying. Fire was the aviators' worst fear. Having seen his newly-discovered cousin –

Chas's Oxford friend, Cedric – roasted alive in an aeroplane crash, Jack and Chas always took along their revolvers when flying. Just in case.

The Zepp was exploding as well, from the ammunition on board. The city was like a stage suddenly illuminated, and they could see people out in the streets. Cheering.

The other Zeppelins must have turned back or headed elsewhere, since they were no longer in view.

"They didn't get very close," Sid said, as if disappointed the Zeppelins hadn't dropped bombs around her house.

Jack found himself perturbed and annoyed by that blasé civilian attitude that some espoused – that war was a fun diversion for a while.

He couldn't help thinking about the aircrew who had just been doing their duty for their country, as he did, and who perhaps had wives and mothers and children awaiting them back home.

His ardour dampened, he knew it was time to leave.

.   .   .

Ria wasn't happy booking into the Randolph in Oxford because it reminded her too sharply of when she and Chas had stayed there last year. But it was a comfortable hotel, and she would be here for only one night.

Although her grandparents lived in Oxford, Alice Lambton attended a boarding school on the outskirts of the city. Her British relatives didn't really know her, so she was closer to Ria, Chas, Beatrice and the others than to her own family. Her father had sent her to England ostensibly to be "properly" educated after her mother had died, but in reality because he had remarried and not wanted her around.

Ria fumed whenever she thought about how careless and indifferent so many were with their children. Granted precious moments of their parents' time from self-indulgent and frivolous social schedules, raised mostly by nannies and tutors, sent off to boarding schools while impossibly young, they must surely feel neglected, even insignificant. Ria had been horrified when Rudyard Kipling had told her about his own childhood. Born in India, he was six and his sister only three when their parents had shipped them off to England to be looked after by strangers, who had treated them quite cruelly for six years, after which Rudyard had been sent to boarding school. For some people, children seemed to be just an inconvenient byproduct of marriage. If she were able to have children, she would cherish them and revel in their company. Being a welcome member of her Uncle Richard and Aunt Olivia's large brood revealed how warm and loving families could be. She had never had more than censure from her own father.

Ria and Alice had become friends aboard the *Lusitania*, and Alice had saved Ria's life. Ria shuddered to think that she had been scooped out of the Irish Sea like the corpses that had become a gruesome haul for the trawler, and piled on top of them on the ship's deck. If Alice hadn't recognized her and insisted she was still alive, she would have been left to perish there, amongst the dead.

For Ria, who had no siblings, Alice had become a little sister. So it was with some trepidation and enormous sadness that Ria went to visit Alice at her school.

Surprised and delighted, Alice threw herself into Ria's embrace. "Oh this *is* a treat! Why didn't you say you were coming, Ria?" Alice was suddenly concerned. "Is something wrong?" She had the uncanny ability to almost read Ria's thoughts.

"Your headmistress has given me permission to take you out to tea." Ria took Alice's hand as they walked to the car.

"Oh dear, I have a feeling you're going to tell me something dreadful. Chas hasn't been wounded has he?" she asked tentatively, fearful to even think the worst. "Or Jack?" The others, as far as she knew, should be safe at the moment.

"No. Nothing like that."

Alice breathed an audible sigh of relief. "Then this is a glorious day indeed!"

Ria thought that Alice was older than her fourteen years. No doubt her experiences in the past couple of years had contributed to that.

Over tea Ria quizzed Alice about school.

"I like most of my classes well enough. Well, not mathematics so much. I don't even mind Latin, although most of the girls hate it, and the Classics Master is very comical. He's as ancient as the Parthenon, and seems completely bored by his subject. He drones on for twenty minutes and then sits down in his chair and promptly falls asleep." She giggled. "He even snores. It's just after lunch, so I suppose he should be having a nap, like my grandfather does. He leaves us translations to do, of course, but today, because it was so lovely and the windows were wide open and one of the girls had smuggled in cigarettes, most of them climbed out the windows and smoked in the shrubbery below. They were back at their desks by the time the Master awoke."

"Are you miserable there?" Ria asked astutely.

"Oh no," Alice countered, not wanting to worry her. "Of course I'd rather be at a day school, like I was in Ottawa, and come home in the evenings. Although my grandparents are rather... old and a bit vague."

"You know that Bovington Abbey always eagerly awaits your holiday visits. And when you're finished school, I expect you'll be going home again."

Alice felt uneasy. "Something's bothering you, Ria. Will you tell me?"

"I don't want you to think that I'm deserting you, Alice." At that moment she wanted nothing more than to take Alice to Canada with her. But her house in Toronto was a convalescent hospital for the duration of the war, and it would be too late in the year to go to the cottage. And she had no jurisdiction over Alice. "I'm going to France with the WATS. Leaving in a couple of weeks. I won't be back for at least six months."

Alice's jaw dropped. "But why?" she squeaked. "You have so much work to do at the Club."

"They manage quite well without me. I need to do this, Alice. For myself. For Reggie."

"Surely Chas doesn't approve."

"It's not for him to decide what I do," Ria said firmly.

"Oh dear. I think you've had a row." Alice put her hand on Ria's. "It's terribly dangerous over there, Ria. I've read about the WATS in the newspapers. I expect it seems rather adventuresome and patriotic and even glamorous, and I'm sure I'd like to go as well, but I would hope that a friend would talk me out of it, because I can't really see subjecting myself to all that hardship and peril when I can quite adequately contribute to the war effort at home by organizing truly useful things and raising pots of money for good causes."

Ria was amused and deeply moved by Alice's earnest attempt to dissuade her. She squeezed Alice's hand. "I will write to you regularly, my dearest friend. And you must promise to keep me informed of what's happening here."

"No, Ria! Must you go?"

Ria felt her anguish. Alice had lost not only her mother, but also several of their friends in the past few years. "Yes. I think that if I don't see what's really happening over there, then I will

never again understand Chas or any of them. What they're
experiencing is alienating them from the rest of us."

Alice nodded reluctantly. "I expect that you're right. But how I
wish you didn't have to go!" She appealed to Ria with her large,
tawny eyes, tears sparkling on her lashes.

"Write to me at the headquarters of the WATS in London and
they'll forward the mail to me. Billets change and units move to
new locations. Address your letters to 'Victoria Wyndham'. I don't
want to be thought of as the wife of a famous Ace."

Alice regarded her shrewdly. "Is that really the reason?
Something *has* happened, hasn't it?"

"Yes to the first question, and nothing-that-you-need-to-worry-
about in response to the second," Ria said with forced brightness.

"I'll get it out of Chas, you know," Alice pronounced
confidently.

It was an emotional leave-taking.

When Alice was back in school, she sat down and penned a
letter.

Dear Chas,

*I hope that you are being careful. I worry about you and the
others. Of course I'm awfully proud of you. The girls here don't
believe that I'm a friend of two celebrated Aces, especially you, since
you are second only to Albert Ball. They don't believe that I know
Rudyard Kipling either. I mentioned that this week when we read
his poem 'If...' in class. Isn't it just ripping? Do you think that if I
show Mr. Kipling my poems that he will give me some literary
advice?*

*Anyway, I don't really mind that the girls don't want to be
friendly, but I do hate being called a liar. One girl said that if The
Countess of Kirkland really were my cousin, then I wouldn't be at
this school but some place more swish. I've told them that she's not
my real cousin, but I call her that because she's my friend, and I
can't just call her Bea because she's almost as old as my
grandmother and Lady Beatrice is too formal. They think that just
because I like to write stories, I make everything up.*

*I'm actually surprised at how narrow-minded so many of them
are. I'm odd because I'm a Colonial with a ridiculous accent –
which I will never try to change! They even tell me that my French
is absurd. I learned it from my first nanny, who was French-
Canadian and hardly spoke any English, but perhaps she would be
considered a peasant here. The girls are very attuned to accents,
and peg people accordingly, so they all try to modify their speech as*

some come from various parts of London and others from Manchester or Yorkshire or wherever. I think their big goal is to all sound the same by the time they graduate, which is to say, more swank than they really are. It's so that they can find themselves Oxford or Cambridge men to marry. Not that many of them want to attend university themselves. Although I think I should like to.

Anyway, I don't want you to think that my life here is terrible. My friend from last year, Mary, didn't return because her father was killed at the Somme and her mother doesn't have the funds to send her back. But I do have a few new friends. Moira is from Ireland, and Dorothy, from Rhodesia – they have 'funny' accents too. And there's Kate, whose mother is a doctor – which makes her weird – and her father was killed at Ypres. She's the smartest girl in the school, and wants to be a doctor, too. She devotes herself to her studies, and doesn't mind what the others think of her or how they tease her. I'm proud to be her friend, and told her all about Blake's sister, Ellie, even though I haven't met her yet.

But my very best friends are still all of you, which also makes my life more interesting. If only you were all safe!!!

And now I have to worry about Ria as well! She was just here, telling me that she has joined the WATS and is going to France soon! I think that something terrible has happened to her, because I saw despondency in her eyes, like when she lost the baby. But she didn't lose another one, did she, because I thought the doctor said she couldn't have more children because of the infection?

She said there was nothing wrong, but she's not a good liar. So I'm terribly afraid that the two of you must have had a misunderstanding. But how is that possible when you've been back in France for six months? I can't bear for you two not to be happy....

And Alice couldn't bear to tell Chas that Ria was calling herself Victoria Wyndham. Surely that was ominous.

Ria meanwhile had left a message for Henry, arranging to meet him in the lobby of her hotel. A student of medieval history at the university, he was wearing his gown, which made the absence of his left arm seem insignificant. Even his scarred face was healing and looked less like the trenches now. "Let's go for a walk," she suggested.

As they wandered towards the River Cherwell, she told him about her plans.

Henry shook his head, "I shouldn't be surprised, but I do think this is your craziest scheme yet."

She couldn't help but smile. Henry had always been straight-laced and proper and critical of many of her activities, like visiting neighbours at the cottage in her bare feet. But as the eldest of her cousins, he had felt somewhat responsible for her, she'd discovered, which had touched and amused her, so she never really minded – or heeded – his rebukes. "Even crazier than flying, and fixing engines?" she teased.

"Marginally. I can't believe that Chas is letting you do this. It's deuced dangerous!"

"It has nothing to do with Chas."

"He's your husband."

"He doesn't own me!" She hadn't meant to be so vehement.

"Hmm. It sounds to me as if you two have had a spat and you're trying to get back at him."

"That would be childish."

"Precisely."

"I'm doing this because I need to. This war is a curse and a challenge for our generation. I want to be a part of it."

"That sounds selfish. This isn't a game you're missing out on. You also need to be a support for Chas. Do you know how tough and dangerous his job is? He doesn't need the added worry about your safety. He needs to know that you will be waiting to welcome him to the 'home fires' and give him some comfort and stability in his stressful life. The reason our lads are over there is to protect women and children and our way of life. The least you can do is to help to preserve that."

Ria felt herself close to tears now, but she said almost flippantly, "You're right, I *am* being selfish." She figured that Henry didn't know about Chas, and for some odd reason didn't want him to. Could it be that she didn't want Henry to think badly of Chas? But that didn't make sense, because she herself almost hated him at this moment. Was it because Chas's affair reflected badly on her, the pathetic wife? Although she hadn't been his wife then, only engaged to him. Perhaps it was because she knew that Henry was a very moral and righteous person, and didn't want to upset his sensibilities. She had never told him about her baby either. In fact, very few of their family and friends had known that she was pregnant.

Henry shook his head again. "I don't think I'll ever understand you, Ria. But I'll still worry about you."

• • •

Sid took Jack to Max Aitken's London pad, a lavish suite at the Hyde Park Hotel.

"So, Captain Wyndham, Lady Sidonie tells me that you are something of an artist."

"Not as a career," Jack was quick to point out. "It's merely a pastime I enjoy."

Max Aitken flipped through Jack's sketchbook and said, "But you *are* talented. Look at this, Sidonie," he said, holding one out to her. It depicted crumbling buildings threatening to slide into a huge bomb crater in some village, while soldiers and artillery mingled with refugees, their carts mounded precariously with their few belongings. "Brilliant! And this one." It showed a squadron of Nieuports taking off against a threatening sky. "What *are* your ambitions, Captain Wyndham?"

Aitken stared shrewdly at Jack, who, at six feet tall, towered over him. But Aitken had an aura of tremendous energy, like a champion racehorse chomping at the bit, which gave him a larger presence than his physical self. And he was the most powerful and influential Canadian in London. As well as being in charge of War Records, he was the official "Canadian Eyewitness", meaning that he was responsible for reporting news from the Front. A Conservative member of the British Parliament, Aitken was also the representative of Sir Sam Hughes – Canada's Minister of Militia – at Allied headquarters in France and the War Office in London.

Jack replied, "To become a millionaire. Like you."

Aitken threw back his head and laughed delightedly.

Jack added, "Otherwise Lady Sidonie won't marry me."

Aitken laughed even harder. When he'd stopped and wiped his eyes, he said, "You're a hard woman, Sidonie."

"Just a realist," she replied with a shrug. "But I also have faith in Jack. He has the same rapacious ambition as you, Max."

That had him in stitches again.

"You could certainly be an asset to me, Captain Wyndham. A decorated flying Ace, a celebrated hero with the sensibilities of an artist. A handsome, strapping Canadian who can hold his own in British society, and who has a sense of humour. That makes damned good press in itself. Didn't I hear that you're Lady Beatrice Kirkland's cousin?"

"That's right."

"We've met through Churchill. Admirable lady. Yes, I think you'll do just fine." He paused. "I had to convince the Canadian government that it was important to document this war. Did you know that there's not a single photograph of the Second Battle of Ypres, where our boys had their baptism by fire? Where the Germans first unleashed that deadly gas and our boys held the line despite everything?" He shook his big, shaggy head. "But we're not about to let that happen again. So it's my job to compile records and eyewitness reports to capture events for posterity. I have photographers and cinematographers going to the front lines to capture the action. But I've been thinking that art is the only true way to immortalize the entire picture – the emotional as well as the visual. You'll be just the chap to paint us some pictures of aerial battles, as well as doing more of these sketches, which I can use for our press communiqués. But I could also use you to fly the media crews low enough and close enough to the trenches to get some good footage and photos. You'll still be near the front lines occasionally, but not in as much danger, I should think." He threw a knowing glance at Sid. "So your colleagues can't accuse you of swinging the lead with some safe desk job at HQ."

"Thank you, Sir. It's a most intriguing offer. If it means that I don't have to give up my RFC uniform, then I'd be delighted to accept."

"I'll see that you're seconded to the staff at Canadian HQ as an RFC pilot. And the Canadian War Records Office will make use of your services from there."

"Max, you'll be the first warrior to have your own pilot-chauffeur," Sid said with a chuckle.

Aitken preened at her reference to him as a "warrior". He had the honorary title – which didn't include a salary – of Lieutenant-Colonel in the Canadian forces. His large mouth broke into a captivating smile.

"Yes, indeed! Are you both free to come to Cherkley Court this weekend?" That was Aitken's country house in Surrey.

"I am, of course, darling Max, and Jack has a few more days of leave, haven't you?"

"I'm due back on Monday."

"You won't be there for long. But keep it under your hat for now, Captain, when you rejoin your squadron. By all means shoot down a few more Huns, but watch your back. I rather fancy having my own pilot. Sidonie, tell Quentin to come down to Cherkley as well, if he's free." Quentin, Viscount Grenville, eldest son of the Earl of Bisham, was Sid's beloved older brother and the heir to the crumbling Elizabethan pile that she so treasured. He had been honorably wounded at the Front and invalided into a staff position in London. "And Wyndham, is your friend Thornton on leave?" Jack realized he had already graduated to the more informal "Wyndham".

"Not yet."

"Ask that pretty young wife of his to come along anyway. The Kiplings will be there, and they're very fond of her. She's your cousin, isn't she?"

"Yes. I think she's visiting friends, but I'll certainly pass the invitation along if she's back in time."

When they left, Jack said to Sid, "I know what you see in Aitken. He's quite charming, but he also radiates power and energy. You come away feeling happy to hang onto his coat-tails, knowing that he's going places."

Sid laughed. "People seem to either love him or hate him. But to those he likes, he's very loyal and generous. He's helped Quentin by giving him sound financial advice and including him in some lucrative scheme of which I have no inkling. I know Max has had an uphill battle to be accepted into society here. Some are rather scornful of Colonials, I'm afraid, no matter their accomplishments. Not I, of course, having married one. I think you're all wonderfully refreshing! Crackling with energy – sexual and otherwise," she said, leaning against him provocatively. "So I admire Max tremendously for having done so well, and yet remaining his own person."

"I expect that he would be a good friend to have."

"Especially if you're on your own way up," Sid said astutely. "Now tell me what Ria's up to. I sense something's afoot."

"It's not something I feel at liberty to discuss."

"Ooooh. Even more intriguing! Is she having an affair?"

"Sid! She loves Chas."

"Don't be naïve, Jack. Bored, neglected wife. Wants a bit of fun and romance. It happens all the time, especially with so many hungry young officers available."

"Well, you're quite wrong there. She's angry with me at the moment, so we're not exactly on speaking terms. I have no idea where she is."

"What did you do?"

"Well, that's the damnedest thing, really. I did nothing. Except be careless."

"And let something slip. So it's Chas who's having a fling?"

"Does everything come down to sex with you?" he asked with amused irritation, wishing she would drop the subject. He didn't want to be the cause for any more blame from Ria.

"Or money. Yes. I told you I'm a realist."

"You'll have to talk to Ria yourself. Now I have a favour to ask. Would you teach me to drive? I do think it's absurd that I can fly an aeroplane but not drive a car."

Sid laughed. "Of course, darling! Despite the fact that you're keeping secrets from me."

"Friends need to be loyal."

"Quite so. I'll be sure to let Ria know that you tried, when I grill her. Shall we start your lessons right now?"

.   .   .

"If you tell me that it's insignificant and that I should just forgive him, then I shall leave," Ria said, clasping her hands to still her shaking. Haltingly, she had just told her friends, Lady Meredith Powell and Theadora Prescott, about finding the letter from Chas that she wasn't supposed to open until after his death. It was to have gone for safekeeping to his lawyer, but had fallen out of Jack's pocket. The letter had tried to explain and apologize for his affair. And the illegitimate child.

They were in the sitting room of Meredith's London townhouse. Theadora sprang up and went to Ria's side, putting her arm about her shoulder. "You poor dear! No one expects you to accept that and just move on as if nothing had happened. Good God, I know how much this must hurt."

Ria barely controlled her impulse to weep. "May I stay here for few days? Jack is at Cousin Bea's, and I don't want to see him."

"Of course," Meredith said. "Stay as long as you like. You can go down to my father's place by the sea near Cardiff, if you want a change of scene. He's in London. I'd offer my own place in Wales, but since Humphrey and I are getting a divorce, it wouldn't be appropriate."

"Are you?" Ria was surprised, although Meredith had told them on the *Lusitania* that hers had been a marriage of convenience.

"Oh it's very amicable. We're both rather relieved really."

"I'm only going to be in London for a few more weeks." Ria told them about joining the WATS.

"What about the Club?" Meredith asked. It was she who had instigated the Maple Leaf Clubs and asked Ria to organize and administer the Thameshill one. They were places where Canadian soldiers of all ranks could have a comfortable bed, hot baths, and good food for a nominal sum. At Thameshill they could also canoe, fish, swim, golf, bicycle, or just rest.

"You know that Mr. Grayson runs it perfectly well without my assistance." Grayson was Ria's butler.

"He's a gem," Meredith admitted. "Well I admire your mettle. It's the sort of thing I wouldn't mind doing myself, if I weren't involved in some exciting work for the Ministry. We're creating women's units with the various forces. They won't be right at the front lines, of course, but just think how many men can be freed up for fighting if women do the clerical work, manage kitchens, drive generals, fix engines, run dispatches and so forth. I'm not saying it's going to be completely safe mind you, since bombs are being dropped behind the lines on supply depots."

"It's not as if women aren't already doing their bit, working in munitions and other factories. Chauffeuring the brass is probably much safer and certainly more fun than stuffing explosives into shells," Ria said.

"I expect this will be more helpful to women's suffrage than chaining ourselves to fences," Meredith observed wryly. She had been an active suffragette before the war, and had even spent time in prison for setting fire to a letterbox. "It just takes men to start killing each other by the millions for them to realize that women can do more than stay at home having children and serving tea. Perhaps *some* good will come out of this brutal war."

"I am definitely going to do a story about you and the WATS," Theadora said to Ria. An American freelance journalist with independent means, Thea was now the editor of *Home Fires*, the newsmagazine that Meredith published. Both women were in their late twenties, and had become best friends since their shared experiences on the *Lusitania*, Thea claiming that Meredith had saved her life. "I have press permission to travel to France. Once you're settled into the job, I'll come over."

"As long as I can remain anonymous."

"Going into hiding, are you?" Meredith asked.

"I need time to think."

.   .   .

Jack and Sidonie arrived at Cherkley Court just before tea on Friday, with Jack driving Sid's car most of the way. It had rained earlier in the day, but the bedewed lawns now sparkled in the shafts of sunlight that had broken through the fleeing clouds.

"Isn't it the ugliest house you've ever seen?" Sid asked.

"I think it's rather imposing." They had come upon it at the end of a mile-long drive through majestic beeches and maples. Squatting large and white, with bulging bays and a battalion of balustrades, substantial and solid, it flaunted itself and was hard to ignore. Much like Aitken himself.

Sid practically snorted. "It's an architectural abomination! Can't make up its mind whether it's a French chateau, Italianate villa, or Victorian Gothic monument to bad taste and the crass ambitions of the *nouveau riche.*"

"You are cruel, Sid."

"Just observant, darling. Anyway, I didn't mean Max. He didn't build the place, just bought it. Mostly for the view, I think. It does have lovely grounds."

"It's a spectacular view," Jack said appreciatively, gazing out over the valley that spread bountifully beyond the cascade of terraces sweeping down from the house.

"You'll have to paint that for Max. He'll be tickled pink."

"Yes indeed."

Their host embraced them warmly, as if they were lifelong friends. They found Lady Aitken most welcoming. Jack had already met the Kiplings through Ria's involvement with the Maple Leaf Club, and they had been frequent visitors to the Canadian hospital at Cliveden, where he and Chas had spent some time recovering from their injuries last summer. Jack was thrilled to be in the company of the famous author of those enthralling stories he had so loved to read in his youth. How sad it was that the Kiplings had lost their only son in the Battle of Loos last year.

Sid's brother, Quentin, arrived in time for dinner, as did a few other young acquaintances of Max, but with no political guests this weekend, it was a casual and relaxed atmosphere. The younger crowd danced after dinner, while the Aitkens and Kiplings played bridge.

Although the house had thirty bedrooms, Jack and Sid's rooms were relatively close. They spent most of the night together, Jack leaving Sid's room just before dawn. Instead of returning to his own bed, he went out to catch the morning light, which flooded the valley below the house, promising a glorious day. He had the painting almost finished by the time Sidonie found him. They didn't see their host until lunch, at which time Jack presented him with the finished work.

"Splendid! You've got it just right, Wyndham." Aitken's face split into a huge grin. During the repast, he told the others about his latest project, the Canadian War Memorials Fund. "I'm going to hire artists to roam the front lines and capture the Canadians' experiences and deeds. I think that art is the only effective way to enshrine those images for posterity. Captain Wyndham is one of my first recruits."

"Cracking good idea," Quentin said. "But don't you have faith in the new technologies of film and photography? Surely there's an immediacy there that puts the viewer right into the frame, so to speak."

"They have their place, of course, for just that reason. And to give an accurate account of details. But it's not enough. What they can't evoke as effectively is emotion. Consider the watercolour that Wyndham did this morning. It conveys more than the sum of its parts – like a good merger," he added with a cackle. "It stirs something in the soul."

"Jack is admittedly a good artist," Quentin said. "I expect it will be a relief to be out of danger."

"He'll still be at the front lines, brute!" Sidonie chided.

"I didn't mean to infer that there was anything cowardly about Jack's new position," Quentin said. "Everybody knows that the RFC is the most dangerous job in the forces. They hemmorhage pilots. You're damned lucky and skilled to have survived this long, Jack."

"You do have a charming way of putting things today, Quentin," his sister observed drily. "Jack's going back in two days. Have you been indulging in Max's wine cellar or is that what happens to intelligent men when they work for the War Office?"

"Paperwork *can* be rather deadly," Quentin riposted, smiling indulgently at his sister.

"Fortunately, you can't draw anything more exciting than a stick person, so you're stuck in London." She grinned back at him.

"Which can be jolly dangerous," one of the young guests opined. "Were any of you there when the Zepps came over last weekend?"

"They didn't get very close to London," Sid said dismissively. "Although I hear there were thirteen of them. What a sight that would have made!"

"You're dippy, Sidonie! I would have been petrified! Fortunately, I was in Devon for the weekend," one of the young women said.

"It just shows how well prepared we are to deal with the Hun invading our home territory," someone else declared. "I heard it was an aeroplane pilot who downed the Zepp, and that he's going to be awarded a VC. What do you think about that, Captain Wyndham?"

"Well deserved, I'd say. I know how difficult it is to shoot down Zeppelins. A bit easier now that we have incendiary missiles."

"Seems to me we've had more casualties in London from our own Archie than from hostile bombs," Quentin pointed out, referring to the anti-aircraft fire.

"Surely not!" someone protested.

"How exciting to think that those fireworks are actually dangerous to the very people they're supposed to protect," Sid said.

"You *are* mad, Sidonie!"

"Just fond of irony," she chuckled.

.   .   .

As they sauntered to the tennis court, Sid whispered to Jack, "Max doesn't like to lose."

"Neither do I," he riposted.

But as it turned out, Jack was partnered with Lady Aitken, and Sid, with Max, so Jack didn't have to decide if he should play his best or let his host win. His hostess was as determined as her husband to win. Jack wondered if that had been done deliberately to test his true skill.

And he played brilliantly. It was a close match, but he and Lady Aitken won.

"You're a damn fine player, Wyndham," Aitken said, his face screwed into a scowl.

"Chas Thornton taught me. He was considering Wimbledon after Oxford."

"Then you've been well taught." The fact that Jack's mentor was a world-class player cheered Aitken.

They had tea in the Italian garden, and then a rousing game of croquet. Champagne and cocktails were served on the terrace.

Max said, "Come for a walk, Wyndham, while the ladies dress for dinner."

"You seem to think we need absolute ages to make ourselves presentable, Max," Sid complained.

"I just appreciate all the effort you ladies exert to dazzle us with your elegance. The beauty, of course, is natural."

"And flattery never fails. So I shall go and luxuriate in a tub."

"Isn't this just a glorious view?" Max asked Jack with pride as they strolled along. "Not New Brunswick, mind you, but about the best spot in the British Isles if you ask me. You did it justice, and I'm most appreciative of the painting." He paused. "So, you're Augusta Wyndham's grandson."

It was more a statement than a question. "Yes, although we didn't know each other until 1914." Jack had already decided how to play this. Aitken liked to talk about his "humble beginnings" in New Brunswick, but he had not experienced the desperate poverty that Jack had, for Max's father had been a Presbyterian minister, albeit with nine children.

"My father was disowned when he married my mother. Being an actress from Montreal, she wasn't deemed an adequate match. My father wasn't trained for anything, although he fancied himself an artist. It didn't pay much and we grew up destitute. Often hungry."

"And Augusta refused to help."

"Even when my father was dying from consumption. She didn't even know that we – my sisters and I – existed. So I introduced myself to her that summer." When he had been a waiter at The Grand Muskoka Hotel.

"And demanded your fair dues?" Aitken asked with mirth.

"Told her I was a hard worker and determined to get ahead, so I offered to work for the family."

"And will you? Work for the family?"

"Not in the mills, which is where my uncles intend to put me. I'm interested in finance. Stocks and bonds. Real estate. I've made some successful investments already."

"So you want to be a protégé of J.D., do you?" Aitken said astutely. "Capitalizing on your friendship with Chas Thornton, so to speak." He chuckled at his witticism.

"I've done some work for J.D. here in England, so he's offered to take me on after the war."

"Capable fellow, J.D." It was a noncommittal observation. Having been an immensely successful bond salesmen in Canada before coming to England, the young Aitken would have known J.D., and probably done business with him. "Did Augusta leave you anything in her will?"

"A fairly substantial sum, but it's to be doled out to me over ten years."

"Ha! Didn't completely trust you with her money."

"I think she didn't want to make things too easy for me. Wanted me to prove myself, work my way up, like my grandfather had."

"But you have some money to invest?"

"I'll have more coming due in January."

"How would you like to buy into my rather lucrative bond-selling syndicate?"

Max seemed impressed by Jack's questions as they discussed details. Jack said, "I'll have $1500 available in the new year, which I could invest." He received $2000 a year from his inheritance, but he wanted to keep some of it to give his family and for other investments of his own.

"It's a start." Max lit a cigarette, after offering Jack one. "You know the problem with the British? They drift along on a tide of privilege. And you know what happens to a tide? It eventually goes out. A cleaning lady at Whitehall once berated me for not being a gentleman, because true gentlemen never show their faces before 11:00 AM. It's preposterous! You can't run a country, and certainly not a business or a war, with that sort of lackadaisical attitude, that deluded conceit and smugness. I've witnessed it at the Front as well – inept generals, the lack of organization for supplies and troop movements. It's maddening! Criminal!

"They need clever, dynamic, visionary chaps like you and me, Jack. It's up to us to wake them up, shake them out of their damned complacency, and drag them into the 20th century. And if we can't be kings, we can at least be king-makers."

Addressed by his first name now, Jack knew he had impressed, and been accepted by one of the most ambitious and capable men in Britain.

.   .   .

Ria had used most of her petrol allowance for the month, so she left her car in London and took the train to Marlow, walking the two miles to Bovington Abbey.

She hadn't seen Jack before he returned to France, and wasn't looking forward to seeing Justin. She was still angry with him for his part in the conspiracy of silence.

She also hadn't visited Sidonie because Sid was first and foremost Chas's friend, and Ria figured that she would receive short shrift from Sid, who was too casual about sex. Sid would probably tell her that affairs were *de rigueur* in society, and that she should just have one herself.

It was a gentle, sunny day, and Ria enjoyed her walk along the narrow country lane overhung with summer-lush trees. But she was poignantly reminded of last Christmas Eve when she, Chas, Henry, Jack, Justin, and Blake had walked back from the church in Marlow in the softly falling snow. They had indulged in a snowball fight, amid much laughter, and had arrived at Bovington wet but exultant. If only they could all go back to that innocent moment.

Justin's face lit with a warm and compassionate smile when she arrived at Bovington. "How are you, Ria?" he asked solicitously.

"I don't want to talk to you, Justin," she replied coldly.

She started to go past him but he grabbed her arm and said, "Then *listen* to me."

She was surprised by his intensity. Justin had always been so gentle and easygoing.

"You know that I would never hurt you, Ria. But sometimes one is caught in an impossible situation, and there is no easy answer. I interfered once because I thought it would help you, and will forever regret that. If I hadn't written to tell Chas about the baby, you and Vivian wouldn't have been on the *Lusitania*. But I had wanted to spare you the scandal and disgrace of giving birth to a bastard." He used the harsh word deliberately to make her see what an untenable position she had been in, and why he had wanted to help. But how much better it would have been if she had stayed in Canada and had the baby, which would probably have lived. Always ready to flout the rules, she would have been perfectly capable of handling the social censure. And his beloved sister, Vivian, would still be with them.

His frustration was evident as he said, "Chas swore me to secrecy. And if I had persuaded him to tell you the truth, you would have been just as hurt as you are now. And that's the last thing that any of us wanted, Ria." He noticed that she had softened a bit, and wished he could take her into his arms and ease her pain. But surely that would be too dangerous.

He thought that she didn't realize he was in love with her, although her grandmother had wanted them to marry, knowing they enjoyed each other's company and thinking that he would be a steadying influence on her. And he had promised Augusta

Wyndham that he would look after Ria, no matter what happened. He regarded her ruefully as he said, "I'll go up to London, if you'd prefer not to have me around. I'm having my Medical Board next week anyway, and expect I'll be pronounced fit for duty."

"No, I'm only staying the night. I leave for France on Monday." Her expression was defiant.

Justin knew there was no dissuading her. Lady Beatrice had already told him of Ria's intention to join the WATS. "I'm sorry you feel the need to do something so drastic. But if you ever need help, you know how to get in touch with me," he said, and walked away before he revealed his own despair.

Ria was surprised that he hadn't questioned, argued, protested, or cajoled. He would have once. Of course she knew it had been unfair to take her rage out on Justin just because he had been here when she'd read the letter, and had tried to state Chas's case.

So although she still felt let down, she was also angry with herself for rebuffing his help, practically repudiating his friendship. She wanted to scream or throw something, but instead, decided on a punishing ride, being careful not to overtax Calypso. He was a wonderful horse, and had been an extravagant present from Chas before he'd left Canada. And Chas had persuaded his brother, Rafe, to bring Calypso to England at Christmas. So the horse had twice been a cherished gift.

She finally ended up at Thameshill, and informed Grayson of her plans.

"Yes, of course we will manage, Mrs. Thornton. Forgive me for speaking out of turn, but I'm concerned for your safety," Grayson said. Having known her all her life, he had developed a fatherly affection for her. But he was still her butler, and careful not to overstep his bounds. "I've read about the WATS, and the ladies do admirable work. But there is a large element of danger."

"Who's to say that a Zeppelin won't drop a bomb on us in London, or even here? You and I have already experienced some of the horrors of this war." Grayson and his wife had been aboard the *Lusitania* as well. His wife's body was never recovered, and he would forever bear the scars of his ordeal, both physical and mental. "We can't hide from it. We see it in the broken bodies of the men in the hospital, and the frightened eyes of the boys at the Club who know they soon have to return to some indescribable hell. I need to use my skills, to feel that I'm doing my bit in every possible way."

"You've done more than most already. But you always were the adventuresome one, Miss Victoria," he said fondly, slipping into his old form of address. "You *will* be careful?"

"Of course! You mustn't be concerned. I will keep in touch, and you must let me know how things are going with the Club."

He seemed pleased that she wanted him to write to her. "By all means."

When Ria returned to Bovington, Cousin Bea handed her two letters, saying, "This is the one that came for you two weeks ago." Beatrice had told Ria about it when she'd called from London, but Ria had asked her not to bother forwarding it. "And this one arrived today."

The sight of the familiar handwriting, slightly flamboyant, made her eyes prickle with tears. She went to her room and opened the first letter reluctantly, for it would seem as if Chas were there, talking to her.

My Darling Ria,

I can't even begin to express how deeply sorry I am and how much it hurts me to know that I have caused you such pain. You're right that it was cowardly of me not to tell you, to let you discover the truth in such a shocking way.

There never seemed to be a good time. At first you were so frail and wounded and mourning our son's death. Then we were so happy together that I wanted nothing to jeopardize that, just to leave that mistake behind me, pretend it had never happened.

Of course it shouldn't have happened in the first place. I was thinking only of my immediate needs at the time. But I never meant to hurt you, my darling. I was shocked by the gruesome deaths of my friends, in a funk, convinced that I was soon to join them and would never see you again. I was grasping at pleasure to make me forget, to make me feel that I was still alive. I've since seen many more men die, and am hardened to the slaughter. A sad commentary on this life, isn't it? I need you more than ever to give me hope and to keep all this craziness from making me lose faith in humanity.

I am not like my father, as you suggested in your letter. I don't need or want any woman but you. My parents have a marriage of convenience. We would never be like them.

Nor am I like your father, wanting sons to carry on his dynasty. We can be happy together, just you and I, if you'll give me another chance. I don't want to live without you.

Do you remember we once talked about different kinds of love? It was that evening when you were in disgrace for running away, and alone at the cottage while the rest of us were enjoying ourselves at the Oakleys'. I came round because I realized, when I didn't see you at the event – a play by Oscar Wilde, I think – that the evening would hold little pleasure for me. I was already falling in love with you. Or more correctly, realizing that I had been in love with you for a long time. We had hot cocoa and I sang love songs to you at the piano. I – pompously, probably – said that there were different kinds of love. And I realize now that that is true.

At first my love for you was selfish, physical, centered more on my need for you as an adorable, adoring, and available young woman. Hoping to give you pleasure, impress you, make myself indispensable to you. When I went so brashly off to war – to slay dragons – I was the knight, impressing my lady-love, but still thinking too much about myself.

But after almost losing you on the Lusitania, I realized that my love for you ran much deeper than even I had expected. So when I pledged myself to you at our marriage, I meant it with all my heart and soul. I haven't betrayed you, Ria. I and my love for you have matured.

Please find it in your heart to forgive me. I want us to sit on those two chairs on the dock when we are old and wrinkled, comfortably, abidingly in love. Two halves of a whole.

I ache for you, my darling. Your loving Chas

My Darling Ria,

I miss you, dream of you, long to hold you in my arms again, to taste your lips, hear your laughter, run my fingers through your silken hair, lose myself in your beautiful eyes.

And I would be happy merely to have a letter from you. Ecstatic if you were to forgive me, or even just say that you will try.

Alice tells me that you have joined the WATS and will be going to France. Please, my darling, don't put yourself into danger. If you must punish me, don't do it by harming yourself. Your silence is torture enough.

I should be able to get leave by the beginning of October. Please wait for me, Ria. I want to show you how much I love you, how desperately I need you.

Life is empty and meaningless without you. Your loving Chas

When Ria didn't come down for dinner, Beatrice went to her room. Curled up on her bed, hugging herself, Ria had obviously been crying for a long time. Bea sat down beside her and stroked her back, completely at a loss for words. It was no good telling someone who was grieving that they would get over it, that things wouldn't seem so bad in time. Bea's cousin and Ria's grandmother, Augusta, would have told her to buck up and get on with things. Bea, who had never had children, found herself with a bevy of young people who had come to seem like her own, all of them already damaged by this war. She didn't have the heart to be stern and judgmental. Although she had been content and often happy in her marriage, she had never had the kind of love that Ria and Chas shared. But she could empathize, and lamented this rift between them.

"Will you join us for dinner?" Beatrice asked.

Ria shook her head. "I'm not hungry."

"I'll send up a tray, in case you change your mind."

"Do you think I can ever feel the same about Chas again, Cousin Bea?"

"I think that you still do in the way that truly counts. You love him. In the first flush of passionate, romantic love, it's too easy to be blind to reality and think that you will forever be afloat on a sea of euphoria. But life isn't like that, and love has to be strong enough to survive difficult times. You have to accept that Chas isn't perfect, that you've both made mistakes and will continue to make them – hopefully not the same ones.

"When I first met Chas I found him a delightful boy to whom things came easily. Handsome, athletic, charismatic, impeccable manners, with an immense fortune behind him, he'd had a charmed and carefree life. When I saw him at your bedside in Ireland – when that fool of a doctor had pretty well given up on you – Chas was a changed man. That was perhaps the first time in his life when money and privilege weren't going to help. He was terrified of losing you. He spoke to you constantly while he was sponging you to bring down the fever."

Bea recalled how poignant it had been, watching Chas minister to Ria when she had been unconscious and close to death, all the while reminding her of good times they had shared. "We have to build up your strength, my darling, so that we can defend our title in the canoe race at the Regatta next summer. And we'll change the rules of the tennis tournament so that you and I can be a team again. We're unbeatable, Ria. Remember that. Remember that we have good Karma. You must be strong, my darling. You have to fight. I know you can survive this. Think about the cottage, about those mornings at the Shimmering Sands. We'll still do those, even when we're old and grey. We'll take a picnic breakfast – croissants and café-au-lait, remember? – and watch the mist run across the lake as the sun tries to catch it. Please don't give up, Ria. I need you."

It seemed to Bea that it had been the sheer power of his love that had pulled Ria through. She said, "I believe his love for you is much deeper now than when he had the affair. I truly believe that Chas won't do that again."

"I wish *I* could believe that. I wish I could trust him. I wish I could forgive him. But I don't feel it in my heart."

"Give it time, my dear," Bea said, patting Ria's shoulder.

"What if we don't have time? Sometimes I'm so scared! If something happens to Chas, how will I live without him? How will I ever forgive myself? And yet, right now I can't live with him either." She started crying again, and Bea didn't know what to say.

"Dear God, but this is a frightful situation!" Bea said later to Justin, before they went to join the others in the dining room. As part of her war work, she hosted Canadian officers on leave or during their transition from hospitals back to the Front, some staying with her for many weeks, even months.

"I don't suppose there is anything that I can do," Justin said disconsolately. "I seem to have become *persona non grata*."

"You're a bit of a whipping boy, I'm afraid." Bea knew that Justin was enamoured with Ria and had already advised him to move on. She smiled reassuringly at him. "She'll get over that once she has a chance to think straight, so don't take it too much to heart. She still needs your friendship, hard as that may be on you, dear boy."

"Not at all." He would do anything to make Ria happy.

She didn't join them for breakfast the next morning, although Bea was glad to see that Ria at least ate something from the tray that had been sent up. She hadn't touched the dinner one.

She came down with bags packed, and Justin offered to drive her to the station in Bea's car. She looked into his warm hazel eyes and saw the friend of her youth with whom she had once been infatuated and who, although three years older and already a lawyer, had always treated her as an intelligent equal. It was obvious that he still cared for her. She almost burst into tears.

"Thank you," she managed to say.

Having resolved to be supportive and treat her like he would his younger sister, Lydia, Justin said, during the short drive, "Be sure to take lots of warm things along. Conditions can be quite brutal. I've seen some of the WATS in fur coats, so your mink won't come amiss. Things like jam and cocoa, even Bovril are luxuries, so take lots with you. Do you know where you're going to be stationed?"

Ria hesitated. "No"

He sensed the lie, but didn't press her. "You can always write to me and let me know. Perhaps I can visit you when I have local leave. It's too bad you won't see Zoë. I hear she's arriving Friday."

It was heart wrenching to think that she was missing her beloved cousin by a matter of days, but she had no choice now. She was part of the war machine. "Give her my love. You can tell her what happened. I don't think I could."

Justin gripped the steering wheel tightly. She sounded so disconsolate. So unlike her usual exuberant self. He worried that in her fragile state she might be careless of her safety. "I know that you can do this, Ria, and I'm proud of you, even if it terrifies me to think of you in situations and conditions that you can't even imagine. Take good care, my friend. We have a lifetime of memories still to make in our Muskoka."

She looked out the window and hastily brushed away tears.

At the station, they stood awkwardly together as the train arrived. Ria turned to Justin and was suddenly overcome by the fear that she might never see him again. She hugged him impulsively, tightly, saying, "You take care as well."

As the train pulled away, she shouted out the window, "I'll be in Calais. But don't tell Chas."

Chapter 3

"Make yourself useful and grab that rope," a young woman barked at Ria. She dropped her bags and helped the three women secure the guy ropes on a tent that the ripping wind threatened to snatch away. They struggled against the willingness of the flapping canvas to take wing, but finally managed to tie it down. A fox terrier was rushing about as if trying to help snag the ropes.

"Blasted wind!" the young woman said, turning her back against the stinging sand that was whipped up. "I shall never get used to it. Grit embedded in my teeth and eyes and pores. Sybil Fox," she added, extending her hand to Ria and giving her a firm shake. "Foxy. And you must be Wyndham. Boss told us about you. What do say girls? I think she should be 'Windy'."

Ria was puzzled as one of the others said, "Righto. Came on a blast of wind as well, didn't she? Lucinda Ashby-Grey. Cinders. I don't answer to Lucy or Cinderella. Just so you know."

"And I'm Carly Stratton. Always have been, although I was christened Caroline," the other one said.

"Carly's father started a motor works just so she could live up to her name," Lucinda Ashby-Grey said drolly.

"Stratton Motors," Ria said in recognition.

"Righto. Absolutely nuts about cars is Carly. Even won a Ladies' race at Brooklands – that's a motor racing circuit in Surrey. Her brother's a race car driver as well."

"And this yappy little fellow is Boots," Carly said, giving him an affectionate rub on the head. "He helps to keep the mice and rats out of our tent."

"But unfortunately not the earwigs," Lucinda bemoaned.

"Seems you're mucking in with us, Windy, so let's get out of this sandstorm and show you your Royal suite, courtesy of the King," Sybil Fox said, leading her into the bell tent. "Ex-Indian army surplus, and better suited there than this perishing place with gales constantly howling off the Channel. That's your cot over there. Hope you brought a nice warm fleabag. The army ones aren't much to write home about."

It was a Spartan space with an oil stove in the middle, some ropes strung up for hanging uniforms and towels, crates as bedside tables with oil lamps and framed photos on them, and trunks that seemed to serve as dressing tables with pitchers and basins for washing, and pins and hair brushes lying about.

"Not exactly the Ritz, is it?" Lucinda said. They all seemed to be waiting for Ria to burst into tears or run screaming from the tent.

If Ria wanted to cry, it was not because of these minimal living arrangements, but because she was exhausted from the journey, and because she realized that she was now truly committed to this job. And another step further from Chas. Steeling herself, she said, "I'm not fond of the Ritz, actually. Reminds me too much of the *Lusitania*," She hadn't intended to reveal anything about herself. At least, not yet. But she would not allow these women to make her feel inadequate or intimidated. Everyone knew that the term "windy" referred to soldiers who were apprehensive, though not necessarily cowardly. Although it was a logical nickname for Wyndham, it also had this rather unflattering connotation.

The others seemed a bit shame-faced as Carly said, "Boss told us that you were on board. Did you... lose anyone?"

"Yes." But Ria didn't elaborate.

After a long pause, Carly said, "Do let me give you a hand with your trunk."

Carly was a pretty girl with mahogany hair looped back and a fringe across her brow, which accentuated her large brown eyes. She had a cheerful smile as she – and Boots – accompanied Ria back to her car.

The WATS camp was outside Calais, nestled in the sand dunes overlooking the English Channel. The dunes seemed to flow and change under the capricious sculpting of the wind. Beyond them, a broad silvery beach stretched away in both directions, with steep cliffs and headlands visible to the west and a busy harbour to the east.

There were several more tents, a large canvas hut – the mess Carly explained as they walked by – with an iron shed behind it, which was the cookhouse. A few bent and stunted pines gave a bit of shelter there.

Carly said, "The Red Cross promised us proper barracks. I expect you saw that the office is finished, and the mess will be soon, and we should be able to move into our 'posh' new accommodations before the snow flies." Workmen were hammering away at an L-shaped building. "It's rather fitting that German prisoners are doing the construction. There's a Prisoner of War camp near Marquise, and the Royal Engineers are supervising this project, so it should be fine. We don't acknowledge them. The Germans, I mean."

Lining the road into the camp were nearly two dozen ambulances of various makes, as well as a lorry and a couple of motorcycles. Behind them was a workshop shed.

"Ah, a Silver Ghost! Jolly nice. Electric starter, I'll wager," Carly said appreciatively.

"Yes."

"It's the only one then. We have to hand crank the others. Oh, it'll be a shame to convert this into an ambulance!"

"I'm only lending it, so it will be kept as a staff car and to drive medical personnel around, fetch supplies, and so forth. I have an ambulance coming as well."

"That's topping then! What do you call her? The car. We have names for each of our beasts."

"Dragonfly," Ria said automatically.

"I brought Nessie," Carly said of a Stratton that was now an ambulance. The back seats had been replaced by fittings for stretchers with a canvas box overtop, the roof extending over the front seats. Red crosses were prominent on all sides, and "WATS" was painted on the hood.

"They don't have windscreens," Ria observed.

"Oh no. Yours will have to be removed as well. We can't have any light reflecting from them and attracting enemy fire. Or injuring us if the glass breaks. It can get jolly dangerous around here." They each grabbed an end of Ria's trunk as Carly said, "You've missed supper, but we'll scrounge something from the kitchen. I expect you must be famished."

Ria didn't feel hungry these days. Sometimes she was positively nauseated by the thought or smell of food. It was as if her insides had knotted up and refused sustenance. All she'd had today was a very early breakfast of a boiled egg, half a slice of toast, and tea, and a chocolate bar on the drive. "Not really."

"We may have a busy night, so you need something to keep your engine ticking over. ComRad – that's what we call the Commandant, Fanny Radstone – asked me to show you the ropes for a few days. Some of us were working for the Belgians before we were sent here in January. You can't imagine how cold it was then. I'm dashed glad we won't be spending another winter in the tents."

When they'd deposited the trunk at the foot of Ria's cot, she opened it and took out some of the food she had brought. There were biscuits and cheese, which she thought would be as much as she could manage at the moment, and which she offered to share with her roommates. She also brought out cocoa and sugar.

"Oh, and you have Bovril. Let me make some for you," Carly offered.

"You're all welcome to some," Ria said.

"I'll have cocoa. With lots of blessed sugar," Lucinda yelled after Carly who rushed off to the kitchen for hot water. "What other treasures do you have hidden in there?" she added as Ria took out cookies and bottles of jam.

"Strawberry! Black current! Not a sign of the ubiquitous army apple-and-plum. How heavenly," Lucinda enthused. "Peppermint humbugs and caramel kisses! You are my new best chum, Windy."

"Cinders has a sweet tooth," Sybil said drily. "Feed her cakes and candies and she's as devoted as a hound. Ah, a bottle of very fine cognac. And a whack of cigarettes. You certainly know how to make friends, Windy."

Ria passed her both, and took a cigarette for herself.

"I smell goodies," a willowy, pretty girl said, entering the tent.

"Windy, this is Lady Antonia Upton – Tuppy – whose parents go by the name of Netherton, Lord and Lady, which is what the ruling class does just to confuse all us commoners. Tuppy can sniff out treats for miles. Always finds the best *patisserie* in town, although you wouldn't know it to look at her. And here comes Betty Haydon-Wicks. Hayrick we call her, but not because she resembles one."

Betty had coarse and wild straw-coloured hair that refused to be tamed. She grabbed a pillow and tossed it at Sybil.

"And Baby. Winifred Turville. 'Baby' because she lied and is only twenty-one, and so *by far* the youngest."

"Hogwash! You and Carly are only twenty-two, and Carly's been here for well over a year. It's all rather silly, really," Baby complained. "They changed the age requirement from twenty-one to twenty-three in January, just before I joined up. What's the sense of that?"

"To keep out all you immature youngsters, of course," Sybil teased.

"I think it's because we're working for the British now, and the Red Cross VADs have to be twenty-three," Carly said. "Have to play the rules, don't you know. Or at least be seen to comply."

"Well, we haven't ratted on her, so she's still here," Sybil said to Ria. "And never far away when there's mention of food."

"I'm a growing girl."

"You may have aspirations to grow some more, Baby, but the reality is that you will forever be a little person," Sybil told her. "Cute, but short. So unless you intend to grow sideways, you should leave the sweets for those of us who have more statuesque frames to sustain."

"You're batty, Foxy."

Henrietta Maltby – Hennie – blustered in, carrying mugs. Carly followed with a kettle of hot water. "Black clouds rolling in. Pray for rain," Henrietta said in a singsong voice as she helped dish out Bovril.

"It means that there won't be any bombing raids," Carly explained to Ria. "The Boche prefer moonlit nights."

The young women, none over twenty-five, sat around on the beds and plied Ria with questions, when all she really wanted was to lie down for a rest.

She had stayed overnight in Folkestone, but could barely sleep for the excitement and trepidation of going to France. She had realized on her crossing to Ireland a few weeks earlier, with some surprise, that she was no longer terrified of being on the sea. As she had gazed into the dark and busy waters of the Channel, where U-boats were a constant threat, she thought she would even welcome death.

On board she had met several distraught parents and anxious young women. One of them had asked her if she'd also received a dreaded telegram summoning her to her husband's bedside. Ria had felt a shiver of fear then. She knew that those cables only went to the families of severely wounded men who were not expected to survive. For those who couldn't afford the passage, the Red Cross helped out. But often these pitiable families arrived too late.

She had landed at Boulogne before, but then she had been with Chas and Jack, and they had boarded a train for Paris. This time she'd had to negotiate the Rolls through the congestion of army lorries and tenders, drafts of silent, grim soldiers returning from leave, the brash, tidy first-timers, and the exuberant, dirty ones going home for a brief respite. Some of the men, noticing her in khaki, had saluted or blown her kisses. All had had a smile for her.

Boulogne was a bustling military base, with supply depots and camps that sprouted a variety of tents and huts and sheds on the outskirts. Makeshift hospitals of canvas and wood were strung along the coast to Calais.

It was a dramatically beautiful coastline, Ria thought, with breathtaking vistas suddenly appearing at the top of challenging hills, the mostly treeless terrain undulating for miles in all directions or dropping precipitously into the sea. But there were also stretches of cemeteries, astonishing fields of wooden crosses like a gruesome crop. This enormity of death had somewhat unnerved her, for she knew that these were just a few of the thousands of cemeteries sprinkled about the French and Belgian countrysides. The detritus of war, like empty shell casings.

Ria had noticed several plain wooden coffins being carried by uniformed men to waiting graves, and heard the haunting lament of The Last Post.

And she had driven through her tears then, thinking how vulnerable they all were. Her cousins and friends. Chas. She didn't want any more of them buried here, so far away from all that they had loved and those who loved them. She would find out where Archie Spencer was buried and make a pilgrimage to his grave, she suddenly decided. Someone should be there, just to give him some connection to home.

She had been almost run off the road when she'd encountered another vehicle, and had forgotten to drive on the right, which was backwards from England.

She'd been given excellent directions by London HQ, and had had no difficulty finding the WATS camp, fortunately this side of Calais so that she didn't even have to go into the town. Some of the women had been washing or fixing their ambulances when she'd arrived, and had directed her to the office.

Commandant Fanny Radstone was in her early thirties and, like Pat Bosley-Smythe, had been with the Corps since before the war. She had a long, serious face and large hands. She had told Ria that her ambulance was almost ready for delivery, and that Boss would bring it over from England. In the meantime, she needed to learn the routes and routines.

"I say, I *do* like your hair," Betty Haydon-Wicks now said to Ria, bringing her out of her reverie.

The others laughed. "You like everyone's hair but your own," Sybil Fox pointed out.

"But Windy's is particularly fetching. Perhaps I should cut my hair short."

"Would you dare?" Antonia Upton asked. "My mother thinks I'm already most unlady-like. She'd disown me if I cut my hair."

Ria laughed. It was absurd to think that these intrepid young women doing "men's work" should be concerned about what people thought of their hair.

As if reading her thoughts, Carly Stratton said, "It's rather ridiculous to worry about that. Short hair seems so much more practical. I, for one, am tired of not being able to keep mine properly clean."

"And free of lice," Sybil stated. "I'm all for cutting mine off. Shall we find ourselves a hair salon in town next time we're there?"

"Yes, let's! And we'll take Windy along to show them how we want it done," Carly said.

"Does your husband like it short?" Lucinda Ashby-Grey said.

"Yes." Ria rummaged in her trunk to avoid meeting anyone's eyes. Trying to change the subject, she said, "I cut it because it's easier to wear my leather helmet for flying."

There was a moment of stunned silence. "You can fly an aeroplane?" Carly said with awe.

"Yes."

"I take back what I was thinking about you," Sybil said with a guffaw. "You are no butterfly chauffeuse. That's what we call the girls who think this is a great lark, but run home to Mummy after the first week or two. So tell us what it's like to fly!"

They listened with glowing faces to Ria's descriptions.

"I would love to do that!" Carly said eagerly.

"*Après la guerre*," Sybil said.

"Is your husband a pilot?" Betty Haydon-Wicks asked.

"Yes."

"So is my brother, Eddie," Carly said. "I wonder if they know each other. What's his name?"

Ria groaned inwardly. She hesitated only a moment before she said, "Charles," which was true, of course, though surely no one had called him that since his christening.

"Is his aerodrome nearby?"

"No. He's been involved in the Somme."

"Oh." They'd had enormous casualties come through from the Somme for months now, so they were suddenly subdued. Only ten days ago the Prime Minister's eldest son, Raymond Asquith, had been killed in a new Allied offensive at the Somme.

"Do you have a photo of him?" Sybil asked.

"Oh yes, do let's have a gander at him!" Henrietta Maltby said. She was a rather large girl who moved awkwardly, but bubbled with enthusiasm.

Ria had lost everything on the *Lusitania*, of course, but Zoë had sent her copies of all the photos Ria loved most, especially of Wyndwood. She had brought a few with her, and now showed them, with great reluctance, the one that Zoë had taken of her and Chas that magical evening when he had treated her to a romantic, intimate dinner aboard the Thornton's yacht, and had given her the engagement ring. It was her favourite photo of the two of them – she, leaning her head towards him, her arm wrapped around his, laughing at something he'd said, and he, looking lovingly down at her.

"Wow, he's a knock-out!" Henrietta said.

"Peachy!"

"You *are* a lucky girl."

"There's something familiar about him," Sybil said.

"Probably the man of your dreams," Carly jested.

"You should both have stayed in Canada and be making beautiful little babies now," Lucinda said.

"Cinders, really!" Betty Haydon-Wicks chided.

"Well, it would be a terrible waste if they didn't."

Ria had to bite her lip.

Carly noticed her distress and said, "Now girls, Windy looks dead beat, so we should let her rest a bit before the fun begins."

"Righto! Come on girls," Lucinda Ashby-Grey said. "Let's retire to the mess. We should practice our routines anyway. I expect that you have some talents other than flying, Windy. We put on shows for the chaps occasionally."

It was now completely dark and the lamps had been lit. When the others had departed, Ria lay down on her cot. She had left all her jewellery behind save for her RFC wings necklace, which Chas had given her last Christmas, and her wedding band, which she wore on a chain around her neck. Her engagement ring, which had saved her life in the *Lusitania* disaster by alerting the sailors to her presence, was too large to have brought along.

She held her wedding ring as she gazed at the photo, and couldn't suppress her tears.

.   .   .

Ria struggled to emerge from her dream. She was swimming at the Shimmering Sands and Chas was sitting on the beach, urging her to come back. She was shivering and longed to be with him, but icy waves kept sweeping her farther into the lake.

She woke with a start, realizing that someone was shaking her. She was chilled, and could feel the dampness of rain.

"Sorry, Windy, but a train's coming in," Carly told her. "You'll want your coat. And don't forget your tin hat. In case there's an air raid." This was the steel helmet that they and the soldiers now wore when in action.

They doused the lights before going out into the stinging, gusting rain. With the wind whipping off the Channel, it felt colder than England, and it was only late September.

Ria cranked Nessie's engine, which was strenuous work, and then hopped in beside Boots, who sat in the middle as if to attention, obviously used to the routine. "Does he always travel with you?" Ria asked with amusement.

"Can't leave him behind, although it's really against the rules. Clever little blighter makes himself scarce when he senses someone who's likely to disapprove of his presence. But he's so small that he doesn't interfere – we often have sitting cases in the front if the back is filled. Then Boots crawls under the seat. He's good company when I'm returning alone late at night."

The phalanx of ambulances crept into the road.

"What about your headlights?" Ria asked. They had only small sidelights burning.

"Oh no. We can't have lights on. Can't let the Boche know where we are. And they couldn't see the red crosses on our roofs in the dark."

"But you said they wouldn't be flying in the rain."

"Regulations."

"Bloody hell!"

Carly laughed and said, "Absolutely. But don't let ComRad or Boss hear you talking like that, or you'll end up cleaning the latrines for a month. *Always remember that we are ladies, if unconventional and feisty ones,*" Carly quoted in a pretty good imitation of Boss.

Once they were on the main road to Calais, Ria was amazed at how quickly they drove through the thick darkness.

"ComRad always leads. We think she's a bat, because she seems to be able to see in the dark. Some of the girls call her ComBat."

Ria felt somewhat panicked as they pushed relentlessly through the molasses of the night, the rain blowing at them across the bonnet and dashboard.

"Is Boss often here?" she asked, trying to take her mind off the harrowing drive.

"She regularly makes the rounds of all the units, but also spends time in England raising money and recruiting and trying to land new jobs for us. It was a great achievement for her to finally convince the army and the British Red Cross to accept our services here in Calais. Unpaid, of course, which puts the Red Cross's male drivers' backs up, since they *are* paid and think that they're losing jobs because of us. The sad reality is that there's too much work for us all. Anyway, she managed to keep us as an independent corps, but we do get army rations, which are better than what we're usually able to scrounge. She's very plucky, is Boss. Never takes 'no' for an answer and doesn't hesitate to use influential friends. But I think her favourite thing is still driving, which she does whenever she can. Now do watch this railroad crossing. Trains come barreling out of the tunnel, but there are French sentries monitoring it, so be on the lookout for them.

"Sometimes it takes hours for the trains to actually roll in," Carly informed her when they arrived at the station. "They always have to give way to troop trains going *toward* the war. That's the first priority you see, not the sick and wounded who are now useless as far as the army's concerned," she added snidely. "Fortunately the canteen's open tonight, so we can at least warm ourselves with a cup of tea."

Although they weren't supposed to smoke in public, Ria noticed that most of the girls, including ComRad, puffed on a cigarette. Ria mentioned it to Carly. "We don't smoke when there are officers visiting or when we're trying to make an impression. But at other times, no one really notices or cares. We WATS already have a rather brazen reputation anyway."

They had several cigarettes with their tea as Carly filled Ria in on some of the details of life as a WATS.

"Gird your loins. Here they come," Carly said, as a train pulled into the station. Ria could see her drawing herself up to face whatever horrors were about to erupt from it. "I'm never quite prepared for all the misery."

They returned to the ambulance and awaited their turn to accept cases. When Carly had backed up to the train, orderlies slid four stretchers into the racks and said, "35 General."

"You'll soon get to know the locations of all the hospitals," Carly told Ria. "I'll show you tomorrow. At least we're not transporting Blighties. I hate going to the pier, but it's worst of all on a rainy night. You'll see why when you have to do it."

But Ria thought that driving through the liquid darkness wasn't easy either. It was like swimming underwater at night.

"Hello, lads. We'll be as gentle as we can," Carly told her occupants. Their heads were just behind the front seats, so it was easy to talk to them through the canvas curtain.

"Bless you, Sister," one of the boys said.

"Friggin' 'eck, can you hurry?" another asked. "Sorry, but the morphine's wearing off."

Another groaned. The fourth one muttered softly to himself. Some of them cried out occasionally.

Ria noticed the stench almost at once. It was an intense, nauseating, rotting smell. She swallowed hard to keep from retching, and of course she couldn't say anything.

She hoped she didn't actually have to look at whatever was causing that putrefying stink. But when they arrived at a nearby hospital, she and Carly helped unload the stretchers. One boy had his head and most of his face bandaged, as well as a foot. Another had a bloated leg covered in a suppurating bandage, which seemed to ooze the gut-wrenching stink. One chap had two stumps for legs. They all had grateful smiles. A boy with bandages around his chest gasped, "Luvely ride, ladies. Ta very much."

"It's gas gangrene, before you ask," Carly said to Ria when they were once more underway. "You do get somewhat used to the smell. You did very well not to throw up."

"Gangrene means he'll have his leg amputated?"

"Yes. He may survive if it hasn't spread. Gas gangrene is caused by the dirt that gets into wounds. It comes from old farm fields with lots of manure. The lads sometimes lie wounded in no man's land for days, so even a minor wound can get badly infected if it's not treated quickly. We get a lot of these. Some, of course, have already had a limb or two removed, as you saw. Poor souls!"

"Why did that fellow call you Sister?" Ria asked.

"The boys think we are VADs. Nurses are the only women who are supposed to be on this side of the Channel, don't you know."

With all the ambulances running but over four hundred injured to unload from the train, Carly and Ria did three more trips to various hospitals. The last was the longest. "Canadian #3 General. Mind how you go."

"Which means we have to drive extra carefully because of the nature of the injuries. And we'll be most of the way to Boulogne," Carly said, but with no hint of annoyance in her voice. This was all part of the job. "The hard part is trying to miss all the shell holes and bumps in the road. You get to know where the worst ones are." Louder she said, "Boys, you'll be happy to know that I have a bona fide Canadian girl here with me. From Toronto. She's come all the way to help you."

"I'm from Guelph, Miss. I expect you know it," a strained voice mumbled slowly into the darkness.

"Indeed I do! Some of my best friends live there. Do you know the Carringtons?"

"Know of them. My sister's working in their factory. Making uniforms. We have a farm..." His voice caught on a sharp intake of breath.

Ria could feel his pain, a physical reality like the wind and rain that drove sharply at them.

"I'm from Winnipeg," another voice said.

"I'm afraid I've never been there," Ria said.

"You probably don't know Launston Mills," another voice said. "Just a small town in Ontario."

"The Carringtons' grandparents live there, and I see them every summer," Ria told him. "Keir and Megan Shaughnessy."

"Well I'll be buggered! Sorry, ladies. But everybody knows them! He was mayor once, and owns the newspaper. Didn't I hear that one of his granddaughters was on the *Lusitania* and drowned?"

"She was with me. We were good friends."

"Holy smoke! That must have been terrible for you."

"Yes."

Winnipeg said, "It's not right that you girls should be risking your lives like this. I wouldn't want my sisters or sweetheart here."

"I'm glad to hear a Canadian girl's voice," Guelph managed to say haltingly. "Will you keep talking?"

Ria was at a loss. He sounded so needy, so she said, "Have any of you ever been to Muskoka? It's a lake district about a hundred miles north of Toronto. We have a summer home there."

"Camped once," Guelph said. "Beautiful."

"I love the granite, how it sparkles in the sunlight and absorbs the warmth of the sun. Islands of all shapes and sizes, some merely a giant rock or big enough for a golf course. Some with sandy beaches or sheer cliffs rising a hundred feet above the water. Some with funny names like Old Baldy and One-Tree-Island and Ouhu. That belongs to Professor Carlyle. His son is a doctor and he's here, at one of the Canadian hospitals." In fact, at the one they were going to. But she wasn't ready to see Blake yet. "My favourite place on our island I named The Shimmering Sands."

She told them about the Regatta, the Stepping Stone Marathon, the tennis tournament. About blueberry picking, excursions to waterfalls, canoeing up the mystical Shadow River, and moonlight cruises. About the costume balls and parties and picnics, fascinating Carly as well as the men, who occasionally exclaimed or chuckled.

"I like canoeing too," Guelph said, his voice tight, barely above a whisper now. "Go on."

She painted a vivid picture of the Northern Lights, and a moonless night shimmering with an immense canopy of stars, some of them falling to earth. She described storms whipping across the lake, and early morning swims with the mist dancing across the water. Whenever she stopped, someone urged her to go on. So she was hoarse and tired by the time they finally arrived at the hospital, an hour and a half later.

When they unloaded the stretchers, they discovered that Guelph was dead. Most of his body was heavily bandaged, his face obscured. "Burns," the Medical Officer said, reading his tag. "RFC. Poor chap."

Ria burst into tears.

"First day on the job?" the doctor asked wryly. "You'll get used to it, more's the pity."

The boy from Launston Mills said, "You helped him, Miss. He heard about home. And a voice from home. God bless you, Miss."

Carly put her arm about Ria's shoulder and said, "He's right, you know. And I think about my brother, Eddie, too, every time I have a flyer. Come on. Let's go home."

Carly gave Ria a cigarette and a sip of brandy from a hip flask. "I carry this for emergencies."

When they had slipped back into the engulfing darkness, Carly said, "What you described sounds too lovely. I shall come and visit you in Muskoka, if I may. *Après la guerre.*" To distract her, she questioned Ria about her family and friends, and told her about her own.

The rain was pelting down, but at least the wind was now at their tail. The rumble of thunder mingled with distant guns in the Channel, and lightning forked around them, illuminating momentarily the shiny trail that was the road. Ria felt chilled to the bone, despite her leather coat, her fingers stiff, her eyes sore from straining to see into the darkness. She wondered how she would ever manage to drive with such assurance yet caution, as Carly did.

"I have four older brothers. No sisters. Harry's in the War Office, Giles is designing aeroplanes, Grant is at the Front, with the Engineers. And then there's Eddie, who's two years older than me. I have three female cousins, but they're in their thirties and we've never really been close. And I have fifteen male cousins with whom I did share a very active childhood. I've always been a bit of a tomboy, so no one was surprised that I joined the WATS. I was already driving and fixing my own car. One of my uncles is an Admiral, and most of my cousins are in the forces somewhere. Robert was killed at the first Ypres. Michael went down with Kitchener in June." She was referring to Lord Kitchener, Britain's Secretary of State for War, whose ship had struck a German mine off the Orkney Isles, with almost all hands lost.

"I'm so sorry."

Carly shrugged. "You can't talk to anyone who hasn't lost at least one relative or close friend. It's rather telling, that."

"Like these fields of death we're driving through," Ria said.

"Yes. I get a bit spooked sometimes when I'm doing this run alone at night, especially when there's a moon and you can see the silhouettes of the crosses. Or like now," Carly added when a brilliant blast of lightning fractured the blackness around them. "When I'm tired, I have bizarre visions of all these dead rising from their graves, demanding to be taken home to England. Cinders swears she saw a ghost once, at dusk. A chap walking along the road. He turned to watch her approach. He had his head and one eye bandaged and his arm in a bloody sling, his uniform, torn and dirty. She thought he must have been from one of the hospitals, out for a stroll, gone too far or gotten lost. Although that didn't make sense, since he wouldn't have been in khaki, but the blue hospital uniform. She was going to stop and give him a lift anyway, but he just disappeared!"

Ria shivered.

"The next day Cinders had a cable from her mother informing her that her eldest brother had been killed at the Somme."

"Good Lord!"

It was four in the morning when Ria and Carly returned to the camp. Lucinda was already fast asleep and Sybil staggered in shortly after they dropped into their beds.

.   .   .

Reveille woke them at nine. Sybil put her pillow over her face and muttered, "Go to hell."

Carly was quite chipper as she said, "Get up lazy bones. ComRad let us sleep in this morning. I'm going to try and bag me a bath. Breakfast in half an hour," she told Ria.

It was a beautiful, sunny morning, the air still and surprisingly warm. The high dunes, seeming so fluid yesterday, looked comfortably settled, and trapped the radiance of the sun. The water was calm and opalescent, fluctuating between blue and green.

So Ria was puzzled by the distant rumbling of thunder. Carly noticed and said, "That's Ypres. There's always fighting going on there, even when there's no major offensive. And when the wind isn't howling, we can hear the guns. And feel the disturbed air, I fancy. It reminds us how close we really are to the action."

Ria's fatigues after breakfast included helping in the kitchen. "Good luck," Carly said to her. "I almost burnt the place down, so they haven't allowed me back in, except to fetch water. I get to chop wood today, after I clean Nessie." The cooks, laundry staff, and the secretary were the only non-driving WATS, so the drivers all had chores to do to keep the place clean and tidy. Ria washed dishes for the first time in her life – and managed not to break anything.

After that, she was sent out with Carly to learn the lay of the land. Ria drove Nessie as Carly directed her to each of the hospitals, showed her where to load or unload the stretchers, and introduced her to a few of the staff who were about. The Stationary Hospitals were housed in old buildings – a casino, a monastery, a hotel, a villa. But the General hospitals were huge cities of tents and hutments, some accommodating 2000 or more wounded, and Ria felt she needed a map to find her way around them.

They had brought sandwiches and a thermos of tea, which they enjoyed in the generous sunshine atop Cap Blanc-Nez, a spectacular crumbling headland spilling into the sea far below. The Channel was busy with ships plying between Calais and

Dover, Boulogne and Folkestone, destroyers keeping guard. Boots dashed happily about, running to the edge of the cliff and barking, as if ordering the vessels on their way.

The chalky white cliffs of England seemed surprisingly close, and yet a world away. Aeroplanes flew overhead in the cloudless blue sky, leaving white puffy trails that broke apart and diffused. A group of uniformed riders raced their steeds across the broad, pale sands below them.

"That's the Cavalry," Carly said. "They're stationed nearby, and often come to visit us for tea or entertainments. They also let us ride their horses, if you're interested."

"It all sounds so jolly and civilized."

"We do try. Have to, don't we, to keep sane."

At their last stop, they were to evacuate men to a hospital ship for transport back to England. They were walking wounded, meaning they could at least hobble and sit up, so Nessie was able to take ten at a time, sitting in the back.

One of the boys said eagerly, "Hey, Sister, wasn't it you brought me here t'other night? I got a Blighty, see? Broken arm, but it's still mine. Maybe the war will be over by the time it's mended, and they won't send me back. Caught a bullet in the shoulder last year, but I was back in six months. Didn't even send me home when I got one in the arm. Flesh wound they said, and kept me here till it healed. Third time lucky, don't you think?"

One of the others said, "Bob Carter's been wounded five times and is still here. They'll keep sending you back until they plant you in the mud."

Another voice said, "I'm going to marry me girl. Lost me toes, but I can still walk up the aisle."

"Shot them off, did you?" someone teased. Men were known to inflict wounds upon themselves that would ensure a 'Blighty'.

"Trench foot, rotter. Fell off on their own, didn't they?"

When they arrived at the quay, Ria said, "Good Lord!" She caught herself, realizing she mustn't alarm the patients.

Carly looked over at her and grinned. "Told you." The pier was barely wide enough for two cars to pass. "Rule is that empty cars take the seaward side," Carly said as they watched another ambulance turn around at the end. Ria held her breath, as it seemed impossible for it not to plunge off the quay. A front wheel stopped barely a foot from the edge. A moment later, the ambulance scooted toward them at a fair clip.

It was Henrietta Maltby, who waved to them energetically as she passed.

"Hennie's a good driver," Carly said, reading Ria's thoughts.

Ria picked her way through the throngs of elated men heading home on leave, and felt relief when she reached the hospital ship. But once they had helped the men limp on board and bidden them farewell, she had to turn the suddenly monstrous vehicle around. She wondered whether she wasn't a butterfly chauffeuse after all. Maybe she just didn't have the kind of courage and sang-froid that these veterans had.

"You could back up the quay," Carly said sympathetically. "I did for the first few times, but it's a neck-wrenching job."

"I'd better learn how to do it right."

"There's only one way to do it. See that dip over there? You have to back into that, but first you have to go as close as possible to the edge of the quay. I know that there are only inches to spare, but you do get the hang of it after a while."

Ria crept forward. She could see no edges at all, just the sucking sea thirty or more feet below.

"That's perfect there. Now back up carefully. You don't want to hit the edge of that platform or it will catapult you right over the side."

Ria was white-knuckled as she followed Carly's directions.

"Well done! You can breathe now," Carly said with a chuckle.

They heard applause from some of the men on the ships and pier, and Carly said, "I'm sure they're always astonished that we don't take a nose-dive. It's even worse when we have to do this at night or in fog."

"Hell's bells!"

Carly laughed. "We consider it rather a test of a girl's suitability as a WATS. And I'd say you passed admirably. We've had male Red Cross drivers tell us that they don't try to turn around even on quays that are wider than this one. So it's become part of our mystique, that we are fearless and foolhardy Englishwomen."

Ria still had to squeeze back along the pier. The jaunty leave-men, kits slung over their shoulders, waved and whistled at them, and sometimes patted the ambulance as it passed, making it hard for Ria to do more than crawl along.

Carly said, "When Sybil comes charging along here, she has them jumping in all directions. We have two more runs to do to the ship before we head home for tea."

Ria was grateful that Carly didn't ask her if she was up to the task, just assumed she was, although Ria found it a strain to be driving in unfamiliar territory, in a vehicle that handled differently from her own, and on the other side of the road to what she had become accustomed to in England. And having to do two more breath-snatching turns on the quay.

As they drove, Carly explained the organization of the medical services. "Think of it as a river of sick and wounded that has to keep moving to make way for more to come. So they get a few hours here, a few days there until they're finally back in England. An injured man gets first aid at his Regimental Aid Post where he's assessed by his Medical Officer, and a tag with his name, number, and nature of his injuries is attached to a button on his tunic, as you saw. The walking wounded then go on foot to the Advanced Dressing Station; the others are carried by stretcher. When the fighting is really fierce, this can only be done under cover of darkness. From the ADS they are taken to the Main Dressing Station by ambulances. Not ours though, since they don't allow women that close to the front lines, because the ADS is still in the fire zone. Only emergency operations are performed at the MDS, From there the men move on to the Casualty Clearing Station. Wounds are properly dressed at the CCS, and operations for the most critical cases are carried out there. That's the closest that nursing Sisters get to the action. The wounded are then put onto the ambulance trains, which also have emergency operating theatres. And that's when we get them. If a man is likely to recover within a few weeks, he's kept at a base hospital and stays in France to convalesce. If he needs longer to heal, he's sent back to England as soon as possible. All the boys want Blighties, of course – an honourable wound that gets them safely home."

Their next two loads were stretcher cases. "You're already becoming more comfortable on the quay," Carly observed after they'd unloaded their last passengers.

When they returned to camp, they cleaned and refueled Nessie, and washed up for tea. Ria was rather surprised to see several officers in the mess talking with the girls who were already back.

Carly shrieked with delight. "Eddie!" She ran to him and embraced him joyfully. "This is my brother!" she explained to the others.

"Oh sure, that's what all the girls say when they want to hug a handsome man in public," Sybil teased.

There was a strong resemblance between brother and sister. "I'm being 'rested' at the aerodrome near Marquise, which is only about ten miles from here," he told Carly. "And I've brought a friend with me. This is Jonathan Telford."

Carly introduced all the girls, and then said, "You won't believe this Eddie, but Victoria is a pilot."

"Good Lord! Where did you learn?"

"At an aerodrome near Henley. On the Avro 504."

"Her husband is in the RFC as well. Do you know Charles Wyndham?"

Eddie seemed disappointed. Ria had noticed the admiration in his eyes. She was used to men flirting with her, even as a married woman. It was all part of normal social interaction. But she was disillusioned with men right now, and didn't feel like playing games.

"No. Canadian, are you? Jack Wyndham's an Ace. Any relation?"

"I don't think so," Ria lied calmly.

"Which squadron is your husband with?"

Hell's bells! "He started out with the 2nd. Now he's down at the Somme. I've heard you're a race-car driver. Do you plan to do that as a career? I have a cousin who intends to race boats."

"You should hear about their cottage on a lake in the Canadian wilderness," Carly said. "It sounds rather jolly!"

"'Cottage' meaning summer home," Ria explained, thankful to Carly for helping her change the subject.

And so she was called upon to describe summer in Muskoka. Meanwhile several more officers strolled in – a couple of doctors, sailors, cavalry.

Lucinda Ashby-Grey sat down at the piano and began to play very competently as the others talked over tea and cakes. Then she said, "The new girl has to show her stripes, so the floor is all yours, Windy."

Here was another test of her suitability as a WATS, but Ria had grown up giving entertainments. It was one of the ways they amused themselves at the cottage. With aplomb she sat down at the piano and accompanied herself as she sang the tongue twister, *Sister Susie's Sewing Shirts For Soldiers*. She had already entertained the boys at Thameshill with this piece.

Sister Susie's sewing in the kitchen on a Singer,
There's miles and miles of flannel on the floor and up the stairs,

And father says it's rotten getting mixed up with the cotton,
And sitting on the needles that she leaves upon the chairs.
And should you knock at our street door, Ma whispers "Come
inside,"
Then when you ask where Susie is, she says with loving pride:

Sister Susie's sewing shirts for soldiers,
Such skill at sewing shirts our shy young sister Susie shows!
Some soldiers send epistles, say they'd rather sleep in thistles
Than the saucy soft short shirts for soldiers sister Susie sews.

She invited the others to join her in the final chorus, but no one was able to get through it, and they all convulsed with laughter as they tripped over the words.

There was appreciative applause.

"Well done, Windy!" Carly said.

Someone put a record on the gramophone, and people started dancing. Ria wished she could just go to her tent, but an officer invited her to dance, and it seemed that this was also part of the WATS' duty.

"That was splendid, Miss..."

"Mrs. Wyndham."

"Lawrence Chadwick. I'm with the Cavalry. Do you ride?"

"Oh, yes."

"Then you must come out for a gallop on the beach some day."

"Thank you, Major. I'd enjoy that." Ria didn't want to commit to anything, but she had thought, seeing the riders earlier, that it would be invigorating to race along the miles of empty beach. If only she could have Calypso here.

When Ria danced with Eddie, they fell into easy conversation, and, fortunately, he didn't ask about Chas again. He had the same cheerful, easygoing manner as his sister, and Ria found that she was actually enjoying herself.

"I should like to see your boats and meet your cousin. I expect that it would be quite exciting racing across open water," he said.

"Oh yes. The lakes can be serenely calm. Like glass. But you have to know where the rocks and shallows are." She told him about various mishaps on the lakes over the years, like Lionel Camford running his launch onto a rock on a moonlit night. "Even the big steamers have been grounded on shoals."

The secretary, Mildred Elmsley, rushed into the mess and announced, "Barges!"

The girls scrambled, bidding hasty farewells to the guests.

When they were underway, Carly explained to Ria, "The barges bring the worst cases, the ones who can't stand the jolting of a rail journey. Usually we don't have to take them far, thank God. That can be an unnerving drive. They don't mean to, but some of the boys can't help screaming with the pain. We have to drive extra carefully, to make the trip as smooth as possible."

One of their cases, who was unconscious, had drainage tubes extending from his abdomen. Another was heavily bandaged and the other two had serious fractures. Ria was nervous after what Carly had told her. The road sloped up from the canal, and it was hard not to stall the engine while trying not to jerk the car. The trip seemed endless as the darkness settled around them, making it even more difficult to drive. Not used to the roads, she hit a hole that caused anguished cries from the men. "I'm so sorry!" she told them, gripping the wheel tightly and peering hard into the encroaching blackness.

"Well done," Carly said to her when they had unloaded the poor wretches at the hospital. "Now we do another run."

Although her muscles burned from the strain, Ria nodded and drove back to the canal.

When they returned to the camp at nine o'clock for a late dinner, Ria was in pain and not hungry. Her back and legs ached from the driving, from carrying the heavy stretchers, from the unaccustomed stress. "I just want my bed," she told Carly.

"Nonsense! You have to keep up your strength. We may well be called out again tonight."

Ria said nothing, although she wondered how she would survive. Carly said, "Don't worry, it does get easier."

Ria did manage to swallow some of the roast pork and vegetables, and then gratefully donned her silk pajamas. She had brought flannel ones as well, for the colder weather, but noticed that the others also wore fancy night apparel. It was like an antidote to the decidedly unfeminine khaki.

"Let's have a tot of that cognac of yours, Windy, to toast your lasting the first full day as a WATS," Sybil suggested.

"And doing it brilliantly," Lucinda added. "*Sister Suzie* was cracking good."

When Ria had poured them each a measure into their mugs, Sybil raised hers and said, "Welcome Victoria Wyndham, Colonial aristocrat, aviatrix, show girl." Sybil grinned. "In other words... one of us."

"Righto!" Lucinda agreed.

Carly said, "Hear, hear!"

"And now, if Fritz will let us, I will bid you all a fond good night," Sybil said.

"No moon," Lucinda pointed out.

"But no rain and lots of stars," Carly said. Seeing Ria's quizzical expression, she explained, "Air raids. We've had a lot of them lately."

Ria must have slept in an instant. But she awoke to a heavy droning noise and then a klaxon. Explosions shattered the air and shook the earth. They were all up in an instant, pulling their clothes on over their pajamas, grabbing steel helmets and torches.

"Off to the dugout," Carly said to Ria.

It was built into the side of a hill at the edge of the camp – just a tunnel with benches lining both sides, and a few hurricane lamps shedding meager light. It was 4:30 in the morning and the girls streamed in wearily, too accustomed to these raids to feel the fear and excitement that Ria did. "Hennie's on duty this time. She stays and mans the telephone. Let's hope we don't get called out," Carly told Ria.

Although the whining noise of bombs was muffled in the shelter, they could still feel the shuddering impact.

"They're close tonight," someone said. Nobody voiced the obvious concern for Henrietta. An hour later, she pushed her way through the heavy curtain and said, "The supply depot. My team." Henrietta was one of the three Sergeants, each having nine girls beneath her. Dora Pettigrew, alphabetically the next in line, went to man the phone. "We've been a bit shot up," Henrietta told them.

When it finally came, the sudden silence was eerie. They could see the damage as soon as they emerged from the shelter. Bombs pock-marked the perimeter of the camp. Shell splinters had sliced through tents, ripping up sleeping bags, imbedding themselves in the walls of the unfinished barracks, and denting some of the ambulances. Ria marveled that Henrietta had seemed so composed in the midst of a deadly rain of metal.

"Hell and damnation!" Sybil swore. "Don't anyone come any closer. There's an unexploded bomb outside our tent."

They all stopped chatting, as if their voices might detonate it. It was firmly imbedded in the sand and only noticeable because of the new depression. Thank God Sybil had spotted it. They moved quickly away.

"I'll call the army," ComRad said. "All of you take your vehicles to the Casino. Scrounge some breakfast," she added with a grin. The Casino was the nearest hospital, just a few minutes away along the beach.

Ria laughed when she alighted from her car. "How do I explain the turquoise pajamas hanging below my skirts?" she asked the others.

"I'm burgundy, Carly's pink, Cinders is green," Sybil said. "Surely we could perform a stage show."

"I wish I could at least wash," Ria said.

"Get used to feeling grimy," Lucinda said. "I look forward to heavenly baths. Do you know what Sybil and I did on our last day off? We went to a resort hotel just down the coast, rented a room with a bath for the day, and took turns lounging in the tub. Isn't it frightfully pathetic that that's become the height of luxury and decadence?"

"Napping in real sheets on a real mattress was the truly decadent part," Sybil said. "Hell, just being able to sleep without people and Huns constantly disturbing me was glorious!"

They were treated to a very fine breakfast, all in various states of disarray but with the composure of debutantes sporting ball gowns – as befitted their surroundings in the Belle Epoque grandeur of the Casino. Crystal chandeliers dripped from frescoed ceilings, and the ornate, gilded walls conjured visions of baroque chateaux. If it weren't for the rows of beds filled with suffering men, Ria could easily have imagined the suave and glittering people who usually graced these sumptuous rooms.

A message relayed to the women two hours later assured them that they could return.

"Our new mess ornament," ComRad told them, pointing to the seven-foot tall aerial torpedo that was now deactivated. "A hundred pounder. Quite the trophy. Now you girls had better don proper uniforms. We have a busy day. Wyndham, you'll be looking after the medical staff."

For the next few days, Ria and Dragonfly ferried nursing Sisters and doctors to and from the leave ships. She also took visiting brass to hospitals, and on her fourth day, was required to chauffeur a Brigadier-General to various encampments.

ComRad made her memorize a map beforehand and said, "You need to show complete confidence in where you're going. I don't think I've misjudged you, Wyndham. I expect that you will be quite capable of handling Brigadier-General Bulmer and impressing him with the competence and charm of the WATS. Perhaps I should be sending a more senior member, but I know he likes a pretty face. And you have the newest and smartest uniform," she added with a grin. "He'll be tickled pink that you're an aristocratic Colonial. Bring him to tea afterwards. He happens to be my Godfather."

She chuckled at Ria's surprise, and then said, "We women have to use all our wiles to get what we need. Your captivating smile and wit are weapons in our battle for acceptance and respect. We're counting on you, Wyndham."

"Thank you, ComRad. I'll do my best."

Ria picked up the General at the area HQ in Calais. He was accompanied by his Adjutant and two Staff officers.

"Delightful as it may be to have a pretty girl driving me, I don't hold with women being here," the General stated firmly as he greeted her. "But I understand you WATS have hoodwinked some bureaucrats in the War Office."

"Be assured that I will take good care of you, General."

"I daresay you will, my dear. But you *should* be at home having babies."

"Rather difficult to do when my husband is in France," Ria said lightly, swallowing the lump of pain that thoughts of Chas and children always gave her. "I consider that this is my war as much as his."

"You modern girls! You'll forgive an old man for wanting to keep beautiful young women safe. It's why we're fighting this war, after all – to preserve the status quo."

Ria drove confidently and skillfully, and was pleased that Calais was becoming familiar and she didn't lose her way. When a tyre blew, she cursed under her breath, but managed to keep the heavy, swaying car on the road and bring it safely to a stop. They were just outside the Cavalry camp, where they were expected for lunch.

"If you gentlemen would be so kind as to step out of the car, I'll have it fixed shortly," Ria told them.

"Emerson," the General barked. "Give the girl a hand or go and find someone who can change a wheel."

"That won't be necessary, General. I'm quite capable of doing it on my own," Ria assured him. "Do go ahead, if you'd prefer not to wait, and I will meet you there."

But the General was determined to watch as Ria pulled the jack out of the trunk. Fortunately, she had a spare tyre. She kept her tyre iron beside her seat at ComRad's advice. She and Boss had once been accosted by two drunken French soldiers. Boss had whacked one with the iron, and the women had made their escape unscathed.

One of the officers said, "May I offer some assistance?"

"Not at all, but thank you, Sir."

Several officers on horseback on their way back to the camp stopped to watch. Ria heard the General refuse the offer of a mount. She knew she was being tested as a WATS now, but was also comfortable with the task, so she managed to make it look easy. There were several amused chuckles and many approving glances when Ria had finished and was wiping her greasy hands on a cloth.

One of her admirers was Major Lawrence Chadwick. He winked at her and pointed surreptitiously to his cheek to indicate that she had a smudge on her face.

General Bulmer said, "A damn fine job you've done there, girl."

"Thank you, Sir. Shall we continue?" She pulled out her handkerchief and quickly wiped her cheek.

The Brigadier-General climbed back into the car, although the others opted to walk the short distance. "I'm not going to miss the opportunity of arriving with such a lovely young lady at the helm," he said with a chortle.

Finding herself the only woman in the Cavalry mess for luncheon was easy now that she seemed to have received the General's approval. Major Chadwick was seated across from her, at the General's table.

"It's a great pleasure having you here, Mrs. Wyndham. You've ensured that all the men are on their best behaviour," the Commanding Officer said with a grin. "Perhaps it's not such a bad idea of the government's after all, having women join the forces as drivers and so forth. What do you think, General?"

"I would have said you were cracked, but Mrs. Wyndham has proven herself capable as well as ornamental. Rather sit next to her than some hairy chap."

The others laughed politely.

"I heard that Mrs. Wyndham can also pilot an aeroplane," Major Chadwick said.

Amongst the exclamations of surprise and disbelief, the General said, "The devil you can! Whatever next? You Canadians are certainly a dynamic lot. I have nothing but praise for the

Canadian forces. But I draw the line at allowing you to take me for a flight, young lady."

"I'm sure I can keep the wheels of the Rolls on the ground, General," Ria said to his amusement.

Major Chadwick spoke privately to her while the General was being shown around. "That was very well done, changing the wheel, and with a skeptical audience," he said.

"I can clean the carburetor, too," she replied with a grin.

He laughed. "I have no doubt! And when do you have time off? For a ride?"

"Goodness, I don't even know. We seem to be perpetually busy. We're supposed to be off-duty by tea time, but jobs seem to come in at all hours." She had accompanied Carly again the previous evening to unload a train, so they hadn't seen their beds until midnight.

"I'll ride over tomorrow around five with a mount for you. If you're free we can stretch their legs on the beach. Otherwise, I'll just enjoy some WATS hospitality."

The rest of the tour that afternoon went without further problems, and the General was delighted to accept an invitation to tea. He kissed ComRad's cheek and said, "You're looking well, my dear. This military life seems to suit you."

"It's partly your influence, Uncle Lucius. All those stories about soldiering when I was a child."

"Ha! Blame me for your tomboy ways, eh? Let's see what you've done here then."

ComRad took him on a tour. Several of the women were fixing cars, clad in overalls and headscarves. Tuppy explained to the visitors what she was doing.

"Antonia plays a splendid violin when she's not mending cars," ComRad told her Godfather. "Her parents are Lord and Lady Netherton."

The General shook his head. "Modern girls! Can't say I understand them, but there you have it. You've done a damned fine job here, Fanny! All ship-shape and Bristol fashion."

The General was quite jaunty while he had his tea and talked to the girls as they trickled in. A few played piano. Tuppy obliged with a virtuoso performance on her violin.

When Ria drove the General and his entourage back to HQ, he said, "It's been a delightful day, my dear. Perhaps next time I'll let you take me up in an aeroplane." He grinned broadly at her.

"I'd be delighted. I do so love flying."

"Damn me, but your husband's a lucky chap!"

The tears held off until she was once again alone in the car.

.　　　.　　　.

"You have a good seat," Major Chadwick said to Ria when they stopped galloping along the beach.

"I have a very fine horse back home. Actually he's in England now. At my cousin's. I do miss him."

They walked their mounts to let them cool down. "You're welcome to ride ours anytime."

"Thank you, Major. You, of course, are a splendid rider."

"I grew up with horses and have been in the Cavalry since I graduated from Sandhurst twelve years ago."

"You're a career soldier then."

"What's the youngest son of a viscount to do but join the Cavalry? Except that we're rather an anachronism in this war. Sure, we do our stints in the frontline trenches as infantry, but they're still hoping to see us in a glorious charge." Facetiously he said, "Going over the top, avoiding the muddy shell holes, jumping the fifty feet of barbed wire fences of no man's land, capturing enemy machine gun nests and heavily fortified trenches while bombs are blasting all around our poor steeds. So we've been mostly relegated to reserve lines, digging communications trenches, that sort of thing. Waiting for the big day when we get to shine. Some of the men have given up and joined the RFC. But I'm not complaining, mind you. I have no great desire to gallop – or fly – into the jaws of hell."

He smiled and she thought that his trim moustache accentuated his good looks. His dark hair, unrestrained by a hat, curled onto his forehead, making him look younger and more carefree than a veteran soldier at least a dozen years her senior.

"Ironically, my eldest brother, the heir apparent, joined Kitchener's Army and has not only attained the rank of Major in the infantry, but has distinguished himself by winning a Military Cross." He chuckled, although Ria sensed his annoyance. "I think perhaps I'll give up the military *après la guerre.*"

"And do what?"

"Breed horses."

"My brother-in-law breeds horses and races them. Mine comes from his stables."

"I should like to meet him some time. Your horse, I mean."

She laughed.

"We're having a polo match on Sunday, if you and the ladies would care to come and watch."

"I'd like that. You'll have to mention it to the Commandant, and see if we're allowed out."

"We're also planning some races on the beach. The Rifles are resting here and have challenged us. Some of the doctors have mounts, and many of the RFC are keen horsemen. I thought I'd suggest that we hold a Ladies' Race as well. What do you think?"

"That would be super! I doubt that I'd have a chance against Sybil Fox. She's apparently a very accomplished show jumper. Won all kids of cups."

"As, undoubtedly, have you," he said astutely.

She chuckled. "Swimming, canoeing, tennis. But never equestrian."

"You'll just have to practice, won't you? I'll race you over to that headland."

The tide was out and the beach seemed a mile wide, the silvery sand, hard. There was almost always wind but it wasn't fierce today, and the waves rolled in gently. Thrusting up over four hundred feet above them, the chalky Blanc-Nez cliff was an imposing sight.

Ria was exhilarated by the ride. The Major was only a length ahead of her when he pulled up. She was flushed and laughing as she dismounted. He caught her by the waist and helped her down.

"You're certainly fearless," he said.

"It's almost as good as flying. I do miss that."

"I shall have to try it some day."

"I don't expect the RFC will allow me to borrow an aeroplane as readily as you offer your horses," she said with a laugh.

Ria accepted a cigarette as they walked side by side.

"I'll take you up on your offer of an aeroplane ride, if we survive this war."

"I don't recall having made the offer."

"And here I thought you wanted to borrow the plane for me."

"You find one and I'll fly it for you."

"It's a deal. Now I'll race you back."

He won by more than two lengths this time, obviously putting more effort into his riding. "You were holding back," she accused him.

"Only a little," he said with a grin. "So you'll just have to work harder at catching me up, won't you?"

When he had gone, Ria picked up her mail. Included in a letter from Cousin Bea was one from Chas. She was grateful that she was alone in the tent as she read.

My Darling Ria,

Jack tells me that you think my wanting to return to France was because of Madeline and the baby. They had absolutely nothing to do with it! Nor did I want to leave you.

When I was posted back to work, I had to overcome my sometimes paralyzing fear of flying. I didn't tell you about that, of course. I realize I should have.

It was good to have that time at Upavon to reassure myself that I could still fly – and do it with some skill.

Perhaps I have a perverse nature, but you know that I don't like to be bested by anyone or anything. So when Boom Trenchard complimented me on my flying skills at Upavon, I instantly suggested to him that I would be of more use at the Front than teaching in England.

I needed to go back and continue the battle alongside my comrades, to make a difference and help us win. And my success in recent months has revived my confidence. Perhaps selfish of me again. I am but a fallible male, needing to prove myself worthy.

Blake says that my compulsion to win – regattas, races, the war, whatever – stems from my subconscious perceived failure as a worthy son and successor to my father. I don't analyze my motives that deeply, knowing only that I feel chuffed by my successes, and thus compelled to compete and win.

As John McCrae's poem suggests, we must keep faith with those who've died. Otherwise their deaths become meaningless. Futile. Too many of my friends have fallen, and need me to carry on their fight. And I don't feel that I can abandon the chaps who are still here and counting on me.

Please write, even just a few words, my darling. I love you unreservedly, passionately, completely. I long to make you smile again.

Your loving Chas

Ria hastily brushed away tears as Sybil and Carly came into the tent. "What's wrong, Victoria?" Carly asked.

"Nothing."

"A letter from hubby?" Sybil said, as Ria tucked it away quickly. "Already missing him, are you?"

"I haven't seen him for six months."

"More fool you for coming to France when he's about due for leave then."

"Yes."

Sybil seemed puzzled by Ria's meek acceptance of the criticism. "Anything you want to talk about?"

"No."

Sybil and Carly exchanged glances, and Sybil said, "Tuppy's just taken Baby off to hospital with a fever. So you're to take over Baby's bus if we're called out tonight. Dinner awaits."

"I'm not hungry."

"Suit yourself," Sybil said with a shrug. "I'll wrestle Cinders for your dessert then."

When they had gone, Ria put on her coat and walked into the gathering darkness. She found shelter in the lea of a dune where she sat down and wept.

.   .   .

They were awakened near dawn by an intense shaking, as if the earth were splitting apart beneath them, and a cacophony of explosions. Boots was jumping about and barking in agitation. But instead of going into the dugout this time, they were called out. They had word that the ammunition dump near Audruicq, south of Calais, had been bombed. Ria had taken the Brigadier-General there only two days earlier.

Ria struggled to start Baby's Siddeley-Deasy ambulance, 'Sadie'. She felt as if her arms would drop off from all the cranking, and was careful to avoid backfires, which could easily break her wrist. Each vehicle handled differently, and it took her a while to become accustomed to the clutch and gearshift. But they had to travel about nine miles, and, with ComRad leading, the convoy raced along the road.

She could see the destruction well before they arrived – flames shooting into the air under a thick cloud of smoke, shells exploding like fireworks. From as far as five miles away they had to avoid live shells that littered the road. As they drew nearer, they noticed trucks that had been blown, by concussion, into nearby fields, as if they were no more than children's toys tossed away after play.

And in the middle of the depot was a crater large enough to swallow a village, lined with hills of spent bombs. And still shells were detonating from the raging fires that spread from shed to shed, raining shrapnel about, and narrowly missing the ambulances as they streamed in.

"We didn't expect you so soon," the harried CO said. "Bless you! We have some severely burnt men, and a lot of broken bones."

This time they needed to apply their first aid training, bandaging wounds and applying splints. Ria was horrified by the state of some of the men. The stench of seared flesh was nauseating. She was bandaging one boy's chest, arms, legs, and face – most of his uniform burnt away, with bits of charred puttees stuck to him, feeling his pain as he stoically tried not to cry out, wishing she had something to give him for it. Officers carried morphine, but there wasn't enough to go around.

And then Major Chadwick was beside her, and offering the victim a morphine pellet. "Cavalry to the rescue," he said to her. "But not as quick to respond as you WATS."

He suddenly pushed her down and threw himself on top of her as a shell whizzed overhead. They could hear the shrapnel violently hitting something metallic and Ria wondered if any of their ambulances had been destroyed. He helped her finish the bandaging and lift the boy onto a stretcher she had placed beside him. They carried him to Sadie and then went to treat another man – burns first, since they were the most critical. When they had four of them in the ambulance, Major Chadwick said, "I'm your orderly, so drive on."

ComRad had been on the telephone to various hospitals to ascertain how many casualties each could take, and now stood calmly in the hail of shrapnel bullets giving orders to the drivers. Ria had already discovered that the WATS were so well organized that there were always beds available and staff awaiting them at their destinations.

With dawn making the road easily navigable, she sped to Calais. The men had been unconscious, but then one of them started screaming in pain. Ria gripped the wheel tightly. Major Chadwick, seeing her distress, said reassuringly, "Hang on there, soldier. Sister's doing what she can to get you to hospital."

"Where's Mummy? Please, where is she? I need her," the boy sobbed. "It hurts! Oh, Christ Almighty, it hurts! Help me. Please! Oh, God, please make it stop!"

Major Chadwick had no more morphine to offer.

Another voice started singing, "It's a long way to Tipperary, It's a long way to go..."

His song was interspersed with screams from the other lad. Ria was tense with anguish for these poor souls. But she concentrated on her driving and was relieved when they finally arrived at the hospital in Calais.

While the one Tommy was still mumbling the words to *Tipperary*, the boy who had cried for his mother had died. Ria didn't weep this time, although she easily could have. It was part of her job to be strong.

Major Chadwick lit two cigarettes and passed one to her as they dashed back to Audruicq. She accepted it gratefully. "I'll never be able to think of *Tipperary* the same way again," she told him.

"Yes, I know what you mean." After a long pause he said, "You're very capable. Forgive me, but am I right in thinking that you're as young as you look?"

"Which is?"

"No more than twenty-one. I promise I won't expose you."

"Twenty. But just don't tell me that I shouldn't be here or you'll be walking back."

He chuckled. "You should be sent home immediately – for lying. But I believe that people should be judged on merit and not by some arbitrary parameters. The WATS are lucky to have you."

Their next load was the walking wounded. With all the ambulances running, they had now dealt with the burns, broken bones, and the ragged wounds from shell fragments. ComRad told Ria that she wouldn't need to return.

When the last patients were unloaded, Major Chadwick took Ria's arm and said, "Come along. I'm taking you out for breakfast. You look just about done in."

She realized that she hadn't eaten anything since lunch yesterday, and allowed herself to be ushered into a café. She ate her omelette with relish, despite everything.

"I don't understand how we can do ordinary things, like eat, in the midst of all this," she said.

"The eating part is easy. Because we need to. Whether we need to dance or play tennis or have horse races is another matter entirely," he said wryly. "But I believe we do, so I'm going to challenge you to a tennis match this afternoon. Duties permitting."

"You mean your duties as an orderly?" Ria teased.

He laughed. "I'd already ordered my men to help fight the fires and evacuate the nearby villagers. I was damned if I was going to stand around and watch you ladies in the thick of it!"

She chuckled. "I'm not sure if that is chivalrous or chauvinistic."

"Chivalrous, of course," he said with a grin. "I have no doubt about your abilities. But I *am* surprised your husband allows you to do such dangerous work."

"He doesn't own me, Major!"

"How foolish of me. But you won't mind if *I* worry about you just a little? You already seem to be battle-scarred," he said, looking at her forehead. "How did you get that?"

"The *Lusitania*."

"Good God!"

She turned away to hide the anguish that was never far below the surface.

"I'm sorry, Victoria. I expect it was a horrendous ordeal. I didn't mean to remind you." He gazed at her with compassion. "I think you're damned plucky. You ladies all deserve medals for what you did today. I wonder if you realize quite how dangerous that was? Shells constantly exploding. All that shrapnel dropping around us. It's a miracle that none of us was hurt."

Ria recalled how he had shielded her, and wondered if she might well have been injured but for his quick reflexes. "I think you probably saved me from harm. Thank you."

"All in a day's work," he quipped. "You do know that you have to throw yourself to the ground when a bomb or shell detonates nearby, because the concussion alone can stop your heart, even if you're not hit by shards of metal. Anyway, I'm going to make sure that the WATS' courage and the skillful handling of today's crisis gets into the Dispatches."

"Mentioned in Dispatches. Isn't that almost like receiving a medal?"

"Indeed it is."

As they left the café, he said, "I'm afraid I took the liberty of calling you Victoria. So will you reciprocate and call me Lance? I'm only Lawrence officially, not to my friends."

"Lance of the Lancers?"

"Yes, a bit much that, isn't it? I suppose I could have joined the Hussars or Dragoons."

They passed a flower shop on their way back to the ambulance, and Lance said, "Hold on for just a minute."

They walked into the shop where a little girl of about six jumped to her feet and said, "Bonjour Monsieur et Madame Soldat."

"Sophie!" her mother scolded with an indulgent smile. "Cette demoiselle n'est pas une soldat. Elle aide les blessés. Une WATS. Pardon, Mademoiselle."

"Ça ne fait rien," Ria said. Continuing to speak in French to them, she added, "What a lovely child." She had curls the colour of maple syrup, sea blue eyes, and a fair complexion.

"Thank you, Mademoiselle. She is a big help to me in the shop, and already has a flair for arranging flowers."

"You like flowers, do you?" Ria asked Sophie while Lance gave his order.

"Oh yes, they are the most beautiful things in the world! Maman says they come from God and since Papa is with God, they come from him as well. They make me happy."

Ria threw the child's mother a sympathetic look as she said, "I'm sorry for your loss, Madame."

"C'est la guerre, n'est ce pas? I am lucky I have Sophie." She gave Ria a conspiratorial smile as she handed Lance three dozen red roses.

Ria offered a coin to Sophie and said, "Do you think you can find some chocolate with this?"

"Oh yes! I can get lots of chocolate with this!"

"She knows her sums," her mother said with a laugh. "She'll be running the shop soon."

"Thank you, Mademoiselle WATS," Sophie said.

"Vous êtes la bienvenue."

When they were out in the street, Lance offered the roses to a surprised Ria. "One for each of the ladies. And any extra ones for you," he said with a warm smile. "A token of my respect and admiration for the WATS."

"They're beautiful, Lance! The girls will be thrilled. Flowers do brighten the world, as young Sophie says. Thank you. This is very considerate."

"I'm sure the men you helped today would be only too happy to do the same."

The girls *were* delighted. Sybil said, "I think Windy has a *pursuitor.*"

At Ria's puzzled expression, Carly clarified. "That's what we call men who are trying to woo us."

"Don't be silly!" Ria said. "I'm married, and he knows it. I thought that being sociable was part of the WATS image."

"Oh, it is, and flirting is quite harmless, and does us all good," Carly said. "Boss once had a Belgian Count fill her ambulance with roses. It's nothing more than fun."

"Then who wants to come and play tennis at the Cavalry camp this afternoon? That is, if we can get away."

Both Sybil and Carly were happy to go. Lucinda said she planned to sleep, as she felt she might be coming down with the influenza that had Baby laid up. ComRad allowed Ria to use her car to drive them over to the camp in the late afternoon. They stopped at the Sick Sisters' Hospital in Calais to visit Baby and give her the extra roses. She was touched.

Lance had no trouble rounding up two more officers to play with Carly and Sybil. He and Ria sat out the first round, and then played the winners of the other match.

"You *are* good," Lance said to Ria when they all sat on the sidelines sipping champagne.

"She has a cup to prove it," Carly said.

But she shared that cup with Chas, and felt such a stab of longing for him that she almost doubled over in pain. What was she doing in France without him? Sitting here, overlooking the Channel, with these virtual strangers, as if they were just indulging in a country house weekend by the sea. It was as if she had suddenly found herself in a bizarre dream where nothing really made sense.

Ria was saved having to describe the tournament at Thorncliff as they all watched an aeroplane spin out of control and crash into the waves. With no enemy about, the plane had obviously had some sort of equipment failure.

"Oh, dear God!" Carly cried.

"It was one of the Navy planes," Lance reassured her. "Not your brother's squadron."

She looked immensely relieved, but everyone felt the tragedy of yet another young life snuffed out.

Ria said, "I think we should head back."

On the drive, Sybil said dreamily, "I think I'm in love. Captain Adam Bentley is a cracker, don't you agree? Thank you, Windy, for being a magnet for attractive men. Once they know *you're* married they become fair game for the rest of us."

Ria laughed. "Happy to oblige!"

.   .   .

"If I sit down, I'll never get up again," Ria said as Carly handed her a cup of tea. Her hands shook from fatigue as she raised the cup to her lips. They were waiting for yet another train to arrive. It was two in the morning and rumbles of distant thunder mingled with the incessant booming of guns in the Channel. "Oh God, it's going to rain as well!"

They had been working round the clock, taking time only to grab some food. Sybil was stretched out in the back of her ambulance, fast asleep, but Ria thought it would be harder to get up again after only twenty minutes.

There was another big push on at the Somme, involving the Canadians as well, the boys talking about trying to take the Regina Trench, the Sudbury Trench, about such intense fighting that they sometimes ran out of Mills bombs and ammo, and had to retreat. There were a lot of casualties.

"Better than air raids," Carly said. They had driven through one the previous night, which had been harrowing, but not much worse than their experience at Audruicq. Ria had discovered, sadly, that two more of her burn victims from that explosion had died.

At least she now had her Rolls-Royce ambulance, and was particularly pleased that it had an electric starter. The others were envious. She had named it "Calypso Two", since it was her steed here.

The rain arrived just after the train. Cold, slicing, it was as if the wind had sucked up the icy sea and was spitting it out in disgust. It blew into the open cab, freezing her fingers, dripping from her face and the wet curls plastered to her cheeks. Ria thought she would never be warm again, though it was only early October. And it was even harder to see in the watery darkness with rain blowing into her eyes. It would be easier on the return journey, but now she was driving westward into the throat of a ferocious storm with not even a windscreen for protection.

Thunder obliterated some of the moans emanating from the back. Although she didn't think she would ever become hardened to the terrible injuries she had seen and stories she had heard from the men, she felt herself going a little numb, able to shut out the sounds of pain and concentrate on her driving.

It was when she slept that her mind assimilated the horror, and she would wake in a cold sweat or with pounding heart, gasping for breath. It was Chas and Justin, even Lance Chadwick, who figured in her dreams of shattered, limbless bodies.

This week had been exceptionally busy, and they had rarely been able to get a full night's sleep. If it wasn't trains arriving, it was aeroplanes buzzing and bombing that kept them from their beds.

It was almost impossible to summon the strength to keep going. When she had safely delivered the patients, Ria headed back for yet another load. Because she didn't need to focus so fiercely on her driving, she found herself nodding off at the wheel, almost veering into the fields. Or graveyards. She started talking to herself, singing, shouting into the storm, anything to stay awake. Her last load was to the Canadian #3 General, and Ria babbled on to the men during that seemingly endless journey.

When she had finally unloaded them, a familiar voice said, "Ria?"

She turned to see Blake, and almost collapsed into his arms.

"Good Lord, you look exhausted!"

"I could sleep standing up. But it's wonderful to see you!"

"You're freezing. Come along. You need a cup of tea. Lots of sugar." He took her into the reception hut, and asked one of the orderlies to fetch a mug of sweet tea. "I haven't long, since I'm on night duty."

"And I need to get back and hopefully bag some sleep before we have more casualties arriving. I don't even know what day it is anymore." She accepted the steaming cup gratefully, but shook so much that she spilled some of it. Blake put his hands around hers to steady her, and help her drink.

"When *did* you last sleep?"

"We were roused around midnight on Thursday. After about three hours of sleep."

"It's now Saturday morning. We sometimes operate for days at a time as well. Welcome to hell." He handed her a towel so she could dry herself a bit. "Justin wrote to me," he said meaningfully. "I thought you might have come to see me before this."

"I... couldn't. It's been too painful. And I've been here less than two weeks, although it already feels like years!"

"We can't talk now, but we will soon."

Seeing him had shattered the barrier she had erected between herself and her Muskoka friends. She had avoided them because they reminded her too much of Chas, but realized how much she needed them. "It's really good to see you, Blake."

As no one was watching at that moment, he gave her a swift kiss on the cheek. "I'll visit as soon as I can get away. In the meantime, look after yourself."

The strong, syrupy tea helped her on the return journey, but she was so wound up, despite her exhaustion, that it seemed to take ages to fall asleep, her muscles twitching, her body plummeting, convulsing every time she drifted off. But then she must have slept like the dead, for it was noon before she regained consciousness.

Carly said, "Sorry, but we have to go out again."

Ria tried to drag herself from her cot, never comfortable, but seeming like paradise after only six hours of sleep in days. Her body ached, but was at least warm again. Her sleeping bag was down-filled and cozy. She dropped back to sleep, and Carly shook her. "Buck up, Windy. It's barges."

"Oh God, no!"

There was no time for breakfast, just a sip of watery tea. Once she saw the men who were in the most fragile state, she lost all self-pity and got on with her job as best she could.

It was teatime before they were finally able to grab something to eat.

"I've aged decades," Sybil said. "See these wrinkles? They're from lack of food to bolster the skin. We'll soon be walking skeletons if this keeps up."

"I don't even feel like eating," Betty Haydon-Wicks said. "I feel ghastly."

She looked flushed so Sybil put her hand on Betty's brow. "You're burning up, Hayrick. Good lord, there'll be a conflagration," she jested. "You should go to the Sick Sisters' for an assessment. I'll bet you've picked up what Baby has. Come along, I'll take you."

Betty barely had the energy to follow Sybil. And didn't come back with her.

"My kingdom for a hospital bed," Sybil declared. "What bliss that would be just to stay in one for a week!"

They had one more train to unload that day, and several transfers from the hospitals to the ships, but then managed to get a full night's sleep.

Things slowed down enough the following days so that there was once again time for teas and dances, tennis and riding. As a consequence, Ria saw quite a lot of both Lance and Carly's brother, Eddie. She enjoyed their company, and managed, for a while at least, to forget about how miserable she really was. Every moment that she wasn't occupied with strenuous, stressful work or a bit of levity, she thought of Chas. Recalling wonderful, intimate moments that often had her crying herself to sleep.

One quiet afternoon, Sybil and Carly managed to find time to have their hair done in town. They dragged Ria along with them, and planned to have tea afterwards.

While the others had their hair cut, Ria had hers properly washed and coiffed, which felt wonderful. Then she visited some of the nearby shops.

There was a surreal moment when the street was completely empty save for a solitary staff officer walking towards her. He seemed absurdly young and oddly familiar, but she couldn't place him. She eyed him curiously, wondering if he had been at one of their teas, but surely she would have remembered him, as he was rather dashing and had a dignified presence, despite his youth. As he walked past her she suddenly realized that he was the Prince of Wales. Astonished, Ria turned to look at him just at the instant that he also turned around. He smiled broadly and saluted her. She did the same, and then heard him chuckle as he walked on.

When she returned to the hair salon, she said to Sybil and Carly, "I've just been saluted by our future king! How bizarre!"

"How exciting!" Carly enthused.

"I heard that the Grenadier Guards were resting at Beau Marais," Sybil said. "I had tea at the Sauvage the other day and the proprietress was all aflutter as she told me that the Prince had ordered their largest room to entertain his fellow officers to dinner. According to her 'Ee eez très charmant, très chic!'"

"Strange to think he's in the army like any other chap," Ria said.

"And not even as a General," Sybil quipped.

"Surely they don't let him go to the front lines."

"It's dangerous enough away from there," Sybil said. "I heard that he had a near miss last year at Loos, when his car and driver were blown to bits. Ironically and luckily, he had just left the car to venture closer to the trenches."

"Maybe we'll run into him at tea time," Carly said.

"And invite him to share a pot?" Sybil teased as they went out into the street. "Especially as I feel fabulous! Carefree! Liberated!"

"She'll be demanding the vote next," Carly said with amusement.

"And why not, pray tell?"

"Why not, indeed. Yes, it does feel marvelous," Carly said, shaking her head. Her straight hair was cut to chin length and swayed like silken strands, the geometrical bangs giving her a Cleopatra-like look.

Sybil's hair, relieved of its weight, was thick and curly, which de-emphasized the thinness of her rather equine face.

"You both look stunning," Ria said, and meant it. "And ready to tackle the world."

"Or at least the men in it," Sybil said. "I actually feel more sexy."

"Sybil!" Carly chided.

"It's true. So Captain Bentley had better beware!"

They laughed, and Ria said, "Now you can see why it's considered 'fast' to cut your hair."

"We'll just have to start a new trend," Carly said. "The look of the modern woman who is no longer chained by her hair to a life of domestic boredom and relegated to some inconsequential role."

"I'm not sure you can be chained by hair," Sybil jested.

"Metaphorically. We should have brought Cinders. And Tuppy. Did you know that she was considered one of the most beautiful debutantes in England, after Lady Diana Manners? Her parents were very much against her coming here, but since Lady Diana is doing her bit as a VAD, Tuppy's parents relented. Wouldn't you love to hear what Lady Netherton had to say if Tuppy cropped her hair? She's got Tuppy destined to marry the Prince."

"Can you image Tuppy as the future Queen?" Sybil asked.

"She would transform the monarchy," Carly replied. "And we could all be her ladies-in-waiting – me driving her car, Windy flying her aeroplane, and you in charge of her stables."

"And all of us, including 'Her Majesty', jumping up to respond to cries of 'Barges!'"

When they had finished laughing, Sybil said, "And all this from cutting our hair!"

Ria stopped suddenly and said, "What's that smell?" It was sulphurous, throat-catching.

Sybil replied, "Gas. They must be using it at Ypres again. We get a whiff of it when the wind's in the right direction."

"Good Lord! It's not dangerous, is it?"

"Not this little bit. Just stinky. We'd best prepare ourselves for some nasty casualties. They don't always have their gas-masks handy."

Their exuberance was curtailed as they thought of the boys with liquefied lungs who might soon be riding in their ambulances.

As they passed the flower shop where Lance had bought the roses, Ria said, "We need something cheerful and fragrant. Let's go inside."

"Ah, Mademoiselle WATS!" Sophie cried when she saw her. "You should see how much chocolate I bought! Maman and I were eating it for a week."

"Good! Now can you put a little bouquet of flowers together for me? I want something to brighten our tent. You choose. And Madame, a dozen roses as well, please. For our mess," she said to the others. "And one white one." For Reggie.

"Oooh you are extravagant," Sybil said. "Will you buy me some chocolate as well?"

Ria was impressed with the bouquet of pink carnations and white daisies accented with purple chrysanthemums that Sophie created. "You do have an eye for design. Thank you, Sophie. What is your favourite flower?"

"Carnations. All their petals live happily together for a long time. And they don't have thorns like roses, which always bite me."

Ria pressed another coin into the child's hand and said, "More chocolate, don't you think?"

"Oh, thank you, Mademoiselle WATS! Maman says you are like an angel. Are you one?"

"No, ma petite. But your Maman is very kind." And seemed slightly embarrassed. "I'll see you again soon."

Out in the street, Carly said, "I take it that's where the last batch of flowers came from. Seems you're rather popular there."

"I think Windy's broody," Sybil said. "Wants children of her own."

Ria held up the single white rose. "This is for my baby. He's buried in Ireland. I can't have more children."

They were stunned. Sybil's face drained of colour. "Oh, Victoria, I'm so sorry! I had no idea. How tragic. How bloody unfair!"

"I can't risk disgracing myself in public. Do you mind if we just go back now?"

Ria let Carly drive while she sat in the back, gazing numbly at the flowers. Once they were ensconced in their tent, Sybil poured her a large shot of brandy, and said, "Will you tell us about it?"

Reluctantly she talked about the *Lusitania*.

"You shouldn't be here, Victoria," Carly said, looking stricken. "You should be home with your husband."

When Ria didn't say anything, Sybil said, "There's more to this infinite sadness, isn't there? You never talk about your husband either. I thought you'd bore us with 'My husband did this or said that'. But you don't mention him at all. And that's not normal. You're married to a chap who looks like a Greek god and you have nothing at all to tell us about him? What's wrong?" Sybil added with a note of compassion.

Coming from her, this kindness seemed to open a dam. When Ria had finished her tale, Sybil said, "The bastard! But if he's truly contrite, then I think you need to accept that and forgive him. Otherwise someone else will snap him up. At the rate our chaps are going west, there won't be many men left, decent or otherwise."

"It's easy for you to be flippant about things. You don't understand!"

"I understand that you may lose a good thing by expecting a man to be a saint. If you've noticed the goings-on in London and here, you might realize that there probably aren't many fellows who *haven't* been indulging in pleasures of the flesh. Fear of dying can do that to people – make them a trifle lax in their morals. I'm ready to give myself to any intelligent man who wants to live life to the full. Preferably Captain Bentley."

"Sybil!" Carly chastised.

"I mean it! God knows if you or I are going to survive this war, Carly. I'm not ready to die a virgin. The moment Adam Bentley asks me to sleep with him, I'll say 'damn the torpedoes' and be prepared to be chucked out of the WATS for inappropriate behaviour."

Lucinda came in swearing. "Bloody, bloody, bloody hell! Mother has summoned me home. Absolutely *insists* that she can't cope any longer without me. The servants are deserting her, she's prostrated by George's death, the food is terrible and difficult to obtain, and a dutiful daughter should be at her parents' side in such dire times and not indulging herself in false heroics. Apparently the war can get along quite well without me, but they can't." She burst into tears.

"Oh dear God, it's a weepy day," Sybil said. "Here's a tot of brandy for you, too, Cinders."

"Go and organize them, Cinders, and then come back," Carly suggested.

"They'll never let me," Lucinda wailed disconsolately. "Father would stop my allowance, and I certainly can't manage without that. I have no other income. My widowed aunt will leave me something eventually – quite a fortune actually – but she's still hale and hearty."

"It's damnable that parents expect us to subjugate ourselves to their needs. As if we've been raised merely to be servants," Sybil said. "Let's agree that we shall *never* treat our own daughters this way." She threw an apologetic look at Ria.

"Can you persuade your aunt to ante up, so to speak, with at least enough to give you some independence now?" Ria asked.

"Good idea!" Sybil said with a guffaw at Ria's witticism. "Convince her that what you're doing demonstrates that the modern woman can hold her own in a man's world, while still being a lady, and is not just some empty-headed flapper who likes to show her knees."

"Hear, hear!" Carly said.

Lucinda looked a bit more cheerful. "I could certainly try. Auntie doesn't approve of suffragettes, but she also doesn't approve of girls being idle and self-indulgent."

"Tell her that we've impressed noblemen and Generals," Ria said. "And have been Mentioned in Dispatches."

"And that our teas and entertainments are legendary," Carly said.

"She'll be *sending* you back soon," Sybil added. "Just remember that you're a WATS."

.   .   .

A feeble dawn was creeping over the hills as Ria delivered her last load to the Chateau Mauricien in Wimereux, a summer estate now housing wounded officers. She liked the village with its ornate Casino, villas, and hotels, some of them turned into hospitals. Once when she had descended towards it from the Boulogne hill, she had witnessed fierce waves pummeling the stone wall that defied the sea, washing over the promenade and threatening the stalwart Victorian buildings that huddled along the seafront. But the Channel was relatively calm this morning and appeared to be a mile offshore. A few locals strolled along the exposed seabed with buckets, harvesting shellfish. A solitary bicycle perched in a stranded pool of water amid the receding tide.

Ria stopped as she joined the main road just shy of the bridge. A mounted officer passed, acknowledging her with a nod. She recognized Lieutenant-Colonel John McCrae, whom she had recently met, riding his horse, Bonfire. He was second in command at the Canadian #3 General, which occupied the buildings and grounds of an old Jesuit college nearby. Ria had thought him a charming, handsome man with impeccable social graces who, nonetheless, seemed faintly remote. Perhaps that part of him was only revealed in his poetry.

She watched him turn to follow the river valley, which looked tantalizingly arcadian beyond the tall arches of the railway viaduct. For an impulsive moment she wanted nothing more than to accompany him on horseback in companionable silence.

But the luxury of independence was not hers at this moment. Still, she was in no hurry to return to camp, so she drove leisurely, enjoying the picturesque, hilly route already so familiar to her. At low tide, broad, shimmering beaches appeared. Massive, grassy dunes gave way to scrubby moorland and colourful downs. The narrow road snaked through sleepy villages and around headlands, the most impressive being chalky Cap Blanc-Nez, which could already be glimpsed from the heights of Gris-Nez.

It was in a twisty valley that another vehicle came up quickly behind her. Ria was astonished when it began passing, since it was impossible to see far enough to do so safely. When they were side-by-side Ria realized two things in quick succession – that it was another WATS ambulance, and that a military truck was suddenly approaching from the other direction. There was no shoulder and no time for anyone to stop, so Ria swerved into the ditch and ploughed through the gorse bushes that grew thickly along this part of the road. In that instant, she could discern that the lorry also took some evasive action so that the other ambulance sailed unscathed between them.

She cursed under her breath when she realized that her car was stuck fast in the muddy ditch. Because the steering wheel was on the right in the open cab, the spiny gorse branches had sliced through the arm of her leather coat and scraped her cheek.

The truck had stopped and a couple of soldiers rushed to her aid. The British Corporal said with concern, "Are you alright, Miss? Nasty scratches," he added as he helped her climb out of the tilted car. "Lucky you didn't put an eye out."

Ria dabbed a handkerchief to her burning cheek, but was relieved to see only a little blood. "I'm quite alright, thank you, Corporal. I hope the same can be said of my ambulance."

"We'll haul her out in no time, Miss. Good of you to ditch her as we couldn't take the chance. Carrying ammo, you see."

"Hell's bells!"

"Quite right. We all owe you a debt of gratitude, especially that reckless driver. One of yours, wasn't she? Eager for her breakfast, do you think?" he added sarcastically. "Didn't even stop to see if you needed help. I'll have to report this, Miss..."

"Mrs. Wyndham."

Ria had recognized the bus – it was Dora Pettigrew's. She had already sensed that Dora disliked her. Not that that bothered Ria. She had enough friends, and didn't care what others thought of her. But she resented hostility and, in this case, outright, dangerous belligerence.

The soldiers had Calypso II back on the road in a few minutes, and the ambulance seemed undamaged save for some tears in the canvas and a punctured tyre. The men ignored her contention that she didn't need help, and replaced her tyre, the Corporal saying, "Gives the lads a boost to come to the aid of a pretty girl. It'll be the highlight of their week, I daresay."

They waved her cheerily on her way, but Ria was fuming and no longer enjoying the scenery. She raced back to camp.

The others were already at breakfast. Ria noticed that Dora and her friends stopped twittering amongst themselves and now eyed her challengingly.

'The Pod' Sybil called that clique because their names, first or last, all began with a 'P' – so, 'Ps in a pod'.

Ria marched up to Dora and demanded, "Why the hell did you run me off the road, Petty?" Ria knew that Dora hated that moniker, preferring 'Pet', but Sybil enjoyed it vastly.

"Oooh, do watch that Colonial vulgarity, Windy! Not at all acceptable here, don't you know."

"But not as bad as homicidal lunacy," Ria countered. "I should have let you encounter the lorry."

"You were ambling along as if you were asleep at the wheel. Or nervous about the winding road, *Windy*," Dora sneered. "I despise having my time wasted. You should have moved aside."

Ria suddenly chuckled. "You must have great faith in my humanity, Petty, to rely on my driving into a ditch to save your neck. By the way, that lorry was carrying explosives." She flounced away with a smirk, leaving Dora looking rather shocked.

"What was that all about?" Sybil asked as Ria joined her friends.

When Ria had explained she added, "I don't know what I've done to earn such resentment from The Pod."

"Pure jealousy," Carly informed her. "Major Chadwick had once – and only once, mind you – invited Petty to ride on the beach."

"Hell, Windy, you're so beautiful and accomplished that it's surprising you have any friends at all!" Sybil quipped.

"Well, Petty's going to be even more annoyed with me, because I'm reporting this."

"ComRad already threatened to send her back to England once," Carly said. "We all hate the Germans, of course, but Petty despises them with maniacal fervour. Her fiancé was killed early in the war, and that's why she joined the WATS. In any case, she was constantly trying to run down the POWs who've been working on constructing our new digs. Went out of her way to charge towards them, and laughed when they had to jump aside to avoid being hit. The guards complained and Petty was chastised. But I think she's just become more sneaky about it."

"She has a decidedly nasty streak, so watch your back, Windy," Sybil said. "She'll hate you even more now, since there's nothing worse than having to feel grateful to someone you dislike."

When Ria went to speak with her, ComRad had already received a complaint from the transport division about one of her drivers. And praise for Mrs. Wyndham's quick thinking.

"I do so relish irony," Sybil enthused as she painted iodine on Ria's scratches. "Petty's been chucked out of the Corps in disgrace, and she's inadvertently made you a heroine. I hear you're going to be Mentioned in Dispatches."

·   ·   ·

Ria was delighted to see Blake walk in to their tea social that afternoon. She wanted to embrace him, but since he was neither her husband nor brother, it wasn't appropriate.

"You're certainly looking better than when I last saw you," he said with a warm smile. "Except for those scratches. What have you been up to now?"

"A bit of a catfight," she joked. "Actually, an unwelcome encounter with gorse." She told him what had happened.

"You've been here just a matter of weeks and already you're receiving accolades."

"Or getting into mischief, as Grandmother so often said."

"Quite right. So I shouldn't be surprised."

For a happy moment, memories of childhood escapades in Muskoka overwhelmed them.

"Not hubby from what I remember of the photo," Sybil said, joining them.

"A very old and dear friend of mine, Dr. Blake Carlyle," Ria explained, and introduced him to everyone else there, including Lance Chadwick. "He's at the Canadian #3 General."

"Are you one of the summer friends?" Carly asked him.

"Yes indeed."

"Ouhu," Ria said to Carly. "Remember?"

"Your father's the professor with the telescope! I'll have you know that I plan to look through that one day."

Blake laughed. "I do hope so."

After he'd accepted a cup of tea and chatted amiably with the others, he and Ria excused themselves and went for a walk along the beach. The light was failing fast these days.

"I can imagine what you're feeling," Blake said to her after an awkward silence.

Ria paused. "I've been through a range of emotions, but now I feel almost numb. Still crying, though there can't be much left in the well. It helps to have these intense experiences to jolt me into realizing I'm still alive. Mostly I feel like I'm floundering in some nightmare."

"You seem to have an intellectual grasp of your feelings. That's a good sign."

"You mean I won't go loopy or top myself?"

Blake took her hand. "Chas wrote to me as well, Ria. He's profoundly sorry for what he did. I *can* understand it. But I know it's hard for you to accept that and forgive him. He wanted me to look out for you. God, I wish this hadn't happened! There was nothing more uplifting to the rest of us than seeing how happy you two were together."

Ria bit back tears.

"You can recapture that. I believe Chas when he says he's been faithful to you since your marriage."

"Do you think that a ceremony makes such a difference?"

"Yes. It's a psychological state we get into, telling ourselves that we're no longer looking after only ourselves, but are now part of a unit, a relationship that requires our dedication and nurturing and respect. And definitely loyalty. He really does love you, Ria. He's matured a lot since he came here. And we all make mistakes. We shouldn't have to pay for them forever."

"I can't put it behind me so easily. There's a child, Blake! Do you know how much that hurts?" She hugged herself tightly, as if to keep from falling apart. "Sometimes I do wish I were dead, just to stop the pain."

He held her. "I don't know what else to say except that children don't define you, Ria. You have so much to offer. And if you want little ones to raise, there are enough orphans out there who need parents. Especially now."

"I wanted Chas's children," she said quietly.

.   .   .

The day of the horse races began as a dud, according to the RFC. Which meant that the clouds were too low and thick for any effective flying – the kind of lazy day when the pilots were soon bored trying to amuse themselves with billiards or card games or tennis. That's why going into town or visiting the WATS was usually in order.

But by the time the races began, the clouds had thinned and ripped apart, and weak sunlight flooded the beach. Hundreds of people from the various hospitals and military camps, as well as the town, sheltered among the dunes to watch or picnicked on the cliffs farther along, where they had commanding views over the long stretch of sand.

"You can't be the best at everything, Windy. So if you beat me, I'll be jolly annoyed with you," Sybil warned Ria.

"Boss will trounce you both," Lucinda said. "I'm glad I'm not a horsey type." It was her last day, and she was trying to be cheerful.

Ria had been practicing with Stardust, the horse that Lance always brought for her. He wasn't the calibre of Calypso, but still a fine steed.

"You can't intimidate me, Foxy," Ria told Sybil. "And I don't give up easily."

"*En garde* then, Wyndham!" Sybil had taken up fencing in her very limited spare time. Captain Bentley was a good teacher.

Ria rode flat out, but Boss won, Sybil and ComRad tied for second place, and she came a close third.

"Very diplomatic of you," Sybil said.

"Not a bit of it! You had a better horse," she teased.

There were so many officers racing that they had heats. Ria sat with her WATS friends and Blake, who had managed to take the afternoon off. Eddie and Jonathan Telford were soon disqualified and joined them.

"We hadn't a hope against the Cavalry. That's all they do all day," Eddie said in feigned disgruntlement.

Ria had seen, at the polo match the previous week, that Lance was an expert horseman. He made it to the last round, and she cheered loudly for him. He came in third as well.

"The story of my life," he said in jest, when he joined them. "Third in line to the throne, so to speak, as well." He was referring to his father's title.

"This was jolly good fun," Henrietta Maltby stated. "Isn't it lucky that the clouds lifted?"

But suddenly, as if to mock her, there was a drone of engines and they looked up to see a couple of German bombers flying over Calais and dropping their load. It was so unusual for them to do this during the day that everyone watched speechlessly.

The strange silence of the spectators contrasted with the sharp explosions that shook them.

Anti-aircraft fire suddenly peppered the sky.

"Bloody hell!" Eddie said as he and the other pilots jumped to their feet and raced to the lorry they had driven over, although they all knew that the Germans would be long gone before they were even in their cockpits.

The WATS, too, rose as a body and hurried back to their camp. "I'll come with you," Blake said to Ria.

Secretary Mildred Elmsley was already taking a phone call for help with civilian casualties, but only half the ambulances would be needed, so the others stayed behind in case something else came in.

The German bombs had probably been intended for the harbour and railroad station, but missed key military installations and destroyed houses and shops instead. The cinema had been flattened, but fortunately, a movie had just finished and most of the patrons had left. Lucinda and Sybil would handle this scene.

Ria was directed by the authorities to a street a few blocks over. Her blood ran cold when she realized where she was. The café, the hair salon. The flower shop. All lay in ruins.

"Oh dear God!" Ria cried.

People were being dug out of the rubble. Blake hurried over to examine them. Some were still alive.

Others stood or sat on the street looking dazed. One woman, blood streaming down her face, crooned to the baby in her arms.

Ria put pressure on the wound to stop the bleeding, and bandaged her head. She looked to see if the baby was hurt and realized with horror that it was dead. She told Blake.

"Don't try to take it from her. Let them deal with that at the hospital. This woman is alive, but has both legs and an arm broken. Do you have any splints?"

They never seemed to have enough supplies. She handed him two splints and a broom she found in the rubble, and rounded up some more potential splints.

She did a quick assessment of the walking wounded, many hit by flying glass and debris, and applied bandages and slings. She asked everyone if they had seen a little girl. "Sophie, from the flower shop."

The lady who had only a few days earlier washed Ria's hair, had gashes on her arms and probably a broken wrist. "Sophie? Mais oui. Mme Bertrand at the boulangerie took her away when the soldiers came. She was screaming for her Maman."

"Thank God she's alright."

"But I have not seen her mother."

They pulled a few bodies out. One of them, Ria recognized as Sophie's mother. Her heart stopped when she heard Sophie come running, screaming, "Maman! Maman!" An elderly women hobbled behind her as quickly as she could, calling, "Sophie, come back!" But the child was frantic. Ria tried to grab her before she could see her mother, but she wasn't fast enough. Sophie fell onto the prostrate body and shook her. "Maman! Please wake up, Maman!" Her mother did look as if she were just sleeping, although covered in yellow dust. There were no marks, other than some superficial cuts, so her injuries must have been internal.

One of the soldiers picked Sophie up, although she tried valiantly to squirm out of his grasp.

Ria took her from him saying, "Come Sophie. Let the doctor have a look at your Maman." She blocked the child's view as Blake examined the mother. He shook his head at her.

"Come to my ambulance and I'll clean that cut on your head. Remember your Maman said that I help the injured?"

The sobbing child nodded and said, "Can you help Maman? Can the doctor?"

"Sometimes no one can help, ma petite," Ria said as she put iodine on the wound. Sophie didn't flinch. It would need stitching. "Sometimes only God can."

The old woman caught up to them, breathless. "I couldn't keep her away, Ma'mselle," she said to Ria. "Can you look after her now?"

"Where's her family?"

"There is no one."

"Grandparents? Aunts?"

"Not that I know of. Madame never spoke of them. It was just the two of them. Ah, pauvre enfant! You do what is best, Ma'mselle. Take her to the authorities."

"What does she mean?" Sophie demanded. "I want Maman! Please, Mademoiselle WATS."

"I'm afraid your Maman can't see you just now, ma petite. Would you like to ride in the ambulance with me?"

Sophie nodded as large tears created rivulets through the brick dust on her face.

The soldiers had already moved her mother's body, so Ria let the child look at the detritus of her shop and home, which had obviously been in the rooms above. Ria saw the arm of a rag doll sticking up and pulled it out of the debris.

"Delphine!" Sophie cried, hugging the doll to her. "She has a cut on her head as well, Mademoiselle WATS. Can you fix her?"

"Yes. We'll take her in the ambulance with us. Now you sit up here, and look after Delphine. Why don't you bandage her while I get some blessés into the back? D'accord?"

"Oui."

Ria left her with a small length of bandage and went to help Blake load four stretchers, all fractures and one with probable internal injuries. Carly and Henrietta arrived and took the shuffling wounded in their ambulances. Carly said, "The bombs only just missed the civilian hospital. I've had mostly minor injuries, surprisingly."

"Some dead here," Ria told her. "Including the child's mother."

"Oh no!"

Blake cradled Sophie on his lap as Ria drove to the hospital. They had to detour through several streets to avoid the rubble and a fire. When they had unloaded the stretchers, Blake offered to stitch up patients, since there was a stream of them being brought in by the ambulances. The overworked doctors accepted his help gratefully, and dealt with the more severe cases. Ria stayed with him to help clean wounds and apply bandages.

Blake lifted Sophie onto the table and said in passable French, "Will you be brave for me? I'm going to stitch your head, and

Madame WATS is going to stitch Delphine's. Then you'll both look like Madame. See?" He pointed to Ria's scar.

Sophie nodded. "Will you stitch up Maman as well?"

"If I could, I certainly would. You are a very brave girl. Your Maman would be proud of you."

"She's with Papa, isn't she?"

"With him and God, yes," Ria said reluctantly.

"Maman said she would never leave me unless she had to be with Papa."

Ria thought her heart would break as this little girl, who seemed too young to have any real notion of death, looked bleakly at her with overflowing eyes. "Why does he need her more than I do?"

"I don't know, Sophie. God has reasons we can't always know. But He knows that you are strong and good and will be everything that your Maman and Papa taught you. You will be the flower girl now. And the flowers will remind you of your parents. When you look into the face of a daisy you will remember your mother's smile. When you smell the roses, you will recall the scent of her. When you count the petals of a carnation you will remember all the happy times you had."

Ria held the sobbing child in her arms, with her own tears running unchecked down her cheeks.

Blake said to Ria in English, "Beautifully said, if heartbreaking."

Sophie wouldn't leave Ria's side, although the Sisters tried to pry her away. "Never mind, I'll look after her for now," Ria told them.

They shrugged. "Take her to the orphanage when you're ready. Someone there will check to see if there is family."

"What are you going to do with her?" Blake asked as she drove him back to his hospital. Sophie was sitting between them, hugging her doll. Silent.

"I don't know. Poor mite! I can't just dump her at the orphanage. Not yet. She needs people around her she knows, and oddly enough, she seems to have taken to me."

"Not odd at all. She must sense that you truly love children."

"I can't exactly bring her into the camp, like a pet. But maybe I can keep her with me tonight and then find a good place for her. Oh God, this bloody war is destroying so many lives, devastating so many futures! You should have seen how happy she and her mother were. How close. She'll never be the person she would have been. How can she ever recover from this?"

"People are remarkably resilient. Look at you. No mother. An indifferent, even hostile father. A stern grandmother. And yet you are a warm and caring and joyful person."

"Because I had people like you and Zoë and the rest."

"You can keep in contact with Sophie. Perhaps even adopt her." Blake gave her a sidelong glance.

"What? No! How can I? I have a job to do."

"Think about it. You don't have to quit the WATS. Cousin Bea would take her for now, don't you think?"

Ria thought about Blake's suggestion as she raced back to the camp in the twilight. Much as she liked Sophie, she wasn't ready to take on such an enormous responsibility. And Chas would have to be consulted. If she stayed with him.

Boss said, "This is highly irregular, Wyndham."

"Just for tonight. The child is devastated."

"One night then. No more."

"Thank you. And I'll do duty this evening." Someone always had to stay behind to take telephone calls while the others went to the entertainments. It wasn't her turn. The dance at the Cavalry mess was still on, but she wouldn't have had the heart for it anyway.

She set up a bed for Sophie in the office and brought her own in as well. The mess was now operational in the new building, adjacent to the office, so Ria took Sophie in there once the others had left, and played *Ragtime Nightingale* on the piano, while Sophie sat next to her on the bench. The piece was both hauntingly poignant and cheerfully uplifting, and taxed Ria's skills. She taught Sophie some simple phrases, which delighted her, and soon they were playing a duet.

"Well done, Sophie! Isn't it fun to make music?"

"Oh yes."

After a while Ria asked, "Where were you when the aeroplanes came?" wondering how the child had escaped the devastation.

"Maman said I could go and buy chocolate with the money you gave me. Madame Fortin always lets me have it cheaper on Saturday, before she closes the shop. I was coming back. And the house fell. Maman was inside."

Ria made hot cocoa, with real milk, and tucked Sophie into the makeshift bed. She told her stories about Canada to distract her, and Sophie eventually fell asleep, tears glistening on her cheeks.

Ria was writing to Zoë when Lance suddenly appeared. "I heard about today. Poor tyke," he said, looking at Sophie. Opening a bottle of champagne, he added, "I've come to say goodbye. We've been given marching orders. Back to the Somme. We leave tomorrow."

"So soon!"

"We don't have much to pack," he said with a grin. "But we are taking our horses, so I wonder if they're expecting a breakthrough. I can hardly imagine it. The war has begun to feel like it's a way of life, like it will never end." He clinked glasses with her. "I hope you're still here when we return. We may be back by Christmas."

"I don't get leave for six months." She added, "Except that I might be sent home in disgrace. Do you know it's against regulations for us to be alone, now that it's dark?"

"In case I do this," he said, pulling her into his arms and kissing her.

Caught off guard and realizing that she enjoyed the kiss, Ria hesitated momentarily before pushing him away. "Please don't. You know I'm married."

"So am I," he said to her surprise. "But don't you think this war has changed things?"

"Not in that way. Not to make infidelity normal or acceptable."

With a wry smile he said, "But it already is in some circles. My wife was chosen for me by my family. Just like they chose my career. She had the right lineage. We rub along alright, and have two children who I believe are mine. But my wife amuses herself with fox hunting and weekend house parties. I don't know how many lovers she's had. We don't expect fidelity."

"Well *I* do! I love my husband."

"Do you? You never talk about him." His gaze both challenged and invited her.

"I think you should leave, Lance."

Regretfully he said, "Perhaps I should. Look after yourself."

"And you."

Chapter 4

"Is Ria at the Club, Cousin Bea? I didn't see her car," Chas said after hugging Beatrice and presenting her with a bouquet of flowers.

He looked hopeful, worried, and slightly shamefaced, Beatrice thought. She took his arm and led him into the sitting room. "I'm afraid she's gone, Chas. To France with the WATS." Bea poured him a scotch and handed him the glass.

He gave her a dozen red roses, saying, "Then you'd best have these as well.... Bloody hell! Alice told me about Ria's intentions. I sent her a letter, trying to dissuade her, asking her to wait for me. I tried to get leave earlier!" He downed the whiskey and ran a hand agitatedly through his hair. "God, I've made a mess of things!"

"I'm rather afraid you have, dear boy. But I believe there's still hope for you two."

"Where is she, Cousin Bea? I'll go back to France and talk to her."

"I don't know, Chas. She seems to have gone into hiding. She tends to do that when she's upset."

Chas recalled Ria's running away that summer of 1914 when her father had announced that he was engaged to a woman young enough to be his daughter. It was when he had found Ria that Chas had realized he was in love with her.

Bea said reluctantly, "You should know that she's calling herself Victoria Wyndham now. All her letters are to be sent to the WATS office in London."

"Oh, God!" he said, putting his hands over his face and pressing his fingers into his forehead in an effort to stave off tears. She hated him so much that she'd even renounced his name. That was more of a blow than her silence had been.

"Perhaps Ria is better off without me," he said disconsolately.

"If you really believe that, then you don't know her at all. Or is that a convenient, noble-sounding excuse to get out of your marriage?"

"Of course not! I love her. I need her. I want her back. Desperately."

"Then fight for her."

"I don't know how! She won't write back to me. I've tried to explain to her in my letters, but I don't even know what foe I'm fighting anymore."

"Ria wants and needs to be cherished. She never had a mother and had no love from her father. Augusta loved her, of course, but doled out her affection sparingly. No doubt she thought it would give Ria backbone. That was probably a reaction to Augusta's having indulged and cosseted Alex, only to have him turn against her. Albert is rather a cold fish and Phyllis is antagonistic toward Ria, as you know. Thank God for Richard and his family! They are the only ones who've loved her unreservedly. They are the family that Ria has always wanted to be part of – especially being so close to Zoë and Max. It's why Ria so desperately wants a large family of her own."

"Which she can't have," Chas said.

"But she'll have you. And you can always adopt children. So what you need to do is to reassure her that you *do* cherish her, that you are her family. That you will always be there for her. Don't accept her silence. She's afraid to trust you right now, afraid that if she lets down the barrier she's erected between you she may be hurt even more."

Bea's face softened when she saw the misery in Chas's eyes. She laid her hand reassuringly on his. "You two can make this work. Her love is too deep to be easily lost."

He nodded, not trusting himself to speak. Finally he said, "I never thought I would ever rely so much on someone else for my happiness. It's rather disconcerting."

"Remember that when you two have your disagreements, as all couples do."

"I'll go to London, to the WATS headquarters and find out where she is. Then I'll return to France."

Bea poured him another drink. "Right now, you take this along to a hot bath and have a nap before dinner. You're exhausted, dear boy, and no good to anyone in your present state. Take a week at least to rest. Ria needs time to think things through. Give her a chance to see what it's really like over there. She might be more willing to forgive you."

But going into their bedroom was difficult. It was a lovely room overlooking the lawns and gardens that flowed down to the river. Chas opened the wardrobe and saw Ria's clothes hanging there. Flaccid silk. Lifeless. Left behind as if she were dead. He drew out one of her favourite evening gowns and hugged it, breathing in a faint lingering scent of lavender. He buried his face in it as he wept.

· · ·

Chas woke with a start to find his bath had gone cold. Yet again. It seemed he couldn't get enough sleep or hot baths. He refreshed the tub with steaming water and lay back, gazing out at the Thames. Thinking about the times that he and Ria had canoed or rowed along the river.

God, how he ached for her!

Although he hadn't encountered the ghost that reputedly haunted Bovington Abbey, Chas found the *absence* of a person more disturbing than meeting a spectral presence. The many rooms in the house seemed to contain a palpable void that unnerved him.

But then he was easily startled these days and sometimes felt as if electricity was crackling along his nerves and tingling his skin.

He seemed to be drifting between agitation and somnolence, finding himself in places and not knowing how he got there, or suddenly in the midst of a conversation and not recalling what was being discussed or even whether he had participated. Perhaps it was a reaction to the intense concentration required when he was flying that he could now not focus his thoughts.

Or perhaps it was mild shell-shock. He had seen it often enough in his men. Some shook and sweated uncontrollably, stammered, vomited, couldn't sleep, burst into tears, or, like Ria, had gasping, heart-pounding panic attacks. One of the boys had stopped speaking altogether, as if he could no longer put voice to the fear and horror he had experienced. It was then that Chas remembered how young most of them were – eighteen, nineteen – and felt decidedly old at twenty-four.

Major-General "Boom" Trenchard, who was in charge of the RFC in France, had recently said to him, "Can't afford to lose good pilots like you, Thornton. Twenty-four victories under your belt. What would people say if we lost all our heroes? Time to let other chaps have a go at the Hun. You're a talented leader and teacher, so I'm giving you a choice."

He could either train fighter pilots somewhere in darkest Scotland, or become the Commanding Officer of a new fighter squadron. Chas had intended to opt for the safest course, which would also give him and Ria a chance to be together, for she could set up a home for them near the base. But now that she was in France, he could hardly go to Scotland. He had thought of telling her about the option, hoping that she would come back to be with him. But he was afraid she would refuse, and couldn't deal with that kind of rejection at the moment.

At Bea's insistence, Chas had slept for most of three days. When he lifted his hands out of the water, he was pleased to see that they hardly shook today.

After he was dressed, he sat at the small writing table by the window.

My darling Ria,

Your silence is like a physical blow, your absence, as if you've been carved away from my flesh. That you have renounced your status as my wife has poured salt on my wounds. But I know that you suffer as deeply from what I have unintentionally done to you. How I wish I could take all that anguish away from you!

When you hovered on the brink of death with the fever, I made pacts with God, the devil, and every divine being who might be able to spare your life. I was haunted by visions of having to live without you. I saw only a bleak stretch of lonely, joyless days.

I am once again gripped by the fear of losing you. My own fault, you will say. But I believe that if we talked, we could help each other through our pain and become whole again.

My 'prostrations of love' as you called them were never empty words. You can blame me for keeping things from you, but never that I lied about my feelings for you.

We can't resolve things with silence. Please write, at least to let me know that you are safe, my darling....

.   .   .

"You're looking better," Beatrice said to Chas as he drove them to Cliveden in her Rolls. Although Bea had learned to drive before her chauffeur had resigned to join up, she wasn't entirely comfortable behind the wheel. Horses were more her style.

They were going to see Zoë, visit the wounded, and lunch with the Astors, who owned the magnificent Cliveden estate and had so generously given over part of it to the Canadians as a hospital at the outbreak of the war.

"I feel a bit more able to face the world, thanks to your ministrations, Cousin Bea."

Chas had to admit he was rather nervous about seeing Zoë. She was one of those touchstone people whose opinion he valued. Devoted to Ria, Zoë would undoubtedly be furious with him.

Cliveden perched like a crown atop a commanding terrace high above the Thames. The house was immense and beautifully proportioned in a classical Italianate style. Strewn about the more than twelve hundred acres of gardens and parkland were ornamental pools and fountains, statues and sculptures, an ancient Byzantine chapel, transported from Asia Minor, an elaborate clock tower, a nine-hole golf course, and tennis courts.

There was also a Canadian cemetery in a sunken garden, flat granite stones marking each soldier's grave. And in what had once been the Astor's indoor tennis court and bowling alley was the Duchess of Connaught's Canadian Red Cross Hospital, much expanded with endless wings which housed several hundred wounded, mostly Canadians. The hospital was better known as *Taplow*, named for the village nearby.

As Zoë was still on duty, Chas and Beatrice distributed chocolates and cigarettes among the patients, and stopped to chat. When questioned about the wound stripe on his sleeve, Chas admitted that he had spent some time in the hospital the previous summer, and could attest to its excellent reputation.

When Zoë, a coat thrown over her uniform, appeared at his side, Bea waved them off saying, "You two have a lot of catching up to do, so I'll see you at luncheon in half an hour. The grounds are lovely for a stroll."

Chas and Zoë walked out silently, and then he said, "It's wonderful to see you again, Zoë." He looked at her apprehensively.

When Zoë had arrived in England, just days after Ria's departure to France, she had stayed with Bea before beginning work at the hospital. Justin had still been at Bovington and had told her what had happened, as Ria had requested.

Zoë stared hard at Chas as she said, "I've been through a gamut of emotions about you, from surprise and disappointment to anger. But right now, I'm delighted to see you whole and well, if tired." She smiled sadly at him and gave him a hug. He clung to her gratefully.

She could sense a certain frailty in him, which moved her. The invincible, easygoing friend of her youth was also being torn apart by this war, perhaps not physically, but mentally. Having studied psychology and discussed it at length with Blake when they had both been at the university, she feared for Chas. She knew about shell-shock and about how dangerous flying was even without that added complication.

She entwined her arm in his and led him down to the river walk. The autumn here was gentler, less intense than in Canada, where the brilliantly colourful fall leaves would already have been sliced from the trees by ice-edged winds. But the rich, earthy smell of crumpled and decaying vegetation was similar.

"Do you think Ria will ever forgive me?" Chas asked. "I swear I never meant to hurt her, Zoë! Perhaps I was too casual about intimacy before, and didn't think of it as a betrayal. Sometimes sex is just a hunger that needs to be appeased. Or a temporary escape. Not connected to emotions." Angry with himself, he said, "And here I am, constantly trying to make excuses for being a cad and an fool! But when I almost lost her, I would have sold my soul to the devil himself to keep her alive. I've changed. How can I make her understand that, Zoë?"

Not having seen him for two years, Zoë was struck by the difference in him. He was no longer the flippant, flirtatious bon vivant, but uncharacteristically intense and serious. It was encouraging to see that he had matured, but also somewhat sad to see the demise of hedonistic gaiety and innocence. "I don't know, Chas. Somehow you have to reassure her that she is the most important person in your life, and that you *will* be faithful to her."

They had reached the river's edge. Among the venerable trees providing a golden canopy, Chas said, "I'm going back early to find her. If... I can't persuade her, will you be sure she knows how much I love her?"

He said it as if he wouldn't be coming back, which sent a shiver down Zoë's spine.

Chas leaned his head against a massive oak and was embarrassed by the tears he couldn't suppress. "I'm sorry," he stammered as Zoë put her arm about him.

Damn this bloody war, she thought. "Let Ria into your thoughts and feelings, Chas. I'm sure she'll understand."

They stood silently for a long time, looking out over the murky river. Chas finally roused himself and said, "We mustn't be late for lunch."

As they walked up to the house, he said, "One of the things I find really difficult now is coming back to some sort of normality. Life going on as if hell weren't raging just across that narrow strip of channel. Just fifteen or twenty minutes away by air. I expect you've already seen enough of the casualties to know what I'm talking about.

"I particularly detest the 'hero' label I've been getting in the press. Of course I'm glad I've been successful, but it's not like winning a race at the Regatta. I'm not proud of the fact that I've killed valiant men. I do it because it's my job, because if I don't, I know that chaps on our side will be killed. That's the madness of war. Do you know that in the beginning, we used to salute each other – we and the Germans? It was more a contest of skill then, with old-fashioned chivalry. But it's become as bloody as the ground battles."

So when some of the Astors' guests were keen to discuss Chas's 'kills', Zoë felt for him. Knowing him all her life, she could see how tightly he held himself.

"I expect it's a thrill to see the enemy go down in flames," someone observed with vicarious delight.

"Of course one is pleased to win the battle." Chas wondered why he hesitated to admit that he felt diminished causing another man to die in such a gruesome way. It seemed somehow unpatriotic to voice that thought.

"Do tell us, Captain Thornton, what it's like to fight in the sky," someone urged. "I can't even imagine what it must be like to be up there in the first place."

"Extremely cold," Chas said to amused chuckles. He resisted telling them that the Germans had once again gained air superiority over the Somme with their latest Jagdstaffel or Jasta – fighter squadrons – equipped with powerful and tough new Albatros aeroplanes, armed with two machine guns. Oswald Boelcke, the top German Ace since Immelman's death in June, was in charge of a Jasta. He was a clever tactician, and his squadron flew in large, disciplined, aggressive formations, which were scaring the hell out of Chas's pilots. Like a pack of bloodthirsty hounds, the Jasta pilots were no longer gentlemanly in pursuit of their prey. Within this past month of ferocious and deadly fighting, one of his pilots had been killed, one wounded, and another had to be posted out when he lost his nerve. Odds were that the two remaining members of his flight would no longer be there when he returned from leave.

But he felt he couldn't spoil the Astors' luncheon party by relating gritty details that people didn't truly want to hear. He said, "Our job as scouts is to protect our reconnaissance and artillery spotting planes, as well as to prevent the enemy from doing their reconnaissance work. Because those aeroplanes are slow and cumbersome, they're relatively easy to shoot down. I know, as I started out by flying them myself. You have to be a skilled pilot to survive, and I think that those chaps are not given enough recognition. They and their observers are the true heroes, taking photographs and relaying strategic information to the ground forces, all the while knowing that they're sitting ducks for the fighter planes."

"So you engage the enemy fighters, allowing the others to dash away smartly. Just how do you manage to fly an aeroplane and shoot a gun at the same time?" someone asked.

"It takes practice. Our machine guns are now mounted so that they are synchronized to shoot through the propeller blades."

"Good Lord! Aren't you afraid you'll shoot them off?"

"That has happened, but we're getting better equipment all the time. Have to keep up with the Germans, you know," Chas added wryly.

"Yes, but I want to know how you actually manage to hit the enemy and not your own men when you're all flying about higgledy-piggledy shooting at each other."

"It's not easy. And occasionally planes even crash into each other. But my men know my strategy, and we work as a team. In addition to our RFC roundels, we all have some sort of personal design painted on our aeroplanes. Mine's a dragonfly." For Ria. "It's how we recognize individual pilots. One of the new German fighter pilots is so confident that he's painted his entire aeroplane red. The lads are calling him The Red Baron."

"Ha! Easy target then. Fool! You'll make minced meat of him quickly enough," Lord Moulsford snorted.

"Is he a Baron?"

"So I hear. Von Richthofen."

"Do tell us what you did to earn your medals, Captain Wyndham," The Honourable Miss Eugenia Willoughby urged, blushing prettily.

Zoë was amused, for the young woman was evidently smitten by Chas. He undoubtedly left plenty of love-struck women in his wake, since he was astonishingly handsome, congenial, debonair.

"I shouldn't like to bore people," Chas demurred.

"Not at all," Nancy Astor said, adding astutely, "We all delight in experiencing the war from the safety of our drawing rooms."

He told them briefly, downplaying his heroics, which actually impressed the others much more than if he had bragged about them.

The inside of Cliveden was even more spectacular than the exterior. Visitors were invariably awed by the magnificent baronial Great Hall, and the dining room was exquisite. It had once belonged to Madame de Pompadour, been brought over from France, and installed at Cliveden. Tastefully Rococo, the gilt-edged wall panels were powder blue, as were the long table, chairs, and buffet. Beautiful leaded glass doors at the end of the room opened onto the extensive terrace that overlooked the Thames.

Zoë was glad that a few Medical Officers and Sisters had also been invited. She was one of only two VADs working here, since the Canadian Army Medical Corps didn't approve of volunteers. Many of the professional nurses were scornful of them, thinking them frivolous socialites who were playing at nursing, but secretly afraid for their own jobs, since girls like Zoë were competent and learned quickly. The fact that Zoë had aristocratic connections alienated her even more from narrow-minded staff, who, unfortunately, had the power to make her life miserable.

But Nancy Astor had already taken a shine to Zoë. Smart and curious, an American by birth, Mrs. Astor was interested in Zoë's experiences at university and her volunteer work with indigent immigrants at the Settlement House in Toronto.

The Astors were teetotal, so only fruit juice was served. It appeared that a few favoured guests, including the doctors, were discreetly served glasses of whiskey by the butler, who asked Chas quietly, "Would you like something more sustaining, Captain?"

"Thank you," Chas replied gratefully, hoping it would take the edge off his unaccustomed tension.

"What do you think of this negotiated peace nonsense?" one of the guests asked.

"Nonsense indeed. Unconditional surrender, I say!" Lord Moulsford declared. "What do you say, Captain Thornton?"

"I shouldn't like to see a few more million men die just to prove a point."

There was an awkward silence. Chas realized that they probably didn't know that troops were being mown down like so much hay. Propaganda, censorship, and a reluctance of the men themselves to talk about the horrors when they were home on leave all contributed to a comfortable sense that the Allies were winning the war, and the conviction that Germany must pay for the audacity of having started it.

While people were still proud and eager to send their sons to be slaughtered for the perceived good of the Empire, democracy, even humanity, it seemed churlish to tell them that their progeny might die barbarically. Possibly to no avail.

"It does seem to have become a war of attrition," one of the doctors said. "Which leads one to speculate that the war will be won by whichever side has the most young men to sacrifice."

"We just need to get the slackers and conchies to do their duty and the war would be over in no time," Lord Moulsford said dismissively.

"Ah, but wait until the women are mobilized," Nancy Astor said. "You know that the Ministry of National Service is organizing women's auxiliary troops to replace men in non-combatant roles."

"Stuff and nonsense!" Lord Moulsford snorted. "Women shouldn't be interfering, playing at being soldiers! They'll just distract the men and we'll end up with a generation of *war babies* – what we used to call bastards."

"Really, Mortimer!" his wife chided.

"Well, it's an absurd idea. They'll have women in trousers next. Chopping off their hair. Flying aeroplanes."

Chas had to suppress a grin, since the indignant aristocrat had just described Ria. Nancy Astor noticed and said mischievously, "Have you met Mrs. Thornton then, Lord Moulsford? She took me for a thrilling flight over the countryside this summer. What fun to see Cliveden from the air! A most accomplished aviatrix, and a delightful and beautiful young woman. With very attractive short hair. She's just gone off to France to drive a motor ambulance. Young women these days are so adventuresome. I admire them tremendously."

Lord Moulsford grumbled. The Honourable Miss Eugenia Willoughby wilted noticeably.

Coffee was served in the more intimate atmosphere of the library rather than the enormous drawing room that could comfortably seat sixty. Zoë noticed that Chas, who was usually a witty conversationalist and completely at ease in any social situation, was quiet and pensive. He seemed relieved when one of the doctors announced that he needed to return to work, effectively breaking up the party. Chas offered to walk Zoë back to her lodgings while Beatrice and Nancy Astor said that they would visit with the patients. From experience, Chas knew that Nancy not only enjoyed cajoling and badgering the patients into getting well, but also that they adored her. She was the best medicine for them, one of the doctors had told Chas during his stay.

"I feel as if I can breathe again," Chas said to Zoë as they strolled through the gardens. The nurses were billeted in a Georgian mansion that belonged to the estate, across the road from the hospital. "Not like me to eschew a social occasion, is it?" he asked with a self-deprecating chuckle. "I find that I have so little I really care to discuss these days. Certainly not the war. And idle chatter almost puts me into a coma. So now let's talk about something cheerful and important. I want to hear all about home – how everyone is, what summer was like in Muskoka. Fliss sends me photos of herself and I feel that I'll hardly recognize her when I get home. She's going to be seventeen soon. Good God! I've missed out on her childhood!"

Zoë laughed. "She's an accomplished young lady already. Did she tell you that she planned the Labour Day Ball at Thorncliff virtually by herself? Your mother made suggestions, but Fliss carried it off beautifully. We all enjoyed it, even if we did miss absent friends."

She talked about his family and hers, and the neighbouring islanders, even though she had spent only a few weeks at the cottage this summer.

"So Max and Lydia are affianced, and Edgar and Daphne are spooning. I suppose Daphne's grown up as well," Chas said.

"The same age Ria was when you... got engaged." Zoë had almost said "seduced her", but knowing Ria, it may well have been the other way around. "Ellie and I were astonished at how quickly that happened. They danced at the ball and suddenly became inseparable. I wouldn't be surprised if they married soon." Ellie had been disappointed to discover that her little sister had no greater ambition than that. Daphne had refused to attend the university, assuring her family that it would be a waste of time and money.

"It's good to know that some of us are able to carry on in some sort of normal fashion," Chas said. "Realizing that's still possible keeps us going and gives us hope."

He paused and then confessed, "Do you know what I want more than anything in the world? To take Ria back home, squirrel ourselves away at Wyndwood or Thorncliff for the winter and emerge in the spring feeling healed. I know it's a stupid thought, since neither place can be inhabited in the winter. But I can imagine what the lake must look like when it's frozen feet thick and topped with snow sculpted into fantastic shapes by blizzards. We'd listen to the wind howling about our fire-lit island of warmth or watch the softly, endlessly falling snowflakes on gentle days. The evergreen boughs would be muffled with fluffy snow, tree branches encased in ice, and everything would sparkle in the pale winter sun. I see this pristine whiteness everywhere. Good God, I must be tapped, spouting such nonsense!"

"It sounds wonderful to me. I think you've missed winters at home," Zoë said, since Chas had spent the four years previous to the war at Oxford. All that whiteness must be an antidote to the mud and blood of the trenches that she had been hearing about from the patients. Chas's life in the RFC would be cleaner to some extent. But the blood was everywhere.

"Look after yourself," Zoë said when they arrived at her lodgings.

"It's not official yet, so don't pass this along. But I'm being offered my own squadron and promotion to Major."

"Chas, that's wonderful! Does it mean that you won't be in the front lines, so to speak?"

"Technically, Commanding Officers are only supposed to fly recreationally, to train, or on special missions. So it *is* less dangerous."

"'Technically' meaning that most of them don't adhere to the rules?"

Chas laughed. "You always were quick. Our present CO loves a good scrap. It's hard to keep him on the ground. But because he was wounded, I was Officer Commanding for the past two months. It's why I didn't have leave until now."

"But you flew. Didn't you just get another medal?"

"And a bar. I was Fight Commander as well as OC. It'll be easier just being the CO."

"And you *will* play by the rules?"

Chas smiled at her concern. "I'm not out for glory anymore. I can do my bit by making sure that the boys I send up are trained well enough so that they come back again."

"And you, too."

Chas kissed her cheek. "It's good to have you here, Zoë."

She was back on duty from 4:00 PM until midnight – part of her penalty for a good lunch.

Hastily she penned a letter.

Dearest Ria,
    *I saw Chas today. We and Cousin Bea were invited to lunch
with the Astors. I'm concerned about him. The war seems to be
taking its toll. I'm convinced that he is somewhat shell-shocked,
which worries me since he's soon going back.*
    *I can see that he is truly devastated by what has happened
between you. Don't close your heart to him. You need each other. We
can't always take the moral high road. We must take circumstances
into consideration.*
    *God, how trite and preachy that sounds! I mean to say that I
believe that Chas loves you deeply, devotedly, and deserves another
chance.*
    *Already I miss the healing power of Muskoka. I wish the two of
you could just go home.*
    And I wish I could see you, my dearest friend and cousin!
    Love, Zoë

·   ·   ·

Chas sent a telegram to Alice's headmistress. "Request
permission take Alice Lambton out Sat. PM. Also invite her
friends Moira, Dorothy, Kate to lunch, if amenable. Arriving noon.
Capt. Chas Thornton, BA (Oxford), DSO & bar, MC"
    To Alice he cabled, "Request pleasure of your company for
lunch and tea Sat. Please extend invitation to your 3 friends for
lunch. Love, Chas."
    Alice shrieked with delight when she read it.
    The headmistress, Miss Sedgeberrow, asked Alice, "Is this the
Ace pilot we keep reading about?"
    "Yes, Headmistress."
    "Are you related to him?"
    "No, Headmistress. He and his wife, Ria, are my friends. She
and I met on the *Lusitania*, and we, well... sort of saved each
other's lives. Cousin Bea, that is, Lady Kirkland, is really Ria's
cousin, not mine, but I'm like a part of the family now."
    "I see. Well, it's a great honour to have Captain Thornton visit
our school. A most distinguished young man. It's not every day we
see heroes like him."
    Alice's friends were excited, and Moira couldn't resist making
the rest of the school aware of their special treat.
    So when Chas arrived promptly at noon on Saturday in Bea's
Rolls Royce, he was the focus of most of the upper school and the
staff – as he had planned. He knew when credentials and celebrity

were useful. Alice should gain a bit more respect from the other girls now.

He hugged her warmly, and she whispered, "You look so dashing that all the girls will be green with envy."

He whispered back, "Good."

The headmistress and some of the staff stood at the entrance like a welcoming committee, so Alice said, "Miss Sedgeberrow, may I introduce my very great friend, Captain Chas Thornton?"

Chas's warm blue eyes engaged hers and he could see a blush rise in her sallow cheeks. "A great pleasure to meet you, Miss Sedgeberrow. This is an impressive establishment you run." It was an immense, pseudo-Gothic country house that had outgrown the needs and means of its previous owner.

"Thank you, Captain. May I say how delighted we are to meet one of England's heroes?"

"We Canadians are rather fond of our Mother Country," he said with a grin.

"To our great benefit. Do allow me to introduce our staff."

Chas charmed them all, as he did most people, just by being himself. There was no artifice involved. He answered questions with his usual wit, and gracefully extricated himself.

The four girls clambered eagerly into the Rolls. As they drove off waving, Alice said to Chas, "I feel like royalty."

Chas laughed. "Well, Princess Alice, your chauffeur is ready to whisk you off anywhere."

"Bovington?"

"How about The Randolph?"

The other girls were awed by its elegance, but Alice had dined in the best hotels in London with Ria and Chas and the others. He soon put Alice's friends at ease, and they had a delightful, long lunch with much laughter and Chas promising he'd take them all for an aeroplane ride some day. Afterwards, they did a short tour of the Ashmolean Museum, which was just across the street.

When they had dropped her friends back at the school, Alice said, "That was such great fun, Chas! Thank you so much for asking my friends along. None of them gets treats like that, especially Moira and Dorothy, who aren't close to home or family. But I am glad that you and I have some time together. Just by ourselves."

"I thought I'd take you punting on the Cherwell. Would you like that?"

"Oh, yes!"

It was a beautifully warm day for late October, and there were a few other boats out. But not like the days when Chas had been here, for most of the able-bodied students had gone to war.

He said, "So you have ambitions to attend Oxford?"

"I think so," Alice said, wrinkling her brow in serious contemplation. "I was wondering what I should do when I'm finally liberated from school. I can't really go home, because I don't even know my stepmother and she and my father have a new baby – my half-sister, I guess – which is a rather bizarre thought. And I can't just live with my grandparents forever. So I need to look after myself. Which means I need a career. I couldn't be a doctor like your friend, Ellie. I don't like blood. I'd hate to be a teacher. I can't imagine constantly struggling against indifference and ignorance and rebelliousness. So I don't really know what I could do that I'd actually *like* to do. Oh, dear, I'm afraid I'm rather hopeless."

Chas smiled. "You like writing, don't you? Poems and stories?"

"I love it! But do you think anyone would actually pay to read my stories? Because I will have to pay for lodgings and food."

"I most certainly do think you could make a go of it. You could start in journalism, like Thea. Why don't you write an article right now for *Home Fires* about something – the schoolgirl's view of the war, for example. I'm sure that Thea would give you helpful advice. And publish your story."

"Do you really think so?" Alice asked excitedly. "Could I interview you? Ask the famous Ace what keeps him going, what he looks forward to when he's home on leave."

Chas winced slightly, but Alice noticed and said, "Oh dear. I seem to have touched a sore spot. There *is* something wrong between you and Ria, isn't there?" She felt terrified in that instant, hoping he wouldn't say something that would shatter her world. She loved Ria and Chas, and wanted them to be forever happy. Just like in the story she had written for them last Christmas.

Chas steered the boat over to the bank and sat down. "I'm afraid I did something stupid that makes Ria think I don't love her enough. It's not true, of course."

Alice had seen in Ireland, when she had first met Chas, how much he loved Ria. "I know it's not. Can't you convince her?"

"I will," he said with a determined smile. He didn't want to spoil Alice's day or have her worry about him and Ria. "And I *will* give you an interview. One day, when you're a famous author, I'll be able to tell everyone that I gave you your big break."

Alice laughed joyfully. Somehow she knew that Ria and Chas would be alright.

.   .   .

"What's happened between you and Ria? Why has she suddenly gone off to war?" Henry asked Chas over dinner at The Randolph that evening.

"What did she tell you?" Obviously not the truth, and Chas was grateful for that small mercy.

"I had the sense that she feels she's missing out on the ultimate adventure if she doesn't actively participate. I would have thought that *you* could control some of her crazier notions."

Chas smiled ruefully. "You know your cousin. When she gets an idea..."

"She's as stubborn as a mule. And revels in being unconventional. Yes, I know only too well. And she'll stick with this no matter how horrible and difficult it is. Even just to prove that she can. I both admire and detest that trait in her. I can see you have your hands full with her, Chas."

.   .   .

Chas didn't have to go to the WATS headquarters to try to find Ria. He received a letter from Blake in response to his own in which he had confessed everything to his friend.

Dear Chas,

Justin also told me what's happened so that I can keep an eye on Ria, since she is actually stationed nearby, on the outskirts of Calais. We're both worried about her. I've seen her a couple of times. She is shattered, and I fear, rather negligent of her own safety.

What she's doing is tremendously taxing, both physically and emotionally, and often dangerous. We seem to be getting more air raids in the Calais area, and you know how inaccurate dropping bombs can be. The WATS often have to drive through the raids.

I do understand how you could have drifted into a relationship when in a funk, as you say. I don't understand how you could have been careless with protection, however. I think it would have lessened the impact of the liaison had it not resulted in a child. Of course, Ria would never have found out otherwise, would she?

I trust you're not going to make a habit of cheating on your wife.

As you can imagine, Ria has no lack of admirers. In her fragile state of mind, she may be ripe for seduction – she is in her own funk right now, especially as she feels severed from you, and is emotionally adrift. I do think it would be a good idea for you to see her as soon as possible and try for a reconciliation.

This war has already taken so much from us. I don't want to see your marriage as another casualty.

Good luck, my friend. Blake.

.   .   .

Chas was frantic now to get to France, and frustrated by the delay in obtaining his travel documents and a local pass for Calais. The War Office wasn't used to men choosing to return to France before their leave was up, and Chas was grilled about his reasons for wanting to stay in Calais for a week.

"They think I'm a bloody spy," Chas complained to Quentin. He had gone to his friend's office to see if Quentin could expedite matters.

"You have to admit it looks suspicious," Quentin said. "I'm surprised they're letting you go back at all. It wouldn't be good for morale if one of our great heroes gets killed."

"Rubbish! There's nothing more heroic in what I do than any other poor sod who has to face the Huns."

"Nevertheless, it's how you're perceived, old chap. So I would have thought they'd be parading you about and having you make patriotic speeches to inspire young men to go enthusiastically to the slaughter."

Chas grinned. "I'm not sure that having a Canadian tell you Brits that you ought to fight for the glory of the Empire would go over all that well."

"You're an Oxford man so they'd forgive your impertinence," Quentin jested.

When Chas finally secured his papers, Quentin invited him to dinner.

"I'm not good company these days. I find the frenetic social life of London rather irritating," Chas said.

"I felt like that when I came back as well. It's as if the war is just an excuse for a never-ending party. People don't really want to know what it's like over there. And the men who are on leave are desperate to drink, dance, and make love to willing young women before being shipped back to hell. You feel that you've stepped through the looking glass, like Alice, into a bizarre world where nothing makes sense anymore. Do you realize that they bring the hospital trains in at night so that there aren't many people about to see the maimed bodies being unloaded by the thousands? It's all part of the propaganda machine that's trying to make us believe that our boys are dying cleanly and valiantly for a noble cause. Anyway, you have to eat, so let's make it just you and me."

Beatrice kept a minimal staff at her London townhouse, which no longer included a cook. The kitchen maid provided a simple breakfast, but otherwise he needed to dine out. "Yes, alright."

"The Ritz at 8:00?"

"Let's make it 7:00. I want an early start tomorrow."

Chas didn't betray his annoyance when Sid sauntered into the restaurant with her brother. He rose gallantly to his feet to greet her, and she gave him a peck on the cheek. "Don't be angry with Quentin. You know that I always get my way." She allowed him to seat her. "You are a rat, Chas! You haven't even come to see me since you've been home! And Quentin tells me you're leaving tomorrow. What's the hurry to return to France?"

"You have an active social life, Sid, and all I've wanted was sleep."

"You see how deftly he ignored my question?" Sid asked her brother. "I can't believe how incurious you men are. When I asked Quentin what you were planning to do in Calais, he said he hadn't asked! Good thing he's not in Intelligence!"

"I have every faith that Chas isn't a German spy, so what he's planning to do in Calais is none of my business."

"It must be a woman," Sid said flippantly.

"Yes. My wife," Chas replied, staring her down.

She had the grace to blush. "Of course. Jack mentioned something about Ria joining the WATS. Has she really? Whatever is she thinking? Tell her that I'm hurt she didn't come to see me before she left. I do think that there is something going on here which neither of you wants to discuss."

"So we won't," Quentin declared, and changed the subject, for which Chas was grateful.

They reminisced about their Oxford days and Chas's visits to Blackthorn – that carefree time when Sid and Quentin's younger brother, Sebastian, had still been with them. He had recently been killed at the Somme.

Sid lamented, "I loathe this war. What is the point of saving England or democracy or anything else if one's family and friends aren't here to share it? Thank God you're safely in London, Quentin."

"I might be knocked down by a crazy cab driver on my way home," Quentin pointed out.

"Then I suggest you not stagger along the streets after a debauched night at the Cavendish," Sid retorted.

Quentin guffawed as he reddened. "Whatever are you on about, Sid?"

"You should know that you can't keep anything secret in London. Mrs. Lewis is renowned for her *entertainments*. Or as Diana Manners calls them – orgies."

"Sid! You're impossible!"

Chas suppressed a grin at his friend's embarrassment. He had heard about the Cavendish Hotel where the ebullient, large-hearted Cockney proprietress, Rosa Lewis, a favourite of Edward VII, was famous not only for her cooking, but also for providing approved gentlemen with a 'nice clean tart'.

Chas found that he actually enjoyed the evening, for both Quentin and Sid were lively and witty conversationalists. But he wanted an early night, and excused himself around 10:00.

"Chas will walk me home, won't you, darling?" Sid said. "You owe me that at least for ignoring me."

Quentin gave Chas an apologetic look, but Chas laughed and said, "I expect I'll never be forgiven if I don't."

"You could accept the offer more graciously and say it would be your great pleasure," she said with mock indignation.

"Chas prefers not to lie," Quentin quipped.

"You're horrid, Quentin!"

"Come along, milady," Chas said, offering his arm. Sid's townhouse was nearby in fashionable Gosvenor Square, and on his way back to Bea's place.

Sid clung to Chas as they ambled down the dark streets. Street lamps were shielded so that there was only a faint circle of light directly below them. Taxicabs without headlights careened about them, among the throngs of revelers stumbling off to nightclubs and emerging from cinemas. "Are you going to tell me what's wrong between you and Ria?"

"There's nothing wrong," Chas replied, trying to sound nonchalant.

"Don't be evasive, Chas. That insults my intelligence. Your loving wife should be at your side, seeing to your *needs* in the little time you have together. Not off risking her life in France. Jack didn't say anything specific, but I gather that something's happened. She's left you, hasn't she?"

He was glad for the darkness, and fought the tension in his body. "She's off doing her bit. You know that Ria is adventuresome."

But she ignored his excuses. "Did you have an affair? I understand, of course. Life is too short not to enjoy oneself at every opportunity. And I know that Ria isn't particularly worldly. I expect she's taken it rather hard."

"Sid, stop!"

"I'm right, am I not? You just don't want to admit it."

They had arrived at her front door, and stood facing each other in the dim aura from a nearby streetlamp. She stroked his cheek provocatively as she said, "I can see it in your eyes. The confusion, the sadness. You can come in, if you like."

He knew what she was offering and said firmly, "No thank you, Sid." He didn't feel in the slightest bit tempted, much as he had once enjoyed her body.

"We had fun, you and I. We're good together."

He recalled the first time they had made love, whispering, giggling in his room at Oxford. She had stayed the weekend with Quentin, disguised as Sebastian, and had sneaked into Chas's room next door. He'd been twenty and she, eighteen. He'd been surprised that she had already been experienced, but soon realized that Sid was uninhibited and very much a creature of impulse and pleasure. Whenever he had visited Blackthorn, she had managed to find time alone with him. They had made love in the summerhouse, the hedge maze, his bedroom.

"I value your friendship, Sid. But I love Ria. I realize that I did before I even knew you."

"So I never had a chance?"

"I'm afraid not."

"I wish I didn't like Ria so much. Then I could really hate her."

Chas kissed her cheek and said, "Take care, Sid."

"You'd better make it up to her, whatever you did, Chas. You're bloody lucky to have such love. I'm not sure I ever will."

"You just haven't met the right man."

"Oh, I think I did. Once," she said wryly.

Chapter 5

Chas felt intense joy and relief to see Ria's face light with a smile when she first noticed him. Her luminous eyes seemed even larger than usual, but the anguish that then clouded them was like a stab to his heart, especially since he knew he was the cause.

Ria was astonished to see Chas dismount from the motorcycle. For a moment she wanted to throw herself into his arms and never leave him again. But his betrayal was still too raw.

"What are you doing here, Chas?" she challenged, making no move to embrace him.

He was shocked by how thin she was. She had a smock over her uniform and was cleaning the engine of her ambulance. Some of the others were in overalls and under their cars, but all paused to look at him.

"I was worried about you, Ria. You haven't answered my letters."

"I had nothing to say."

"I do. Will you walk with me?"

Ria cleaned her hands vigorously, trying to keep them from shaking. Technically she was already off duty. She shed her smock and fetched her leather coat as Chas waited outside her tent. Seeing him again brought a flood of memories. Happy times. She realized how much she still loved him, and wondered how she could ever stop, despite the pain.

They walked to the beach, but she didn't accept his outstretched hand, which he shoved into his pocket.

"We can't resolve things if you won't talk to me, Ria."

"I'm not convinced talking will help. You did enough of it before, but it wasn't all sincere, was it? You lied to me, Chas! You didn't tell me things you should have!" She turned to him angrily.

He wanted desperately to take her into his arms. She looked so hurt, so vulnerable. But he realized he couldn't rush her. "You don't know how much I've regretted that," he said, holding her gaze. "Almost as much as I've regretted having slept with Madeline. But I never actually lied to you, Ria. I just didn't tell you the entire truth."

"It results in the same thing. Deception. Did she really have nothing to do with your wanting to be posted back to France?"

"Absolutely nothing! I saw her once, just to give her the information about the trust fund. Of course I liked her, but I don't love her, and I know it was terrible of me to have used her. What more can I say except to tell you that I wasn't in my right mind? I was depressed, afraid of losing my nerve. Convinced I was going to die. She helped me through that, and I gave her some companionship and financial security. Sometimes people's lives intersect for just a short while and then they move on."

"You can hardly move on when you have a child," Ria said bitterly. "You'll always be tied to her. Why couldn't you have shared your feelings with *me*?"

The wind tormented the cold sand among the smashed boxes and crates that littered the beach and washed back and forth in the waves – debris from yet another supply ship that had been sunk. The WATS had managed to salvage a barrel of rum, and had decided that it was the King's contribution to their party stores.

"How could I tell the girl I adored, whom I wanted to protect and impress, that I was scared? That I had been a damn fool to think that war was a glorious game? That I was sure I would never hold her in my arms again? That I had seen one of my best friends – her cousin – burnt to death? That I'm haunted by that grisly image and terrified of the same fate?"

Ria touched his arm tentatively, moved by his distress. "I would have understood and sympathized. I would have come over sooner. You know how much I wanted to be here with you, right from the beginning. But you kept pushing me away."

Encouraged by her touch, Chas turned to her, but she dropped her hand and moved away from him and the brooding, grasping sea.

By the sea, by the sea, by the beautiful sea,
You and I you and I, oh! How happy we'll be...

"I'm sorry about that as well, but if I'd known you were pregnant, I would have asked you to come sooner. We've both made mistakes, Ria. Our intentions were good. How could we anticipate the consequences?"

She knew he was right, but it was almost unbearable to think that if she had told Chas as soon as she knew about the baby, she could have been with him by Christmas, and Reggie would surely have lived and Vivian wouldn't have died and she herself probably wouldn't now be sterile. And Chas may not have had an affair. That was what she wasn't certain about.

"But we can't change the past. So what do you want me to do, Ria? What can I do to earn your forgiveness?"

"You'll have to slay the dragons that you unleashed. The dragons of doubt and distrust."

"But I can't do that in isolation. You can't keep ignoring me. You have to want to make our marriage work."

"Can it?" she asked, suddenly terrified of the answer.

"If you mean do I love you enough and want only you, then yes. If you want it to."

Tears ran silently down her cheeks. She made no move to brush them away. "It's all I've ever wanted. It's what I thought we had, what I feel I've lost."

"Oh, God, Ria! I can't bear to see you so unhappy!" This time he wrapped his arms about her, grateful just to touch her, suppressing his own tears as he kissed the top of her head. "I would do anything to take away your pain, my darling. You are more important to me than life itself. I don't want to live without you."

Much as she longed to abandon herself to his caress, to allow him to wipe away her tears and fears, as he always had, she pulled away from him. "I'm hesitant to give myself to you so completely again. Not until you're willing to let me into your mind and soul. I'm not just another trophy you've won. And you have to stop treating me like a child who needs to be protected from unpleasant truths. I know the charming Chas that the rest of the world sees. I want to be allowed to know the one beneath that brave and flippant façade. We've already made a terrible mess of things by not being completely honest with each other."

They had reached a sheltered spot behind the dunes, and Chas said, "Let's sit down." He lit two cigarettes and offered her one.

"I would never jeopardize our love again, Ria. You're right that I've been trying to protect you from the gruesome reality of my life. I wanted to be your knight. I wasn't sure you'd really like the fallible creature that I am."

"How can you think that? Do you believe I'm so shallow that I only appreciate being cosseted and entertained?" She hugged her drawn-up knees.

"Of course not! I wanted to be strong for you. You'd had a bad time of it with your father and grandmother, and then on the *Lusitania*. And losing Reggie."

"Being strong meant you were shutting me out. I wanted to share your nightmares, to ease the torment that you didn't want me to see. I wanted to know how terrifying and stressful your life in the RFC is, and to help you cope with it all. I should have been the first person you turned to. Not the last. If something had happened to you, did you really mean to leave me with that cruel, shocking letter as the only truth between us? It's almost destroyed me, Chas, and you're still here with me. We might be able to redeem our love. If I had lost you and then found out..." She couldn't even finish the thought.

Chas ran his hands agitatedly through his hair. "You see what a coward I really am? Do you think you *can* still love me?"

In that raw moment of fear and misery that showed in his eyes, Ria was certain. "Oh, yes. More than you realize. I've never stopped loving you, Chas. I just have to stop hating you for what you've done to me."

She shivered. Chas put his arm about her and drew her close. She didn't protest. He said, "Bea told me that marriage is a journey, with lots of bumps along the way. If we overcome them together, then we'll be stronger."

He paused. "Do you know what I want more than anything right now? To be sitting with you at the Shimmering Sands looking out over our lake. Then to paddle over to Thorncliff for a candlelight dinner in the tennis pavilion. Instead I can offer you dinner at my hotel and we can watch the hostilities in the Channel. I'm staying at the Auberge de la Plage, just a couple of miles down the coast, until my leave is up in five days."

She drew away from him. "You have to give me time to see if I can come to grips with all this." She knew how easily he could seduce her into resuming their previous relationship. Talk of summers, their courtship, just the way he looked at her and touched her could melt her resolve. But her heart hadn't forgiven yet.

Chas felt immensely lighter. Happy, hopeful. "I will, my darling. "

"I still can't get over the idea of your having a child. Especially as I can never have any." She moved away from him again and stood up. "I can't do this anymore right now, Chas."

He tried to pull her back into his arms, but she ran off, weeping.

He caught up to her. "Ria! Charles means nothing to me!"

"He's your son."

"Only by accident. Of course I'll ensure that he is well provided for, but I have no interest in him other than that."

"You say that now, but some time you will see him as your legacy."

"I'm not your father. It would have been wonderful for us to have children as an expression and extension of our love. But we don't need them to make us whole." He looked beseechingly at her. "You are all I desire and need, my darling."

"When I truly believe that, then I may be able to forgive you."

"Then give me a chance to show you. I don't expect you can get leave, but may I at least see you? Have dinner with me."

"I'd have to bring someone as a chaperone."

"Even though we're married?"

She shrugged. "The WATS have to keep up an image of respectability."

"Bring your friends then. I just want to be with you, Ria."

He sounded so desperate that she was reminded of what Zoë had written about him being shell-shocked. "I have a half-day off the day after tomorrow. But I have plans."

"May I be included?"

"If you like."

"Thank you." He was so relieved that he wanted to embrace and kiss her, but still felt the wall of resistance around her.

"Be here at 1:00. I can probably get the car. And if you can find a bouquet of flowers, would you bring one? Preferably carnations."

"Of course."

When he had gone, she wept bitterly.

"If you keep crying like that, there won't be anything left of you. Just a desiccated shell," Sybil said as she came into the tent.

"That's all I am anyway."

"Tosh! That was the wayward husband, was it? Handsome devil. And I recognized him this time. Chas Thornton. Britain's number two Ace. How could you keep that from us, Windy? And what's with all this Wyndham nonsense?"

"My maiden name."

Carly had walked in on the conversation. "Chas Thornton's your husband?" she squeaked. "He was one of Eddie's teachers at Upavon, and he's always bragging about him. He'll be devastated."

"Why?" Ria asked.

"Because he fancies he's in love with you. He thought you had a dud husband, because you avoided talking about him. But he admires Chas Thornton immensely. You really shouldn't have deceived us, Windy."

Ria was stung by Carly's criticism. What right did Eddie have to assume that she was fair game? "I don't see what difference it makes who my husband is! I never gave any man the impression that I'm available."

"Well, a slew of them have fallen for you," Sybil said. "What about Major Chadwick?"

"What about him? He's married as well."

"You see what I was telling you earlier, Windy?" Sybil said. "This war has changed things. People take each day as it comes. *Carpe diem*. The one expression that I actually found useful from Latin class."

Their new tent-mate, The Honourable Cordelia Hazlett – known as Hazy, which she despised – flounced in angrily. She had been with them for a week. She was wearing a frilly pink silk blouse with a plunging neckline instead of the plain, white, high-buttoned uniform one. Sybil had already declared her a butterfly chauffeuse.

"Ridiculous! ComRad says I'm not allowed to wear this blouse. And she's saying that I can't do what I like in my time off. Absolutely absurd! Billy Farthington is an Intelligence Officer and an old friend. We're going out for dinner, and I'm definitely not taking any of you with me. How public school to put such restrictions on us! Bad enough I have to suffer these primitive conditions, but I'm certainly not giving up my friends!"

"You'll be sent back to England," Sybil said with satisfaction.

"Let them boot me out! I expect Mummy will withdraw her rather substantial support. I don't care! This has already become a howling bore, and I have better things to do. So, I'm off. Billy's picking me up at the end of the lane. He's all for a bit of subterfuge. Don't rat on me, girls."

When she had gone, Sybil said, "I don't understand how creatures like that ever get by Boss."

"I expect it was her Mummy's 'substantial support' that got her here," Carly said. As a Sergeant, she could have imposed punishment on Hazy for breaking the rule about being alone with men in the evenings. But they all felt constrained by this, and rules were often broken, or at least bent. "I do hope Cinders comes back soon."

Although the curfew was 10:00 pm, Hazy sneaked back into camp just before midnight, as the summons came to meet trains.

As some of the wounded were to be moved right through to Britain, Ria was on the quay behind Hazy. She hated this part, especially on a rainy night, so she watched somewhat nervously as Hazy turned her ambulance. But Ria could see that Hazy was too close to the edge, and held her breath as the vehicle suddenly teetered and plunged over the side.

Ria ran onto the quay. Lights were played into the frigid black water to illuminate the sinking ambulance while several sailors prepared to jump in. The rear canvas was still rolled up and Ria could see Hazy scrambling up through the back as the water poured in. A life preserver tied to a rope was expertly thrown to her and she managed to grab it as the car sank. The sailors hauled her up, dripping and quivering.

"Thank God!" Ria said as blankets were being draped around Hazy. "Are you alright?"

She seemed a bit dazed. "I think I hit my face on the steering wheel."

"That was very quick thinking, climbing out the back like that."

A Medical Officer from the ship came to examine her and said, "You've had a lucky escape, young lady. I expect you'll have a black eye, but nothing seems to be broken. Dashed clever of you to get yourself out so quickly."

Ria took Hazy into her ambulance, and wrapped another blanket around her. When she had dropped off her patients, she said, "I'm taking you home now."

The words seemed to jolt Hazy out of her stupor. "Home? Not that dump! You're damn right I'm going home! I was almost killed! Take me to the Hotel Maritime. You're all crazy to stay!"

But Ria took her back to camp and settled her with a stiff brandy, although she realized that Hazy had already had too much champagne. She was asleep almost instantly, and snored lightly.

"God preserve us," Sybil said.

"She could have been killed," Ria said.

"She should have been sober. She's not up to the job. Let her go back home and sleep her way through the war," Sybil said snidely, with double entendre.

"Don't be cruel," Carly said. "She's had a terrible experience, and didn't break into hysterics. She was rather plucky."

"And she will dine out on this for years. Can't you just hear her now... *Oh, darling, it was just too too ghastly! Army rations and outdoor latrines and broken, bleeding, stinking men and not being able to wear my silk blouses. And taking a drunken dive off the quay. You can't imagine what horrors and agonies I've endured!* It irks me to think that she'll be calling herself a former WATS, and basking in our achievements."

Sybil didn't have to rat on Hazy, although she was prepared to. The Honourable Miss Hazlett resigned first thing in the morning and couldn't wait to get away.

·   ·   ·

Chas noticed that Ria was wearing her wedding ring today, which made him tremendously hopeful.

She had waffled for a long time about whether or not to wear it on her time off. It was a declaration that she truly was married. The first step perhaps to forgiving Chas.

"It's odd to have our car here in France," Chas said. "Can you drive it when you like?"

"Not really, although I do donate money for the petrol I use. We're not supposed to joyride, but we do need transportation to events for our free time. Today I'm going to bring back some medical supplies, so the Commandant can justify my having the car for the afternoon."

"Where else are we going?"

"First to meet with my lawyer."

Chas went cold. But then Ria told him about Sophie.

It had been difficult to part with the distraught child the day after the air raid that had killed her mother. But Ria had had no choice. She had first investigated the old orphanage in Calais, but found it overcrowded, and the children, thin, ragged waifs. There was no way she would leave Sophie there. Ria had discovered through the lawyer she had hired that there was a refuge run by nuns near Wissant, not that far from the WATS camp. It was for unwanted children whose relatives could pay for their upkeep. And Ria had soon realized that many of the children were bastards. But the nuns were taking in war orphans as well.

"How have your investigations been going Monsieur Lemieux?" Ria asked the lawyer after introducing Chas simply as "my husband" without giving his name. She could see that it could become complicated trying to explain why she wasn't Mrs. Thornton.

"You'll be pleased to know, Madame, that I have located the child's grandmother." He beamed. "Dominique Rousseau, the actress! Undoubtedly you have heard of her?"

"Yes, of course. She's almost as famous as Sarah Bernhardt. But surely she's too young?"

"Ah, the artifice of the theatre, Madame. She gave birth to Alayna twenty-five years ago when she was seventeen." His brow wrinkled as he went on. "But I regret to say that Mademoiselle Rousseau is not interested in the child. She said that she sacrificed much to raise Alayna, and had great hopes for her daughter. She started her quite young on the stage, but Alayna was not interested in the theatre. Terrified of the stage, in fact. Then she married beneath her – as Mademoiselle said, 'a mere flower seller, a peasant'. Alayna had spurned liaisons with wealthy men, even a Compte. Mademoiselle says her daughter was a fool and wants nothing to do with her offspring."

"It's unfortunate for her, but I daresay, much better for the child," Ria declared, thinking that Dominique Rousseau had undoubtedly been trying to make a courtesan of her daughter, and would do the same with her granddaughter if she took an interest in her at all. The French still considered those high-priced whores as acceptable members of society. "What about Alayna's father?"

"A Marquis who showered Mademoiselle with lots of baubles, as she called them, and helped her to pursue her career. She had no use for him otherwise, and I believe he was married in any case."

"And Sophie's father's family?"

"An ancient mother who still works her small plot of land. Not so old in years, you understand, but weary of them. Two other sons killed in the war. One who is rather simple and lives with her. A daughter, married to a farmer, with ten children of her own and not willing to take another. And the other daughter, married to a wealthy merchant, who gives herself airs and will have nothing to do with her family. So, Madame, it seems the child is unwanted."

Ria's heart bled for Sophie. "Have you settled her mother's affairs?"

"There is very little. Enough to help the nuns clothe and feed her for a year perhaps. I have retrieved some books and photographs and such from the cleanup of the rubble. They are in that box, Madame."

"Thank you, Monsieur Lemieux. You've done very well, and so quickly."

"My pleasure, Madame. Is there anything else I can do for you? Would you care to arrange for an adoption of the child?" he asked shrewdly.

"I shall let you know, Monsieur. For now, I will pay your bill, if you'd care to present it to me."

"Most assuredly, Madame."

When they were outside the office, Chas said, "Do you want to adopt the child, Ria?"

"I don't know. This has all happened so suddenly. I just feel so sorry for her. She's bright and charming and lovely. And she seems to have attached herself to me."

"That's what Blake said as well." Chas had visited his friend at the hospital yesterday, and they'd had a long talk. He stopped walking and faced her. "Ria, you know I like children. If you want to adopt her, I'd be delighted."

"You haven't even met her yet."

"If you like her, then I'm sure I shall as well. We can still have a family."

She started walking again. "I don't know." This seemed to be forcing her hand.

When they'd put Sophie's box of treasures into the car, they went into various shops where Ria bought pastries, ham, cheese, croissants, milk, and oranges. Chas was amused to see her dicker over the price of the dozen boxes of chocolates she was purchasing.

"I'll give you half that," she said to the proprietress.

"But, Madame! C'est impossible! With this war..." She shrugged. "Sugar is so dear and the cocoa... Well, you know the difficulty we have obtaining supplies with so many ships sunk."

Ria's wedding band was inlaid with small diamonds, which reflected the light brilliantly. Chas saw that the proprietress had noticed it, and must have judged Ria to be wealthy.

"I understand, Madame Fortin. But my friend, Sophie Dumont, tells me that you give her a special price on Saturdays. These chocolates are for the poor orphans, Madame. I'm trying to bring them a little joy in these sad and difficult times. I may do this more often if the price is acceptable."

"Oui, les pauvres enfants. D'accord, I will give you a special price today." Madame Fortin smiled, not at all upset by the negotiation, and Ria knew that she was still making a tidy profit.

Outside, Chas laughed and said, "Well done, my darling!"

"I resent being taken advantage of and asked to pay double what the French do. War profiteers!"

He laughed again. He had paid an exorbitant price to rent the motorcycle. "I expect that we would be accused of being that as well, with all the investments we have in armaments and bully beef."

"But we're not gouging the buyers. We're merely supplying a need. That's just business. The French should be grateful that we're here helping them."

"A rather Imperialist notion. Some of them resent the fact that they need our help. And they haven't forgotten that the British controlled this area for a few hundred years."

"But surely that was in the Middle Ages!"

"People in Europe have long memories. And it must seem as if we're invading them again. Anyway, I think we're here to protect the doorway into Britain more than liberating Belgians or saving the French. Imagine if the Germans had control of the coastline. Already they're bombing England with the massive Zeppelins, but once they have harder-to-detect aeroplanes that can easily flit across the Channel and protect warships sailing from Calais, invasion becomes a real threat."

"Do you think that's likely?"

"God, I hope not! It's why the Ypres Salient is so important. It's not that far from here, and is blocking the Germans' advance to this part of the coast. You know how close Dover and Folkestone are from Calais."

"We get men sent in from Ypres all the time."

At her grave look, Chas wondered what sorts of terrible injuries she had already seen, and wished he could take her away from all this. He knew that they would never be able to forget the monstrosities that were daily being seared into their brains. To lighten the mood, he said, "I sense a picnic brewing."

"I visit Sophie whenever I can. It hasn't even been two weeks since her mother was killed. The nuns say that she is morose when I'm not there. So I'm... we're taking her out for the afternoon."

"Splendid! In that case, I'll procure some wine for us."

After they had picked up the medical supplies and dropped them at the camp, Ria drove to the convent. Wissant was tucked into the valley about halfway between the two dramatic capes, Blanc-Nez and Gris-Nez. The convent was a grey-walled fortress in spacious grounds overlooking the ever-changing panorama of sea and sky.

Ria introduced Chas properly to the Mother Superior, and declared nonchalantly that she was working under her maiden name while in France. She had learned young that if you didn't make excuses and remained unruffled, you could get away with plenty.

"She misses you, Madame. Her Maman, too, of course. She cries for her every night. But she speaks little except to ask if you are coming."

Ria told her that no relatives had been located, so Sophie would stay there for the time being and Ria would cover her expenses. And she wanted to make an extra donation to the children's home. She handed Mother Superior a cheque. "This is more than generous, Madame, Monsieur!"

"I... we may wish to adopt Sophie. I'm not in a position to do so at the moment. But you will let me know if anyone is interested in her? And you will look after her well." It was more a command than a question. Chas thought her magnificent, and could see traces of Augusta – Ria's grandmother – in her demeanor. Ria was less than half the age of the rather formidable Mother Superior.

"Most assuredly, Madame."

"Très bien. I will have Sophie back before supper. And here are some chocolates for the children. And yourselves, of course."

Sophie's face glowed when she saw Ria. "Oh, Madame WATS!" Ria squatted to accept a big hug. Sophie didn't want to let go.

"Shall we take Delphine for a drive and a picnic?" Ria asked her. Delphine went everywhere with Sophie. Ria had discovered that her mother had made the doll.

"Oh yes please!"

"Good. Now I want you to meet Captain Thornton. He is my husband."

Sophie looked seriously at him as she said, "Bonjour Monsieur Capitaine Thornton. Are you a new husband?" To Ria she said, "Is the Major not your husband?"

"No, ma petite, only a friend."

Chas gave Ria a quizzical look, but she could sense his unease. She explained to Sophie, "Major Chadwick is with the Cavalry, and he helped me with the blessés."

Chas's earlier joy was considerably dampened by a new fear. Ria was an exceptionally beautiful woman, and men were invariably attracted to her. He was used to that, but had been confident in her love for him. Now he wasn't sure where he stood with her. Hadn't Blake warned him about her vulnerability in his letter?

Blake had told him yesterday, "You may find this hard to believe, Chas, but your *betrayal*, as Ria sees it, has damaged her self-esteem. By turning to another woman for emotional support and intimacy, you've made her feel she wasn't enough for you or important enough to you. Telling her you love her isn't sufficient now. Your actions belied the words."

"It wasn't like that!" Chas had countered. "I didn't realize I was in a serious funk. And I didn't look for a woman or pursue Madeline. It was just... circumstance. Opportunity. An immediate need easily fulfilled."

"To have a meaningful relationship that's going to weather difficult times, you have to be open with Ria. Perhaps if you'd poured your heart out to her in a letter or asked her to come to England where you could have seen her during your leave, you wouldn't have been so depressed. Or even if you'd confessed your lapse to her immediately, she wouldn't have taken it so hard. Now you have to regain her trust. And because her ego is battered, she may seek validation for herself through others."

Chas recalled her question in response to his assertion that his affair had been insignificant – would he consider *her* having sex with another man as insignificant? He didn't think she would do it just to spite him, but, if Blake was right, she might become involved with another man who made her feel needed and cherished. He cursed himself yet again.

When they reached the car, Sophie exclaimed with delight at the bouquet of flowers Chas had brought. "They are for your Maman," Ria told her.

She drove first to the cemetery on the fringe of Calais. It had been deemed inappropriate for the child to attend her mother's funeral, so Sophie hadn't yet seen the grave. It was heart-wrenching watching the little girl take the heavy bouquet of flowers to the dirt mound. She knelt down and laid them gently on the ground. "Can you see them from heaven, Maman? They are beautiful. Like you."

Ria wiped away tears, trying to be strong for Sophie. Chas put his arm about her reassuringly, and she wondered if he was thinking about Reggie as well.

Sophie said, "Maman is not here, in this ugly dirt. I have felt her. But not here. May we go now?"

"Yes, of course. But take a carnation with you."

Sophie sat between Ria and Chas and brightened considerably on their journey. Ria stopped at the top of Cap Blanc-Nez, where they spread out the blankets and food and the dishes that she had borrowed from the mess. It was not a particularly warm day, but for once there was only a gentle breeze, so it was pleasant to sit in the sunshine. Ria had already bought some clothes for Sophie, so she was warmly dressed. They all became cheerful as they ate the very fine fare, Ria and Chas indulging in a glass of Veuve Cliquot. Ria was teaching Sophie some English, so she pointed out various things to her and Sophie was quick to pick up the words. Ria and Chas told her about the picnics they'd had in Muskoka.

"Remember the time that Ellie started to climb up the cliff at Indian Head Point and got stuck?" Ria said. "And you were the only one brave enough to attempt a rescue. Blake kept yelling instructions at her and she hollered back that he was worse than useless."

"I didn't really know what I was doing, so we were lucky we didn't both fall and break our necks."

"She fell alright. In love with you."

"Good Lord, did she? When *was* that?"

"I was fifteen, Ellie was sixteen, and you were all of nineteen and just back from your first year at Oxford. And rather pompous. Fortunately, the British accent disappeared after a few weeks."

They laughed, and realized by Sophie's curious look that they had lapsed into English. Ria explained, "We're talking about the sister of Dr. Carlyle. She is also a doctor."

"Dr. Carlyle is very nice. He came to take out my stitches and said that he found a ribbon growing there and that I had better wear it in my hair rather than on my forehead." She giggled. "Of course I knew he was teasing! But look, isn't it pretty?"

It was velvet, in a rich blue that matched her eyes.

"Very pretty," Ria agreed.

"Do you have many friends?" Sophie asked.

"Yes, we do."

"May I meet them also? I have only Delphine and you."

Chas caught and held Ria's gaze. They didn't need words to communicate, she realized, which was another reason why she couldn't just cut him out of her life. He was too much a part of her. Soul mates, their friend Edelina had called them. "I expect that you will meet them, Sophie," Ria said. "Let's go for a walk."

They ambled along the cliff path towards Wissant, Ria and Chas each holding Sophie's hands. The tide was out and the broad beach below them was deserted. Trapped seawater created pools and streams on the flaxen sand that were anxious to rejoin the beckoning sea.

"I wish I had my sketch book with me," Ria said, and realized that she hadn't done any painting since she'd been in France.

Sophie was flagging on their return journey, so Chas gave her a pickaback ride. She fell asleep and Chas laid her gently on the blanket. Ria covered her with the other blanket as he poured them each another glass of champagne.

"She is a delightful child, Ria. I would be happy to be her father."

Ria nodded. "Life sometimes overwhelms you, doesn't it? I must be getting old if I can't deal with unexpected events!"

"This isn't an easy decision. It's a lifetime commitment. For all of us. But we have to take advantage of opportunities and gifts."

"I'm not ready yet, Chas. I need time."

She accepted a cigarette from him as he said, "Will you tell me about Major Chadwick?"

He was jealous, she realized with some satisfaction. "He's a career soldier with the Lancers. We constantly have officers from the area – including the RFC and the navy – come to our teas. We're renowned for our hospitality. Lance took me riding."

So they were already on a first-name basis, Chas thought with trepidation.

"We WATS also play tennis at the Calvary camp." She told him about the horse race.

"Can I meet Major Chadwick?"

He tried to hide his anxiety, but Ria saw it in his eyes. "His regiment has been sent back to the Somme. He's married and has two children," she added.

Knowing the ways of the upper classes, Chas wasn't reassured by that. He also knew that the intensity of shared wartime experiences could make people bond in ways that they wouldn't otherwise.

She told him about the air raid at Audruicq, and how Lance may well have saved her life.

He was appalled. "Blake tells me that you work through the air raids. What you're doing is incredibly dangerous, Ria! How can I not worry about you and wish you safely in England?"

"Do you think that I've worried any less about *you* these past two years?" she asked heatedly.

They stared each other down. Chas drew her into his arms and kissed her passionately. She groaned as she pulled away. "It's not that easy, Chas!"

He got up and walked to the edge of the cliff, lighting a cigarette. She could see him running a hand through his hair, as he did when he was distraught.

When he returned, he said, "I love you, Ria. That will never change, no matter what happens. So forgive me for wanting to keep you safe for my own selfish reasons."

The anguished look in his eyes almost made her relent.

Sophie awoke and Ria realized it was time to take her back.

Ria promised to visit her soon, but felt torn when she saw the misery on the child's face.

Chas broke the silence on the return journey. "I've just been gazetted Major. They're giving me command of my own squadron, a new one being formed in England."

"That's wonderful, Chas!" He would be safer, she thought instantly.

"I was going to ask Jack to be one of my Flight Commanders, but he's been recruited by Max Aitken." Chas explained Jack's new position and said, "It certainly takes advantage of all of Jack's talents, and will undoubtedly be less dangerous. Nothing wrong with that. But I find Sir Max too rapacious for my liking. Anyway, I'll miss Jack. We've been flying together for two years." And it almost seemed as if they were each other's talisman. Pilots became superstitious, and Chas realized that he felt more secure when Jack was around. Talking about the lake had always lightened their mood.

"So I'm soon going to England for a few months to train my crew. Will you come home, Ria? Bring Sophie with you."

"I made a serious commitment when I joined the WATS. And I can't go back to waiting anxiously on the sidelines, grateful for a few crumbs of your time. I'm not sure I can be that kind of wife again." Her look challenged him.

He smiled ruefully. "I should have known that. I would be exultant if you would at least *be* my wife again."

"I have to feel it. And I can't. Not yet."

Blake had told her, "Don't hold it against Chas forever. When you forgive him, you really must forget. Otherwise it will eat away at you both and destroy something precious."

"I'll wait, Ria. However long it takes. But you must let me know what I can do."

"Be honest with me."

"I am! I will, but you must as well. And don't downplay the dangers or you'll be doing just what I did."

When they arrived at the WATS camp, Chas said, "May I see you tomorrow?"

"You can come to tea, if we don't have a job on."

When Ria entered the tent, Carly looked up from her book and said, "Have you read this novel? *The Doomed*, by Montgomery Seaton. It's about a Canadian female ambulance driver, and it's uncanny how this character reminds me of you. Just listen to this description. 'Eyes like deep azure pools... daringly short, moonlight pale hair... a smile so surprising, so beautiful that it both wrenched and gladdened his heart and lingered in his thoughts long after she had gone.'"

"It *is* me," Ria said grimly. "We met Monty at Cap d'Antibes while he was working on the book. I feel as if his story has jinxed us." It really was uncanny how their lives were becoming more like those of their characters in the book. When Ria had read the novel in the summer, she hadn't yet known about Chas's affair, nor had she decided to come to France to drive an ambulance. It was as if, by appropriating their personalities, Monty had also written the script for their lives.

"And your husband is the pilot. Of course! Oh hell. He didn't have an affair with Monty's wife, did he?"

"Definitely not. He doesn't even like her."

"But I'm afraid they're going to come to a sticky end. Oh dear!"

Ria shivered when she recalled that both of their characters are killed.

"And what cheek!" Carly continued. "Although it is rather flattering. Especially as the main character, the journalist, seems to be in love with you – her."

Sybil said, "I expect that Montgomery Seaton is another of Windy's conquests. Or victims, depending upon how you look at it. Slain by a smile."

"Now do tell us about Monty!" Carly said.

As she did, Ria was reminded of how perfectly wonderful their time at Cousin Bea's Riviera villa had been while Chas and, for the first while, Jack were recovering from their wounds.

"We've made Windy sad. Thinking about hubby again, aren't you. Why don't you just admit that you love him, go home for some good sex, and make up?"

"Shut up, Foxy," Ria said.

Sybil shrugged. "You know you'll never forgive yourself if something happens to him."

There was an air raid that night, which woke Chas. He had fallen asleep to the almost nightly booming of guns in the Channel, but the more intense sounds of bombardment nearby worried him. He got up to look out the window, wondering if Ria was driving her ambulance through this fiery metal storm.

It was his fault that she was here, no matter what she might say about wanting to take a more active role. Although Blake was still concerned about Ria's recklessness, he thought that the child, Sophie, had awakened some sense of responsibility in her that was bringing her out of her funk.

"Ria is not only devastated by your affair, but also by the fact that she can't have children," Blake had told him. "She doesn't blame you for that, of course, but she does hold it against you that you didn't tell her. She's mourning the loss of her baby and all the children she had imagined having, and you weren't there to support her. You had chosen to return to France, where you would be close to your son and his mother. To Ria it seems that you had abandoned her yet again. And the fact that *you* have a child and she doesn't – and can't – has created an immense gulf between you, in her eyes."

Chas felt powerless to do anything. And he would soon be safe in England while she remained here, in the line of fire. It was damnable! He leaned his forehead on his clenched fist.

.   .   .

It was two in the morning when Ria dropped off her last casualties at the Canadian #3 General, and she hated the lonely drive back. She was getting "stretcher face" – a drawn, haunted, exhausted look – from the stress of peering into the darkness and the tension of trying to avoid jolting her patients.

As she passed Chas's hotel, she thought it bizarre that he was there without her. For a moment she was tempted to go to him, climb into his bed and arms, and seek oblivion in his lovemaking. But the vision of him with a faceless French girl always intruded on those thoughts.

She drove faster toward the exploding night.

.   .   .

Ria was delighted to see Blake arrive with Chas for tea the following afternoon. Aside from being a bit of a buffer between them, Blake was also a reminder of their circle of friends, and a return to the normality of fond times.

She'd had to confess to the others that her husband was the famous Ace. Some had been annoyed with her for her secrecy and deception.

"You don't deserve him if you're not even using his name!" Baby had declared.

"She didn't want to be 'Thorny'," Sybil had quipped.

"If you call me that, I'll live up to it and become prickly," Ria had threatened.

"I don't blame Windy for keeping him to herself," Antonia Upton had stated, "when you have girls like Baby drooling over his photo in the newspapers."

"I would be so chuffed if he were mine!" Betty Haydon-Wicks had said, her eyes sparkling. "You really must tell us all about him!"

"Enough, girls," Carly had said. "You see why Windy's kept quiet? None of you was much interested in her husband before this. I don't expect she's prepared to share him or her marriage with you."

Ria had given her a grateful look.

"That's terribly selfish of her," Baby had said. "I'm sure I would be bragging about him constantly."

"And boring us to tears," Sybil had added. "I do hope you find yourself a decent, unaccomplished man whom you can appreciate for his real qualities and not just his fame or fortune."

"You are wicked, Foxy!" Baby had retorted.

ComRad had looked at Ria sternly over her desk and said shrewdly, "Well *Thornton*, I'm not interested in your marital problems. But I wonder what else you've been lying about. Your age, perhaps?"

"I think people should be judged on merit. Not by their name, their family, or their husband's fame. And if they can do the job, surely age becomes arbitrary."

"I tend to agree with you, and since we have a reputation for boldness and initiative, your very act of 'stretching the truth' to get yourself here is exactly the sort of quality that makes you a good WATS." ComRad had smiled. "But I expect you've not considered the consequences. Your documents, for instance. If they don't match with your passport, you could be arrested as a spy. Really, Thornton, you've been rather silly, but also lucky. I've asked Captain Farthington to deal with this. He's an Intelligence Officer in Calais."

"Cordelia Hazlett's friend." Billy Farthington.

"Is he? Oh well. He'll straighten out your paperwork. Permits and so forth. And you will answer to Thornton from now on."

Now the girls were swarming around Chas, plying him with questions. As punishment, Ria figured, she was expected to entertain the guests.

"You're becoming very good at that piece," Chas said when she'd finished playing *Ragtime Nightingale*. He had managed to extricate himself from the others and sat down beside her. He started to play *That's A Plenty* and she joined in, since they often played it as a duet.

When they finished, someone clapped, and Chas looked up to see Eddie Stratton. "I say! If it isn't my star pupil! How are you, Stratton?"

"I'd be a hell of a lot better if you didn't have prior claim to this delightful young lady, Sir," Eddie retorted. Carly had cornered him when he'd arrived and explained the situation to him.

"My lovely wife does rather have that effect," Chas said. "I am both envied and hated."

"But I have great admiration for you as well, Captain Thornton. Good to see you!" They shook hands warmly. "I tell everyone I can that you were my mentor."

"Good Lord, I hope they forgive me!"

"I'll have you know that I can do a perfect three-point landing almost as consistently as you, Sir."

"So aren't you swinging the lead a bit, Stratton?" Chas teased. Marquise was one of the Aircraft Depots and, as Chas well knew, the Reception Park for machines flown in from England. It was also where machines were overhauled, reconditioned, and tested, along with any captured enemy aircraft.

"I've lasted seven months at the Front, so this is instead of Home Defence or, God-forbid, teaching," Eddie said with a grin. "I rather enjoy being a test pilot. There isn't anything I can't fly now, including Fritz's busses. Ferrying brass and machines back and forth across the channel, and delivering planes to squadrons is just a joy ride. Best of all, it gives us a chance to spend time with these lovely ladies."

"When you tire of your seaside holiday, I'd be happy to have you on my team, Stratton. I'm forming a new fighter squadron."

"Thank you, Sir! There's no one I'd rather fly with."

Before the summons to meet trains interrupted the tea, they had already decided that Ria, Carly, Sybil, and Antonia would dine with Chas, Blake, Eddie, and Jonathan Telford the next evening at Chas's hotel. Ria would pick up the others in the Rolls.

Some of the girls were miffed that they weren't invited, but Sybil said that they didn't want to see Baby gushing over Chas all evening.

"What *shall* I wear?" Sybil said facetiously the following afternoon. "My uniform, don't you think? Positively sexy. Blast it! Sometimes I do long to slip into something soft and pretty and sensuous. Especially as I intend to seduce yummy Captain Carlyle."

"Hands off!" Ria warned. "He belongs to my cousin Zoë."

"Does she have a tether around him? A ring? A promise, a commitment, an understanding? If not then he's fair game."

"I thought you were in love with Captain Bentley?" Carly said.

"I am. But he's not here at the moment. *Carpe diem*, remember?"

The Auberge de la Plage was only a few kilometres from the WATS camp, so Carly offered to drop off the others while she went to collect Eddie, Jonathan, and Blake. Once a private seaside estate for some aristocrat, the inn was elegant and sumptuous with rich colours and textures, but not quite large enough to have been commandeered as a hospital.

"I'd forgotten what real food tastes like," Sybil said. They all agreed that it was exceptionally good. "On my next day off, I'll book in here and just eat, bathe, and sleep. Hell, maybe I'll just stay here for my next leave. Two heavenly weeks of indulging myself! From what I hear, the food in England is terrible."

"Nothing new about that then, is there?" Eddie quipped.

There were about a dozen tables, all occupied by at least one person in uniform – most of them high-ranking officers. It wasn't cheap, and Chas had offered to pay for everyone.

Coffee was served in the double cube drawing room, half of which had been cleared as a dance floor.

The proprietor, looking more like a Compte who was entertaining friends, made sure his guests were comfortably settled with cognac or champagne, and then turned on the gramophone.

Ria had hoped to avoid such proximity to Chas as he took her into his arms for a waltz. She didn't want to respond to him on just a physical level, which was too easy to do. That resolved nothing.

Sensing her reticence, Chas tried to keep the conversation light. He told her about his visits to the Canadian hospitals in his free time these last few days. "I was really touched by how cheerful the men became when they found out who I was. They think of me as a great Canadian hero, which is both flattering and embarrassing. But I'm glad that my fame is of some use. Blake told me I'm good medicine."

"Some of our boys really get homesick, especially when they're wounded and so far from loved ones. They always tell me how much they enjoy hearing my Canadian accent," Ria said.

Chas asked her about her duties and experiences. He laughed at the story of the General and the flat tyre. She finished by saying, "ComRad told me I'm lucky I haven't been arrested as a spy. So I'm Mrs. Thornton again."

She didn't look at him because she didn't want him to think it meant anything more than that, but Chas felt heartened. "I'm glad," he whispered, pulling her tighter. She didn't protest. "I saw Sophie today. I took her some chocolates and carnations, and we sat for quite a while in the garden, talking. That is to say, I did most of the talking. I told her about the lake and the islands. She particularly liked the name Ouhu. It was nice to see her laugh."

"That was very thoughtful of you, Chas."

"I wanted to get to know her. Just in case."

When she danced with Blake, he said, "I'm glad to see that you two are at least talking. It makes me hopeful."

"Do you care so much that Chas and I reconcile?"

"Hell, yes! You're both too intensely involved to see what the rest of us do – that you are a natural fit and madly in love with each other. I think your heart has already forgiven him, Ria. So you need to listen more to it than to your mind."

Although they switched partners regularly at the outset, they were soon in couples. Carly with Jonathan; Antonia with Eddie; and Sybil with Blake. But Ria wasn't worried, since she knew that Blake really was in love with Zoë. He was excited to be going on leave soon, and seeing her in England. And she felt oddly bereft to think that Chas and Blake would be leaving her behind.

Because they were a group of four, ComRad had given them an hour extension on their curfew. But Carly and Antonia left at ten to take the men back. Sybil ordered herself a large cognac as she watched Ria and Chas dance.

They were the only ones on the floor, as there hadn't been many women here in any case – an elderly aristocrat and her daughter who were staying at the hotel and had entertained a French General to dinner, and a few stylish young women with officers. Ria hadn't wanted to speculate on those relationships. But now the room was empty.

Yet Ria didn't really notice Sybil's presence. She was enveloped in Chas's arms, her head on his shoulder. And she wanted to stay there.

But the proprietor put on the popular *If You Were The Only Girl In The World*, and Ria was instantly transported to Upavon the night Chas had told her he would be going back to France. She had been upset, but he had made it seem that he'd had no choice, and had crooned that song to her. She went rigid.

"Ria?" Chas could feel her distancing herself from him. Things had been going so well that he'd begun to hope that she might spend the night with him. Always resourceful, she would find some way to sneak back into camp, or otherwise explain her absence.

"You could have stayed with me in England."

He knew right away what she was talking about. Their tiny billet when he had been teaching at Upavon. Ria accusing him of always putting her second. And she had been right. He *had* wanted to come back to France.

"You explained that you needed to prove yourself. And I obviously wasn't that important. So what's changed?" She looked stricken.

"I *have* proven myself, done my bit for the war. And I've realized that I need to stop thinking so much about myself or I'll lose the most precious thing in the world. You."

But she moved away from him. "Easily said. Until the next time."

"Ria!" He tried to draw her close.

"No, Chas! I need to get back."

But he didn't let go of her. "I wouldn't have had much longer at Upavon anyway. You know that Home Establishment is just a respite. But I wanted to come back as a fighter pilot, not flying reconnaissance."

He felt her resistance ebb somewhat, and said, "I have to report back to my squadron tomorrow. I don't know when I can see you again. But it'll be hell until I do." He looked longingly into her eyes, and gave her a tender kiss. "I love you, Ria. You hold my life in your hands. Take good care, my darling."

Chapter 6

Justin thought he couldn't see much worse than he already had at the Ypres Salient earlier that year, but arriving at the Somme more than three months after the battle had begun, he was stunned by the destruction. Ceaselessly pummeled by millions of shells, the landscape as far as the eye could see was a wasteland of tortured earth liquefied into slimy, sucking mud, studded with the amputated ghost trees of annihilated woodlands and the brick rubble of once tidy villages. Pastoral fields now sprouted a gruesome crop of bodies in varying stages of decay. Corpses had been used like sandbags to try to shore up trenches. Some became landmarks. Who could ever forget the two who must have bayoneted each other simultaneously, and were propped upright by the tree stump against which they had fallen? Surely it was hideously symbolic, Justin thought. Two enemies locked forever in a macabre dance of death. Neither side a victor.

Continued explosions churned up more bodies and pulverized others, mincing and mixing men and mud until they became inseparable. Dust to dust. What did it matter now, the colour of the uniform, when there were only shreds of flesh and shards of bone remaining?

The stench, as thick as the muck, was almost unbearable.

Cold rain or icy sleet hammered the troops relentlessly. The constantly battered trenches were no more than crumbling ditches knee-deep with cloying, putrid water, and shell holes had become cesspools. But there was no other place for shelter, so the men rigged up their waterproof sheets to form roofs. They were never dry. They lived on cold rations, everything polluted by the clinging mud and the odour of putrefaction.

It was almost impossible to bring in supplies, the horses and mules labouring to pull the wagons and artillery often sinking belly-deep in the treacle. Their bodies added to the lunatic landscape and became stepping-stones through the mud.

Mud that seemed to undulate as if men squirmed to surface from their premature graves. But it was only the thousands, perhaps millions of rats that feasted on bloated flesh. Some had grown as large as cats. Impudent, contemptuous, they owned the shattered earth.

Justin was revolted when they sometimes jumped on him in his dugout. He could understand why one of his boys had had an unnatural fear of them. Sweating, shaking, the kid had confessed that he'd rather face a Hun than a rat. Justin should have realized the severity of the boy's phobia, and sent him out with a case of nerves. The poor kid had started screaming when he'd awakened to find a rat nibbling his cheek, with others scurrying around him. In mad desperation, he had scrambled over the parapet and dashed into no-man's-land. A sniper, always on the alert for a target, had put a bullet through his eye.

Justin had made sure the boy was decently buried. He would have hated feeding the rats.

For over a week his battalion had been seesawing back and forth, capturing trenches, losing them again, running out of ammunition and having to withdraw as the Germans reclaimed their territory.

And this morning they were going over the top yet again. But it was madness to send troops to trudge through the tenacious sludge, thus providing easy targets for the enemy machine guns.

The concussion from a nearby shell-burst threw him violently to the ground, a heavy rain of mud pummelling him down. Justin had a moment of blind terror as he found himself sinking into the bottomless mud. He fought desperately to gain some purchase and push and pull himself out of the glutinous morass. The rush of blessed icy air into his starved lungs stilled his panic.

But some of his men hadn't been so lucky. The wounded and exhausted had already stopped struggling.

·   ·   ·

"What *are* you doing, Sybil?" Ria asked as Sybil ran the hem of her skirt over a candle. "Trying to set yourself on fire?"

"Trying to kill these blasted chatts."

"Oh hell!" Carly said. "You haven't brought us lice again? They really seem to like you."

"It's my sweet blood."

"I'm afraid this isn't an auspicious welcome," Ria said to Theadora, standing behind her. The other two hadn't noticed her at first. Ria made the introductions. "Thea's here to do a story on the WATS for *Home Fires*, and ComRad has said that she may kip in with us for a few days and accompany me."

"I've enjoyed your articles, Miss Prescott," Sybil said. "So let's plunge you right into the harsh realities. The lice abound on the men in the trenches, because they can't wash themselves or their clothes for days or even weeks at a time. If we get them before they've spent time at a Casualty Clearing Station, they haven't yet been cleaned up and de-loused, so the hungry little blighters like to jump onto anything else they get close to – like me. And they're the devil to get rid of."

Thea laughed. "By all means let's make this story authentic. Show me the worst."

"You'll have seen enough in a few days. I say, why couldn't we have a uniform as stylish as your suit?" Sybil said appreciatively.

Always chic, Thea was wearing a greenish-brown tweed suit, the skirt fashionably short, moss-green tailored shirtwaist, and smart knee-high leather boots, all of which gave her the air of an energetic and forthright businesswoman. She had also cropped her hair.

"If we looked like Miss Prescott, we could probably be accused of distracting the men," Carly pointed out.

"Aha! So that's why we wear this drab, shapeless khaki," Sybil said. "Don't want to arouse men's desires. I'd say it works. Well, except for Windy. I'm sure her uniform was created by Worth."

"It seems to me that your split skirts are most practical, though," Thea observed.

"Yes, I can leap onto a horse and not worry about showing petticoats," Sybil quipped. "Makes us somewhat sexless, don't you think? Neither trousers nor skirts, but something in between."

"Modern women!" Carly said.

"I'd like to be modern *and* sexy," Sybil said. "Now, Miss Prescott, if you want to be one of the girls, we have to give you a nickname. What do you suggest?"

"I was named after Theodore Roosevelt. He's a friend of the family. So how about Teddy? Although he himself hates that name. I call him Uncle Teedy."

"Perfect!

"You should see what Thea... Teddy's brought us!" Ria said. "A trunk full of goodies."

"Caviar!" Sybil exclaimed as they delved into it. "Raisins and nuts and real coffee! How heavenly! And shortbread. Rich, creamy, buttery, decadent shortbread!"

"Lavender bath salts, and lotion," Ria said. "You certainly know what we need."

"I've brought lots so that all you ladies will have a treat or two. And something special for you," Thea said, handing Ria the latest copy of *Home Fires*. "Turn to page 9."

Ria read:

A Hero For Our Time – The School Girl's Viewpoint
by Alice Lambton

As we descend into our third dark winter of the war, it is important to find a flicker of light to comfort and sustain us. The soldiers at the Front think about the "home fires" awaiting them. We at home admire the courage and fortitude of all those striving towards victory, from the munitions worker who deals daily in poisonous and dangerous chemicals, to the men facing a barrage of bullets and hail of shrapnel. Although we are proud of them all, it's the heroes that focus our attention on the many acts of valour. Among these, the daring aviators are perhaps the most visible.

The very act of climbing into a fragile machine and defying gravity is already an act of great courage. It has been just over a dozen years since man even achieved the ability to fly in heavier-than-air machines. In 1909 it was considered a great feat when Louis Blériot was the first to cross the twenty-two miles of the English Channel from Calais to Dover. And it's still so dangerous that many young men don't even survive the training. But once they have mastered the skills, they must then face an enemy trying to shoot them out of the sky. Whereas a badly wounded man in the trenches may be helped to safety by his comrades, a pilot who has lost the ability to fly his machine has no hope of survival.

The Aces are masters who can out-fly, out-maneuver, and out-shoot the enemy. One such is Captain Chas Thornton. He is one of the many Canadians who has come willingly to the aid of Mother-country England, and he has been with the Royal Flying Corps for two years. Britain's second-ranking Ace, just behind Albert Ball who is also in his squadron, Captain Thornton currently has twenty-four victories to his credit.

The story went on to encapsulate Chas's heroics and awards.

On a recent home leave, Captain Thornton was kind enough to grant me an interview. He is a modest hero, who claims that his victories were merely achieved in the course of his duty, which is primarily to protect our important reconnaissance aircraft and to drive off the enemy ones. Ensuring that his own men are well trained in aerobatics, gunnery, and tactics is why he and his flight are so successful.

"Team work is crucial for pilots to survive as well as prevail," he stated. "One can easily extend that team to the ground crew who maintain and repair our aeroplanes, as well as to those who design and build them. We trust our lives to these machines. And if we can have faster and more responsive ones than the enemy, then we *already have the advantage. So let me say how much we appreciate the work being done on the home front."*

About his celebrity, Captain Thornton states, *"I'm pleased if it helps people to understand what we do, and appreciate how many young men put their lives at risk several times a day when they lift off from the ground."*

Unassuming he may be, but he has become the heart-throb of many a young woman, and the idol of boys. He exemplifies the very best of the young men from the British Empire who do all in their power to help us triumph. So we applaud all these intrepid birdmen.

Captain Thornton is married to his beautiful and accomplished childhood sweetheart, Victoria Wyndham. Mrs. Thornton, an aviatrix herself, is currently volunteering in France with the WATS as an ambulance driver.

"This is astonishing," Ria said.

"Alice did a terrific job," Thea agreed. "Especially considering she's not yet fifteen. I'm going to encourage her to pursue her dream of becoming a writer. And I think that she can start by being a regular contributor to *Home Fires.*"

"That's splendid! She must be thrilled."

Sybil started scratching. "I think I'd best go and de-louse. Apparently the bathrooms are ready, and we should be able to move into our new digs in a few days. Blast it!" she added as a bell interrupted them. Two rings for a train, which meant they all had to turn out.

"Your adventure begins," Ria said to her friend.

Their first load was to the Canadian #3 General. Ria told Thea about Lieutenant-Colonel John McCrae working there.

"I should arrange for an interview with him while I'm here."

"Blake said that he's down with pleurisy and bronchitis and will be sent to a convalescent home on the Riviera."

Ria left a message for Blake to inform him of Thea's visit. Their next delivery was the Harvard Unit. Ria was delighted to see Troy Roland on duty, helping her to unload the stretchers. He had come to see her a few days earlier, shortly after his arrival in France. Although he wasn't an officer, he was so obviously a gentleman – and irresistibly charming as well as handsome – that no one had protested his presence in the WATS mess.

And although he and Ria hadn't been close friends, he was part of her summer life, and caught her up with the latest news from Muskoka. She had been surprised at his obvious fondness for Ellie, but secretly wished him luck.

Ellie might still be in love with Jack, but Ria was beginning to think that he was an opportunist, latching onto rich and influential people whenever possible. Working for Max Aitken, sleeping with Sid, friends with Chas when it suited him. But not enough to stick out the war with him. Jack would never marry Ellie, she was sure.

Troy was delighted to meet Thea, a fellow American. "A pleasure indeed! I've read your articles, Miss Prescott, and have been most impressed. I must say that your descriptions of the *Lusitania* were truly harrowing. You had us caught up in the tragedy, as if we were watching a moving picture. Of course it was especially relevant to us, since Victoria and Vivian were aboard. I thought the story of the young woman who was left for dead, but was then discovered by a child she had befriended and later lost her baby, especially poignant. And your own experience of being sucked into a funnel and then blown out again was unbelievable!"

Ria felt decidedly uncomfortable about him referring to her ordeal, but Thea hadn't used her name so only a few knew that she was the young woman who'd lost the baby. A lot more of them knew about Alice's role in saving her life, and might eventually realize that the stories meshed. But how many people remembered incidents they had merely read about as clearly as Troy had?

Their last load was "sitting" cases destined for the Duchess of Axminster's Officers' Hospital.

"Welcome aboard gentlemen," Ria said. "You're all in for a treat, being looked after by Her Grace. But I won't spoil the surprise. There are cigarettes and ashtrays behind the front seat, so please do help yourselves, and I'll try to make the ride as pleasant for you as possible."

"Is that the lovely voice of my favourite Canadian?" someone inquired through the canvas curtain.

"Lance? Good Lord! What happened to you?" Ria asked in astonishment.

"I decided that a break from hostilities would be welcome."

"You didn't get a Blighty?" She knew he couldn't be too badly injured, because the Duchess's hospital only took illnesses and minor wounds – those who would return to active duty after a few weeks of convalescence.

Lance had been home on leave in September, but had found himself even more distanced from his wife than before. She had an active social life, which seemed frivolous to him, and had been as relieved as he when he'd declined to participate. The boys, aged eight and ten, were at prep school, so he hadn't seen much of them. He'd been glad to return to France, so now he'd volunteered for light duty during his convalescence. "Not much more than a scratch, so I expect to be back at it in a few weeks."

He felt absurdly happy to be near Victoria again. He had thought at first that they might just have a civilized dalliance, not wanting an emotional attachment to anyone. Much easier were mind-numbing encounters with amenable and forgettable women. But Victoria had invaded his thoughts and being in an exhilarating if perturbing way.

"So what's the secret about the Duchess's hospital?" one of the others asked.

"All that I will reveal is that Her Grace converted her villa at the beginning of the war. The place is privately funded, and she has friends who help her with the administration and raising funds. There's a woman doctor on staff, as well as two nursing Sisters and several VADs and orderlies. It's a beautiful place on the cliffs at Cap Gris-Nez, and I expect that you will all feel like privileged guests enjoying a country house weekend."

"Sounds cracking good to me," someone said.

To Thea she said, "And you, too, will be interested in the Duchess's hospital."

"You have us all intrigued now," Thea replied.

The villa was chateau-style and commanded a splendid panoramic view of the sea. As she pulled up, Ria said, "I've been told that this is the closest spot to England in France, and that Dover is only twenty miles from here."

"As close as I'm getting to Blighty this time then," one of the men said disconsolately.

When she helped them out, she smiled warmly at Lance. His thigh was bandaged.

"It doesn't look that minor," she said as she offered her shoulder as a crutch. "My husband had a bullet wound in his leg and it took him four months to recuperate."

"This is just a surface wound, so I'll be walking in no time. Although it might take a bit longer before I can beat you in a race."

Orderlies met them and took the men's kit bags. They were dressed in black suits, looking like guests ready to attend a dinner party. When the wounded in their battlefield-grimed uniforms shuffled inside, they were greeted by music from a gramophone, a giant wolfhound, and four women dressed in lavish evening gowns and diamond tiaras. They shimmered under the twinkling chandeliers.

"Welcome, gentlemen," the Duchess said graciously, as one of the orderlies handed round a tray of champagne-filled crystal glasses. She was in her late thirties, and somehow managed not to look ridiculous in her evening regalia. "We'll just take down your particulars and then you'll be shown to your rooms. I'm afraid we can't offer you private accommodation, but we will certainly make you comfortable."

Ria chuckled at the stunned expressions on the men's faces. The ladies, hoping to keep up the men's morale at such a low ebb in their lives, always dressed in their finery when they were informed of a new convoy arriving. Ria knew that silk pajamas or nightshirts, depending upon their wounds, awaited the men – blue for junior officers and burgundy for the senior ones – along with black and gold brocade dressing gowns.

"I think I've arrived in heaven," one of the officers said. "Who needs Blighty?"

As it was their last stop, Ria introduced Thea and asked the Duchess if they could be shown around. As the tour started, Thea whispered, "You're absolutely right that this will make a fabulous story!" The wolfhound accompanied the Duchess everywhere.

Except for a few men who were laid up with fever, the patients were ambulatory. So they ate in the splendid blue and gold dining room that overlooked the sea – calm at the moment, the clear afternoon allowing a glimpse of the white cliffs of England. The tables were already laid for dinner, with starched white linens, polished silver, and sparkling crystal. In one corner stood a grand piano and a harp – apparently one of the ladies always played during dinner. There was a billiard-cum-smoking room, and the conservatory, which acted as a sitting room. The chandelier-hung ballroom and drawing room had been turned into dormitories for the junior officers, while senior officers shared bedrooms on the upper level. The women and the female staff had their quarters in a private wing that included the morning room and library for their exclusive use.

Some of the men braved the cold to lounge on the terrace overlooking the sea, and a foursome was playing tennis on a sunken lawn sheltered by walls and hedges from the perpetual wind.

The Duchess stopped one of the orderlies and introduced him. "I expect you've read his poetry. John is quite brilliant. And you must meet Zachary. He's an artist and did all the exquisite sculptures in the garden, which you really must see. You may have heard of Bill Wylie. He was the Wimbledon champion three years running, back in the 90s. He's still a brilliant player and gives the men tennis instruction when he's off duty. I've been most fortunate with my staff."

The Duchess was delighted to be interviewed by Thea, so Ria went to visit Lance. He had been settled into his bed in a spacious second floor room overlooking the sea, which he shared with three others.

"They're very efficient here. I've already been assessed, bathed, and bandaged. I feel quite spoilt," he said when Ria sat down in the visitor's chair.

"Isn't it rather telling when we envy someone's bed?" she said, looking at the bright-blue puffy duvet and the crisp whiteness of the sheets.

Lance forbore the temptation to invite her to share it. "I certainly shan't be in any hurry to leave," he said with a laugh.

"How will you manage the stairs?" Ria asked.

"I'm confined to bed for a few days, but I expect the stairs will be good therapy. I'm really not as bad as you think," he assured her, taking her hand in his.

"I have something to confess," she said as she removed her hand from his warm grasp. "I've been using my maiden name. I'm really Victoria Thornton."

It took him a moment, but then he realized. "Chas Thornton is your husband?"

"Yes."

"You should be proud." He tried to keep the bitterness from his voice.

"Of course I am! I just didn't want to be his appendage, I suppose."

Wasn't it significant that she hadn't used her married name? He'd had a sense that there was a problem in her marriage. Was the famous Ace a bit too full of himself and perhaps too free with the ladies? He knew that Thornton was being lionized by the press, and, having seen a photo of him, was aware that he was a handsome devil who surely had no lack of female admirers. But Lance couldn't imagine wanting anyone but Victoria.

"Well, Mrs. Thornton, your company is still greatly appreciated."

"I don't think that there is anything I can bring you," she said with a chuckle, noticing the bud vase sprouting a rose, a package of cigarettes, a snifter of cognac, and a box of chocolates set out on his bedside table.

"If all our hospitals were like this we would probably lose the war. Everyone would be eager to get wounded, and reluctant to recuperate," he quipped.

"I'm glad that you're out of the battle for a while at least."

He was touched by her obvious concern. And couldn't suppress a niggling hope that she might be a widow some day. Pilots didn't have a long life expectancy.

"I just wish my other friends were," she added, thinking of Justin. And Chas, of course, although he was imminently returning to Britain. "Were you at the Somme?"

"Yes. And it was foolishness for us to take our horses. I don't know what Command was thinking we would do with them. I saw mules and dray horses that had to be shot because they were drowning in mud. I feel antiquated as a cavalryman. We're all waiting for that glorious charge that's going to break through the enemy lines, but I can't see that happening anymore. Not in this war. And I never wanted to be an infantryman."

"You'll just have to take up flying."

"Not my style, I think. But I recall that you owe me a flight."

"So I do. I'll ask Eddie Stratton if I can borrow his aeroplane," Ria said with a chuckle. "I really should get back now. But I'll visit when I can."

"I shall look forward to that."

The ladies had changed out of their evening gowns and one of them now appeared in her very chic and surely couturier-designed, nurse-like uniform of scarlet and white. "Would any of you gentlemen like me to write a letter for you?" she asked brightly.

Ria gave Lance a big grin as she left.

On their return journey, Thea said, "The British never cease to amaze me! I'm glad I took photos, because I can hardly believe that place myself."

"I have a fanciful suspicion that the Duchess was entertaining her friends when the war broke out and they all just stayed on to run the hospital. Something to do for amusement rather than play charades. But they *are* doing a great service."

"Where is the Duke?"

"In England, running his ducal estates. They have three boys at Eton, and the Duchess does take leave once in a while to go home."

Thea expelled a bubble of laughter. "How can we not win the war with such dauntless support?"

"You're one of us now, are you?" Ria said with amusement.

"America will come into this war yet, I'm sure of it. Uncle Teedie is determined upon it. And I'm doing my best to get the word out." Thea also sent articles to the *New York Times* and other American publications.

"But isn't that anti-war song, *I Didn't Raise My Boy To Be A Soldier*, really popular in the States?"

Ten million soldiers to the war have gone,
Who may never return again.
Ten million mothers' hearts must break
For the ones who died in vain.

Head bowed down in sorrow
In her lonely years,
I heard a mother murmur thro' her tears:
I didn't raise my boy to be a soldier,
I brought him up to be my pride and joy,
Who dares to place a musket on his shoulder,
To shoot some other mother's darling boy?
Let nations arbitrate their future troubles,
It's time to lay the sword and gun away,
There'd be no war today,
If mother's all would say,
"I didn't raise my boy to be a soldier".

"Yes, and if we women had our way, there wouldn't be war, would there? But since we have to deal with reality, it's important to fight for our beliefs. Uncle Teedie says that there should be a companion song called, *I Didn't Raise My Girl to Be a Mother*," Thea said with a chuckle. "Americans are certainly divided on the issue. Besides the pacifists and isolationists, the German- and Irish-Americans oppose our participation in the war."

"Troy's mother is German, so it was probably difficult for him to decide to help the Allies."

"I don't see how we Americans can think that the 'European' war doesn't affect us. Just look at the *Lusitania*."

They were both silent for a moment and then Thea added, "If America can help to win this war sooner, before too many millions more on *both* sides are slaughtered, then surely that is worth fighting for."

"Can it really be that many? Millions? It's unfathomable."

"Yes. I've been doing some digging, which isn't easy with censorship, but I've gathered that British casualties just on the Somme alone amount to some 400,000 so far. Add to that the French and the Germans and you've got a staggering number of dead and wounded just from the last few months."

"I'm terrified sometimes, Thea. It's as if our men won't be freed from this war until they're either dead or maimed."

"It must be very hard on you, Ria, with so many of your friends involved."

"Practically everyone I love, especially now that Max and Freddie are soon to come over."

It was at moments like this that Ria almost capitulated, because she couldn't imagine what life would be like without Chas.

A fine day usually heralded an air raid, so Thea experienced shivering in the dugout in the middle of the night, and then being called out to a train before the bombing was over.

"Something is always falling out of the sky here," Ria told her. "Rain, ice, snow, or metal."

"You sound so blasé about it," Thea said.

"I've driven through quite a few of these now. You can't remain scared all the time. Perhaps we just get fatalistic."

When they had dropped off their last load of patients at the Canadian #3, Thea said "I'm exhausted, unnerved, and thoroughly impressed, Ria. What you ladies are doing here is nothing short of heroic. I will ensure that everyone knows it!"

Dawn was just beginning to lighten the horizon. The black grave markers in the cemeteries were taking shape, as if the night were congealing into crosses and leaving behind a sombre grey detritus of sky.

"You do this run alone all the time, don't you?" Thea asked.

"Yes."

"Do you get spooked at all? I can't get over the endless fields of crosses. Of the dead."

"I do find it eerie." She told Thea about Lucinda's "ghost".

"I can't imagine how all this violent death *wouldn't* leave some sort of impression. People should never be allowed to forget the enormity of this, Ria. It's absolutely mind-boggling. How many potentially brilliant artistes and academics, scientists and leaders have we lost and will we keep losing? Maybe the very people who would ensure that this sort of cataclysmic war never happens again are being annihilated as we speak."

"I'm afraid that this is somehow *our* war," Ria said. "Our generation. I'm certain that nobody who hasn't been here will ever understand this."

"Yes, we have been cursed, haven't we?"

There was a cozy fug about the tent, with the oil stove burning, but the wind had picked up again, and worked hard at sucking out the warmth. They managed to snatch a few hours of sleep and then, after a quick breakfast, Ria was sent out to the Prisoner of War camp not far from the Marquise aerodrome. She was to transfer men to a hospital in Boulogne. She didn't like this job.

On this load she had half a dozen who were down with fever and coughs, perhaps deadly pneumonia or tuberculosis. They were sitting in the back with an armed guard, although some of them should surely have been stretcher cases.

When she helped a grey and drawn boy out of the ambulance at the hospital, he said to her, "Thank you, pretty lady. I worked in London before the war, in a restaurant. I will be a chef and come back to London one day, and you will come to my restaurant and I will give you a meal for free. Ja?"

"Danke schön."

His face lit up. "Sie sprechen Deutsch!"

"Ein bisschen. Ich hoffe dass Sie bald wieder nach London gehen können."

"Please, you look for Hans Schröder. I will make you the best schnitzel in London!"

"Move along," the guard said. Hans began coughing violently and Ria noticed the blood on his handkerchief.

"Viel Glück, Hans," she called after him, thinking he might well be dead before long.

"Do you feel odd wishing him luck?" Thea said astutely.

"I hate feeling sorry for them. But he's just a kid. Surely not even eighteen. Hell's bells, Thea, they don't seem like monsters!"

"I expect that they, like our boys, are just doing what their government asks and requires of them. They're not evil or bloodthirsty killers like the propaganda posters want us to believe. How can anyone be persuaded to go and kill another person whom he perceives is really no different from him? We have to hate them to do that."

"I thought I *did*."

"So did I, but it's the cold-blooded machinations of war I hate, those commanders sitting at their desks figuring out how many men they're prepared to sacrifice to gain a few hundred yards of mud. It's not the individuals who carry out their orders. And you know what happens to anyone who doesn't obey."

"Shot at dawn. The lads don't have a chance, do they? Kill or be killed – by the other side or your own. Take your pick. Bloody hell, Thea, that song is right! If we could persuade women on both sides to stop sending their sons and husbands willingly to slaughter, the war would have to end."

"But you know it's considered unpatriotic for women to do that. It's their sacrifice to the cause, and they're expected to be proud of their fallen men, stoical in their mourning. Do you know that a friend of Nancy Astor has just lost all three of her sons? But she still believes in helping out, so she takes in Canadian officers, like Lady Beatrice."

"That's terribly tragic!"

"Yes. There's so much tragedy that one more or a thousand more deaths hardly seem to make an impact anymore. We can't mourn them all. It's too overwhelming."

.   .   .

My Darling Ria,

To prove to you that I love you and want to share the rest of my life with you, I'm going to write to you every day, even if just a few lines.

I'm back with my squadron, but have an entire flight of novices, the others having either been invalided out, or sent back on Home Establishment. It's stressful having to train a new batch of pilots, and I don't like to take them up for combat until I judge that they are completely comfortable with their machines and well versed on my strategy. Fortunately, the clouds have been too low to go up today, so I've been drilling my team on technique and making them do gunnery practice.

On dud days, many of the lads think it's a holiday, but they get easily bored and tend to drink too much and then behave like hooligans, breaking up the mess, smashing dishes and chairs, rough-housing, and falling down dead drunk. I know that some of that comes from abject terror, so I don't give them too much time to think about their situation, other than to reinforce the fact that what I'm teaching them can save their lives.

I expect by now you're laughing that I should be such a fuddy-duddy, curbing the adolescent exuberance of boys already officers at eighteen and rather full of themselves – you see, I am an old fogey. They'll mature quickly, if they get the chance. I consider it's part of my job to make sure that they have a fair shake at survival.

I suppose I was lucky that I started flying when there was still chivalry, and we had a chance to perfect our skills before starting to shoot each other out of the sky.

I'm only here for two more weeks, and Jack is leaving in a few days. He wonders if you're still miffed with him, or whether he can visit you some time. You mustn't blame him for my transgressions.

But also remember that I want to make things up to you, Ria. I *can* be the man you thought I was. I *am* the person you married.

I live for the day that I can see you and hold you in my arms again, my darling.

Lovingly yours, Chas

My Darling Ria,

Thinking about what I wrote to you yesterday, I realize that I was wrong. I am much more flawed than the person you thought I was. Obviously, or I wouldn't have hurt you and alienated you. Perhaps I don't deserve you, but I'm not noble enough to set you free.

I don't want to live without you, Ria. I love you so desperately that I've been weeping whenever I think of what I've done to cause this rift between us. It's hard for me to write words like this, to admit that I am weak and scared and not the hero that the world thinks I am. That I wanted to be for you.

Please think of all the days since you arrived in England and our wedding as a new beginning to our relationship. We can recapture those happy times, that exuberant sharing of our love.

I cherish you, my darling. Is your love generous enough to forgive me?

Hopefully, your loving Chas.

Dear Chas,

I never thought you were an infallible knight. I didn't fall in love with you because you're heroic or stoic, but because you're thoughtful, generous, unpretentious, witty. Because you always made me laugh. Because you made me feel like the most important, desirable, beloved, special person in your world. Because I was elated whenever you were around.

I knew there had been other women – Edelina and Sid, at least, I suspect. But they were in the past and you didn't seem to have any lasting attachment to them, other than friendship. Lance Chadwick pointed out to me that in society it is not uncommon for people to have discreet affairs. But I didn't want a marriage like that, nor did I expect that you would ever desire anyone but me. Was that foolish or naïve of me?

If you feel any of the anguish that I have for the past two months, then perhaps we can find each other again.

Love dies hard. Ria

My Darling Ria,

You <u>are</u> my world – all that is good and desirable and joyful. Happiness has eluded me since our separation. The only way that I can keep darkness at bay is to hope for a reconciliation and dream of our future together.

I think about us walking hand in hand down the leafy lanes around Bovington or the cobblestoned streets of Antibes or the wind-swept beach outside your camp. But mostly I envision us together at Wyndholme and Wyndwood, waking up with you in my arms, gliding through the early morning mist in our canoe, sitting beside you on our rock at the Shimmering Sands sharing a picnic breakfast, entertaining our friends at tennis or tea, swaying together on the dock as the moon's reflection shimmers across the water and kisses the hem of your gown, skinny dipping under the stars, making love to you.

Oh God, Ria! I can't bear to be away from you, especially knowing that you are so hurt and unconvinced of my love for you. Please be assured, my darling, that I have devoted myself to you, body, mind, heart, and soul. Let me show you.

Your loving Chas

My Darling Ria,

I dreamt of Thorncliff again last night, of dining with you in the tennis pavilion and taking you to my bedroom as I did that day of your father's wedding. But when I awoke and reached for you, I realized that it had been just a glorious dream. I felt myself plummeting into despair.

So I suppose it's good that I have work to keep me busy and unable to dwell upon my loss.

Sometimes I'm gripped by such terror that I feel as if the blood has drained from my veins. The fear is not of my own death, but of something happening to you. I can't relax knowing that you are in danger and that I am not there to protect you or to take you away completely to someplace safe.

And warm. I expect that you are also freezing in your flimsy tent, or have you moved into the hut yet, and is it much warmer? Ours certainly aren't, and it's terrifically cold a few miles up. If we're out patrolling for an hour or more we can't feel our limbs by the time we return. How can anybody be expected to fight efficiently when the icicles that once were fingers can barely be induced to move?

I must admit that I am envious of all those officers who come to your teas, the lucky men who hear your voice, your delightful laugh, who may be tempted to lose themselves in your stunning eyes and be enslaved by your beautiful smile. I've always been terrifically proud to have you on my arm, but now I selfishly, jealously want you all to myself.

If I keep on in this vein you'll think me cracked and be glad to be rid of me! I don't own you, Ria, but I do want to be the most important person in your life.

Longing to be your husband again, Chas

Dear Chas,

One of the things that I regret profoundly is that the laughter has gone out of our lives. Yes, the war is much to blame, but in our personal torment we have lost the wit and humour that sustained us even in difficult times.

I do believe that you are suffering as well. If you weren't then there really would be no hope for us. Although I would never deliberately hurt you, I cannot honestly say anything yet to alleviate your distress. Except to tell you that I do still love you, as I had mentioned. The forgiving part is harder.

It's like trying to believe in God when you really don't anymore. Much as you may want to, the certainty that once sustained you is no longer there.

I think I find that as frightening as you. I do want us to reconcile, but feel a wall between us. You laid the bricks and I have added the mortar. So can we ever reach each other? I am in despair. Ria

My Darling Ria,

You may no longer believe in God because you can't see his hand in any of the horror and madness around you. But I can show you my love.

And a wall can be reduced to rubble with determined effort.

But how hard it is to break this wall when we are apart. If I could be with you every day, I would demonstrate my love and devotion. I would scrub your back as you soaked in the tub, let you drive the boat, car, aeroplane, massage your feet as you lounged on the veranda after I beat you at tennis – I won't just let you win, you know.

Have I raised a smile? I dearly long to make you laugh again.

I know now that we can never be the people we were – those hedonists whose lives were easy and fun-filled. We've seen and experienced too much to ever again be so innocent. But we can and should find pleasure and joy in the world and in our friendships. And particularly in our love.

I am nothing without you, Ria.

Your loving and ever hopeful husband, Chas

. . .

Thornridge, Toronto,
October 24, 1916

Dear Jack,

Your last letter was awfully disturbing. How terrible it must be to be relaxing in London and see German Zeppelins bombing the city! Silly of me, I suppose, since you are in far greater danger when you're in France, but I think the idea of the war coming right to your doorstep, to the place you think of as sanctuary from the war, is chilling. That would be like the Germans bombing Toronto!

Daddy is rather concerned about your working for Sir Max Aitken. He says that Sir Max is a sharp dealer, a rather shady character it might be best not to associate with, especially if you hope to have a career in Canadian finance. I don't know what he did before he left Canada – Daddy didn't say, as he thinks business is not something that girls should be troubled with. But I don't suppose there's anything you can do anyway, Jack, since, as you say, you've been seconded to HQ, which surely is an honour and not something to be ashamed of. I really don't understand Daddy sometimes. Anyway, I'm terribly glad that you are no longer flying over enemy lines. I do worry so about Chas! I hope that the war ends before Rafe gets over there, but it seems to be dragging on forever. Will it only end when there are no more young men left to kill?

Oh dear, I am sorry to sound so gloomy, but you don't know how hard it is to sit here and wait for God-knows-what to happen! I feel rather as if life is on hold, even though we're all getting older. When can we go back to those summers in Muskoka when all we had to worry about was whether it would rain on our tennis tournament, or whose boat we'd be taking on cruises?

And I'm worried about Ria now as well! I expect she wanted to be near Chas, but isn't it terribly dangerous for her to be in France? She sent me a photo of herself in her WATS uniform standing in front of her ambulance. I say, doesn't her short hair look absolutely spiffing? It's made quite a hit at school – her photo I mean.

She's given me an exciting mission. I'm to collect toys and clothes for the orphans in Calais, for Christmas. So Claire and Esme are helping me to organize the "Teddy Bears' Concert". I managed to secure the Massey Music Hall. As it can seat 4000, we will hopefully have a good turnout. People are to bring a teddy bear or children's clothes as well as $1 for the Soldiers' Christmas fund. It's an amateur production, and we have lots of talent. Lady Eaton has even agreed to sing – she has quite a lovely voice. Claire is shy about her voice, but she sings well, so she, Esme, and I are going to do "Three Little Maids From School" from The Mikado. Your mother is making us the most fabulous costumes! She really is talented with her designs. I'll send you a photo of us.

So many of my school friends are keen to take part. Odd how popular I've become – no one else has a brother and sister-in-law who are so famous and accomplished as mine!

Claire came up with a ripping idea for the finale. All of us performers will be on stage holding candles while we sing, "Keep The Home Fires Burning". Isn't that clever?

Do you know the most exciting news? Claire said that Emily might be able to come home for our concert! She would be our special guest star. Can you imagine it? She's already gaining a reputation on Broadway, so people would surely turn out to see her. Oh, I do wish you could be here as well. Don't they ever let you come home for a rest?

Please do take care.

Your friend, Fliss

●   ●   ●

Rosedale, Toronto,

October 24, 1916

Dear Ria,

Daphne and I are going to be married on Dec. 27. I wish that you and the others could be here! It will seem very odd to have so many of my favourite family and friends absent.

I'm taking Daphne to California for our honeymoon, and then we'll come home via Vancouver, where I have some business to conduct, which gives us a few more weeks away from dreary, wintry Toronto. So we'll be gone for over two blessed, blissful months!

I can't tell you how excited I am to be getting married! Daphne is such a delightful surprise. How could I have been so unaware of her all these years? Blinded by the glare from Ellie, no doubt. Unlike her sister, Daphne is very much a homebody. She's so grateful and genuinely thrilled with every little thing I do for her. How could I get so lucky? I'm strutting about like such a proud peacock these days that you can barely tell I'm limping!

I've just bought a house close by. I couldn't go too far away for Phoebe's sake. She says she already misses me, so we're going to be within a ten-minute walk from her and from Wyndholme – something of a triangle. Daphne is absolutely ecstatic about 'our house'. I never thought it could feel so good to make someone else so happy. If you can't already tell, Daphne and I are both overjoyed!

Of course, Mama doesn't approve. She thinks I should be marrying someone of my own "class", and says that Louise Oakley is much better suited to being a Wyndham wife! She's pretty enough, but still a giggling schoolgirl, and I feel absolutely no attraction towards her. Mama pooh-poohed my contention that Daphne and I are in love, maintaining that breeding is what counts. I replied that breeding wasn't necessarily wrapped up in wealth, because that's what it seems to mean to her. As if I need any more money or that it will make me any happier! Papa has said very little because I think he envies me my love. Grandmother arranged his marriage, of course, which is so old-fashioned! I feel sorry for my parents, actually, because I don't think they've ever been particularly happy. I will ensure that Mama is not unkind to Daphne, but I know it will be difficult for my poor darling.

Damn, I wish you could all be here for our wedding. What fun that would be!

Here's a bit of a wrinkle though, which might amuse you. I expect you've heard that the Ontario Temperance Bill passed in September, and booze is no longer allowed to be sold in bars, clubs, and stores, although we may keep and drink it at home. How we are to buy it when no one is legally allowed to sell it, remains to be seen, but, of course, bootleg liquor is readily available. In any case, seeing this coming, we all laid down vast quantities of the stuff, and sold our shares in Gooderham and Worts, although they're still permitted to manufacture and export alcohol. Oh, and doctors can prescribe it for medicinal reasons. Wine is exempt and good thing too, as we are serving it at our wedding. But we're having the reception at home in any case, and will offer our friends a good choice of beverages.

Phoebe is tickled pink with the new project you have given her and spends all her time knitting mittens and mufflers and socks for the orphans.

I sometimes think that Phoebe is improving – being more mature and growing out of her strange delusions. And then she'll surprise me again with something that I would never have conjured up in my wildest imagination. Yes, I know I don't have much of an imagination to begin with. But a while back she told me that she was concerned because the birds were singing in French! I teased her a little and said that perhaps the Quebec birds had gotten lost and maybe our English birds were now in Montreal. She, of course, took it quite literally, and fretted about how the birds would manage if no one understood them. I reassured her that many of us can speak both languages, which at least calmed her down.

I have to tell you that she's been showing signs of an amorous attachment to a boy from the lake. Someone new. Which is very odd to me – the fact that you don't know some of the summer people anymore! The Millers had a small foundry before the war, but are now turning out lucrative armaments, and have bought the Farleys' island.

I worry that Bobby Miller is taking advantage of Phoebe – I don't mean in the sexual sense! At least he'd better not be! But using her to gain more status and influential friends like us and the Thorntons. She is flattered, since boys have rarely paid her much attention. Mama, of course, has done her best to discourage any sort of friendships for Phoebe, which I believe adds to her problems. But in this case, I think she's absolutely right. Phoebe doesn't see it that way. She tells me she wants to marry so that she can be free of Mama. I can't really blame her.

Ellie told me that Rosie Miller snubbed her at the Country Club. Most of the Miller kids – there are five of them – are arrogant *little rotters, so I don't want Phoebe associating with them either. The problem is that they live in Toronto, and thus are nearby in the winter as well.*

As Phoebe is virtually a prisoner at home, I suppose she isn't in too much danger from them at the moment. But she's been down in the ravine a lot to 'commune with God'. Mama doesn't like that, even though it's still our property, but Phoebe gets very angry with her – which is rather surprising. She says that God wants her to go there, that it's the only place that He can truly reach her, not in the church and not in the parlour, endlessly reading the Bible. He told her that He wants her to be happily married even if Mama doesn't. I wish she could be, but I wonder if that would ever be possible. I think she's upset by my forthcoming marriage, and has now decided that she needs to do the same. She does worry me.

And if that swine, Bobby Miller, ever lays a hand on her, I swear I'll do him an injury!

Uncle Richard and I have being doing really useful work with the Military Hospital Commission, which is in charge of men returning from overseas. I was chuffed that I was invited to sit on the board, because it means I'm doing proper war work. We deal with the logistics of ensuring that the men have clothes, meals, transportation home, their pay and discharge papers, as well as helping them find employment. We also look after the wounded and crippled, providing them with therapeutic treatment and occupational training, and so we have taken over or set up convalescent homes and hospitals for them across the country – including your place, which means that Aunt Olivia no longer has to worry about raising funds for the Wyndham Hospital.

We have facilities dedicated to orthopedics, shell-shock, tuberculosis, and so on. We've set up classes in carpentry, motor mechanics, tailoring, typewriting, accountancy, and anything else you can think of including bee keeping! I've visited a lot of these places, Ria, and have seen some terrible injuries. Makes me rather ashamed to hobble about so obviously with this bloody silly ankle, I can tell you!

And it makes me wonder what the hell you see and experience so close to the front lines! I worry about your safety. We have no real idea what's going on over there, except that it seems to be something akin to an indescribable and unfathomable hell.

Do you always have to be so... adventuresome? (To put it mildly. Headstrong and impulsive, your father says.) Chas seems neglectful of his duty – you should be home having kiddies by now.

I know you won't listen to reason in any case, so do look after yourself. I'm awfully proud of you and tell everyone I can about your being a WATS, and that you can even fly! How will you ever settle down in Toronto when the war ends? Actually, you probably won't. I can just see you zooming all over the place, terrorizing the populace in your car or aeroplane.

You'll be amused to know that your wicked step-mother (sorry, I couldn't resist!)... Helena, seems determined to become a "Lady". That is to say, she's striving to procure some sort of position for your father that will earn him a knighthood. John Eaton did, and she's convinced that Joseph Flavelle will, since he is now in charge of the Imperial Munitions Board, which is replacing Sam Hughes's scandal-ridden Shell Committee. Flavelle is a terrific choice, since you know how capable and honest he is. Did you know he was at the Front recently? He told us that he was absolutely appalled by what he saw on the Somme battlefield. He's so incensed by inadequate and overpriced equipment for our troops that he's imposed strict profit margins, and I'm sure will reform our war industry. And he doesn't get paid for this, which might put to rest some of the profiteering accusations that have been leveled against many of us businessmen over everything from boots to the now-notorious Ross rifle.

Unfortunately, too many innocent people are tarred by the same brush. You know that the Carringtons are honourable and conscientious people. Simon has aged a decade trying to get orders for uniforms, blankets, etc. filled quickly and with their renowned quality, but some manufacturers are skimping, and so we hear stories of uniforms shoddily made and falling apart. Simon and his father are doing their damnedest to ensure that their name is not associated with those despicable practices. I think that Simon would prefer to go to France rather than to have to deal with the pressures of supplying the troops.

So, back to Helena's mission. I don't think she has a snowball's chance in hell of getting your father knighted. He's just not that ambitious or much of a philanthropist, although he allows Helena to host lavish events, ostensibly as fund-raisers. She is currently planning a big ball at the King Eddie. You'll also be amused that she talks about you and Chas constantly and with such affection that it's all I can do to stop myself from roaring with laughter. She thrives on your celebrity. I expect that you never thought you would be doing Helena a good turn by being your usual audacious self!

Take care! You have to come back to us. No martyrs for Helena to mourn, if you please!
Affectionately, your euphoric cousin, Edgar

Ria told Blake about Edgar's letter when he came to tea that afternoon.

"I'm glad that Edgar is so enthralled with Daphne," he said. "She needs someone like him, and he's a decent chap. Unlike the rest of our family, she's never had a whit of ambition, so at least we don't have to worry about her future."

"We girls aren't supposed to have any ambitions beyond marrying well," Ria said sardonically.

"Not in my family! You know how much Ellie likes to push the boundaries. For a while she couldn't decide whether she would attempt to become the first female physics professor at the university, or the first female engineer. But since she wasn't inordinately fond of math we persuaded her that she would still be on the forefront by becoming a doctor. Of course she soon became passionate about medicine, and I can't imagine her doing anything else. But I think she was counting on Daphne having an illustrious or avant-garde career that she – Ellie, I mean – could also enjoy vicariously. My little sister will instead become an unabashed lady of leisure."

"We aren't all cut out to be brilliant doctors or scientists. Ladies of leisure and means do all kinds of good works. Just look at what Fliss is organizing for our orphans, and she's only sixteen."

"You're right, of course. I shouldn't be so judgmental. I despise that in others. I truly am pleased for Daphne. Now for *my* news... I've just sent a telegram asking Zoë to marry me."

Ria was astonished. "That's wonderful, Blake! So you've finally realized that you're in love with her?"

He laughed. "Was it so obvious?"

"Ellie and I have long thought that you and Zoë are perfectly suited. You just got sidetracked."

"By an overwhelming passion for Vivian that was primarily fantasy on my part, I know. Although we did kiss a few times, before she fell in love with someone else. I've always thought of Zoë as a best friend. There wasn't that same sexual attraction – more a meeting of minds. But I realize that I care deeply for her, want to look after her, spend time with her. My life, if this war allows. That's a good kind of love. Not meteoric, but I know that we will never disappoint one another."

"Do make it seem a bit more romantic when you talk to her," Ria said wryly.

Blake grinned. "I didn't mean it to sound so prosaic! I treasure her. She is an absolutely wonderful person. I'll feel a lucky man if she accepts me."

"I have no doubt that she will. She's crazy about you. Just remember that," Ria said, staring hard at him.

"I do know. And, fortunately, she's very persistent. I've been finding myself humming that song, *You Made Me Love You – I Didn't Want to Do It*. I've always enjoyed being with her, but kept pushing away any sort of romantic attachment. Until last year, when she convinced me not to close my heart to possibilities."

"Good for Zoë!"

"She's been writing to me at least three times a week since I left. Not trivial gossip. She'd mention issues from her psychology and philosophy classes, talk about the political and social implications of events, engage in medical discussions with me. And I've realized that I couldn't live without someone who is so passionate about important things, so dedicated to whatever she undertakes, so giving and caring. Ellie keeps telling me that Zoë is my soul mate, and I believe her now. So I can hardly wait to translate that into a physical relationship."

"No romantic dinners and cuddling, but right into the marriage bed?" she teased.

"I've already wasted too much time, Ria," he said, suddenly sombre. "I'm going to be sent to a Field Ambulance soon."

Ria shuddered. A Field Ambulance was a mobile medical unit and a Medical Officer pool in the forward area, supplying MOs to regiments, Dressing Stations, and Casualty Clearing Stations as needed. As a regimental MO, Blake would be in the front lines with the troops, and the Advanced and Main Dressing Stations weren't far behind.

"It's what I've wanted from the beginning. Until now." He snorted. "You have to be careful what you wish for. I realize now that I don't need to be on the front lines to make a difference. But someone has to be, and I have to take my turn. I haven't told Zoë yet, so don't mention it to her."

Ria put her hand reassuringly on his shoulder. "You'll have even more reason to be careful."

"Yes, indeed! If Zoë agrees, we'll get married when I'm on leave next week."

"I wish I could be there! I expect that Cousin Bea will manage to do quite a spread for you, despite all the problems with food supplies that we've been hearing about."

"Oh, hell! I just realized that I'll be marrying above my station." He gave her a wry grin. "Zoë's something of an heiress isn't she? I certainly can't support her in the style that she's accustomed to. I'll be seen as a fortune hunter."

"Applesauce!" Ria said with a laugh. "Although I expect that Grandmother wouldn't have approved. But times have changed, and Zoë would never have let that stop her. And she's never been materialistic. She would live in a tent with you. But since she *does* have her own money, you'll just have to become comfortable as a kept man."

He hooted with laughter.

. . . .

"Do hurry up with those beds, Wyndham," Sister Stone snapped. "You'll have to help with the dressings, or we'll never get through everything before our guests arrive."

Zoë hid her amusement at Sister Stone's agitation. This was no time to tell the nursing Sister in charge of this ward that Zoë had met – indeed, had dined with – their illustrious guests on several occasions in Canada. Field Marshal His Royal Highness the Prince Arthur, Duke of Connaught and Strathearn, third son of Queen Victoria, had just finished a five-year term as Canada's Governor General. The hospital was named for his wife, the Duchess, who worked for the Red Cross and other organizations to support the war effort. They would be visiting, along with their youngest daughter, Princess Patricia, who was Colonel-in-Chief of Canada's Princess Patricia's Light Infantry.

"Gonna have us all ship-shape as well, Sister?" one the boys asked.

"Aye, no bleedin' into your bandages, mates," one of the Australians quipped.

"That's enough of that now. Best behaviour, lads," Sister Stone reprimanded.

"We'll be good, Sister," another promised. "No cussin', spewin', or dyin'."

"Ouch! Don't get her riled up, lads. She's getting rough." The young fellow was having a particularly deep wound irrigated, and

Zoë knew it must hurt like hell. Although the treatment usually made him deathly pale and raised a sweat on him, he rarely complained.

"Nonsense!" Sister Stone said. "Come along, Wyndham, I need you for the next one."

Zoë's back was aching from changing all the linens in the ward of forty beds. She had already scrubbed the floors, helped the men wash and shave, served meals to those who weren't ambulatory, taken temperatures, and sterilized bedpans. After assisting the boy who had lost a leg back into his freshly made bed, she went to help Sister Stone.

This one was a particularly nasty wound, and Zoë could see the dread on Billy's face as Sister approached him with the dressing trolley. They always gave him a glass of brandy before *and* after his treatment. He was nineteen, and had had his genitals blown off. There was only a gaping hole, which had to be cleaned, disinfected, and repacked with gauze around the catheter every day. They had the screen up, of course, and the others couldn't see the tears streaming down Billy's face, but he couldn't stop the occasional gasp or anguished cry.

It seemed so cruel to have to inflict such suffering on these boys who had already gone through so much, but there was nothing aside from aspirin or morphine to give them, although not for changing dressings.

"I understand that Their Royal Highnesses enjoyed their stay in Canada and were sorry to leave," Zoë said so that they could all hear and be distracted from Billy's suffering. That was the official word, at any rate. From her father she had heard that the public enmity between the Duke and Canada's hot-headed and erratic Minister of Militia, Sir Sam Hughes, had precipitated the Duke's departure. "They're proud of you all, I'm sure."

"Even us Anzacs?"

"Of course. We're all part of the Empire."

Sister Stone looked rather disapprovingly at Zoë, but said nothing. Zoë wondered if she would be in for it later. Giving herself airs? Pretending that she knew what Royalty was thinking?

"Sister, can't you close the blasted windows yet?" Someone yelled. "My nostrils are freezing shut!"

"Fresh air is good for you," she announced as she left Zoë to finish the bandaging.

And temporarily cleared the air of the smell of carbolic and Lysol and that peculiar blood-and-infection stench that could never be dislodged.

"But rain's blowing in. You wouldn't want the Royals slipping."

"Goodness! What a lot of complaints from you boys today."

"It's not right that you should have to see this sort of thing, Miss," Billy croaked in a strained whisper to Zoë. She knew he would be exhausted for at least an hour now.

"It's not right that *you* should have to suffer this sort of thing, Billy," she said gently as she covered him up. She wiped away his tears before removing the screen.

Because Bea was invited, Zoë knew that the Connaughts were lunching with the Astors. She was grateful that she hadn't been invited. Nancy Astor must have known it would be awkward for her.

Sister Stone went pink with delight when the guests were shown into her ward. The men, who had feigned indifference, were equally thrilled, their wounds now less painful and more noble.

"There's Miss Wyndham," Princess Patricia said, noticing Zoë.

The Duchess said to her, "I am pleased to see you here." There was a twinkle in her eyes, for it was through her influence that the RAMC had relented and allowed both Zoë and Martha Randall, whose Ottawa family the Duchess also knew, to be taken on. "How lovely for you that Lady Beatrice is nearby. How are you finding things, my dear?"

"I'm extremely impressed with the organization and efficiency of the medical services, M'am. This must be so difficult to do well in these uncertain and dire times."

"Well said," the Duke observed. "And well done."

The Royals spoke briefly with the men and moved on.

"Sister Wyndham knows the nobs," one of the boys said with awe.

"It's *Nurse* Wyndham," Sister Stone pointed out frigidly.

"Yeah, but Sister, she's probably had tea with them."

Zoë grinned at him.

"She has!" he crowed in triumph. "Tell us, *Nurse*."

"There's no time for this nonsense! Nurse Wyndham has to scrub the lavatory."

"Oooh. Being put in your place now, *Nurse*."

Later, Sister Stone said privately, "Surely you should have addressed the Duchess as 'Your Royal Highness'."

"Since I've met her before, it's perfectly acceptable for me to call her, *M'am*."

"*Have* you had tea with them?" Sister Stone couldn't resist asking.

"A few dinners, actually. And the Duchess took an interest in my cousin's Convalescent Hospital in Toronto that my mother is running. Is that all, Sister?"

When Zoë returned to the ward, she did some massage on the patients recovering from fractures and operations. She had realized how beneficial it was while working at the Wyndham hospital, so she had taken a course and done some additional study of anatomy on her own. She often discussed her theories in letters to Blake and asked him to clarify medical conditions.

Early on she had suggested to the CO that she could help rehabilitate some of the patients, and had been transferred from a Medical to a Surgical ward. Some of the professional nursing Sisters were not pleased that she had received the approbation of the doctors, but Zoë ignored their petty jealousies. They were all here to help the men, and her methods worked.

"Next time I'm wounded, I'm getting whatever he's got," one of the lads quipped. "So that I can have Nurse Wyndham run her hands over me."

The boy being massaged took offence and said, "Shut up, Lindsey, or I'll have to challenge you to a duel! Nurse Wyndham is an angel, and I'll not have you lusting after her."

"Hear hear!" someone else added.

"No offence, Miss!" Lindsey said. "Just doesn't seem fair that they get all the attention."

Lindsey had a head wound that was healing nicely, so he was mostly an up-patient now. But he had embedded shell splinters that were inoperable, so no one really knew what his long-term prognosis was. He would soon be sent back to Canada.

"Say, Nurse, did you really have tea with them Royals?"

Zoë described, to a rapt audience, a fund-raising dinner and ball in Toronto the previous winter.

"Blimey! Nurse is a toff as well!"

"Not a bit of it!" she protested. But she knew that in their eyes she was, no matter what she said. And if it gave them pleasure to think that she was waiting on them, then so much the better.

Zoë was in a rather jaunty mood as she returned to her room. And was astonished to find a telegram awaiting her. She had to read it twice to believe it.

Friend of my heart and soul, will you marry me? If yes, can you make arrangements for wedding? Am on leave Nov. 15 – 29. Longing for you. Love, Blake

She wrote back, *Yes! And yes. All my love, always, Zoë.*

She cabled her parents with the news. Olivia replied:

Of course we are happy for you! Wish so much we could be there. How we miss you, my darlings! Hope Max can give you away. Papa will put part of wedding present into your bank account, which you can draw on there. Will have a big celebration when you return, and you can choose yourselves a house. Love from all.

Things didn't go quite so smoothly with Matron.

"You're not entitled to leave for another five months, Wyndham."

"Yes, Matron, but I'm getting married next week." She made it a statement rather than a request for permission. She was, after all, a volunteer.

"Are you indeed? It's precisely this unprofessional attitude that makes us balk at taking you volunteers. You're here on sufferance as it is, Wyndham. You're doing yourself and other VADs a disservice to treat this so lightly, to think that you can arrange a wedding as if you just needed to add it to your social calendar and everyone else should accommodate your plans."

"Not at all, Matron. I am committed to whatever I undertake. I shall work longer shifts, and do without my days and half-days off to make up for the time, if necessary."

"Of course you may break your contract if you have no intention of working for us in the future. What happened to your determination to be sent to France? You realize that as a married woman, you'll never be sent over?"

Zoë hadn't. She had hoped to get there after the requisite three months in England. Although the Canadian Army Medical Corps definitely wouldn't take VADs in their front line military hospitals, the British did, and she was part of the British Red Cross anyway. "I have no wish to break my contract, Matron, but I do need two weeks special leave of absence to be with my husband." There was nothing to stop her from leaving, but the Red Cross would probably not take her back. Yet there were other places, like private hospitals, where she could work. She gazed determinedly at the Matron.

"Her Grace mentioned how pleased she was to see you working here, Wyndham. She had much praise for your family. I understand that both your parents are actively involved in the care and rehabilitation of our men back in Canada. And I know that Mrs. Astor is fond of you."

And had probably put in a word for her, because Cousin Bea would be pulling strings to help out.

"I don't intend to make a habit of this, but I will grant you ten days leave."

"Time is precious, Matron. I do need fourteen days."

There was a moment of silent struggle, but finally Matron said, "Very well, Wyndham. But you *will* make this up."

"Thank you, Matron. I have one more request. I'd like Nurse Randall to be my Maid of Honour. May she have Thursday night and Friday off?"

"You're stretching my patience, Wyndham. She may have Friday. One more thing. What are we to call you when you return?"

"I believe you may have met my fiancé, Dr. Blake Carlyle."

"Indeed I have! He comes to visit the patients when he's on leave. A very personable young man. I suppose that explains your enthusiasm for medicine." There was a hint of a smile on her face. "I wish you both well."

"I'm most grateful, Matron."

The telegram from Ria said: *Knew you were meant for one another. Take anything you like from my closet. Wish I could be there. Be happy.*

Zoë arrived at Bovington the evening before Blake. Beatrice had already made all the arrangements, so she said, "You must pamper yourself before the wedding, and what you probably need most is a good meal and a long sleep."

"I'm too excited! I have to choose a dress, and just look at my hands. Whatever shall I do with them?" They were red and rough from all the cleaning and washing.

"I have some lotions, and cotton gloves you can wear overnight."

Zoë hadn't brought much in the way of formal evening gowns, so she looked eagerly through Ria's dresses, none of which she had seen before, since Ria had lost everything on the *Lusitania.*

"Her wedding gown is beautiful," Zoë said. It was lilac silk with a hip-length white lace coat that dipped to knee-length in the back.

But for herself, Zoë chose a simpler pale blue dress and tried the lace coat over it.

"That's perfect for you," Beatrice said. "Matches your eyes."
Because it was an unadorned, yet sophisticated frock with sleek lines, Zoë could wear it for other occasions, and would take it along on her honeymoon. "I really will have to pick up a few things when I'm in London." Blake had suggested they spend their first few days in the city and see the sights like any old-fashioned tourists. The rest would be a surprise.

"Are you ready for this, my dear?" Beatrice asked hesitantly. "Your mother said that I should talk to you about... wifely obligations. Since she doesn't have the opportunity."

They both blushed and couldn't meet each other's gaze.

"That's quite alright, Cousin Bea. I'm not totally ignorant of what happens." At least in the purely biological sense. "When I first had to bathe and bandage the wounded, we were all rather embarrassed, but it's nothing to me now to see a naked man or to touch his private parts. Once you've had to help them deal with the calls of nature, there's not much left to be modest or prudish about."

"Quite so. I do admire what you're doing, Zoë. I know that I never could. And I don't even see the raw wounds like you do. I just know that some abominable things lurk beneath the bandages."

"The body is an absolutely marvelous creation. What we can do to mutilate and destroy it is appalling. And what people can survive is astonishing. It's what keeps me from completely losing faith."

Zoë managed to sleep well after all, and was brought breakfast in bed. "What luxury!" she said to Beatrice, who handed her some telegrams.

"We all need some pampering now and again," Bea replied.

"I always have a moment of panic when I see a telegram these days," Zoë said. But one was from the Carlyles. *Couldn't be more delighted! Welcome to our family, Zoë. Looking forward to having you all home again. Much love.*

Ellie said simply, *At last! Well done, sister-in-law!*

The Thorntons wrote, *Heard the good news. Setting up a medical scholarship at the university in your names. Best of luck!*

"How thoughtful!" Zoë exclaimed.

Edgar said, *So you and I will be twice related? Daphne and I will be there in spirit.*

Zoë indulged in a scented bath and then packed a suitcase. She was excited and yet somewhat terrified. When Blake arrived, she searched his eyes to be sure that it hadn't all been a bizarre mistake. And was relieved to see more than the usual affection.

He crushed her in his arms and kissed her hair, her cheek, her lips. "God, how I've been longing to do that!"

Zoë couldn't stop the tears of joy. Beatrice left them alone.

They talked for hours, both of them gazing at each other as if astonished that they should be lucky enough to be together. Although they had poured out their hearts to each other on paper these past seventeen months, they hadn't seen each other since the previous summer. Or touched. Blake held and caressed her hand.

Chas, who was at Farnborough and had weekends free, arrived on the same train as Max and Freddie, who had come up from Shorncliffe. They walked from the station and breezed in just in time for dinner.

A fierce November gale blew on the day of the wedding. It uprooted trees, flooded roads, overturned buses. At Bovington, it rattled the ancient windows, raising thoughts of the ghost rampaging through the house, and felled a four-hundred-year-old oak, which lay splayed across the formal lawns that sloped down to the Thames.

The men had planned to walk the two miles to the church in Marlow, but instead, Chas had to make several runs in Bea's Rolls to ferry everyone there. "So much for my carefully arranged hair!" Zoë laughed when he and Max helped her battle the ferocious wind into the church.

The vicar's daughter, Enid Robertson, who assisted Grayson at Thameshill, played the organ with great gusto, yet it barely drowned out the screeching of the gale.

Zoë would have been saddened to realize that those closest to her were unhappy as they witnessed the ceremony. Max, who had walked her up the aisle, was wishing that he had married Lydia and brought her along. Chas, the Best Man, was recalling poignantly his own wedding here, and praying that he still had a marriage. Freddie, who had come only because he knew he should support his friends, was disconsolate that Zoë was now lost to him. He had been forever hopeful. Henry wondered if he would ever be fortunate enough to get married, although he was glad for Zoë and Blake.

But they all put on a cheerful front.

And for once, Zoë was oblivious to their needs.

At such short notice, it was a small affair, but the Astors had come to the church, although they had another commitment and regretfully couldn't join them at Bovington Abbey for the reception. They had brought Martha Randall, the Maid of Honour, and Chas would make sure that she was back at Taplow in time.

Grayson was there, looking proud. Beatrice had arranged for Alice to have time off school, so she had come down with Henry this morning, and would stay the night.

"I'm so pleased to meet you!" Alice said to Zoë and Max. "I've heard so much about you all that I feel I already know you."

"It's a pleasure to meet the author of those wonderful stories and poems," Zoë said, referring to the book that Chas had had printed of Alice's literary Christmas gifts to them the previous year. Justin's poem had been about his sister, Vivian. Zoë found it strange to think that Alice had been with her in her last moments. "Ria has told me about you as well, so I think you should call me Zoë and I will call you Alice."

"Thank you, Zoë. May I ask you about university some time? Blake told me how clever you are, and I do think I should like to attend university as well, so I'd like to know more."

"Of course!"

"But not right now," Chas interrupted with a wink at Zoë. "I'm going to monopolize you, Alice, because I want to hear all about how your headmistress and the girls reacted to that splendid article you wrote. I hardly recognized myself," he teased.

Alice giggled, so happy to be back with her friends. She found a moment later to tell Blake, "I do like your wife. I think she is very much Ria's cousin, even if they are different."

"They do have a few things in common. Daring, willfulness, rebelliousness, stubbornness, the inability to take *no* for an answer," he teased as Zoë joined them.

"Is he extolling my virtues already?" Zoë quipped. She entwined her arm in his and murmured, "Aren't you glad I didn't take *no* for an answer?"

He kissed her briefly and said, "Very, Mrs. Carlyle."

Thea and Meredith had also managed to attend. Thea took Chas aside and said, "I'm not going to be sanctimonious, Chas. I expect you realize that you made a dreadful mistake. I'm heartened by the fact that it all happened before I knew you. What I saw of your love for Ria in Ireland and since has been genuine. I also know that Ria finds it much harder to understand that than the rest of us do. I've just come back from seeing her, and realize that you haven't yet reconciled. But I did notice your letters arriving. And making an impact. I do believe there is hope for the two of you yet." She smiled at him. "And I'm very glad." She patted his arm.

Alice had overheard most of the conversation, but didn't let on. She was observant and well read enough to imagine what the problem might be between Ria and Chas. She could hardly imagine Chas having an affair, but if it had taken place before they were married, it was probably excusable. Strangely, it didn't make her think any the less of him. The man *she* knew loved Ria too much to hurt her like that. Perhaps the old Chas had not been so thoughtful and deeply in love. The war had changed a lot of things. And people.

Zoë introduced Freddie to Martha Randall saying, "Her father is in lumbering in the Ottawa Valley. Her three brothers are all engineers, and all here. One's in your Corps, one's with the mining division, and the other's with the Forestry Corps. And you'll be most interested to know that Martha wanted to study architecture at U of T, but the School of Practical Science wouldn't admit her because she's a woman!"

She was glad to see them in animated conversation, and would be happy if they hit it off. If Freddie could find someone else to love. She was really so fond of him, and hated to think that she might be causing him pain. But realized that there was nothing she could do to help him.

After a delightful meal with much toasting and jollity, Chas and Max drove the newlyweds to the station to catch the train to London. Max and Freddie, both being in reserve units, didn't know when they would be sent to France.

"Thank you for coming, Freddie," Zoë said before leaving Bovington. "Be careful, my friend." He smiled sadly at her.

At the station, Zoë held onto Max for a long time. "Look after yourself, Max. I can't be a twin without you, you know."

"Don't worry about me, Sis. You and Blake enjoy yourselves. *Carpe Diem*, as Ellie keeps saying."

She brushed away tears as the train pulled out of the station. Blake put his arm reassuringly around her. She explained, "I can't help wondering how many of us are going to meet again. It terrifies me, Blake!"

"I know." He hugged her tightly. "So we can't dwell on the future. We can only deal with the present. And right now, you and I are going to be completely selfish – for once! – and indulge ourselves. Although I'm not sure I can get used to all this largesse. Your father cabled me £1000 for the 'honeymoon and immediate expenses'. That's $5000! I might earn that in three years, once I'm out of the army."

"You'll just have to get used to it. He put $20,000 into my account."

"Good God! Ria said I would be a kept man."

Zoë laughed. "She would! It means we have freedom – to do what we want, help whom we choose. But all the money in the world couldn't make me happier than I am right now with you."

Zoë hadn't had a chance to see Bea's London townhouse yet, and was delighted with its aspect over Kensington Gardens. Bea had arranged for a light supper to be sent in from the Carlton, prepared by the famous chef, Escoffier. Zoë was completely enchanted by the beautiful Victorian townhouse and the delectable meal. That they were safely ensconced in this island of warmth with gentle firelight playing over them while a storm still raged outside was somehow symbolic of how they would weather the other storm – the war – she thought. And felt terrifically optimistic.

Zoë, legs tucked up beside her, leaned against Blake as they finished their champagne. "This is bliss," she said.

"Yes, and I'm afraid I'm already being corrupted by wealth," Blake quipped. "I could get used to this lifestyle." He kissed her. "But right now, I think it's time for bed."

"Are you nervous?" he asked her when they were in their bedroom. She stood before him in a flimsy lace-edged silk nightgown, which shimmered in the firelight. She was flushed and quivering, but not from cold.

"A bit," she admitted, staring at him wide-eyed. "I don't know what to do."

He laughed as he took her into his arms. "Stop thinking, and just do what feels good. Let me show you."

He was a considerate lover, and soon had her feeling comfortable with her own body and his. When she lay in his arms afterwards, she said, "I never knew anything could feel so exquisite. I can't imagine anyone ever being happier than I am at this moment."

He hugged her. "That makes two of us."

"No regrets?" she asked him.

"Only that I didn't come to my senses sooner. I love you, Zoë Wyndham Carlyle."

"And you didn't marry me just to keep me out of France?"

He laughed. "Would I be so devious?"

"Yes. To protect me."

"I married you because you are the most beautiful, intelligent, kind, and thoroughly good person I've ever met. And because I want to do this," he said, rolling her onto her back and kissing her. "Over and over..."

They had a couple of days in London, visiting the Tower, Westminster Abbey, St. Paul's Cathedral, strolling through Hyde Park. They had no desire to see shows or moving pictures, or dance at nightclubs. They wanted only to be alone, talking, touching, stretching out the moments that they had together.

Blake would sometimes awaken from a nightmare, momentarily surprised to find her beside him. He'd gather her into his arms and gratefully breathe in the scent of her.

Zoë would wake to find herself ensconced in his strong embrace and sigh contentedly. Sometimes they made love yet again.

"Where are we going?" she asked him as he advised her what to pack for their trip.

"It's a surprise, but something of a pilgrimage. Take lots of warm clothes and good walking shoes. Not many evening gowns."

"Oxford!" Zoë cried when they boarded the train.

"For a few days. You've always wanted to go there, haven't you?"

"Yes! Oh how wonderful! And we can see Henry."

"In his full glory. You'll notice how well he fits in there."

Zoë was impressed with the golden, spired city. But it was peculiar to see uniformed men at the university. RFC ground training was being given here, so there were lots of eager and brash young recruits swaggering about.

"Not many of us civilians here," Henry lamented. "Anyone fit left years ago, and the rest of us are mostly crippled or convalescent. And a few women, of course," he said with a smirk.

Their next stop was Yorkshire, where they wandered the Brontë moors in the appropriately bleak and bitterly cold November days.

"How easy it is to imagine Heathcliffe striding these desolate hills," Zoë said when they stood on a blustery crag gazing at the bronzed bracken, bleached grasses, and dusky, purple-tinged heather undulating to the horizon in all directions. The only hint of civilization was the acrid coal smoke that coalesced above the tiny villages in the distant valleys.

Lowering clouds skimmed overhead, scraping the frozen crests, spilling streamers of darkness lacerated from the vast, brooding sky. It was starkly beautiful. Forbidding.

On the higher, even more remote reaches of the moor, a lonely farmhouse resembling a rocky outcropping huddled next to the black skeleton of a solitary tree. "I can certainly understand the inspiration for Wuthering Heights, and how that kind of isolation could breed intense, destructive emotions," Zoë said.

"Then we won't approach the house in case Heathcliffe's vicious hounds are still about," Blake replied with a grin.

"You read Wuthering Heights?"

"Ellie did when she was fifteen, so I got the abridged version. I recall her annoyance and impatience with Catherine for being spineless, and her fascination with the delightfully menacing Heathcliffe, whom she psychoanalyzed. I was in my first year of med school and Ellie insisted I diagnose Catherine's fatal illness."

"What did you conclude?"

"That she died of a broken heart, of course."

The chill wind tormented the withered grasses and flowed across the furry sea, which lapped against islands of squat shrubbery, infusing the wintry moor with life. Writhing leaves swished a soft symphony. The world became timeless here, the rhythms of nature uninterrupted by the fleeting passage of mankind.

Zoë gripped Blake's hand tighter. She could feel his warmth through their leather gloves, glad for his strength and vitality. Surely at this moment they were invincible in their youth and love.

"So, do you think our landscape defines us?" he asked.

"Well... I suppose we have split personalities," she jested. "For the best part of three seasons we're in the city, hunched over books, scribbling in drafty classrooms or silent libraries, scurrying from one building to another..."

"...crunching through leaves, struggling through snow, trudging through mud," Blake interjected.

"Especially mountains of snow. But we are undaunted! And then we spend three months at the lake frolicking in perpetual sunshine."

"Of course it never rains there."

"Just the occasional invigorating storm to clear the air."

"So you conclude that we are gay and frivolous, but also hard-working and studious. And tenacious."

"Precisely!" Zoë laughed and hugged his arm. "Isn't this fabulous, though? It's how I imagined it, only better! So much more dramatic and sinister. It feels as if we're the last people on earth."

"Yes, very evocative. But I think that's snow sweeping towards us, so we should head back smartly. The landlord warned me how dangerous fogs or storms could be, and that darkness descends quickly these days. Said we could end up falling into bogs or wandering the moors for eternity."

"Alongside the ghost of Catherine Earnshaw. No thank you!"

They had some tense moments on their return to the village as the sudden, blinding snow obliterated paths and landmarks. But they were cozily ensconced by the fire at their inn by the time the blizzard muffled the countryside.

When they ambled along the River Avon in the gentler climes of Shakespeare's Stratford two days later, Zoë said, "It's a literary pilgrimage, isn't it?"

"I thought you'd enjoy that."

"This is absolutely perfect! You're so thoughtful, Blake." She grinned joyfully at him.

He squeezed her shoulder, overwhelmed with love for her. "I think you've bewitched me, Zoë Carlyle. I seem to be falling ever deeper in love with you."

Zoë couldn't imagine that she could feel any happier, but those words finally put the spectre of Vivian Carrington to rest.

Bath, evoking Jane Austen, was a quick stop. Then they spent a couple of days exploring Thomas Hardy's "Wessex", wondering if they might even encounter the famous author in their rambles. But at Stonehenge, the war couldn't be forgotten, since the military was present everywhere and pilots received training in the skies overhead.

They arrived back in London for the last day of their leaves.

When they lay in bed that night, Blake said, "Promise me something." She was resting her head on his chest and he was stroking her hair.

"Anything."

"That you won't cut your hair. I know you'll be tempted when you see Ria, and she'll convince you that it's chic and carefree and very *modern*. But I love running my fingers through it."

She laughed. "Goodness! I never give it much thought, but I won't cut it if it gives you pleasure."

"Mm, it does." He lifted it in the firelight. "It's like... you know I'm not very poetic, so let me ponder this."

Zoë, Max, and Rupert had all inherited their father's dark hair, while Esme and Miles were blonde, like their mother.

"Mud," she said.

"Poppycock! Chocolate syrup," Blake announced jovially.

She laughed. Raising her head to look him in the eyes, she said, "So what colour will our children's hair be?"

"I'll have to work out the Mendelian genetics," he replied with mock gravity. "But I expect that we'll have three redheads for every chocolate one. I'm sure red hair dominates."

"It's not red. It's like a wheat field at sunset."

There was such a tender look in his eyes that she said seriously, "How will I get through the days without you?"

"By remembering this. By anticipating our next meeting." He stroked her face reverently. "Promise me one more thing. That if something happens to me, you'll move on with your life."

"Stop, Blake! You mustn't even think that!"

"I'm being sent to the front lines, Zoë. At least, within target range. I'm not being pessimistic, but we can't ignore the possibilities. Don't cry, my love." He held her tightly.

.   .   .

"I feel that I'm swinging the lead," Lance confessed as he and Ria sauntered along the cold, wind-swept beach below the Duchess of Axminster's Hospital. A heavy pewter sky crushed the distant shore of England into the quicksilver sea. He fought the temptation to reach for her hand.

"You're still limping," Ria pointed out.

"I'm a charlatan! Look, I can do this," he said, suddenly taking her into his arms and waltzing her smoothly about the deserted beach.

She laughed as they twirled and dipped.

He was exhilarated, holding her in his arms. And reluctant to release her. "We'll have to invent a new step," he said, buying time. "The *Invalid Hug.*"

She laughed. "You've just proven you're no longer an invalid."

"The *Convalescent Shuffle* then," he suggested as he slowed the pace.

Ria began to feel uneasy as they swayed back and forth in rhythm with the waves washing ashore. He was drawing her closer, physically and emotionally. She pulled away hastily.

"I do think you're on the mend, Major," she stated.

He was pleased that she seemed disconcerted, as if she had been tempted.

"I hope we'll be galloping across the sands again soon," he said.

They sat down on a tumble of rocks that spilled from the cliff, but these weren't pretty, like Muskoka granite. They were blistered grey boulders tortured by the ruthless sea. He lit cigarettes for them both.

A squadron of aeroplanes suddenly emerged, as if condensing out of the clouds. They were flying low, undoubtedly planning to land at the Marquise Reception Park where the pilots would refuel themselves and their machines, and then head to wherever they would be stationed. This was how Chas and his squadron would arrive in France when they were finished their training in a few months.

"That's where we should be," Ria said enthusiastically. "I didn't realize how much I've missed flying."

"You really do like it?"

"When I was a child, I used to imagine myself soaring with birds, picturing what the world looked liked from their vantage point. I even had wonderful dreams about skimming over the treetops and dipping over the lake, and remember being dreadfully disappointed when I woke up and found I was tucked up in bed. I've always liked being up high, in my tower window seat, on a cliff, at the top of a tree. So the first time Chas took me flying was a dream come true, only better than anything I had envisioned." That had been on their wedding day, she recalled poignantly.

He saw the shadow cross her face at the mention of her husband, and tried to lighten the mood. "I'm looking forward to my flight."

"And I'm itching to go aloft! I do think I will coerce Eddie into letting me. Somehow."

•   •   •

My Darling Ria,
Mumsy once told me that you were such a beautiful child that she told Pater she wanted one just like you. I gather that nine

months later, Fliss was born. (I know what you're thinking – it seems bizarre to imagine our parents actually having sex!)

I think what I admired most about you, even when you were young, was your pluckiness. Remember the time that Pater hired a professional tennis player to teach us all? You and Zoë and Max (the Three Musketeers, I always thought), Henry and Edgar, Blake and Ellie, the Carringtons and the Spencers all participated in the week-long lessons. I was thirteen, I recall, because that was the summer I became passionate about tennis. So you must have been nine.

Rafe was ten and his usual devilish self. He was always able to taunt you into doing something daring. This time it was to climb trees and see who could get up the highest. Simon and Blake were playing against Justin and Henry, I think, when we all realized that you two monkeys had clambered up different trees next to the court – you, of course, choosing the tallest. Our nanny, who was ostensibly keeping an eye on you younger nippers while actually minding Fliss in the pavilion, suddenly started shrieking hysterically when she heard a branch crack and spotted you up in the treetop. It startled you so much that I thought you were going to fall. (You see, even then I was already concerned about you!)

Calmly I said, "Ria, you're frightening the birds as well as Nanny, so I think it would be a kindness for you to come down now."

You, looking rather wide-eyed, like an owl, replied equally calmly, "I do think it's easier to climb up than down."

I knew you were scared, but didn't want to show it. I think you were prepared to stay there pretending you were having a jolly old time gazing at the world from such a height. I remember you sitting there swinging your legs oh so nonchalantly.

So I climbed up to within a few feet of you, not being able to go higher since I was heavier and the branches were thinning by that point. We passed the time of day in the leafy bower, commenting on how the lake looked from this height, and then I started directing you on how to climb down, keeping close to you and ready to catch you if you slipped. But you did splendidly.

Nanny was terrified of losing her job, so we all, of course, swore we would never tell the adults. Henry was a bit harder to convince, as I recall, because he never did approve of your "waywardness". I gave Rafe a wigging, telling him there was nothing valiant about challenging a younger girl to silly competitions.

The next day you were up the tree again, but not so high! When I in my older-and-wiser tone ticked you off, you replied that you now knew the technique and needed to practice it if you were ever going to be good at tree climbing. I think I called you an "incorrigible minx", but I was secretly amused and impressed that you hadn't been daunted.

Not so amusing was the time you came to Thornridge to practice horse jumping. What were you then, thirteen? Rafe, as usual, was showing off, taking jumps riding bareback. So, of course, you had to try it as well. I arrived just as you fell. We were all terrified when you lay there unconscious and deathly pale. I carried you to the house, for which the doctor later hauled me over the coals, saying you might have broken your back and shouldn't have been moved. What a relief it was when you opened your eyes and said, "Did I go over?" I think that's the first time I really took note of what an unusual and mesmerizing colour your eyes are. I replied, "Yes, ass over tea kettle" for which Mumsy pi-jawed me, but you laughed, even though you had a beastly headache and were almost in tears. You stayed with us a few days, but as soon as you felt better, you would have hopped back onto the horse and tried it again if the doctor hadn't absolutely forbidden you to ride for a month. And Pater had threatened to sell the horses if Rafe even let you think about jumping bareback again.

I was seventeen and interested in girls my own age, but I do recall thinking what fun it was having you stay with us. You seemed to belong there, like a cousin or such a close friend that one could just be natural and relaxed around you. Not surprising, I suppose, since we've known each other from the cradle.

I've been trying to think about when I actually started falling in love with you. Maybe the summer when you were fifteen and so infatuated with Justin. Did you think the rest of us didn't notice? I found myself rather jealous of the starry-eyed looks you gave him, and the disarming ways you made opportunities to be near him. Yes, I think that was when I began trying to win you over, "flirting outrageously" with you, as you've often accused me of doing. Remember the first time we were together that summer of 1914? You all came to Thorncliff, and it was you I took into my arms for a sensual tango when we went into the music room. But it was your unhappiness when you ran away that make me realize that I did actually love you and want you more than anyone else.

If only you could believe that I've been falling ever deeper in love with you since then.

I could go on and on with memories that I savour and that cheer me immensely. They make me realize that you are such a large and important part of me, Ria, that I'm not whole without you.

I love you and need you, my darling. Chas

.　　　.　　　.

"Lieutenant Wyndham is taking the Major up for some reconnaissance," Eddie Stratton told the ground crew at the aerodrome. "That BE2c ready to go, is it?"

It had taken considerable cajoling to get Eddie to agree to the scheme, more because he was afraid of what Chas would say if he found out than the thought that he was breaking rules. But there was good reason why pilots had the reputation of being devil-may-care adventurers, and he soon fell in with Ria's audacious plan.

Lance Chadwick had another momentary qualm. This was undoubtedly stupid, certainly risky, and possibly dangerous. But after more than two years the war had become a terrific bore. And with the spectre of death constantly on the horizon, he, like others, had become both fatalistic and blasé about it all. And he no longer cared about playing by the rules. He would snatch whatever moments of amusing diversion that he could, and to hell with his career. He would happily resign his commission tomorrow if it didn't mean that he'd just be recruited again for Kitchener's army through the new conscription law, and end up in the infantry.

"Lieutenant Wyndham" strode boldly over to the aeroplane. Ria was surprised at how well the uniform fit, and being in trousers, it was easy to swagger like an arrogant young pup. She knew from playacting that you had to affect the manner, and people would be taken in. Her hair was completely hidden beneath the fur-lined flying helmet, and the roomy leather coat helped to disguise her figure even more. She wore a fake moustache, which tickled. If the crew thought she looked terribly young, they at least didn't seem to suspect that she was a girl.

"So you're letting me take up 'Fokker Fodder'," Ria said wryly. The BE2c was a two-seater biplane, with the observer's cockpit in front of the pilot. "I thought we'd have something better by now. Chas was flying these when he first came to France. So tell me the strengths and weaknesses of the machine."

Eddie looked at her in surprise and said with a chuckle, "I've only ever heard Captain Thornton talk like that, so I shouldn't be surprised. It's very reliable, stable..."

"And therefore rather un-maneuverable."

Eddie laughed. "Good enough for what you want to do. We're not about to engage in a dogfight, or do any stunts."

"How is she in a dive?"

"Not bad. You can push her a lot before the wings are in danger of coming off."

"Speed?"

"You can get her up to 70 or so miles per hour."

Ria checked the rigging the way Chas and Peggy had taught her.

"You won't need any ammunition," Eddie said, referring to the Lewis machine gun.

"I hope not," Ria said. "Chas gave me a small pistol when I started flying, but I didn't bring it to France."

"Why a pistol?" Lance asked.

She looked at him askance. "In case of fire."

He raised his eyebrows. "I see. I have mine."

"And you'll be prepared to use it?"

He was perturbed by her determined gaze. She was asking him if he'd shoot her, should it become necessary. He laughed uncomfortably. "I trust your flying skills, *Lieutenant*. But, yes."

She grinned. "I'll look after you, Major. But the machines sometimes don't co-operate. You'll be happy to know that I have had training in forced landings. And now that I've thoroughly disconcerted you... shall we?"

Eddie said, "We'll fly south, along the coast."

"Couldn't we go towards Belgium? I want to see the front lines, at least from a distance. Just a glimpse of Ypres, Eddie? Please?"

Eddie and Lance exchanged glances. Lance shrugged. Eddie laughed. "Alright! I expect you'd probably do it anyway, once we're aloft."

She flashed him a smile. "You're a brick."

"And likely to get cashiered if anything happened to you. Not very close. Understood? And once we're up, you obey my commands."

"Yes, Sir!" She saluted him.

Eddie and Jonathan Telford were flying Nieuport scouts, which were, of course, much faster fighter planes. They flanked Ria as they flew along the coast to Dunkirk. At over a mile up, they could stay well behind the lines but still see the brown, cratered corridor of the trenches – a wasteland between the frost-tinged green fields of a divided country. But the puffs of shells looked innocent from up here, Lance thought, the nether regions insignificant as he and Victoria flitted through the grandeur of the sky. Clouds that looked heavy and ominous from below were soft, gossamer fields of dazzling white snow. The sky was a brilliant, endless blue, while the mere mortals far below them existed in the passing shadows. Lance could certainly understand Victoria's fascination with flying. Surely up here, men – and women – unencumbered by gravity, soaring higher even than the birds, became a breed apart. They transcended the ordinary, seeing what only God had hitherto seen. Amidst all the radiance and purity of air and colour, the mud and blood and anguish far below them no longer seemed to exist. They were alone in this celestial sphere with a freedom that one could never feel when tethered to the earth.

Ria looked about her, remembering what Chas had said about constantly having to scan the infinite sky for a sign of the enemy. They were on their way back when she saw them, thinking they must be Allied planes, but she waggled her wings to let Eddie and Jonathan know that she had spotted aircraft.

They were obviously astonished when they noticed the bomber with an escort of three Albatros fighters. Eddie motioned her to return to the aerodrome, as he and Jonathan flew off to engage the enemy. One of the Albatroses, probably thinking that he wasn't needed in combat with the British scouts, peeled off and came after her. The slower two-seaters were usually easy kills and were how most Aces accumulated their victories.

Ria was surprised at how composed she was despite the fear. Chas's tactics for fighting came back to her in an instant. *Never fly in a straight line. Never let the enemy get behind or beneath you.*

"Get down!" she yelled at Lance as she saw the trails of the smoky tracer bullets. But he couldn't hear her over the noise of the engine and the wind. She banked and turned.

But the Albatros was much faster and more maneuverable than the BE2, and Ria couldn't out-fly it. As bullets whizzed past her ears and ripped through the canvas wings, she felt real terror. It could be so quick, she realized. A bullet in the head and she and Lance would both be dead. What would Chas think?

She tore off her moustache, goggles, and leather helmet, feeling the icy wind whip through her hair. The bullets stopped. She looked over as the Hun pilot pulled up alongside her. She saluted him, and was amused at his astonishment. "No!" she shouted to Lance, who cocked his revolver. She banked away so that Lance couldn't get aim. The German pilot saluted her and laughed as he flew off.

Ria had almost stopped shaking by the time she landed the plane.

"A bomber and three Albatroses heading for Calais," she shouted to the crew. "Stratton and Telford have engaged them." Having watched her battle with the Hun, the crew had already been alerted, and there was a scramble to get other pilots up. But they noticed smoke on the horizon and Ria prayed it wasn't one of her friends who had crashed.

"You should have let me shoot him," Lance said.

"No! Chas told me about chivalry among the pilots. The Hun spared us, Lance. I hadn't a hope of getting us safely away."

"So we let him go back to shoot down one of our friends."

She was angry. It was unfair of him to make her feel guilty. "You can't blame me for doing the honourable thing! Whatever the consequences."

Her distress weakened him. "I'm not blaming you, Victoria. In fact, I'm damned grateful to you for your skill and quick thinking. And I'm glad that you're not ruthless enough to be a combatant," he said, stroking her cheek gently. God, how he wanted to take her into his arms then! Make love to her. She was so beautiful, so vulnerable, so feisty – it was a heady mix.

After getting three more scouts airborne, the ground crew were milling about, not making much of an effort to hide their astonishment at "Lieutenant" Wyndham's sudden transformation into a woman. Ria was thankful to see Eddie land, but the CO marched onto the field.

She hadn't bothered to cover her hair, as everyone who had seen her land now knew that she was a woman. She felt only slightly awkward in her male uniform, thinking, actually, that it was more practical than skirts of any description, and surely one way that men were keeping women out of their active and powerful realm.

"What's the meaning of this?" the CO barked.

Lance said, "A bit of a lark, I'm afraid, Major. The *Lieutenant* is actually a licensed pilot."

"But not with the RFC! What the hell's going on here? Stratton, is this one of your hi-jinks?" he asked as Eddie joined them.

"Sorry, Sir. It was intended to be a brief ascent until Fritz came. I have no doubt that the bomber was aiming for Calais," he pointed out. "But we downed it. Telford's plane was badly shot up but he managed to put it down near Audruicq. He waved that he was alright. The military from the supply depot were already heading out to the two crash sites. I think we gave them a good show."

Ria breathed a sigh of relief. Eddie winked at her.

"Fortuitous for you to intercept them, but no excuse for this sort of... of... Well, I don't even know what to call it! Allowing a civilian woman to take up one of our aircraft. What *were* you thinking, Stratton? You should be court-martialled for this."

"Yes, Sir."

"It's my fault, Major," Lance said. "I'm afraid I couldn't resist the idea of being taken aloft by a beautiful young aviatrix. I pulled rank, so don't blame Stratton."

Which was a lie, of course, but Ria was grateful for his chivalry.

But Major Goodwin ignored Lance's confession. He turned to her. "And you, young lady, should be spanked and sent home to your parents."

Hiding a grin, Ria couldn't resist saying, "I don't think my husband would appreciate your spanking me, Major."

"You're married?"

"To Chas Thornton."

"Good God! Chase!"

"You were with him in 2nd Squadron?" Ria said in surprise, for only there had Chas had that nickname.

"Yes, and you must be the fiancé who was on the *Lusitania*. My God, I remember how berserk Chase went when we heard about that. The CO almost had to shoot him to keep him from taking off for Ireland in his aeroplane. Well, I'll be bug...! Now that I think on it, I do recall Chase telling me that his wife was taking flying lessons. You must have picked up some techniques from him, since you did some damned fine evasive flying. I could see it from my office window."

"Chas told me his strategies when he was teaching."

Major Hal Goodwin laughed. "Boom Trenchard's going to rake us over the coals when he hears about this." He was referring to the commander of the RFC in France. "I expect it'll be impossible to keep this quiet, but let's try, eh? You're grounded and confined to base for a week, Stratton."

"Yes, Sir."

"I will still have to mention you in Dispatches for a job well done."

"Thank you, Sir."

"May I suggest, Major, that Wing adopt a new policy? Women pilots would distract the Germans," Ria said with a grin.

He guffawed. "I daresay! But Chase would have my hide if I suggested it."

Eddie said, "If Mrs. Thornton hadn't drawn the attention of the one Albatros, Telford and I wouldn't have had a chance of shooting down the bomber."

Major Goodwin harrumphed. "That's as may be..."

The adjutant rushed onto the field. "Sir, we've had news that an LVG had a forced landing outside Boulogne. The French have captured the crew, but it seems that they just bombed London!"

"The hell they did! What's up with Fritz suddenly attacking us in daylight? An LVG?" It was a relatively slow reconnaissance two-seater, Ria knew.

"Dropped six bombs on London. The RNAS didn't catch a glimpse of them." The Royal Naval Air Service patrolled the coasts. "If the Boche hadn't had engine problems, they would have made it back undetected."

Major Goodwin frowned. "Is this the Hun thumbing his nose at us after we shot down two of their Zepps last night? Telling us that even if we can get the big guys, they can still flit in and out of Britain dropping bombs from aeroplanes? It doesn't bode well." He shook his head.

Jonathan arrived in a tender before Ria and the others left. He hobbled over to them. "Bit of a rough landing. Twisted my ankle, but I'll be fine."

As Ria drove Lance back to his base, he said, "That was exhilarating. You've made me seriously consider joining the RFC. Of course, it was more enjoyable before the sky became a battlefield, but I can see how that kind of one-on-one warfare has such tremendous appeal. You're pitting your skills and wits against another, not being blasted from miles away by artillery or mown down by unseen gunners as you struggle through the mud."

"But the bullets are just as deadly," Ria pointed out.

"Yes, but I'd rather die up there in a fair fight than at the bottom of a shell hole, never even having seen my enemy. It's more like the cavalry used to be. Besides, it seems to me that when pilots aren't flying, they're living a rather genteel life – dining well, sleeping undisturbed in clean beds well behind the lines, and greatly enjoying their leisure time."

"Rather like you at the moment," she said with a chuckle.

"Only because I'm convalescing. The others are still at the Somme."

When Ria stopped the car, Lance said, "You're an incredible girl, Victoria. If Goodwin hadn't sworn us to secrecy, I'd be telling everyone how brave and clever and talented you are."

He had to restrain himself from taking her into his arms when she flashed him one of her bewitching smiles.

My Darling Ria,

What have you been up to? My first suspicion was when I read a newspaper account about a female pilot from the German press, reprinted in our papers via the American press. I've added it below. I should have known it was you!

Boom Trenchard recently took me aside and said, 'Spunky lass, your wife, but you have to keep her under control, Thornton. Won't do for her to make a laughing stock of the RFC.' Whereupon he hid a grin. 'Would have given anything to see the look on the Hun's face! Secret weapon, indeed. Should have thought of it myself.' And he went off chortling to himself.

From the German Press:

The British are using a new, secret weapon in their air battles. Women pilots! We believe this to be unfair, since no gentleman will fire upon a lady. Much as our pilots may appreciate seeing a pretty face in the skies, they cannot be distracted from their objectives.

Our Aces say that if the pilot who claims he saw a beautiful blonde angel flying, and most skillfully, wasn't suffering the aftereffects of too much schnapps, then they want to give fair warning to the British. Keep your women at home or they'll be treated like any other combat pilot.

· · ·

Zoë devoted herself to her work when she was back at the hospital, more to stop herself worrying about and longing for Blake than to make up for her absence. While she had once thought a career was important, she now wanted nothing more than to be Blake's wife, look after him, have his children, create a happy home environment, as her own family life had been. She felt a little shamefaced for thinking her mother had given up too easily on a potentially brilliant musical career.

On her return to Taplow, she was transferred to an officers' ward, and wondered if that was because of her connections. Was it deemed more appropriate for her to look after the men who were usually from the upper classes?

She missed "her" boys and went to visit them on her time off. Most of them were still there, and doing well. She was glad to see that Billy was looking less strained. "It's healing nicely," he told her. "I'll be going home soon." He looked at her uncertainly, and she knew what he must be thinking. What woman would want a man who could never be a proper lover or father children? Her heart went out to him.

"Lindsey's not doing so well, Sister.... *Nurse*," one of them said. "He told Sister Stone that something exploded in his head the other day, and he's been kinda queer ever since. Rambling sometimes."

Lindsey lay there looking waxen, plucking at his sheets. "How are you feeling, Joey?" she asked him.

"Can you hear that buzzing? Someone should get rid of the bees before they sting us. Or maybe it's a new bomb the Huns are using. Bzz, bzz, bzz, bzz, bzz, bzz. Make them stop!" He covered his ears and started thrashing about.

Zoë held onto his hands gently but firmly. "It's alright, Joey. Shall I give you a bit of massage to relax you?"

"Is that you, Sister Wyndham?" He looked at her as if he couldn't reconcile her face with her voice.

"Yes." She didn't want to confuse him, and when one of the other lads started to say something, she interrupted with, "That's alright. I expect I'll always be Nurse Wyndham to you chaps. Try to relax, Joey." She took one of his rigid hands away from his face, laid it down beside him, and began to massage his arm. It seemed to soothe him and he took his other hand away from his face and laid it calmly across his chest. She massaged his shoulders, neck, and around his ears and jaw, which brought a smile to his no longer frozen face. "That *is* nice. Finally I get it too." He chuckled. "Didn't need to get shot up again after all."

He was asleep when she left him. One of the others said grimly, "We thought he was going home soon, but he's getting worse, poor bugger! Shrapnel must have shifted."

Joey Lindsey, who had lied about his age to enlist and wasn't yet eighteen, died in the night.

Chapter 7

Having grown up in the slums of Toronto, Lizzie Wyndham knew how to look after herself. So when a strong hand grabbed her arm as she left the stage door, she swung around on her assailant with a sharp punch to the jaw, which he just managed to deflect.

"Hey, Lizzie! Hold on. It's me."

She could make him out now in the dim aura of light from a nearby streetlamp. "Christ Almighty, Rafe! What the bloody hell are you playing at?" He had her wrist imprisoned in his hand, and she jerked angrily away from him.

He chuckled wickedly. "Nice greeting. Showing your roots a bit, aren't you?"

"If you've stopped by to insult me as well as assault me, you can just kiss my... derriere!" She marched away, annoyed that he had forced her to abandon her upper class poise. Pleased that he had sought her out.

He pulled her to a stop and said, "Delicious thought! But let's begin again. How delightful to see you, Miss Wyndham. May I have the pleasure of your company at dinner this evening?"

"Mr. Thornton, what a pleasant surprise to see you in New York. I had no idea that you were lurking in the shadows."

He laughed. "How I've missed you, Lizzie! Take pity on me and dine with me. I'm staying at the Plaza."

It was one of the most opulent hotels in New York, overlooking Central Park and next to one of the Vanderbilt chateaux. She particularly enjoyed having tea in its elegant Palm Court under the Tiffany stained-glass skylight. "Emily, Hugo, and I go there sometimes to meet with George Cohan. He's producing Hugo's musical, and has his own booth in a corner of the Oak Room. He likes his afternoon cocktails before the curtain goes up." If Rafe thought he was going to impress her and make her feel she was getting a special treat, then he was about to be put in his place.

And he was taken aback by this. He fell into step with her. "I saw the show yesterday. Your sister is astonishing."

"Yes, she's making an impression on Broadway. This musical is already a hit."

As if responding to her unasked question, Rafe said, "I arrived late yesterday, and just managed to catch the performance. But I didn't know how to get in touch with you, other than by lying in wait. What do you say then?"

"I'd be delighted to dine with you, Mr. Thornton. I'll meet you at the hotel in an hour."

"You look fine the way you are." She looked quite chic, in fact.

With her mother's eye to fashion and a superb figure, Lizzie knew how to dress well. She had sent her mother sketches of the latest designer fashions, so she and Emily had exquisitely made replicas. "But not for dining at the Plaza."

"An hour then. May I hail you a cab?"

"As long as you're paying for it," she said with a smirk.

When she walked into the Plaza lobby less than an hour later, Rafe was impressed. She was not only dressed in a beautiful and flattering gown, but carried herself as if she had always trodden these marble and gilt halls. "You look fabulous," he said.

When she smiled at him, he saw Ria for a moment. It was something of a shock to him. Otherwise, they didn't look much alike, but in some of her movements and certainly in her brash behaviour, she was very much Ria's cousin. Because he had always fancied Ria, he felt irresistibly drawn to Lizzie.

She drew stares from men and haughty glares from their women.

"I enjoyed the musical," Rafe said as they sipped champagne. "Garrick obviously based it on his visit to the Oakleys' back in '14. Almost autobiographical, I'd say. Moonlit summer night at the lake. A lovely ingénue with an untapped talent. An up-and-coming composer who falls desperately in love with her. I found myself humming the signature tune all night." Which was *Under the moon, I'm over the moon for you.*

"Hugo *is* rather taken with Emily. I wouldn't be surprised it he asked her to marry him. He's twice her age, but she's enthralled by him. Understandably, since he's given her what she's always dreamed of. And when she does marry him, I'll be able to go home again."

"Is that what you want? To return to Toronto?" He tried not to sound hopeful.

"New York is certainly fascinating. The Americans do everything on a grander scale than we do. Imagine if Toronto had even one hotel like this one. And look at the mansions of people like the Vanderbilts." She was subtly pointing out that Thornridge and Wyndholme weren't even in the same league. "But I don't really feel at home here." In fact, never having had a decent home until the one that Uncle Richard had bought for them two years ago, Lizzie just wanted to go back there to enjoy it. And wait for

Rafe to marry her. Having lived as a maid in the homes of others since she was thirteen, she wanted something that was truly her own. The flat that she and Emily rented in a rundown brownstone in Greenwich Village worked for the moment, but was not where she wanted to spend much more of her life.

And having tasted this extravagant lifestyle, she wasn't about to settle for even the middle-class respectability that her family now had. She wanted the kind of flamboyant, glittering, exciting life that only someone with Rafe's wealth could provide. And she'd never move in those exalted circles here. So if Rafe didn't come through, she'd pick up another millionaire in Muskoka, where she was now an accepted member of the illustrious Wyndham family and their social set. "I'm intimate with Toronto, and feel I have more control of my life there. Here, I'm insignificant. Not something I relish," she added with a grin. "Especially as Emily is bound to become New York's darling, and I'll just be the superfluous older sister."

"So you'd rather be a bigger fish in a smaller pond?"

"Precisely." Mrs. Rafe Thornton, renowned society hostess, philanthropist – because giving money to worthy causes was the ultimate expression of wealth and power – talented in her own right, glamorous, saucy, beguiling, desired by men, envied by women.

"We went home for a few days last month," she told him, "before *Under the Moon* premiered, because your sister had organized a fund raiser. Emily sang at the concert, which was a huge success. Fliss was delighted with the turnout."

"So I heard. That was good of you both."

"We have to do our bit as well."

"So you're staying here just to look after Emily?"

"Yes. She's very ambitious and dedicated to her work. And she's no fool. She does have a head for business. But she's only seventeen, so I'm here to make sure that no one takes advantage of her, in any way. She is a bit of a dreamer, and sometimes not the best judge of people. But I like Hugo, and think that he *will* take care of her."

Rafe was impressed that she was so responsible and mature, considering that she was only nineteen. And felt oddly protective of her. He'd like to take her home and make her happy. But, hell, he wasn't prepared to marry her. Set her up in a love nest somewhere, spend fun days and especially nights with her. But he didn't want to be tied down to one woman. Unless it were Ria.

He'd coveted her ever since he'd had his first adolescent yearnings. But Chas had charmed her, and she had only ever repulsed his advances.

"What brings you to New York?"

"I've just finished my flight training in Texas, so I thought I'd stop in to see you on my way home." Having taken private lessons from the Stinson sisters, he was now eligible to join the RFC and go overseas right away.

She met his eyes and could see the desire there. And felt triumphant. "So now you're going to war."

"Yes. Have to try to keep up with big brother," he said with a smirk. "And yours. Bloody celebrities!"

When they had finished a leisurely meal, Rafe said, "Do you have to go back to the theatre?"

"No. Hugo will take Emily out for supper – she doesn't eat much before a performance – and then bring her home. And I have to get up early for work."

"You work?"

"For Anders Vandeburgh, the photographer. And he's teaching me. So when I return to Toronto, I'll set up a studio."

"You're good, are you?"

"I have an eye, so I've been told. So yes, I'm damned good!"

He laughed. "You'll have to show me. In the meantime, why don't we go to a nightclub?"

His gaze was intense, intoxicating. She wanted to dance with him, be held in his arms, be seduced – up to a certain point. "I'd like that." She smiled coyly.

And she did like it. He ran his hands provocatively along her back as they danced. He drew her close so that she could feel his desire. They danced until two in the morning, when Lizzie finally said, "I have to get home or Emily will worry about me. And I have to be up by six."

When they were outside, he drew her into the shadows and kissed her.

"Stay with me tonight," he whispered.

"I must have missed the part where you asked me to marry you," she said sarcastically.

"Is it just me you won't fuck, or are you still a virgin?"

He anticipated the slap and caught her hand. "Lizzie, You're a vamp. You're driving me crazy! Let me make a woman of you."

His caresses had aroused her, and she was tempted. But if she gave herself to him, she no longer had an ace to play in this game in which he held most of the cards. "I don't trust you, Rafe. Look at what Chas did – got Ria pregnant, went off to play soldiers, and promptly knocked up another girl. I don't blame Ria for leaving him." Jack kept her well informed.

"Has she?" He was surprised. Of course that explained Ria's joining the WATS. He wondered if that meant he had a chance with her, but knowing his brother, he figured that Chas would win her back. Chas always got what he wanted. "You're cruel, Lizzie, sending me off to fight and maybe die without fulfilling my desire for you."

"I have no intention of ending up like either of Chas's playthings. You'd just mock me and say that it served me right for growing up poor. Because that's how you think of me, isn't it? A lower class tart, naughty, unprincipled, perhaps a bit dangerous for someone of *your* upbringing. Exciting, is it?

"Very. But I do respect you, Lizzie."

"Bullshit!"

He grinned. "How can I convince you that I need you?"

"I might entertain a proposal of marriage. *Might*. I'm not convinced that you Thorntons are entirely respectable."

He threw back his head and laughed. "I do love you, Lizzie Wyndham."

.   .   .

Lizzie was surprised to see Rafe walk into the photography studio a few hours later. The little sleep she had managed to snatch had been disturbed by thoughts that she might have been playing *too* hard-to-get. Perhaps she should let him take her virginity. Perhaps that would make him feel responsible for her. Perhaps he would realize that they were good together, and he would be tied to her even more by his physical need of her.

Yet he might consider her just another conquest and move on. She knew that some men relished the hunt as much as the kill. She also realized that Rafe didn't have the same upright moral character as his brother, and yet look at what Chas had done, no matter how sorry he now claimed to be.

She needed to be careful. Rafe might even damage her reputation if things didn't work out between them, warning off one of his friends who might otherwise take an interest in her. Someone like Lionel Camford, heir to Pittsburgh Plate Glass. She had once told Rafe that she thought Lionel a buffoon and wasn't at all interested in him, despite his immense wealth. But that had been merely a ruse to make Rafe feel that she wanted *him*, and to make herself *not* look like a gold-digger. But, hell, why was she different from any upper class girl who expected to marry well?

She would ensure that he never discovered that she had served him at Wyndwood when she had been disguised as the Irish maid, Molly. He would be vastly amused, but when he realized that she was an easy liar and a consummate actress, he would feel justified in his initial contempt of her. She had worked hard to win him over with her charm and sexual allure.

Now here Rafe was asking to have his portrait done by her. "We're old friends," he said to her boss, winking at her.

"She'll do a good job," Anders Vandeburgh said.

"Talented, is she?" Rafe asked.

"Yes. And hard working. Not the frivolous socialite I thought she was when she first approached me." Anders grinned at her.

Bless him, she thought. It was important that Rafe be reminded that she truly was a Wyndham, descended from a long line of aristocrats.

She took time with the lighting, and positioned Rafe so that the camera flattered him. Not that he needed much help there, she thought, for he was rakishly handsome. She felt a thrill of pleasure that he considered himself an intimate friend. And knew she would desire him even if he weren't rich.

"And now, Mr. Vandeburgh, would you take a photograph of Miss Wyndham for me? As I need to return to Toronto tomorrow, would it be possible for me to have these later today?"

"Certainly, Mr. Thornton. For a premium, we can have them ready by 5:00 o'clock."

She felt awkward sitting for Anders while Rafe watched, but tried to look pure, yet sophisticated and sultry enough to enthrall Rafe whenever he looked at her photo. Surely that was a sign that he really did like her.

Before he left, Rafe murmured to her, "Dine with me again. Will you meet me at Delmonico's at 7:00?" Delmonico's, the oldest and most renowned restaurant in New York, was frequented by the rich and famous. Hugo had taken her and Emily there once.

"Make it 7:30."

Lizzie was glad that she had several decent evening gowns, so when she was shown to Rafe's table she noticed that he was once again impressed. As was *she* to realize that he had booked a private dining room on the third floor, near the ballroom. When the maitre d' had left them, she said, "This is lovely, but rather reeks of seduction."

He laughed. "I wanted you all to myself. No old men ogling you."

"I don't think only old men ogle me," she replied archly.

"Even more reason to keep you away from the lascivious masses. Besides, you can smoke here if you want."

She took the proffered cigarette.

"I had a run of luck at cards today, so I thought we'd really celebrate."

"You've been to one of the gambling dens?"

"Not much else to do on a cold winter's day in New York by myself. I sense you don't approve."

She took a sip of champagne and said, "I have more respect for money than to risk it on something with very little chance of gain. So mine is invested in various ventures, all of them paying handsomely at the moment. Jack is looking after that for me, and seems to know what he's doing."

"He is rather adept," Rafe admitted reluctantly. He still hadn't warmed to her brother, although Jack and Chas were great chums. "And I keep forgetting that you are something of an heiress yourself. Although I expect I've lost more money on the horses than old Augusta left you."

"That's unfortunate." He probably knew that her grandmother had left her $12,000, which was a small fortune. But the bulk of the money was to be doled out over ten years once she reached twenty-one.

"I trust you're not like Ellie or Zoë who tell me I should instead be feeding the poor or housing unwed mothers."

She laughed. "Not at all. Although that's also important. I suppose if it gives you pleasure to lose money, and you have more than you need, then someone else will be happier at the end of the day."

He chuckled. "You do have a way of cutting to the heart of things, Lizzie. You're also a good photographer." He had come back just before closing and picked up his photos. He'd given her one of himself, and a few of herself to pass along to her mother and Jack, which she had considered thoughtful of him. He had ordered a large one of her and a pocket-sized one that he said he'd take overseas as good luck. The other ones of himself would go to Fliss and his mother.

"I enjoy the work. It allows me to be creative. Anders also does landscapes, which are his real passion."

"I take it that you approached Vandeburgh for a job? I understand he's the premier society photographer in New York."

"I decided that I wanted a career. So I offered my services as dogs-body to Anders in exchange for learning the business."

"So you don't even get paid?"

"I make enough as Emily's manager to more than cover all my living expenses," she said dismissively. "But Anders is so pleased with my work that he's insisted on paying me."

She was clever as well as beautiful, Rafe thought. And faced with the rather daunting menu, she chose wisely from the ten different categories of food, beginning with consommé and caviar and ending with brandied pears and brie, with, of course, the legendary Delmonico's steak as the centerpiece.

"I'll have the same," Rafe told the waiter, "but with Parisienne potatoes instead of sweet potatoes, and mushrooms. Inform the sommelier that we'll have a bottle of his best Beaujolais."

They conversed easily during the meal, and Rafe thought that she had admirable poise and wit, and was bright and articulate. She could swear like a fishwife, which amused him, but her English was impeccable, and he had discovered that she was fluent in French, since it had been her mother's first language. He had already admired her determination and skill at learning and mastering tennis and riding. So he wondered why he still thought of her as a jumped-up opportunist. Except for her harsh upbringing, she was as much a Wyndham as Ria. His own father had started out poor, so it wasn't really her impoverished childhood that bothered him. In fact, he gave her a lot of credit for surviving and overcoming all that with such aplomb. She was a hell of a lot more interesting than most of the vapid girls he had met.

Perhaps he didn't quite trust her. She had accused him of moral paucity, but he wondered how sincere *she* was, and how much was just a role that she played all too well.

But he did enjoy her company, and was determined to savour her luscious body one of these days. He felt certain that although she claimed to be a respectable girl, she had the instincts of a whore. And that was a heady combination.

He put a blue box in front of her as they sipped the champagne that accompanied dessert. "This is so that you don't forget me while I'm off fighting the Boche."

Lizzie was surprised and delighted. No one had ever given her a present like this before. It was a gold locket, from Tiffany's. "You can put miniatures of us into it."

"Rafe, it's exquisite! Thank you."

He thought that the sheer joy on her face was real, and felt a bit ashamed of himself for his uncharitable thoughts earlier. For a moment he saw the girl who had never had much in her life and appreciated small things and kind gestures. He became even more enamoured with her.

"If I put your photo in here, everyone will think that you're my boyfriend."

"Good. Then perhaps they'll leave you alone. Will you write to me, Lizzie?"

"Of course!" She almost relented then, for she sensed his fear. She put her hand on his.

"I'll tell all the chaps that you're my girl."

"Am I?"

"You know I'm *over the moon for you*, Lizzie."

"But not enough to want to marry me."

"I'm not ready to settle down."

"You can't have it both ways."

"Can't I?"

"Not with me," she said reluctantly. "I think I should go."

When she stood up, he pulled her into his arms and kissed her passionately. "I want you, Lizzie."

"And I'd come to England to make a home for you, Rafe. We could be together when you were on leave." She kissed his cheek, and said, "I do love you. And I'll wait for you. If you want me to."

He kissed her hungrily. "Don't leave yet, Lizzie. I don't know when I'll see you again. Dance with me. Please."

After Delmonico's closed, they went to a private club, where Rafe paid the membership fees so that they could dance until dawn. Lizzie had told Emily not to worry about her if she didn't come home. If Rafe had proposed to her, she would have stayed with him.

By the time he dropped her off at her flat before breakfast, she was hopeful that he would one day. They'd had fun together, laughing, dancing, drinking champagne, being outrageous by kissing in public and singing as they staggered, slightly inebriated, down the streets.

Damn him for making them wait to consummate their relationship until he returned from the war! And damn him for not giving her the opportunity to be his rich widow if he didn't.

Chapter 8

When she first saw the soldier, Ria felt a shiver of fear. She swore he hadn't been there a moment earlier, but seemed to have risen from one of the graves in the field of crosses. She recalled Carly's story about Lucinda seeing a ghost the day her brother had been killed, and prayed that this wasn't some omen for her. Surely Chas was safely in England.

But the figure didn't fade away. He was very real – mud-encrusted, a tag attached to his tunic. When a company marched, soldiers sometimes fell ill and couldn't go on. The Medical Officer would scribble a diagnosis on a piece of paper and attach it to the invalid as proof that he wasn't a deserter. He'd be left sitting by the roadside, waiting for the first ambulance to come along and pick him up. Perhaps that was why this soldier seemed to have materialized from the cemetery.

Ria hadn't seen any troops marching in the area today, so she did think it rather odd to find him there, but of course she stopped. He hopped in beside her, bringing with him an overpowering stench of putrid trench mud and sweat-encrusted clothes.

"I'll be buggered! Never thought to see you again, Victoria fuckin' Wyndham. Oh, begging your pardon, M'am. Fuckin' Thornton it is now."

Ria's blood ran cold. It was Tom, their former footman who had been dismissed for molesting their maid Molly the summer of 1914. She recalled, with increasing trepidation, how Tom had manhandled her last Christmas when he had been at the Club. Chas and Jack had been there then to protect her. Now she was in the middle of nowhere in the thickening darkness with a vile, possibly deranged character who held a grudge against her family. She needed to keep her head.

"Tom. Are you ill? I'll drive you to a hospital."

"The hell you will! You'll take me to the nearest fishing village. I'm getting me a boat for Blighty. And don't try any tricks, bitch. This is loaded." He pointed a Webley at her.

"Deserting isn't a good idea, Tom. They'll find you and execute you."

"Let them try! Do you think that's any worse than being sent over the top time and time again? Into fuckin' hell? You can't imagine it. Seeing your mate's head get blown off, having his brains all over you. Or some other pal's guts squishing under your feet."

"If you're shell-shocked, you'll get help. You don't have to do this."

"Shut up and give me a cigarette. No, the whole pack!" He grabbed it from her and lit one. "Christ, that tastes good! Fancy you, driving an ambulance. Should have known you'd do something crazy like this. You've got guts, girl. Always did like your spunk. And your style. Nice coat, that. Expensive." He ran his hand along her fur-covered thigh.

Ria jerked her leg away and stiffened when the cold barrel of the gun stroked her cheek.

"That's an officer's service revolver. Where did you get it?"

"Off his body, of course. My Captain. After I shot him. He was going to court martial me for shooting a bunch of fuckin' Jerries!" He laughed. "Can you see how crazy that is? We're supposed to kill the bastards, but when they become our prisoners, they're treated like fuckin' royalty, and get to sit out the war while the rest of us are blown to pieces. I'm not the only one who's done it. Strafed by machine gun fire, blasted by their own artillery is what we say officially. But the Captain wasn't having none of it. We were in the middle of a big push so he told me I'd better show what I was made of or he'd have my guts for garters. I already had it in for him after he'd given me fuckin' Field Punishment Number One for telling him to bugger off when he accused me of being drunk. Betcha don't know what that is, eh? They tie you to a wagon wheel, bloody well crucify you, and leave you there for hours, day after day. Doesn't matter if it's pissin' rain or snow. You just about go berserk not being able to scratch when you feel the bloody fleas crawling all over and biting you. So this time I hung back and plugged him after he'd threatened to shoot me for cowardice right there in the shell hole. He was a fuckin' arse bandit anyway."

Ria was shocked. And scared, but felt that she had to keep him talking. "Where did you get your label?"

"Stole it from a guy I met. Pneumonia it says. Useless toe-rag was spewing his lungs out. Didn't have long anyway."

"How did you manage to get this far without being stopped?"

"What's with all the questions? Fancy me, do you?" He laughed. This time the gun stroked her breast. "I always fancied you. Loved the smell of your silk undies. Told you, didn't I, that I used to go into your drawers? Ha! Bit of a wag, aren't I? I'd like to get into your drawers. Properly this time." He squeezed her breast and Ria swerved the car so abruptly that he was thrown sideways and almost out, the door stopping at waist level.

"What the fuck are you doing?"

"Avoiding a shell hole."

"Pull over."

"We're almost at Wissant." Ria tried to keep the fear out of her voice.

"Pull over, I said!" This time the gun poked into her breast. "I don't think *Mr. Chas* would fancy a wife with no tits. Over there, behind the shrubs."

Ria's heart thudded so hard she was sure he must be able to hear it.

"Good girl. Now climb into the back. Handy having this ambulance. Means we don't have to fuck out in the snow. Go on! Move! I've been dreaming about this for years! Then you're going to give me that nice fur coat. That'll buy me a boat outa this sodding country."

Ria reached surreptitiously down beside her seat and closed her fingers gratefully over the tyre iron, unfastening the clasp that kept it in place. She wouldn't have much room to swing it from her seat. With the gun pointing at her, she had to be quick as well as accurate.

"I can't climb over the seat. I have to go around the back."

"Then do it, but don't try to run or I'll be fuckin' a corpse."

Ria hid the bar behind her as she stepped down from her seat. He slid out beside her. As he motioned her to the back of the ambulance with the pistol, she swung the iron at his head with all her force. She shuddered as she heard the crack of his skull and a grunt as if of expelled life. He sank to the ground. Ria tried to control her panic as she leaned over him and grabbed the revolver from his flaccid fingers. She was terrified that he was faking and would suddenly pull her down. She didn't check to see if he was alive, but jumped into the car and started it up, thankful that it didn't need to be cranked. Still petrified that he might suddenly lunge at her, she slammed the ambulance into gear and sped off, shaking, gasping for breath.

Scared that he might have hopped into the back before she actually got away, she kept looking behind her, expecting a hand to suddenly thrust through the canvas curtain and grab her. Despite regulations, she turned on her headlights, which gave her some comfort and allowed her to drive faster.

At the Cavalry camp she pulled in, leapt from the ambulance, and ran into the officers' mess. Seeing the men at dinner, she felt suddenly safe, and tried to pull herself together as she stammered, "I need help."

Lance was at her side in a moment. "Victoria, what's happened?"

She was still quivering and unable to catch her breath. He escorted her to a chair and she was handed a glass of water and a tot of brandy. A few others crowded around, like Adam Bentley, who had recently returned from the front lines.

"Have you had an accident?" Lance asked with concern as he stroked her arm.

She shook her head. "I think I've killed a man."

"How? What happened?"

Brokenly, she told him.

There was shocked silence.

"Christ!" Lance swore, appalled at how close she had come to being raped.

"He may not be dead," Adam said. "Can you tell us where it happened? We'll go and look for him."

"Just south of Wissant. I... can show you."

"Are you sure?" Lance asked. "You've had a terrible ordeal."

"I need to know."

Lance insisted on driving the ambulance. Ria sat between him and Adam, while four others were in the back. All were armed. There was a stopped lorry at the spot where Ria thought she had left Tom. Adam and the others went to see what was going on, leaving Ria and Lance in the car.

Taking advantage of this moment alone in the darkness, Lance put his arm about Ria's shoulders and hugged her reassuringly. His lips on her temple were warm. "You've been very brave," he said.

She laid her head gratefully against his shoulder. "He told me about a field punishment he'd had."

"Number One, I expect."

"Is it true that the offender is lashed to a wheel?"

"Yes or a stake. A couple of hours a day for whatever the length of the sentence, up to twenty-one days."

"It seems so barbaric doing that to our own men."

"We need to enforce discipline. If we don't have every soldier doing his job properly when ordered and without hesitation, then every other man's life is in jeopardy."

"War brutalizes us in so many ways."

Adam came back and said, "The lorry hit a chap. They say he staggered out of the bushes right in front of them. They tried to stop, but hit him. He's dead. Can you come and identify him, Victoria?"

"Yes."

Lance steadied her as they walked to the front of the truck. The driver had turned on the lights so that they could see the scene. Tom lay several yards ahead, one leg twisted awkwardly under him. Looking like a crumpled marionette. Something darker, blood surely, on his matted hair and dripping out of his ear.

"It's him," Ria managed to say and turned away, covering her mouth and forcing back the bile. She had seen plenty of dead men by now, but knowing that she had contributed to Tom's death made her body seize and stomach rebel.

Lance seemed to have read her mind as he said, "It wasn't your fault. You were defending yourself, and as far as I'm concerned, the bastard deserved court martial and the disgrace of an execution."

She nodded, but couldn't keep back the tears. Lance took her gently into his arms.

He held her reassuringly, wishing that she were free to be loved. Because he was certain now that he loved her. It was a heady, consuming emotion that he had never before experienced, too intense to ignore, too rapturous to relinquish. In the absence of a possibly wayward husband, he could perhaps win her over. Slowly.

"Let's get you back to camp. I'll drop the others off and Adam can send the staff car for me."

Ria sat numbly beside him, so cold that she was sure her blood had frozen in her veins. The wind hurled icy needles of sleet at them. She was shaking so much when they arrived that Lance carried her into the WATS mess. He settled her next to the woodstove.

As he was rubbing her hands, ComRad joined them, saying briskly, "What's going on, Major Chadwick?"

"A large brandy, please, Captain Radstone. Make that two. Mrs. Thornton has been assaulted."

"Good Lord!"

He related the facts briefly and succinctly.

"I used the tyre iron, like you said," Ria managed.

"Well done, Thornton! I think what you need now is some rest. And a day off tomorrow. You go and get some sleep."

Sybil and Carly, along with some of the others, had come in during Lance's recitation, and now took her in hand.

They had moved into the new building several weeks earlier, and each girl had her own cubicle off a central hallway. Ria missed the convivial atmosphere and warm fug of the tent. But her friends now squeezed into her tiny space. Henrietta clattered in with a mug of hot cocoa for her as she gave them a more detailed account of what had happened.

Carly said. "Good for you, Windy, taking the tyre iron to him!"

"I'm glad it wasn't me!" Baby said. "I left mine in the back the other day and haven't replaced it."

"That'll teach you to keep your bus ship-shape," Sybil chided.

"I may never look at our footmen the same way again," Antonia remarked.

"You mean you'll see them as men. With desires?" Sybil said.

"Jolly creepy," Antonia said. "They're always in the background, watching, waiting..."

"Imagining you naked and fantasizing about ravishing you," Sybil said. "It's no wonder that the ancient civilizations employed eunuchs."

Henrietta said, "Just remember, girls, a well-aimed blow to the nether regions will instantly reduce a man's desire and ability for mischief."

"And might very well turn him into a eunuch," Sybil said with a guffaw.

The following day was anything but restful, despite Ria's time off. The Military Police came early to take a statement from her. She couldn't even supply them with Tom's last name, so she told them to contact Grayson. Later that morning a telegram arrived from Chas.

Grayson phoned, concerned about why MPs wanted to know about Tom. In relation to incident with you. What's happened, Ria? Anxiously, Chas.

She replied: *He's dead. I'm OK. Ria.*

Not OK. Something's happened. Please tell me, my darling. Love, Chas.

Tom went AWOL. I thwarted his efforts to escape. He was hit by a lorry and died. Drama over. Ria.

Lance visited her in the afternoon, arriving with a bouquet of roses. He was still limping slightly, and on light duty at the Camp, so he had plenty of free time. As it was another bitterly cold day with ice crystallizing out of the damp sea air, walking along the beach was not a pleasant option, so Lance took her into Calais for tea.

"You look tired," he said to her. And haunted.

She was touched by the concern in his eyes. "I'm trying not to let it bother me. But Tom worked for my family for four years. He lived in our house. He was efficient, helpful, pleasant when I encountered him. Was he always this monster underneath? Is that what people who are dependent upon us for their livelihood think of us beneath the deferential façade? That hatred and contempt?" She shivered.

"There'll always be some, I expect. But this fellow was obviously a bad lot. And perhaps the war stripped the last thin veneer of decency from him. You mustn't feel responsible for any of this, Victoria," he said gently, stroking her hand. "He would have been executed for killing an officer. And who knows what other crimes he might have committed before being caught, had you not stopped him."

His next words cost him dearly. "Have you thought about going back to England?" She would undoubtedly be lost to him, but she'd be safe.

"Have *you*?" she challenged. "You men seem to think that we women lack moral fibre. We're as capable of dealing with hardship as you!"

He laughed with relief and admiration. "My apologies for being patronizing."

She smiled. "But thanks for bringing me out of my funk." She couldn't hold his gaze, since there was such tenderness there that she was flustered.

Blake was waiting for her when she arrived at the camp. She had already seen him since he'd returned from England, and been delighted to realize that he was deeply in love with Zoë.

"Ria, what's happened?" he asked with concern. "Chas sent me a rather cryptic telegram and wanted me to be sure you were alright. Carly told me there'd been an incident yesterday."

Lance took his leave, reluctantly, and Ria told Blake what had happened.

"Good God! He didn't hurt you?" He looked at her searchingly.

"I didn't give him a chance. And don't you tell me as well that I should go home!"

"You should. But I won't tell you," he said. "Chas can do that."

"He's forfeited the right."

"Don't punish him by being reckless."

"I'm not reckless! I'm just doing my job. And just because he's my husband, doesn't give him the right to tell me what to do!"

"I don't think anyone could ever tell you what to do, Ria," he said with amusement. "But let me just give you one more word of advice. Don't get back at Chas by doing what he did. It will only make things worse, and everyone will get hurt."

"What are you talking about?"

"Your friendship with Major Chadwick seems to be drifting into dangerous territory."

"Blake! I haven't done anything inappropriate! How could you think that?" she demanded indignantly.

"You've bewitched him. I can see how he looks at you. Be careful, that's all." He kissed her cheek and added, "Now don't be angry with me, because I'm leaving in a few days."

"They're sending you away before Christmas?"

"The chaps at the front lines want to come home, so yes."

"I don't want you coming for a ride in my ambulance, so be careful."

My Darling Ria,

I know that this incident with Tom is not as simple as you maintain. I recall last Christmas when he assaulted you, nasty blighter. I fear that things are more dire than you're letting on.

I know how dangerous it is out there and am in constant fear for your safety. Won't you please come back, my darling?

And be honest with me. It's what you expect of me.

Worried and unhappy without you. Chas

.   .   .

There was lots of activity at the WATS camp in the days before Christmas, but fortunately, little work. Of course there were always wounded, and troops were killed even on "quiet" days, but most of the cases arriving now were men ill with nephritis, bronchitis, trench foot, trench fever, rheumatism, and other ailments. And most of these were being sent right through to England, which also gave some relief to the base hospitals.

So preparations were being made for concerts and dances and Christmas dinners. The WATS would be performing in several of the hospitals and camps, so the girls spent whatever free hours they had rehearsing and making costumes.

Several enormous parcels arrived for Ria from Fliss. There were nearly a thousand teddy bears, and dozens of crates of children's clothing. Ria thought she could supply all the orphanages in the Pas-de-Calais region with these. As a special treat, she set aside a teddy for each of the WATS, who she felt deserved the comfort of a furry cuddle.

Boss gave her, Carly, and Sybil permission to take the lorry and distribute the items to communities between Boulogne and Dunkerque and as far south as St. Omer. Boots went along as well, of course.

Despite the exceedingly bitter cold, there was a party atmosphere about their outing. Carly claimed, "I feel like Santa Claus!"

In St. Omer they visited with the WATS unit stationed there, but Ria declined their offer of makeshift beds and paid for a hotel room for the three of them. "Bless you, Windy, for providing us with real beds!" Sybil said.

As if agreeing with her, Boots was on his best behaviour and curled up contentedly beside Carly.

Because Chas had often come here, Ria was curious about the old town with its sizable market square, ancient cathedrals and abbeys, a hodgepodge of medieval, Flemish, and classical architecture, and its important canals that led to the sea. It was a bustling place, which had a relaxed atmosphere despite being overwhelmed by the military. Noticing the many pretty young women on the arms of cheerful officers, especially those from the RFC pilots' pool stationed here, Ria couldn't help wondering if Chas had strutted about like that with Madeline. The anger and despair that had begun to recede threatened to choke her.

She was happy to get away, and relieved that she hadn't run into Jack. She would have been in no mood to forgive him.

Three days before Christmas, five huge hampers arrived for the WATS from Fortnum & Mason, courtesy of Chas. There were turkeys and caviar, smoked salmon and Stilton cheese, pheasant in aspic, brandied fruitcake, nuts, chocolates, champagne, and other delicacies. The girls were thrilled.

"There really is a food shortage back home?" Henrietta asked in awe.

"Must have cost a king's ransom," Antonia said.

"Just what does your husband's family do?" Betty asked Ria.

"More importantly, does he have brothers?" Sybil wanted to know.

The WATS first performance was at the Cavalry camp on Christmas Eve. They were invited to stay to dinner afterwards.

A dozen of the girls sang as a chorus, some sentimental tunes, like *Roses of Picardy* and *There's a Long, Long Trail*, and others humorous, like *Another little drink wouldn't do us any harm* from the immensely popular London musical, *The Bing Boys Are Here*, which most of the men had seen when they'd been home on leave.

The songs were interspersed with Antonia playing her violin, Henrietta doing an amusing recitation, and several skits.

Easily pleased, the audience laughed heartily. With the boredom of military routine and tedious stretches of waiting interspersed with intense, terrifying engagements with the enemy, any sort of lighthearted interval, especially with women present, seemed more acutely enjoyable.

Carly began her performance saying, "We know that you gentlemen have special relationships with your horses. As do we with our cars. Mine is named Nessie."

Sybil bounded onto the stage with a hat that looked like a steering wheel. She sat on the floor in front of Carly, who was seated in a chair. "Nessie" had a flashlight in each hand, representing the headlights. With their facial expressions and slick delivery, the girls soon had the audience in stitches.

"I eat better than you do," *Nessie* said smugly.

"You just eat the same boring, smelly thing all the time."

"So do you. Bully beef, bully beef, bully beef. Lots of bull in those army rations."

"Eggs and chips would be a nice change." That was the ubiquitous meal available in France for troops who dined out.

"Does it ever stop raining in this blasted country?" *Nessie* asked.

"Yes. When it starts snowing."

"It's all very well for you to be blasé about the cold. You at least have a room. Where's the garage I was promised?"

"My sponge was frozen this morning, so it's not much warmer inside."

"Well, the POWs built your barracks didn't they? So they're Jerry-built. Ouch, watch the shell-holes! You'll break my axle." Sybil turned on the flashlights.

"Nessie, turn off your headlamps."

"Shan't."

"Toot sweet!"

"Shan't."

"If the Boche don't get us then the Red Caps will," Carly said, referring to the Military Police.

"They have to catch me first! I'm a Stratton, and I've won motor races."

"Stop bragging. Thornton's Rolls is twice as powerful."

"Hoity toity. San fairy ann. See, I can speak French."

"You mean *ça ne fait rien*."

"Trez beans. Oh look, there are those lovely cavalry chaps." As if in an aside to Carly, *Nessie* said, "You know what I don't understand? Why those blokes are so chuffed about the one horse they have, while I have twenty!"

And so it went on to the delight of the audience.

Accompanying herself on the piano, Ria sang the first verse and chorus of *Sister Susie's Sewing Shirts For Soldiers*, and then substituted her own lyrics:

> *Cousin Katy's driving on the wrong side in Calais,*
> *She responds to calls for help with never a delay,*
> *Bombs and shells may fall but she'll keep driving through them all,*
> *She's a WATS and that's what WATS do – heed the battle call.*
> *But in her scratchy khaki she still likes a dance or two,*
> *For she's a lady fair and there is nothing she can't do.*
>
> *Cousin Katy cleans the carburetor,*
> *Vulcanize, decarbonize, oil, grease, and then much later*
> *She dances and she sings until the telephone rings, then*
> *Cousin Katy cranks and cranks and cranks the cranky car again.*
>
> *She drives and drives through darkness that is dangerous, undaunted,*
> *Taking troops and top-brass anywhere where they are wanted,*
> *Meeting ships and trains, soon she'll be flying aer-o-planes!*
> *She'll defeat the Hun with her grease gun and never she complains.*
> *But when she's not in breeches, and underneath her car,*
> *She likes champagne from crystal, and a taste of caviar.*
>
> *While...*
> *Sister Suzie's sewing shirts for soldiers...*

Ria finished with the tongue-twisting chorus.

There was tremendous laughter, cheering, and applause. Ria took her bows and went behind the improvised stage.

"You were terrific!" Lance said, giving her a quick but ardent hug.

"Yes, you were."

Ria was shocked to hear that familiar and beloved voice. She moved guiltily away from Lance as she turned around. "Chas! You didn't tell me you were coming!"

There was something in his rueful smile that touched her heart. She could imagine how it must appear to him to find her in another man's embrace, brief though it was. And she suddenly realized that she had slowly, inexorably been drifting into an intimacy with Lance that was in danger of becoming emotional infidelity – which is what Blake had warned her about.

Chas felt a sharp stab of jealousy and pain, seeing Ria in Lance's arms. He hid his fear of rejection as he said, "I have a few days off, and didn't want to spend Christmas without you, Ria." He was grateful to see her smile.

"Do forgive me! Lance, allow me introduce my husband, Chas Thornton. Chas, this is Lance Chadwick."

They shook hands, and eyed each other resentfully. "You're a lucky man, Major Thornton."

"Yes, I'm well aware of that, Major Chadwick." Turning to Ria he said, "Will you join me for dinner tonight?"

She could see his anxiety, but also that tender look that had always been there for her. "Yes."

She looked regretfully at Lance, suspecting by his disappointment that he was at least a little infatuated with her.

Ria found Boss and ComRad together, and stated, "I'd like permission to dine with my husband this evening. Alone."

Pat Bosley-Smythe said, "And if I refuse to give it?"

"I expect you'll have to send me home for insubordination."

Boss chuckled. "Let us know where to contact you. I expect to see you at breakfast. Merry Christmas, Thornton."

"Thank you, Boss." The CO's smirk convinced Ria that she had just been given tacit permission to spend the night with Chas. She wasn't sure that she was ready for that yet.

When she bid the others a hasty farewell, Sybil said, "If you're smart, you won't come home. And we won't rat on you, Windy. Actually, I should take my own advice."

Carly said with a laugh, "I fear for Captain Bentley's honour."

Lance waylaid her, saying, "I'll miss you tonight, Victoria. Or is it Ria?"

"Lance, I'm sorry if I ever gave you the impression that there was or could be more between us than friendship. I do value that, but..."

"As do I." He flashed her a smile, and then kissed her wrist. Rather sensually. "Merry Christmas." His own joy disappeared with her, but he was damned if he was going to let her go that easily.

Chas had once again rented a motorcycle, so Ria clung to him as he drove the short distance to the Auberge de la Plage. It was bitterly cold, and the snow was being whipped by the wind into a blinding blizzard. She pressed her face against his back, having refused his leather helmet. It felt so good to hold him, even as she shivered.

With its rich colours and soft lighting, the inn was welcoming. They warmed themselves by the crackling fire. Chas ordered a bottle of champagne and told the innkeeper that they would dine at eight.

A couple of officers had been sitting in the bar lounge, but no one else was in the drawing room at the moment, so it seemed as if she and Chas were having a quiet evening at home.

"It's wonderful to see you again, my darling," he said, clinking glasses with her. "I've missed you dreadfully."

His eyes held hers but she finally looked away from the intense need in his.

He said, "Hal Goodwin heard that I was training a new squadron, so he came to see me when he was on leave. And told me about your stunt. I'll have to tear a strip off Stratton when I see him."

"Please don't. I coerced Eddie into helping me. He feels bad enough as it is."

"Major Chadwick is considerably older and should have known that it was not only wrong, but dangerous. He should have been cashiered."

"It was my fault, Chas. I was determined to take Lance for a flight, and you know how I always get my way." She gave him a quick smile.

He stroked her cheek as he said, "Goodwin told me your plane was shot up. This isn't a lark, Ria. If I'd lost you..."

"Major Goodwin said that you taught me well."

"He told me that I had a remarkable wife. I think he's smitten with you as well."

She didn't pursue that, but knew that he was referring to Lance.

"I wish I'd seen the look on the German's face," Chas said.

She grinned. "It was priceless."

"I can imagine! And you're incorrigible. Which is one of the reasons that I love you so." He took a small wrapped box from his pocket and handed it to her. "Merry Christmas, my darling. I think you need this more than ever."

It was a dragonfly necklace to match the one she had given him for good luck, except that this one was made of white and yellow gold. "It's beautiful! Thank you, Chas. But I'm afraid I don't have anything for you."

"There is only one thing that I want from you, Ria. Your forgiveness."

She put her hand tentatively on his cheek as she searched his eyes for some assurance.

He pressed his own over hers and then kissed the palm of her hand. "Can we start again, my darling?"

She thought of all the letters he had sent her these last months, of his reminders of their shared youth. He was the friend who had always cared about her, the lover who had brought her breakfast at the Shimmering Sands and waltzed with her on the dock at Wyndwood, the husband who anticipated her wishes, knew her thoughts, was part of her soul.

And there was something in his beseeching, wounded look that finally shattered the wall.

"I don't want to live without you, Chas," she said brokenly.

"Thank God!"

Then she was crushed in his arms, weeping. His own tears wetted her curls. When he kissed her, she felt weak with desire. He took her to his room and their lovemaking was hungry, intense. Overwhelmed with emotion, they both wept again.

"Please don't ever hurt me like that again, Chas. I couldn't bear it. And I couldn't forgive you next time."

"I want only you, Ria," he said, kissing the tears from her cheeks. "I've had a taste of what it's like to be without you, and I never again want to feel that pain and emptiness. Will you stay with me tonight?"

"Yes. Oh yes."

"Then let's go down for dinner and resume this later." He chuckled. "I'm reminded of a letter that one of my ground crew sent to his wife. You know that I have to censor them? Well, he was forewarning her about his upcoming leave and said, 'Prepare yourself, Mary, because when I get home you won't be seeing anything but the ceiling for a week'."

They laughed. "I know how he feels," Chas said, kissing her and pushing her back down on the bed.

Ria wriggled out from under him. "Dinner first," she said with a giggle. "I'm famished."

"So am I," he said suggestively. "But I'll contain myself." He noticed that she wasn't as painfully thin as she had been when he had last seen her. She was muscular, like a sculpted athlete. He knew that the work she did was physically demanding. Her body was more womanly now that she had lost the girlish softness. "You're so beautiful," he said in wonder, stroking her bare breast.

"Stop, or we'll never make it to dinner!" she laughed.

The duck a l'orange was tender and tasty, but they didn't linger over their meal, and took the unfinished wine up to their room. They made love more slowly this time. The snow-breathed wind howled and tugged about the windows.

Chas propped his head in his hand as he gazed down at her. He ran a finger across her shoulder and down her arm. "Will you tell me now what really happened with Tom?"

When she had finished recounting the facts, Chas was upset and once again frustrated by his inability to protect her.

Seeing his distress, she said, "It was a bad scare, but I'm really all right, Chas. He didn't hurt me. In fact, I feel somewhat responsible for his death." She didn't tell him that Tom, reeking of the grave, came to her in dreams and that she often woke in the middle of the night, shaking and panicked.

"I wanted to spare you all the atrocities of this war, Ria."

"I realize that, Chas. But none of us should have to endure this. And if I didn't have some idea of what you're going through, how could we ever again speak the same language? We may never want to talk about it, but we'll have a common base, an understanding far deeper than if I attended garden parties and raised money. I think the war will divide people – those who've been here and those who haven't."

"I expect you're right. But I'd still rather you were safely in England."

"I wish you were, too. I know you're coming back soon."

"Will you come to England with me, Ria? My squadron's not being posted to France until March or April. We can rent a house near the base. Officers often do. We can adopt Sophie and bring her along. We can be a family, Ria."

She felt a strong commitment to her job as a WATS, but Chas and her marriage meant more to her than anything else in the world. "On one condition."

Chas was surprised and delighted. "Anything!"

"That you won't object to my coming back when you do."

He could see the determination on her face. "You *are* incorrigible! And taking after your grandmother."

"Good! You said that you liked her," Ria pointed out with a grin. "Feisty, you called her."

"Yes indeed."

"And don't start planning ways of keeping me in England."

"OK, I give in!" he laughed.

"I do have to finish our engagements this week, though. We're performing in all the local hospitals."

"I won't keep you from your illustrious stage career. I do have to be back in three days."

Adopting Sophie had been more and more on Ria's mind, since she visited the forlorn child often, and they had established a deep bond. She really couldn't leave her behind in France. With joyful determination she said, "Sophie and I will be there by New Year's Eve. I'll have M. Lemieux start the adoption proceedings, and ask Cousin Bea to find a reliable young woman to act as nanny, preferably one who can speak French."

This time Ria brushed a tear from Chas's cheek, and was moved by his emotion.

"God, how I love you, Ria!"

She pulled him down to her breast and ran her fingers through his hair.

•　　　•　　　•

"I can be a WATS representative in England for the next three or four months. I'll raise money, give talks, recruit volunteers, whatever is necessary," Ria said to Boss the following morning, after her request for an extended leave had been denied.

"And if I don't agree, you'll leave anyway, I expect," Pat Bosely-Smythe replied.

"I would hate to give up being a WATS, but I expect I can drive ambulances for the Red Cross in London. Or even persuade the Duchess of Axminster that she could use a skilled driver for her hospital. My car is just on loan here, after all."

Boss eyed her wryly. "We'd hate to lose you, Thornton. So, yes, I think you could be an admirable spokeswoman, and I know that you have connections. In the meantime, you can do night duty until you leave."

"Every night?" Ria squeaked. It was an onerous and exhausting job, which the women took in turns. Nor did it excuse them from doing their regular work during the day.

"The others will be more likely to forgive you for deserting them. So you can do your next two months' duty all in one week."

"Yes, Boss," Ria said, discouraged by the fact that the next few days would be hell, and she obviously couldn't go and stay with Chas at the hotel tonight. Boss had probably considered that as well.

When Ria had left the office, Fanny Radstone said, "That was a bit harsh wasn't it, Pat?"

"She's tough and can handle it. I don't want her thinking she can just dictate to us."

"A bit like you then, isn't she? I recall you not exactly playing by the rules, which is how you managed to take over the Corps," ComRad said with a chuckle.

"You mean it's how I got us where we are today. I'm not concerned that Thornton has any aspirations for my job. She'll actually be a perfect representative for us. Exceptional beauty, charm, courage. She should convince people that we're not a bunch of crackpot suffragettes or unfeminine women." Or lesbians, she could have added.

．　　　．　　　．

"She's been very melancholic," Mother Superior said. "I expect that the loss of her mother feels even sharper today. Last year she had only her at Christmas."

"We're going to adopt Sophie, and take her to England with us at the end of the week," Ria announced.

The nun nodded and then looked at Ria as she said, "It concerns me that you are not of our faith."

"We will ensure Sophie's spiritual well-being. Nor will she want in affection or in any other manner. In Sophie's name, I would like to continue my patronage and pay for a child who has no sponsor." It was a reminder to the nun that Ria was paying for

Sophie's keep and therefore had some right to her. Of course it all had to be formalized in law.

"You have been very generous to us, Madame," Mother Superior said. "The children were excited with their new clothes, and the teddy bears have brought much comfort. And Major, we are all grateful for the turkeys which you sent us."

"Our pleasure," Chas replied. "Now I think we need to speak with Sophie."

"But of course."

When Sophie appeared, Ria thought her heart would break. She looked so despondent, but managed to smile at them.

"We've brought you some presents," Ria said.

The first was a copy of *The Tale of Peter Rabbit*, by Beatrix Potter, which Ria had ordered from England. "You and I shall read this together, until you can read it yourself in English," Ria said. "When we have books, we are never alone for then we always have friends."

The other was a watercolour painting set. "The other thing that is important is to express ourselves. I'll teach you to paint as well."

Chas gave Sophie a silver locket and said, "You can put pictures of your parents in here."

She was delighted with the gifts, especially since it meant that she would be spending time with Ria.

"Your Maman and Papa will always be a special part of you, Sophie. We could never take their place. But would you like to come and live with us?"

She stared at them wide-eyed. "Forever?"

"Yes. First we will be in England, and when the war is over, we will go home to Canada."

"That is the best present of all," Sophie said quietly as a smile lit her face. Then she threw herself into Ria's arms.

•   •   •

The WATS did only one performance on Christmas Day, at the Casino. Then the girls had the afternoon off, to take turns bathing and pampering themselves in preparation for the Christmas feast. They were each allowed to bring one guest.

Since Antonia, Carly, and Sybil had, weeks ago, invited Eddie, Jonathan, and Adam, Ria had felt it appropriate and almost expected to invite Lance, the other member of their group of friends. She was greatly relieved when Adam Bentley brought

Lance's regrets that he couldn't attend after all. She blessed him silently for his diplomacy, and liked him all the better for it. Thanks to Chas's generosity in sending all those Fortnum & Mason hampers, the dinner was magnificent. There was much laughter and jollity, and exuberant dancing after the mess had been cleared. Boss allowed the party to go until midnight, and then they returned to routine.

Sybil was on duty with Ria for the night. It was still bitingly cold, with wind whipping off the hostile sea. Draining the radiators and carburetors didn't keep the engines from freezing, so all the cars had to be warmed up at hourly intervals on such cold nights. Since all but the two Rolls-Royces had to be hand cranked, it was arduous work. The cars were notoriously difficult to start in this weather. They coughed and groaned as if protesting the injustice of having to work under such harsh conditions, which meant that each ambulance took endless cranking to splutter to life.

"I'm never going to be able to play the piano this week if I have to keep doing this," Ria complained to Sybil after the second round. "I think my arms are going to drop off."

"I do think that Boss is cruel," Sybil said. "You won't want to come back after this."

They heard the noise of an engine and were apprehensive as a motorcycle pulled into the yard. Especially since Ria's encounter with Tom, the girls were all cognizant of the fact that their only protection was a pistol that ComRad kept in her desk. As a group of young and attractive women, they knew they were vulnerable. And during a war, normal social and moral restraints were too easily lost. But Boss had absolutely refused to have any men in the camp for so-called protection. Ria and some of the others kept cricket bats under their beds.

She was elated to see Chas alight from the bike. "What are you doing here? You should be tucked up in your cozy bed."

"Not without you," he said, giving her a passionate kiss, despite Sybil's presence.

"You did say he had a brother?" Sybil quipped.

"I thought I'd give your CO time to retire before I returned. So I'm here to help," Chas said. "For the night."

He managed to start twice as many cars as they did, so they had more time to rest and warm up in the mess between stints. Although the building had central heating, it was not well insulated, and the hot water pipes were never very warm. The girls froze in their cubicles. Sybil stretched out on one of the couches with her fur coat thrown over her. She had the knack of taking catnaps and was soon asleep, leaving Ria and Chas cuddled up on another couch.

"This is how it should always be," he said as she rested her head on his shoulder. "The two of us doing things together."

"Mmm. But soon there will be three of us," Ria said in some astonishment at the realization. "Are we doing the right thing by adopting Sophie?"

"You can't believe that she would be better off if we left her at the orphanage?"

"No, of course not. But I won't be in England long to look after her. I've always been disdainful of people who don't participate much in their children's upbringing. Even I had Grandmother."

"We'll give Sophie everything she needs to feel loved. And the war won't last forever. Then we'll be a proper family. In the meantime, we'll have a few months together. It'll give us all a chance to get to know each other. And I'm sure that Cousin Bea will look after her well when we're back in France."

"Of course." Ria stroked his cheek. "We're awfully young to have a six year old."

He laughed. "We certainly are! But never mind. We'll pretend we're kids too, and just have fun."

"I do love you," she murmured.

"Good," he replied, nuzzling her neck. "Because I've never been happier than just being here with you in this damnably miserable place."

She smiled contentedly.

At the end of the shift, they all managed to snatch a few hours of sleep, but Chas wasn't about to miss spending any time with Ria, so he arrived at the Harvard General Hospital shortly after the WATS. Following the ladies' performance, he and Ria managed to talk with Troy and his brother, Kurt, who had a few days leave from the Lafayette Escadrille. He plied Chas with questions about his flying and fighting tactics. Still a student, Kurt had not yet encountered the Hun.

With a sly grin, Troy said, "You should ask Victoria, too. She managed to evade an enemy scout while flying a two-seater."

"How did you know?" Ria asked in surprise.

"You didn't think you could keep a story like that quiet around here, did you? You weren't mentioned by name, but when I heard it was one of the WATS, I just knew it had to be you."

Kurt was wide-eyed with admiration when Ria reluctantly told her story.

"Who would have thought that the Thorncliff tennis champs of 1914 would become such heroes?" Kurt said astutely.

"Don't forget that we beat you at croquet and won the canoe race at the Regatta as well," Ria said with a laugh.

"Oh, perfect training for war," Kurt observed drily.

"In any case, we're not supposed to tell anyone about the incident," Ria said.

"You've got to be kidding!" Kurt said. "That's just too swell a story! You'll become a legend, Victoria."

"Oh dear," she said.

Chas smiled lovingly at her as he said, "Ria's renowned for her antics anyway."

"When we're all back at the lake, we can do aerial stunts for the neighbours," Kurt suggested.

"And give rides to the kids," Ria added.

"And fly people up from Toronto and Pittsburgh," Kurt said.

"And give lessons."

"And soon everyone will be pulling up to their docks in hydro-aeroplanes instead of boats!"

Chas and Troy shook their heads in amusement, Troy saying, "I can just imagine how peaceful the lake will be with you soaring above us!"

"Have to move with the times, big brother. Hey, Victoria, we'll drop water bombs on Troy when he's out sailing," Kurt said with a mischievous grin.

She laughed and replied, "You're on your own there, Kurt. And you two really must call me Ria."

When the WATS finished their next performance at the #14 General, they were to stay for dinner. But Sybil and Carly urged Ria to sneak off with Chas. "We'll cover for you until you're back on duty at 11:00," Sybil said. Since Boss and ComRad had come in the car and the others in the lorry, it was possible that they wouldn't notice Ria's absence.

Ria needed no persuasion. Chas paid the proprietor well to serve them dinner in his room. While they were waiting for the food to arrive, they climbed into a steaming bath together. Ria was almost too tired to eat, but Chas made sure she finished her meal. She fell asleep in his arms and he was reluctant to wake her after only a few hours.

"Come along, my darling. I can offer my assistance again tonight, but tomorrow I have to return to England." He hated the thought of leaving her, worried that now that they had found each other again, something would happen to keep them apart. Crossing the channel was never safe, and he didn't trust the quirks of fate that spared you on the battlefield only to fell you in a motor accident back home.

When they arrived at the WATS camp just in time for her night duty, Ria didn't bother to go inside to put on extra layers of clothes just yet in case Boss or ComRad saw her going in.

Antonia, who was on duty with Ria tonight, said, "Pratt noticed your absence and ratted on you." Mabel Pratt was one the Pod, who blamed Ria for Dora Pettigrew's being sacked. "Foxy was magnificent in her fury to protect your snatched moments of rest when Boss wanted to check your cubicle." Antonia chuckled when she added, "And I don't think Pratt's ever been called such colourful names! But I expect Boss will be out here at any moment to check up on you."

"I'm tempted to chuck it all in, Tuppy, and just go home with Chas. But I promised I would stay until the end of the week."

"I'd better hide out in the back of your ambulance until she's gone," Chas said to Ria. "I'm not leaving before I have to."

Pat Bosley-Smythe did indeed appear just as Ria and Tuppy began cranking cars. She said to Ria, "Managed to get some sleep, did you, Thornton?"

"Wonderful sleep, thank you, Boss."

"Major Thornton, I do hope you're leaving tomorrow so that you stop disrupting my Corps," she said loudly enough for Chas to hear. "Your wife won't be given any more concessions just because you are here. I won't allow the discipline of my Corps to be jeopardized by suspicions that a girl can go AWOL and get away with it."

Chas felt rather shamefaced as he stepped out of the ambulance. Boss said, "Surely you didn't think that I was unaware of what's been going on? And it's chivalrous of you to help out, Major, but I find that men tend to disturb the status quo. You *are* leaving in the morning?"

"Indeed, Major."

"Then the next time I see you will be in England, I expect. Goodnight."

"I feel like a kid who's just had a wigging from the headmaster," Chas admitted when Boss was out of earshot.

The girls giggled. "She is rather formidable," Ria conceded.

Unlike Sybil, Antonia didn't nap between bouts of work, so the three of them conversed during their breaks, Ria snuggled up against Chas. They discovered that Chas had been at Oxford with Antonia's cousin, who was now in Gallipoli. They chuckled over Tuppy's apprehension at going home on leave in February, since she had bobbed her hair as a Christmas present to herself and didn't know what her mother would say. Ria thought that she looked stunning with her dark hair cut up high in the back and slanting dramatically down below her attractive cheekbones.

Despite the hard work in the numbing cold, neither Ria nor Chas wanted the night to end. He left her reluctantly in the grey dawn.

"I'll talk to the lawyer about the adoption before I leave. And visit Sophie," he said.

Ria clung to him. "I don't want to be away from you for even a few days. I'm suddenly scared."

He hugged her tightly, and despite his own misgivings said, "It's not like you to be afraid of anything, my darling. I'll meet you at Bovington on Saturday."

Ria managed only a couple of hours of sleep, since today they bracketed lunch with performances at hospitals. When they arrived back at the camp, she was delighted to see Justin waiting for her, and embraced him warmly. "It's so good to see you!" she said.

"Tut, tut. Hubby has just left, and already you're in the arms of another handsome man," Sybil teased.

Ria introduced him to the others.

"They all come from this Muskoka of yours, your bevy of Adonises," Sybil observed.

"And you haven't even met them all yet," Ria quipped.

"Be warned that I do intend to. In the meantime I'd best push off and let you get caught up."

"Chas was here?" Justin said. "And judging by your jaunty demeanor, am I to understand that you've reconciled?"

Ria wrapped her arm about his eagerly as she steered him to a secluded corner of the mess. "Yes," she said with quiet joy. "We were both miserable without each other. And I think we've matured in our love."

"I am happy for you."

She knew that he meant it, and smiled gratefully. "I'm so glad to see you. How long can you stay?"

"I have to catch a train back tonight."

"So soon! You look tired."

"France will forever remind me of perpetual fatigue," he said.

"You'll have to go to Cousin Bea's Riviera villa for a proper rest and an antidote to all this."

"I expect a kinder climate would do us all good. I've heard that this is already proving to be the coldest winter in decades."

"Then I feel both thankful and guilty for deserting my comrades and returning to England."

Justin was relieved when she told him her plans. He had been concerned by Blake's reports about her during the past months.

Sybil approached them saying, "Boss is allowing Carly, Tuppy, and me to take you out for dinner in Calais, since you're leaving in a few days. So we'd like Captain Carrington to join us." She winked conspiratorially at Ria.

"Do you have time?" Ria asked him.

"Certainly."

Once they were in the Rolls, with Carly driving, Sybil said, "This was just a ruse to give you and Captain Carrington a chance to be alone so you can talk."

"Much appreciated. But once Justin and I have caught up on our news, we'd be delighted to join the three of you."

"Absolutely," Justin agreed.

So he and Ria sat in the Hotel Maritime lounge and talked for an hour over drinks before they went in to dinner.

Although they tried to steer the conversation away from the war, the girls did mention humorous incidents like Ria's aerial battle and Hazy's dunking at the pier, which nonetheless had serious undertones that left Justin uneasy.

But by the time they finished dinner, they were all lighthearted, having promised each other that after the war they would cheer Carly on as she raced at Brooklands, fly over the English countryside with Ria, attend Ascot to watch one of Sybil's father's horses compete, sail in Muskoka with Justin, and lounge about Antonia's castle home persuading Lady Netherton that Tuppy wasn't cut out to be the Queen of England.

When they dropped Justin at the railway station, Ria said to him, "I expect you won't see your bed tonight. Thank you for coming all this way to visit me. I don't know what I've done to deserve good friends like you, especially after the way I behaved..."

"You were understandably upset, and I was more concerned about how I could help you than with your reaction to me. But I'm glad that's all behind us." He hugged her gratefully. "We're all lucky to have each other. And I like your new friends as well. Regards to Chas. I'm looking forward to meeting Sophie when I'm back on leave. I'm really proud of you, Ria. You always manage to bounce back from adversity with compassion and humour." He kissed her cheek.

She couldn't fail to see the love in his eyes, and bit back tears as she said, "Please be careful, Justin. I seem forever to be saying that, because I'm terrified for you and the others."

"The same applies to you. I don't think you realize quite how dangerous your job really is. But we've invited guests to Muskoka, so we'd better be sure to be there," he added with a grin.

On their return journey, Sybil said to Ria, "Unless I'm very much mistaken, I'd say that Captain Carrington's love for you is more than neighbourly."

"My grandmother wanted us to marry. And I do love Justin, but more like a brother. If I hadn't fallen in love with Chas, I suppose things might have been different."

"So he's fair game then," Sybil declared.

"Absolutely."

"How many chaps do you actually need, Foxy?" Antonia asked. "Especially now that Captain Bentley is back."

"When I'm shopping for a hat, I don't try on just one," Sybil stated.

"I don't think we should examine that statement too closely," Carly said amid the laughter.

When Ria was due to begin her onerous night shift yet again, she was astonished to see most of the other WATS prepare to leave the mess with her.

"What's the meaning of this?" Boss asked in annoyance.

Antonia, flanked by Sybil and Carly, replied with her formidable aristocratic aplomb, "We WATS work as a team and as such, are going to help Thornton. None of us should be required to bear an unequal burden of the work."

Ria was deeply touched.

"You don't think that Thornton's swinging the lead by spending a cozy winter in England?" Boss asked.

"We're delighted that she plans to return here at all," Antonia assured her. "And wouldn't blame her if she changed her mind after this gruelling week."

There was a moment of tense silence as Antonia haughtily stared down Boss. ComRad, looking up from a letter she was writing, tried to hide her amusement.

Then Boss chortled and said, "You're lucky to have such staunch friends, Thornton. And girls, I'm pleased to see that you *are* a team, and willing to stand up for one another. Well done. We'll return to our regular rota then." When she rejoined ComRad she whispered, "Don't you dare say 'I told you so'."

"You're a true leader, Pat. The girls will respect you even more now for having the grace to admit you were wrong."

"It's called democracy, isn't it?" Boss said wryly.

Meanwhile, Ria was ushered back to her room by her three closest friends. "Thank you," she said simply when they sat down on her bed and Sybil poured them each a small cognac.

"I detest unfairness," Antonia said.

"So you mustered the troops," Ria said.

"It wasn't hard," Carly replied. "Well, except for a few."

Ria had noticed Mabel Pratt's sneer when the others had stood with her friends.

"What do you expect from The Pod? Jealous cows," Sybil commented. "And if they were *smart,* they'd be clinging to Windy's coattails. After all, she seems to have a slew of these lovely men friends who are unattached."

They all laughed.

"I'm going to miss you," Ria said. "And I do feel guilty leaving you all behind."

"Never mind that," Antonia assured her. "You'll be back soon enough. And *après la guerre* we'll descend upon your summer home and stay until you'll be glad to be rid of us."

"Then you'll never leave!" Ria replied with a grateful smile.

.　　　.　　　.

Lance waited until Chas had left before visiting Ria again. He hadn't wanted to create an awkward situation where Ria would feel she had to make a choice. He, of course, would have lost.

But those few days had been hell. He couldn't stop thinking about her, and imagining her in Chas's bed. He'd heard through Bentley that Ria was going to England for several months, and hoped that he himself would be sent back to the Front where the rigours of survival would help to distract him.

He had considered transferring to the RFC so that he could be in England, training, while she was there. But he couldn't see himself virtually starting over, in the company of rowdy eighteen-year-olds, and thought it unlikely he could match Thornton's achievements in any case. So he would stick with what he did best, and angle for promotion to Lieutenant Colonel.

He felt absurdly happy when she smiled warmly at him. "I haven't had a chance to give you your Christmas present," he said, handing her a flat parcel.

She took it reluctantly. "I can't accept this, Lance."

"Why not? We're friends, aren't we?"

"Our friendship is perhaps a dangerous thing," Ria said with regret.

"Surely not!" he replied with a grin, trying to lighten the mood.

"I enjoy your company, Lance. But I love my husband. I'm afraid that our friendship could end up hurting you both."

"Look, Victoria, I respect your marriage, and promise to stop flirting with you, if that's what you want. Would you be saying this to Captain Carlyle?"

"No, but..."

"So is it your own feelings that you're afraid of?"

"Of course not!"

"Good!" he said with a quick smile, before she had a chance to become truly indignant at the implication. "Then there's no problem, is there?"

"As long as you don't expect too much of me."

"I expect us to carry on as we have been, with perhaps the exception that I may call you Ria, like your other friends do."

She had intended to keep her two worlds separate, but that obviously wasn't happening. "Yes, of course," she replied with relief, pushing away any thoughts that she was being disloyal to Chas. Lance was right to say that neither she nor Chas would be concerned about her spending time with Blake, or Justin, or any of their other friends.

"Open it then," Lance urged. "Since you're going away, I hope it will remind you – in a pleasant way – of your time here."

"Not a German helmet or a shell casing then," Ria replied with a chuckle. The girls had been given many such souvenirs by officers.

It was a wonderfully evocative watercolour of the beach and cliff at Cap Gris-Nez, a shaft of sunlight breaking through the brooding clouds to kiss the sand. Lance had commissioned Zachary, the artist-orderly at the Duchess of Axminster's Hospital, to paint it. He hoped it would remind Ria specifically of the walks they had taken together along the seashore during his convalescence.

"It's beautiful, Lance! Zachary captured it just right! Thank you."

Her disarming smile made him want to gather her into his arms. It took all his willpower not to touch her.

. . .

Since they needed to be on the ship very early on Sunday morning, Ria had decided that she and Sophie should stay overnight at the Hotel Maritime, near the wharf. The girls had given her a delightful send-off tea after their last performance, Sybil spiking the tea with plenty of rum. A fierce gale had already blown up when Carly had driven Ria and Sophie to the hotel in time for dinner. It howled and wailed all night, and Ria prayed that it would subside before they were due to leave.

She was anxious about crossing in a high sea, as she still hadn't shaken the fear that something would keep her and Chas apart. But she took comfort in Sophie's presence. The child clung to her all evening, and cuddled up to her in bed.

Ria slept very little and rose in the darkness of the early morning to see the wind now driving sharp snow before it. If she hadn't promised Chas that she would be at Bovington for New Year's Eve, she would have been tempted to stay put until the blizzard was over. But surely the ship's captain would know when it was too rough and dangerous to cross.

She ordered her trunks to be taken to the ship while she and Sophie ate a light breakfast, but the manager interrupted, saying, "Pardon, Madame, I regret to inform you that your ship will not be sailing today. And perhaps not tomorrow. The storm has set mines adrift in the Channel." He threw up his hands in a very Gallic gesture. "And the storm caused a grain ship to smash into the Boulogne pier and sink, blocking that harbour. It will take many days or even weeks to clean up the mess, so there are no ships to England."

Ria's heart sank, despite the fact that the decision she had dreaded to make had been taken out of her hands.

"You wish to retain your room, Madame?"

Deciding she had needed to indulge herself and Sophie, Ria had taken the best room.

"Yes, indeed. Thank you, Monsieur LeBlanc. I would also like to send a telegram."

"But of course." He bowed to her.

No ships sailing possibly for days due to loose mines. Impatient to see you, my love.

Chas's reply read: *Terribly frustrated, but thankful you are safe. Surely we'll be together in a few days, my darling. All here send their love.*

Chas was right, of course. They were safe, and lucky that the problem had been discovered before a ship – theirs perhaps – had hit a wayward mine. Somehow it seemed even worse to be blown up by one's own bombs.

So Ria tried to be cheerful, and not dwell on the disappointment of not being in Chas's arms tonight. She and Sophie had a restful day, playing games, drawing, reading.

As there was a New Year's Ball in the hotel that evening, Ria decided that she and Sophie would have an early dinner. Coming out of the dining room, she almost collided with Lance.

"Ria!" he said with delight and some embarrassment. "What are you doing here? I thought you'd be in England by now. Bonjour, Sophie."

"Bonjour, Monsieur Major."

"Hello, Lance," Ria said, glancing at his alluring companion. The young woman looked her over with the kind of royal disdain that only chic Frenchwomen could express at a khaki-clad female. He made no move to introduce them. "We're stranded." She explained about the mines and Boulogne harbour.

"You should have told me."

"Isn't there a dance in the mess tonight?"

"Yes, but it didn't appeal to me." But he was suddenly happy. "Look, I can get rid of her," he said quietly. "And we can spend the evening together."

It was tempting, but Ria knew that it would only re-ignite his hopes. She couldn't resist a smirk as she said, "I can't offer you what she can, Lance."

He seemed a bit shamefaced, but held her eyes as he said, "You can offer me much more. A truly delightful evening."

She smiled, rather sadly he thought, as she said, "With the luxury of sleeping in a real bed, I was planning to have an early night."

"See the New Year in with me," he pleaded. "Think of it as rescuing me from a night of debauchery."

Ria laughed. He could sense her hesitation. "Just friends, remember?"

"If you'd really rather spend the evening with a child and a decidedly unglamorous woman in uniform..."

He smiled. "Absolutely! Wait here."

He took his impatient companion by the elbow and steered her to the exit. Ria couldn't overhear them, but could tell from her petulant look that she was extremely annoyed. Lance discreetly pressed something into her hand. Money, of course. After glancing at it, she gave him a seductive smile and walked out without further protest.

"So, what were you planning to do?" he asked as he rejoined Ria and Sophie.

"Sophie and I were just going to sit in front of the fire here in the lobby and read *Peter Rabbit*. She's learning English – and quite quickly."

"She's a bright spark. Has she been introduced to Ratty and Mole and Toad and Badger? My children couldn't get enough of them."

"I adore *The Wind in The Willows* as well," Ria confided with a grin. "I discovered that the author lived quite near to my cousin Beatrice when he was young, so I can easily imagine her stretch of the Thames as Ratty's riverbank. I even wonder if Bovington Abbey was the model for Toad Hall."

"Were you emulating Toad when you decided to drive cars?"

"'The poetry of motion! The *real* way to travel! The *only* way to travel! Here today – in next week tomorrow!'" Ria quoted Mr. Toad.

"What dust-clouds spring up behind you as you speed on your reckless way?" Lance paraphrased Toad.

Ria laughed. "You *do* know it well." To Sophie she said, "Major Chadwick is going to tell you a tale about a naughty toad who drives his car much too fast. And he lives in Cousin Bea's house where you and I will soon be staying."

Sophie was astonished, and then enthralled as Lance related part of Toad's adventures on the open road.

Ria was impressed with his story-telling expertise, even in French. She said, "Your children must miss you."

"They're beyond my reading to them now. I did enjoy those times, although they were all too rare."

"You're never too old to have someone read to you." Ria didn't tell him that she and Chas had read that book together in bed at

Bovington Abbey. But that reminded her with a sharp pang that they had agreed to read it to their children there as well.

Lance wondered what had brought a shadow across her face, but they were interrupted as Troy Roland suddenly appeared beside them. "Hello, Ria. Chas cabled me you were here. I'm off duty and came to see if you and Sophie would care to celebrate the New Year with me."

"Of course! How delightful. I don't believe you've met Lance Chadwick."

Lance's joy diminished somewhat. So hubby was keeping control of Ria's life. Of course it was thoughtful of him to ensure she wasn't alone, but wasn't Thornton concerned that this ruggedly handsome American might woo his wife?

"A great pleasure to meet you, Major," Troy said. "You were the co-conspirator in the legendary flying escapade, I believe."

"Indeed!" Lance said with surprise. "So we're already legendary."

"I'm afraid so," Ria replied with a grin.

Lance found it rather comforting to have his name associated with hers in such a daring adventure.

"Imagine if Toad had seen aeroplanes," Ria said to him.

"Good Lord, yes! He'd be skimming over the rooftops, terrorizing the populace. You'll have to write a sequel, Ria – *The Wind in the Wires*, or some such thing," Lance suggested, much to her amusement.

"I may well do that. It will be a story for Sophie." They explained to a bewildered Troy, who hadn't read the book. "You'll just have to when you come to Bovington," Ria insisted. "I'll make sure that there are copies in the spare bedrooms."

"I'll look forward to that."

Ria was astonished to see Jack walk into the lobby. He seemed both happy and apprehensive as he joined them. They hadn't communicated since she had angrily dismissed him at Bea's London townhouse back in September.

"Hello, Ria." He squatted down in front of Sophie and put out his hand, saying in French, "You must be Sophie. I'm your cousin, Jack, and I have three sisters who are going to be excited to have a new member in the family."

Sophie shook his hand gravely and replied, "I like to have cousins, Monsieur Capitaine Jacque."

"So do I, Sophie."

He glanced up at Ria, and she could read the question in his eyes. Was he forgiven?

Jack patted his jacket pocket in mock surprise and said, "I'd completely forgotten. I found this little stray today." He pulled out a small plush kitten as if it were alive, stroking it and making it jump in his palm. He had often entertained his young sisters with that trick, using the dolls his mother had made from fabric scraps.

Sophie giggled. The kitten settled down when she petted it.

"She likes you. Will you look after her, Sophie?" Jack asked as he handed it to her.

"Oh, may I?"

"She needs a good home and I can't look after her properly," Jack replied with a wink.

Sophie hugged the stuffed cat and said, "I will call her Fleur. She is beautiful, n'est ce pas?"

"Mais oui. Très jolie."

Jack had figured that one way to reach Ria was through the child, whom Chas had told him about, and was pleased to see that he had been right. She embraced him warmly when he stood up. "How wonderful to see you, Jack!"

As he hugged her, he whispered, "I'm so glad that you and Chas have reconciled." Aloud he said, "Chas wired me that you were here. I managed to scoff the staff car, as the others took the train into Paris." Jack had been planning to go along with them for a few days of carousing, but knew that this was more important. "It's taken me all day to drive here from St. Omer. The roads are appalling! Narrow, rutted, icy. More than once I was convinced I was going to slide into a canal. Then I was held up by those who did. Sometimes I couldn't see beyond the wall of snow. So I have a new appreciation for what you do, Ria." He shook hands with Troy, whom he had met at all the major events the summer of 1914, and said, "Good to see you, Troy. Ellie told me you were here."

In that instant Troy realized who his competition was for Ellie's affections. He was only momentarily daunted.

Ria introduced Lance, who said, "Another of our illustrious Aces." And another guard dog sent by Chas.

Since none of the men had eaten, Ria insisted that she and Sophie would be happy to sip wine and cocoa while they dined. But first she sent a telegram to Chas. *How thoughtful of you to marshal the troops. But wish so much you were here, my love.*

His cable must have crossed hers, since it arrived shortly afterwards. *Hope you're not alone tonight, my darling. The narrow channel that divides us has become an ocean. How I chafe at this delay. Longing to start our new life together.*

Throughout the evening Lance noticed that Ria was pensive, despite her convivial manner, and he realized that she was far away in Britain with Chas. For a fleeting moment he thought that he should have stayed with his companion. The brief sexual pleasure that would have ensued might have assuaged this overwhelming desire he had. But he would only have longed for Ria.

When the New Year's Eve dance commenced at ten o'clock, he was at least able to hold her in his arms, even if he had to share her with Troy and Jack. And when they swayed to *The Roses of Picardy*, Lance was reminded of the first time they had met and danced to that song in the WATS mess. It was *their* tune, he thought.

> *Roses are shining in Picardy,*
> *In the hush of the silvery dew,*
> *Roses are flow'ring in Picardy,*
> *But there's never a rose like you!*
> *And the roses will die with the summertime,*
> *And our roads may be far apart,*
> *But there's one rose that dies not in Picardy!*
> *'Tis the rose that I keep in my heart!*

But Ria was oblivious to his sentimental reminiscences and tender embrace. Laughingly, she said, as she took a break from the dancing, "I'm sure I'm the envy of every woman here, being with three such handsome and attentive gentlemen. Please don't feel obliged to stay with me when so many girls are eager to dance. Perhaps we are celebrating the beginning of the year that will see an end to the war, especially if the Americans join us, don't you think, Troy?"

"Wilson was just re-elected President, narrowly, and partly on the strength of his having kept us out of the war. But from what I hear, it appears that if he can't negotiate a peace between the warring factions, and if Germany reneges on the 'Sussex Pledge' and reinstates unrestricted submarine warfare, which seems ever more likely, then I'd say we'll definitely go to war soon." Troy was referring to the torpedoing of the French passenger ship, the *Sussex*, in the Channel last March, which had caused Wilson to issue an ultimatum to Germany. Trying not to alienate the Americans, Germany had promised to stop the indiscriminate sinking of ships, which had already resulted in the loss of many civilian lives, Americans among them, most notably on the *Lusitania*.

With thoughts of the war once more intruding upon the festivities, Ria wondered if the night would be fractured by the clanging of the claxons and the cacophony of shells. Surely the Germans wanted a few days of rest from hostilities as well. But this was the third winter of the war, not that first optimistic Christmas of the truce, so why not strike when your enemy least expected it? That thought gave an edge to the evening.

They were interrupted by shrieks of delight as an elegantly clad woman rushed to their table and smothered Sophie with kisses. "Ah, mon p'tit chou! Mon cher p'tit pigeon! But what are you doing up so late and in such illustrious company? Bonjour, Madame," she said to Ria.

"Madame Fortin," Ria said, recognizing the proprietress of the chocolate shop. She was amused to see how prosperous Madame Fortin looked in her finery, obviously not suffering from Ria's discounted chocolates.

"My best customer! Is it true what I hear, that you and your distinguished husband have adopted Sophie and are taking her to England?"

"Yes, indeed. And to Canada when the war is over. Allow me to introduce my friends."

"Enchanté!" Although in her late thirties, Madame Fortin fluttered her eyelashes at the men. "Ah, Sophie, you are fortunate to have found such a fine new family. But I shall miss you, mon p'tit chou. I expect you will be strong and beautiful like your Maman, and I hope you will visit me sometimes, d'accord?"

Sophie looked at Ria, her eyes brimming at the mention of her mother, and Ria squeezed her hand saying, "Of course we shall, Madame Fortin. How can we resist your delectable chocolates? They rival the famous Belgian ones," she added mischievously.

Drawing herself up, Madame Fortin stated dismissively, "Far superior, I should say! So you must come to my shop before you leave, to show your friends in England what delicacies, what delights they are missing."

"Thank you, Madame. We shall certainly take advantage of your generous offer." She was amused by the woman's slight shock at this, for she had probably not intended to give the chocolates as a gift. Relenting, Ria added, "And I shall put in a standing order for chocolates to be sent to the orphans while I'm away, if you can manage that, Madame. At our special price, of course."

"But of course!" her equanimity restored, she said warmly, "You are a generous young woman, Madame, as well as a courageous one. I daresay you are also très chic when not in uniform." She grinned. "And now I will bid you all a Happy New Year." She kissed Sophie again and glided off to rejoin her party.

Troy noticed a group of nurses from his hospital and excused himself to go and dance with them. Some other officers who had been entertained by the WATS, driven by Ria, or met her at the various encampments came to pay their respects and dance with her. So Lance regaled Sophie with more of Toad's misadventures, and jealously guarded the few moments that he had alone with Ria, leaving Jack to teach a flagging Sophie to dance.

As more people stopped by, including the lawyer, Monsieur Lemieux, Billy Farthington, and a party of staff from the Duchess of Axminster's Hospital, Jack said, "You seem to have quite a circle of acquaintances here, Ria. But I shouldn't be surprised."

"You haven't even met most of my new friends yet," Ria replied.

At midnight, the mood was both solemn and hopeful. People kissed each other, in the French fashion, on both cheeks – acquaintances and strangers alike. Lance gave Ria a more lingering kiss, which he fought hard not to turn into a passionate one.

Sophie had managed to stay awake, but now drooped onto the table. "I really should take her to bed," Ria said.

Before Lance could offer, Jack said, "I'll carry her up."

They bid the others goodnight. Not knowing when he would see Ria again, Lance asked, "May I write to you?"

She hesitated for a moment and then said, "I'll look forward to hearing all the news about my cavalry friends."

He didn't dare attempt to kiss her again, and said, "You will no doubt have interesting stories from England, which I shall look forward to. Most particularly, the further adventures of Toad." His lighthearted grin reassured her.

Jack had managed to procure a room, but only by generously greasing the manager's palm, which he had resented, but felt powerful being able to do. And with the disdain that it deserved, which earned him even more respect.

When they were in the elevator, Jack said, "You are a heartbreaker, Ria. I'd say that Major Chadwick is in love with you."

She avoided his eyes as she replied firmly, "He's married, Jack. And he knows that we can only be friends."

"I'm glad to hear that. I wouldn't want to have to challenge the Major to a duel over your honour, as any good cousin should be willing to do."

"Especially as Lance is quite a swordsman," Ria riposted. "As is Chas, so I have no doubt that my honour is well protected." With a grin she added, "But thank you for being willing to sacrifice yourself."

He laughed. "No reveille in the morning for either of us. So we'll meet for a late breakfast and have a leisurely day."

Although she woke early through habit, Ria luxuriated in the soft bed. She was glad to see that Sophie had slept well and not cried in her sleep as she had the previous night. Ria soaked in a hot bath until the water went tepid, and by the time she and Sophie joined Jack in the dining room, he had already done a sketch of the harbour and was on his third cup of coffee.

Over breakfast, Jack told her about his work. "I'm not doing as much flying as I'd like, but of course I'm safer on the ground. Aitken is arranging for an art exhibition in London in February, so I'll be there then. Did you know that he's been granted a peerage? Lord Beaverbrook. Scuttlebutt has it that he was instrumental in bringing down Asquith and putting Lloyd George in as Prime Minister, and that this is his reward. He's also bought the *Daily Express*, so I expect he'll be wielding even more power." Jack hadn't thought of the press as a way to further his career interests, but he could see that influencing public opinion was a powerful tool, especially for those who had no ambition to enter politics, but preferred to manipulate them from the sidelines. And if well run, the papers could also make money. Something he'd have to consider.

Jack did a portrait of Sophie as Ria finished her coffee, which delighted the child. She told him about her painting kit, and he promised to give her lessons whenever they were together. She glowed with happiness. "Monsieur Capitaine Jacque, you are a very great artist, and I will be a very good student."

"I'm sure you will. But first you'll have to call me Cousin Jack. D'accord?"

"Oh, yes!"

"I have a terrific idea," Ria said. "I will write a story about Mr. Toad's aerial adventures, and you and Jack can help me illustrate it. What do you think, Sophie?"

She was bouncing in her seat, and Ria was glad to see some of her old spirit return. "Could we, Cousin Jack?"

"Absolutely! I read *The Wind in the Willows* to my sisters when they were young, and I think it's quite natural for Mr. Toad to take to the skies." He sketched quickly as he talked.

"And I will have Thea and Alice on my editorial team," Ria said. "Then we'll publish the book and give it to all our friends for Christmas next year."

"You'll be starting a publishing company soon," Jack quipped, referring to Alice's book that she and Chas had printed the previous year.

"Perhaps." Exuberantly, Ria said, "Do you know what's so wonderful? Being young and able to do anything we want! *Après la guerre* I might teach flying, or open an art gallery and display your and Edelina's works, or build aeroplanes, or design more flattering uniforms."

Jack laughed. "All it takes is money."

"And initiative and determination."

"And connections and luck and talent." He showed her the sketch he had just made of Toad flying a Sopwith Pup.

This time she laughed and Sophie clapped her hands in glee at the comical picture of Toad in goggles and helmet and fluttering scarf. "That's brilliant!" Ria said. "You see, you have all the ingredients for success, Cousin Jack." She regarded him wryly.

"Yes, I believe I do." If he could survive the war, he added to himself.

Aside from a chilly walk, they spent the day in the hotel lounge, Ria writing and reading her evolving story to Sophie and Jack, who added their suggestions. Jack sketched appropriate scenes and showed Sophie how to colour them. They laughed and joked and enjoyed the day, so that by the time they went in to dinner, Ria felt that they had established a new and stronger bond.

Jack, relaxed and thankful, decided that the journey had been well worth the effort.

· · ·

They were awakened shortly after 2:00 AM by the shrill voice of "Mournful Mary", the air-raid warning. Jumping out of bed, Ria looked out to see the frantic twitching of the searchlights and the scintillating, coloured showers of the star shells that illuminated the sky in the hopes of picking out the invaders. The roar of aeroplanes and the whine and thunder of falling bombs augmented the boom and chatter of the anti-aircraft guns.

Ria threw on her fur coat and hastily dressed Sophie in her warmest things. Sophie screamed and clung frantically to Ria. Jack was already banging on their door.

"We can take shelter in the basement," he assured her as they joined the general rush down the dark corridors, lit only by the explosions outside. Jack had picked up Sophie, and she hid her face against his shoulder, trying to burrow into him whenever another explosion shook the night, reaching for Ria, afraid to be even inches away from her.

The bombs were close tonight, no doubt targeting the harbour and naval installations. Ria and Jack were both keenly aware of the danger of shattering glass, and hastened through the lobby, where the manager was directing his guests to the basement via the kitchen.

Lanterns were lit in the windowless cellar, which housed an extensive collection of wine and endless shelves of supplies. There was also a monstrous coal-fired boiler that supplied the hot water and heating. Ria thought it wasn't a particularly safe place to be if the hotel sustained a direct hit, especially if it was an incendiary bomb, as there was a mountain of coal here to fuel an immense conflagration.

Having a similar thought, Jack secured them a spot under the stairs, thereby ensuring a quick escape. If the stairs weren't blocked.

Reminded of the raid that had killed her mother, Sophie was sobbing, so Ria hugged her, sandwiching the child between herself and Jack. He could smell the subtle lavender fragrance of Ria's soap, and thought it was probably a good thing that Sophie separated them. He really didn't want to lust after his best friend's wife.

Ria said, "It's different somehow, driving through this sort of thing. I suppose because I'm moving and have some control. I don't usually feel this scared."

"It's too easy to imagine being entombed here, if the hotel's hit," Jack replied. "At least we have wine," he added with a grin.

As if he had heard, M. LeBlanc began opening bottles and chivvying his nervous staff to offer glasses to the guests.

"Surely only in France," Jack whispered to Ria as they sipped champagne.

"I'm glad you're here, Jack," she confessed. "I've been feeling jinxed by Monty Seaton's book, and keep thinking that Chas and I are destined never to be together again. Silly, I know. But I can't honestly convince myself of that. So I feel as if your presence is preventing anything truly bad from happening."

"I'm glad that helps. But remember that you and Chas have good Karma. Cling to that, and forget about Seaton's book. It was damned cheeky of him to use you like that."

"He should be paying us royalties," Ria quipped.

They hunched together as another nearby explosion shook the earth, rattling the bottles and knocking jars from the shelves. Ria stroked Sophie's hair and began crooning a lullaby to her.

By the time the "all clear" sounded, Sophie had fallen asleep on Jack's shoulder.

"Your arms must be ready to drop off," Ria said to him.

"Not at all. She hung on so tightly that it was no effort to hold her. I expect she'll sleep soundly now."

They emerged from the cellar surprised to find no damage to the hotel. Word came in that even the city had been mostly spared – a few buildings destroyed, along with an old woman and a dog. It could have been much worse.

Sophie didn't wake when Jack laid her on the bed. He said, "I have to make an early start, but the two of you should sleep in. I'll inform M. LeBlanc to rouse you in good time if the ship is able to sail."

"Thank you, Jack." Ria hugged him. "How lucky we are to have you as a friend."

He recalled how he had once viewed her as merely someone to be used to further his ambitions, and had been surprised to realize that he truly cared for her. If anything ever happened to Chas, she would be an immensely wealthy and desirable widow.

Unfortunately, she was barren, and Jack definitely wanted to establish a dynasty. So Fliss was still his best bet.

Chapter 9

It was two more days before Ria and Sophie could leave for England. The ship that normally carried eight hundred passengers now held twelve hundred, of which only a few others were women – nurses going on leave.

It was a nauseatingly rough journey as they scaled watery mountains and plummeted into liquid valleys. Ria was glad that she'd had no more than tea and toast for breakfast, although her stomach still threatened to rebel. Of course she and Sophie were well laced into their lifebelts, but Ria felt again that paralyzing fear of being on the sea, and held tightly to the child, who bravely didn't cry or complain, although she looked terrified. Ria tried to distract her, and herself, by playing word games and telling stories.

It was as if they were crossing the River Styx. Returning from hell. If that was allowed. She was somewhat reassured to see their escort of destroyers.

Profoundly relieved to finally dock at Folkestone, Ria was astonished and overjoyed to find Chas waiting for them. They kissed unabashedly and Ria was reluctant to let go of him. It was Sophie tugging on both their coats that made Chas laugh and pick up his new daughter in an exuberant embrace. And suddenly everything was alright.

"It's heavenly to be here," Ria said as they sat down to tea at Bovington Abbey some hours later.

Chas had managed to take a few days leave, and she and Sophie would stay at Bovington for a week until the house that Chas had rented near his aerodrome at Farnborough was ready for them.

"And how wonderful that you're still here, Alice!" Ria said. Alice had come to Bovington after Christmas, and wasn't due back at school until the following Monday, so her grandparents had allowed her to stay on. "You must catch me up on all your news."

Which Alice did over an animated tea, concluding with, "Ever since Chas came to visit and I wrote the article about him, I seem to have become the most popular girl in the school. Not that that means a thing to me, since I have my loyal friends. But," she added with a smirk, "it is rather fun *not* to be the pathetic Colonial anymore. You should see how envious they are whenever I tell them that I'm going to London to visit my editor!" Alice was still writing pieces for *Home Fires*, and occasionally visited Thea and Meredith for the weekend.

"Your articles are very thoughtful and well written," Ria said. "None of the WATS believes that you're only fourteen."

"Almost fifteen," Alice corrected.

"In two weeks, isn't it? Which explains why you're such a sophisticated young lady," Ria said.

Alice giggled. "Now I'd like to write an article about you, Ria. What Theadora wrote was amazing..."

"And terrific publicity for us," Ria interjected.

"So I'd like my article to be complementary to that one. Now that we know what the WATS do and under what severe conditions they work, I want to know what your impressions of the war are."

"You probably wouldn't be able to publish those," Ria said seriously. "Because of censorship. The government can't have us telling too much of the truth, or people would revolt."

"And we've already told Wilson we're not willing to enter into peace talks until Germany agrees to what amounts to unconditional surrender," Chas added.

"So we fight to the bitter end," Ria stated sadly. She had hoped that the American President would be the voice of reason at a peace conference that he had been trying to arrange.

"Rather gloomy talk for a homecoming," Bea said. "Now tell me how you found Calypso."

"He's splendid, Cousin Bea! Thank you for looking after him so well. I've missed him so. Will I be able to take him along, Chas?"

"I'll see what I can do."

Sophie had already been introduced to the horse, with some trepidation on her part. Now she sat pressed up against Ria, who was leaning against Chas. Beatrice was relieved and delighted to see that the rift between them had healed. And amused to notice that they were holding hands in a rather sensual way, as if barely able to contain their desire for one another.

"I think it's time for you to meet Johanna Verbruggen," Bea said. "She's only sixteen, but has been looking after her two younger sisters for years, especially since the family's been in England. They're Belgian refugees. Her father was a schoolteacher who was killed in the early days of the German invasion. Her only brother was taken away. The family has no idea whether he's still alive. Johanna has two older sisters who are working as land girls on farms in the area, and her mother is keeping house for the local doctor. She speaks Flemish and French, of course, and has picked up English very quickly. A bright girl, amenable, well-mannered, unassuming, and conscientious, I'd say."

"She sounds perfect, Cousin Bea. Thank you for finding her," Ria said.

"You can thank Enid Robertson, who recommended her to me." Bea rang for Johanna to be brought in.

Ria's first impression was that the girl was astonishingly tall, but that was because she was so thin. She had a pert, elfin beauty with large, dark eyes and a generous if nervous smile.

Ria was mostly won over when Johanna, after being introduced, squatted down in front of Sophie in a very natural, child-like gesture and said to her in French, "I do hope we'll be able to play together later, Miss Sophie."

"I would like that," Sophie responded with a grin.

In English Ria asked, "You like children, do you, Johanna?"

"Oh yes, Madame. I had hoped to be a teacher of small children. My Papa taught the older ones."

"What would you do with Sophie if you were looking after her?"

"I know that I must see to her baths, and dressing, and putting to bed, and if she is not going to school, then we would enjoy some lessons. And we will be reading and taking exercise. I would like very much to play tennis and notice that Lady Kirkland has a court."

Already won over by her eager, guileless manner, Chas said, "Sophie won't be going to school just yet, so what would you teach her? I expect your father taught you well."

"Oh yes, Sir! He was a very great... scholar, I think the word is. Learning was fun. He had many games for mathematics. We would study the globe and learn about the countries and their history. When we walked in the woods or by the sea or looked at the heavens at night, he told us about the science of the world. We discussed philosophy at dinner and the new events that might change civilization. Every night we read books."

"What are you reading now, Johanna?" Ria asked.

"*The Doomed*, by the American writer, Montgomery Seaton. I think it will be very sad."

Oh, Lord! Not Monty's book again!

Chas noticed Ria's dismay and said, "What other English books have you read, Johanna?"

"*Oliver Twist, Little Women, Alice's Adventures in Wonderland, Tess of the D'Urbervilles, Jane Eyre, Peter Pan, Wuthering Heights* — but there was much difficult English in that. I like very much Jane Austen's books also."

Ria and Chas looked at each other, then Ria said, "We'd like very much for you to be Sophie's nanny. Come and I'll show you both your rooms and we can unpack."

"Oh, thank you indeed, Madame!" Johanna smiled broadly and almost bounced over to Sophie and stretched out her hand, which Sophie took without hesitation.

"Why don't you come along, Alice?" Ria suggested.

She did gladly, and Ria took her fervently by the arm, saying, "I so enjoyed your letters, but how much better to see you again, my dearest friend!"

When they had left the room, Chas said, "Joanna's truly charming, Cousin Bea."

"I do think they will be good for each other."

"I agree. But I warn you that Ria is apt to adopt Johanna as well."

They both laughed. "And with Alice being a part of the family, I expect you'll feel as if you have three daughters already, Chas."

"Good Lord, that's sure to age me!"

"Quite the contrary. Having young people around keeps you young. As I have discovered, much to my delight."

"You're very good to us, Cousin Bea."

"Nonsense! I can tell you that I shall feel quite bereft when the war is over and you all return home again."

"You'll just have to come with us. We'll spend time at the cottage, at your villa in Cap d'Antibes, here, London, Toronto."

Bea chuckled. "That's certainly tempting."

Upstairs, Ria took the girls to the nursery, which hadn't been used in decades. It was clean, if a bit shabby, and cozy with the crackling blaze in the fireplace. Johanna's small bedroom was off the main room, which would serve as Sophie's bedroom, sitting room, and classroom. A private bathroom was off it as well.

As they unpacked, Ria chattered on, sometimes in English, sometimes in French, trying to make Sophie relax in this strange new environment. "We'll have to go shopping in London for some more winter clothes for you, ma petite. And we'll have to make sure there's a piano in our new house, because I'm going to teach you how to play. You enjoyed our duets, didn't you?"

"Oh, yes..."

Ria had noticed that Sophie didn't know what to call her now that "Madame WATS" was no longer suitable, so she said, "Would you like to call me Mummy Ria?" Being "Mama" or "Mummy" would probably be too soon for the child.

"Oh, yes."

"And Daddy Chas. And Lady Kirkland can be Aunt Bea. And Alice will be like your older sister. Tomorrow you will meet my cousin, Zoë."

"She will be mine also, like Cousin Jack?"

"Mais oui! And there are more, you'll see. Now you'll want to have a little rest, because we don't dine until much later." And Ria had decided that Sophie would not be confined to the nursery until she was practically an adult. At the cottage, the children, once out of nappies and able to speak, had been allowed to eat with the adults, except on formal occasions. It was how grandmother had ensured some control over training them, but Ria and her cousins had enjoyed this unusual privilege, even if silliness and lax manners had been quickly trounced.

"Here's a lovely warm dress for you to wear to dinner, after your bath. But first we're going to cuddle up in front of the fire and start reading *The Wind in the Willows*."

Ria read her the first couple of pages, but translated loosely as she went along so that Sophie could understand the story.

She didn't realize that Chas was leaning against the doorjamb, listening and watching. Admiring them, marvelling at the fact that they were his family. Feeling slightly choked up to see his beautiful wife so animated with joy as she explained about Mole giving up his spring cleaning to wander down to the river.

"This very river outside your window," Ria said to her rapt audience, which included Johanna, who had finished putting Sophie's things away. "Which we will explore when the weather is warmer, just like Ratty and Mole. Alice can tell you about that. And now I must go for my bath and will see you later. Oh, Chas! How long have you been standing there?"

"Long enough to know that Mole is about to embark on an adventure," he said with a wink.

Sophie seemed a bit distressed at Ria's leaving, but Johanna took her in hand, saying, "I will sit here by the fire and read while you rest, Miss Sophie. But first we will talk a little, and get to know each other, d'accord?"

"Oui."

"I'll stay for a while as well," Alice said.

Sophie's face lit with a tentative smile.

"Perhaps Miss Alice will tell us what she likes about England," Johanna said. "I have been here for two years now and find it very beautiful. Many more hills than back in Belgium, where we lived...."

"I think those three will get along famously," Chas said as he took Ria by the hand and led her to their bedroom.

"Yes. Isn't it delightful that Johanna is still so child-like, even if she does read Seaton and Hardy. Almost like an older sister."

Chas laughed. "She really is too old for you to adopt, Ria! Besides, she has a perfectly fine mother."

"How do you know she's fine?" Ria quipped.

"Just look at how her daughter turned out."

"If you applied that logic to me, I'd be like my father, God forbid, or Grandmother."

"Whoever said that you're *not* like your grandmother?" he teased.

"You'd best watch what you say," Ria cautioned as they went into their room. "I don't expect that she would have approved of doing what I think you have in mind as an après-tea activity."

He laughed again. "OK, I take it back!" He pulled her into his arms and kissed her hungrily. "Much more delicious than tea."

.   .   .

Ria was thrilled to be on Calypso again as she and Chas rode to the Club after breakfast the following morning.

"Mrs. Thornton!" Grayson said with obvious delight. "How splendid to have you back with us. I've enjoyed your letters, but they haven't always reassured me that you weren't in some peril." He regarded her as if certain that she had been holding back. Grayson knew her well.

She smiled. "Adventures are rife with risks, aren't they, which make them that much more exciting."

"Not too exciting, I trust."

"Nothing I couldn't handle. You should see how strong I've become, carrying all those stretchers. And I can even make tea and toast."

He grinned and said, "Oh, dear. We shall all be out of jobs soon."

"Not in the least! Cousin Bea tells me that things have been running smoothly here, as expected. Oh, and I must thank Miss Robertson for finding a nanny for me."

"Do come through to the office. Miss Robertson is most capable and dedicated. Makes me feel quite superfluous at times."

"Then we'll have to find something else to keep you occupied," Ria teased.

As they interrupted her bookkeeping, Enid Robertson said, "Major and Mrs. Thornton, what a pleasure to have you here! We have tried to do you proud, Mrs. Thornton."

"And you certainly have," Ria assured her.

After a brief discussion with Miss Robertson, Ria and Chas chatted with the men and entertained them for an hour. There was especially wild applause for *Sister Suzie*. Ria was in uniform, and one chap cried, "I rode in your ambulance a couple of months ago! Doesn't that beat all! See, I'm all better now, Sister, and heading back soon."

"Then be careful that we don't meet again, Private," she said with a grin. He laughed joyfully.

"You're really good for them," Chas said when they rode back to Bovington.

"Don't..."

"I'm not trying to influence you, Ria. Just stating a fact."

"Ha! I can see the machinations going on in that Oxford brain."

"Wouldn't you want me to stay here if I had the choice?"

"Tell me honestly that you couldn't have stayed in England if you'd chosen. That they'd rather risk your life at the Front than have a brilliant pilot like you teaching."

With his new policy of openness and honesty, Chas hesitated for only a moment, but it was enough.

"I knew it!" Ria said angrily.

"Listen, Ria!" he said, grabbing Calypso's reins and pulling her up short. "Last October Boom Trenchard gave me a choice. I could have gone to Scotland and spent the rest of the war teaching fighter pilots. But I didn't want to be there when you were in France."

"You didn't tell me!"

"You didn't give me a chance! You wouldn't even respond to my letters. Why should I have thought that you would give up the WATS and move to Scotland with me?"

"You would have been safe."

"Perhaps. But what good is that if you're not?"

She looked stricken as she said, "Can't you change your decision?"

"It's too late. We desperately need more squadrons at the Front. I have a crack team, hand-picked. I'll have so much administration to do that I won't even have much time to fly myself."

Ria was shaken, despite Chas's attempts to cheer her up. It wasn't until they were on their way to pick up Zoë later in the afternoon that she managed to throw off the ominous foreboding.

Ria and Zoë hugged and laughed and wept a little. Having not seen her for almost two years, Zoë thought that Ria had been noticeably toughened by her war experiences. The scar on her forehead gave her an almost piratical look, and her bobbed hair was incredibly flattering and daringly modern. She understood now what Blake had meant. "I can't believe I haven't seen you for so long," she said.

"Especially since we've never been apart for more than about four days, the year I had the measles," Ria said. For they had seen each other daily at school and, of course, at the cottage all summer. "Once *you* got them we were able to share a sickroom."

"Which was rather fun, come to think of it."

"Marriage suits you, Mrs. Carlyle," Ria said with a grin. "And nursing, I expect. Although you're probably as glad to get out of your uniform as I was of mine."

They talked easily, endlessly, almost desperately trying to catch up on the past two years. Chas interjected the odd comment but was happy to listen to their sisterly banter. Zoë was able to stay to dinner but had to be back before 10:00. On the return journey she recounted some of the news from Blake.

"He told me how unnerving it was the first time a bullet whizzed past his ears. He tells me about the shells exploding around him as he assesses the wounded, how he's been ankle-deep in blood after an offensive. I get rigid with fear sometimes, so cold I feel my blood has turned to ice."

Ria squeezed her hand reassuringly. "Surely he tells you some good things as well."

Zoë sniffed back tears. "Yes of course! And funny incidents. As MO he has a horse so that he can ride up to the front lines. You know that Blake and horses don't have a great affinity with one another. His nag, as he calls her, seems to have a mind of her own and is quite contemptuous of his needs. So she takes a dinner break whenever she finds a juicy patch of grass, and can't be budged. But when the shelling becomes particularly intense, she suddenly becomes a racehorse."

"Clever old girl," Chas said. "A survivor, I'd say."

"Like Blake," Ria added.

. . .

"The girls and I will accompany Chas as far as London tomorrow, Cousin Bea," Ria said. "They need some more clothes, and I long for something new and decidedly feminine. Will you come with us?"

"Thank you, my dear, but I will decline," Beatrice said. "I don't have the energy to keep up with you. Besides, you'll want to meet with your friends. I'll look forward to visiting your new home once you've settled in."

"Everything's worked out so well, hasn't it? And you won't mind looking after Sophie when I go back to France in the spring, will you, Cousin Bea?"

Beatrice hesitated before replying, "She's a delightful child, so of course not. But you are her mother now, Ria. Perhaps you should reconsider going back. Sophie has already lost her parents. Is it fair to subject her to constant fear for your safety, the loneliness of your prolonged absence, the very real possibility that you might not return?"

Ria was dumbfounded. "But I have an obligation to the WATS, to my colleagues."

"So you must decide which obligation is more important. But rest assured that Sophie will be well looked after by us all."

Later in bed, Ria said to Chas, "Is Cousin Bea right? Am I being selfish and unfair in wanting to return to France? I already feel that I'm letting the girls down by being warm and comfortable here while they now have even more work because I've left."

"I know exactly what you mean – that feeling of guilt and needing to be with one's comrades. It's mostly what keeps us going back. Certainly not for any idealistic reason anymore. At least not for me. Don't worry about it tonight, my darling. We have at least two months before that becomes an issue," he said, as he began kissing her.

But Ria lay awake after their lovemaking, wondering how to resolve her dilemma.

. . .

London was hectic and fun. They shopped at Harrods and Selfridges, Ria buying Sophie and Alice muskrat coats and fur hats. As nanny, Johanna inhabited a limbo between upstairs and down, but Ria knew that it would be awkward for the girl to be treated too differently from the other servants. So she bought Johanna a warm but still stylish wool coat, much to the girl's delight. They all got new dresses, jumpers, hats, scarves, and cozy boots. "We have to be appropriately dressed for our walks," Ria explained.

From her usual dress shop, Ria ordered some clothes designed in the latest style of the House of Chanel fashions that she had heard about in France, which offered sleek and comfortable lines that allowed freedom of movement.

She stocked up on books and phonograph records and piano sheet music. She also bought presents for Zoë and Max, whose twenty-first birthdays were in a few weeks.

It was bitterly cold, but used to Canadian winters and properly clad, she and the girls wandered in Hyde Park and Kensington Gardens, across the street from Bea's townhouse, and along the frozen Serpentine, which Ria and Alice agreed would make a splendid skating rink. When Sophie and Johanna looked at each other in puzzlement, Alice said, "Ria, we'll have to teach them to skate!"

"Indeed we will. You can't be a Canadian without being able to skate."

They had a delightful lunch with Thea and Meredith at her townhouse just a short stroll from Bea's. After the meal, Ria suggested that the girls go for a walk in the park and then return to the house for a rest, since they would be out late this evening.

"They're lovely children," Meredith said. "Rather like sisters."

Ria laughed and said, "I know I'm not treating Johanna at all like a servant, except that she is being paid. But I feel so badly for her as well. War is hell for the strongest men. For children it is horrific."

"I don't expect anyone has ever accused you of being conventional, Ria," Thea said. "So you are Johanna's mentor, which I find quite charming. I think the days of the traditional servant are coming to an end, thanks to this war. Young men and women find that they can do much better for themselves by working in factories and such. Not necessarily the security of a roof over their heads or regular meals as in service, but the chance to do even better for themselves with hard work and wise economies, while having some sort of life of their own."

"So you're saying that I'd better learn to cook," Meredith said with a chuckle.

"With chefs like Escoffier around, we can always dine out. But we might have to start making our beds and preparing our own tea. Ria's already learned to do things like that in France."

"I can even wash dishes without breaking too many. But I have to admit I hate doing them," Ria said. "At the cottage we didn't have as many servants as in the city, so we were expected to put away our own clothes and run our baths. But it does rather make you feel more independent, not having to rely on someone else to supply you with a cup of tea or lay out your evening gown."

Ria had managed to procure four tickets to the immensely popular musical, *Chu Chin Chow,* which surely every soldier on leave and every resident in London had seen at least once. Alice had already seen it with Thea and Meredith, but was happy to go again. The fabulous costumes and sets and the live animals, like a camel and snakes, had the girls absolutely enthralled, and even if Sophie didn't understand much of it, she was mesmerized.

Ria telephoned Sidonie the next day, somewhat reluctantly, and they agreed to meet for lunch at the Savoy Grill. Ria decided it was prudent to leave the girls at Bea's townhouse, arranging for the kitchen maid to prepare a light luncheon for them.

"Darling, you look fabulous!" Sid exclaimed, giving her a peck on the cheek. "I was expecting you to be haggard and hollow-eyed, but the exciting life of driving ambulances must suit you. Do tell me all about it."

Ria gave her highlights, amusing and shocking her.

"I have to admit that I'm almost envious. Especially as there must be a bevy of luscious and lonely officers there. Anyone of particular interest?" she asked slyly.

"I have Chas, Sid. Any other men in my life are merely relatives and friends," she said pointedly.

"Yes, you are a lucky girl."

"Is there anyone in *your* life, Sid?"

"Oh, there's always someone," Sid said airily. "Rarely the right one.... So you want my help recruiting more WATS or at least some money?"

"If you could arrange a tea for some suitable candidates of your acquaintance, then I'd be delighted to tell them about our Corps. But we don't want to give anyone the impression that this is easy and fun or, God forbid, glamorous. It's damned hard work. And dangerous."

"I will do that."

"Thank you, Sid. Chas and I would love for you and Quentin to come visit us once we've settled in."

The following day they accompanied Alice to Oxford. Amid tearful goodbyes, Ria realized that the three girls had already established a deep bond. Perhaps the fact that they had all suffered hardships and lost at least one parent gave them common ground. Ria was interested to see that Alice didn't treat Johanna like a servant either. She had heard them discussing literature like classmates.

"I wish I could stay with you as well," Alice said to Ria as they hugged, suddenly feeling terribly envious of Sophie and even Johanna.

"You'll have to come to visit us whenever you can."

"I'm allowed one weekend away each month."

"Good! And you'll spend some of the summer at Cousin Bea's again, won't you?"

"I do hope so."

"Perhaps you can look after Sophie as well, when I'm back in France."

Alice bit back her protest, knowing that Ria would do what she felt she must. But hopefully she would change her mind. "Yes, of course. I'll teach her tennis and canoeing and riding, and we'll write even more adventures for Mr. Toad," she said with a grin. She'd been impressed with the little book that Ria and Jack and Sophie had created.

"Why does Alice have to go to school so far away?" Sophie asked. "You said she was my sister. Why can't she stay with us?"

"This is where her grandparents live," Ria explained.

"They are very old. I do not have grandparents."

"You have two grandmothers, but you can't live with them."

Sophie let out an audible sigh. "That is good. Aunt Bea is old, but she laughs." Sophie gripped Ria's hand tightly.

They stayed and dined at the Randolph that evening, Ria having invited Henry and Rafe to join them. Rafe was obliged to attend the School of Military Aeronautics at Oxford before being allowed to fly.

"Which is ridiculous," he said over dinner, "since I had perfectly good training in Texas."

"Then you should come top of your class," Ria said.

"Theory is all very well, but what you do with it is more important," he replied.

"Not top of your class then," Ria said astutely.

"Not like you, eh? Chas confirmed what I had suspected when I read about the Germans being outraged at our *women* pilots. I'm surprised they didn't lock you up or ship you home for masquerading as an RFC pilot."

Henry looked scandalized. "Ria! You didn't!"

Rafe chuckled wickedly. "Of course she did, Henry. You must know your cousin by now."

"Confound it, I should! But she always ventures beyond the bounds of my imagination."

Rafe insisted on her telling the story and laughed fulsomely. Henry looked appalled and said, "What *were* you thinking? But, of course, you weren't. Being impulsive and reckless as usual."

"I really miss flying. And Chas tells me that Peggy had to shut down her aerodrome because of fuel restrictions. I wonder if I can persuade Chas to let me fly," she said mischievously.

Henry started to splutter, but Ria laughed and said, "If you let me take you up for a flight some time, Henry, you might think differently. Now tell me what you've heard about Edgar and Daphne's wedding. Ellie sent some lovely photos. Daphne certainly has grown up, and Edgar was positively beaming from the pictures."

They talked about news from home during the rest of the meal. Ria suggested that Johanna take Sophie up to bed while they had coffee.

When the girls had gone, Henry said, "She's very well-mannered, your *daughter*, but surely it's most unusual for the child let alone the nanny to dine with us here."

"Scandalous, I should say," Ria conceded with a grin. "You should have seen how many eyebrows we raised in London. They gave us a nice, quiet corner table at the Carlton."

Henry shook his head and said, "I must be off as well, before Ria shocks everyone by smoking in public or something equally fast. Anyway, I have papers to write."

"I'll keep my sister-in-law company," Rafe said. "I only have papers to read."

"I hope you can manage to stay out of trouble for a while, Ria," Henry said. "If not, at least be careful."

She laughed as she kissed his cheek. "Goodbye, *Uncle* Henry," she teased. She had decided that he was much too staid to be anything but Sophie's "uncle". Rafe, of course, really was.

He ordered himself a large cognac to be served in the lounge. When they were seated in the overstuffed leather chairs by the fire, and both smoking cigarettes, Rafe said, "You shouldn't be giving that girl airs above her station, Ria. Your Belgian peasant."

"If you're going to be hateful, then you can drink alone!"

"Don't get your knickers in a twist. I don't think you're being fair to her. When Sophie no longer needs a nanny, what will your little refugee do then? Too posh to be a regular servant. Not the right lineage or education or enough money to be in society. She'll be neither fish nor fowl, and damned unhappy, I expect. Even if she's going to be a corker when she grows up, and will have plenty of men after her."

"Just make sure you keep your hands off her."

He chuckled. "No guarantees if she's going to be sitting at our table like any other guest. But not till she fills out a bit. In a few years, who knows?" He shrugged.

"You haven't changed, have you Rafe?" Ria said angrily.

"I say what I think, unlike too many people I know. Makes for fewer misunderstandings," he said meaningfully. "*You* should know that you can't have it both ways, Ria. Honesty *or* politeness. Friend *or* servant. Wife *or* mistress."

She glared at him. "Don't you dare throw that in my face!"

"I'm just surprised that you forgave your adulterous husband."

"I'm not prepared to discuss this with you, other than to tell you that I love Chas and I know that he loves me more than you will ever realize."

"Sit down, Ria. I wasn't planning to gloat. I saw red when I found out about Chas's affair. And I was concerned about you. So I'm glad that you and Chas are lovey-dovey again, as long as you're happy. You may find this hard to believe, but I wouldn't deliberately do anything to hurt you." His sincerity didn't take him the next step – revealing that he had always fancied himself in love with her. "Let me tell you about meeting up with Lizzie and Emily in New York. Your cousin is quite a hit on Broadway, and Lizzie's an accomplished photographer."

He went on to tell her about his flight training in Texas, and Fliss's latest undertakings, so they ended the evening amicably.

"When you come to visit us, will you help me buy a pony for Sophie?" Ria asked.

"Oh no, you must allow Uncle Rafe to buy one for his niece."

"That's very kind, Rafe. She was rather intimidated by Calypso, but I'm sure she'll be more comfortable by something more her size."

"And I'll start her on lessons. Can't have a niece of mine afraid of horses. I say, it's decidedly odd to be an uncle, especially since I can barely converse with her."

"Your French not up to snuff then?" Ria asked with amusement.

"I imagine I can just about talk myself into some Mademoiselle's bed."

"Vous êtes scandleux!"

"Je sais."

·   ·   ·

"Oh Chas, it's smashing!" Ria said when they arrived at the house. "Our very own English country estate!"

"It's called Priory Manor because monks lived on this property in the 12th century," Chas explained. "You'll enjoy the stone ruins in the garden. There's still the odd Gothic arch standing. This house wasn't built until the 1750s."

"Quite modern then," Ria jested.

It was an elegant and substantial Georgian house of mellowed red brick trimmed in white. The three-storied central section was flanked by tall one-storey wings. Ivy scrambled about the walls, softening the rigid symmetry of the design. It sat in park-like grounds whose massive beech trees rested pendulous branches on the ground.

"The widow who owns it found it too large, what with the fuel and staff shortages, and has moved in with her daughter for the duration of the war."

"So you're saying that I'm going to have to cook and clean?" Ria asked.

Chas laughed. "There's an ancient cook, an even more ancient gardener, and a somewhat slovenly and sullen girl from the village."

"Charming!"

"But I'm sure you'll whip them into shape, my darling. And I've found a young lad to look after Calypso. There are stables here. Clive is only twelve, but he mucks out for one of the local farmers, and seems to have a way with horses. And, by the way, he has a perfectly fine mother," Chas teased.

Ria laughed. "This is too exciting! Do you realize that this is our very first house?"

"So it is!" They were already out of the car, so Chas scooped her into his arms.

"What are you doing?"

"Carrying you over the threshold, of course."

But they both laughed when Chas fumbled with the door handle, saying, "Damn, it's stuck!" and had to put her down on the wisteria-vined portico. But once he had the door open, he insisted on carrying her inside.

Their passionate kiss was interrupted by a disapproving voice saying, "This is the new mistress, is it?"

"It is indeed, Mrs. Skitch," Chas said nonchalantly, setting Ria down gracefully. "Ria, Mrs. Skitch is the cook-housekeeper."

"You have a daunting task then, Mrs. Skitch."

"I manages. My mistress never complained, I'm sure," she sniffed.

"No, I'm sure she didn't," Ria said, already noticing the patina of neglect on everything. "But I will see what I can do about finding more help for you."

The old lady snorted. "Chance would be a fine thing. Gels these days are too uppity to work at decent jobs anymore. Off doing men's work. Won't be a one of them'll know how to cook, you mark my words. Then who'll be wanting them, I ask you? It's lamb for dinner, Madam, if that suits."

"Lovely! This is our daughter, Sophie, and her nanny, Miss Verbruggen. They'll be dining with us at all times."

Mrs. Skitch harrumphed and shuffled off.

"Oh dear, I think I've scandalized her twice already," Ria said.

"I'm sure you'll have charmed her in no time, my darling."

"It's chilly in here," Ria said, noticing long-dead ashes in the hall fireplace, elegant though it was.

"We have electricity and hot water, but no central heating, I'm afraid," Chas said.

"Oh Lord, the English are either hardy or masochistic, but they really need to be hauled into the 20th century." Bovington didn't have central heating either, but then Beatrice and her husband had spent most of each winter on the Riviera. "I suppose I should be grateful for hot running water. And who is that dour and uncharitable looking fellow glaring at us from over the mantle?"

"Judge Prendergast, the deceased husband."

"Hell's bells! I wouldn't have wanted him to pass judgment on me. But I'll feel that he does whenever I look at him. And find me wanting. Do you think we could relegate the judge to the attic?"

Chas laughed. "Absolutely! We'll just be sure to haul him out whenever the widow plans to stop in."

"Let's think of something really suitable to hang there."

"You could do a large painting of the lake from one of your sketches."

"I'm not that good! I'll put mine somewhere else, but you haven't added anything to your art collection lately, have you?" Chas had begun collecting art when he was at Oxford, and had Monets, Renoirs, Van Goghs, Picassos and others. Not everyone liked his taste in "modern" art, but Ria found the paintings impressive and moving.

"No, and I do want to."

"Then I'll contact some of the galleries in London."

The broad central foyer was paneled in oak and had a grand staircase swooping past a landing lit by a massive stained-glass window. The main hall led to the back of the house, and Ria caught her breath. Like a beautiful flower on the apex of a stem, a small, semi-circular sunroom blossomed beyond double French doors. She rushed over to it, and cried in delight as she saw the tumbled ruins of the priory through the many tall arched windows. Gardens had been cleverly laid out to appear natural and to enhance the romantic ambiance of the ruins. With the low winter sun streaming in, the room was remarkably cozy.

"Oh, Chas, it must be beautiful in summer! Those look like roses clambering over the stones."

Chas was amused and pleased by her enthusiasm. "You can just see the roof of the summerhouse, which sits on the bank of our own five-acre lake. I expect it's frozen hard enough for skating."

She gave him an ecstatic hug and another kiss, oblivious of the girls, who were entranced by the garden in any case.

"I agreed to take the house, fully furnished, on a year's lease – it was only £200 – so there may be a chance for you to see it in summer after all…. Stop giving me the evil eye."

"I can see what you're plotting, trying to seduce me with all this beauty into staying in England."

"Darling, you're much too strong-minded to succumb to that. So I couldn't possibly be held responsible if you became enamored of our modest little home."

She laughed. "You're devious, Chas Thornton!"

"Can we play there?" Sophie asked.

"Of course, ma petite. It looks like a magical place for children." She gave Chas another mock scowl.

He said, "Come and look at the rest of the house."

"I hardly need to as I expect I'll spend most of my time here."

Ria was delighted with the grand piano in the drawing room. The ornamental medallions, decorative details, and two mantelpieces were in the Adam style, and floor-length windows and doors opened onto a balustraded stone terrace that swept along the back of the house. Across the hall was an equally elegant dining room also overlooking the garden. The morning room had a breakfast table, sofa, several wing chairs, a lady's writing desk, and presumably the morning sun streaming in the large windows. There was an office, a cloakroom, a butler's pantry with a dumb waiter that hauled trays up from the kitchen, a lavatory, and back staircase, which also led down to the basement. One wing housed the library, the other, the billiard room. On the second floor – or the first floor as it was called in Britain – were half a dozen generous bedrooms, two baths, and a nursery suite. Servants' quarters were collecting dust in the attic above, and the kitchen, servants' hall, butler's quarters, pantry, scullery, wine cellar, and laundry were in the raised basement. The house wasn't as large as either Ria's Gothic, towered Wyndholme or the Thorntons' rambling Thornridge, but it was more than adequate.

They came upon the maid, Beryl, carrying an empty coalscuttle. She was a disheveled young woman, streaks of coal dust on her face and uniform, her cap and apron askew – neither very clean to begin with. She had a sharp nose but might still have been relatively comely if her hair weren't greasy and her sallow skin grey with old dirt. She bobbed a sketchy curtsey when Chas introduced her, but barely looked at Ria as she said, "I lit a fire in your bedroom, Major Sir. And the nursery, like you asked." She bobbed again, growing alarmingly mottled in the face, and hastened away.

Ria smirked and whispered to Chas, "I think you've made a conquest there."

"Ha! If it means that the house is dusted and floors swept, then I'm glad."

Two of the bedrooms each had a dressing room attached, with a bathroom shared between them. "The master and mistress appear to have had separate rooms," Ria said.

"And I told Beryl to prepare only one."

"Then I expect Mrs. Skitch will be even more scandalized."

The nursery suite occupied one corner of the house, with a bathroom and two bedrooms off the day nursery, the small one obviously for Johanna while the other was big enough for three beds. "I can see the garden!" Sophie said with glee as she looked out the window.

"And the edge of the lake," Ria added. "Do let's go and look at it right now."

"Unfortunately, I have to return to work," Chas said. "But I'll leave you three to explore, and see you by dinnertime."

Chas had bought a second-hand Stratton motorcar for them, as new cars of any make were hard to obtain with wartime production focusing on military vehicles and aeroplanes. He'd also purchased a motorcycle, which was much easier on petrol, and perfect for his six-mile commute to Farnborough.

They accompanied him to the graveled circular drive and waved him off before setting out to explore. The house had sixty acres of grounds – the same size as Wyndwood Island – which included tennis and croquet lawns, a walled kitchen garden with greenhouses and espaliered fruit trees, meadows and woodlands, the lake, with a charming glassed-in summerhouse perched on a knoll above it, and the mystical ruins. Ria wondered if the ghosts of long-dead monks roamed the grounds.

She was also reminded of Frances Hodgson Burnett's novel, *The Secret Garden*, which she decided that Sophie should read when she was a bit older, and that Johanna would undoubtedly enjoy now.

When Johanna took Sophie up for a rest, Ria, grateful to see that there was a telephone in the office, called the Club. "Grayson, might I borrow you for a couple of days? I'd like you to organize the staff here. It's one thing for me to be the mistress, but quite another to have any credibility with the servants."

"Why of course, Mrs. Thornton."

She could hear his smile. "Then perhaps you can advise what I should do to find capable help. I expect that a decent wage is helpful, but I don't want to alienate the neighbours by stealing their servants."

They discussed what salaries should be offered and what advertisement Ria should put into the newspaper. Grayson would come down to interview the candidates in a few days.

"In the meantime, I'd advise that you not exercise any of your new domestic skills, Mrs. Thornton. Servants resent anyone treading on their territory, and would feel insulted by offers of help, no matter how well meaning or even practical. Nor would they respect you for it."

"Point taken, Grayson. I shall be suitably disdainful of physical labour," she jested.

Ria next phoned the local paper to place an ad, and also spoke to the vicar. Prompted by Grayson's suggestions, she said, "I'm willing to consider youngsters, elders, crippled soldiers, unwed mothers, full or part-time, living in or out, whatever suits, so long as they're honest, willing, and able to do a decent day's labour for a fair wage. I'll hire and pay them for a year, although the house may not be used much after April."

Then she went down to the basement, She could hear the servants chattering, and, although her grandmother had always admonished her for eavesdropping, she stopped outside the kitchen to listen.

Beryl was saying, "She don't even got no lady's maid! Wot proper lady ain't got no maid? She'd better not be expecting me to be doing that for her! And they sleeps in the same room."

"Not quality then," Mrs. Skitch declared disparagingly. "I reckoned she was common."

A male voice chuckled and ended with a phlegmy cough. "Must be a corker then."

"Oooo, the Major's dreamy right enough," Beryl said. "A war hero, he is, so I heard in the village. One of them Aces, wot flies about shooting down Germans "

"That's as may be, but they're Americans," Mrs. Skitch said as if the word burned her tongue.

"Canadians," the old man corrected.

"From North America, so Americans an' all. Any road, wot's the difference, I ask you? They all talk funny and give themselves airs. Swanking about like they's all lords and ladies and not a title between them."

"The American's don't like our tea, do they? Threw it all into Boston harbour, going on a hundred and some years ago now."

"Get away with you, you old fool! They're rough Colonials no matter how you dress them up," Mrs. Skitch intoned. "Why, our mistress has more breeding in her little finger... Mind, she said we was to do right by them, but she would, being such a fine lady and all."

"She don't have to live with them, do she?" Beryl bemoaned.

"Young mistress must be a real looker with you two jawing away when you've barely clapped eyes on her," the old man said.

"Get away with your foolishness, Enoch!" Mrs. Skitch berated.

Ria decided it was time to announce her presence.

"I see the entire staff is assembled," she said, breezing into the room.

They jumped, for obviously no one had heard her coming. Wondering if Ria might have overheard any of their conversation, Beryl mottled again and Mrs. Skitch became tetchy. "You could have rung if you was wanting something, Madam."

"I'm aware of that, Mrs. Skitch. However, I wanted to see the kitchen and to have a word with all of you. I've decided that more help will definitely be necessary to make the place comfortable for us and our visitors. My cousin, the Countess of Kirkland, will be coming within the next few weeks. I'm also expecting friends to drop in frequently. I've consulted with my butler, Mr. Grayson, who has advised that we at least find a kitchen-scullery maid, and a hall boy or footman. Another parlour maid, if possible. As Mr. Grayson is supervising one of the King George and Queen Mary Maple Leaf Clubs on my behalf, he can't join us here, but will nonetheless be in charge and make monthly visits to ensure that the household is running smoothly."

Mrs. Skitch scowled, but Ria didn't give her a chance to complain. She said, "Because of the coal shortage, I've decided that we shall take all meals in the morning room, which we will also use as our sitting room, along with the sunroom. There's to be a fire lit at all times in the morning room and main hallway, Beryl, as well as our bedrooms and bathrooms, of course."

"The hallway, Ma'am?" Beryl asked.

"That's correct. Some of the heat will find its way into the sunroom," which had no fireplace, "and give a welcoming warmth to the house." And also drift up the stairs. Ria had no intention of scuttling down icy corridors between lukewarm rooms.

"Until the weather is warmer, we'll only use the dining room and drawing room when we have sufficient guests to warrant heating them. I'd like fires laid in the office, library, and billiard room, ready to be lit at a moment's notice. I expect that the butler's quarters are down here, so you can prepare them for Mr. Grayson."

"Them's my quarters now," Mrs. Skitch announced huffily. "No need for me to be traipsing up three flights of stairs to be up in the frosty attic now, is there, when I can sleep next to me warm kitchen."

"An' me an' all," Beryl said. "I'm never staying up there on me own, wot with them monks walking about! I got the footman's room."

"Then you can prepare one of the guest rooms for Mr. Grayson's visit, Beryl. Does anyone have any questions?"

"Will Mr. Grayson be dining with you as well, Madam?" Mrs. Skitch inquired sarcastically.

"Of course not, Mrs. Skitch. He'll be dining with you."

Enoch was working his lips around his pipe as if trying to keep them from springing apart in laughter.

"These are difficult times, so we must all do what we can to preserve resources, make do, help out. It won't be necessary to serve meat at every meal, Mrs. Skitch. We enjoy a well-balanced vegetarian fare as well. You and I will discuss menus tomorrow. We'll serve ourselves at table, except for formal meals. So you can leave the dishes on the sideboard, Beryl."

The staff had been having their tea, and Ria had noticed that Beryl's hands were none too clean as she gathered the crumbs on her plate and shoved them into her mouth. So she said, "Nevertheless, I'll expect you in a clean uniform and hands properly washed when you're bringing the meals. Hygiene is extremely important when dealing with food, isn't that so, Mrs. Skitch? Well, if there are no other questions, then we'll have our tea in the sunroom in an hour, Beryl, and look forward to a fine repast tonight, Mrs. Skitch. Oh, and Enoch, you may want to have that nasty cough seen to."

Ria gave them a brilliant smile and left the room. She grinned as Enoch's explosive laugh rang up the stairwell. They were in no doubt now that she had overheard them.

Oh, Lord, they were going to be a challenge, Ria thought. And if Beryl and Mrs. Skitch between them didn't poison the household then it would be luck more than anything.

In the kitchen, Beryl was saying, "Hygiene? Wot's that when it's at home? Washing hands? I'll spit in her soup, I will, and see how she likes that!"

"You'll do nothing of the kind, my gel, or you'll be out on your ear!" Mrs. Skitch warned. "The Countess of Kirkland, coming here? We never had a Countess afore. Get yourself smartened up, for pity's sake, or you won't be here much longer. Butler's coming, and they're right sticklers. Haven't had one here since ours died. That was just after the master did. Ten years gone, give or take."

"And we haven't had much going on since, have we?" Enoch said. "Maybe the place will come alive again with the new mistress."

Mrs. Skitch grunted, but was obviously anticipating that as well.

Ria did another quick review of the grounds, and went to look for Enoch. He was gathering the twigs that had come down in the last windstorm, and moved stiffly, as if in pain. Possibly being crippled by rheumatism or arthritis. "The gardens are fabulous, Enoch. You should take great pride in them."

"Thank you, Ma'am. I've been working here, one way or another, since I were a lad of ten."

"I expect that with little or no help these days, you haven't been able to cull the trees in the woodland anymore. It's obvious that it was once well looked after." At his surprise, she said, "My family is in lumbering so I do know a bit about wood. And the caretaker on our island is always cutting out saplings to give us good views of the lake and keep the best trees healthy."

"I had a staff of three once, but can't manage all this on me own. And we had a load of trees come down in that big storm last November."

"Yes, so I was thinking that if we could find a strong lad to help you out, perhaps you could supervise him chopping up the deadwood. It seems such a waste to see it rotting when we could burn it in the fireplaces. It may have dried out sufficiently by now to be useful, do you think?"

"I reckon it's still a mite green, but, aye, useful."

"And in summer, you'd have more help with the kitchen garden. I'm sure you get a good crop there."

"Would do with more hands."

Hands that weren't becoming deformed like Enoch's. "Then I think we definitely need to find a boy who'd like to apprentice under you. We still need beautiful and fruitful gardens to get us through this war," Ria added with a smile.

"By gum, it'll be a breath of fresh air having you about. Begging yer pardon, Ma'am."

Ria laughed. "Now I'd like you to give some thought to where we can build a hen coop, for I intend that we have chickens to supply us with eggs. And a cow, which can share the stable with the horses. We'll have to fence off some of the pasture for her in summer. What about a couple of sheep to keep the lawns trimmed?"

Ria realized she was making long-term plans when she fully intended to return to France in a few months. But it wouldn't hurt to make the household more self-sufficient. After all, she and Chas would get leaves, and since the place was theirs for the year, they needn't always impinge upon Cousin Bea's hospitality. Much as she loved Bea, she was already enjoying having her own place.

She was surprised that the dinner was quite good, and summoned the cook to the morning room afterwards. "Thank you, Mrs. Skitch. You've done remarkably well with the food, considering the shortages these days."

"Much obliged, Madam," Mrs. Skitch replied, drawing herself up proudly. "I does me best."

"Indeed. We shall look forward to more such delightful meals. Good night."

"Good night, Madam. Major."

When she had gone Chas said, "You've won her over, my darling. As I knew you would."

He had a good laugh when she told him about her earlier encounter with the staff. But Ria said, "I hate always having to pull out the big guns. *My cousin, the Countess...*"

"You at least have some guns. I'm at an even further remove from greatness."

"Hardly that! You're a hero, Chas."

"If so then a very tired one."

"Then I'd best get you to bed."

"My thoughts precisely."

.   .   .

"They're not an ideal staff," Grayson said to Ria, "but I believe that they will get the work done." He had interviewed candidates all morning. "First we have Matilda, or Tilda as she prefers to be called, whose father was a postman but was killed at the Somme. She was recommended by the vicar. Her elder sister works in a munitions factory and her mother takes in washing to make ends meet. The girl is sixteen and affianced to the local greengrocer's son, who's in France. They're going to be married whenever he gets leave, which may not be for six months to a year. She seems clean and well spoken. And she's three months pregnant."

"Oh dear. How will that go over with the rest of the staff?"

"It will depend upon your attitude, Mrs. Thornton."

"You know very well what that is, Grayson. My heart goes out to her, but I don't want to work her too hard in her condition."

"She's well and strong enough to do a proper day's work as parlour maid, and eager and grateful for the opportunity, which makes her even more valuable. She'd appreciate living in for now, but not once the baby comes. But it will be looked after by her mother and younger sister, if you need her to keep working after it's born. No need for the staff to know just yet, since it doesn't show. Give them a chance to know her before they pass judgment."

"I think it was very honest of her to tell you, Grayson. Not many would."

"My thoughts as well. Which is one of the reasons I like and trust her. Next we have sixteen-year-old Gareth and his mother, Branwyn. She is also a war widow, her husband having been a farm labourer. They live in a small tied cottage on a neighbouring estate, but expect to be evicted soon. She's been making a pittance selling herbs, about which she is very knowledgeable, but which has earned her a reputation as a witch. That and the fact that she is Welsh and has a livid birthmark on her face, which simple people sometimes attribute to the sign of the devil."

"Oh dear. You are bringing me a challenging crew."

Grayson suppressed a grin. "I haven't finished. Gareth is a healthy, strapping lad who loves the outdoors and has a great affinity with nature, according to his mother. He has an uncanny knack with plants and animals, and a sense when the weather's about to change..."

"Don't tell me... he has two heads, right?"

Grayson chuckled. "Fortunately not. But he is deaf. He had measles as a young child and completely lost his hearing. He can read lips amazingly well, and he and his mother have developed a type of sign language, but it means that she's the only one who can really help him communicate with the rest of the world."

"Aside from the more astute creatures of the forest. So we take them both."

"Branwyn is fiercely determined and will put her mind to anything that will help her son. She'll be the scullery and kitchen maid, and is happy to look after the cow and chickens. Gareth will apply his skills in the garden and help out with heavy work in the house, like hauling coal and wood to the various fireplaces. They are very grateful to have a new place to live.

"And lastly, there's Patrick, who's an experienced footman, and, having been a batman in the army, he'll be an excellent valet for Major Thornton. He worked his way up to Corporal. I'm most impressed with him, and will feel comfortable leaving him in charge of the staff. He'll make a good butler one day. He..."

"No! Let me guess. A footman without a foot!"

"Without a leg, actually. He lost it in the Battle of Loos."

"I'm sorry," Ria said, trying to stifle her laughter. "I realize it's not at all humorous, but the situation is rather. I'll have a menagerie of the maimed and the dispossessed."

"And because no one else will give them the time of day, you will have a loyal and hard-working staff."

"You've done splendidly, Grayson, as I knew you would. But how will Patrick manage stairs and such? I won't need him to wait at table except when we have guests."

"Which will be helpful. He admits that he can't be on his feet for extended periods of time, since his stump starts to ache. But some of his duties can be done sitting down, like polishing the silver, and he can pace himself with breaks. Fortunately, trays can be sent up via the dumb waiter. I expect that once he becomes more proficient with his artificial leg, he'll find things easier."

"I have to admit that I'll feel much happier with an experienced footman wearing clean white gloves handling the dishes and serving the food rather than Beryl, who seems to be allergic to water."

"So I've noticed. I will talk to her. I've asked the new recruits to wait in the hall so you can meet them."

They did seem a cheerful and eager lot, Ria thought. She found Branwyn momentarily shocking, for if viewed on her good side, she was a very attractive woman. The other half of her face was port-wine coloured, some with the texture of a strawberry, which made her look as if she had two faces. Ria felt terribly sorry for her, knowing how cruel and superstitious people could be. Her son, Gareth, on the other hand, had not even a freckle to mar his handsome, sun-bronzed young face.

"Welcome to Priory Manor," Ria said. "Together we are going to make this place sparkle and hum. If any problems arise, I hope you'll let me know."

Grayson sent them all home to pack and told them to arrive by 7:00 the following morning, when they could take breakfast in the servants' hall before beginning their training. Then he ordered uniforms for them from London, to be delivered by the next post. He also arranged for a stock of wine and other liquors.

He evicted Mrs. Skitch and Beryl from the men's quarters in the basement. "Patrick will take the butler's rooms, and Gareth, the footman's. All the women will be in the attic. You will have the housekeeper's suite, Mrs. Skitch, and be able to keep an eye on the others."

She was none too pleased, and snapped at Beryl. "You make sure you cleans it proper, gel! None of your blowing on the dust and sweeping just up the middle."

"I'd like to go through the accounts now, Mrs. Skitch, while you order some more supplies. Mrs. Thornton has given us a very generous budget for the household."

"Why, I can do us right proud with this!" she said in surprise. "Shortages or no. There's always some to be had for them wot can pay."

Grayson had everyone organized and comfortable with their duties by the time the servants sat down to supper the following evening. They were rather awkward with one another. Mrs. Skitch kept looking askance at the newcomers, as if in disapproval. Beryl couldn't stop sneaking slack-jawed looks at Branwyn's face.

Seated at the head of the table, Grayson said, "We've had a very productive and busy day. Now that we have a few minutes to ourselves, I'm going to tell you something about the family you're serving. I've been butler to Mrs. Thornton's family, the Wyndhams, since before she was born. They and the Thorntons are among the most prestigious and important families in Canada." By the time Grayson had finished, none of them was in any doubt that their Master and Mistress were anything but Canadian aristocracy.

Mrs. Skitch was as puffed up as a pigeon. "Fancy the Master knowing the Prince of Wales at Oxford, and the Mistress being related to the Earl of Leamington and the Marquess of Abbotsford! I knew she were quality the moment I clapped eyes on her."

Enoch, the gardener, chuckled at this about-face.

"Fancy her flying aeroplanes and driving ambulances in France!" Patrick, the footman, said in awe. "And the Master being the Ace I keep reading about in the newspapers! It was my lucky day when I came to visit my old auntie in the village."

"Mrs. Thornton must be quite a compassionate young woman as well," Branwyn said. "With her adopting a French orphan."

"Indeed she is. You should also know that Mrs. Thornton was on the *Lusitania*, where she lost several friends," Grayson said.

"Bless me!" Mrs. Skitch cried. "The poor lass!"

"Were you on board as well, Mr. Grayson?" Branwyn asked.

"Yes. I lost my wife."

"How tragic. I am sorry."

"Unfortunately, there are very few of us these days who haven't been touched by tragedy."

"Will you tell us more about the lake and the islands, Mr. Grayson? They sound ever so lovely," Tilda asked shyly.

"Yes, do, Mr. Grayson," Patrick urged.

He had them wide-eyed with his descriptions of the theatricals and balls, the Stepping Stone Marathon and Regattas, the motorboats, canoes, and moonlight cruises.

"I'd like to see that some day," Tilda said quietly.

"And me!" Patrick said.

"I expect it's not as much fun for the servants," Branwyn said astutely.

"You're quite right," Grayson agreed. "We even have trouble finding staff willing to spend the summer there."

"Maybe I'll emigrate after the war," Patrick said. "Have you ever regretted going there, Mr. Grayson?"

"Never. It's a grand country. Young and exciting. Truly a land of opportunity. So... I hope you'll all remember that we are a team, working together to make this household run smoothly and efficiently, to make it a place where the Major and Mrs. Thornton can be proud to entertain their family and friends. As Mrs. Skitch will have her hands full with cooking these excellent meals and seeing to the household linens and such, you'll all be answerable to me, through Patrick. I'll be in touch with him by telephone frequently, and will visit every few weeks."

Grayson stayed on another day to make sure that they all understood their duties and were able to execute them. Ria was amazed at how quickly the house was transformed. Even Beryl had been spruced up. Not the brightest or most ambitious girl, she seemed content to let Tilda take the lead, and *she* was fastidious, Ria was glad to notice.

It was just at the end of the week, as Ria was accepting a pre-prandial glass of sherry from Chas, that they heard what sounded like an explosion.

"Hell's bells! Is it an air raid?" Ria asked.

Chas opened the French doors off the sunroom and stepped out onto the terrace. "I don't hear any Zeppelins or aeroplanes. It was a bit too loud to be the guns from France." He scanned the heavens. "There's a curious glow from the direction of London."

As there was no additional noise, they didn't think much more about it until they read the papers the next day. The Silvertown munitions factory in London had caught fire, exploding tons of TNT, killing over seventy people, destroying nine hundred properties and damaging seventy thousand more.

"It blew out the windows of the Savoy," Ria read to Chas. "There's speculation that a German spy might have set the fire. Good Lord! I hope that Tilda's sister wasn't at that factory."

She wasn't, but the staff was worried about the threat of espionage. Beryl skittishly went about the house as if she expected Germans to pop out of the woodwork at any moment.

But things had settled down and every room in the house was spotless by the time Beatrice arrived a few days later. Having two officers convalescing at Bovington, she stayed only a few days.

Mrs. Skitch was gratified to be able to entertain Miss Mason, Beatrice's lady's maid, who told Mrs. Skitch about her travels with Lady Kirkland, and all the important people her mistress knew.

During Bea's stay, Ria received a visit from a neighbour, Lady Darlington, whose footman had ascertained that Mrs. Thornton was "at home" before escorting his elderly mistress to the door. She stayed the requisite fifteen minutes, and left her visiting card.

"I presume that means I'm invited and therefore obliged to make a return call. Do advise me, Cousin Bea, since you know how hopeless I am with formalities. I was never 'finished', as you know."

Bea went through the minutiae of rules governing visits and calling cards and other upper class etiquette. "So you need to return Lady Darlington's call within three or four days, otherwise she will consider that you are snubbing her."

"Oh dear. Do you think that if I scandalize her with my flying and ambulance driving, I'll be excused from further visits? I'm really not good at making small talk."

Bea laughed. "You can certainly try."

But as it turned out, Lady Darlington was a bit of a feminist, and most impressed by Ria's adventures. She agreed to host a luncheon with influential friends so that Ria could tell them about the WATS. Surprisingly, Ria raised £100 for the Corps, and one of the young women at the luncheon was interested in joining.

The staff at Priory Manor was thrilled with the succession of illustrious guests. Lady Meredith and Theadora. Lady Sidonie and Quentin, Viscount Grenville. Chas's officers often came to dinner, and Major-General "Boom" Trenchard joined them once.

Ria had to admit that she was rather nervous at his presence, but was soon put at ease when he said with a laugh, "Damn me, but how could we possibly lose the air war if we let beautiful young women like you go up? No man in his right mind would shoot at you."

She said, "I have to tell you, General, that it's as much as I can do to keep my feet on the ground when I hear our aeroplanes overhead." Which she did every fine day. "I would love to try out the new S.E.5 that Chas's squadron is being equipped with. He tells me it has a 150 horsepower engine and goes 130 miles per hour, which means it should be able to out-fly the Albatros. So you see, I'd be quite safe up there," she added with a grin.

The General laughed again. He had a huge voice – and thus his nickname "Boom" – which reverberated throughout the house. "I've heard nothing but complaints about the S.E.5 from these chaps. They'd be going over sooner if Thornton didn't insist on changing the windscreen design."

"It's a greenhouse, not a windscreen, and interferes with forward visibility," Chas said. "And with that rough metal edge so close to the pilot's face, it would be bloody dangerous in a crash."

"Thornton would be designing the ruddy aeroplanes if we gave him half a chance," the General complained.

"And who better than a pilot to tell the engineers what's needed?" Chas riposted. "The S.E.5 will be unbeatable when it gets a bigger engine."

"It's just come off the assembly line..."

"And obviously didn't even get to the Testing Squadron, or they would have rejected it. You know that air superiority inevitably goes to the side that has the best aeroplanes."

The men discussed the pros and cons of the new fighter plane, all agreeing that it was sturdy and reliable, if a bit unwieldy. It could be looped, rolled, and dived without breaking up. Chas made sure his pilots knew the machine intimately, and were skilled at aerobatics.

Over coffee in the billiard room, Trenchard said to Ria privately, "Your husband is not only a brilliant pilot and instructor, but he's also an inspired leader. And we badly need those. You know how pilots are – cocky, reckless, even foolhardy..." He gave her a sidelong glance and a smirk. "... So they don't always make good commanding officers, especially the Aces. But Chas balances that daring with sense and shrewdness. He channels his pilots' high spirits and sets an admirable example, trains them rigorously, and then lets them blow off steam, but not get too wild." He chuckled. "Damn me if I didn't wonder about his sanity when I heard he was scouting for top-notch men who also played an instrument. But now he's got a band as well as a crack crew! And he's got the pilots and most of the ground crew playing cricket as well. He's built a real team. I don't think there's one of them who wouldn't fly into hell itself if he asked them to. That's how much they trust and admire him. Deuced glad he didn't take up my offer of teaching."

"Will you be able to keep Chas from flying missions?"

"He knows the rules."

"But he's also an Ace," Ria reminded him.

"So it'll be your influence more than mine that will keep him grounded."

Watching Chas with his officers, Ria was aware how he had taken all these younger men under his wing, although he himself was only twenty-four. She wondered, as she always did these days, how many of them would be here next year, or the year after, or whenever the war ended. It would be even harder than usual on Chas when any of these bright and eager boys didn't return from their sorties.

If she couldn't fly aeroplanes, Ria was at least exhilarated to be out on Calypso again. The stable lad, Clive, was indeed a natural with horses. Ria asked, "Shouldn't you still be in school, Clive?"

"I can read and write well enough, Ma'am, and do me sums. What would I be needing any more book learning for when I only want to work with horses?"

He put Sophie at ease right away with her pony, Buttercup, which Rafe had brought her. Ria gave her riding lessons, but noticed that Sophie and Johanna spent more time at the stables, talking to the pony, grooming him, learning from Clive. She was glad to see Sophie not only take such an interest, but appear to be blossoming into a happy child.

Max and Freddie, both having been recommended for additional training courses, were still in England and free most weekends. Ria was ecstatic to see them, and Sophie was excited to have another charming cousin. There hardly seemed enough time to catch up on all their news, so the boys promised to visit often.

Ria received a treasure trove of supplies – parcels from Fliss and from Olivia. So they were able to enjoy Mrs. O'Rourke's jam made from Wyndwood Island blueberries, her canned tomatoes, pickles, and relishes, many jars of honey and maple syrup, soda crackers, wheels of cheddar cheese, Quaker Oatmeal, Kellogg's Corn Flakes, plenty of canned tuna, jars of peanut butter, pots of canned meats, a hundred pounds of flour, and several of Mrs. O'Rourke's rum-soaked fruit cakes. Fliss also sent Coca Cola,

Juicy Fruit Gum, Hershey's Kisses, Oreo Cookies, and Life Savers for her new niece.

Olivia wrote, "We've heard how bad the food situation is becoming over there, and hope that this will help. I'll send more next month, so let me know what else might be useful."

Ria persuaded a skeptical Mrs. Skitch to serve pancakes with maple syrup not only to the family, but also to the staff. Most of them took to it, marvelling that sap from trees could taste so delectable. Sophie and Johanna were also introduced to peanut butter and jam, and were soon addicted. Mrs. Skitch was almost scandalized that Ria and the girls sometimes required nothing else for their lunch. She was, however, impressed by the very fine "Canadian jam", which all the staff enjoyed.

Ria regularly received letters from Lance. He kept the tone light and caught her up with acquaintances, weather, activities – all the things that she was "missing". She'd felt awkward writing back to him at first, but he seemed to enjoy her account of domestic trivia because she put such a humorous slant on everything.

Ria read Chas snatches of Lance's letters as she did from her other friends', and he never said anything. He felt once again secure in her love for him, but it did bother him that the fellow wouldn't give her up.

Ria corresponded frequently with her WATS friends, and was surprised by Sybil's letter.

A French lorry, indifferent as they always are to weather, courtesy, and logic, tried to pass Tuppy, who was sensibly crawling along the icy road. It lost control and skidded into her, causing her to somersault into a ravine. Her bus was pretty badly smashed up, but fortunately, not so Tuppy. She does, however, have a black eye and a fractured collarbone, so the poor thing has had to go back to boring old Blighty for at least three months. I expect you'll console each other over watery tea and hardtack, the best food, of course, being sent to us and the troops.

Within a week, Ria had a telephone call from Antonia. "Windy, you must come and rescue me or I shall go mad. Mummy fusses over me and insists I stay in bed, although that isn't at all helpful. We have no interesting visitors, are miles from civilization, my brother and sisters are all away, Mummy refuses to go to our townhouse in London in case of air raids, and there's no one I can talk to who understands!"

So it was arranged that Ria would go and meet Lord and Lady Netherton, stay overnight, and bring Antonia back for a prolonged visit to Priory Manor. She drove the eighty-five miles to Quincy Castle, built by the De Quincys in the 13th century. Some of it lay in ruins, "from the Civil War," Antonia explained. With its towers and crenellations and Elizabethan addition, it was picturesquely beautiful, but rather a forbidding and decidedly chilly place to live. In contrast, Lord and Lady Netherton were warm and charming, if a bit vague. But Ria and Antonia were glad when they were able to escape.

They had agreed that calling each other Tuppy and Windy was fine when they were with the Corps, but that, as friends, Toni and Ria was much preferable. Antonia said, "My mother was always hopeful of producing the requisite son and heir, so we girls were given names that shortened to the rather masculine Georgie, Ronni, and Alex. And Toni, of course, although Mummy never uses anything but our full names. Our brother Bernard we call Bunny." They laughed.

Ria came home to find a new tenant in the house – a beagle puppy that Chas had brought for Sophie. She named him Ace, since he came from Chas and the aerodrome. They were already fast friends, with Ace sleeping on her bed.

"Unlike cats, dogs are needy, and will make her a good companion. Especially when we are gone," Chas explained.

"You're always so thoughtful, Chas."

"I remember how comforting it was to have Snoopy by my side in France. I actually found it a wrench to leave him and Josephine behind, but one of the other chaps took them on."

Antonia stayed for two weeks and then was obliged to return home for a while, but swore she would be back as soon as possible.

Meanwhile, Beatrice called to say that Zoë was quite ill. She'd developed a septic hand, which had required lancing to release the infection, but she was still feverish and in pain, and needed several weeks of nursing care, which Bea couldn't provide. Zoë had refused to go into a civilian hospital.

Ria drove immediately to Bovington. She was shocked to see how swollen Zoë's hand and wrist were beneath the thick bandages. Her temperature had come down a bit from 104°. Ria bundled her up warmly, made her as comfortable a bed as possible in the back seat, and drove cautiously to Priory Manor.

Zoë said weakly, "I was always careful to disinfect my hand whenever I got a cut or a prick, but it's almost impossible not to become infected by all the wounds that we have to deal with. We're sometimes wrist-deep in someone's pus. And I'm not allowed to wear rubber gloves like the Sisters do."

"For God's sake, why ever not?"

"Perhaps because I'm not supposed to be dealing with wounds, but the Sisters can't manage all the dressings without me."

"So to make it look as if you're sticking to the rules, everyone can pretend that you're not encroaching on the professional nurses' territory."

"It does seem rather stupid."

"Well, now they'll just have to do without you for a month or two."

"And I get to ride in a WATS ambulance," Zoë quipped.

Ria put Zoë to bed in the room adjoining hers as soon as they arrived. She was even more distressed when she unbandaged Zoë's hand. It was red, hot, and distended like a balloon that seemed about to burst. There was a deep incision on her wrist, left open to drain the yellow pus.

"I'm supposed to soak it in a saline bath for a few hours a day," Zoë said.

When Ria had her bandaged up again, Zoë said, "Thank you, Nurse Thornton. You're very gentle."

"It's wonderful to have you here, Zoë. I just wish you weren't so ill."

"I'll be better in no time. Don't worry, Ria."

But her fever was still 103° and showed no signs of abating, so Ria called the local doctor, who had nothing new to offer, but told her to keep bathing the wound and giving the patient aspirin and plenty of fluids. Ria was concerned about septicemia, which could be fatal. She checked Zoë carefully to see whether telltale red streaks were moving up her arm. If that happened, amputation would be the only way to stop the deadly spreading of the bacteria. She sent a telegram to Blake.

He wired back, *Irrigate with hypochlorous acid ¼ % solution. Can't leave without going AWOL. Tell her I love her. Keep me informed.*

The acid solution was extremely painful, as Zoë knew only too well for she'd had to use it on men with terrible wounds. Unable to stop her tears, she had a new appreciation for what they suffered.

Branwyn approached Ria and said, "Excuse me, Mrs. Thornton, but might I offer a herbal treatment for your cousin? I can assure you that it will do her no harm, and should help."

"I'm open to all suggestions at this point, Branwyn."

"St. John's Wort reduces swelling and heals wounds. I'll make up a poultice. Also, I have a tea that should give Mrs. Carlyle some ease, and strengthen her system. It contains catmint, dandelion, chamomile, and echinacea."

Ria didn't know whether it was the herbs or the acid or a combination, but was mightily relieved to see that the following day Zoë's hand was less inflamed and that her fever was down. A few days later, her temperature was normal and the swelling was almost gone.

She cabled Blake. *Zoë on mend. St John's Wort and catnip tea also used. You choose. She loves you too.*

"So, now that you really are on the mend, you'll be able to enjoy your convalescence. Blake wired to say that you need at least two months off – doctor's orders, he said. Oh, and once again that he loves you."

Zoë smiled contentedly. "I can hardly wait for him to come back."

Ria thanked Branwyn for her intervention. "Not at all, Ma'am. It's a gift to have the knowledge of the healing herbs, so I share it gladly."

Beatrice and Alice came for a weekend, Alice kipping in with a delighted Sophie. Max, Rafe, and Freddie were also able to come, as well as Jack who was in London for the war art exhibition that Lord Beaverbrook had organized. They would all go up and see it when Zoë was stronger. So the house was filled with activity and laughter. With the new supply of wood for the fireplaces, it wasn't too difficult to keep all the rooms relatively warm, despite the unusually cold and snowy winter.

They skated on part of the lake that Gareth had scraped clean of snow, Ria having bought a supply of blades that could be attached to anyone's boots. She had discovered a hill that made a terrific toboggan run and occasioned much merriment. There was enough packing snow to build a gigantic "snowmonk" under the Gothic arch of a doorway, which was all that remained of one wall of the priory. There were, of course, the inevitable snowball fights. Afterwards they gathered round the drawing room fire for hot toddies and cocoa.

The servants were excited by all the activity, for theirs was a popular and young household, with interesting people coming and going.

Grayson managed to time his visit with Beatrice and the others, and was pleased to see the esprit de corps that had developed among the staff. Even Beryl had become cheerful and took more care and pride in her appearance, perhaps because she had to answer to handsome Patrick.

Grayson took Branwyn aside and said, "I want to thank you for helping Mrs. Carlyle."

"You're fond of your Mistress and her family, Mr. Grayson." It wasn't a question.

"Indeed, I am. I feel an almost fatherly affection for her." He didn't know why he had confessed that, but there was something in Branwyn's hypnotic, gold-flecked green eyes that seemed to invite confidences.

She put him at ease when she said, "I expect that perhaps Mrs. Thornton needed a father figure. I'm not one to think that all the rich are necessarily privileged, nor the poor, disadvantaged, Mr. Grayson."

"Then you are very wise, Branwyn."

She smiled at him and excused herself to go and wash the dinner dishes.

In the drawing room, Ria and Chas were playing piano. Except for Bea and the girls, they all stayed up much too late, talking and reminiscing.

Chas said to Ria, as she lay in his arms later, "You've made this a truly happy household, my darling."

"And until we can go home again, I'd be truly happy to stay here like this, if *you* could."

Ria lay awake long after Chas slept, imagining what it would be like to remain behind once he and the others had returned to France. Torn between her comfortable domestic role and the compulsion to be in the thick of things with her friends.

.   .   .

It was the juxtaposition of the photos that made Eleanor Carlyle realize who Jack's latest lover was. There was the stock picture of Max Aitken, now Lord Beaverbrook, and below his, a newer one of Jack looking handsome and dapper in his uniform. Beside it was a portrait of a sophisticated flapper with sculpted dark hair and a seductive smile. The headline read, "Toronto's RFC Ace Artist Exhibits in Beaverbrook Show".

The story confirmed her speculation. "Captain Jack Wyndham attended the opening of the Beaverbrook War Art Exhibition in

London, England yesterday accompanied by Lady Sidonie Dunston. Lady Sidonie, a renowned society beauty, is the widow of Lieutenant Percy Dunston, son of Montreal shipping magnate, Sir Montague Dunston. Lt. Dunston was one of our many heroic young men who gave his life on the battlefields of France for King and Empire. The event was well attended..."

Rich, aristocratic, and classically beautiful, Lady Sidonie would be just the sort of woman Jack would want as a wife, Ellie thought despondently. She brushed tears away angrily and opened her pathology book.

.   .   .

Antonia returned to Priory Manor for another extended visit. She was still wearing her sling, but was able to take it off for short periods. She and Zoë soon felt like old friends.

Sybil wrote:

Greetings, lead-swingers. I expect that Tuppy is there as well, so will address this to you both. I just wanted to be sure you know what you're missing. Our blankets are sheets of ice. The water pipes have burst from the cold, so we can't wash, let alone bathe. Water is as precious as fuel, and there's hardly enough for tea, so I resorted to taking some out of my radiator the other day just to make a cuppa. You doubt me, do you? Hennie was looking for some relatively clean snow to melt. The roads have heaved from the frosts, making driving even more treacherous. You can't possibly walk on the streets of Calais, as 'efficient' housewives keep chucking their wash water and God knows what other unmentionable effluence out into the street, which is now feet thick with ice. Our coal is at the bottom of the channel again, as is our food. So we subsist on bully beef – did I ever think it was good? Half of us are down with flu, bronchitis, plague, pustules, and hangnails, while you two are lollygagging in your elegant civvies over cream teas and champagne dinners. By God, how I hate you! And wish I were there with you!

They went up to London to stay a few nights at Bea's townhouse and see the war art exhibition. For propaganda purposes, only paintings that depicted the glories of war were exhibited – like Jack's squadron of Nieuports symbolically highlighted by the dawn light against a threatening sky, which he had turned from a sketch into a large canvas. Another of his paintings was an aerial view of skirmishing planes, which nonetheless implied British air superiority. Ria was really proud of Jack, whose work rivaled that of the more experienced and renowned artists. The paintings weren't for sale, but were to become part of Canada's heritage.

Ria commissioned Jack to do a painting for Chas. "Something that will always remind him of the thrill of flying," she stipulated. She would present it to him for his twenty-fifth birthday in June.

Ria and Toni wore their uniforms when they attended a tea given by Sidonie for the WATS. They raised over £300, and Ria felt as if she had earned her time off. They also attended a function organized by Nancy Astor at Cliveden, raising an additional £360.

When they returned to the now familiar comfort of Priory Manor, the women were rather sombre at the thought that this would soon end and they would be thrust back into their hectic and often gruesome war work.

Not that the war was ever far away, even here in the relative peace of the countryside. Chas's squadron constantly flew overhead, which Ria actually found reassuring.

At the end of January, Germany had announced she was resuming unrestricted submarine warfare. On February 3rd, the United States had severed diplomatic relations with Germany. Merchant ships were constantly being sunk – over a hundred and thirty of them in February alone – reducing the food supplies to Britain even more. At the end of the month, it was discovered that Germany had been trying to make an alliance with Mexico, offering Texas, New Mexico, and Arizona as a reward. Ria wondered how much longer the Americans would wait before entering the war.

And she wondered how much longer Chas could remain in their little paradise before his squadron was declared ready for combat.

Max spent every weekend with Zoë, either staying at Priory Manor, or taking her to London to see the popular musicals, like the *Bing Boys*, or to Oxford, to visit Henry. Freddie came occasionally, Ria suspecting that his excuse of wanting to explore England while he had the opportunity was only partly the case. It was undoubtedly difficult for him to see Zoë now that she was lost to him, but she was pleased to hear that he often stopped at Taplow to visit Martha Randall.

Meanwhile, Justin fell into an easy friendship with Antonia during his leave. They chatted about anything and everything like old friends. They went for long walks that Justin said helped to clear the sounds and smells of France from his senses, and Toni maintained were building up her strength. She always insisted on hearing stories about Canada over dinner, and the others never tired of telling them.

"Heavens, I think the Oakleys have more servants at the cottage than we do at Quincy Castle," Antonia said in amazement after hearing about the more than two-dozen staff that tended to Oaktree. Oswald Oakley, one of the Stepping Stone neighbours, was a Pittsburgh steel magnate.

"Oswald will be thrilled to meet you. He kept calling Cousin Bea 'Countess'. And you're the daughter of an Earl, not just the wife. And destined to marry the Prince of Wales," Ria added wickedly.

"Oh, Lord, don't remind me! Not that he isn't a decent chap and all that, but I feel no spark in his presence. Surely we all deserve that, don't we? That spark? Even Earls' daughters?"

Ria noticed Toni glance quickly at Justin, and wondered if she had felt that spark with him. It was his last night of leave, so they had spent almost two weeks together.

"So being the Queen of England and her vast, global Empire doesn't ignite any sort of passion, never mind a spark?" Chas quipped.

"It makes me numb with dread. I couldn't live that kind of rigid, formal, public existence. That's one of the things that appeals to me so much about your life in Canada, especially at the cottage. That sense of freedom. Being able to talk or dance with whomever you choose, and not see it written up in the gossip columns the following day. Fortunately, Diana Manners' parents, the Duke and Duchess of Rutland, have Diana slated to marry the Prince as well, and she is much more suitable than I. Even my sister, Georgina, would be better for him, since she doesn't mind all the pageantry. But I really doubt that the Prince wants a car mechanic for a wife."

"King Edward and Queen Georgie does have a certain *je ne sais quoi*," Zoë said.

Amid the laughter, Ria said, "We'll just have to whisk you off to Canada after the war is over, Toni, to kibosh your mother's schemes."

"I'd be so grateful! Besides, I'd like to win a cup at the Regatta," she said with a grin.

"You mean after we teach you how to canoe and sail," Ria said.

"Of course! I *can* swim. I'm not sure that I'm brave enough to try diving, though."

"It's less dangerous than driving through shell-fire," Justin said with a smile, even more attracted by her self-effacing manner. He had been rather surprised to find himself smitten by her. She was no vapid beauty, but an intelligent, vivacious, and plucky young woman. Not unlike Ria.

.   .   .

"Are you fucking Jack as well?" Rafe asked as he lit a cigarette for Sidonie.

She snorted and said, "You are vulgar and insulting, Rafe. Which both amuses and annoys me." She drew the silk sheets up around her nakedness as she moved away from him.

"Good. Then you won't easily forget me."

"You always were needy. Trying to outdo older brother. Which, I have to tell you, is virtually impossible."

"Even in bed?" he asked, stroking her arm.

"I don't make comparisons."

"But you wanted him, didn't you?"

"Did you want Ria?" she asked shrewdly.

"Hell yes!"

"Then we've both been disappointed."

He laughed. "I think I could love you, Sid. We should get married."

It was her turn to laugh. "You want me to give up my life of solitary, independent luxury for someone who's in love with another woman?"

"Do you think you couldn't make me forget her?"

"More to the point, do I want to try?"

He took the cigarette out of her hand as he moved on top of her.

Rafe didn't stay at Bea's London townhouse, but at the Royal Automobile Club, which was a popular place for Canadian officers. He didn't want anyone keeping track of him, since he'd intended to spend most of his embarkation leave with Sidonie.

He'd thought her a cracker when Chas and Quentin had taken him to Blackthorn during his first year at Oxford, but she had been all starry-eyed for Chas, and he knew that they'd had a passionate affair. Even though Chas obviously and unaccountably hadn't wanted her, Rafe never could understand why Sid had married good old Percy Dunston, who had always hung around on the fringes like an eager puppy waiting for the leavings.

So Rafe had lost no time in contacting Sid when he'd arrived in England. He'd taken her to a nightclub, and she had invited him into her bed. He'd come to London whenever he could.

He'd been livid when he'd seen the photo of Jack and Sid in Beaverbrook's *Daily Express*, and realized that they had been having an affair even before he'd arrived. Damn Jack for having gotten to Sid first! It both disgusted and excited him. He'd show that upstart bastard who was the better man!

He thought momentarily of Lizzie, recalling their passionate kisses. And dismissing her from his thoughts. Breeding did tell. Getting a woman like Sid to marry him would be a coup. She was, after all, touted as being the most beautiful young widow in England.

Rafe was reluctant to leave London, especially as he felt he was making progress with Sid. He had been wooing her with expensive jewellery and promises of what they could do and have together after the war – winters on the Riviera, summers in Muskoka, shopping in Paris.

"We're not in love, Rafe. You want me because other men do. Like Jack. I gather there's no love lost between you, so 'winning' me would be a way of thumbing your nose at him."

"How could you think that, Sid? I long for you when we're not together. You're incredibly beautiful and desirable and I'm proud to be at your side. We have fun together. I want to lay the world at your feet. Isn't that love?"

"That's lust and acquisitiveness. I'd be like one of your prize race horses."

He laughed. "I swear I love you more than my horses."

"I suppose that's saying a lot. In any case, I couldn't live in Canada. I'd miss Blackthorn too much."

"I could become an English gentleman, buy a country estate where you'd be the most sought-after society hostess, and I'd breed horses that would win Ascot every year."

"We could restore Blackthorn," she said hopefully.

"That pile of rubble? It would gobble up even my rather considerable inheritance."

"Pity."

"It's not yours anyway, Sid. Quentin needs to do what he can with it if he really wants to squander his money. With any luck, the Germans will drop a bomb on it."

"You're hateful!"

"And you're foolish to think that that decrepit old house is your life. Grow up."

"You *are* hateful!" she said.

Sex after that was even more intense.

So Rafe went reluctantly to Priory Manor to say goodbye.

Chas hadn't been allowed to recruit his novice brother for his squadron, which he had wanted to do just to keep an eye on him. Rafe was being posted to Chas's old 60 Squadron, but there was probably no one left from his time with them. He said to Rafe, "I'm surprised that you were posted to a fighter squadron without first having to pay your dues as a recce pilot."

"Who the hell wants to be a sitting duck? Anyway, it seems that my training in Texas has given me an edge, and I'm top of the class in aerobatics at least." He smirked at Ria.

"I'm not happy that you'll be flying the Nieuport," Chas said. "It's already obsolete, underpowered, and its lower wings have a tendency to break off in a high-speed dive."

"I know. I've been training on it," Rafe said laconically. "It is pretty nimble, though."

"Which is its only advantage over the Hun scouts. So watch your back. Remember what I've taught you. Don't get cocky. And don't ever go up hung-over. That's deadly."

"I see you have a very high opinion of my character and abilities, dear brother."

"It's my responsibility as an older brother to lecture you." Chas was afraid for Rafe. He was just the person to lose concentration when he had a victory or otherwise indulged in hubris.

"And mine as a younger brother to outdo you."

"Just stay alive. That's hard enough to do these days." Chas hadn't meant to be so blunt, but Rafe sometimes needed shaking up.

Rafe laughed. "Take your own advice, big brother."

.   .   .

Ria was giving Sophie a piano lesson when Patrick came into the drawing room and said, "Might I have a word, Ma'am?"

"Yes, of course."

"Mrs. Skitch has caught Clive stealing from the pantry. She's given him a cuff round the ear, but thinks he should be dismissed. Shall I bring him up?"

"I'll come downstairs and find out what this is all about. Clive seems such a nice boy."

"He is very good," Sophie said, alarmed that her friend was in trouble. She already had quite a command of English. "The horses like him very much."

"I'm sure there's a misunderstanding," Ria assured her. "You keep practicing, ma petite."

As they walked down the hallway, Patrick said to Ria, "I heard that Clive's father was killed last month. He was a merchant seaman. His ship was torpedoed by a German sub."

"Poor lad."

In the servant's hall, Clive was sitting in a chair, head down, red-faced, while Mrs. Skitch was standing over him berating him as she waggled a wooden spoon at him. "I've never seen such ungratefulness! Stealing from people who's giving you a fair wage and a decent meal! Whatever is the world coming to, I ask you?"

"What's happened, Mrs. Skitch?" Ria asked.

"Oh, Madam! I caught this little blighter stealing a loaf of bread and a hunk of cheese from me larder!"

"Why did you do that, Clive?" Ria asked. "If you were hungry, I'm sure Mrs. Skitch would have given you something if you'd asked her." Ria wasn't at all sure, but thought that Mrs. Skitch might get the message.

"T'weren't for me, Ma'am," Clive said quietly. "T'were for me family. They're starving, Ma'am, and here's me getting a fine feed every day."

"And not eating half of it," Branwyn said as she joined them. "I've seen you squirreling a goodly portion of it into your pockets."

Clive was stick thin, with ragged, unwashed hair that stood up like random porcupine quills, and soft brown eyes that rivaled the beagle's.

Ria pulled out a chair and sat opposite him. "Tell me about your family," she coaxed.

"I've got two brothers and four sisters, all younger. Baby died last week cause me Mam said there weren't enough milk. She's been right poorly, Mam has, and with Dad gone there ain't no one but me working. We're that worried about our Jenny now as she's got a right terrible cough."

"What have they been eating?"

"Bread and scrape or marg mostly, potatoes when we can get them. So I've been bringing bits of cake and sausage and such from me dinner here. There wasn't nothing wrong with that, was there, Ma'am? It was on me plate."

Ria could see him holding back tears.

"No, Clive. But you should have told us how bad things were at home. We're going to put together a basket of food for you to take, and Mrs. Skitch will see that you have one every day."

Mrs. Skitch nodded. "Bread and scrape! And here's the government telling folk to cut down on the bread they eat as if they had anything else!" she said, referring to the new Food Controller's appeal for voluntary rationing.

Branwyn said, "Clive's family aren't the only ones here abouts who are going hungry, what with bread being double the price now."

"We'll just have to do something about that!" Ria declared. "What would be a nourishing and relatively inexpensive meal we could put together for the poor?"

Branwyn said, "Most folk aren't used to anything fancy and wouldn't thank you for it. A thick stew with a bit of meat and plenty of potatoes and veg would go down a treat."

"Cabbage soup with bacon," Mrs. Skitch added. "And oxtail soup."

"Excellent! I'll leave you to plan some meals, Mrs. Skitch. Then you can order ingredients while I talk to the vicar about setting up a soup kitchen. I'm sure he can find some women to cook in the village hall at least three or four times a week."

Branwyn said, "May I point out, Ma'am, that folk are too proud to admit that they're starving, and won't take kindly to charity."

Ria felt that Branwyn was speaking from experience. "Then we'll charge a penny per meal."

"There are some who can't even afford that."

Ria was truly shocked. "I'll have to think about that. In the meantime, I'm going to send the doctor to see to your mother and sister, Clive, and I'll make sure that he's paid, so you're not to worry about that."

Clive burst into tears. Branwyn put her arm about his shoulder and said, "I'll send some herbs for your sister to ease her cough. You make her up some tea with it, alright?"

He nodded, and she handed him a handkerchief before he could wipe his nose in his sleeve.

Sophie, who had been anxious about Clive, was reassured by Ria's news that he wouldn't be dismissed, but sad to hear about children going hungry. She asked, "Can't they grow their own food? Have a cow and chickens, like we do?" She liked to watch

Branwyn milking and to help feed the chickens, which were silly and funny.

"Of course!" Ria said. "How clever you are, Sophie!"

They joined Zoë, who was reading in the sunroom, and discussed the idea with her.

"We'll buy more animals, and as soon as the weather allows, we'll turn some of the flower gardens and parkland on the estate into vegetable plots," Ria said. "The village children will be invited to help and be able to take home a share of the produce and a small wage. We'll call it the Children's Victory Farm. And as part of their payment, the children can bring their families to the soup kitchen for meals, starting right away. Anyone can come, of course, as I expect there will be some families where the children are too young to help out."

"And there'll be the elderly," Zoë pointed out. "It's a terrific idea, if you can make it work,"

Ria discussed it with Enoch. He guffawed. "Cor blimey, Ma'am, but you have some strange notions! What will Mrs. Prendergast think of you turning her lawns into veggies?"

"Not strange at all, Enoch. Even the King has decreed that potatoes and cabbages will be grown instead of flowers at Buckingham Palace and the royal parks. We can't allow the Germans to starve us into defeat, can we?"

"Course not, Ma'am."

"So we must make the best use of the land and other resources. We'll hire more help for you. I'm sure there are boys and girls who could work after school and in the summer. Once you've trained them, they can supervise the younger volunteers. What would be reasonable to pay them?"

"Farm workers earn about a pound a week, but thems long days. So youngsters can't be making more than a penny for an hour's work. A ha'penny for the wee ones."

"It seems so little."

"You and the Major have been right generous with the wages, Ma'am. I expect Mrs. Prendergast won't be thanking you for that, since she weren't paying us anywheres close."

"So you'll all quit once we leave?" Ria asked with a grin.

He chuckled. "I reckon we'll be looking on this as a war bonus. It's right decent of you to be doing this for the young 'uns, Ma'am."

"Not at all! Now what about rabbits? We must have plenty. We should set traps."

He chortled. "Aye, and invite the local poachers to come and help."

"If necessary. We don't want rabbits eating all the vegetables."

"Right you are, Ma'am."

So rabbit stew was added to the menu.

Ria and Zoë went to the vicarage to make arrangements, the vicar assuring them that he would find parishioners to run the soup kitchen. Then they called upon Ria's more affluent neighbours, like Lady Darlington, to enlist their monetary support. A few of the ladies were eager to help out as well.

Not so Mrs. Lyddle, whose husband was a squire, which meant he owned lots of land which was leased as small acreages to farmers who earned a pittance after paying the squire his dues. She said, "You mustn't indulge the poor, Mrs. Thornton. They take advantage. Always whining about something. There's no excuse for country families to be starving, as you call it. If there's not enough food on the table it's because of their laziness or because they drink it away in the pub. You'll get no support from me! It's enough that we're struggling to get the rents out of our tenants, especially with so many of the men gone to war and the women thinking they can just sit pretty."

"I'm sure you have no idea what it's like to be hungry, Mrs. Lyddle," Ria said sarcastically, for the lady was bursting her ample corsets. "But I would expect some compassion for those less fortunate."

"Then you are deluded, Mrs. Thornton. And you needn't regard me in that sanctimonious, self-righteous manner. Who are you to come into our community and criticize us? I will thank you to leave."

"Gladly, Mrs. Lyddle."

When Ria had calmed down on the journey home, she and Zoë laughed, Zoë saying, "Who would ever have accused you of being sanctimonious and self-righteous?"

While they had been gone, Sophie and Johanna had been to the stables, and given Clive rolls of Life Savers, Oreo cookies, and maple sugar candy that Fliss kept sending her.

"He said he shouldn't ought to take any more from us, but I told him he must, because I have too much," Sophie told Ria.

"That was very kind of you, ma petite."

Sophie smiled happily.

When Chas came home that evening, Zoë said to him, with a grin, "Ria's adopted an entire village now, Chas."

He burst into laughter and replied, "Why am I not surprised?"

"I'm terrifically proud of her," Zoë said. "Just wait until Ellie hears."

"I never thought I'd be lauded for my social conscience. But really, how can people survive with so little? I've already cabled Fliss and asked her to send even more supplies." Unfortunately her last shipment had gone to the bottom of the ocean, but Fliss continued to send weekly food parcels nonetheless.

Ria took the girls with her the day the soup kitchen opened. Mrs. Skitch was there for the first day to supervise the cooking. They added the new war bread, which was made with various grains and potatoes to make the scarce wheat go further. It wasn't at all popular, or particularly appetizing, but it was wholesome and filled the stomach.

The villagers were animated as they discussed the communal farm, having committed themselves fully to the idea, especially after Ria made a brief speech. They were a community, pulling together, doing their bit for the war effort, refusing to be defeated by the Germans. Children loved the idea of being able to help, especially when Ria called them "home-front soldiers". She gave each family who signed on a shilling, worth twelve pennies, which she claimed was a special bonus for all her new employees.

A stooped, elderly man shuffled up to Ria and said with a chuckle, "I ain't exactly a young 'un, but I'd be that pleased to help out at the farm. Spent all me life working on one. Reckon I can teach them a thing or two."

"By all means," Ria replied, happy to see such enthusiasm. A couple of his cronies also signed on.

On the fringes were some teenaged boys who nudged each other and laughed insolently.

· · ·

"A letter from Fliss and one from your mother," Ria said to Chas over breakfast. "Which shall I read first?"

"Let's hear Fliss's version," he replied with a grin.

Dear Chas and Ria,

Just dashing off a line so that I can add this to Mummy's letter. PLEASE can you convince her that she and I are desperately needed there? So many of my classmates have stopped coming to school because we're not learning much that's useful in this last year – except for those few who are trying for university – and war work is so much more relevant and important! And some of the girls HAVE gone to England to be with their brothers. Penelope Dupont and her sister are there right now with their parents and staying until their brother is out of hospital. Four months at least, she thinks. Venetia Norton and her mother decided to spend the rest of the war there, since she, Venetia that is, has two brothers at the Front. She and her mother are doing their volunteer work in IODE canteens and the London Maple Leaf Clubs, serving meals alongside Princess Patricia. We could do that too!!!

"They certainly could, you know," Ria said, interrupting her reading.

Marjorie Thornton was on the national executive committee of the Imperial Order Daughters of the Empire. Ria had always been impressed with how modest her mother-in-law was about her very able leadership in this, the largest women's organization in the British Empire. Quietly capable, she had contributed much to their success over the past decade, despite her frail health. Fliss, also heavily involved with the IODE, had learned well from her mother.

"I can imagine Fliss throwing herself wholeheartedly into the war effort here," Ria added. "Aunt Olivia will send us parcels, and a change of scene might be good for your mother."

"I agree, but Mumsy doesn't like to stray too far from home or the cottage. She has great ideas and enthusiasms, but limited energy."

Marjory became winded and tired easily, with debilitating pains in her joints and muscles, which baffled the doctors. It seemed as if her energetic children had sucked some of the life force from her at their births. Ria had already discovered that her mother-in-law greatly downplayed her disability, and masked it with humour and admirable strength of character.

She read on.

Pater says we're doing valuable war work here, and that England, with the food shortage, doesn't need more mouths to feed, but that's a lame excuse!

I long SO MUCH to see you again, and to meet my niece before she is much older. I'm sure you could convince them to let ME, at least, come over. Won't you try?

Your desperately sad, frustrated, anxious, and extremely impatient sister, Fliss!

"Oh dear, I do wish Fliss could join us," Ria said. "Let's try to persuade your parents to let her come!"

Chas smiled. "Yes, alright."

"So let's see what your mother has to say."

My dearest darlings,

To tell you yet again that we miss you dreadfully will be no news to you, so let me say that we talk joyfully about when you will be home again and we can resume our lives.

Fliss continues to pester that we should go over to England. I know that we could do much good work there, but I do not think that I am up to the ocean voyage, and I would be devastated if Fliss were to leave me as well. My anxiety about you rather preys upon me.

"Which means that it's making her more ill," Chas explained with concern.

"So we can't help Fliss after all."

But we mustn't be gloomy! So let me tell you about our latest venture. The IODE is setting up a club for Canadian nurses in the London townhouse of Lady Minto. I expect you children won't really remember when the Earl was Governor General, but he and the Countess were such dears, and enjoyed their time in Canada so much.

The Daughters felt that there are hundreds of nurses, so far from home, who would benefit from having a safe and congenial place to stay and meet fellow Canadians. They don't all have the benefit of having relatives like Lady Beatrice to look after them, and we've heard that hotels in London charge outrageous prices.

Pater and I are supplying the furnishings, so be a dear, Ria, and organize this, as you did such a tremendous job with Thameshill. I heard that the Duke and Duchess of Connaught were most impressed when they visited it last fall. We could certainly use someone with your experience to run this place, so do consider that as well, my dear.

"Did you tell her?" Ria demanded.

"I may have mentioned it. Meredith and Grayson both told me what the Royals had said," Chas replied.

Ria eyed him suspiciously. "And did you put your mother up to this? Trying to keep me out of the trenches, so to speak?"

He laughed. "Mumsy is quite capable of her own machinations. She cares about your safety, you know."

Ria was somewhat mollified. "I can certainly put things in place before I return to Calais." Her challenging look assured him that she *was* still going back.

It's propitious that the Minto townhouse is virtually next door to Lady Beatrice's.

*I heard from Olivia that Zoë is not having an easy time of it at
the Taplow hospital, so I do think she should consider working at
our Red Cross officers' hospital, which is also not far from
Beatrice's townhouse. We've been told it's one of the finest in
London! I have it on good authority that Zoë's skill at massage
would be most appreciated there. Do persuade her to at least
consider the move.*

"Well?" Ria asked Zoë.

"I have no loyalty to Taplow. It's quite evident that Matron
doesn't want VADs on her staff, especially ones with influential
friends who pulled strings to put us there. She was most annoyed
with me for getting a septic hand, ranting on at me about the
carelessness of do-gooders playing at nursing. A place where I
would be appreciated would be a nice change," Zoë said wryly.
"But with the understanding that I want to work in France, and
that London may just be temporary."

*And be a dear, Chas, and visit there when you're next in
London. It would be so good for the morale of the patients. I know
you somewhat dislike your celebrity, but it helps many people by
inspiring them and making them proud Canadians. As a "hero"'
you have responsibilities, my dear boy, whether you like that or not.
Another of those is to come back to us. We need to know that we
really are winning the war and not losing all our best and brightest
in the process.*

Your loving and devoted mother

Ria sent a cable to Marjorie, and she and Zoë went to London
the next day to begin the transformation of Lady Minto's
townhouse into a hostel. They also visited the Daughters of the
Empire Red Cross Hospital, and were impressed with the facility.
Zoë thought she would enjoy working there.

As they ambled through Hyde Park on their way back to Bea's,
Ria said, "I know that you had ambitions, Zoë. But what would I
have done if this war hadn't happened?"

"Had fun?" Zoë suggested.

"And less work."

"And a Grand Tour."

"How we'd looked forward to that! It can never be the same
now, can it? We'll be touring battlefields and cemeteries instead."

"Why don't you consider staying here and running the nurses'
club, Ria?" Zoë suggested. "You don't have to endanger yourself to
feel that you're contributing. Blake says that a lot of the chaps at
the Front are disdainful of those who have safer jobs behind the

lines, but they're important too. How would the soldiers carry on if they didn't have capable people supplying them with food, ammunition, clean water, and so on?"

Ria laughed. "Did I not distinctly hear you say that you were determined to go to France?"

"Not because I think nursing here is less important." Zoë grinned. "Just so that I can be closer to Blake."

"Precisely!"

"But don't tell me that you don't relish courting danger," Zoë challenged.

"I loathe this war and hate admitting that I also find it thrilling. Have you noticed how gay and lively London is?"

"In the face of death, we live more intensely."

"And take nothing for granted. Let me tell you how much I've come to appreciate a soft bed and a hot bath! Do you think we'll look back on these as the 'good old days'?"

"I sincerely hope not!"

.   .   .

Ria was awakened by the shrill voice of Mournful Mary, but it was impossibly difficult to extricate herself from the seductive warmth of her bed.

"It's barges, Windy!" Carly said. "Buck up!"

Ria groaned. Barges in the middle of an air raid!

By the time she pulled on her uniform, the others had gone. She plodded into the frozen pre-dawn darkness, and saw the last of the phalanx of ambulances swallowed by the night. Why hadn't they waited for her?

Hurry, it's barges! The men will die if you're not quick enough, careful enough.

She peered through the eerie twilight as she coaxed Calypso II down the road. Which way had they gone? She would take the left fork. Not so fast! She couldn't see far enough ahead. She might plunge into the canal.

The silence was creepy. Where were the planes? The bombs? The other ambulances?

Where was the road? She was suddenly careening between the black crosses that stretched to the horizon. She couldn't stop, and panicked as she pumped the unresponsive brake pedal.

Finally the ambulance stalled in mud. Emerging from the colourless gloom ahead was Priory Manor. Thank God she was home! They would help her push Calypso II out of the churned up lawn. She had to get to the barges. The others would be expecting her.

Patrick perched like a stork on the portico, unable to move, looking helpless with his one trouser leg empty and tied up behind him. Clive was digging among the crosses in the garden, oblivious to her presence as he foraged for rotten potatoes and carrots, tossing away the skulls and bones that oozed up from the graves.

Beryl peered out from behind Patrick and yelled, "Shut the door! She's a spy! Don't even speak proper, she don't."

Gareth was pushing Sophie on the rope swing he had made for her, suspended from an ancient oak tree. Sophie was shrieking with fear as she flew too high, but Gareth couldn't hear her or Ria's cries to stop.

She tried frantically to get out of the ambulance but the doors were stuck fast. She'd have to climb out the back. But when she raised the canvas, Tom, her former footman, leered at her. Blood was dripping from his ears and from the gash that split his skull. "Thought I was dead, eh? You can't get rid of me, bitch, although you keep trying."

"Mummy Ria! Make him stop!"

"Barges, Windy! Barges!"

A squadron of aeroplanes flew over. Was Chas coming to help her?

"Look, she's brought the Huns!" Beryl cried as the planes dropped bombs on Priory Manor. It collapsed like a house of cards.

"Noooo!"

Tom grabbed her. "You can't escape this time."

She fought to free herself from his punishing grasp, sobbing, gasping.

"Ria! It's alright," Chas said, holding her to still her thrashing. "It's just a nightmare."

She stopped struggling and relaxed against him. "Thank God!"

Chas stroked her soothingly as he cradled her in his arms. "Do you want to tell me about it?"

"Priory Manor was being bombed," she said, not caring to elaborate.

"I ensured that it was sufficiently far away from military targets before I rented it, so we should be safe here, my darling."

"Yes." But sleep eluded her as she pondered the dream.

·   ·   ·

Freddie had a week's embarkation leave. Ever the architect, he visited medieval villages, castles, and cathedrals, stopped in to see Martha Randall at Taplow, and then called Ria to ask if he might spend his last few days at Priory Manor.

The bitter winter was relinquishing its icy grip on the lengthening days. Zoë was regaining her strength and the dexterity in her hand, which had been somewhat numb and clumsy. So while Ria went riding, she and Freddie wandered the country lanes.

He always sketched buildings that he found interesting – "for future reference" – and explained the architecture to Zoë. His fervour and reverence for his craft were infectious.

"I expect that you and Martha have lots to talk about. She seems determined to become an architect," Zoë said.

"She's certainly keen and already well read. Having grown up around clever and ambitious women..." like you, his glance said, "I'm sympathetic to those who are thwarted in their goals. Although, I have to say that Martha would find it a vulgar environment, being the only woman amongst all those puerile, boorish engineering students. I expect that's what the university thought as well."

"We delicate women mustn't be subjected to coarse language or ribald humour," she said wryly. "But I doubt that Martha would let that deter her. Remember that she has three brothers who are engineers. And it's probably not much worse than what Ellie had to put up with in medical school."

'True enough. What about you, Zoë? Will you finish your degree when you return to Toronto?"

"Perhaps. Although I find providing massage therapy both medically interesting and truly helpful to patients. It seems to me that lots of men will need physical rehabilitation for some time after this war ends. More important than having someone reading to them in German or French," she added with a self-deprecating grin.

He chuckled. "Particularly German. Although Goethe did refer to architecture as 'frozen music', which I've always liked."

"What *frozen music* are you longing to create?"

He leaned against a fence and looked across a greening field toward the distant village and church spire. "Beautiful buildings that give people pleasure to took at, and are practical and comfortable to use. Something that I hope will be around and enjoyed long after I'm gone. That's what I love about England – all the picturesque and exquisite buildings that have stood for centuries and yet are still functional. Or even the ruins, like those in the Priory Manor garden, that hint at former grandeur and elegance. I feel some odd connection to the craftsmen who put not only their skill and artistry into their work, but also their passion, their very souls. Isn't that a rather grand legacy to leave?"

"It certainly is! Not many of us can aspire to that."

As if extracting himself from a self-indulgent reverie, Freddie said, "I expect that sounds terribly arrogant. But I don't want to end up with just my name on a cross. Like Archie. If he even has a grave."

Sensing his sorrow and trepidation, Zoë put her hand reassuringly on his arm.

"I'm sorry to have become so maudlin," he apologized. "But I always thought that Archie was going to achieve great things. Become a learned judge or Prime Minister or someone who was going to make a difference in the world. He was the most fair-minded, logical person I've ever met. It's such a bloody waste!"

"Archie did achieve something great – he inspired you, and, I daresay, Emma and Arthur and Maud and Hazel as well," she said, referring to his siblings.

"And Cliff Sinclair. It was because of Archie's enthusiasm that Cliff took up law, not just because he was expected to step into the family business." Zoë had met the Sinclairs often in the summers, since Cliff's father was Senator Spencer's law partner. "But now we've lost him, too. Emma's devastated, of course. They were to become engaged when he finished his law degree. Instead, he's lying somewhere on the Somme."

Zoë allowed herself only a brief, terrifying moment to imagine being in Emma's shoes – losing a brother and her sweetheart. She knew that Emma had been in love with Cliff for years, and would have been surprised if they *hadn't* planned to marry. "How is she coping?"

"She's buried herself in her studies. I wish I could be with her, but I don't suppose there's much any of us can really do to help."

"Except that you have an added responsibility to come back to us."

Freddie smiled gratefully at her.

Max was the next to go. He spent his entire leave with Zoë.

Then Chas received his orders. Ria spent every moment of that last week with him. And it disappeared too quickly, no matter that she hardly slept.

It was infinitely harder to think of his leaving after they received a letter from Troy informing them that his brother Kurt had been shot down and died of his wounds before reaching hospital. Ria recalled how they had joked at Christmas about their proposed flying escapades in Muskoka after the war. She spent most of that day bursting into tears. Kurt had not even turned twenty yet.

As they lay in bed on their last night, Ria said, "Don't be heroic anymore, Chas. Sophie and I need you. Just do your duty and let the others achieve glory as Aces."

"In my great maturity, I realize I have nothing left to prove, either to myself or to my father or to anyone else. But you know that I also lead by example. I can't stay safely behind the lines all the time. I need to be sure that the men are flying strategically, that they don't forget their training." When she started to protest he stopped her with a kiss and said, "But I promise I won't go on patrol more than necessary."

"Beautifully vague way of getting out of that argument," she said sarcastically.

"And what's your excuse for deliberately putting yourself in danger by returning to France?"

"So that we can be together when you have time off." She couldn't voice her superstition that by being as close as possible to him, she could keep him safe.

"Not good enough. If you want to make Sophie and me happy, you'll stay here. Then I won't have to worry about you."

He was hopeful in that moment when she didn't instantly respond.

Ria was terribly tempted to remain at Priory Manor. Quietly she said, "You and all my friends will be in France. I don't want to be left behind."

"We all delight in the sanctuary you provide here, my darling, whether we're on leave or convalescing. You know how important that is, and so is what you've done at the Club and for the children in the village. And you're a mother now."

"I know, Chas. But I feel as if I'll be letting my friends down if I don't return. I'm good at my job. Surely you understand. It's why you left me once."

He winced, although she hadn't said it in an accusatory way.

She put her hand on his cheek and promised, "When you come back, I will too."

Her sleep was once again disturbed by a nightmare. This time she was sitting in her ambulance on the shore of the lake in Muskoka, near the Country Club. The Stepping Stone islands stretched away from her towards Wyndwood. Ellie paddled by, but didn't see her. All her other friends and family skimmed happily about in sailboats and canoes. She had no boat, so she would have to swim to Wyndwood. But her heavy uniform pulled her down, and the islands hovered perpetually, tauntingly out of reach. She was losing her strength, flailing in the water. Suddenly her feet touched bottom and she was back in the shallows along the mainland shore. Edgar zipped past in his speedboat, laughing, ignoring her wild waving and shouting.

"They can't hear you," Montgomery Seaton said smugly as he perched on a rock nearby, smoking a cigarette. "You should have taken heed. I warned you."

Ria awoke with a start and reached gratefully for Chas. He didn't awaken as she nestled against him. He was the only one she hadn't seen at the lake.

Sleep eluded her, but she dreaded the dawn.

· · ·

Ria took Zoë and Sophie along to see Chas off. Grayson, who was staying for a few days, said to her, "I would very much like to see the Major flying. Might I accompany you to the aerodrome, Mrs. Thornton?"

"Why, of course, Grayson," Ria said in surprise. She didn't know that he had planned his visit to be at her side when Chas left. Quietly, unobtrusively, he looked after her, so that she was rarely aware that his concern and affection were more parental than custodial.

At the aerodrome, Chas and the eighteen pilots in his squadron, dressed in their leather coats, sheepskin boots, fur-lined flying helmets, and silk scarves, were doing the final checks on their machines. Chas had instructed them all to be well rested and sober, because he was determined that they would be the first squadron to arrive at their overseas aerodrome without losing a single machine. It wasn't necessarily pilot error that caused broken planes to be scattered along the route, but they had fine-tuned their machines and had become one with them.

The aeroplanes were lined up in three groups, each in the charge of a Flight Commander, whose machine was identified by the streamers attached to its rudder. They would have been even more beautiful had it not been for the pair of deadly machine guns aboard each that reminded her what these scouts' true purpose was.

The squadron called themselves "The Flying Dragons", and each aeroplane had a red and black dragon painted on the side, as well as the RFC roundel and each individual pilot's insignia. Chas's, of course, was a dragonfly.

He hugged Sophie and Zoë, shook Grayson's hand, and gave Ria a long and passionate kiss. The crew clapped and whistled. His eyes held a promise as he stroked her cheek and said, "I'll see you in France, my darling."

Then he and the others climbed into their cockpits and adjusted their goggles. The mechanics spun the props. Chas signaled for "contact", and there was a sudden roar of engines and vibrating wires, and the sharp smell of smoky oil as the 'dragons' sprang to life. Chas opened up his throttle and taxied down the runway. The others followed, lifting gracefully into the air where they took formation – three arrowheads following one bold leader. In unison they dipped their right wings as a salute, a final farewell, and grew ever smaller as they flew into the sun.

In the rude silence of their departure, Ria stood with tears glistening on her cheeks, thinking of the magnificence of the squadron in their shiny new aeroplanes, the fresh-faced, eager boys who had often sat at her table for lighthearted evenings, bursting with pride for her beloved who mentored them like a caring older brother. And praying for them all to return.

Sophie squeezed Ria's hand and said, "C'est magnifique! Daddy Chas is a good pilot, Mummy Ria."

Ria tried to choke back her tears. Zoë put her arm about her shoulder. "Sophie is right. Chas is a good pilot. He'll be careful."

Grayson said, "That was a thrilling sight. We're all very proud of the Major. Now, perhaps I might be so bold as to offer to drive us back, Mrs. Thornton." He chuckled at her surprise. "I've learned to drive. A most useful skill."

"Thank you, Grayson. What would I do without you?" She gave him a grateful smile.

"You won't have to concern yourself with that until I'm put out to pasture." As he was only fifty-two, he hoped that would be a long time in coming.

Ria had decided to delay her return to France until the end of April or even May – at least until the Victory Farm was well established and all the crops had been sown.

But she didn't have much time to brood after Chas left. The following day Tilda, the parlour maid, was informed that her fiancé had been killed. Ria suggested she go home for a few days, but the girl ran tearfully to her room.

The next morning, as Ria was heading for the sunroom, she heard a scream and a commotion from the back stairwell. She rushed over to find Branwyn and Patrick bending over Tilda, who lay crumpled at the bottom of the stairs. Ria thought how child-like she looked.

"Tilda?" Patrick touched her gingerly.

"Can you take her into the morning room?" Ria inquired after she had examined her and ascertained that nothing was broken.

Patrick picked Tilda up easily. "I can carry her upstairs."

"Are you certain?"

"Yes, Ma'am."

"Then take her to one of the spare bedrooms. That way the doctor won't have so far to go."

He struggled up the stairs, and Ria held her breath, expecting him to tumble down. But he made it to the second floor. By now, Zoë was there as well, so she made Tilda comfortable while Patrick was instructed to telephone the doctor. Who was out on a call.

Zoë said, "I expect the poor girl is suffering from shock and exhaustion, as I expect she cried all night." Tilda's face was swollen and stained with tears. "I can't bear this, Ria! Seeing all this misery. Hoping it will never be me lying there prostate with grief!"

Ria and Zoë clung to each other as if they could forever hold on to this moment of safety.

Branwyn offered to sit with Tilda, saying to Ria, "I'm aware that Tilda is five months gone with child. She came to me for advice. I fear for her at the moment."

It was a few hours later that Tilda miscarried. When the doctor arrived, he prescribed bed rest, affirmed that she hadn't broken anything, and took the fetus away.

Branwyn secretly disposed of the bloody sheets, and if some linens went missing from the household inventory, Mrs. Skitch would attribute it to her lax housekeeping and just buy more.

Ria wondered if Tilda had deliberately thrown herself down the stairs, or whether it had been, in some ways, a fortunate accident.

. . .

There was another tearful farewell when Zoë returned to Taplow. She had already requested a transfer to the IODE hospital in London to coincide with Blake's leave in May, allowing her two weeks off between jobs. She and Blake would stay at Priory Manor, and supervise the farm project. Children came daily to help out with the three new cows and dozens more chickens. They mucked out the barn, learned how to milk, fed the animals, and were grateful for the ha'penny and the "Canadian" candies or cookies that were sent home with them. Usually there were eggs to take as well, and always a bottle of milk, fresh from the cow. The older ones, who had been hired on for a few hours a day, had already built more chicken coops and were helping Gareth work the new garden that Ria had had ploughed up on the extensive front lawn.

Having decided that Enoch mustn't bother too much with flowers when there was so much else to do and supervise, Ria was in the "ruins" garden one sunny afternoon cutting down the dried tops of perennials. She was alarmed to hear a child's shrill scream, and jumped to her feet. As she bolted towards the stable, Sophie came running from it crying, "Mummy! Mummy! They're hurting them!" Ace was bounding along beside her, barking furiously.

"What's happening?" Ria grabbed her for a quick, reassuring hug.

"Big boys. They hit Clive and they're hurting Johanna!"

"Go and fetch Gareth. He's in the front garden. Then get Patrick. And you stay in the house!"

What Ria saw when she entered the stable sent a shiver of fear down her spine. Clive was lying unconscious in a corner, a graze on his cheek, while one of three boys, aged about sixteen or seventeen, had Johanna pulled up hard against him, her arm twisted behind her. He was saying, "All French girls are whores, so we've heard. Let's see what you've got." The others laughed. Ria was horribly reminded of Tom the footman, and felt that familiar and paralyzing panic threatening to snatch her breath.

Calypso was whinnying and stomping in agitation.

"Release her this instant!" Ria demanded angrily, trying not to show her fear.

But the ruffian just laughed. "The bountiful Lady Muck, is it? Swan around like you owns the village now. But you can't tell *me* what to do. I might let the little French tart go if you was to fork over some of that luverly brass you're rolling in. But not till I've had me kiss."

Johanna tried to struggle out of his grasp. Ria grabbed a pitchfork just as Gareth stormed into the barn. His rage was all the more powerful for being silent. Tall and strong, he was more manly than the weasely boys who were his age. They were suddenly less cocky and backed away as Gareth strode up to the chief offender and grabbed his arm with lightning speed, pushing it painfully up his back. He'd already released Johanna, who fled to Ria's side with a sob.

"Let go! You're hurting me, you fucking moron!"

"He can't hear you," one of the others said nervously. "It's that deaf and dumb lad wot belongs to the witch. We'd best get outa here afore she puts a spell on us."

"He's breaking me sodding arm! Tell him to back off."

"I will if you swear you'll never come here again," Ria said. "Or molest girls."

"T'were just a bit of fun."

"He was trying to rob us," Johanna said. "Told us he'd cut off our hair if we didn't give him a quid."

"Wot's a quid to you anyroad? Owwww! I swear I won't do it again!"

Ria went to Gareth and gestured for him to let go. He did, but kept a wary eye on the delinquents.

Patrick hobbled in and assessed the situation quickly. "I see we have some troublemakers here. Shall I call the constable, Ma'am?"

Ria knew that he was an elderly man, a special constable taking over for the one who had gone to France. She wasn't sure that he'd be able to do much.

"If Clive is alright, we'll report them, but not press charges. Instead, they can show that they're reformed characters and decent citizens by cleaning out the ditches in the village. And if they don't or if they ever show up here again, we'll make certain that they're locked up until they're old enough to be sent into the trenches." Ria went over to Clive, who was regaining his senses. She knelt beside him and gave him a quick examination.

"I never meant to knock him senseless. He were like a dog nipping at me heels."

"You're despicable bullies, and should be ashamed of yourselves, picking on girls and young boys! Fortunately for all of us, Clive seems to be OK. And if he doesn't stay that way, we'll know who's to blame, won't we?" Ria warned them.

"Your names, boys!" Patrick snapped in fine military fashion. They almost sprang to attention.

"Jack Horner," the most belligerent one said.

"Pull the other one. It's wooden," Patrick said.

"Clive knows us anyroad," one of the others said, so they gave their names.

As they walked past Patrick, "Jack Horner" said, "Fritz got your leg, did he, peg-leg?"

Patrick stuck his prosthetic leg out and tripped him up. "Guess I can walk as well as you. And you'd better hope the war is over before you're old enough to leave bits of yourself in France, mate. I've seen boys with no legs at all, or no face, or no manhood. Boys who sacrificed so much so that little shits like you can be safe over here."

The ruffian jumped to his feet, trying to brush off the muck, looking alarmed now.

"Don't show your faces around here again," Patrick warned. "I won't hesitate to use my pistol against vermin."

They scampered from the stable, "Jack Horner" yelling back, "Fuck you!"

Patrick said, "I apologize for my language, Ma'am. I'm afraid that young hooligans like that bring me to a boil."

"Major Thornton once told me that some men don't respect you unless you talk to them at their level. Sometimes politeness and kindness just don't get the job done. You will keep an eye on things around here, won't you, Patrick?"

"I will, Ma'am. I'll get right on to the constable."

Johanna went over to Gareth and said, "Thank you," as she put her right hand to her heart and gave a slight nod.

He put his hand to his lips and then motioned to her, as if sending a kiss. His way of saying "you're welcome".

"You've been learning his sign language," Ria said in surprise.

"Yes, Madame. It's not difficult and Gareth likes to talk to me. Thank you, too, Clive. You were very brave, tackling those boys."

"Yes, thank you all," Ria said. "Let's take Clive inside and clean him up."

They had no more trouble while Ria was in residence. She was pleasantly surprised that the miscreants did make an effort to clean the ditches. It turned out that the special constable was a great uncle to one of them, and appalled at his nephew's behaviour, so the trio didn't get off lightly. He told Ria, "There's too many lads these days as don't have a father keeping 'em in line. And some never will again, more's the pity."

．　　　．　　　．

It was relief when the United States finally declared war on Germany just before Easter.

．　　　．　　　．

Ria sat alone in the sunroom, gazing out at the ruins garden but not seeing the rivers of daffodils that were basking in the early April sunshine. Its warmth wafted in the open windows and touched her like a physical presence, but left her chilled. The ticking of the grandfather clock in the hallway seemed inordinately loud, muting the trilling of birds and the distant chatter of children.

It would be so easy not to return to France.

But she had received a rather plaintive summons that morning from Boss, saying that many of the girls were down with measles, and if she could see her way to coming back as soon as possible, she would be a Godsend. Ria had had measles as a child, and so wouldn't be susceptible during this epidemic.

The pervasive sound in the tranquility of Priory Manor became the booming of guns and crashing of bombs in her head. She was caught up in the war machine and its insatiable appetite. Chas and her friends were consumed by it. How could she not be?

．　　　．　　　．

Ria was terribly sad when they left Priory Manor. A shipment had just arrived from Fliss. Ria had planned a village feast for Easter, so the dozens of smoked hams, several hundred pounds of potatoes and carrots, tins of baked beans, and crates of cookies arrived just in time. She was sorry to be missing the event.

She said to the staff, "We shall be back, and all our friends are free to come and go as they please – you already know most of them. I'm counting on you all to keep this place alive for us, and the children's farm going. You've helped to make this a warm and welcoming home, and we're grateful for your hard work and dedication."

Even Mrs. Skitch was teary-eyed to see them go.

Ria and the girls spent Easter at Bovington with Alice, who tried to cheer up Sophie.

"Why do you have to go, Mummy Ria?" Sophie asked between sobs.

"You know all my WATS friends? They are sick and need me now. I will be back in the summer, ma petite chérie," Ria assured her, for she had agreed to return to France only on condition that she have leave every three months. She had convinced Boss that as the only married WATS and mother, she wasn't "setting a dangerous precedent."

"We're all free to quit at any time. I don't think that any of us are staying there merely because of some arbitrary rules," she had added.

Boss had replied wryly. "Rules are all we have to keep us going sometimes, Thornton."

They celebrated Sophie's seventh birthday on the day before Easter, Ria making it a gay occasion. It was warm enough so that she could give Sophie and Johanna a tennis lesson, with Alice eager to help out. They went for a row on the river, all the while on the lookout for Ratty and Mole. A treasure hunt evoked squeals of joy and laughter. There was a telegram from Daddy Chas, and a birthday cake, and charades, and tall tales by the fire.

It was easier for Ria to leave knowing that Sophie had formed unshakable bonds with Johanna, Alice, Ace, and Buttercup. Bea would look after them with love and compassion. But it was a terrible wrench for them all. Ria wrote her first letter from the train, and swore to herself that she would find a few minutes every day to write to Sophie.

She arrived on a cold and snowy day in France, just after another major Allied offensive had been launched – one at which the Canadians would distinguish themselves at Vimy Ridge.

Chapter 10

Phoebe Wyndham liked the feeling of churches. She loved watching light transformed by the coloured fragments of the windows, and the soaring Gothic arches that prayed to heaven. She enjoyed the grandeur of the echoing music, and singing the hymns with the congregation, knowing that her voice rose higher, drifting away from the heavy, earthbound others.

What she didn't like about church was the minister, who was up there quacking like a duck. Talking about what God wanted them to do and be and feel as if he actually knew. What nonsense! *She* knew how God felt, right into her core. He didn't need to use words to make her understand His power and the joy He bestowed upon those He favoured.

Phoebe almost giggled aloud when she felt that curious fluttering in her stomach. Butterflies, she thought joyously, wishing that the congregation were singing so that she didn't have to suppress her mirth. She had noticed them months ago. It had been a bit scary at first, feeling something move inside her. But then she had realized what was happening. God had truly favoured her and was turning her into an angel. Like a butterfly in its cocoon, her angelic self was preparing to burst out of her body. It was why her stomach was growing. She knew it wouldn't hurt because her belly button would just open up and the Angel Phoebe would be free of this shell and of Mama's constant badgering. She would fly up to the high windowsills above the arches, where she would perch, and look down with pity on all those who never really saw or understood, despite their piousness. All those who would never be privileged to sit up there with her where the music gathered.

Of course she hadn't told anyone in case Mama did something to keep her forever imprisoned in their hateful house. But surely God was stronger than Mama, and she really wanted to tell someone!

It should be Daphne, her new sister. She loved having a sister. Of course Daphne wasn't Sarah, who had died when she was little. But Sarah approved of Daphne – so Maryanne had told her. The doll often relayed opinions and observations from Sarah, who was with Grandmother and warned Phoebe when the old lady wasn't pleased with her.

Daphne would be happy for her, since she was a soft and warm pink, unlike her sister, Eleanor, who was an energetic and vibrant red. Phoebe thought of people as colours, for they were each enveloped in a glow. Edgar was a cheerful butter yellow. Her father, Albert, was a calm blue that sometimes became rather a dreary indigo. Her mother, Phyllis, was a boring, muddy grey, while she herself glowed white and gold. Like an angel.

No one else in the church did. That's how she knew that she was the only blessed one, and marveled that all these people emanating moss green and midnight blue and purple had such a long way to go to achieve a state of grace.

Another thing that Phoebe liked about church was that it got her out of the house. Mama had never allowed her to attend school, so she'd been incarcerated with a succession of governesses and tutors. Her family rarely attended concerts or balls in the city, and unless it was with family, Phoebe was never invited along on the infrequent occasions her parents dined out. So it was only in summer, at the cottage, that she felt truly alive and somewhat unfettered.

Chatting with friends and family after church was usually the highlight of her week in the city. Today it was gloriously sunny with the warm breath of spring sighing away the frigid isolation of winter. Phoebe wondered how long it would be before she could meet Bobby Miller in the ravine again. She'd had not a word from him since the cold autumn winds had shivered the trees into dropping their leaves, allowing gimlet eyes to follow her everywhere.

"You must see the photographs that dearest Ria sent us," Marjorie Thornton said to the Wyndhams. "Zoë takes such delightful pictures. Priory Manor is absolutely charming, and our granddaughter is such a sweet, darling little thing. Oh, I do hope they come home soon before she's quite grown up! Felicity is thrilled to be an aunt."

"I do wish you'd let me go over, Mummy," Fliss said. "I could look after Sophie when Chas and Ria return to France."

Marjorie put her hand to her heart. "Dear God, I'm already a bundle of nerves worrying about your brothers and Ria!"

"Don't distress yourself, dear," J.D. said consolingly. He was ten years older than his wife, but slender and fit, so that they seemed of an age. "Civilian women are no longer being allowed to travel overseas. It's too dangerous with the renewed submarine warfare."

"Do forgive me," Marjorie sniffled into her handkerchief. "I was just thinking how long it's been since I held my dear, darling Chas in my arms. Almost three years! And Rafe has already been gone for four months! I know I mustn't complain, since there are too many mothers who will never again be able to hold their precious children. Oh, dear, I'm afraid I'm all in pieces."

Fliss, although once again annoyed that she wasn't allowed to go to England, put her arm about her mother and said, "Did you bring a picture with you, Mummy? I'm sure I saw you slip one into your bag."

"Yes, yes, I did." She took it out and handed it to Albert and Phyllis, saying, "Do look at what a splendid little family they are. Isn't Sophie quite the prettiest poppet? I'm not sure whether she or the beagle has the most beguiling eyes."

Helena hid her annoyance that she and James had received no photos as yet of their 'granddaughter', although she wasn't surprised. Ria only sent them a brief formal letter at Christmas, and all the other news came through occasional letters from Beatrice, and whatever Ria had written to the Thorntons or Olivia, with whom she corresponded frequently. With a forced laugh Helena said, "It's rather bizarre to think that baby Cecilia is already an aunt to a six-year-old."

"Actually Sophie turned seven yesterday," Marjorie pointed out. "Felicity sent her the most splendid tennis racquet and outfit with the weekly food shipment."

"I do wish Victoria would keep us apprised of such things," Helena snapped.

"Now, Helena, don't fret," Marjorie said. "I'm sure Ria has more than enough to do, so I shall keep you informed of any important developments."

Olivia suppressed a grin. Always kindly and generous, Marjorie seemed sometimes vague and discombobulated, but Olivia never underestimated her shrewdness or strength of character. Of course Marjorie was aware of the friction between Ria and her father and stepmother, so she took on her role of mother-in-law with great relish and true devotion.

James seemed disinterested in the photograph, which irritated Olivia. She could never forgive him for the way he had always treated Ria, especially since he now doted on his new daughter. So when all the Wyndhams adjourned to her house for Easter Sunday lunch, she made sure that Ria and the others were freely discussed.

But Helena never allowed herself to be upstaged. She announced, "James and I are going to become parents again in October."

After the usual sentiments were espoused, Phyllis said, "Should you be driving, Helena? It's dangerous enough at the best of times."

Helena was proud of the fact that she had learned to drive, although they had managed to find a chauffeur. James had been unhappy with her driving, until she had reminded him that Flora Eaton – now Lady Eaton – had been driving for years, and that it was the "smart" thing for modern women to do.

"Yes, do make her see sense," James said. "What is it with women these days that compels them to take on men's jobs, and even those of servants?" He softened his words with an indulgent smile at his wife. As if she were a wayward, but innocent child.

Helena took no offence from his words. She knew how to keep him sweet and more than contented. She smiled back as she said, "We can't allow you men to have all the glory. Or fun. I find it quite exhilarating being able to drive. I will have to stop when we go up to the island this summer in any case, and I doubt that I'd fit behind the wheel by September."

"I expect this will be quite a different summer in Muskoka," James observed. "Oswald says there won't be a Regatta, what with the U.S. involved in the war now, and fewer people coming to the lake." Oswald Oakley was president of the Summer Residents' Association.

"Most of us haven't the heart for such gay events in any case," Olivia said. Since the war had begun, people had been torn between not allowing the Germans to spoil their fun, and showing proper respect for the gravity of the situation, especially for the many bereaved families.

"Does that mean we're not having the Dominion Day Ball either?" Esme asked.

"I do think that we still need entertainments," Helena assured her. "Nothing extravagant, of course, but we *are* celebrating Canada. That will give us all a boost as this wretched war drags on." Not that Helena truly cared. In fact, the war worked to her advantage, with Ria off in England and the Wyndhams escalating their considerable wealth through investments in war-related industries.

She herself was heavily involved in raising money for the Patriotic Fund, which put her in good company with other influential society ladies. "And we can offer respite and some cheer to the officers who must go back to all that. We have several coming to dinner this evening, as a matter of fact. They do so enjoy a family atmosphere, being so far from home." She had taken her lead from Flora Eaton, and invited British, American, and Canadian officers to dine with them. Many of them were pilots, here to teach or train at the Leaside airfield. One of Helena's regulars was an aristocrat whose parents had already invited her and James to stay whenever they went to England.

And Helena planned to do just that after the war. With regular visits to Paris to refresh her wardrobe, like her best friend, Letitia Oakley, did. And Beatrice had a villa on the French Riviera that Helena fully intended to use. She sighed inwardly in contentment at the quirks of fate – helped along, of course, by her clever machinations – that had brought her all this luxury and security. Even though their house wasn't as large and grand as the Eatons' Ardwold, or the Pellatts' immense Casa Loma, they were at least neighbours. And from the heights above Spadina, they looked out over the city in a proprietary manner. It was so easy to be amenable when she had all that. She smiled broadly.

Phoebe was twitchily eager to take Daphne aside, and almost exploded with impatience before there was finally an opportunity. After the luncheon party broke up, Edgar and Daphne accompanied his family to their house to spend the afternoon, because Phyllis complained that she rarely saw them these days.

"You mustn't tell anyone, Daphne," Phoebe whispered, gripping her sister-in-law's hand tightly as she led her to her room on the pretext of showing Daphne something she had knitted.

The only thing that Phoebe liked about her bedroom was that it looked out over the ravine. Heavy, rusty brocade draperies enshrouded the four-poster bed, with matching curtains smothering the windows. Once, she had hated the fact that she didn't overlook the street so that she could feel a part of whatever little activity occurred in the quiet neighbourhood. But now she could see, through the sleeping trees, those sacred places where she and Bobby Miller had met and communed with God. And felt again that powerful surge of ecstasy and energy.

"I'm going to be an angel!"

Daphne was shocked despite the fact that she knew Phoebe experienced the world differently from everyone else. Schizophrenia, Blake had called her condition. It meant crazy, which scared Daphne. But she had known Phoebe almost all her life and thought her just quirky and unpredictable.

"Don't look so worried!" Phoebe said on a laugh. "I don't mean that I'm dying. Just being reborn!"

"What makes you think that?"

When Phoebe explained, Daphne grew even paler. "Have you... had relations with a fellow?"

"Sex, you mean? Of course, but what does that have to do with it?"

"It sounds as if you're with child."

Phoebe was stunned. Surprised that Daphne thought her flutterings were not extraordinary. Sad that she might not be an angel after all. But with a mounting excitement that she would have her own precious little baby to care for and love!

"Is that truly how it feels? Having a baby?"

"That's what Ellie told me. Oh Phoebe, we should go and see her to be sure."

"A baby!" Phoebe hugged herself and twirled around, stopping suddenly. "Oh dear. I hope that Maryanne won't be jealous. She's used to having all my attention."

Daphne wasn't about to step into the quagmire of unwed motherhood. Or the expectations of two-faced dolls. "Edgar will take us to see Ellie. You mustn't say anything to anyone just yet."

Back in the sitting room, Daphne looked meaningfully at her husband and announced, "I promised Phoebe we'd take her for a drive in your new car, Edgar."

Reading her expression, Edgar responded immediately. "Terrific idea!" He was always amazed at how quickly he and Daphne had become attuned to one another.

"I don't understand why you have to go out. And on a Sunday! We see so little of you as it is," Phyllis complained.

As if she hadn't spoken, Albert said, "It's a lovely day for an outing. Mind you're back in time for tea, or your mother will worry."

"Of course."

They all breathed more easily outside. "So what's the mystery?" Edgar asked as he helped them into the car. "Where are we going?"

"To see Ellie," Daphne explained. "Phoebe needs some medical advice."

"Can't I tell him, Daphne? Please?" Phoebe entreated, practically bouncing in her seat.

"Wait until we get there, Phoebe. Edgar has to concentrate on driving."

He was even more mystified, but the pleasure of driving his McLaughlin-Chevrolet soon diverted his curiosity. He'd been so pleased with the car that he had invested heavily in General Motors shares.

The Carlyles had a respectable, roomy, red brick Richardson Romanesque house in the Annex, close to the university where Daphne's father was a professor of physics.

As soon as they stepped out of the car, Phoebe grabbed Edgar's arm and said, "I'm going to have a baby! A real baby!"

Edgar was momentarily speechless. But seeing the truth in Daphne's eyes, he struggled to control his anger as he said gently, "Who's the father, Phoebe?"

She looked at him curiously, but replied, as if explaining to a child, "God, of course. He's our creator."

Trying not to upset or blame her, he said firmly, "Of course. But for procreation, God created men and women, like Adam and Eve."

"God was Jesus's father."

"Did a boy... touch you?"

"Well, of course! They have to to dance with you! You *are* being silly, Edgar! You mean did I fuck with a boy? It was how I knew that God truly loved me, touched me, because nothing else on earth could feel like that! Mama said that women get the curse because we are being punished for the sins of Eve. So when it stopped coming, I knew that I had pleased God. He made this baby for me."

Edgar and Daphne exchanged bewildered glances. Edgar said, "Was it Bobby Miller who you had intimate relations with?"

"Yes. But I haven't seen him for ages, and I do want to. Can you tell him, Edgar?"

"I'll do more than that," Edgar muttered under his breath, clenching his fists.

Ellie confirmed that Phoebe was pregnant, and already seven months gone.

"She's always been a bit chubby, so no one noticed," Edgar said. "Good Lord! What will we do now?"

"There are only three choices," Ellie said. "She gets married. She's allowed to keep the baby without marriage. Or it goes up for adoption."

"Not much to choose from!" Edgar said. "I hate to see her shackled to Bobby Miller. He's a jumped-up little swine."

"She won't give it up for adoption. Not willingly or easily," Daphne said astutely.

"She sure as hell can't keep it!" Edgar said. "The Wyndham name would be tarnished. None of them would stand for it."

"Someone should be thinking about how Phoebe will be affected by this," Ellie pointed out. "As Daphne realizes, Phoebe wants and possibly needs this baby. It will be something of her own, and some control she can exert over her life. I'm sorry to say this, Edgar, but Phoebe has been damaged by your mother's suffocating oppressiveness and religious fervour. She's been hovering on the edge of sanity. Not handled properly, this could well tip her over that precipice."

"God, what a mess!" Edgar said. "I can't imagine how this could even happen!"

Ellie suddenly recalled seeing a blissfully vague Phoebe at the Thorncliff Ball last September. "I can! And I'm mighty impressed at Phoebe's ingenuity in finding an opportunity for love. Too bad no one explained anything about boys and sex beforehand, though."

"Not my place!" Edgar said quickly.

Dressed again, Phoebe joined them, saying, "I heard the baby's heartbeat! Eleanor let me listen to it! This is even better than becoming an angel!"

"Phoebe, we can't tell anyone but Mama and Papa at the moment, and they won't be happy. Girls aren't supposed to have babies until they're married."

"Bobby will marry me," she said dismissively. "Then we can have our own house, and fuck whenever we like!"

Edgar winced. "You mustn't use that word, Phoebe. It's vulgar and demeaning, especially for girls. And it upsets people."

Phoebe shrugged. "As you like. But it is just a word."

"*Make love* is more appropriate, and so much nicer," Daphne suggested.

There was no easy way to break the news to their parents. Phyllis began shrieking, so Albert shook her angrily, saying, "For God's sake, pull yourself together, woman! The servants will hear!"

Phoebe said, "Don't worry, Mama. You won't have to look after it. It will be *my* baby."

"How could you, Phoebe? How could let a boy do that disgusting thing to you? Haven't I told you that God wants you to be pure? That he reviles Jezebels? Haven't I?" Phyllis ranted.

"That's enough, Mama!" Edgar intervened. "Phoebe didn't know what you were talking about. You never explained anything to her."

"So now it's my fault that she's behaved like a common slut!"

"Mama, I was making love. That's a good thing, isn't it? People are always singing about it. And everyone wants babies. Just look at how happy Uncle James and Helena are, and everybody was congratulating them. Why isn't my baby being celebrated?" Phoebe looked crestfallen, and Edgar's heart went out to her. She was such an innocent, but one who seemed to see through hypocrisy to the very core of things.

"Phoebe will just have to get married," Edgar stated.

She clapped her hands joyfully and spun around to her parents. "Oh yes, please may I?"

Phyllis started wailing.

Albert, looking suddenly a decade older, replied, "It seems the only way. Come along, Edgar. You and I are going to pay a visit. Phyllis, you should go and lie down, and don't say anything else until you've had a chance to consider the consequences."

The Millers had recently moved into one of the big Victorian houses on Jarvis Street. They were entertaining guests, but Albert insisted that he had important business with Bobby and his father, Josiah. They were shown to a dark, stuffy office.

"We don't usually have the pleasure of your company, Mr. Wyndham," Josiah said. "May I offer you some whiskey?"

"No, thank you. We're here on a rather delicate matter."

Edgar noticed the decanter smack nervously against the glass as Bobby poured himself a hefty measure.

Albert went on. "Your son, Robert, and my daughter have been having relations. She is now with child. So it's his duty to marry her."

Josiah looked horrified, but Bobby burst out with, "I think not! She's the one who asked me to fuck her and kept begging for it."

Albert had to restrain Edgar from rushing over and punching Bobby, who lounged mockingly against the bookcase and took a deep drink.

"How dare you! You are no gentleman," Albert declared before Edgar could vent his wrath. "You admit taking advantage of an innocent girl."

"Hardly taking advantage! I gave her what she asked for. I never said I loved her or intended to marry her. You can't condemn me to marriage with someone who's off her onion."

"Robert!" he father admonished. "You've already behaved dishonorably and will refrain from further insulting our guests. You *will* make amends."

"I'm going to war, Dad. I've just made up my mind. I doubt that the Wyndhams want me for a son-in-law anyway, since I have every intention of sampling what other women have to offer."

"You're drunk, boy! I'm sorry, Mr. Wyndham. I'm ashamed of my son and terribly distressed by his caddish behaviour. He might well be right that he wouldn't make a good husband for your daughter."

"I certainly wouldn't have allowed a marriage between them under other circumstances," Albert stated unequivocally. "But now she bears the burden of shame for his seduction."

"That is indeed regrettable." Looking totally baffled, Josiah admitted, "I don't know what to say, except that we are profoundly sorry."

"You might consider disinheriting your spawn, if he doesn't comply," Edgar suggested. "I doubt he'll be so attractive to other girls when he doesn't have money to back his unfounded arrogance."

"He's going to war, Mr. Wyndham. I expect that will be punishment enough."

Edgar snorted in disgust. "Be sure you do, Bobby, or you'll have me to answer to. And if the world is lucky, the Germans will blast off your balls."

Edgar stomped out of the room, leaving Albert to say, "I trust this won't go any further than this room. If there's any hint of scandal, I'll know who's to blame. And you can be assured that your family and your business will be discredited. Good day to you!"

Driving back, Edgar said, "I should have ploughed him one in his smirking face!"

"Some of us still have to behave like gentlemen."

"So where does that leave Phoebe? She'll be devastated that Bobby doesn't want her. And she'll never give up the baby."

"Then it will have to die."

"Papa! What do you mean?"

"We'll put it up for adoption, but Phoebe must think it's dead."

"That's cruel! Ellie said this could devastate her. You know that she is mentally... fragile, Papa."

"That's why we've been protecting her. Ever since Sarah died, she's been sensitive, fearful, plagued by disturbing thoughts."

"Visions, voices. Ellie says that she *can* be helped."

"By putting her into an asylum?" Albert looked stricken. "She's also bright and loving and refreshing. I can't bear to think of her stigmatized and marginalized like that."

"I wish she could keep the baby."

"You know that's not possible. Reputation is everything. Without it you have no respect, no friends, no business."

"But we still didn't force Bobby to do the right thing."

"Do you really want Phoebe tied to that lout?"

"It's what she wants."

"Until he breaks her heart. Imagine how that would affect her."

"I expect we'll find out in a few minutes."

As soon as they walked into the sitting room, Phoebe jumped up and said, "When am I getting married?"

Edgar said, "I'm afraid that Bobby is going to war, so he can't get married just now."

"Oh dear. So he won't be the baby's father after all. Do you suppose there's another boy who makes love as well as Bobby who'd like to marry me?"

"We'll have to see, won't we?" Edgar said, vastly relieved she had taken the news so lightly. It obviously wasn't Bobby she was in love with, but perhaps the fun and freedom that he'd shown her. "In the meantime, you and Mama and Daphne and I are going to have a bit of a holiday. Mama needs some sea air, so we're going down to Boston or some such place until we can go to the cottage. Would you like that?" Edgar felt such a Judas.

"Can we really? Go on a trip? To the United States? But what about poor Papa? Can't you come as well?"

"I would like nothing better, my dear, but I have to work. You can write every day and tell me all about it."

"I will! Thank you, Papa! Is this a special present for me and the baby?"

"Yes, it is. But you have to keep the baby a secret."

"Daphne told me, and I do know that the baby would be shunned if she didn't have a father, so we really must find her one. I don't care so much for myself, and being notorious might be rather fun. Better than being ignored or sneered at, like Rosie

Miller did last summer. But I don't want all of you to be hurt. I
don't think Ria or Zoë would mind, though. I'm so glad that you
and Daphne are coming along to the seaside, Edgar. Will that
really help Mama feel better about me and the baby?"
"One can only hope." Albert said.

.   .   .

Dear Ria,
Bloody hell and damnation! I won't be coming to France after
all! Numerous people have pointed out to me that I'm needed here,
and it would be terribly self-indulgent of me to want to go to war!
They've taken advantage of my overly developed sense of social
responsibility. In other words, they've made me feel guilty as hell
for seeking the "glamour and glory" of war work. As one of my
professors pointed out, more than ninety percent of Canadians are
NOT in France, and are as deserving of medical care as our brave
soldiers. One of my female colleagues thought I was nuts to want to
go overseas when there are so many opportunities for us women at
the moment – a chance to obtain a good position somewhere before
all the male doctors return. Did you know that many of them were
able to leave university early and do their internships in the
military hospitals?
I saved a young woman's life the other day. She came into the
hospital with severe abdominal pains, which did not appear to be
appendicitis, and were dismissed as a bellyache or a bit of hysteria
as her new husband had just departed for England. But I thought
she was suffering too much for it to be that, and know how women
tend to downplay their problems – to their own detriment, I must
add. I asked her a few probing questions and after prodding her a
bit, suspected that she had an ectopic pregnancy, meaning that the
child was developing outside the womb. Which, of course, it can't do
for very long. She was slowly bleeding to death and had mere hours
left to live had we not whipped her into the operating theatre and
stitched her up. We managed to save one of her ovaries and a tube,
so she will still have the opportunity to have normal pregnancies.
My mentor was most impressed with me, saying that ectopics
are relatively rare and difficult to diagnose in time. He said to me,
"I hope you think that saving that young woman's life is as
important as saving her husband's when he's wounded. And what
about all the other women who are reluctant to talk about their
'female problems' with male doctors? At least fifty percent of the

population desperately need your help here, Dr. Carlyle. I do hope you will consider taking on a Residency at the hospital."

What could I say at that point, being so honoured as to be invited to work at the Toronto General? So why am I not jumping for joy? Why do I feel as if I'm being left out of all the world-changing events that all my friends are experiencing over there? My brother-in-law (bizarre thought) and I commiserate with one another about this all the time. Edgar and Daphne, by the way, are sickeningly besotted and surprisingly well suited.

Which brings me to the other reason that I want so desperately to come over – I miss Jack. I expect that he's having a grand old time with all those French Mademoiselles, and English ones as well. Tell me honestly that he and Lady Sidonie Dunston are not an item! I'm not certain that he and I have any sort of future together, but it's hard to explore the possibility when we're so far apart. Damn it, Ria, I miss the sex! Stop laughing.

But I've been left in no doubt that the best way I can do "my bit" is to stay here. I've been told that I'm also freeing up the male doctors to go overseas, since the CAMC won't take women medics anyway – unless we want to work as nursing Sisters. I didn't go to school all these years to empty bedpans, and I'd make a lousy nurse in any case. I like medicine because it's an intellectual challenge, not because I'm particularly nurturing.

I was terribly sad to hear about Kurt Roland. He was so young and eager. I've heard that his younger brother, Stuart, has signed up now that the U.S. is at war. But maybe it will be over before he has a chance to get to France.

Give my love to my friends there. I will feel closer to you all when I'm at the lake this summer.

Your disappointed and heartsick friend, Ellie

Chapter 11

Even if he hadn't been informed, Chas would have known that a major offensive was about to happen. The Allied guns had not been silent for a week.

Chas's aerodrome was only about ten miles north of Filescamp Farm, where Rafe and the 60th were stationed. After their arrival, his ground crew had spent a couple of weeks setting up. The pilots, who had set a precedent by not losing a single plane en route from England, spent their time learning the lay of the land. It was one thing to study maps and quite another to recognize landmarks when flying overhead. In squadron strength, with Chas leading them, they crossed the lines to do their own reconnaissance. Chas also considered it a bit of psychological warfare, since he hoped that the Germans would take note of the new scouts. And they did, but since there were only six Albatros fighters against the nineteen S.E.5s, the Boche watched warily from a distance and flew off smartly. Chas had no intention of engaging them just yet, but hoped he had made them sweat.

Once the Flying Dragons began operations at the beginning of April, Chas found it difficult to send his men on offensive patrols without joining them.

It was Easter Sunday before he took the time to fly over to Filescamp, where he was warmly greeted by the ground crew. They crowded around and plied him with questions about his S.E.5, since this was the first one they had seen.

His former mechanic, Corporal Burkett, said, "You've been missed, Sir, but now I have the privilege of looking after your brother."

"Then he's in good hands," Chas replied sincerely. A pilot's survival was as much due to the skill and thoroughness of his mechanic as to his own abilities.

There was a howling from the sheds and a sharp barking as a beagle charged onto the field and jumped up on Chas. "Snoopy!" Chas rubbed his head as the dog barked happily at him.

Burkett laughed. "He knew you'd come back one day. He's been moping about here, always on the lookout for you. You'd do us a kindness if you took him along, Sir. None of us can stand his sad looks and whimpering any longer. I'll have one of the lads take him over to your aerodrome in the tender."

"Where's Josephine?" Chas asked. The cat had adopted him last year as well.

"Over at the farm, last I saw her. I don't think she liked the fact that chaps come and go so much, so she's attached herself to one of the daughters."

Chas had met Major Jack Scott before. He had been crippled in a crash early in the war, and now struggled to hobble about with two canes. But he refused to be grounded, although many, including his close friend Winston Churchill, had encouraged him to take an HQ job. Scott had been drafted in just weeks earlier when the previous CO had been killed behind enemy lines.

"Your brother seems to be taking after you, Thornton," Scott said. "Got his third kill today. I'm just bloody glad he's managed to survive so well. I've lost five men this week alone," he added grimly. "Three dead, two captured. Have you engaged Richthofen yet? His Albatros fighters easily out-fly us, but hopefully your S.E.5s will level the playing field. His entire squadron is now bright red, so we can't single him out so easily anymore, but you sure as hell can't miss them. Thought we'd cramped his style when 100 Squadron dropped nearly a hundred bombs on his aerodrome at Douai the other night. Made a mess from what I've heard. But it hasn't stopped him."

"I tangled with him last autumn, so I know he's a brilliant and aggressive pilot," Chas replied. "'C' Flight encountered a *Flying Circus* this week, and downed one of them. We were a bit shot up, but I haven't lost anyone." Because the Jagdstaffel squadrons, or Jastas – like Baron Manfred von Richthofen's – had painted their scouts bright colours, they had become known among the RFC as *Flying Circuses*. And greatly feared.

"Well, the Red Baron's already outdone you, Thornton. Has about thirty-seven kills." Chas had twenty-seven.

"Even more than Ball."

"We were damned sorry to lose him to 56 Squadron," Scott said. Albert Ball was Britain's leading Ace and Chas's former colleague. He was fanatically religious and intensely private, so Chas had never warmed to him, although he admired Ball's courage and skill. "It was you and Ball who made this the most famous fighting squadron in France."

Chas wondered if his own success made him appear as bloodthirsty as Ball. Yes, he was angry at the loss of so many of his comrades, and he enjoyed the thrill of victory. But he also had respect for fellow aviators of whatever stripe, and felt that every man's death diminished him. He recalled Ball playing his violin in the evenings after downing as many Germans as he could on his lonely sorties, perhaps as a lament to the dead.

"So I'll have to see what I can do with this new crew, although I'm not happy with the turnover rate. You're lucky that you have well-trained pilots. They take my best chaps away to become Flight Commanders of other squadrons, and COs, like you, and then send me boys who've had less than twenty hours of flying experience. So they can hardly fly, let alone fight." Scott shook his head in disgust. "Your brother had better training, and I'm sure he learned a lot from you. I expect he's in the mess. He's very fond of poker."

"Any sort of gambling. And drinking. Do keep him in check, Scott. He's a bit too brash."

"Which of us isn't? You didn't get your ribbons by being cautious, Thornton. They're daredevils, the lot of them, so why be surprised that they're wild and cocky on the ground as well? Speaking of brash, you'll have to meet Billy Bishop, another Canuck. He's just become an Ace. Shot down at least three today, so he has six confirmed kills. And a sausage, for God's sake. If I recall, you flamed one once, so you know how bloody difficult they are to down."

"Bit of a lone wolf, is he? Like Ball?"

"Can't keep him out of the air."

"I don't allow my men to do solo forays."

Scott shrugged. "Boom Trenchard wants results."

But Chas wasn't willing to endanger his men. Flying in well-rehearsed formation and watching each other's backs while deflecting the enemy from the RFC strategic military operations, and keeping the Germans from doing reconnaissance were what truly mattered. It was how Richthofen's Jasta did so well. The individual glory of Ace status was mostly vanity for the pilots and propaganda for the war effort.

Scott led Chas into the officers' mess where an intense young man was dancing with a bottle of champagne atop the piano, while a fellow officer banged away on the keys of the out-of-tune instrument. The room was thick with cigarette smoke and the fumes of spilled wine and whiskey.

Rafe was playing billiards, and raised his glass to Chas. "Hey, big brother, come and celebrate. I flamed my third Hun today."

"Major Scott's been telling me how well you've done," Chas said, noticing that Rafe was well into his cups. He recalled when, in the early days, he himself had often drowned his fear and sorrow and disgust in champagne.

"Thought I bagged the bloody Red Baron today, but he faked a death spiral and scarpered. Still, I put the wind up him."

Scott said, "And he almost nailed you. Half a dozen bullets missed you by inches."

Rafe shrugged. "But he did miss."

Chas, too, had returned from patrols wondering how he had survived when his aeroplane had been so badly shot up, the bullet holes evidence of close shaves. But he was more worried about Rafe than he had been about himself.

The tap dancer on the piano now began to sing one of the pilots' favourite ballads about a dying aviator. The booing and foot stomping didn't discourage him. When he'd finished he proclaimed, "We can't have a dry piano in this mess," as he poured champagne into it.

"Bish, come down and meet our number two Ace," Scott said to him.

"Top Canadian Ace," Bishop retorted as he jumped off the piano. "Your brother never lets us forget that, Major Thornton."

"Put a sock in it, Bish!" Rafe called.

"Major Thornton, allow me to introduce an appalling pilot, but excellent marksman," Scott said.

"That's what counts, isn't it? Major Thornton, you've been an inspiration," Billy Bishop said as he shook Chas's hand vigorously.

Chas said, "You've done remarkably well in your first three weeks, Bishop. You're Margaret Burden's fiancé, aren't you?"

Surprised, Bishop said, "Yes indeed. You know the family?"

"The Eatons." She was Timothy's granddaughter. "You can't expect something like that to remain private in Toronto, can you?"

Bishop laughed. "Not in Toronto. But here?"

"If you keep shooting down Germans at this rate, Bishop, you can't escape celebrity," Chas warned him. With a grin he added, "My mother thought I should keep a brotherly eye on you."

The adjutant interrupted to say, "Boom Trenchard's flying over from HQ to congratulate Bish."

"Better get into a clean uniform" Scott told Bishop.

Chas had a drink with Rafe as they discussed news from home. Then Chas said, "There's a big offensive starting tomorrow. I know that your squadron as well as ours has an important role in this." They had been ordered to strafe the trenches, as well as do contact patrol, which meant keeping the infantry commanders apprised of the progress of the battle. It also meant that the pilots had to fly dangerously low over the action, dodging the screaming arcs of artillery fire from both sides and the peppering from German machine guns and rifles. "Be careful, Rafe. The odds are against us with so much lead in the air."

"I expect you'll be safely behind your desk," Rafe said. He hadn't intended it as an insult, but because he did care about Chas. He had always been awkward at expressing his emotions.

Chas scowled as he said, "I'm not letting my men do anything that I'm not prepared to."

"Very noble of you," Rafe replied. "But daft."

Chas rose to leave. "Lay off the booze so that you have a clear head in the morning."

Rafe snorted. "Glad I didn't get posted to your squadron, big brother."

.   .   .

Justin Carrington was thankful to be out of the deep subway and cave where the slimy chalk walls had begun to close in on him, reminding him of the suffocating mud of the Somme, making him ashamed of the panic that he had to force back into the pit of his belly. By now he should have been used to the sweat and latrine stench of war, but with men packed so tightly together in these underground tunnels grey with cigarette and candle smoke, the oxygen seemed to have been used up. So he breathed deeply of the cold, pre-dawn air.

Like most of the men, he hadn't been able to sleep, even if it had been physically possible to find a comfortable place to rest. For months the entire Canadian Corps had been training for this day. Over and over they had practiced behind the lines – their objectives carefully laid out, the timing of their advance coordinated to the split-second – so that every last man knew exactly what to do.

Their Corps commander, Lieutenant-General Sir Julian Byng, unlike most of the other British generals, had taken lessons from the Somme and Verdun failures, as had the Canadian divisional commanders, like Major-General Arthur Currie. So this battle was not only intricately planned, but also employed new tactics, a scientific approach to gunnery, more reliable intelligence and communications, and a less hidebound approach to war – which suited the cocky Canadian character. The men weren't expected to follow orders blindly, but to think for themselves and to use their initiative when called upon. Justin was pleased to see how this attitude and expectation had boosted the morale of his troops. In a decision unheard of among the Allies, every group of half a dozen men had been given a detailed map of their sector. So each soldier was not only aware of the battle plan, but also felt he had an important role in achieving its success. And he knew how to take over the job of a comrade or superior if necessary. The platoons had become tight-knit teams who weren't about to let any of their pals down.

The men had had their rum ration, and boxes of Canadian Lowney chocolate bars had miraculously appeared. Justin savoured every bite of his, while relishing the reminder of home.

So now they all stood silently in the trenches, in the rain that was turning to sleet, many up to their knees in icy sludge. 30,000 Canadian infantry strung along the four miles of Vimy Ridge. With another 70,000 soldiers in support roles behind – the gunners, engineers, medics, cooks, and so forth – it meant that the entire Canadian Corps was here, together for the first time.

Justin thought about his friends who were nearby. Max, as a Forward Observation Officer with the artillery, was in the front lines. Freddie, with the engineers, would be building strong points and laying tramlines as soon as the Germans had been swept out of the way. Blake was waiting at a Dressing Station for the first trickle of casualties that would undoubtedly become a bloody river. They had all met earlier that week for a leisurely, convivial dinner in an officers' club well behind the lines. He wondered if Chas and Rafe, who were not too far away, would be flying overhead today. He'd heard that even Jack was here, sketching the activity. He didn't know that "Father" Paul was close by with the stretcher-bearers.

Justin checked his watch yet again. 5:15. Almost Zero Hour.

His company of four platoons would go over in the second wave, leap-frogging those leading the assault at a predetermined line. The first battalions were already in the shallow jumping-off trenches and craters in no-man's-land.

After a week of constant shelling that had pummeled the German trenches and defences with a million shells, the silence now was eerie. And taut. Every one of them knew only too well that the Allies had tried and failed to take this strongly fortified and tactically important ridge during the past two years, the French suffering over 150,000 casualties. In the few months that the Canadian Corps had been here, holding the line and gaining vital information through almost nightly trench raids, they had already had more than 9,000 casualties. So it was little wonder that the disdainful French and British didn't expect the Canadians to succeed in their part of the Battle of Arras, especially within the eight hours that the generals had planned. Despite some trepidation, Justin felt confident that their intense preparation and unprecedented bombardment would surprise and overwhelm the Germans.

And he felt buoyed by the latest letter from Antonia Upton. She had written, "We have been evacuating the wounded from the base hospitals in large numbers recently," which, in the parlance of censorship, insinuated that she realized space was being made for an onslaught of new casualties. She went on to say:

We often hear the remorseless guns, and I wonder how you can stand the diabolical noise that surely threatens the very sanity of civilization. When we have air raids here, I sometimes find it difficult to muster the courage to keep going, cherishing the sanctity and preciousness of life too much to lose it. There is so much yet to experience, so much promise to fulfill. It seems almost treasonous to admit that I don't want to sacrifice myself or any of my friends to the dubious glory of the Empire. Forgive my womanly heart, for I do not mean to diminish what you men are trying and dying to achieve.

I expect you will soon be preoccupied, and trust you will be careful as well as lucky. I enjoyed our perambulations about the Hampshire countryside, and hope we can repeat those when the wildflowers are in bloom and the trees, lushly green. And perhaps you will take me sailing and canoeing when I come to visit your magical Muskoka. I have presumptuously included a photograph of myself in the event that you may wish to recall your correspondent.

Fondly, Toni

He had chuckled at the formality of that last sentence, which was no doubt intended to make the gesture appear less intimate. But he was delighted by the photograph and studied it frequently as if he could delve better into her psyche. To him it was evident that she was transparent, her inner beauty reflected in her outer attractiveness. From her perceptive, forthright gaze shone humour and a joie de vivre that captivated him. He had the picture tucked into his breast pocket, and felt the intoxicating stirrings of love.

Joyfully he had replied to her:

Your photo has brought me much cheer, but I hope that I may see the real you before long. Not in your capacity as an ambulance driver, however!

I applaud your womanly heart, and agree with your sentiments. I have done much soul-searching over the past two years, caught between my civilized conscience and the dictates of war. I have seen both the best and the worst that human beings can do, the many and ever more mechanized ways we can slaughter one another, although we are more alike than dissimilar.

Your friendship has revived in me the determination to survive this war and to make a difference in a world changed forever, but open to new possibilities. Our generation must try to right the wrongs that brought us here and for which so many, as Rupert Brooke so aptly said, 'poured out the red sweet wine of youth'.

Be assured that your thoughts and words comfort and sustain me, Toni. I long to sit in the sunshine with you, listening to the birds, but without the guns which now disturb their songs. The larks here seem forever hopeful. So shall I be.

Affectionately, Justin

It was snowing now, the wind whipping up a blizzard.

5:28. Two minutes to go. After a passing whisper, the tiny clinks of bayonets being fixed to rifles coalesced and tinkled down the line.

Suddenly, with an indescribable, earth-shattering roar, more than a thousand guns of all calibres vaulted a sizzling, screaming cascade of steel overhead. Explosives hidden in tunnels under the German lines erupted as if hell itself were vomiting mud and debris and bloody bits of bodies in protest. Even though he'd been expecting it, Justin was unnerved by the violent tremors and unearthly cacophony that reverberated in every cell of his body. The ceiling of red-hot metal seemed a palpable entity that would surely melt the relentless snow and decimate the enemy.

Like tightly wound springs grateful to be released from the tension and the frigid trenches, the first wave of troops sprang into no-man's-land and began their measured march – a hundred yards every three minutes – close behind the protective shield of the creeping artillery barrage. The "Vimy Glide" the men called it.

For a few mesmerizing and spectacular moments the entire ridge scintillated with multi-coloured fireworks as the Germans sent up hundreds of SOS flares. But because of thorough intelligence work and aerial observation, and well-calibrated guns, much of the German artillery had already been silenced, so the answering barrage was sporadic.

Justin wondered that there could be any Germans left on the other side of this fearsome, nerve-shattering curtain of fire and destruction.

But within minutes some of the advancing troops were being felled like marionettes with severed strings or ripped apart by machine gun bullets and trench mortars. Their comrades walked on without a pause, as they had been trained. The wounded, when able, stuck their rifles into the ground to indicate that they required help. Those who could crawl, snaked their way back to their own lines, knowing that help could be long in coming, although stretcher-bearers were already making their way onto the killing fields.

Dawn was elusive in the blinding storm, but when the snow finally abated, Justin could see the pockmarked, churned-up slope of Vimy disgorging its gruesome bloody stew from beneath the deceptive, melting white blanket.

It wasn't long before confused and terrified Germans stumbled across the debris toward the Canadian trenches. There was little manpower to escort prisoners, so unarmed POWs were sent back on their own, some helping as stretcher-bearers or supporting the walking wounded, and others rushing eagerly toward what they hoped was safety. Some were felled by their own shells.

The forward troops sent up white Very lights to indicate that they had achieved their first objective, capturing the three front line German trenches. Justin was impressed that they had done it exactly on schedule and in only half an hour.

Now it was time for his company to set out, to pick their way through the churned up earth and pulverized trenches, around the bloody, water-filled shell holes and deep mine craters, past the stranded tanks that couldn't get through the honeycombed porridge of mud. Ignoring the moaning, screaming, mutilated, drowning, dying wounded whom they couldn't stop to help. One boy, pleading for water, sat waist-deep in it, the top of his head missing, exposing his brains. A legless man calmly smoked a cigarette as his life's blood pumped out of the ragged stumps. They had to ignore the carnage or they would become impotent.

They assembled at the Black Line, taking over from the forward troops, and at exactly 6:55 the creeping barrage began again with Justin's company among those following behind. The enemy shrapnel burst around them, but even some of their own shells fell short, blowing a few of Justin's men to pieces. They took cover in a crater when an obdurate machine gun post strafed them. Justin sent men off on both flanks for a three-pronged attack on the gunners. Mills bombs and bayonets cleared out the machine gun nest without too many casualties to his company.

Most of them reached their objective, although they could recognize no landmarks. Entire woods had been annihilated by the intense bombing, with not even a tree stump to indicate they had ever existed. Nor was there anything but dust where a village had once stood.

Justin was startled as a group of about fifty Germans suddenly popped up out of a crater. One of his men pulled the pin on a Mills bomb and was just about to lob it at them when Justin shouted, "No! Stop!"

The Germans had quickly raised a white flag. They threw down their guns and clambered out of the hole, pulling off their watches to offer as souvenirs in a good-will gesture. "Kamerad! Kamerad! No shooting!" a few yelled. In almost perfect English, another one said, "Have mercy on us! We surrender!" Several were barely dressed, as if they had just awakened.

The boy with the armed grenade shrugged. It would explode in four seconds once he released his grip, so he tossed it as far as he could over the heads of the advancing prisoners. It landed in another pit from which a dozen more Germans scrambled, some bleeding from the explosion, all raising their hands in defeat.

The English-speaking German began jabbering nervously, "Are any of you fellows from Toronto? I lived there for seven years. I shopped at Eaton's. I went to baseball games at Hanlon's Point. Boy oh boy, I sure like baseball! I was apprenticing with my uncle to be a jeweller. Does anybody know his store, Bergdorfs?"

One of the Canadian sergeants laughed. "Damn right I do! I bought my wife's wedding ring there. Hey, Fritz, why didn't you join the Canadian army?" he joshed.

"I wanted to be a Canadian. Sure, I did! But my mother said I must return to Germany when the war started. So I went to New York and took a ship home."

"Well, you'll be with us for a while now," the sergeant said.

The German went happily with the guards detailed to take the prisoners back to the Canadian front line. Justin could hear him telling one of his captors, "I took my girlfriend to the CNE, and on Sundays in summer we went on the ferry to Toronto Island. Boy, I sure miss Toronto. And my girl...."

Justin's company began to secure the line, consolidate, reverse the trenches so that they were prepared for a counterattack. Meanwhile the next wave of the assault was assembling and waiting for the barrage to begin rolling forward again. By early afternoon, most of the Canadian Corps had achieved their objectives. Justin met up with his battalion and brigade commanders later as they stood in the emerging sunshine at the crest of the ridge surveying the vast Douai plain that spread before them. Justin was already mentally writing a letter to Antonia.

I think what struck me and surely the others most of all was the contrast. The countryside to the east looked so normal and unmolested and green, the towns and villages whole and complaisant, while the slope behind us was a sea of mud and blood and devastation, with only khaki and brown as far as the eye could see to the west. I was also shocked by the fact that we had actually managed to gain the ridge, since from this height I can truly understand what an advantage the Germans had. The odds were against us, but we really had taken them unawares. One German officer hadn't even had time to pull on his trousers. Another left a rather splendid breakfast for us. The intense preliminary shelling had also done a lot of damage to their trenches and fortifications, and most particularly to the morale and nerves of the German troops. The Week of Suffering, they called it. So as I watched the retreating enemy, I felt a true glimmer of hope.

What he wouldn't tell her was that the euphoria of finding himself still alive made him eager and impatient to embrace all the sweet joys that life had to offer. He had a sudden burning desire to see her, touch her, make love to her.

Justin was jolted out of his daydream when a Forward Observation Officer swore as he watched the fleeing Germans. "Christ Almighty! We can't get the blasted artillery close enough to target them because our barrage churned up the earth so badly that the horses can't pull the guns through the quagmire. How's that for irony? And where's the bloody cavalry when you need them? Shit, what a wasted opportunity!"

It seemed that no one had truly prepared for the eventuality of success.

In a few more days, Vimy Ridge would be and stay securely in Allied hands. But with over 10,000 more Canadian casualties, that victory had been dearly bought. A third of them would never return home.

It would later be said that the Canadian nation was born on the battlefields of Vimy. A bloody birth indeed.

For Justin, it was an exciting rebirth.

.   .   .

It was one thing to engage enemy aircraft in a duel, and quite another to shoot men on the ground, Chas thought. He could see the frightened faces of the boys who manned the guns as he swooped low over them and opened fire. God, he had no stomach for this kind of warfare!

His only consolation was that the Canadian troops who had been pinned down by these stubborn machine gun posts were now able to keep advancing.

It was a tricky day for flying, not only because of the weather, but also because of the constant jolts from the bursting shells. He had seen one plane, flying too close to the deadly canopy of missiles, explode like a clay pigeon – not one of his squadron, thank God, and hopefully not Rafe's.

It was an impressive sight from the air – the Vimy offensive. The Canadian troops seemed to be out for a Sunday stroll, some occasionally dropping down as if to rest, but the remainder eventually congregating well behind the German lines. Meanwhile, grey-clad Germans were streaming in the opposite direction, toward the Canadian trenches, as if it were a game where the opponents were switching ends at halftime.

There was a message from Boom Trenchard when Chas returned from his foray. "Major Chas Thornton is ordered not to fly combat missions without express instructions from HQ."

.   .   .

Like angry wasps, Richthofen's blood-red Jasta was all over them, and Rafe felt a moment of panic, which he knew could be deadly. Chas had told him, "You have to remain detached, unemotional. Cold-blooded." But Rafe had just seen his third comrade go down, including his Flight Commander.

He could still hear Chas's voice in his head. *Focus. Don't let him get behind you or under you. Pull up in a loop and dive down on him.*

The machine shuddered and groaned as he pushed it heavenward at full throttle. Then he went over on his back and plummeted like a hawk towards his prey. At thirty yards he fired on an Albatros, watching his smoky tracer bullets slam into the fuselage and break the wing struts. The plane spun crazily out of control.

Don't get complacent or sidetracked by a victory. You can celebrate later.

Damn! He had to change his ammunition drum, so he tried to dodge away from the dogfight, but a Hun was hard on his tail. Bullets whizzed past his ears, smashing into the instrument panel, which spewed oil into his face. He tore off his goggles so that he could see. More bullets riddled his plane. A hot pain slashed through his arm. The engine sputtered and died.

.　　.　　.

"Chas..," Jack Scott hesitated, but Chas knew with icy dread what he was about to tell him, since Scott had called him by his first name. "'B' Flight was in a fierce scrap with Richthofen over Monchy-le-Preux. Only one of them returned."

And it wasn't Rafe. "Is he dead?" Chas asked.

"Rutherford saw him go down with a smoking engine, although he seemed to be in some control... But it was Richthofen who followed him."

And Chas had heard that the Baron sometimes showed his victims no mercy.

"We haven't yet received a confirmation of how many have been taken prisoner."

Or if they were all dead. Chas wondered how he would tell his mother.

"I'm sorry, Chas. I'll let you know as soon as I hear anything. I've lost thirteen pilots in the last two weeks!" Scott said with mournful anger. "How do they expect us to fight Fritz when our machines are so inferior?"

Chas had a cognac that helped to ignite some fire inside the cold numbness. 'B' and 'C' Flights were still out on patrols, so he said to his adjutant, "Tell 'A' Flight to prepare to go up again. We're going hunting!"

Cruising at 15,000 feet, they were far behind the enemy lines, nearly at Douai, before Chas spotted a Jasta a couple of thousand feet below. He signaled to the others and dived down at full throttle. He opened fire on the first plane at ten yards and saw the unsuspecting pilot slump forward. The Albatros turned turtle and spiraled earthward. In the ensuing melee with the other fighters, Chas put another one into a fatal spin, its engine damaged and spewing out black smoke. The remaining Albatroses tried to flee, but Chas pursued them, his men staying in practiced formation with him.

Suddenly there were a dozen more gaily coloured scouts dropping out of the clouds at them, and Chas realized that he mustn't endanger his men because of his own anger. He broke off the fight and headed back. But the Huns weren't about to let them go that easily, especially since the Flying Dragons were now about twenty-five miles behind the enemy lines, and heavily outnumbered.

They used all their aerobatic skills to outmaneuver the Germans. They had been well drilled on marksmanship, so his men shot down four while Chas got another one.

But he also noticed that one of his boys was hit and falling out of control. As a green and yellow Albatros followed him down, the others broke off the battle and flew away.

Chas led his men back before any more Hun scouts could be mobilized. When they landed at the aerodrome, he discovered that Jensen had been badly wounded. He'd managed to land his plane before losing consciousness.

"You all did splendidly," Chas told his men, but wondered, while he was writing up his report, whether he himself had. Had his judgment been clouded by his anxiety about Rafe? Had he potentially lost two men because of that?

It was a relief to hear later that evening that Jensen was out of danger, although he would be out of commission for many months. And they had word that the downed pilot had been taken prisoner.

"Fine bit of work today, Thornton!" Boom Trenchard barked as he suddenly appeared in the mess. "Thirty victories now, have you? But I thought I ordered you to stay out of the action."

"Like Jack Scott?" Chas asked wryly. Scott had even allowed himself to be used as bait in a stunt that had given Billy Bishop another two victories.

Trenchard laughed. "Can't keep you fellows on the ground, can we? I just came from 60 Squadron. They've received a note, signed by Richthofen. Seems that three of our pilots were captured, two of them slightly wounded. Your brother is one."

"Thank God!" Rafe would hate being a prisoner, but at least he was alive. And would now be relatively safe for the duration of the war. Chas was amused as he imagined Rafe cursing that he hadn't paid more attention to languages at school.

"He had a confirmed kill before he was shot, but it only gives him four, so unfortunately, we can't call him an Ace," Trenchard said. "You, on the other hand, should be content with the medals you've won, although I'll have to mention you in Dispatches again. But I imagine that there are plenty of chaps who wouldn't mind seeing that pretty little wife of yours as a widow."

In response to Chas's telegram, Ria wrote back, *Delighted Rafe OK. Heard from Eddie you now have 30. Love you anyway.*

.   .   .

Ria had known it was going to be bad, but had conveniently forgotten how gruelling it was to work for days with little sleep and barely time for a meal. A quarter of the WATS were in the Sick Sisters' Hospital with measles – a few with added complications of painful eye ulcers and one with pneumonia, which meant they would be away for many weeks or months. With the big Arras offensive on, casualties were continually streaming in, so the others had an almost impossible workload.

Ria hadn't been out of her uniform for a week, too tired to do anything but collapse into bed, with no more than a splash of water on her face and a quick brushing of teeth. She longed for a hot bath and undisturbed sleep. But the nighttime air raids on Calais were relentless, and some of the WATS, like her, refused to sit in the shelter when they had only a few precious hours of rest available. After a close bombing, Sybil had discovered a sizeable chunk of shell fragment that had come through the wall and imbedded itself rather low in her door. They had all marvelled at how closely it must have skimmed over her bed – while she was in it. But Sybil had grinned and said, "Another souvenir for our 'narrow-escape' shelf!"

Fortunately, Lucinda Ashby-Grey had been allowed to return, since she had settled her parents into a small but comfortable flat to minimize the workload for the one very capable woman she had managed to find, and had rented out their large house to a wealthy Canadian family for the duration of the war and a sizable profit. Her aunt had been so impressed with her no-nonsense organization and with the increasing fame of the WATS, that she had insisted Lucinda return to France. Cinders couldn't have been happier, and cheerfully embraced the long, arduous days.

But Ria groaned as she heard one of her passengers vomiting for the third time. There would be a stomach-churning mess for her to clean up before she could make the next run. But she berated herself for her selfish thoughts as another boy yelled, "He's spewing blood this time, Sister!"

"We're almost there, lad. Hang on."

But he was dead when they arrived at the hospital. No matter what the reports were saying about how well the Canadians had done at Vimy Ridge, they'd paid a high price in casualties.

It wasn't until her fourth week back that Ria felt clean and rested again, and able to spend time with her friends. Lance was involved in the Arras offensive as well, but Eddie Stratton and Jonathan Telford stopped in for tea when they could.

Sybil breezed into Ria's cubicle one evening, dropped onto her bed, and said, "I'll have some of that very fine cognac that you brought, Windy. I'm feeling a bit wobbly, but that should help."

"You're not coming down with measles, surely?"

"Had them as a nipper. Just worn out, I think. After all, I didn't spend the coldest winter in eternity in warm luxury like you did."

"Aren't you due for some leave?"

"I went to Cannes in March, remember? Mummy will never forgive me for not coming home, but it was fabulous. I told you Adam Bentley was there, convalescing from bronchitis." She ginned suggestively.

"And most appreciative of your company."

"Of course. If he'd been feeling stronger I would have seduced him."

Ria laughed.

"Windy, that's where we should be working! Imagine driving all those lovely officers who are only recovering from nicely healing wounds or non-fatal illnesses. No bodily effluences fouling your ambulance. No shrieks of agony over every bump. No bombs exploding around you or keeping you from your sumptuous, soft, clean bed. Beaches. Mountains. Sunshine. Romantic villages. Soft, moonlit nights..."

"Sounds heavenly," Carly said, joining them. Boots jumped onto Ria's bed and sat listening with his head cocked to one side. "What are we talking about?"

"Paradise," Sybil said with a happy smile. "Instead, we're in a primitive shelter constantly bombarded by nasty Huns, battling perpetual winds off the frigid North Sea, plagued by chatts..."

"Again?" Ria asked.

Sybil scratched and said, "Whenever the men come straight from the trenches, their lice just delight in finding me. Actually, the bites look like measles so perhaps I can get away with that excuse and relax in the hospital for a few weeks."

"I don't mean to be rude, Foxy, but would you kindly take your lousy self off my bed," Ria said.

"Well! I can see who my real friends are!"

As Sybil rose, she staggered and fell against the bed.

"Are you alright?"

Sybil had barely touched her drink. "A bit woozy. And my shins hurt something wicked. That endless driving, I expect."

Ria could feel the heat emanating from Sybil even through her sleeve. She put her hand on Sybil's brow. "You're on fire, Foxy!"

"Am I? I just feel dead beat. And I have a crushing headache. It's silly, but even my eyes hurt."

Ria and Carly took her to the Sick Sisters' Hospital in Calais, where Sybil was diagnosed with trench fever.

"But that's absurd," she said to them when she'd been settled into bed. "Not that I'm complaining about being here. Not as nice as the Riviera, though. But how could I have trench fever when I've never been near a trench?"

"No one seems to know what causes it, so perhaps it's contagious, like the measles," Carly said.

"You're out of it for a while," Ria said. "So enjoy your rest."

It was quite late and pitch-black when Ria and Carly returned to camp, so Carly said, "At least there won't be an air raid tonight."

But suddenly there was a deafening screech and a swoosh of wind that made their hair blow straight up and a tornado of pebbles smack painfully against their legs.

"What the devil was that?" Carly asked.

"Devil, indeed!" There was no sound of aeroplanes.

Another shell whined overhead, but this time Ria had seen a flash of light from the sea. "There must be a destroyer out there!"

They had never been shelled from the sea before, but these screaming, whining, whizzing projectiles were obviously aimed at Calais, most of them skimming over the camp in an unnervingly low arc.

The other girls had been roused by the cacophony, and hurried into the dugout.

"This is worse than bombs plopping down from aeroplanes," Antonia said. "Some of them sound like a blood-curdling roar from a mad animal."

"Gives me the shivers," Baby agreed.

Although there was a gas curtain over the entrance, the smell of gunpowder was nauseatingly strong. The earth shook as several shells must have landed nearby.

"I'm praying that they don't hit the hospital in Calais. Half our girls are there," Carly said.

By the time the German destroyer slipped away, it had lobbed over three hundred shells onto Calais, several landing on the WATS camp, imbedded in the bank behind the dugout and one that had exploded the incinerator. They quickly ascertained that the hospitalized girls were safe, and that there were remarkably few casualties considering the destructive battering the city had taken.

They wondered if the booming of guns in the Channel that night, louder and closer than the usual background rumbling, was a naval battle with the cheeky German invader.

ComRad chuckled as she told them at breakfast, "Rumour has it that the 'plucky lady drivers' have finally 'copped it'. Seems the German destroyer was only a hundred yards offshore here. *Stores* even took bets to see if any of us would show up today!" she added, referring to their military supply depot.

"Very sporting of them," Carly commented dryly.

Everyone she passed that day gave Ria big smiles and hearty waves. The people of Calais had taken the WATS into their hearts, and were rather proud of these eccentric English Mademoiselles.

. . .

It came to be known as Bloody April, with the RFC losing over three hundred men, a third of them taken prisoner. Scott's 60 Squadron alone lost nineteen, and Billy Bishop, who had been a novice only weeks earlier, was now a Captain with nineteen victories, a Military Cross, and the Distinguished Service Order. The highly trained Flying Dragons with their swift scouts had only three casualties and one taken prisoner. Of the two wounded, one had already returned to the squadron at the end of the month.

In early May, Albert Ball died in a crash. And Chas inherited his title as top British Ace.

Only a few days later, McPherson walked into the officers' mess accompanied by a German pilot. McFearsome, as he was called by his colleagues, was a tall, thin fellow, refined and delicate looking, but a crack shot and absolutely fearless in combat. He was Chas's favourite among his pilots. Cultured, and charming, self-assured but not boastful, he hailed from Elora,

Ontario, and was the son of a Presbyterian minister. McPherson had, however, confided in Chas about his loss of faith and how it affected his relationship with his father.

He was trying to communicate with his companion in gestures, since obviously neither spoke the others' language beyond some rudimentary phrases.

To Chas and the others, McPherson said casually, "I've brought a guest to dinner. Shot him down not a mile away, so I thought we might as well feed him before the army comes to fetch him. I've established that he's one of Boelcke's former squadron, and he knows Richthofen."

It struck Chas that the tall, fair German could easily have been McPherson's brother. The captive nodded as if understanding what McPherson had said.

Chas said, "Willkommen, Oberleutnant."

"Ach Sie sprechen Deutsch, dann bin ích ja hier genau richtig!"

In German, Chas said to him, "I do speak a bit of German. Do sit down. May we offer you a glass of wine?"

"Thank you. You are all most gracious."

Introductions were made, and Oberleutnant Stefan Tauner was astonished to meet "the famous Major Thornton, the dragonfly pilot!" Excitedly he said, "Rittmeister von Richthofen has great respect for you, Major. He says that you fly and hunt like a dragonfly. You are a master of the air."

"And, of course, he is hoping to shoot me down," Chas said with a grin.

"Naturally," the young lieutenant replied with a bigger one. "Either that or sit down and talk with you over a glass of cognac. He encountered you when he was still an inexperienced pilot last year. You shot up his machine and engine very badly so he dove for safety, and was surprised that you did not follow him down to finish him off. One of his comrades reported that you had gone instead to the aid of one of your men."

Chas was shocked to think that if he had pursued and killed Richthofen that day, there might now be dozens more of his colleagues alive. It was one of the reasons that Wing Command liked to see enemy planes and pilots destroyed, if not taken captive. But Trenchard's aggressive, offensive policy ensured that most of the aerial battles were fought behind the German lines, which left little option for the British pilots. Shooting an aeroplane out of the sky was one thing, but deliberately killing the pilot was an act that Chas had always balked at. One of his COs had once commented, "You're damned competitive, Thornton, but you don't have the killer instinct. You'd be top Ace by now if you didn't let so many of them get away. Aeroplanes are easier to replace than trained pilots. Next time, he might get you."

If Rafe had been killed, how would he have lived with the knowledge that he might have prevented that?

Tauner looked suddenly sad as he said, "Your Albert Ball was a worthy opponent. But he was like an avenging angel. Had us all scared, I don't mind admitting."

Chas had been translating and could see by his men's faces that they had a fellow feeling for this erstwhile foe. Weren't they all just daring young adventurers enjoying the freedom of the skies while trying to do their duty to their countries? And weren't they all terrified at times?

McPherson said, "Can you ask him what he was doing so far behind the lines, Sir?"

Tauner looked sheepish as he explained that after a skirmish near the lines, he'd been separated from his squadron. His engine was misbehaving and he began looking for a place to land, but the wind was from the east today, and kept driving him farther over the British sector. With his compass smashed, he got rather lost. McPherson had been out stunting and came across him by chance. A few more bullets put Tauner's engine completely out of commission.

"You will let my squadron know that I am safe?" he asked.

"Yes, of course," Chas replied. "McPherson will drop them a note first thing in the morning. You may write one yourself, if you like. But no military information."

"Of course not, Major. I am quite aware that I'm lucky to be alive. Also, I have always wanted to see England." He gave them a broad smile. "Perhaps now I will learn English. A colleague in my Jasta has cousins in the United States of America, in Pittsburgh. His English is very good."

Chas asked, "What's their name, these American cousins?"

"I must think. Row…"

"Roland?"

"That is it! You know them?" He was as astonished as Chas.

"They are friends! We have summer homes on the same lake in Canada."

"Dear God, but the world is a small place, is it not? I wish I could tell him."

"Put it into your note," Chas suggested. "His cousin, Troy, is working at a hospital in France. Troy's brother, Kurt, was with the Lafayette Escadrille. He was killed recently."

"How sad. I must let Guntram know." Stefan Tauner shook his head in disbelief. "It has occurred to me that you are the Ace that has Guntram's blood up. You shot down his brother last year."

"Good Lord!" Chas wondered if Troy knew. This really was a damnable war!

"We'll have to watch your back, Major, with him and Richthofen gunning for you," McPherson said.

Over a delicious roast beef dinner and plenty of champagne there was much animated conversation and laughter. Stefan told them that he had been studying philosophy when the war broke out. Now he thought he might want to be a diplomat some day. "And hopefully stop this from happening again," he added. "You will allow me to visit you, Major?" he asked Chas.

"*Après la guerre*, all things will be possible," Chas responded.

They were all rather sorry when the army came to haul away their guest, and wished him luck. He had managed to pen a few words to his squadron, and to his family, which Chas, of course, vetted. McPherson dropped the letters on a quick sortie with 'B' Flight first thing in the morning. On the way back, they encountered another Jasta and managed to flame one of the scouts over the German lines. War was anything but logical.

Baron Manfred von Richthofen went on leave with fifty-two victories, and the Flying Dragons realized that much of the aggressiveness suddenly went out of the other German fighter pilots. Perhaps it was because they, too, had suffered enormous, though fewer losses in April that they now opted to scuttle away instead of engaging the British more than necessary. The Hun two-seater recce planes had developed new tactics of flying low over their own lines in groups of three or four, and diving down and away whenever the RFC scouts came close, exposing them to deadly accurate enemy fire. So it became almost as dangerous and difficult to get the two-seaters as the observation balloons, and the S.E.5s often returned from forays badly shot up.

Chas noticed a serious case of fatigue and nerves affecting his men, so he started sending them on leave. Now that the major spring offensive was over, Wing reduced the patrols to two a day from four. Chas declared that his pilots were also to have one day off in every three. To make sure they stayed fit and didn't indulge in too much social drinking because of boredom, Chas had a tennis court made, and a nearby field was turned into a cricket pitch. He also encouraged them to fly during their off-time, just to practice their aerobatics and fight mock duels over home turf. They needed little encouragement to go up for fun.

Summer-like weather finally won the battle against a cold and tenacious winter, skipping spring altogether. One fine day, Chas was surprised when an F.E.2b landed and Jack emerged from the cockpit. He helped Lord Beaverbrook down from the forward nacelle.

"I didn't realize until now how much I've missed you," Chas said as he shook Jack's hand warmly.

Jack was pleased. He, too, had missed Chas's company, but he'd been damned glad he hadn't been involved with Bloody April. How long would his luck have held?

"Lord Beaverbrook, may I offer my congratulations on your peerage," Chas said graciously.

"Not all it's cracked up to be," Max Aitken said with a dismissive wave of his hand. "Look here, Thornton, we're all proud of you as Britain's top Ace. We Canadians are constantly showing our mettle, surprising the Brits – Vimy and all that. Now there's talk in the War Cabinet about forming a separate Canadian Air Force. I like the idea, so I want to discuss it with you."

Once they were comfortably settled in Chas's office with a glass of very fine Scotch, Beaverbrook said, "Did you know that a third of the RFC is Canadian? We're now training pilots in Ontario – and a damned sight better than in England!"

Chas had no qualms about being part of the British military, but it was exciting to think that Canada could have its own Air Force.

"I thought there was talk of amalgamating the RFC and RNAS into an independent Air Force," Chas said.

"That's being examined as well. But if we Canadians get our own, you could be top dog, Thornton," Beaverbrook said. "Have the whole operation under your control. What do you say?"

"Do I get to design aeroplanes as well?" he asked mischievously.

Beaverbrook laughed delightedly. "I don't see why not!"

"Then yes, I'm game."

"Knew I could count on you, Thornton. You're a man of foresight and ingenuity, like your father."

"Thank you, Sir."

Beaverbrook and Jack stayed to dinner, and one of the pilots, who hailed from New Brunswick, spent a good deal of time reminiscing about home with Beaverbrook, who delighted in his Maritime roots.

That gave Chas and Jack a chance to talk.

"I feel rather like I'm swinging the lead, especially with the losses last month," Jack confessed. It was true, which surprised him, but he was also not prepared to risk his neck again if he didn't have to. His conscience would just have to accustom itself to his greater need to survive. Intact, unscathed.

"You're helping to document the war. That's useful work as well. How do like the F.E.?"

"A damn sight more than the B.E.! Great forward field of vision, which is what we need when we're filming and photographing. And fighting." Jack ginned. "And I can do perfect landings now, with those telescoping legs." He'd been nicknamed "Bouncer" in 2nd Squadron because of his bumpy landings.

Chas laughed. "I think it's virtually impossible to land it badly. I'm sure his Lordship appreciates that."

"He's quite chuffed having me fly him about, although he's not in France much these days. He likes me to take foreign journalists and visitors about, especially the Americans." Jack knew that it was a subtle form of propaganda, showing the best of Britain's war effort, which would then be glowingly reported back home. Not all the visitors were interested in a flight just behind the lines, but Jack was expected to exercise his charm while he escorted them to key sites. Sid laughingly called him Max's whore. "But sometimes I long for a flip in a scout again, do some real flying."

"Stunting, you mean. I go up as often as I can, just for the sheer joy of it. When the war is over, I'll definitely have to buy an aeroplane. Ria is itching to fly as well."

Somewhat reluctantly, Jack said, "I have to tell you that I ran into Madeline recently. She's living in St. Omer now. And seems to be rather fond of pilots. I'm not saying she's a tart, Chas. I think she's looking for someone – like you – who will marry her, but she's got the wrong end of the stick if she thinks it's going to be one of our chaps. They're only out for a good time, as you know. Your son, by the way, is a handsome child."

Chas grimaced. "Odd, isn't it, how something so innocuous at the time can become such a *bête noir*?" She had been inexperienced when he had made love to her. Having then abandoned Madeline, he felt responsible for her. And he hated that burden. It was a hard lesson to learn that throwing money at a problem still didn't make it go away.

"She's doing well, Chas. Your support is obviously giving her and the boy a comfortable life. I hardly recognized her at first, she was so chic and sophisticated. Not the frightened girl you knew."

"Did she say anything to you?"

Jack hesitated, not wanting to tell Chas, but thinking that any sort of advantage that he had over him would be helpful. "That she still loves you, and is proud of your achievements. That she will ensure that Charles knows about his illustrious father. That she hasn't found anyone like you."

"Christ!" Chas said, running his fingers agitatedly through his hair. "Will this haunt me forever?"

Jack couldn't offer any reprieve.

. . .

Chas managed to take a couple of days off, so he flew up to Marquise, borrowed a motorcycle from the aerodrome, and visited Ria. He had timed it to coincide with her day off, and ComRad allowed her to stay one night with him at the Auberge de la Plage.

As it was a hot, sunny day, they borrowed horses from the Cavalry camp and explored the countryside. They followed an inland trail through wildflower-sprinkled meadows, woodlands carpeted with bluebells, primroses, and violets, past rose-entwined manor houses and tranquil farms. In a secluded valley they came upon an ancient mill that had been turned into an estaminet, where they enjoyed a delightful lunch on a terrace overlooking the stream. As they lingered over their wine, Ria said, "This is heavenly. Just this minute, I could believe that there isn't a war."

He squeezed her hand as he said, "One day we will be able to truly enjoy Europe. We still have to do our Grand Tour."

"But first I want to go home. Sometimes I miss it so much! Right now the ravine behind Wyndholme is sprinkled with trilliums, and the orchard's in glorious bloom. My favourite memory of spring is walking under the fragrant apple boughs when they shower downy petals on me. You and Sophie will love it there, Chas! From the tower you can watch the leaves unfurling on the trees until the whole valley is a sea of fresh, energetic green in a thousand different shades and hues."

"I see you're pining for your paintbrush as well as home," Chas chuckled. "But you've made is sound so enticing that I can hardly wait to move in." He added wryly, "Although it's the man who's supposed to provide his lady-love with the castle."

She laughed. "It's strange and exciting that you're going to be there with me!"

"In the meantime, let's plan your leave in July. I should be able to take a few days and be here with you before you head back to England. Unless you'd rather meet in Paris."

"Paris is filled with soldiers and war. I'd prefer this."

"Good! The French army is actually having some problems right now, so I'm glad you're not anywhere near the French sector. They had over a quarter of a million casualties in this last offensive, and the men are rebelling. Some of them haven't had home leave since the war began, so tens of thousands have been deserting from the trenches. Entire divisions are refusing to obey their Generals. I've heard that as much as half the French army is in revolt. And I've seen some of them. Drunk and disorderly and destructive, they make dangerous mobs."

"Hells bells! Does that mean we might lose the war?"

"Let's hope the French High Command can re-establish control. Fortunately the Americans are coming over soon. And we've let the war intrude again. I'm sorry, my darling." Chas kissed her hand. "I have an overwhelming urge to take off my boots, roll up my trousers, and wade in the stream. Care to join me?"

She laughed. "It'll be freezing cold! But of course I will."

After a blissful day, she was desolate when he had gone again, and said to her friends, "What I hate almost more than anything are the perpetual 'goodbyes', because each time you wonder if this will be the last time you see a friend or loved one."

Ria was still somewhat distracted when she returned from the Calais pier after her last evacuation run early the following morning. She noticed Nessie in front of her as she approached the railway crossing, and saw Carly stick out her arm and wave to the French gunners as she passed the anti-aircraft battery, the men cheerfully waving back, as usual. Ria received the same enthusiastic greeting a moment later.

Suddenly, just as Carly started across the rail lines, a train shot out of the tunnel. Ria slammed on her brakes and held her breath as she instantly realized that Carly could neither stop nor speed up to avoid a collision. The train clipped the front of the ambulance, dragging it along as the train squealed to a halt.

Nessie, mangled and steaming, finally fell away to one side after a hundred yards.

Terrified, Ria turned her ambulance along one of the parallel tracks and drove to the wreck. She almost wept with relief to see that Carly was conscious, if pale.

"I can't see Boots," Carly said as Ria tried to yank open the door, but to no avail.

Some of the gunners came running, and the train engineer rushed over.

"Are you in pain?" Ria asked.

"I do think I might have broken my legs," Carly said. "Beastly excruciating, at any rate."

"Where was the sentry?" the engineer barked angrily. "There's supposed to be a sentry on duty!"

"I'll have his hide!" one of the gunners said as the men struggled to pry open the door. Carly had a head wound that was bleeding profusely, but Ria knew that even minor cuts could look worse than they were, and hoped that that was the case this time. She chafed at the delay in getting Carly out.

One of the gunners crooned, "Mon pauvre p'tit chou! We will have you out of here in no time. You are so brave!"

"Do you see my Boots anywhere?"

"They are on your feet, n'est ce pas?" he said in bewilderment.

"Non, mon petit chien. Boots."

"Sapristi! You are worried about your dog?"

"Mais oui."

He shook his head. "We will worry first about you."

With Ria's tyre iron, they managed to pry open the door, but Carly's legs were trapped beneath the crushed metal where the engine had been rammed into the cab. Ria hastily bandaged Carly's head, but could now do nothing else but hold her hand. Whenever they freed her a bit more, Carly gasped in agony and crushed Ria's hand.

A British ambulance train stopped along another track, and a Medical Officer hurried over, along with a nurse and two orderlies. He gave Carly an injection of morphine, saying, "This will hurt a bit."

She managed a laugh as she replied on a gasp, "Not anything like as much my legs do, doctor."

She couldn't stifle a scream as they finally freed her, although the morphine had already taken effect.

Ria tried not to show her shock as she realized that one of Carly's legs was practically severed below the knee, and the other was badly crushed. The doctor immediately tied a tourniquet to stop the hemorrhaging. Until now, the pressure of the broken metal had prevented bleeding.

"Merde!" one of the gunners expostulated.

"Not as bad as all that, I hope," Carly said, wide-eyed, afraid to even glance at her legs. "I'm sure it looks worse than it is. Windy, you're so pale. Tell me I'll be alright! I'll be able to drive again, won't I?"

The doctor said, "You're going to be resting in hospital for a while."

The orderlies and gunners lifted her out as carefully as they could, but even with the morphine, she felt the slightest jar. "I have a new appreciation for the men I drive," she managed to say.

They put her into Ria's ambulance, and the nurse went along. Ria drove as quickly and carefully as she could to the Casino, but with every unavoidable bump, she heard Carly cry out. The hospital had already been alerted, and staff were waiting to receive her. She was wheeled right into an operating theatre.

Ria could no longer stop her tears. The CO of the hospital, who was a frequent guest at the WATS teas and had been among those meeting them, gripped her shoulder and said, "We see this all the time with the men, don't we? But somehow it's harder when it's a woman. And a friend."

"Will they have to amputate?"

"It doesn't look good for one leg. Let's hope they can save the other."

Ria was horrified. And suddenly icy cold as she realized that if the train had arrived a moment later, she would now be the one on the operating table. Or dead. She accepted a cup of tea but refused the proffered food while she waited. ComRad and Eddie joined her as soon as they could, he, pacing nervously.

It was a relief to finally know that Carly would pull through. One leg did indeed have to be amputated below the knee but the other, badly broken in several places, would heal in time.

"We have to tell her eventually that Boots was killed," Ria said.

It was what Carly cried about most at the beginning. Then she went into a severe depression, confessing that the unrelenting pain and frightening future made her want to just curl up and die.

Jonathan Telford was the best remedy for that. He truly cared for her, and spent even more time at her bedside than her brother and friends. Her room was constantly filled with fresh flowers, always some from him. When he proposed marriage, she rejected him, telling Ria, "It's a gallant gesture that he'll regret when he has a chance to ponder it. What man wants to be tied to a woman with only one rather wonky leg?"

The nerve endings of her severed leg felt raw and caused her immeasurable pain. "It's as if someone suddenly yanks on my stump with terrific force. Knife-like pain shoots up my body. I dread it, Windy. And it's worse at night, when there are no distractions." She wept again. "I'm sorry! I feel such a coward when I know the men endure this and much worse!"

"Don't underestimate what you're going through, Carly. And don't dismiss Jonathan so easily. I think he's completely in love with you, and doesn't care a jot about your having only one leg. You'll be able to dance again one day."

Carly had to undergo another surgery to fix the problem with her nerves, but there seemed no immediate benefit. She tried to be cheerful, but it sapped her energy and she fought melancholia.

The French gunners who had assisted her came to visit and explained that the sentry on duty had been caught up in the revolutionary zeal of the mutinous French army and decided to celebrate with an excessive amount of wine – and had promptly fallen asleep. Summary justice had been dispensed, and he was nursing a broken nose. But he would also be court-martialed. The punishment for sleeping on sentry duty was execution.

· · ·

Ria would have completely forgotten her twenty-first birthday had she not received telegrams from family and friends. The cable from Helena read,

Your father, sister, and I wish you every happiness on the occasion of your twenty-first birthday. Hope care package arrived. Not safe to send diamond brooch, which had been your mother's. Love from all.

Not a word from her father, but then he had never celebrated her birthday, since that had been the day her mother had died. There had been the perfunctory gift for her, but he would go to the city for a few days – since they were usually at Wyndwood then – to avoid her company. It had become a habit long after grief must have faded, but Ria expected Helena had cured him of that.

She was moved by Sophie's card made of dried flowers –
bluebells, violets, primroses, and lilies-of-the-valley – which the
child had collected.

Chas sent roses with a note.

*We will celebrate when I see you in a few weeks. Much as I
would love to show you your present, it will have to wait even
longer, I'm afraid. Freddie has sent this preliminary sketch.*

Ria was puzzled by the drawing of a boathouse. The layout
showed a generous second floor room lined with French windows
giving onto a deck, some of it under cover, with a bathroom, a
small bedroom, and a tiny kitchen behind. Off the boat slip on the
lower level were two change rooms.

*Now imagine this overlooking the Shimmering Sands. I bought
ten acres of that corner of Wyndwood from your father and uncles,
because I wanted you always to have that special place, Ria. This
will be our very own private retreat. Won't it be fun to picnic there,
stay overnight on a whim, indulge in a midnight swim, watch the
sunrise from the balcony? Sophie and the half-dozen other children
that we'll undoubtedly adopt will just have to cope without us
occasionally.*

Happy Birthday, my beloved darling!

.   .   .

There was a terrific explosion early in the morning of June 7th
that practically shook Carly out of bed and set her leg afire with
pain. "I thought we were being bombed, but I've since heard it's
just a new offensive that started near Ypres," she said to Ria later
that day.

"Our engineers blew up the Messines Ridge," Ria told her.
"Apparently the explosion was heard as far away as Dublin."

"Good Lord! Then I expect you'll be busy again."

"Unfortunately. And Sybil's not coming back anytime soon."
Foxy had such crippling rheumatic pains in her legs from the
trench fever that she was barely able to walk. She was now
convalescing at home in England. "I'll read you her latest letter."

*Tell Carly I'm looking forward to her coming to England, as
I'm feeling quite forlorn without my dearest friends about. We'll
both zip about in our wheelchairs, and perhaps instigate races.*

*If my favourite cavalry chaps are back, I trust the girls aren't
flirting with Captain Bentley. Be sure they know that I'm now an
excellent fencer, thanks to him. He's actually written to me a few
times, concerned about me! Said he'd take me to see the Bing Boys*

in London (ooo! la! la!) when he's on leave this summer, if I'm still here. Rest assured that I'm not at all fit to return just yet.

It's actually not so bad being home. Living as we do near Canterbury, there are any number of lovely officers about. Mater likes having them to tea, so that she feels she's doing her bit and staying connected with news from the Front. The cavalry chaps in particular are keen on Pater's stables. I wish I were able to ride, though. I miss that even more than driving. But sometimes I can barely take the weight of the blankets on my legs.

One of the problems with being in the military zone is that we're close to strategic targets. You'll have heard of the surprising and devastating daytime aeroplane raid on Folkestone recently. All those poor people out shopping! And they got some of your lovely Canadians in the Shorncliffe Camp as well. There were nearly a hundred killed and two hundred injured. You have to hand it to the Germans – they have incredible gall! Mater – and everyone else – wants to know where the RFC is when they're needed. She thinks they should be here guarding us rather than messing about in France.

It was only a week later that Ria was visiting Carly when Eddie and Jonathan arrived. "You're looking in the pink today, Sis," Eddie said, kissing her cheek.

"I'm just beastly hot! And this cast is so tiresome." Her "good" leg was encased up to her hip in plaster.

"The doctor says you can go to England as soon as he finds a place to send you. Seems the military hospitals don't know what to do with wounded women. But we'll be visiting you wherever you are," he added with a grin.

"You're going on leave?"

"Transferred to Home Defence. Seems everyone's in an uproar since Jerry bombed London the other day. In broad daylight, cheeky blighters!"

"Was it a bad raid?" Ria asked.

"Yes. They hit the Liverpool Street station, a train, which caught on fire, shops, restaurants, and a school, killing a bunch of kiddies. Over a hundred and sixty dead and more than four hundred injured. Seems that Jerry's Gotha bombers are slipping past all our defences with ease. We didn't shoot down a single plane."

"Hell's bells!" Ria didn't have to voice her fears that if the Germans could so easily attack by air, the war became even more dire for Britain.

"Precisely. We're going to be stationed just outside of London, but I won't be happy if you're sent there," Eddie said to Carly.

"But surely they wouldn't bomb hospitals!"

"Presumably they wouldn't bomb schools, knowingly. Although a lot of people aren't giving the Huns that much credit. There've been riots in London. Mobs have been smashing and looting shops of anyone with a German name or connection."

"Good Lord!"

Ria was worried about Zoë, who was working at the IODE hospital overlooking Hyde Park.

"When are you leaving?" Carly asked sadly.

"Tomorrow," Eddie replied. At a meaningful glance from Jonathan, Eddie said to Ria, "Perhaps you could help me bring something in from the car."

Once they were outside, Ria said, "I hope this diversionary tactic is to give Jonathan time to propose again."

It was another sweltering day. Eddie leaned against the wall in the shade, which wasn't much cooler, and offered Ria a cigarette. "Spot on. The champagne is on ice in the boot. I don't think he'll accept 'no' for an answer this time."

"That's ripping! I expect this will pull her out of her funk. I think she should meet our footman. He's an inspiration." She told him about Patrick.

"Good idea. When are you going on leave?"

"In a few weeks, if things don't get too hectic here. But I don't think Carly will be up to visiting Priory Manor just yet."

Suddenly serious, Eddie said, "You should stay home, Ria. You girls shouldn't be here."

"Neither should you fellows."

"I *am* going to England, remember? Jonathan and I are both being promoted to Flight Commanders. But it's a hell of a lot safer over there than here. We had almost a hundred planes up in the raid on London, and not a single one of our pilots even saw an enemy aircraft."

"So you think it's going to be a cakewalk?" she said with amusement.

"Our aerodrome is half an hour by train to the best seats in the house for *Chou Chin Chow*."

"And all the other earthly delights of London. Carly won't be pleased if Jonathan spends his evenings in London nightclubs."

"He won't. He'll be at her bedside if she's there, and writing reams of letters if she isn't. He's absolutely besotted by my little sister."

"I should hope so! And Chas will be pleased to hear that you've been gazetted Captain," she said astutely. "Haven't you?"

He laughed. "Yes. I was holding off on that since it's not as important as the engagement. Shall we go and see how that's progressing?"

When they went to fetch the wine and glasses from the car, Ria told Eddie that they had a Stratton motorcar at Priory Manor. "I was thinking that you'll need some useful occupation after the war, so you should design a car that doesn't require a clutch, so that Carly can still drive. With an electric starter, if you please!"

Eddie laughed delightedly. "You may well be onto something there!"

"She's not the only one, is she? Not to be seen as a war profiteer, but just think of all the chaps who would be regaining independence if they were mobile like that."

"You are priceless, Ria! You'll have to meet Dad and sell him on your ideas." Eddie was still chuckling as they walked into Carly's room.

She was brushing away tears, but they seemed to be happy ones.

"Can I pop the cork?" Eddie asked.

Jonathan was holding her hand and beaming. "As the Americans would so appropriately say... you bet!"

Chapter 12

"It hurts terribly, Mama! It should be so easy. Why does it hurt so much? Am I dying?" Phoebe asked with fright.

"Birth is supposed to be painful. It's God's punishment for our sin in conceiving."

"Mama!" Edgar said, aghast. "Phoebe needs reassurance, not censure. This is all normal, Phoebe, and will feel less painful if you relax and breathe deeply." He hoped so anyway. Ellie had primed him on what to expect and how to help. Damn, he wished she were here now. "The doctor and midwife will be here soon."

His mother declared dismissively, "This is no place for a man."

"We'll be fine," Daphne assured him.

Edgar realized that his wife was not that different from her sister. Despite her contention that she could never deal with sick people, she had been a great support to Phoebe these past months, and didn't balk at the task now in hand. He realized again what a lucky man he was, and was overjoyed and proud that she herself was now pregnant, and bore everything easily with no fuss and a quiet equanimity that Ellie certainly didn't have, but which he appreciated.

He didn't want to think about Daphne going through this agony in six months. And he wished he could do more to help Phoebe now. He left the room reluctantly after kissing Phoebe and saying, "Be brave. It will all be over soon."

He hated, absolutely detested what was expected of him once the baby was born. The doctor had found a family to take the child and had agreed, reluctantly, to tell Phoebe that it had died. The midwife, also sworn to secrecy and generously paid, would see to it.

He couldn't bear to hear Phoebe's cries any longer. All this suffering. In vain. With tears blinding him, he went to stroll along the beach.

When they had first come to Massachusetts, they had stayed in a Boston hotel for a few weeks, while he had scouted out a house to rent. Somewhere quiet and out of the way. Marblehead had appealed to him. With its maritime community augmented by summer resort hotels, it reminded him at least a little of Muskoka. He and Daphne and Phoebe had spent delightful days wandering the streets and beaches, oblivious to the weather. Feeling defiant and daring, he had taken "his girls" to New York for a few days.

His mother – thankfully – had declined to go along, not wanting to be associated with a heavily pregnant young woman, despite the fact that Phoebe wore a wedding ring and told everyone that her husband was fighting in France. She delighted in that, able to describe her brave Bobby, weaving fabulous tales about him and imbuing him with nobility.

They saw Emily Wyndham perform in *Under The Moon*, which excited Phoebe so much that it was hard to restrain her from going backstage to visit Emily. But she insisted on seeing the show twice more, which neither Edgar nor Daphne minded, since it was obviously based on Hugo Garrick's visit to Muskoka, and reminded them of their own summer romance "under the moon".

"This is so much fun!" Phoebe enthused. She had never traveled anywhere besides the cottage, and here they were going to the theatre and exploring an exciting big city. "Mama doesn't realize what she's missing, but I'm glad she didn't come. It's as if a cloud follows her everywhere."

Edgar had to agree. And also that her bitterness and sanctimoniousness and carping were wearing them all down. He wondered, guiltily, how his father could stand to live with her. And actually felt sorry for him.

Now he stood in a cool fog on the beach near their house, wondering how he could help Phoebe survive this cruel blow.

.   .   .

Dear Zoë,

My baby died. I don't understand how God could have taken her away from me when I didn't even have a chance to hold her or know her. The doctor said that she wasn't strong. Eleanor says that happens sometimes. Mama says that it was a punishment from God because I wasn't supposed to have a baby because it didn't have a father because Bobby Miller couldn't marry me because he went to war instead. Mama is just hateful.

I don't understand how the baby wasn't strong enough. She tumbled about so much in the last weeks, and seemed to be trying to kick her way out of my stomach. I heard her cry when she was finally born. She sounded strong, and angry that it had taken so long to come out. I thought I was going to die, it hurt so much! But not her.

I called her Gloria, like in "Gloria in Excelsis Deo" because I thought that God would like that and it's such a pretty name, don't you think? I don't even know where they buried her.

*I'm not supposed to tell anyone about her because it would
cause a scandal, Papa says. But I had to tell someone, and you
won't be ashamed or angry to still be my cousin, will you, Zoë? Can
you ask Blake why my baby died? He's been a doctor longer than
Eleanor.*

*Sometimes I look in the mirror and can see right through
myself, as if I were a ghost. Maybe I am. But then why do I still
hurt so much? I don't want to feel like this for eternity. Gloria is an
angel now. I wish I were.*

Phoebe

.   .   .

Eleanor Carlyle had to admit that as a child, she had always
felt rather special when the big lake steamers had stopped at their
little island to drop off her family and their summer supplies. The
other passengers, eager to get to their own cottages or to much-
anticipated resorts, had had to wait patiently while the Carlyles'
crates of food, books, bedding, clothing, and paraphernalia had
been unloaded.

But this time Ellie had arrived by herself with little fanfare or
delay. Her parents had "opened" the cottage a few weeks earlier,
but had been able to stay for only an extended weekend, since her
mother was working and her father and brother were spending
some of the summer helping out on farms. With so many young
men gone off to war, the farmers were having difficulty sowing and
harvesting crops. Schools had finished early so that boys could
help out, and professionals were being encouraged to spend at
least part of their holidays volunteering their time.

Almost immediately Ellie felt the magic of Muskoka
embracing and relaxing her. And making her feel grateful for the
privilege of sequestering herself in the small cottage with only
kerosene lamps for lighting, a wood stove for cooking and warmth,
no bathtub, and an outhouse, she thought with amusement.

Daphne and Edgar had invited her to stay in Ria's cottage,
which Ria had asked them to look after until she returned. She
had told them that it wasn't good for it to sit empty for so long.
She was probably right, but must have done it to give the
newlyweds some privacy. Ellie preferred to stay here, but had
accepted their offer of dinners, since she had no aptitude in the
kitchen beyond managing to fry eggs for breakfast and throw
together a cold collation for lunch. Daphne, on the other hand, was
an accomplished cook who created delectable meals.

But just now Ellie needed to cool off in the lake and take out the canoe to relinquish the stress of work. She paddled around the neighbouring islands, noticing that the Carringtons, Spencers, and Oakleys had arrived. Tomorrow was Dominion Day, and already three years since their last Stepping Stone Marathon. She was disconcerted by the flood of memories of that summer and of her friends who were now overseas. The feeling that they were all lost to her was intensified when she returned to the empty cottage.

So she was glad to arrive at Wyndwood. Daphne embraced her warmly. "I'm delighted you're here, Ellie. We have some exciting news. Emily is getting married to that composer, Hugo Garrick, and the wedding is going to be at Oaktree at the end of August! Hugo claims it's the most romantic setting and was absolutely determined to have it there, so Letitia agreed, but *we* are to do the preparations. Isn't that smashing? Lizzie and Claire are staying with Richard and Olivia, so they're coming for dinner tonight, along with Esme and Fliss, and we're going to start making plans. Phoebe's coming, and so are Lydia, Louise, Emma, and Arthur."

"That's quite a dinner party," Ellie said.

"It'll be such fun! But *you* must be exhausted, so why don't you take this glass of champagne and sit on the veranda while I finish cooking?"

Ellie allowed herself to be ushered outside, and gratefully accepted the drink. Edgar took a glass as well, giving Daphne a peck on the cheek. She flounced cheerfully off to the kitchen.

"Stop beaming like that, Edgar," Ellie implored. "It's sickening seeing how enthralled you are with my little sister."

Edgar grinned even more. "Jealous, are you? Had your chance, you know, but damn it, I'm glad you didn't take it!"

"Haven't I been telling you all these years that we weren't suited? But you two certainly are."

"Life doesn't get any better than this," Edgar said complacently. "Except to have our friends back."

"You seem to have settled pretty well into Ria's cottage. Last summer it felt so desolate here, but now I almost expect Ria and the others to suddenly appear."

"Daphne's done wonders, and with just one servant. She's borrowed one of Mama's maids to help out tonight. We've been thinking about building our own cottage, but what would happen to my parents' place when they no longer need it? There's plenty of room there, even for our kids. In fact, we and Phoebe would have the entire second floor to ourselves." His parents' bedroom was in a wing on the main floor because Phyllis found stairs difficult. "If Mama would only be a little kinder to Daphne."

"She can't be any worse than your grandmother was, surely?"

Edgar guffawed. "You're right there! By the way, you probably haven't seen what Papa did in the spring. He had the Dragon declawed. Dynamited it, so now the path goes right along the water's edge." The Dragon's Claw had been the narrow cliff-path where his grandmother had fallen to her death.

"Good God!"

"It sure looks strange. And it's upset Phoebe. She mumbles about how she can never escape Mama now."

"How is Phoebe doing?"

Edgar shrugged. "She's grieving. She barely eats and has lost so much weight you'd hardly recognize her. She fluctuates between being miserable, angry, or vacant. She's happier here with us, but Mama won't let her stay. She wants to keep an eye on her because she's afraid that Phoebe is amoral and likely to 're-offend'."

"Oh dear."

They saw a boat pull up to the front dock, and Edgar hurried down to help Fliss. Ellie was impressed with her having mastered both the speedboat and family car, as well as with her easygoing confidence and poise. In that regard, Fliss was very much Chas's sister.

Just as Edgar had secured the Ditchburn, a smaller Minett pulled up, driven by seventeen-year-old Arthur Spencer. His twenty-year-old sister Emma was with him, and they had picked up Lydia Carrington and Louise Oakley en route. As they walked towards the house, Esme, Claire, and Lizzie strolled onto the veranda with Daphne. They had come in the back via the kitchen.

They all exchanged greetings and settled in wicker chairs on the wide, wrap-around veranda. As if by tacit agreement, no one mentioned the war.

"So the Dominion Day Ball isn't here tomorrow?" Emma asked. It had been for over twenty years.

"We did offer," Daphne said. "But Helena insisted on hosting it, and figured that there wouldn't be as many people as usual up here this summer, so her cottage would be large enough."

"I don't see why we can't have the Stepping Stone Marathon," Arthur said, referring to the traditional swimming competition from the mainland to Wyndwood via the smaller islands.

"Because there'd be only you and kids like Rupert for the race," Edgar said with a chuckle.

"Then I might have a chance of winning," Arthur quipped. Like his brother, Freddie, he was tall and lean and amiable.

"But we have enough girls to hold a race," Esme pointed out. "Look at Lady Kirkland's Cup, only won once, just waiting to be snatched away from Ria." The newly-polished silver trophy sat on the mantelpiece next to the men's cup that Jack had reclaimed for the Wyndhams in 1914.

"Ah, but how can you snatch it fairly when Ria can't be here to defend herself?" Edgar asked his sixteen-year-old cousin.

"Ellie almost won, so if we can beat Ellie then we'd essentially beat Ria."

"Impeccable logic," Ellie said. "But leave me out of it. I'm too old for this sort of thing." At twenty-three, she did feel ancient among this crowd that was mostly well under twenty. They already seemed like a different generation, not as directly caught up in the war as their older siblings. It made Ellie even more keenly aware of her friends' absence.

"I'd probably drown," Louise Oakley said. "Why don't we have a croquet match instead?"

"Or tennis at our place," Fliss suggested. "Mummy won't have our regular tournament until the boys are back, but I'd love to play."

"That's because you always win," Esme said. Fliss played almost as well as Chas.

Fliss grinned. "Well, what's the point of competing if you can't win?"

"Spoken like a true Thornton!" Edgar said.

Phoebe suddenly materialized on the veranda, surprising everyone. "Isn't it wonderful that summer has finally begun?" she said serenely as she joined them.

Over dinner they caught up with each other's news. Lizzie was grilled about the photography studio she had set up in Toronto. She had used some of her inheritance from Augusta Wyndham – the grandmother who had wanted nothing to do with her family – to create a professional environment that obviously catered to the upper classes.

"Anders Vandeburgh has quite a reputation in New York, so I've already received some commissions. Any of you would, of course, be a welcome addition to my portfolio."

"I should love for you to photograph me," Fliss declared. Surely Jack would treasure that picture, she thought.

"How delightful!" Lizzie exclaimed. She would do what she could to make Fliss as glamorous as possible. The girl had fine bone structure and an enviable, flawless complexion. Blackened lashes would emphasize her pale blue eyes, and bright lipstick, properly applied, could enhance her thin lips. Not only would her lank, mousy hair benefit from marcel waves and a bit of bleaching, but cut to cheekbone length it would also give her narrow face a less drawn look. Fliss might not have the natural beauty of her brothers, but she had the elements that allowed artifice to make her more alluring.

Lizzie had learned well from Anders, and could do wonders with her camera and lighting. She was amused to think that this would be mostly for the benefit of her brother, who had already decided that Fliss was the prize he needed to further his career. But surely Jack wanted a wife who was also admired for her attractiveness. Lizzie suspected that Fliss was the kind of woman who would improve with age, while pretty girls often turned into blowsy matrons.

She also considered that Rafe would be impressed with the lovingly rendered portrait of his sister that she would send him. She was caught for a sombre moment in speculation of how he was faring as a POW, thankful he was out of the fighting, hopeful he was well treated, delighted that he had written to her. "I have your photo with me and tell everyone that you're my girl. Will you finally let me love you when I come home?"

Although she admired Lizzie's accomplishments, Ellie didn't understand why she couldn't warm to Jack's sister. Claire and Emily were easy to like. But there was something brittle and calculated and unforgiving about Lizzie. A hard life was surely to blame, but even Jack had some sensitivity that had survived that.

Daphne said, "*Under the Moon* finishes in New York at the end of July, and then Emily and Hugo will have two months off until they take the musical to London. They're hoping that it will be a hit with the troops."

"It should be. It was wonderful," Phoebe said, starting to sing the signature tune. "*Under the moon, I'm over the moon, for you...* We saw it three times when we were in New York."

"You did?" Lizzie asked in astonishment. "Why didn't you let us know you were there?"

Edgar went rigid as Phoebe replied, "Oh no, we couldn't. Mama was poorly." After a momentary pause she said, "Arthur, would you like to marry me? Babies need fathers, you know, and I would dearly love to have a baby."

There was a stunned silence around the table. But Arthur recovered quickly and said, "Gosh, Phoebe, it's awfully kind of you to ask me. But I have to go to university and study for a career before I can consider getting married. I might even have to go to war."

"That wouldn't be good at all. You can't have babies if you go to war." Phoebe sighed deeply. "I shall just have to find someone else then."

Trying to divert the conversation, Ellie said casually, "Are you starting university this fall, Arthur?"

"Yes."

The others may not have noticed the tension between Edgar, Daphne, and Ellie, but Lizzie was always attuned to the subtleties. Probably from her years working as a maid, observing, anticipating. Was Phoebe so slim – and actually rather pretty now – because she'd had a baby in New York, and had obviously and regretfully given it up? What a scandal that would make! Of course, she didn't want anything to jeopardize the Wyndham name, since that wouldn't be good for either her or Jack's careers. But it never hurt to know things about people, so Lizzie would have to tuck that away for a rainy day.

In response to Ellie's question, Arthur was saying, "I don't really know what I want to do. I don't have Freddie's passion for architecture. Or Archie's for the law. History interests me. But Dad's hoping I'll opt for law." Now that Archie was no longer with them.

"Admit that you have a passion for news," Emma said. To the others she added, "Art's been editor of his school newspaper for years, and he's sold articles to papers and magazines. He has one appearing in the next issue of *Maclean's*."

"Oh, well done!" Ellie exclaimed. "What's it about?"

"How we all need heroes, especially at times like this," Arthur replied. "But that not all our heroes are the ones with medals."

"It's a tribute to his brothers," Emma said. "And it's terribly moving. He also mentions Ria and what she's done to help the village children, as well as her ambulance driving. And you, Fliss, with all your hard work for the IODE and for the orphans in France."

Arthur blushed at Fliss's surprised exclamation. "Zowie! Won't Chas be surprised that he's not the only hero in the family." She giggled.

"I've told Art that he should become a journalist," Emma said.

"*You* could take over the family law practice, Emma," Ellie suggested.

Arthur brightened. "You could, Em! You're great at arguing." At the others' laughter, he added, "I mean coming up with logical arguments, like when you wrote 'The Trial of Goldilocks'. I can imagine you in court."

Recalling the play that the Spencers had put on for the Midsummer Night's Dream party three years ago, Ellie said, "Exactly."

"You just want her to do something that girls don't do," Daphne accused her sister.

"Only because men don't want them to, not because they're incapable," Ellie shot back.

"Maybe Emma doesn't want to be a crusading feminist like you."

"Emma should make use of her talents and..."

"Be allowed to speak for herself," Edgar interrupted the squabbling sisters.

"I *have* been thinking about it. Ever since Cliff was killed," Emma said, referring to her sweetheart. She could barely suppress her sorrow as she added, "I thought I could carry on for him as well as Archie. Somebody in the family should eventually take over Spencer and Sinclair. Perhaps I can persuade one of Cliff's sisters to join me in the practice." Cliff had no brothers, which was one of the reasons he had looked up to Archie. "Anyway, I could enter the Law Faculty this semester, but Dad hasn't been receptive to the idea."

"There's your first challenge then – convincing the Senator that you have a valid case," Ellie stated.

"I do think you should, Em," Arthur agreed. "And *I'll* study Modern Languages. *You're* my hero too, Em." He grinned disarmingly.

"Flapdoodle!" Emma expostulated.

After dinner, Ellie and Emma challenged Edgar and Arthur to a rubber of bridge while the others made plans for the forthcoming nuptials. Lydia Carrington, having been planning her own wedding to Max, was eager to offer suggestions.

There was a tenacious, sultry glow above a gathering bank of clouds in the western horizon as Ellie paddled back to Ouhu. She had a swim to wash off the heat as the last of the light bled from the day, and then took her cup of tea to the open second story veranda. She could already smell the impending rain as she watched lightning sparring between the clouds.

The lights of Ria's cottage twinkled gaily through the silhouettes of trees and skipped across the water towards her. In the lantern light, she could discern the others on the big front dock at Wyndwood, preparing to leave, chatting and laughing amid the grumbling thunder.

Ellie felt an intense paroxysm of loneliness. At that moment she envied Daphne's domestic bliss.

· · ·

Helena Wyndham was pleased that the high-waisted Empire-style dress hid the five-and-a-half month bulge of her pregnancy. How propitious that this Dominion Day tradition was a costume ball. In fact, she felt empowered by how splendidly her life had been going since she had met and married James three summers ago.

He was a devoted if dull husband. Enthralled by their eighteen-month-old daughter, Cecilia, he was eager to embrace the new child, and solicitous of Helena's needs and whims. She had assured him that this would be the long-awaited son. And took advantage of his largesse. She had already built up a sizable nest egg with his generous allowance. Having grown up under the stress of her father's fluctuating fortunes, she wouldn't miss an opportunity to provide herself with a secure future. One could never anticipate the vagaries of stocks, bonds, or men.

To counteract her husband's staid, aged presence, she surrounded herself with young officers. Although not a beauty, she had always prided herself on looking younger than her years – thirty-two now – and reveled in the exhilarating flirtation that made her feel she still belonged to the young generation.

There was a knock on the door adjoining James's bedroom, and he walked in. "Are you almost ready, my dear? You look splendid as always."

"Perhaps you can help me with my necklace," she suggested as she held up the triple strand of pearls.

As he fastened it, he said, "Now don't overdo things tonight, my dear. You needn't feel obliged to dance with all the guests. The baby might not appreciate all that activity."

She laughed gaily as she gave him an indulgent peck on the cheek, "The baby and I are fine, James! I daresay that some exercise is beneficial. But I promise I won't tire myself. Have you said goodnight to Cecilia?"

He beamed. "I read *Peter Rabbit* to her again, and she kept saying 'wabbit'. She's such a bright child."

"Nanny tells me that she's developing quite a vocabulary. Isn't it adorable how she calls herself Ceci?"

"I think it suits her. I've been calling her that, too."

"I'll just kiss her goodnight and show her Mummy's pretty dress, so I'll join you downstairs shortly."

Helena spent a few happy minutes with her daughter and then went to greet her guests, confident that the ball was perfectly orchestrated.

The officers were enjoying being in a different costume, and were intrigued by the Muskoka ethos. And she had been right in thinking that her spacious cottage would accommodate the reduced crowds.

Of course she wanted nothing to jeopardize her pregnancy, so she was prudent, dancing with the young men and inviting the older ones to sit beside her for a chat.

She was about to rest after a rather lively waltz with her favourite British officer when another man moved in and took her into his arms. She was so shocked when she recognized him that her knees buckled for a moment. But he held her firmly as he said, "It's not like you to be clumsy, Aggie." He gave her a big grin.

Before she could respond he said, "You've done well for yourself, kid."

"What are you doing here, Carter?" she hissed.

He chuckled, "Come to see how my lovely ex-wife is doing. Did you think I would forget you that easily?"

Helena sensed a threat in his words, and felt a prickly rush of fear. They had been married only a few months before divorcing, both having been duped by the other into thinking that they were marrying into wealth. But she knew him well enough to realize that he wanted something from her. "How did you find me?"

"I ran into your father in New York and treated him to a few drinks. My, but he's proud of your achievements!" He looked about the room and added, "And no wonder! My little Aggie, married to a multi-millionaire!"

"I'm Helena Wyndham, not your little Aggie," she said frigidly, hating to be reminded that she had once been Agnes Jenkins.

"OK, *Helena*. So I gather that Mr. Moneybags doesn't know about me. Tut tut, *Helena*, keeping such vital information from hubby."

"What do you want, Carter?"

"I thought you might like to share some of your good luck. But this isn't the appropriate place to discuss this. I'm staying at the Grand Muskoka. Very nice. Your father suggested it and even provided the funds." He chuckled. "I always knew you were going to help me make my fortune, Aggie."

.   .   .

Helena slept little that night. She had managed to get through the remainder of the evening with her usual aplomb, but no enjoyment. So she could hardly wait for the appointed time to meet with Carter.

She tried not to seem distracted during breakfast with her military guests, and excused herself as soon as decently possible, encouraging James to take them golfing at the SRA Country Club. "I shall have a lazy day and see you at tea time," she told them.

As it was a calm and sunny day, they were eager to take up the offer. Helena was vastly relieved when they left.

Shortly before 11:00 she took the shore path that led to the north part of the island. This was not as well maintained as the path to the south, toward Silver Bay and Ria's cottage at the point, nor did acetylene lamps light this section. Along the north shore of the triangular island was a low cliff – the tail end of the rocky "dragon" that dominated the island – and just beyond it, a bit of beach where a rowboat could easily land.

Carter was leaning against a boulder, smoking a cigarette. "The lovely Helena. How many ships have you launched today?" he mocked.

She stared at him defiantly. Her dignified silence seemed to make him uneasy so he blurted out, "I have no inclination to be blown up in this war. So I'm going to try my luck in South America. I've heard that there are fortunes to be made for men with foresight and some capital to back them. Seems your father and the Wyndhams have done well with investments in Brazil. So all I'm asking, Aggie, is a bit of money to get me going."

Although she had once found his smile appealing, it now revolted her. "And if I don't help you?"

"Then I'll approach Mr. Moneybags. He may not appreciate having his wife's past become public knowledge."

"But I haven't done anything to be ashamed of, Carter."

He chortled. "You're a liar, Aggie. Takes one to know one, eh? Hubby wasn't informed about our marriage, for a start. Does he know that Mommy's in the nut house? Does he realize you're a gold-digger?"

"What's wrong with wanting to live well?" she demanded. "He loves me, and I'm a loyal wife. I've paid my dues."

"Don't pretend to be naïve, Aggie," he said dismissively as he lit another cigarette. "He won't love you quite as much when he knows the real you. Just fork over $5000 and I'll go away."

"But it's my husband's money, Carter. I can't exactly tell him I need it because I'm being blackmailed, can I?"

"You're a clever girl, Aggie. Sorry, *Helena*. You'll find some way to wrangle it out of him."

Reluctantly she said, "I knew what you were after, so I've brought everything I've saved from my allowance. $3000. It's all I have, Carter, and I can't approach James for more." She handed him an envelope containing the money.

He whistled. "Impressive, saving all that! He *must* be generous."

She made no effort to hide her anguish, hoping it might move him to relent.

"Ah, Aggie, you're still the love of my life." He embraced her. "We were good together, weren't we? In bed? Isn't ancient hubby about ready to snuff it? Maybe we could help him along a little and you and I could be together again."

Helena pushed him away. "How dare you! Just take the money and leave me alone!"

He laughed. "How touching is the role of the devoted wife. I think you actually believe it yourself. Never mind. I'll accept your offer, and that nice chunk of emerald surrounded by all those lovely diamonds on your pretty little finger."

She was angry and scared now that she had lost control. "No! It's my engagement ring."

"Then you should have taken better care of it. It must be worth a couple of grand at least." He held out his hand, wiggling his fingers impatiently. When she hesitated, he said, "It's not like you to be sentimental, Aggie. Moneybags will buy you another one. And I've taken quite a shine to that one."

His stare challenged her, and she knew he wouldn't leave until he had the ring.

As she yanked it off she said vehemently, "James is a far better man than you could ever be, Carter! I would *never* want to be with you again, even if I were a widow."

He laughed as he clutched the ring. "Ah well, when I have my own money, you won't seem quite so appealing either, kid."

As he climbed into the rowboat, Helena said, "Stay out of my life, Carter."

He winked at her.

As Helena marched away, Phoebe wondered what that scene had been about. She hadn't been able to hear much of the conversation, which had drifted off into the trees, the words catching and quivering on leaves and branches. But she had sensed the conflict between Helena and the scornful, dark stranger. Why had Helena given him her pretty ring?

This promontory had become Phoebe's special place, and no one knew she often came here. She liked the vista of Thorncliff Island, the Grand Muskoka Hotel in the distance beyond it, and a scattering of other rocky, tufted islands to break up the blue expanse of water. There were always canoes and sailboats out on the lake there. Watching all that activity and imagining herself skimming over the water with them helped to take her mind off Gloria. And she liked being high and therefore closer to God and her sweet baby. She really hoped that Victoria would one day take her for an aeroplane flight up into the heavens.

But now she should get back, because Edgar had promised to take her sailing this afternoon. She looked once more at the stranger growing smaller as he rowed toward the Grand. But his darkness didn't diminish.

· · ·

Helena didn't have to exaggerate her distress. Losing the ring to Carter was symbolic of the control that he now wielded over her. She hoped that he would perish in transit or in the jungle, because she didn't trust him not to come back for more money. He wasn't astute enough to become a successful businessman. He took enormous risks without due consideration, and liked to indulge himself as soon as he had spare cash. So he had become her albatross.

She was weeping in her room when James came in from golfing. He rushed to her side.

"Helena, what's wrong? Are you ill?" he asked with concern as he put his arm about her.

She knew that he truly loved her and wept even more. "Oh, James! I've lost my beautiful ring!" She held out her hand to show him its nakedness.

He sighed with relief. "Is that all? Don't fret, my dearest. A ring can be replaced." He hugged her. "I'm just thankful that you and Ceci and the baby are alright. But how did you lose it?"

"I don't know!" She said between sniffles. "Perhaps when I went for a swim. And I had a walk earlier. I don't know, James! I've looked everywhere!"

"Could one of the maids have taken it?"

"Surely not! I hardly take the ring off. Really, James, how could they expect to steal such a thing when they're stuck on an island with nowhere to sell it?"

"Perhaps we should check their rooms."

"No, James. I have every confidence in my staff. I was definitely wearing the ring this morning, and never removed it voluntarily today."

"Our guests are going for a swim. I'll have them scour the beach. If we don't find it, then I'll take them for a walk and we'll see if we can spot it. It's big enough that it should be obvious. Now please calm yourself, my dear. Whether or not we find it is of no consequence. You shall have a ring in any case." He kissed the top of her head.

"You're so good to me, James," she said.

"It's easy when I'm just indulging myself, my dear. Now you rest, and I'll make your excuses for tea. And dinner if you like."

"I should be fine by then. It will take my mind off things to entertain our guests." She smiled weakly as he left her room.

But she couldn't shake the feeling that there was a dangerous crack in her perfect world.

.   .   .

"But why can't I go to the Club with Edgar and Daphne and Eleanor?" Phoebe demanded of her mother.

"Because you'll be exposed to temptation, like last summer. There are boys there, and Edgar can't keep his eye on you all the time. At least he obviously didn't." Phyllis snorted.

"Don't be silly, Mama! I arranged to meet with Bobby Miller last summer. We even made love in the gazebo here, on Wyndwood. And in the ravine behind our house in Rosedale. If I want to make love to a boy, no one is going to stop me."

Phyllis shrieked. "How can you talk like that? You're a brazen hussy! A depraved Jezebel!" Phyllis grabbed Phoebe by the shoulders and shook her violently, as if she could dislodge that depravity. "You have the devil inside you! You're no daughter of mine."

"Stop it, Mama!" Phoebe tried to wrestle out of Phyllis's strong grip. Her mother's fingers grew into claws, digging painfully into her shoulders. Phyllis's face transformed into a mask of hatred — eyes burning, mouth dripping bloody saliva.

"No, Mama!" Phoebe screamed in fear, pushing against her mother with all her might. And suddenly she was free.

Her mother lay on the sitting room floor by the fireplace as if she were a log waiting to be piled atop the dead ashes. Her demonic features had softened back into their familiar pudginess.

"Mama?" Phoebe said tentatively as she knelt down beside her. "I'm not bad. I just want to have someone I can love, someone who's only mine. I want to have my baby back. Did you take her away to punish me? Sometimes I hear her crying. In the night. Sometimes I think she's not dead, that you told me a wicked lie. I don't feel that she's dead. Mama, are you listening?" She shook her mother's prostrate body. "Mama! Would you really be so horrid as to take away my baby? Just because she didn't have a father. Mama!" Phoebe shook her harder. "Stop pretending you can't hear me! You're hateful! Mama!"

Her scream alerted Edgar, who had just come in. "What's going... Dear God!" He knelt down beside his mother. "Oh, dear God!" He couldn't find a pulse. He noticed the blood in her hair. She appeared to have hit her head on the sharp edge of the stone mantelpiece.

"Edgar, tell Mama to stop being cruel to me!"

"What happened, Phoebe?" he asked with trepidation.

"She was angry and shaking me and I pushed her away, and now she's pretending to be dead to make me feel guilty. But I didn't hurt her! She hurt *me* with her vile words. Make her get up, Edgar!"

"She can't, Phoebe," was all he said.

Phoebe was suddenly calm. "Then God must have decided to take her away. He knows that she was spiteful and wanted to keep me imprisoned. Like Rapunzel. She never wanted me to have any fun."

"Where's Papa?"

"He went to see Uncle James."

"Stay here for a moment while I talk to Pringle." Edgar went to the kitchen and servants' wing. Their elderly butler, Pringle, his wife who was the cook, and the maid were having a tea break. Pringle roused himself instantly. "It seems that Mama has fallen, and I fear may be dead," Edgar told them.

"Oh my dear Lord!" Mrs. Pringle clasped her hands over her heart.

Edgar's throat was tight as he said, "I think we'd best not move her until the doctor and constable have seen her. I'm going to fetch Dr. Carlyle, and I'll take Miss Phoebe with me. She's quite distressed."

"Poor child! Of course she is!" Mrs. Pringle said. "That devoted they were. This will be another blow for her, you mark my words. Like when little Miss Sarah died." Mrs. Pringle dabbed at her eyes with a corner of her apron.

When Edgar and Pringle entered the living room, Phoebe was sitting on the floor stroking her mother's hair. "She'll be happy now, won't she?" Phoebe asked Edgar, tears running down her cheeks. "She always liked God better than people."

Edgar choked back a sob. "Yes, Phoebe. Come along, we're going to fetch Ellie."

She jumped up eagerly and took his outstretched hand. "Can we go really fast in the boat, Edgar?"

"We certainly will."

Even with Pringle standing guard, Edgar hated leaving his mother lying there, in the obscene vulnerability of death. They had put a blanket over her, as if that would ease her discomfort or hide the indignity.

As he and Phoebe walked to the boathouse, he explained how she must never tell anyone the details of the accident. "They'll think that Mama just fell and hit her head. Which is true. We don't have to elaborate on that. You found her lying there, and then I came in. Do you understand, Phoebe? It's terribly important."

"Of course I do. I didn't want her to die, so people shouldn't think that it's my fault." Phoebe added sadly, "But it is, isn't it?"

Chapter 13

The men in the front line were becoming totally unnerved listening to the moans and pleas for help from some poor bugger who'd been lying wounded in no-man's-land for the past two days. A rescue party sent out the night before had been unable to locate him in the dark.

One of the stretcher-bearers could take it no longer. Wrapping his handkerchief onto a stick, he brandished it over the parapet for a moment before rising, like a corpse from a grave, he thought wickedly. Boldly, confidently, he ventured into the wasteland of death between the opposing armies. The guns were strangely silent. His comrades, awed at his daring, held their breath.

Godfrey, they called him now. Or "Dad" since, at thirty-nine, he was twice the age of so many of them.

No longer Father Paul. No one knew that he had been a Catholic priest. He was amused that he had once thought his name propitious, a sign that he was to be a servant of God. Ironically, it had Germanic origins, and meant "God and peace". How he had reveled in that as a child, to be born with such an auspicious name! How could he not become the priest his mother had so desperately wanted him to be?

God-free, he thought. That was what he truly was. He knew now that there was no God, and Hell was here, on these battlefields. It was a relief, really. There was nothing to fear anymore. He had seen the worst. Death would just be an end.

So he was making a new life for himself. He had tremendous respect and admiration for the men – their courage, fortitude, even humour in the face of terrible odds and ordeals. Helping them gave him greater satisfaction and joy than he had felt in many years.

At every opportunity he visited churches and cathedrals, not because they evoked God, but because they exemplified the brilliance and magnificence of mankind. The immense Gothic cathedral at Amiens was particularly awesome. There was nothing more uplifting than listening to pure voices echoing among the ancient, venerable stones of these masterpieces.

If his friend Edelina was right and his soul would be reborn according to his deeds, then he would also have good Karma in his next life. There was no longer the need to appease the vanity and temperament of a judgmental God. There was immediate reward in creating and accepting happiness.

He had decided that he would finally allow himself to love Edelina. Already he had begun to express to her the deep affection he had suppressed during the five years he had known her. Unleashed from the guilt of his priesthood, it had burgeoned into a burning, intoxicating passion. If he survived, he would blissfully consummate that love.

So he walked tall and proud, unaware that those watching him felt a reassuring strength and calm emanating from him, which eased their disquiet. Those who had worked with him for a while had already endowed him with Christ-like qualities.

He found Jacobson in a shell hole, and slipped down beside him. The boy – for surely he couldn't be more than nineteen – had been ripped open by a shell. His intestines were exposed, his right thigh split to the bone, the flesh already festering with gas gangrene. Paul was astonished and sorry that Jacobson was still alive.

There was nothing noble in suffering and sacrifice, although he had thought differently once.

"Thank God! Thank God! I can't bear it anymore," Jacobson said. "Water! Please!"

Paul stroked his brow, and offered him a drink.

The boy began to weep. "Christ Almighty, it hurts! How bad am I? The rats have been here, thinking I'm already done for. You'll get me out, won't you?"

"Yes, as soon as it's dark. In the meantime, I'll bandage you up. Here's some morphine to help you." Paul gave him two grains – a potentially lethal dose, as it was four times what they usually administered.

So he was playing God now.

"Where's home?" Paul asked as he bandaged Jacobson's leg. He knew it was a waste, but it would give the boy some comfort and hope.

"Near Niagara-on-the-Lake. We have orchards. Apples, peaches, cherries."

"They must be beautiful in the springtime."

"Oh, yes." Jacobson replied with a smile lighting his grey face. The morphine was taking effect, for his body relaxed. "Gloriously beautiful. And the harvest. Heavy with fruit."

It was in nature that any sort of God-like being resided, according to Edelina. In its amazing architecture and diversity. In the delicacy of a flower, the trilling of birdsong, the kaleidoscope of sunset. In the intricate, astonishing workings of the mind and body.

"How lucky you were to have had such richness around you. I can imagine you clambering about the trees. What kid can resist the crook of an apple bough? I can imagine bees darting among the flowers, the scent of ripe fruit, the crispness of an apple just plucked from a tree. Cherries warm with sunshine."

Jacobson died with a smile on his face.

.   .   .

My Darling Ria,

You may be pleased to know that I'm no longer Britain's top Ace. Fellow Canuck, Billy Bishop, who is with Rafe's former squadron, now has 31 victories. For an audacious and foolhardy solo attack on a German aerodrome recently, he will undoubtedly be awarded a Victoria Cross. Is it perverse of me to feel both relieved and miffed at no longer being top Ace? I suppose it's that irrepressible competitive nature of mine. I would particularly like to best someone like Richthofen. But I remind myself that a victory usually means a kill, and that sobers me up.

Don't worry, my darling. I'm not about to take to the skies to win back my title. But I have to admit that all this paperwork is extremely tedious, and I'd much rather be flying!

The boys send their regards. They still talk fondly about the dinners at Priory Manor....

.   .   .

Thornridge, Toronto
June 16, 1917

My dearest darling boy,

What a relief it is to have heard from Rafe! He says he's allowed to write only two letters per month and four postcards, so we are to pass along information to you and his friends. First of all, he is in tolerable health, having been only slightly wounded – a flesh wound he calls it. He misses good Canadian cooking, which I hope isn't a secret message that he is being starved, poor boy! He says to thank you for the shipment of goodies from Fortnum and Mason. I must admit to being astonished that parcels actually get to the prisoners. We send him two weekly, and you can be sure that Fliss packs all kinds of practical items, like soap and shirts, as well as food and cigarettes. She's just included a copy of the novel The Doomed, *by Montgomery Seaton, since she's convinced he based the*

*main characters on you and Ria. Of course, I know that you met
him in Antibes, but I detested the story, as it is so tragic. The young
woman dying when her ambulance is bombed and her
philandering pilot husband shot down in flames. What terrible
liberties he's taken if he did use you and Ria as models!*

*The officers' POW camp is in beautiful countryside, and they
play tennis, baseball, and football. There's a canteen where they
can buy anything except food, but he says the wine and brandy are
quite good. I do hope he doesn't spend all his pay on drink. They
have British orderlies cleaning their quarters and preparing meals.
Unlike the ranks, he won't be required to work for the Germans,
which is a good thing because I can't see him doing that with any
equanimity.*

*I'm to tell you that it was the Red Baron himself who took Rafe
prisoner, and upon finding out that you were Rafe's brother, the
Baron was most courteous and interested, and entertained Rafe
with a solid meal and generous drinks. I'm confident Rafe feels
that he was well treated, at least initially. But if the Huns are as
vile as they are made out to be, then I fear dreadfully for him. He is
too inclined to be impulsive and somewhat impertinent, as you
know, which may not bode well for his captivity. I've urged him to
behave himself and not do anything foolish, like trying to escape.
I've told him that bravery is also shown in enduring difficult
situations with dignity and fortitude. Oh dear, can you picture me
wringing my hands?*

*No less for you, my darling Chas, since you are still in the thick
of it. You and Ria are forever in my thoughts and prayers. Be safe,
my darlings!*

Your loving mother

.   .   .

Ria was transporting four stretcher cases to the #14 General
when the air raid began. Since there was a full moon, it was to be
expected, but she sighed as she put on her heavy steel helmet. She
had only two more days until her leave, but with everything that
had happened recently, she was unnerved. Fear raced through her
veins whenever she thought about how close she had come to being
hit by the train that had crippled Carly. And Montgomery Seaton's
novel had been haunting her.

When the bombs began to crash around her, Ria was hardly
surprised. The Germans were probably targeting the military
camps and supply depots in the area, but bombing wasn't exactly a

science and the shells fell wide of their mark, uncomfortably close to the road and the Harvard Hospital, which lay just ahead.

She didn't even have time to react to the one that blasted the ambulance into a gully. She heard the groans and screams of the men in the back as she regained her senses. The ambulance was on its side in a tangle of shrubs, but after grabbing her flashlight, she managed to crawl out across the hood, for once blessing the fact that there was no windscreen.

"Get 'im orf me!" one of the Tommies was shouting. "'E's crushin' me bloody leg, for Gawd's syke!"

Ria played her light into the back to find the men tumbled together in a heap. The one on top was silent and motionless. She couldn't find a pulse, and realized he must have been killed by the blast, poor lad. She managed to roll him off, and eased the others into more comfortable positions, but none of them was able to get up.

"Thank Gawd," exclaimed the boy who had complained about his leg. "Bless you, Sister."

By the feeble light of her torch, Ria could see the dingy white gauze that encircled his stump quickly growing crimson and beginning to drip. He was hemorrhaging. Ria grabbed a tourniquet from her kit, and tied it off above his knee. But there was nothing else she could do for him or the others.

"I'm going to fetch help," she said. "Hang on, lads."

Although darkened, the white hospital marquees glowed like amorphous ground mist touched by moonlight. All she needed to do was to walk there. But why did her limbs feel so heavy? Each step was like trying to maneuver through the quicksand of dreams.

She realized that her left shoulder was numb, and thought it might be broken. The tents undulated and flowed away from her. This was no time for silly games, she thought with annoyance.

She became aware of warmth trickling down her arm and breast, and pain prickling through the numbness in her shoulder. Damn and blast, she'd been hit!

Her breathing was becoming ragged. Ria fought against the gravity that was sucking and clawing at her, at the air that was as thick and enveloping as water. How easy it would be to lie down and allow this lethargy to embrace her. To look up at the winking stars and imagine herself at the lake immersed in the calm and soothing... silky... soft... warm... water....

But the patients were her responsibility. She couldn't let them down, or the WATS.

One step, then another. *It's a long way to Tipperary....* No, that was a mocking song, which only reminded her of screaming, dying Tommies.

She mustn't lose consciousness or they would probably all die. She had a responsibility to Chas and Sophie to survive. She pressed her right hand against the now shrieking pain in her shoulder to staunch the flow of blood. Feeling it running down her arm, Ria was suddenly terrified.

Perhaps it was the fear that kept her going until she staggered into a tent and collapsed. "The ambulance was hit," she managed to say to an orderly who rushed to her side. "In the ditch. Not far. Wounded on board."

She was aware of being lifted on a stretcher and carried ever so gently to an operating theatre, where Troy was suddenly looking down at her. "You'll be alright, Ria," he assured her, although he was shocked by the amount of blood that soaked her uniform.

"If not... tell Chas... how much I love him. Tell Sophie... I'm sorry."

"You can tell them yourself in a few days."

"You have to get the wounded!" she cried, suddenly frantic. "In the ambulance."

"It's all in hand, Ria. Just relax. We'll soon fix you up."

"I'm so cold, Troy." She was deathly pale and shaking.

"It's shock," he said, worried now that he could barely find a pulse. He knew from experience that many of those who died would have survived the wounds, but succumbed to hemorrhagic shock. "We need a transfusion here," he said urgently to one of the doctors as Ria lost consciousness.

"Type her blood, Roland," the doctor replied.

With his expertise in chemistry and his growing medical knowledge from studying texts when he was off duty, Troy had already been promoted to Sergeant. He now worked mostly in the laboratory, the dispensary, and even in the operating theatre administering anaesthesia when things became hectic and the doctors were elbow-deep in surgeries. But in his spare time he had been experimenting with blood transfusion chemistry. On the vanguard of a new and simplified technique was Dr. Oswald Robertson, another Harvard grad, who had visited just last week and given a demonstration. Troy did a quick agglutination test.

"It's B," he told the doctor.

"Damn! Which of the walking wounded has B? I expect we'll have to give her O."

"I have B, Major. And Mrs. Thornton, the patient, is an old friend of mine. I would like to be the donor."

"We can't easily spare you, Roland."

"I don't want the special leave, as I'm due for some next month anyway. I'm sure I don't need more than a few hours to recover. Please, Major. This is important to me."

"Yes, alright. Are you confident about Robertson's new method that you've been investigating?"

"There's no chance of coagulation, so it's a much more reliable method. I've already prepared some vials with the correct amount of sodium citrate to make an isotonic solution when mixed with 450 cc. of blood. I expect we'll need two for this case. We just need to add 100 cc. of sterilized water to the flask and we're ready to go."

"Then let's have your arm before she slips away on us."

After an orderly tied a tourniquet on Troy's upper arm, the doctor injected Novocain under the skin above the vein in Troy's elbow, saying, "I must say, I was impressed when Robertson gave us that demonstration."

It was much easier than earlier techniques, which, in addition to being complex and beset with problems, had required minor surgery and were impractical in emergency situations where casualties came in virtually on conveyor belts. With this method, only a tiny cut was made into the skin with a scalpel, and the two-millimeter wide transfusion needle, pushed into the vein.

The blood flowed through a tube into a flask, which the orderly swirled gently to mix the blood with the citrate solution, preventing it from clotting.

Troy glanced anxiously at Ria in the bed next to him. The doctor had given her some intravenous saline to tide her over, but her breathing was shallow and rapid and she looked ever paler. Troy clenched and unclenched his hand rhythmically and vigorously to increase the flow of blood. But it seemed like a long twelve minutes before the flask was filled.

In the meantime, the anaesthetist and a nurse had prepared Ria for surgery.

As the doctor began to work on her he jested, "This transfusion is so easy now that it hardly warrants a two-week leave for the donor." More seriously he added. "And this could actually be done effectively in the forward areas. Imagine how many lives we can save with something this simple and straightforward."

"And we can stockpile blood when we know there's going to be a new offensive that will overwhelm us with casualties" Troy said. "We can keep the blood refrigerated for at least twelve hours. I have to do more tests to see if longer storage is feasible."

"I must say, you've done well, Sergeant, keeping us on the forefront. And ahead of the British," he added with a chuckle. Now that the U.S. was involved in the war, the Harvard Unit had become an American Base Hospital. "Thinking about a medical career, are you?"

"Medical research, Sir," Troy replied, having recently come to the conclusion that he preferred to be in the laboratory, where there were surely all kinds of life-saving discoveries to be made.

"We need all the help we can get," the doctor said. "Now if you could just find something to counteract infections, we'd be able to save at least a million more men."

.   .   .

When Ria opened her eyes again, she stared at him in bewilderment and mumbled through parched lips, "Why do you look like Chas, Troy?"

"It *is* me, Ria," Chas said, squeezing her hand and then kissing it and her lips, carefully, lovingly running his hands through her hair. "Troy got a message through to me after your operation yesterday. I flew up right away. You're going to be alright, thank God!"

"I was so scared. I didn't want to leave you, Chas." A tear rolled down her cheek.

He brushed it away and stroked her cheek, thankful to see that colour was returning to her face. Choking back his own tears, he said, "I'm glad. You've been very strong and brave, my darling."

"How are the others? The boys in the ambulance?"

"One poor chap was killed by the blast, but the others are recovering, thanks to you. I was told that the ambulance wasn't easily visible from the road at night, and probably wouldn't have been found until it was too late." For her as well, Chas thought with a shudder. He squeezed her hand again, overwhelmed with gratitude and relief and the remnants of the terrifying, unbearable speculation of how close she had once again come to dying. "You must stop scaring me like this, Ria."

She smiled weakly. "I promise."

Since the hospital didn't have accommodations for wounded women, they had fashioned a private space for her at the end of one of the officers' wards. When Troy walked in Chas said, "Here is your blood brother and the man to whom I shall be eternally grateful." At Ria's puzzled expression, Chas explained, "He donated blood to you, which is what pulled you through."

Troy sat down on a chair on the other side of her bed. "We both have the more rare B blood type, so I volunteered for the transfusion. Or, rather, insisted upon it. I wanted to be sure that you were getting blood that wasn't potentially infected with anything." Like syphilis, he thought, which was rather too prevalent among the men. "Besides, I've always wanted a sister." He grinned at her.

"I've always wanted a brother," Ria replied happily. "Thank you, Troy."

A nursing sister came into the cubicle and said briskly, "Sergeant Roland, you are supposed to be resting in bed."

"I'm absolutely top-hole, Sister Matheson. I've had more than enough rest and fluids to replace the litre that I donated to Mrs. Thornton."

"A litre?" Ria croaked.

"Nearly."

"This is not to be taken lightly, Sergeant," the nurse insisted. "Now back to bed with you! Twenty-four hours is the rule, as you very well know."

"Not with our new technique, Sister. I don't even have stitches."

"I've never had anyone complain of having to take time off to rest!" With a grin she added, "I'll bring you a glass of port wine to strengthen your blood. Now I have to deal with Mrs. Thornton, so I'll ask you to leave as well, Major."

Chas kissed Ria gently and said, "I won't be far away, my darling."

"You're a lucky girl, in more ways than one," Sister Matheson said when the men had left. "First of all, lucky to be alive, although in a great deal of pain, I expect. I have some morphine here for you."

"Thank you. It does hurt as if the very devil were trying to rip off my arm."

"Unfortunately, you won't be getting much more of this, so you'll just have to grin and bear it. I'm always amazed at how stoical the men are when I do their dressings. Terrible wounds that have to be subjected to the tortures of irrigation or fomentations, and then re-bandaged, usually twice a day. And we barely raise a moan out of them. We had this hulking great Scot once, a huge tree-trunk of a man with a nasty wound on his leg. We had to dig for bits of shell splinters and bone fragments for a few days every time we changed the dressing and without any kind of painkiller. Didn't get a sound out of him. We thought he had gone mute, like some of the shell-shock victims. Then, when he was finally on the mend, he got a bellyache from eating too much chocolate, and we didn't hear the end of complaints and groans. We had such a laugh! There, feeling a bit easier now? I'll do your dressing and then that dishy husband of yours can come back in."

"Troy – Sergeant Roland – is pretty dishy as well, Sister," Ria said with a grin. "And I can vouch for his character."

The nurse laughed. "We women are all well aware of the Sergeant's attractiveness. Moreover, he's the most gentlemanly man I've ever had the pleasure to know. You can be sure that he leaves a good many sighs in his wake. But I have the feeling that he has a girl back home and isn't in the least tempted by any of us."

"I think it may be my friend," Ria admitted.

"Lucky her."

"Yes, I think so." Troy would be faithful to Ellie, Ria was suddenly convinced. Jack... well, much as she liked him, he was too absorbed in his own needs and ambitions to be a devoted husband.

"There. Now the Major can come back," Sister Matheson said when she had seen to all of Ria's needs. "And as the poor man needs some sleep himself, I'll just arrange for a cot to be brought in. Won't do anyone any harm, will it? And it isn't every day we have such a decorated hero with us."

When Chas was once more at her side, Ria said, "I haven't even had a chance to thank you properly for the most fabulous and thoughtful and romantic present you could possibly have given me! The Shimmering Sands. Mine forever!"

"I'm looking forward to it as much as you," he said, happier than he could have imagined at her evident joy. He had already commissioned a builder, and his father and Fliss would oversee the construction, so it would be ready by the time they returned from the war. They would call it The Sands, and talked about it until Ria fell into exhausted sleep.

It was wonderful to have Chas next to her, especially when she awoke in fear and agony. Morphine was doled out sparingly and there was nothing else other than aspirin, so she suffered from the pain of the deep wounds from the shell fragments that had sliced through her left shoulder, fracturing it and tearing ligaments and muscles.

The nurses gave in to Chas's persuasions and allowed him to hold Ria's right hand while they did the dressings. She was sure that she must have pulverized his fingers.

"Have you gone AWOL?" she asked him on the third day he was with her.

"I should. But no. I was going to take a few days leave in any case, remember? I put McPherson in as OC before I left, and check in daily. We haven't had any new offensives, so it's just the routine work. But I will have to leave soon, Ria, much as I will hate that. The only consolation is that I know you'll be going to England soon."

"I wish you were coming as well, Chas! I need to be with you, for us to be safe. I can't stand the thought of leaving you behind to God knows what!" She started to cry.

He hugged her as best he could, feeling tense and uneasy himself. "We'll be together again soon, my darling. And one day we'll be sitting on the deck at The Sands recalling, with disbelief perhaps, how dire life once seemed, in this long-ago, crazy place when the world had gone temporarily mad."

"You're right, of course. I'm sorry," she stammered between sobbing gasps.

He kissed her. "Shhh. It's alright. You have every right to cry. There's been too much sorrow already. I promise I will come back to you, Ria."

"I wish it were that easy," she replied, gazing at him through a veil of tears.

· · ·

Ria was touched by the support from her friends. Antonia dropped in to see her at every opportunity, and other WATS, including Boss and ComRad, came by with flowers and chocolates. There were orderlies and stretcher-bearers with whom she had worked, both French and English. Ria was surprised to see the lawyer, Monsieur Lemieux, and Madame Fortin from the chocolate shop, who brought a generous supply of her finest goods.

Ria and Chas laughed afterwards at Madame's indignation that such a terrible thing could happen to her noble friend, but Ria was deeply grateful for her concern.

Her small space was filled with flowers, which cheered her and reminded her of Sophie.

She was somewhat nonplussed by everyone's assertion that she had done something heroic. It was just her job as a WATS, she explained. But on the fifth day, the hospital CO came in with Troy and said, with a big smile, "You have visitors."

Boss, ComRad, and Antonia entered first, followed by the English Base Commandant and Staff Captain, whom she knew, the French General who was governor of Calais, along with his aides-de-camp – all in full regalia – and lastly, a dashing young officer of the Grenadier Guards. Ria gulped as she recognized the Prince of Wales instantly this time. He smiled at her the way he had that autumn day they had passed each other in the street.

The General asked after her health, and then cleared his throat of emotion and read a citation awarding her the French Croix de Guerre and Silver Star for her bravery, which had saved the lives of three men as well as her own. He was obviously nervous about pinning it onto her thin gown, lest he should disturb her wound, but he managed it, and gave her a quick kiss on each cheek, as was the custom. Then he heartily shook her right hand, which, nonetheless jostled her and caused her to bite back a gasp of pain.

Seeing her go pale, the others were less exuberant in their congratulations.

The Prince said, "Well done, Madam. Brave as well as beautiful. You are a lucky man, Major Thornton."

"Thank you, Sir," Chas replied.

"I've heard that you fly aeroplanes, Mrs. Thornton," Prince Edward said with barely suppressed amusement.

Oh, hell, Ria thought, he knew about her escapade. "I do enjoy it, Your Royal Highness. It's most liberating."

"I can imagine. I'm still determined to learn," he said. "And I'd like you to teach me, Major Thornton. I understand that you are an excellent instructor as well as pilot."

"I'd be honoured, Sir," Chas replied. He would have called him David had they been alone together, for they had often socialized at Oxford, but that was certainly not the protocol in situations like this.

"I must say, I do admire you Canadians. I shall look forward to visiting Canada, *après la guerre.*"

"May we extend an invitation to our summer home on the lake, Sir?" Ria said.

"How delightful. I do recall Major Thornton talking about your civilized wilderness when we were at Oxford together. We were all quite intrigued, I must say. So I shall look forward to that." He smiled again.

Chas said with a grin, "You may wish to bring your banjo along, Sir, for our musical evenings."

The Prince chuckled and said, "But I'll leave the bagpipes behind."

Ria was the only one who understood the joke between them, for Chas had told her about the Prince practicing his banjo at all hours in the residence at Oxford. A group of fellow students had protested under his window one day, and the Prince had driven them off with his even more appalling efforts on the bagpipes.

Chas accompanied the Prince out, as they chatted easily.

Boss said, "Well done, Thornton! You've done us proud, as I suspected you would." With a grin, she added, "I have a new appreciation for you Colonials."

When everyone had gone, Chas kissed Ria and said, "Well deserved indeed, my darling. But I wish you didn't have to suffer all this."

A nurse brought in a glass of brandy, the only analgesic before the inevitable painful dressing. Ria raised her glass and said, "For King and Country. Which takes on a rather bizarre new meaning now that I've spoken with our future King."

. . .

Chas was preparing to leave the following day when Lance walked in with a bouquet of flowers and several other officers, including Adam Bentley. He had brought his comrades deliberately so that Chas wouldn't have any reason to object to his visiting Ria.

He had been shocked to hear about her ordeal, but immensely relieved to realize that she would recover fully and soon be back in Britain. And he felt terrifically proud of her. "I see you got your Blighty," he said with a grin. "And a well-deserved medal... Major Thornton." He nodded to Chas.

"Major Chadwick," Chas riposted, hiding his annoyance as he moved closer to Ria. Chadwick was unrelenting in his pursuit of her, although she, naively, might think they were only friends. It was damnable that he had to return to his squadron today while Chadwick would undoubtedly become a regular visitor.

"Lance! When did you get back?" Ria asked in surprise.

"Last night. And you were the talk of the mess. I understand the Prince is one of your new conquests... Major Thornton, do allow me to introduce my fellow officers, all great admirers of your wife." Which he did.

Ria could sense Chas's disquiet, and wondered how she could reassure him that he had no reason to be concerned about any of these men, including Lance.

Adam Bentley said, "It's jolly good that it isn't your tennis arm that's injured, Victoria. But on the other hand, that might have given me an opportunity to finally beat you in a match."

"Yes, indeed!" one of the others added.

"Chas taught me well," she said, taking his hand. "We're an unbeatable team." She gave Chas a meaningful, intimate look, which cheered him.

Lance noticed, and read the message. That secret language of lovers, which he wished he could share with her. She was obviously more in love with her husband than he had thought. And more than she had seemed to be last year. So Thornton had truly been forgiven. But Lance wasn't about to give up hope. The war wasn't over yet.

· · ·

"Carly says it's dreadful being in a civilian hospital in London," Ria told Lance, who managed to visit most days. "She says that all the best medical personnel are working for the military, and she's getting short shrift. But there isn't a military hospital in Britain that will take wounded women, not even the ones for amputees. I hope they can keep me here until I can actually go home, but I know that isn't likely. I suppose they might send me to the Sick Sisters' hospital in Calais."

Calais was under almost constant bombardment these days, and so not a safe place to be, Lance thought.

He arrived the following day with The Duchess of Axminster.

"My dear girl," she said as she swept into the cubicle. "I've only just heard! How terribly brave and noble of you! But what an ordeal! Of course you must come and stay with us. I've already prepared the guest suite for you."

"Thank you, your Grace. How kind."

"Nonsense! It will be a treat to have you with us, and you must allow us to pamper you. I've already spoken with the CO and he assures me that you can be released into our care within a few days. We'll have you playing tennis in no time! Now... Major Chadwick tells me that Beatrice, the Countess of Kirkland is your cousin. My dear Papa was a member of the Royal Yacht Squadron with the Earl, and I recall him being immensely impressed that Lady Beatrice crewed for her husband and did it remarkably well. It would be Cowes Week soon," she said on a sigh. "Rather odd to think of such an innocuous event happening in the channel when now there's the incessant booming of guns and the occasional ship blowing up! I daresay that we'll be cheering on the sailors and dancing at those balls again some day. But whether with that same innocent enjoyment as before, I can't quite imagine." The Duchess's grave expression brightened as she added, "But we mustn't bemoan the loss of entertainments when there is so much more to concern us!"

Ria suspected that the Duchess was lamenting the passing of a way of life, as so many were.

When Antonia picked Ria up to drive her to the Duchess's hospital, Ria maintained she was not a stretcher case and would sit in front with her. Troy insisted on taking Ria out in a wheelchair, since she had only just been allowed out of bed, and was still weak and unsteady. He hugged her gingerly, but she clung to him, unable to suppress tears of sorrow for Kurt and gratitude for her life. Although they had once been mere casual acquaintances – the Yanks versus the Canucks in their various summer competitions – they had forged a deep and abiding respect and fondness for each other.

"I'll visit when I can," he said, moved by her tears. He stroked her hair reassuringly as she pulled herself together. "And I hope to see you in England soon, little sister," he said with a wink. Oddly, he did feel a brotherly responsibility towards her, and was delighted.

"I shall look forward to that, big brother," she responded with a warm smile.

When they were underway, Toni quipped, "You're beginning to look alike, you and your *brother*. It's such a bizarre thought, that you have his blood in your veins."

"It is rather. I suppose that makes me part American now," Ria joked. "And Troy is such an intimate part of me that I know his very thoughts. For instance, that he's in love with my friend, Ellie."

"Is he?"

"I'm convinced of it. And I would adore for them to be together."

"Your cousins and friends seem to have claims on all the best men."

"It seems to me that Justin has become a regular correspondent of yours."

Antonia blushed. "He has rather. Do you suppose that there's any chance he'll forget he's in love with you and look elsewhere?"

She said it so guilelessly that Ria laughed until a shaft of pain made her gasp.

"Not so much levity for you," Antonia declared with concern at Ria's pale, sweat-beaded face.

When she was able to speak again, Ria said, "I think Justin would be lucky – and happy – to win your affection, Toni. I'm sure he'll always feel a sense of responsibility to me, because of his promise to my grandmother, and we will forever be best of friends. But I think he's ready to find someone who can fully reciprocate his love."

Antonia blushed again. "It's silly, really. Of the endless suitors my mother has put my way, there was only one chap I ever fancied, and he had eyes for no one but my sister Veronica. And she was just disdainful of his affection, which rankled at the time, I can tell you. I had thought that Eddie Stratton and I might click, and he's a decent, fun chap, but not my sort at all, I realized. It took only a few days with Justin at Priory Manor, and a few months of letters to make me feel as if I want to be with him always. Is he truly as wonderful as he seems?"

Ria laughed again, but more cautiously. "Yes. And sincere and trustworthy. He wouldn't be playing games with you, Toni. It would be ripping if you two married and we had summers together on the lake!"

They discussed the prospect excitedly.

When they arrived at the villa, Antonia fetched help before allowing Ria to step out of the ambulance. Zachary, one of the orderlies, took firm hold of Ria's right arm, while Antonia walked carefully on her other side, ready to catch her should she collapse. It seemed a long way up to her room in the private wing of the house.

Once she had been settled into the soft embrace of the bed, Ria felt the nausea and dizziness abate.

"It appears I won't be playing tennis anytime soon," she said, discouraged by her evident weakness, and feeling very weepy these days, as if she had no strength to contain her emotions. It was as if the shrapnel had ripped apart more than her shoulder. She had tried to collect these fragments and reassemble herself, but they kept slipping away. Eluding her.

"It's hardly been two weeks since you spewed a gallon of blood," Antonia chided.

"Only half a gallon," Ria replied with a weak grin.

"And you're still in beastly pain. So this is a rather jolly place to spend the next month or so."

Decorated in blue and gold, the room was bright and cheerful as well as soothing.

Antonia went on. "You can see the cliffs of Cap Blanc-Nez, and the ever-changing sea, and a bit of the tennis court. You wouldn't even know there's a war on."

With Antonia, Troy, and Lance dropping by at every opportunity, as well as others, Ria had visitors every day. The Duchess and her friends invited her to dine with them in the morning room, once she was able to manage the stairs.

But she also relished quiet moments in her lovely room, sitting by the window smelling the warm sea breeze, reading Chas's letters, which arrived almost daily, and writing to him just as often. She delighted in the missives from Sophie, printed in carefully formed letters spaced evenly between the lines, showing her growing mastery of English and penmanship, and then illustrated with carefree childish imagination and wonderful exuberance. Ria couldn't help weeping when the letters always ended, "Please come home soon, Mummy Ria. I miss you. I send you many hugs and kisses."

Her daughter. It was still a strange thought to which she hadn't quite adjusted.

Once she was stronger, she sat in the garden or among the sea pinks and thrift that carpeted the cliff tops, and began painting again, awkwardly, since her left arm was in a sling. Zachary was sometimes with her, which was helpful. With his shoulder-length silver hair but unlined face and trim physique, the artist was anywhere between forty to sixty years old. He had a wry sense of humour, so she thoroughly enjoyed his company. He also gave her plenty of tips to improve her own skills.

Before long she was walking on the beach with Lance, as she had last year when he had been convalescing here, only now the air was warm and a few brave souls ventured into the sea. "I love to swim, but have no desire to do it here," Ria said. "The sea seems... I know this will sound foolish, but *malevolent* is the word that springs to mind."

"With good reason, I expect," Lance replied, thinking of her *Lusitania* ordeal.

"Yes, I suppose that will forever haunt me. But it's more than that. Perhaps the fact that the sea is another venue for the war. Imagine what it must be like when the guns are actually silent for more than a few hours, and all you can hear are the waves and the seagulls." On a laugh, she said, "Henrietta complained that she was stung by jellyfish the other day and it was jolly painful! We don't have anything nasty or dangerous in our lakes."

Her third summer not being at the cottage was almost too much to bear. She bit back tears, for it was silly to cry about something so trivial. But her soul truly yearned for Muskoka and all that it represented. She had some inkling of what her disowned uncle and Jack's father, Alex, must have felt in exile. She kicked at the wet sand, which sent a crab scurrying back into the sea and a bolt of pain through her shoulder.

"I should like to see your lakes some day," Lance said. "Ria, we're being sent back to the front lines imminently. There's another offensive starting."

He tried to shoo off a dozen dragonflies that suddenly zoomed in to hover about Ria's shoulder.

"Don't frighten them away," Ria said.

"You're not bothered by them?" he asked in surprise.

"On the contrary. We have an affinity."

She held out her hand and one immediately landed on her outstretched finger, while two others perched in her hair. The remainder flitted about her wounded shoulder.

Lance laughed as a few settled on her sling. "I've never seen anything like this!"

"They bring me comfort."

"And can they heal you?" he teased.

"Oh, I think so," she replied with a grin. "I feel better already."

"Despite the ministrations of insects, you appear to be flagging. And the tide is galloping in."

Not only would the beach quickly disappear, but the smashing waves also rose many feet up the cliff side. More than once Ria had dreamt that she hadn't been able to outrun the tide, and had been forced to climb the sheer rocky face that seemed to heave and shrug, preventing her from escaping the grasping sea.

They picked their way around the pools and rivulets stranded by the low tide. Gulls circled and dove, all the while screeching as if admonishing the trespassers.

"You should be resting in bed, in any case. Don't be too heroic," Lance said.

She smiled. "I'll save the tennis for Priory Manor. I do think I'll be able to go home soon."

"May I offer my arm as we scale the cliff?"

"Hell's bells, it didn't seem so bad on the way down," Ria said, as she glanced up the long, rugged path. She took Lance's arm and managed to reach the top, but with many breaks and increasing support from him. They sat for a few minutes and gazed out at the white cliffs of Dover, which, by some quirk of the atmosphere, seemed tauntingly close today.

"What will you do when you're back in England?" Lance asked.

"Spend lots of time with Sophie. Give Carly some much-needed support. Ride Calypso once I'm able. You'll be impressed when you meet him, Lance. He's such a beautiful horse, and I've missed him so!"

Realizing that she expected him to visit her in England, he was exceedingly cheerful, despite having to leave her soon. "Come along, my decorated heroine."

He had his arm around her waist and almost had to carry her to her room, she was so exhausted. He was dismissed as a VAD took her in hand, tut-tutting at Ria's overdoing it again.

She threw him an exasperated grimace. He grinned and said, "I'll come to see you before I leave."

Which was the following day. As it was rainy, they sat in the conservatory, but had no privacy. "I'll see you in England, if I may."

"Of course!"

Ria found herself somewhat gloomy at his departure, especially as greyness enveloped them and it rained for days. So she was astonished and delighted when Chas suddenly appeared. "I had no idea you were coming!"

"I wanted to surprise you. I'm taking three days leave, and the Duchess as well as the doctor have given me permission to stay with you."

Ria was ecstatic. They barely left her room, and didn't mind in the least that it poured rain the entire time. They talked for hours, took naps, tolerated visitors, and enjoyed delectable dinners with the others.

On the day Chas had to leave, a notice arrived announcing that King George was awarding her a Military Medal for bravery.

"I'll get leave in the autumn and go to the Palace with you when you receive your medal," Chas said with a grin. "In the meantime, you need to rest."

She was still terribly fragile, both physically and mentally. The doctor had told him that she'd require at least three months to heal, and probably longer to regain her strength. And Ria didn't seem to realize that she was somewhat shell-shocked. She was on edge and cried easily, and suffered from nightmares and mild panic attacks again. He hoped she would settle down to a more domestic role in England, and dreaded the prospect that she might want to return to the WATS.

He stroked her cheek as he began softly singing his own modified version of the new hit tune, *For Me and My Gal.*

What a beautiful day, For a ball at the bay,
See the people all stare, At the lovable pair.
She's a vision of joy, He's the luckiest boy,
In his formal array, Hear him smilingly say.

The bells are ringing for me and my gal,
The birds are singing for me and my gal,
Everybody's been knowing, to a party they're going,
And the champagne keeps flowing, till the dawn is our pal,
They're conversating 'bout me and my gal,
Our friends are waiting for me and my gal,
And sometime, I'm going to build a love nest and more,
On the Shimmering Sands shore,
In Loveland, For me and my gal.

"There's no such word as 'conversating'!" Ria challenged with a laugh. "And don't try the Oxford grad excuse."

"So I'm coining a new word. Oxford grads are allowed, dare I say even encouraged to do that." He grinned broadly and then kissed her. "But 'Loveland' is real. Let me show you."

She cried herself to sleep after he had gone.

Sybil returned to the WATS camp, although she still didn't look well. She confessed that she was inordinately tired, but couldn't stand the tedium of lounging around on her parents' sofa making witty conversation at tea. "Even if there were some rather scrumptious officers." She confessed, with unaccustomed shyness, that she and Adam Bentley had spent several unforgettable days together, travelling to London for a show and just walking about the neighbouring village. "I do think he's stuck on me. And he's a rather splendid kisser."

.   .   .

Antonia arrived in a terribly agitated state one day in mid August. She was practically wringing her hands.

"I don't even know how to tell you this, Ria. Oh, dear God!" She put her hands over her mouth and turned away for a moment.

Ria was panic stricken, thinking something must have happened to Chas. "What's wrong? Toni!"

"It's Justin. He's been wounded. Terribly wounded, Ria. They left him for dead at first."

After the initial immense relief that it wasn't Chas, Ria became distraught. "Tell me!"

"It's a chest wound. One lung badly damaged. They had to aspirate blood from it because it was hemorrhaging and pressing on his heart. He came in on a barge. Henny got him on her bus. He asked for you. And me."

"Can you take me to him?"

"Of course. They didn't want to transport him too far, so he's at the Casino."

Ria was shocked by how pale he was. But he smiled when she dropped down beside him and took his left hand in both hers and hugged it to her cheek. His other arm was encased in bandages covering several wounds.

After their success at Vimy and now under Canadian commander General Sir Arthur Currie, the Canadian Corps had been assigned another difficult task — to take the ruined coal-mining town of Lens. But Currie had decided that they first needed to capture the German strongpoint on the adjacent Hill 70. Using the same precision tactics that had won them Vimy, the Canadians secured their objective after three days of fierce fighting, worse than any Justin had seen so far. It was on one of the forays to drive the Germans back even farther from Lens that a shell had exploded behind him.

"You're out of it for certain this time," Ria said to him. "But you'll be alright. You have to be, Justin!"

His breathing was laboured and shallow, but Ria refused to cry in his presence. He needed her to be strong and give him hope.

But Justin could see the fear in her eyes. "I'm trying," he managed to whisper. "How are *you*?"

"Ready to go home soon. And when you're back in England and well enough to leave hospital, you'll come and stay at Priory Manor with us. We'll be quite a household of battle-scarred," she quipped. She talked to him about pleasant news from home to buoy up his spirits.

She was reluctant to leave him, but he needed rest, and she herself was flagging.

Once again there had been massive casualties, so the WATS were kept busy, but Antonia managed to visit Justin daily, sacrificing sleep when necessary. Ria chafed at not being able to be at his side, but was allowed to telephone daily to check on his progress. Within a few days he was finally considered out of danger, and soon to be shipped to England.

.   .   .

Max was reminded of the game they had played as kids – Ruler of the Castle. Of course it should have been King of the Castle, but the girls had protested. You had to go from one gazebo to the other, across the centre of the island, running a gauntlet of pinecones hurled at you by the others who were hiding in the shrubbery. If your trunk was hit, you were dead. If only your limbs were hit, you were allowed to keep going. Max felt that same heart-pounding mixture of apprehension and excitement now.

But these missiles were all too real.

A couple of the battalion scouts had discovered a perfect observation post in the ruins of a building in no-man's-land. Following them, Max and one of his signallers were crawling through the cornflowers and daisies toward the building, playing out their telephone wire as they went. They crept up the stairs to shelter under a bit of roof, and realized that, through a large gap in the wall, they had a clear view over the new German line. Careful to keep out of sight themselves, they could see carrying parties bringing in supplies, and work parties shoring up new defences. About two dozen Huns were building what was probably a gun emplacement for a Minnenwerfer, which launched the terrible trench mortars known as "Moaning Minnies". Through his binoculars, Max could even see the faces of the men, sweating in the summer heat as they mixed cement.

It was a perfect target. Only yesterday, Max had been careful not to direct fire on the Germans collecting the victims of the gas attack that the Canadians had launched earlier. It was one of the inconsistencies of war to one moment be doing all in their power to eliminate the enemy, and the next, be showing compassion.

But now he had his battery aim a gun at these Huns. The first two shots bracketed them. The third scored a direct hit. Half a dozen men lay unmoving, while a few wounded were crawling away. He kept the gun registered on the spot, and directed another on the carrying parties, scoring a few more hits.

Max hated this job. It was much worse killing a man when you had seen his face. And when he looked like any other boy, too young to be here. Firing the guns from miles away, you could feel detached from all the death and destruction you initiated. But watching men being blown to bits revolted him. He had been considering transferring out of the artillery. Into what he wasn't sure. Asking for a safe job well behind the lines was construed as cowardice by many. But what else was he trained for?

He wasn't scared for himself – not unduly, anyway. Perhaps he could become a front-line ambulance driver or even a stretcher-bearer – anything that helped others rather than obliterating them.

He prudently stopped the guns when he noticed a couple of Germans peering cautiously over their embankment with binoculars, and focusing a little too long on Max's hideout.

He and the others looked at each other in shock as they heard someone running up the stairs, and an officer announcing, "I say, that's a jake view!" as he rashly peered out the opening.

Without a word, the others grabbed their gear and ran like hell, hearing behind them, "I say, what's your hurry, chaps?"

A moment later they dived into the grass as they heard the shell roaring over. It crashed into the ruin, blasting debris about and showering them with grit. The foolish officer was miraculously unhurt, and hightailed it back to the company HQ. Their perfect vantage point was soon pulverized, and the Germans kept bombarding other buildings in the decimated village, trapping a group of officers beneath the rubble of what had been the headquarters.

It was a whiz-bang that caught Max and some others unawares, since it made no sound until the moment before it exploded. The noise was deafening. The concussion blasted him into a ditch.

His ears were ringing but he could hear nothing else. He could only feel the impact of explosions nearby. His entire body seemed to reverberate with them, his heart thumping wildly. He couldn't catch his breath. Men around him roused themselves, and urged him to get up, but his limbs seemed to be paralyzed. He wondered if he'd been hit after all, although he could feel no pain. Only a curious numbness.

He saw the world through scintillating lights, and noticed his signaller had a piece of shell casing embedded in his forehead, like a steel horn. Another fellow was bleeding from his ears. He realized that the chap beside him had been killed. Slowly sensation returned to his shattered senses, and he was able to stand. Had the others not been there to urge him on, he would have been rooted to the spot.

·   ·   ·

Zachary dropped Ria off at the Casino while he ran errands in Calais. Justin did indeed look better. "I can almost breathe," he said with a grin.

"Thank God! How are you feeling?"

"A bit rough, but not in a lot of pain anymore. The lung is healing nicely, but I'll probably be susceptible to bronchitis. I can move my arm now, although there's some shrapnel in it that they're going to leave as souvenirs. So all in all, I'm on the mend."

"That's the best news! I'll cable your family and let them know."

"Thanks. I just hope they haven't received a telegram saying I was dangerously wounded, or they'll be frantic." When they had brought him into the Dressing Station with the hundreds of others, he had been put aside with those "not-likely-to-survive" and given morphine, while those with treatable injuries had been seen to first. Justin vaguely recalled drifting in and out of consciousness, hearing someone saying, "Looks like he's done for... Shell fragment right through the chest," and his Colonel replying, "Damnation! Can't afford to lose men like him."

The next thing he remembered was the painful jolting of the ambulance waking him, the agony of his stretcher being lifted and put onto a barge. Passing out and waking again as he was being transferred to another ambulance. Seeing the WATS uniform. Asking for Ria and Antonia.

Ria was astonished to see Chas walk in. He gave her a swift kiss, and said, "The Duchess told me you were here." To Justin he said, "I can't stay long, but I wanted to see how you're doing, old chap." Ria had sent him a telegram before she had known Justin was expected to recover.

"Better for seeing both of you." And seeing the almost palpably sensual way they looked at each other, he hoped that he might one day know such love.

Chas held Ria's hand as they sat at Justin's bedside and chatted, doing most of the talking so as not to tire him.

Ria told them, "I had a letter from Edelina. Do you remember her friend Tom Thomson? Apparently he drowned in Canoe Lake, in Algonquin Park, last month. Somewhat mysteriously. There's speculation he may have been murdered!"

"Good Lord!" Chas exclaimed. "Who'd want to murder him?"

She shrugged. "Murder in the midst of war seems somehow incongruous. But I'm glad I bought one of his paintings for your collection, Chas. I do think he was a rather brilliant artist."

"How is Edelina?" Chas asked.

"Enjoying the tranquility of the lake. In the winter she rented an old farmhouse in the country near St. Jacobs…"

"That's not far from us in Guelph," Justin said.

"There are many German and Mennonite families in that area, living simply, as she put it, who keep mostly to themselves. She thought it safer to be away from Toronto, for herself as well as Frieda. Which I find outrageous!"

"Anti-German feelings are still running high in London," Chas said. "There've been a few more daytime Gotha raids."

"I do hope you manage to get sent to Taplow," Ria said to Justin. "Too bad that Zoë's not there anymore, but Cousin Bea will visit you. I wish Zoë weren't in London either. Perhaps I can wangle her a job at the Duchess of Axminster's."

Chas laughed. "I expect you will. Blake may not want his wife in France, but she might well be safer at Cap Gris-Nez than London."

"And when he gets posted back here from the Field Ambulance, they can see each other!" Ria said happily.

"I sense machinations afoot," Chas said.

"And they can take their leaves at Cousin Bea's villa on Cap d'Antibes! What could be more romantic? Other than being at the Sands?" Ria added with a smile at Chas.

She noticed Justin's face light up as Antonia walked in, somewhat diffidently. She was carrying a large bouquet of pink and white carnations in a vase made of a shell casing. "I do think that flowers brighten up a room as well as our spirits. Even if the vase is rather ironic." She added these to the several others that she had undoubtedly brought. "What a surprise to see you, Chas!"

"Reluctantly, I must be on my way. I'm just out doing some recreational flying to keep my hand in. You'd be amazed how much we need to practice," he added with a grin.

Ria walked out with him. "You're not strong enough for a motorcycle ride," he said. "And I really must get back, my darling." He took her around a corner and gave her a passionate kiss. Then he was gone.

•   •   •

"Neurasthenia," Blake said to Max. He had come to see his brother-in-law at the Casualty Clearing Station after Zoë's cable had arrived. "That will get you back to England for treatment."

"Which means I'm a coward," Max said ruefully.

"Nothing of the kind! You had a concussion. Autopsies have revealed that shell bursts can produce bleeding in the brain and spinal cord and various organs without any signs of external injury. So there's some thought that minute hemorrhages might account for some of the neurological symptoms, and we're even getting laboratory results that show evidence of a biochemical change in the nerve cells. But that should be transitory."

'Not Yet Diagnosed Nervous' was the official verdict, since the government didn't want to acknowledge the psychological toll the war was taking. 'Shell-shock' was now forbidden terminology.

Max clasped his hands fervently to stop them shaking. He was distressed to think that he had lost control of his body. Upon the slightest exertion, his heart thumped erratically and he couldn't catch his breath. Sometimes he couldn't decipher what was being said to him, although he could see the person's lips move and hear some vague, barely recognizable sounds to which he knew he was expected to respond. He burst into tears for no reason, he was dizzy and his head ached abominably at times, and when he could actually corral the words from his scattered thoughts, he stuttered and stammered and then angrily tried to spit them out. Sleep eluded him, but when it finally came it was accompanied by nightmares from which he awakened with choking, numbing terror. At times he couldn't even move or cry out. That was when he thought he would surely die. Slowly. Excruciatingly. Once again he was gripped by the paralysis that had incapacitated him when he had been splattered with the blood and entrails of the man next to him.

"You need rest and the opportunity to discuss your experiences and thoughts. Once the physical trauma heals and you exorcise the demons, it will be easier to regain your equilibrium. So tell me what happened."

. . .

Ria was distressed by the news of Max's shell-shock, but terrifically pleased that he had been sent to England. He would surely be safe there.

She was deemed fit to travel home, with the proviso that she continue to get plenty of rest. All her friends and acquaintances seemed to have heard that she was leaving and came to see her. It took a great deal of energy to stop herself from breaking into tears at every goodbye. She felt that she wouldn't be back, which made it that much worse.

She had even become a favourite at the Duchess's hospital. They gave her a delightful send-off dinner with no luxury spared. The poet-orderly, John, had written a poem for her. Zachary had done a painting of her on the cliff top, much to her surprise. It showed her gazing pensively out to sea with her sketchbook on her lap, her bandaged shoulder not visible at that angle. It was beautiful and poignant.

Ria mentioned Zoë and her skill with massage and ever-expanding knowledge of physiotherapy, which interested the Duchess and the doctor, who agreed to take her on if she chose to come.

Sybil and Antonia showed up at dawn to take Ria to the hospital ship. Toni had her own bag along and said, "I persuaded ComRad to let me go on leave a few weeks early so that I can escort you home."

"Are you allowed to come on the ship with me?" Ria asked.

"Not officially. But you watch me!" Antonia assured her.

They helped her aboard, a private cabin on the top deck having already been arranged for her. It was filled with flowers sent by various friends, including a big bouquet of red and white roses from Chas.

"This is amazing," Ria exclaimed.

Sybil bid them farewell, saying to Ria, "Oh, I shall miss you, Windy! Be assured that I'm coming to visit you on my next leave!"

When the ship was about to depart, the Captain stopped by and said to Antonia, "Do be sure to go ashore in good time, Lady Upton. I won't be able to turn the ship around should you find yourself still aboard once we sail. And, of course, I haven't seen you," he added with a wink.

"You've blackmailed him!" Ria said with amusement when he'd gone.

"Hardly! I went over on his ship, one of his first female casualties. He's a thoroughly decent chap who has a soft spot for heroines. I just told him how frail you still were and that you couldn't possibly make it back to England without my help."

Which was almost true, as a fierce storm blew up and it was a rough crossing. Ria still found that jolts sent sharp pains through her shoulder. It was as if the severed nerves were like cut electrical wires shooting deadly sparks.

At Dover, she was transferred to an ambulance train where she had a ward all to herself. She and Antonia were brought endless cups of tea, as the orderlies seemed to want an excuse to meet them.

"Good thing I'm here to protect you from the curious masses! You'd think they had never seen women in uniform!" Antonia opined, and they burst into laughter.

"Damn, that hurts!" Ria said between gasps.

They changed trains in London and arrived in Marlow at seven o'clock, having boarded the ship twelve hours earlier. Ria was surprised and delighted to see Grayson waiting for them at the station.

He gripped her right hand in a firm grasp that conveyed as much as a hug, which he would never dare allow himself. "We're so thankful to have you home with us, Mrs. Thornton! And very proud that you've been awarded medals. But not surprised, I should add. You'll be quite the celebrity back home, I think," he said astutely. And Ria could just imagine what Helena would make of that.

He soon had them and their luggage aboard the Club Rolls. Getting into the driver's seat, he said, "I have to admit that I thoroughly enjoy driving." Sitting beside him, Ria noticed his quiet smile.

He caught her up on news of the Club and Priory Manor on the short journey to Bovington Abbey.

It was an emotional homecoming, and a wonderful if tiring evening. Sophie sat pressed up against Ria, holding her hand whenever possible, gazing up at her in grateful wonder. Alice sat across from her, elated, joyful, wanting to know everything, but afraid of tiring Ria.

She laughed when Sophie, Alice, and Toni tucked her into bed. "It should be the other way round," she protested.

"You sleep now, Mummy Ria," Sophie said. "Tomorrow I will tell you a story."

Beatrice was happy to let Antonia drive the Rolls over to the Duchess of Connaught's hospital at Taplow the following day so that she and Ria could visit Justin. They found him sitting in a wheelchair in the garden, where several others also basked in the sunshine. Antonia pushed him close to a bench, so that she and Ria could sit and talk to him.

"You're looking so much better!" Ria said.

"Just jake, as the lads say," he replied with a grin. "It's glorious when you have nothing to do but lounge about in the sun. Makes me wish we were at the lake, though."

"Doesn't it just! Are they sending you home to Canada soon?"

"I've asked to be assigned to duty at the War Office or Shorncliffe – wherever they can use me." He would have stayed even if he weren't hoping to pursue a relationship with Antonia. He wasn't about to desert Ria while Chas was still in France. But he hoped to hell that she would never need his support.

Ria noticed the look that passed between him and Toni, who blushed slightly. "Oh, I *am* glad!" Ria said.

.   .   .

"We're going to play follow-my-leader," Chas said to his latest recruit. "I want to see your aerobatic skills. You do what I do. An hour should suffice. Then you can practice until you're out of petrol. Just make sure you get back here so we don't have to fetch you from some farmer's field," he added with a grin.

"I can manage anything you throw at me. Sir."

Chas sensed the young man's arrogance and replied, "Glad to hear it. But we don't want any broken aeroplanes or damaged pilots, so be cautious as well, Dexter."

Chas itched to wipe that smug expression from the boy's face, but instead, put Dexter though his paces with few concessions. He started with "contour chasing", flying so low over the countryside that they needed to avoid treetops and church steeples. Then he did loops and rolls and death spirals. Dexter kept pace with him. Yes, he was good.

Chas waved him off and landed his plane. 'B' flight, under McPherson, had just returned, so they were walking off the airfield with Chas when Dexter swooped so low overhead that they had to duck.

"What the hell!" Chas expostulated.

Dexter pulled up hard, jerking his plane about. "A bit ham-fisted, isn't he?" McPherson observed.

Once more Dexter dived at them, this time bouncing his wheels along the roof of the hangar. They could see him laughing.

"What's that idiot doing?" one of the mechanics complained as he rushed out of the hangar.

"Fire a Very light and get him down!" Chas said with annoyance.

"Kid showing off, is he?" one of the old hands said.

"Being a silly ass, if you ask me," McPherson replied.

Dexter ignored the signal and roared into a loop.

"Gosh, he shouldn't be doing that so low," McPherson said.

It was obvious that there wasn't enough room for Dexter to level out when he came over the top and plummeted earthward.

"Shit!" McPherson said.

They watched helplessly as the plane dived into the ground. They and other crew rushed over, but hot plumes of fire shot up fifty feet or more. There was no hope for Dexter, even if he hadn't been killed on impact.

"Damnation!" Chas swore. "What a bloody waste!"

Chapter 14

For a few moments it almost seemed like old times to Eleanor Carlyle. The wedding guests, champagne glasses in hand, were milling about the manicured grounds of Oaktree Island. She expected to find Ria and Chas canoodling behind one of the trees. Blake and Zoë would be perched on a granite boulder just along the path, deeply engaged in a meaningful discussion. Max and Lydia would be laughing as they danced to their own tune on the bowling green. Justin and Freddie would be dutifully conversing with the older guests, while Rafe would be chatting up every pretty girl at the party.

Jack was more of an unknown quantity. She would like to think that he would be at her side, touching her surreptitiously and provocatively as a promise for what would come when they managed to sneak away.

He had seemed genuinely disappointed that she had not gone to England, saying in a letter,

I have a studio in London that Lord Beaverbrook rented for me, so I spend a few weeks at the Front, doing sketches, and then some time in London creating the larger canvases. So if you did come over, we would certainly find opportunities to be together.

I miss you, Ellie. Your candour would be refreshing, and shake up some of the toffee-nosed Brits. I often think of what you would say if you were with me in certain situations, or how we'd laugh over the snobs afterwards. Recently I attended a fund-raising event where Lady Sidonie Dunston, whose brother is an Oxford chum of Chas, was wickedly baiting one of the stuffy Brigadier Generals by saying that it took the Canadians to win Vimy Ridge. Blustering, he retorted that the Canadians terrify even the barbaric Huns with their brutality, so it was little wonder the Germans gave in so easily. "The Canadians don't fight like gentlemen," he sniffed, to which Max Beaverbrook responded, "You mean they apply intelligent tactics and treat their men like something more than cannon fodder." Winston Churchill was vastly amused, and you would have enjoyed the Brigadier's outraged reaction as well. Beaverbrook would like you, Ellie. Perhaps a bit too much, as he fancies himself quite a ladies' man.

I, too, appreciate your charms, so in addition to your outspokenness, I also miss the sensual, sexy woman who constantly

*invades my dreams. I long to run my hands through your rich,
titian hair and over your luscious, lithe body.*

*But of course I understand your reasons for not coming over,
and am rather glad, since you won't be exposed to the dangers of
the crossing or the air raids in England.*

And so that he didn't have to worry about juggling his affair
with Lady Sidonie, Ellie thought with a pang.

Yet it was these heartfelt letters that kept her tethered to him.
There seemed to be no artifice on his part. She was his confidante,
chum, lover. And someone who could momentarily remove him
from the arena of war.

Never far from her thoughts was Troy, who also wrote to her
weekly, if not more often. His latest letter had been very odd.

Dearest Ellie,

*I'm deeply revolted with myself. I've succumbed to the needs of
the flesh. I can't call it 'pleasure'. It was more a bodily relief than
something enjoyable.*

*I shouldn't be telling you this, but I feel that I need your
absolution to be free of the crawling disgust that now assails me
whenever I think of what I have done.*

*I do still struggle with my moral upbringing, although I've seen
too much suffering and horror not to understand people wanting to
grasp at every opportunity of pleasure or forgetfulness, to live each
moment as if it might be the last, because for so many it will be. So
I judge no one else.*

*But for myself I want intimacy to be more relevant and
meaningful, to be a true expression and culmination of emotional
love.*

*Are you shaking your head now and thinking that I'm a prude
or naïve? You have been very frank with me about your opinions of
sex. I know you think it healthy and natural, even necessary, but
are you aware of how many men here are afflicted with VD? I'm
glad I hadn't exposed myself to the possibly of disease before
donating blood to Ria. But how can I be certain that I am
uncontaminated now? How can I offer my love untainted?*

Can you forgive me, Ellie?

Yours in abject humility, Troy

She was surprised and yet pleased at this naked honesty. His
letters certainly did come from the heart. It was how he had been
drawing her ever closer.

Ellie was tugged out of her reverie by Rupert Wyndham, who
offered his arm as he said formally, "Dr. Carlyle, may I escort you

to a chair? The ceremony is about to begin." He, along with his younger brother, Miles, and the three Oakley boys, were pages whose job it was to assemble the guests.

"Why thank you, kind sir," Ellie replied graciously as she took his arm. The boys were obviously excited to be dressed in tails and given such an important job. But she had Rupert giggling as she said casually, "You've really shot up this year – almost as tall as your Mum. I expect your appendix had been weighing you down."

The actual ceremony was being held in the gazebo on One-Tree Island, which was little more than a large granite rock connected to the main island by a humpback bridge. Only close family would be seated there, and the rest of the guests would watch from the shore of Oaktree.

Clusters of elegant white calla lilies appeared to grow out of the balusters of the bridge railings. Potted white climbing roses artistically entwined the eight pillars of the gazebo. Large urns of hydrangeas with enormous blue flower heads were scattered about. Ellie thought it was all very tastefully done, unlike that ostentatious picnic of 1914 when everything had been shrouded in white flowers. She had to give Lizzie credit for her decorating flair and restraint.

Lizzie herself was sophisticated in a sleek, copper silk calf-length dress with hip-length jacket. As the official photographer, she was busy.

Claire was the Maid of Honour and Esme, Fliss, and Phoebe were the bridesmaids. Ellie figured that Phoebe had been chosen because it would have seemed unnatural and unkind not to include her. But she had never seen the girl so excited, other than when she had been pregnant. Ellie hoped that this would be helpful to Phoebe, although she was surprised that the girl had dealt so well with her mother's death. Ellie wondered what had really happened there – if Phoebe had been implicated somehow – but the local constable had been satisfied that it was accidental.

There was a unanimous gasp as the bride appeared. Not only was she a natural beauty, but she also looked as though she had stepped out of a Hollywood movie. Her gown was elegantly simple – a sleeveless, narrow, ankle-length white satin, swathed at the hips so that the bodice draped into a long V. It was overlaid by a beaded net cape with a diamante black scalloped edge, which drooped from elbow-length in front to knee-length at the back. Her headpiece was a white satin cap with the same black scallop and fringe dripping onto her shoulders.

"Wow! What a knock-out!" Ellie heard a chap from the groom's side say. Apparently, Hugo Garrick's New England family was old money, and had been very much against his marriage to a Canadian showgirl. Ellie thought it was a recurring theme that might finally be put to rest. The Garricks could hardly fail to be impressed by the Wyndham family. Although Hugo had offered to pay for the wedding, Lizzie had made sure that the Wyndhams picked up the costs. It was as easy as talking to Olivia, who had also elicited support from Helena.

The bridesmaids' blue dresses matched the hydrangeas, and seemed as couturier designed as the wedding gown, although Jack's mother, Marie, had created them all.

Marie Wyndham had been reluctant to come. She hadn't wanted to see the place that her husband had pined for all his married life. His nostalgic reminiscences had always seemed a subtle criticism and huge regret. Because he had defied his parents and married her, Alex had not only been disinherited, but had also been shunned by his family. It was difficult to forgive that.

And yet Richard and Olivia had not only made her most welcome, but had also provided her Toronto house and, consequently, her livelihood, which was renting rooms to university students and young career women. And she could now understand Alex's obsession with Wyndwood. She was immensely saddened to think how different life would have been for them had Alex's parents not taken against them. Never since his death had she longed so much for him as she did now, in the place he had so loved and where she suddenly felt close to him.

Although she had been angry at first, her pride hurt, she was thankful that Jack had taken the initiative to contact the Wyndhams, because her children, already hugely successful, would have a secure and bright future. She shuddered to think that Lizzie would otherwise still be slaving somewhere as a maid, Emily, in a sweatshop, Claire having to leave school to work, and Jack waiting tables or trying to make a living with his art. If only Alex could have seen this! Her tears were not just for the beautiful bride.

After a sumptuous dinner, the guests chatted on the terrace and lawns while the ballroom was being transformed from dining to dancing.

At one point the Wyndwood and Stepping Stone islanders were in a group. Phoebe said, "Oh, Helena, you have a new ring! How beautiful! But why did you give your other one to that rather nasty fellow?"

There was moment of stunned silence. Helena's throat was dry as she said testily, "Whatever are you talking about, Phoebe?"

"I saw you give it to that stranger."

Helena threw James a confused and helpless glance, which didn't quite put to rest his sudden unease. With his wife so much younger than himself, he was always on the alert for interlopers.

"You have a rather vivid imagination, Phoebe," Helena stated firmly.

In exasperation Phoebe said, "People always accuse me of that when they don't want to hear the truth. Like when I told Victoria and Zoë that Lizzie had been our maid, Molly."

There were chuckles and sighs of relief at this obviously ridiculous statement. But Ellie had noticed Lizzie's momentary shock. She wasn't so ready to dismiss Phoebe's observations as those of a demented mind. She tried to recall Molly, and wondered if Lizzie had been in their midst that entire summer of 1914. Ellie could well imagine that Lizzie had the skill and daring to pull that off. What a delightful thought! But why hadn't Jack told her about it? He must have known that she would have been highly amused. Was there something more sinister that they were hiding?

It affirmed yet again her instinctive mistrust of Lizzie.

Phoebe shuffled away muttering to herself, and Ellie caught up with her. "They all think I'm crazy, don't they?" Phoebe said.

"You see the world differently, Phoebe. And sometimes you see things that the rest of us don't, which must be quite scary at times."

"But I *did* see Helena give her ring to a stranger."

"Sometimes it's better if we don't tell everything we know or think. Isn't it kinder to say nothing than to tell Letitia that her gown is rather too tight for her expanding girth?"

Phoebe giggled. "She does look like a sausage about to burst."

"But we won't tell her that."

"Shouldn't someone? Or she won't change – either her dress or her attitude."

"You're very perceptive, Phoebe. Tell me about Helena's stranger."

"I think she was afraid of him. He didn't look like a nice person, although he never stopped smiling at her. Smarmy and superior. Don't you think that Uncle James should be told?"

"I think that Helena has to be the one to do that. It's not up to us to reveal other people's secrets. Well, not unless we can save someone from harm."

"Uncle James might be angry with Helena if he believed me, wouldn't he? And that wouldn't be good for their baby. So I won't say anymore about it. I can tell you things though, can't I, Eleanor?"

"You certainly can. In fact, you'll probably feel better if you do."

"Maryanne says that I'm wicked because I don't miss Mama enough. I do wish she were here. Sometimes. She doesn't visit me like Grandmother does. I guess Mama is happy with God and Sarah, and she's probably still really mad at me. Can you hate someone and love them at the same time?"

"Of course you can. Emotions are very complicated."

"Mostly I don't really want Mama back. At least not the way she was, telling me how bad I am, and being mean to me."

"You're not bad, Phoebe," Ellie reassured her. "Don't let Maryanne or anyone tell you that."

"You don't believe my doll talks to me any more than anyone else does," Phoebe accused.

"I believe that we all have our own reality, Phoebe. I can't know what's going on in your head any more than you can see through my eyes. What I do know is that if you believe something, then for you it is real. But when your reality becomes too confusing or scary, other people can help you to deal with that."

"When it does then I'll let you know. So I don't have to feel guilty for enjoying myself, just because Mama died? I'm having ever so much more fun now," Phoebe added brightly.

After the dancing began in the ballroom, Ellie was glad to see that Phoebe was indeed enjoying herself. She seemed to have blossomed in the company of her cousins and friends, now that they shared the excitement of being bridesmaids.

Ellie was contemplating a dull evening, since there were so few young men in attendance.

"May I have this dance?" a familiar voice asked from behind. He drew Ellie into his arms before she even had a chance to respond.

"Troy! My God, Troy!" Ellie hugged him exuberantly despite all the people around them.

He chuckled. "What an accolade, being your God."

His arms felt so good around her. "Am I dreaming? What are you doing here?" she asked in amazement.

"I couldn't wait to see you," he replied with a broad grin. "How could I stay away after all your entreaties to return safe and sound? And I didn't think they'd mind an extra guest at the dance."

"Have I missed the end of the war?"

"Unfortunately not. But now that we Americans are at war as well, new chaps are coming to France, so our CO decided that the medical students with just a year of study left, who have been acting as orderlies, should return home to finish their degrees. I'm to do some biology and biochemistry courses to help me with my laboratory work. They'll count towards a Masters degree. So I'll be at Harvard until Christmas."

"I can't believe that they actually let you come home! I have this insane fear that the war has consumed all my friends and will never relinquish any of you." As they danced, she drew him tighter. "I'm so sorry about Kurt. God, I weep every time I think about him. It was only a year ago that we all laughed at the Country Club."

Amidst all the gaiety they clung to one another as if they were the only ones who truly felt the impact of the war. But few there were undamaged, Ellie knew. There were parents and lovers who were anxious or already bereaved, everyone carrying on stoically. Determined not to think about the war for a while, she tried to lighten the mood. "I haven't had a decent dance since you left," she admitted.

"Would it be selfish of me to claim you for the entire evening?"

"Terribly. But I'd adore it. I'd much rather dance under the stars, and then no one can intervene."

She took his proffered hand and they ambled out onto the terrace. A few others were enjoying the balmy evening, smoking cigars or cigarettes, talking in pairs or groups.

The musicians were professional friends of the groom, and their lively renditions of popular tunes drifted into the night air, the music at once stimulating and soothing. When *You Made Me Love You* began, Troy said, "Our song, I think," and took her into his arms.

"You play it better," Ellie said lightly as he nuzzled her hair.

"You remember."

"Of course! Have you been entertaining the troops?"

"We all do." He told her about Ria's rendition of *Sister Suzie*, and then caught her up with the latest news about her friends. "Ria should be back in England by now."

Having heard about Ria's ordeal in more detail, Ellie said, "It seems to me as if you all live on a different planet!"

"It's more like Hell." They had wandered beyond the reflecting pool and waterfall to the path that skirted the island. Moving away from the lanterns, they proceeded down to the water's edge.

"Did you receive my letter of the 7th?" Troy asked, somewhat shamefaced. "I mailed it just before I left."

"You mean the *mea culpa*, hair-shirt one?" she asked with a grin.

"Am I forgiven?"

"Troy, you don't owe me any explanations, but if it helps, then yes. I expect that you took precautions, so there shouldn't be any consequences of any kind, medical or otherwise. You really mustn't chastise yourself over a powerful biological urge."

"Perhaps Dr. Carlyle would be willing to provide some therapy."

She laughed. "Do you mean psychological or physical?"

He gazed at her intently in the dim moonlight. "Whatever the doctor recommends."

She kissed him, and he responded hungrily. "That's a good start," Ellie said breathlessly.

"I've missed you, Ellie, more than I could ever have imagined. You're forever in my thoughts, dreams, fantasies. Always more beautiful, intelligent, desirable than any woman I've met. I'm crazy about you, Ellie."

Trying to deflect the conversation from becoming irrevocably serious, she quipped, "You just haven't seen a woman in ages who's not in uniform."

"Au contraire. The French Mademoiselles are a lovely and generally uninhibited lot."

"In that case you must have to beat them off. Ria told me that you are very much admired by the Sisters in your hospital."

He stroked her cheek. "I was oblivious to them all."

"I'm off until after Labour Day. How long can you stay?"

"I also have this week free."

"So what are we doing tomorrow?" she asked. "Tennis, swimming, canoodling?"

He laughed. "Most definitely. Especially the latter."

"I just arrived yesterday. My family's been here for a month, but Mum has to return to work, and Dad and Derek are helping out with the harvest at a farm, so they're all leaving tomorrow. I expect I could manage to put something edible on the table if you'd care to join me for dinner."

"There's nothing I'd like better. As long as it's not bully beef."

She laughed, relieved that he had responded to her mood. She was afraid that he wanted some commitment from her, which she wasn't prepared to give.

Ellie was glad the next day when she saw her family off and now had the cottage to herself. Because it was Sunday and he was only newly arrived, Troy had confessed that he probably couldn't get away until late afternoon.

"I just told my folks that I'm dining with the Carlyles," he said when he arrived. "Mom would be scandalized if she knew you were staying here unchaperoned and entertaining me to dinner."

"I daresay most mothers would," she said. "Mine, however, considers me an adult fully responsible for my actions. And since I have a career, my reputation in the marriage market isn't so critical."

He laughed. "I think that your formidable intellect would intimidate men more than any scandalous reputation."

"I shall take that as a compliment. Let's have a swim before dinner," she suggested.

The perfectly blue sky of yesterday had been bled to a milky white by the humidity. Ellie had already spent a good part of the day cooling off in the lake. They swam to Picnic Island, which perched between Ouhu and Oaktree.

"I love the beach here," Ellie said as she lay back in the shallow water. The island wasn't big enough for a cottage, but as it was easy for canoes and rowboats to pull up on its sandy shoreline, it was a popular spot for picnics. "When we were kids, we sometimes camped over here on hot nights, pretending we were great explorers or *The Swiss Family Robinson*. If I ever have pots of money, I'll buy this island just so that I can always come here. I know that sounds very materialistic of me."

"Not at all. It's a beautiful spot."

"But wouldn't it be terribly indulgent to spend money on something so frivolous?"

"No more so than buying a painting that just hangs on your wall. All you can do is look at it, which is delightful enough. This you can experience as well."

The shallow water shelved gradually, the hard golden sand seeming to ripple in the waves.

Ellie rolled over and propped her head on her elbow, looking down at Troy who lay stretched out beside her, half submerged in the clear water. She said, "I know how to justify it! I'll host a week for impoverished children from the city. They can camp here, learn to swim and canoe..."

"Which is a generous idea, but how about just enjoying it yourself, and keeping it as a place where your children can play? Special things we sometimes only want to share with special people."

The look that passed between them was unbearably sensual. This was not the place to allow a kiss to stoke an unquenchable fire, so Ellie challenged, "I'll race you back."

When they were at the cottage and dressed, Troy offered to help, and Ellie said, "You can build a fire. We're having a cookout. I'm already sweltering again and it would be impossible to fire up the woodstove today." Her father had long ago built a stone fire pit with a large grill laid on top. "I'll have you know that despite the late night, I was up with the birds, fishing for our dinner. And I managed to catch a couple of pickerel."

"Another talent I wasn't aware of," Troy said appreciatively.

"Dad taught me to fish when I was young, and also to clean my catch. I performed my first autopsy on fish," she said impishly.

"No need to elaborate. You're speaking about my dinner."

Which was simple but tasty. "An accomplished cook as well," Troy said, raising his wineglass in a toast to her. They sat at a small table on the veranda. The chairs and table had been assembled from twigs and branches, which Ellie admitted her father had cobbled together, while her mother had caned the chair bottoms.

"I expect anything tastes good after army rations. The potatoes have turned to mush inside their burnt skins, and the carrots are practically raw. The sauce is good because I coerced Daphne into making it for me, and the peas are from a can. I'm actually rather hopeless in the kitchen."

"I happen to like mashed potatoes and crispy carrots, and the fish is cooked to perfection."

"I figure that by foraging for my own food, I'm doing my bit for the war effort. So I spent the afternoon picking blueberries for our dessert. I'm afraid you'll have to eat them as is, since I can't manage to turn them into a pie. In any case, we're supposed to cut down on wheat consumption. And bacon and bully beef," she added with a grin. "I hope you men appreciate that I've sent my portions over to you."

"You can keep the beef," Troy quipped.

They lingered over the wine, watching the misty sunset transform the lake with its softened palette, discussing Troy's research into blood chemistry and transfusions, which impressed Ellie tremendously. She felt inordinately pleased that he was planning a career in medical research.

He insisted on helping her wash up. When he had draped the tea towel over a chair to dry, Ellie said, "You really are domesticated."

"I've learned a lot since I've been away from home," he said as he drew her towards him. She moaned when he kissed her, and then pushed him away.

"Troy, would you think me brazen if I ask you whether you brought some protection?"

"Would you think me presumptuous if I told you I did?"

They laughed joyfully. He scooped her into his arms.

"What are you doing?" Ellie demanded.

"Sweeping you off your feet and carrying you upstairs."

"You will not! You're more likely to put your back out and then I'll spend the rest of the night doctoring you."

He put her down at the bottom of the stairs and took her hand. Suddenly shy, he said, "Are you sure about this, Ellie?"

They could barely contain their passion when she kissed him again. "Oh, yes," she breathed.

His lovemaking was tentative and inexperienced, but she guided him.

"Wow, Ellie, I knew it would be wonderful with you!" he said in awe afterwards. "But I'm sorry. It shouldn't have been that quick, should it?"

Because she had spoken so candidly about sex, Troy had expected that he was not her first lover. He had already struggled with that thought, imagining her with Jack, wishing he could be the only one to know her so intimately, but had decided that it truly didn't matter. He loved her no matter what. His mother's edict about keeping oneself pure for marriage was surely an outdated concept, especially in these uncertain times.

"You just need practice," Ellie advised.

"Ellie...."

She pressed her fingers to his lips to silence him. She could see that he was overwhelmed with emotion, and struggling to put that into words. "*Carpe Diem,*" she said. "And we have all week. How about a skinny dip now?"

The half-moon emerged from the tumescence of the day, spilling a silvery swath across the calm water and transforming the treed shoreline into pewter. They swam over to Picnic Island again, Ellie admitting that she had always wanted to do that in the buff.

"This is delicious," she enthused as they lay in the warm shallows and looked up at an infinity of stars.

"You're delicious," Troy said as he drew her into an intimate embrace.

"You're insatiable!"

"I've just discovered something magnificent and life-altering. You've liberated me."

"Unleashed a beast, you mean" she teased. "Well, you'll just have to contain yourself while I explain all the constellations to you."

"Alright," he agreed as he trailed kisses down her neck and breast.

She laughed. "You have to look up!"

"I'd rather look at you." He rolled on top of her, and she could feel his swelling desire. "And I came prepared," he said, showing her the condom in his hand.

"I expect that making love under the stars is even better than just looking at them."

This time he brought her to a climax just before his own. "You learn quickly," she said.

"You inspire me."

"I wish you could stay the night."

"So do I. Of course, you could marry me and then I could stay every night," he said lightly.

"I shall give that due consideration," she replied equally lightly. "In the meantime, you could just tell your family that you're camping out on Picnic Island."

He laughed. "Is that what we're doing? Mom would be suspicious and probably check up on me. So I really do need to go home now," he added reluctantly.

"Will you come back after breakfast?"

"You bet!"

It was a heady week. They played tennis at the Country Club, dined and danced at the Grand, sailed and canoed, went on picnics, sometimes with others, visited Edelina, and spent many delightful, indulgent hours alone together.

Daphne gave a dinner party for family and close friends on Friday evening, including the newlyweds who were honeymooning in Albert's cottage for a month before heading over to England. Albert was in British Columbia on lumbering business. Since Phyllis's death, he had been rather confused, as if seeking himself and determining what he wanted out of life. Too long he had been under the tyranny of both his mother and his wife.

To everyone's delight, Emily was easily persuaded to sing tunes from the musical, *Under The Moon*, accompanied by her adoring husband. Phoebe was particularly enrapt by the romantic music. Hugo also gave them a sample of tunes from the new musical he was writing, which promised to be just as captivating.

Ellie overhead Felicity Thornton tell Lizzie, "Chas was amazed with the portrait you did of me. He said that I was so grownup he hardly recognized me. And Jack said that you have a talent for exposing beauty." Fliss blushed, and added, "We've been corresponding quite a lot lately."

"Jack mentioned how much he enjoyed your letters," Lizzie lied.

Ellie was somewhat taken aback. Was Jack flattering Fliss because he was hoping to marry into the Thornton fortune?

It was obvious that Fliss was smitten, and so would be an easy conquest. Would Chas allow it? But of course he and Jack were good friends, comrades. Chas had saved Jack's life, putting his own at risk. J.D. Thornton had married into wealth, and had thus begun his empire, so why would anyone object if ambitious and talented Jack Wyndham, with the bonus of aristocratic relatives, did the same? Hadn't one of Chas's Oxford chums been Jack's cousin? And Chas would think nothing of the fact that Jack had had an affair with her and was probably having a fling with Lady Sidonie. Bloody hell!

After she and Troy made love that night, Ellie considered more seriously the possibility of marrying him, for she felt certain that he would ask her again. They had been almost inseparable this past week, so Ellie already dreaded the moment they would have to part.

But she felt incredibly torn. How was it possible to love two men? She had an easy rapport with both. With Troy there was the added piquancy of a shared intellectual interest in medical sciences.

Jack had been her first love, and they had grown even closer through their numerous intimate letters these past three years. From the outset of their romance, they had made no commitments to one another. Hadn't she even told him that she didn't expect him to be faithful to her? Whenever she looked at the stunning portrait he had painted of her, which hung in her bedroom in the city, she was astonished at how he saw her – "strong, sensitive, sexy" he had said. That was seductive in itself, so it was little wonder she had fallen so hard for him.

But with Troy offering himself unreservedly and Jack probably scheming to marry money, why was she unable to let Jack go? Ellie had never been so confused.

On the Saturday of the Labour Day long weekend, Felicity Thornton once again hosted a ball. It was where Ellie and Troy had become enamoured the previous year.

Now Ellie was imagining Jack here, at Fliss's side, the perfect, sauve host. Fliss would be exactly the kind of woman he would want to help his career. Already an accomplished hostess, she also had important connections.

When Troy went to fetch glasses of wine partway through the evening, his mother came and sat next to Ellie. "My son seems to be very fond of you, Miss Carlyle."

"We enjoy one another's company, Mrs. Roland," Ellie replied, feeling suddenly ill at ease with Erika Roland's haughty manner.

"Too much perhaps. He has been neglectful of us this week. And I've heard that your parents are not even here." Her tone was accusatory.

Ignoring the latter statement, Ellie said, "Troy and I have been enjoying time with our friends because we all soon have to return to work or school."

"I don't believe that women should work outside the home. The wife and mother must be the moral centre and strength of the family, which she obviously cannot be if she is out somewhere, making money." She said it as if earning money were immoral. "It goes against nature and God when women try to take over the roles of men."

With anyone but Troy's mother, Ellie would have launched into a much-practiced rebuttal. But she also couldn't stay silent, so she replied, "Women have talents that can be beneficial in many ways, Mrs. Roland."

"I'm sure you do admirable deeds as a doctor, Miss Carlyle, and of course, you can choose to live your life as an independent woman." Again that disdainful inflection. "But don't involve my son. He needs a wife who will be devoted to him and completely supportive. Someone who puts her husband and family above all else. He also needs a woman of impeccable character." She was obviously implying that she didn't consider Ellie to be eligible for that distinction either.

She stopped her diatribe when Troy joined them. When Ellie accepted the glass of wine he handed her, Erika Roland rose regally and said dismissively, "I also don't approve of women drinking. Or encouraging men to do so." She threw Troy a withering glance that seemed to reduce him to a disobedient child.

After she had glided away, Troy looked sympathetically at Ellie as he said, "I'm sorry, Ellie. Was she being supercilious?"

"She thinks I've corrupted you. And she made it quite plain that I'm not suitable for you." Ellie was more hurt than she wanted to admit, and couldn't deal with this blow in her usual feisty manner. Just wishing to escape, she flounced onto the veranda, and hastened across the lawn toward the tennis pavilion, suppressing the tears that unaccountably threatened.

"Ellie! Just ignore her," Troy pleaded as he kept up with her punishing pace. "I've told you how controlling and sanctimonious she is."

He pulled her to a stop, but she wouldn't meet his gaze. "I'd like to go home," she said.

"OK, but first I want you to look at me." When she did, defiantly, tears glistening, he said, "I love you, Ellie. I want you to marry me, come to Harvard with me, and then England when I'm posted back. You can work anywhere as a doctor." When she didn't respond, he said, "Don't judge me because of my mother. We will make our own life together."

She was tempted, and if she hadn't just had this encounter with her possibly future mother-in-law, she might well have agreed. But the insult was too raw. "I don't want to be responsible for alienating you from your family. You may end up hating me for it." She was reminded of what Jack had told her about his parents.

"How can you think that? You are my life. All that I hold dear. All that I want."

She wished that they could just create their own little universe and be happily sheltered within it. But that wasn't reality. And just for a moment she still longed for Jack. "I can't deal with this right now, Troy. Will you please take me home?"

When they arrived at her dock, she didn't invite him into the cottage. "I'm leaving tomorrow," she informed him.

"Ellie, don't shut me out like this!" he pleaded, taking her into his arms.

She wriggled free. "Perhaps your mother is right. You need a charming, socially adept, well-connected girl who will devote herself to you and your career."

"Bullshit! I need a woman who is my equal, someone who shares my passion for science and other things. It's not like you, Ellie, to give up so easily."

"I'm not! I'm being realistic! What can there be between us, Troy, if you're destined for bigger things and better people?"

"Ellie, stop and think about what you're saying. Don't echo my mother." He drew her back. "I love you. The world has changed from our parents' time. We need to make our own way. Marry me. Please."

She couldn't stop her tears when he kissed her. "I can't. I'm not ready. I don't know what I want."

"I can wait. But don't dismiss me from your life."

Troy stayed with her for most of the night, partly in defiance of his mother, but mostly because he wanted to console Ellie and prove his love. He arrived home just as the first light of dawn was rousing the birds. It was not an unusual time to be home after a ball, but of course his mother would have realized he hadn't stayed until the end, even though he'd brought his own boat. She emerged from her bedroom when he tiptoed through the hallway to his room.

"I expect all men must have their whores," she said to him. "Just don't bring her to me as your wife."

She disappeared into her room before Troy could respond. He snatched a few hours of sleep and left without seeing anyone. He was too angry to face his mother across the breakfast table. Ellie was just preparing to boil an egg when he arrived.

"Is there enough for two?"

He was relieved to see her smile. "There's always enough for you."

Troy had convinced Ellie not to return to the city until the last possible moment, but she had to leave early the next morning for the day-long trip back. His family would leave the following day, but tomorrow would be spent supervising the packing and closing of the cottage for the season.

"I'd be happy to have a quiet day here with you," Troy confessed as they sat on the veranda eating eggs and toast. "It could be a year or two before we're together again."

She winced and almost capitulated at the thought of more lonely years ahead with all her friends gone and without either of the men she loved.

It was anything but a quiet day.

.   .   .

"Phoebe Phoebe! Look at me! Look at me!"

Phoebe looked up at her namesake bird that sat on a tree branch squawking at her.

"Phoebe Phoebe! Look and see! Look and see!"

"What should I see?" she asked him.

He flew onto a lower branch. "Phoebe Phoebe! Can't you see? Can't you see?"

The bird hopped about excitedly, laughing as Phoebe noticed her mother's face in the trunk of the tree. Her arms were outstretched, reaching toward Phoebe.

"No!" she shouted. But she couldn't run. It was as if she, too, had grown roots that anchored her in the shadow of her massive mother.

The bird flitted about her mother's waving arms and shaggy hair, cackling maniacally. "Phoebe Phoebe! Come to me! Come to me!"

The foul breath expelled by her mother tugged and shoved and whirled. Her mother's flailing arms threatened to beat her. "You killed me you killed me you killed me!" the bird reiterated.

"No!" Phoebe shrieked. "No! I didn't! Mama, I didn't mean to!" Finally pulling herself free, she rushed up to her mother and beat her fists against the frowning, hostile face. "Go away! Leave me be! You're the one who's evil! You stole my baby! Where's my baby?" Over and over she pummeled the smug face.

Edgar, having heard her screams, rushed to her side. "Phoebe stop!" It took all his strength to pull her away. Her hands were raw and bleeding. "Hell! Phoebe, what are you doing?"

"Make her go away, Edgar! I hate her! Why won't Mama leave me alone?" Phoebe collapsed against him, wailing.

He held her tenderly. In the rising wind he led her into the cottage. As he maneuvered a sobbing Phoebe onto a sofa, he said to Daphne, "Would you give me a couple of clean towels and then fetch your sister?"

He had taught Daphne to drive the boat, and she was at Ouhu in a matter of minutes. Ellie and Troy were still sitting on the front veranda and discussing how war ironically precipitated progress in everything from medicine to aeroplanes.

When they arrived at Wyndwood, they found Phoebe wild-eyed and hysterical. Her towel-bandaged hands looked like bizarre wings, which she had wrapped around herself. She was rocking as she mumbled, "It was better when she went away. Why is she back? Why is she tormenting me? I didn't do anything wrong. Mama shouldn't be mean to me! I want her to hold me and tell me that everything is alright, like when I was little. Why didn't she do that anymore?"

A strong gust of wind rattled the screen doors as if unseen visitors were clamouring to get in. Unseen to most. Phoebe looked over and screamed in terror.

Ellie stroked her head. "Tell those scary ones to go away, Phoebe. You don't want them here. Only you can make that happen. You have the power, Phoebe," she assured the terrified girl. "Your grandmother and mother and sister are all with God. They don't belong here with us anymore."

Edgar put his arm around Phoebe as he said, "Mama always loved you, Beebee. Sometimes she was angry, but that was only for a little while. She would never hurt you. Now you calm down and let Ellie bandage your hands properly."

Ellie was surprised at the damage Phoebe had done to herself, her skin torn and flesh gouged and riddled with splinters. Now that Phoebe was no longer in a manic state, she was feeling the pain. Ellie gave her some chloral and cleaned up the wounds, which was a painful process.

Troy sat down at the piano and began to play *Ragtime Nightingale*, hoping the music would soothe Phoebe. Ellie gave him a grateful look.

When Ellie had finished, Phoebe said, "Troy is pretty good, isn't he?" He had played Chopin and Debussy as well.

"He is indeed," Ellie agreed.

"If he didn't like you so much I'd ask him to marry me," Phoebe confided to Ellie, but not quietly enough.

Troy grinned and winked at Ellie as he said, "Here's a popular new tune," and launched into *For Me and My Gal*.

Sedated, and now enchanted by the music, Phoebe became positively cheerful.

Ellie asked Edgar to accompany her to the library. When he had closed the door, she said, "I would never advocate sending Phoebe to an asylum, you know that." She considered them little better than prisons for people with a variety of neuroses and psychoses, filled with indigents or those abandoned by families who could no longer look after them either financially or with proper medical attention. Thrown into the mix were also the feebleminded, the homeless, and the occasional criminals. "As I've mentioned before, I strongly believe Phoebe would benefit from a few months at the private sanitarium in Guelph. Homewood is expensive – about $40 a week – but your family can easily afford that. They're on the forefront of dealing humanely and sympathetically with psychiatric issues. It's a resort-like environment – lovely grounds by the river, with tennis courts, surrounded by their own farms, which supply fresh produce. Phoebe would be given massage and hydrotherapy in addition to psychotherapy. Think of it as a healing vacation for her. There's nothing shameful in going there, Edgar. It's quite fashionable for neurasthenics to take a rest cure." Ellie didn't say that Phoebe was likely more seriously ill with schizophrenia, and for her it would take much more than a few months of relief from stress to cure her.

Edgar didn't protest this time. "I'll talk to Papa about it."

"In the meantime, she needs some nursing care. With her hands so badly injured, she can't even care for herself at the moment, and you and Daphne can't do everything for her. I know a nurse who may still be between private patients at the moment. Her husband was a doctor but he died a couple of years ago, and she took up nursing again. Her daughter was in medical school with me, so I know how to contact her. I'll do that right away."

Most nurses worked privately after their three years of training in hospitals, but with the unprecedented number of wounded soldiers returning and convalescent hospitals short of staff, nurses were becoming difficult to find.

On the way to the dock, Ellie stopped to examine the tree that had sent Phoebe into hysterics. It was a gnarled and knolled oak. She could see nothing unusual at first, but allowing her mind the freedom to *not* think of it as a tree and just absorb the overall impression of this entity, she was a trifle surprised to realize that she, too, discerned a face in the rough bark. Not Phyllis's, of course, but how easily one could attach a personality to it.

Troy drove Ellie to the Grand Muskoka Hotel so that she could telephone her friend Lorna Partridge in Toronto. Lorna said she would call her mother immediately and one of them would get back to Ellie at the hotel shortly.

"Fancy an ice cream while we wait?" Troy offered.

"Sure." She told the receptionist, "I'm Dr. Carlyle, and I'm expecting an important call from Toronto. I'll be in the ice cream parlour."

The woman asked, in obvious astonishment, "You're a medical doctor?"

"A very fine one, too," Troy interjected.

"Oh, Dr. Carlyle! We could really use your help! One of our guests has snagged his ear on a fish hook!" She was practically wringing her hands.

Ellie bit her lip to stop from laughing, and said, "I expect I can help."

"Thank goodness! We have him in the office."

"I'll fetch your bag," Troy offered.

An elderly gentleman was sitting on a chair, his fishing rod still in one hand, the line tethered to his ear. "I'm in rather a pickle," he said with a twinkle in his eyes when Ellie had introduced herself.

"You weren't planning to catch such a big fish, I expect," she jested. "But you did a good job."

He chuckled appreciatively, but looked alarmed a moment later when Ellie requested tin snips from the receptionist.

"This shouldn't be any worse than when women have their ears pierced," she reassured her worried patient after she cut the fishing line and took the rod from him.

"I've never appreciated how barbaric that really is," he replied.

"Yes, it's hard to imagine that women willingly submit themselves to this."

Troy arrived with her medical bag at the same time the tin snips appeared.

The manager, Mr. Graham, bustled in. Obviously agitated, he demanded, "Do you know what you're doing, young lady?"

"I certainly do. If you're squeamish, you needn't stay."

But he did, and muttered apologies to the victim. "We usually have a doctor here full time, but with the war, it's become impossible. I'm afraid that Dr. Rumbold from Port Carling is probably at church and there's no one else available at the moment. My sincerest apologies, Mr. Rossiter." Mr. Graham was practically groveling.

"I've put myself into the hands of this very pretty young woman," the patient said.

"Who happens to be a doctor at the Toronto General Hospital," Troy explained, sensing Ellie's frustration at being considered first a woman and then, as an afterthought, a professional.

She cleaned around the wound with alcohol and also swabbed down the fishhook. Seeing what she was about to do, Troy offered to take over. He cut off the eye end of the hook. Ellie disinfected it again and then pushed it the rest of the way through the patient's earlobe. "When we can't pull, we push," she said, showing the victim the offending hook.

"Well I never! Hardly noticed a thing!"

"Good. Now I'll just tidy you up a bit and we'll hope that it doesn't become infected. No stitches required, but I'll put a bandage on. I want you to clean the wound for a few days with rubbing alcohol."

"Can you prescribe some for me internally, as well? Since we're not supposed to drink any fine old Scotch unless the doctor orders it."

"A few ounces to get over the shock would be highly recommended," she agreed. "Can you see to that, Mr. Graham?"

The manager was taken aback, but said, "Yes, I can manage that. We keep supplies for emergencies."

In his desk drawer, Ellie was thinking.

"Thank you, young lady. Now what do I owe you?" Mr. Rossiter asked.

Without hesitation, Ellie said, "My usual fee is $10." She had judged him to be affluent, and was taking Richard Wyndham's advice to charge the wealthy more.

The old man pulled out his pocketbook. "A bit extra for the prescription, don't you think?" he said, handing her twenty dollars. "Worth every cent. Now what about your able assistant?"

"I'll buy him an ice cream cone," Ellie replied.

Mr. Rossiter chortled.

When they left the room, Troy said to her, "You probably don't care, but your patient was Jacob Rossiter, the President of one of our major American banks."

"I knew he had money! My normal rate is $5."

Troy laughed. "And you're not a bit impressed by such an illustrious patient," he said with admiration.

"Actually, I thought he was rather foolish to get himself trussed up like that. These weekend fishermen!"

Troy took her arm and said, "You're priceless!"

"Thank you. So now that I am in funds, you may order the biggest ice cream cone they have. My able assistant and champion deserves a reward."

Before they could start for the ice cream parlour, Ellie's telephone call came through. Lorna's mother, Irene Partridge, was free and would be able to catch the train from Union Station first thing in the morning. The overnight train had been dropped this summer for the duration of the war. Ellie assured her that she would earn at least her standard fee, and gave her instructions on how to get here.

"Now that it's already lunch time, let me invite you to dine before we have our ice cream," Troy said, offering his arm.

"How delightful!"

Wine was still served at meals, despite prohibition. Mr. Rossiter raised his glass to Ellie when their eyes met across the room. She smiled and reciprocated the gesture.

"I have a rival, do I?" Troy said.

"He does have pots more money than you," she teased. "I was just thinking what a cakewalk it is for the resident doctor. Perhaps that's how I should spend my summers, living at the cottage and making quadruple fees for soothing sunburns and poison ivy rashes."

"Why not? Someone has to do it."

"What, and leave all those desperately poor and seriously ill in the city in the clutches of the student doctors?"

"The wealthy deserve your ministrations as much as the destitute, don't you think? And there's a great deal of arrogance in thinking that one is indispensable in this world."

"Touché!"

"So don't obsess about doing good. You are. Enjoy yourself as well."

"Oh, I am. I've always liked the Grand." She had no objections to living well as long as it wasn't at someone else's expense. She truly did want to make a difference in people's lives.

Modern, luxurious, with a spectacular setting, the Grand was still touted as one of the finest resorts in Canada. Despite the general decrease in tourists during these war years, the resort was bustling with the affluent who could no longer travel to Europe.

Ellie and Troy sat on the top level of the three-storey veranda while they savoured their ice cream cones. The lake had turned a steely grey under thick, inky clouds, the wind whipping the water into foaming whitecaps. Thunder was growling.

"I do think we should head back before the storm hits," Troy suggested. "I'd much rather be stranded on your island than here."

They were nearly at Ouhu, when another boat approached them and slowed down. It was Fliss, who hailed them. Their boats bobbed violently in the swells, and Fliss had to shout to be heard above the wind. "I was looking for you, Ellie. Can you come and see Mummy? She's hurt herself!"

Ellie nodded and Troy turned the boat around. He put it into full throttle for they could see a wall of water rapidly approaching, so dense that everything behind it disappeared as if annihilated. It was decidedly eerie. The lightning was dangerously close by the time they reached Thorncliff. Thunder shattered the air above them. Troy was able to pull the boat into one of the slips in the large boathouse. They all ran up to the cottage in the first splattering of rain, arriving on the veranda just as the deluge hit. So dense and fierce was the downpour that little could be seen beyond it. The rain and wind pummelled and thrashed the trees and flowers. Puddles of water were already standing on the lawn, as it couldn't sink into the earth fast enough.

"Zowie! That's some storm," Fliss said, shaking droplets off her hair.

They all jumped as a brilliant flash of lightning was immediately accompanied by thunder. Fliss gave a small shriek and covered her ears, and Ellie thought about Phoebe, who was terrified of storms.

Troy said, "One of the fellows who fought at Vimy Ridge told me that the noise of the barrage was like a thousand thunderstorms overhead. We could hear it on the coast. Even the British Prime Minister could hear it from Downing Street in London."

"Golly!" Fliss said in awe.

Contemplating how nerve-shattering that would be, Ellie said, "With the added tension and fear of being killed, it's little wonder men become shell-shocked."

"Convince the military of that!" Troy said. "They think a lot of the chaps are either cowards or shirkers, and try to return them to the battlefields as quickly as possible."

Ellie hoped that Max wouldn't be sent back. But she had another concern at the moment. "Now, Fliss, what's happened to your mother?"

"She went over on her ankle yesterday on the flagstone path, and insisted it was nothing but a bit of a sprain. Now it's terribly swollen and bruised and jolly painful. I'm afraid she might have broken something."

"Thank goodness you're back!" Marjorie exclaimed as they walked into the morning room. Partly a glassed and screened extension at the southeast corner of the massive veranda, the large room was where informal meals were served and where the family lounged most of the time when there were no guests. The two walls of tall windows had lovely south and east views over the lawns and gardens to the tennis pavilion and a large arc of lake. Wyndwood Island would normally be seen, since it was only a quarter mile distant, but the rain seemed to have washed it away. "This storm is rather terrifying. Thank you for coming, Eleanor, but I do think that Fliss is overly worried. Hello Troy. It does reassure me to see that our boys do come home again. I hope the war is over before they expect you back."

"That would indeed be marvellous for us all," Troy agreed.

"It's no problem for me to have a look at your ankle. Mrs. Thornton," Ellie said. "Better to check these things out."

Marjorie's foot was resting on a cushioned stool. Ellie removed the damp towel and was surprised at how swollen and extensively bruised it was. "Fliss was right to be concerned, Mrs. Thornton. I do have to probe a bit, so I'm afraid this is going to hurt."

As Ellie manipulated the ankle and toe joints gently, Marjorie tried to stifle her gasps.

The rain was pelting the windows like hail and thunder was rolling down the lake.

"I don't think that anything is broken, but you really should have an x-ray as soon as possible, just in case. Can you go to the city tomorrow? I'll be traveling down first thing in the morning, and can accompany you."

"Of course we can," Fliss said immediately. "Thank you, Ellie."

"That's quite a bad sprain, in any case. I suspect you have at least a partial tear of the ligament. I'm going to apply a bandage to immobilize it, but if it keeps swelling, you should re-wrap the ankle. We don't want to restrict circulation. Keep it elevated and apply ice for ten or fifteen minutes at a time every few hours to reduce the swelling. You should keep off your foot as much as possible. Do you have crutches?"

"No, but I do have walking sticks."

"They'll have to do until we're in Toronto. I suggest aspirins for pain and to help with the inflammation."

"Thank you, my dear. How delightful to have such expert advice from a young woman I've known since she was barely out of nappies."

"I've been trying to persuade Ellie to become the island doctor during the summer," Troy said. "She could do house calls by boat."

"What a grand idea," Marjorie exclaimed.

Ellie and Troy chuckled at the irony. "Grand indeed!" he said with a wink at Ellie.

"Now let me pay you before I forget, and then we'll have a cup of tea," Marjorie said.

Ellie charged her $10 without hesitation.

As they sipped their tea they watched the wind gather strength. The younger trees were beaten to the ground. Clumps of leaves and dead branches were ripped from the older ones. Great gusts shook the sturdy cottage and hurled buckets of water at the windows.

There was an ominous and hair-raising roaring wail accompanying a whirlwind of debris. They watched in disbelief as a tall maple was plucked from the ground and now lay across the lawn with its massive root ball sticking up helplessly. The cottage had shuddered at the crash. A nearby oak tree exploded, and looked as if it had been twisted open with all its sinews exposed. They could see right through it. Gathering and flinging sticks and branches, the twister sheered off a pine, which crashed onto one corner of the pavilion, crushing the roof. Then it ripped several more trees out of the ground, and skipped across the lake toward Wyndwood. They could see it sucking up the water in a whirling funnel.

"Dear God!" Marjorie cried. Fliss was clasped in her mother's arms. Troy had instinctively put his arm about Ellie and she clung to him. J.D. came into the room looking anxious.

"I think that was a small tornado that just passed by," Troy said.

"We're lucky it didn't hit the cottage," Ellie pointed out, still in shock at the destructiveness of the storm.

"I hope that others are as fortunate," J.D. said.

Almost as abruptly as it had started, the rain stopped and the sun broke through the clouds that chased the storm. A rainbow glowed against the indigo sky in the east. The drenched and battered vegetation was dripping and trying to right itself in the calm aftermath as they stepped outside to assess the destruction.

Judging by the path of uprooted and broken trees, the boathouse – and boats – had also narrowly escaped being hit. The massive pine that the wind had snapped like a twig lay heavily against the pavilion, which could nonetheless be repaired.

"I'd say we were mighty lucky," J.D. declared.

"I hope no one was caught out on the lake in this," Ellie said. "Let's check on Daphne on the way back," she added to Troy.

They could see that the twister had ripped across the northeast corner of Wyndwood and then probably headed across the lake towards Mortimer's Island. There were lots of branches down at the point, but no major destruction. They found Edgar on the veranda, checking for damage.

"How's Phoebe?" Ellie asked.

"She was terrified and hid under the piano, as usual," Edgar replied. "She's finally calmed down, but now she's in pain again. Daphne's just given her more chloral and sent her up for a nap. Ye Gods! I've never seen a storm like that. Daphne's making tea, if you'd care to stay."

"Thanks, but we just had some at the Thorntons'," Ellie said.

Ouhu hadn't sustained any damage either, although the wind had rearranged the furniture on the veranda, sending some of the chairs onto the lawn, which was also littered with debris. "We'll have lots of sticks for the fire pit," Ellie said as she began collecting them.

"I was going to suggest that we could do something more fun, but it seems you have a visitor."

It was the Oakley's boatman. He zoomed up alongside the dock and yelled, "I'm glad I found you, Dr. Carlyle. Madam says could you come quickly? A large tree branch crashed through the kitchen window and one of the maids was cut by flying glass. A real mess she is."

"Yes of course."

Troy looked at her ruefully as she fetched her bag. They arrived at Oaktree a few minutes later, and jumped out of Troy's boat, letting the boatman tie it up as they hurried into the house.

"How good of you to come, Eleanor. I'll show you to the kitchen. I see you've brought an assistant," Letitia added with a sly grin.

"Troy is a most able one. He can turn his hand to anything from administering anesthetics to playing soothing music," Ellie said, smiling affectionately at him.

The injured maid, who wasn't yet twenty, sat calmly on a chair with blood oozing or dripping from the many lacerations, glass still embedded in her face and one particularly large shard protruding from her shoulder. Her uniform and white apron were blood-splattered. Another maid was sobbing hysterically while the French chef was imploring her to be quiet. "Sapristi! You are not the one hurt! Make yourself useful. Go and... make tea!" He waved his arms vigorously to shoo her away.

"This is Anna," Letitia said without looking at the girl. "I'll be in the morning room."

"Let me have a look at you, Anna," Ellie said after washing her hands.

"It's Annabelle, but Madam thinks that's too long a name for a maid."

"It's very pretty." So was the girl.

Or had been. "You're incredibly lucky that you didn't get any glass in your eyes."

"Yes, doctor."

Ellie began extracting the shards and bandaging the less serious cuts. "You're going to need stitches for several of these."

"Yes, doctor."

"I must say that you're very calm," Ellie said as she stitched one of the wounds above the eyebrow.

"My boyfriend is in the army. I reckon he's going to go through a lot worse, so the least I can do is be brave." But she couldn't keep a few tears from escaping. "Will I look ugly?"

"You'll have a few battle scars, but they won't destroy your looks. And I expect that your boyfriend loves you for more than your complexion."

"Yes, doctor."

"I'll leave you with some ointment for the wounds, and something for the pain," Ellie said when she had finished. Now you go and rest, and I'll make sure Mrs. Oakley knows that you're to have a few days off."

"Thank you, doctor."

In the drawing room, after Ellie had given her advice, Letitia said, "Of course, poor girl! I expect she'll be terribly scarred. I'll have to find a different job for her. I can't have her waiting at table, because she might horrify the guests."

Ellie nearly exploded. She had never much liked Letitia. She managed – barely – to control her temper as she said, "I do think a promotion would be in order, don't you, Letitia? Considering Annabelle was wounded in your service. She's a very courageous and thoughtful young woman, and I've heard it's difficult to find good staff these days." Ellie couldn't keep the sarcasm from her voice. "She could become Louise's maid. Surely your daughter has the compassion and strength of character to overlook a few trifling scars. And she'll be constantly reminded how fortunate she is to have just a few adolescent spots that she'll grow out of."

"Do you think so? Louise *is* old enough to have a lady's maid. Yes, perhaps you're right. May I offer you some tea or cocktails?" Letitia asked brightly.

"No thank you. I'm leaving tomorrow and have packing to do. That'll be $25 for the house call, Letitia."

She seemed a bit surprised at this large sum, but Ellie *had* spent considerable time with the patient.

As they walked down to the dock, Troy said to Ellie, with obvious admiration, "You're priceless!"

"Actually, I put quite a high value on my time and expertise. And tolerating stupid people. I would have charged Letitia $50 if I didn't think she would then balk at having me attend to her staff in future."

He laughed.

When they arrived back at Ouhu, Troy took her into his arms and began unpinning her hair. "Now it's finally time for us to be alone," he said.

But they heard a boat slowing down as they kissed.

"Oh, hell! Now what?" he said in exasperation.

It was his brother Felix who pulled up to the dock. Troy and Ellie walked down to meet him. He didn't get out of the boat, but said, "Mom's really angry with you, Troy. You missed church this morning. She said to tell you that you'd better go to evening service and then come home for dinner, or she'll know who to blame for corrupting you, and will make sure that everyone else does too. I expect she means you, Eleanor," Felix said with slight puzzlement.

"I rarely attend church," Ellie said quickly, as if that were the sole reason for the threat. "We each have our own paths towards spirituality."

"Mom should mind her own damned business!" Troy said, barely controlling his rage. "I'm an adult, for God's sake!"

Felix seemed a bit taken aback, but then shrugged. "Do what you like, Troy, but you know what she's like when you cross her." Felix drove off.

"How *dare* she threaten to ruin your reputation!" Troy fumed.

"It doesn't matter, Troy," Ellie said, stroking his arm.

"Don't kid yourself, Ellie. People expect their doctors to be above reproach, just like their preachers and teachers." He gazed at her tenderly. "I can't let you be besmirched like that. I'll have to go." He swore as he pulled her into his arms. "How am I going to manage without you? You can change your mind at any time, and we'll get married the next day."

"Are you sure you want to marry a doctor? Our relaxing day hasn't exactly gone as planned."

"I love you, Ellie."

"I *do* love you, Troy. Give me time. I want to do the right thing for both of us. Will I see you before you return to France?" she asked hopefully.

"I'll try to visit Toronto before I leave."

"You have a standing invitation to stay at the Carlyles', although I expect your mother wouldn't approve."

"Leave that to me." He smiled and said, "You know German, so you know what *treu* means."

It was the same pronunciation as his name. "Yes. Faithful," she replied.

"Exactly."

Chapter 15

Zoë thought she heard the alarm and felt a shiver of fear as she rushed to open a window. On the deserted street below, a policeman pedaled by on a bicycle, persistently ringing his bell and announcing, along with a placard across his handlebars, "Take cover! Take cover!"

She could already hear the distant, ominous drone of German Gotha bombers. The evening sky erupted in a fabulous fireworks display of colourful star shells, augmented by searchlight beams frantically scanning the heavens. Anti-aircraft fire stammered, spewing its own deadly missiles into the vulnerable sky over London.

Zoë would have been off duty shortly, but now it was imperative to help the patients down to the basement. "Air raid!" she announced to warn them and the other nurses.

"Not again!" one of the wounded officers complained. "What's the bloody RFC doing? Sitting on their flaming asses?"

"The hell we are!" a Canadian pilot retorted. "Do you realize how difficult and dangerous it is to fly at night? And how do you locate and then fight enemy aircraft in the dark? It's like finding and killing the mosquito that buzzes by when you're lying in bed. In the pitch blackness," he reiterated to make his point.

It was the sixth raid in the past eight nights, and Londoners were frazzled. Hundreds of thousands were already sheltering nightly in the Underground stations, while thousands more were camping on the outskirts of the city, returning to homes and jobs during the day. At least the daylight raids had stopped.

The Daughters of the Empire Red Cross Hospital for Canadian Officers overlooked Hyde Park, and was considered one of the finest in London. Being in a swank area away from what were generally considered military targets – like factories and the docklands – the patients and staff had felt they should be relatively safe. But bombs dropped only a week earlier had created a large crater in Green Park, dangerously close to the Ritz Hotel and not far from the hospital.

So everyone moved resignedly to the basement. Once she had helped with the evacuation, Zoë insisted on being the nurse who stayed with the patients that couldn't be moved, since she wanted to be with Cecil Rankin. He had been at Upper Canada College with Max, and had come to Wyndwood for a few weeks each summer during their senior years. Cecil had mustard gas poisoning. Areas of his skin were so painfully blistered that he couldn't even tolerate the touch of bandages or the weight of blankets, so he lay under a tent of sheets. His suppurating eyes were glued shut. His breathing was laboured, although his lungs were only slightly seared.

The Germans had started using mustard gas a few months earlier. It was an oily contact poison that polluted the environment for days or even weeks, and gas masks weren't helpful. Although it didn't have a high mortality rate like the inhalant gasses, chlorine and phosgene, it was terribly disabling, and effectively removed troops from the contaminated battlefields.

Another fellow had also been gassed, and a third had just come out of the operating theatre, so Zoë sat with them in the gloomy darkness of the deserted ward.

"You shouldn't be here, Zoë," Cecil whispered. "You need to survive."

"As do you, Cecil. The doctor says that you're making a good recovery. The blindness is probably temporary. Your lungs are healing. We'll be playing tennis in Muskoka by next summer."

"Forever the optimist."

"Realist."

"Hell of war, isn't it?" he chuckled between gasps. "Jerry really seems to have it in for me."

It was almost comical the number of times that Cecil had been under fire since he'd been gassed. The ambulance that had taken him away from the front lines had dodged missiles, Calais harbour had been targeted just after he had been loaded aboard a hospital ship, and bombs were falling close to London Bridge Station when his ambulance train had arrived.

They both cringed at the sound of explosions nearby. He had no blisters on his left hand, so she held it tightly.

They were in what had been the dining room on the ground floor of a luxurious three-storey townhouse. The beds of the three immobile patients were at the edge of the room farthest from the windows and not beneath the crystal chandeliers that swayed and tinkled elegantly with each shuddering blast.

"They're damned close," one of the others opined. "Damned close."

Zoë realized how helpless and therefore anxious they must be, so she tried to distract them. She reminded Cecil of the fun winter weekends he had spent with them at Rosemullion, her family's

Toronto home – the skating and tobogganing parties, the sleigh rides through Christmas-card city streets.

"Remember the blizzard that snowed us in and we couldn't get to school?" Zoë asked. "Ria managed to make it to our house, although Grandmother was awfully annoyed with her for even trying, especially as Ria had to stay over. We built a huge snow fort and had a wicked snowball fight. It snowed for two days and we all had to huddle in front of the fire when the electricity went off because some power lines came down."

Zoë faltered for a moment as another bomb shook them. "The wind was wailing outside and piling huge snow drifts against the windows."

"Got about three feet, didn't we?"

"At least! But I've always loved storms. Wasn't it beautiful afterwards when the soft, fresh snow was sparkling in the sunshine?" She went on to describe hot and lazy summers at Wyndwood.

"Know what I liked best?" Cecil muttered. "The Regatta weekend. Never won a cup, but cracking good fun."

"You and Max almost made it into the final round of the canoe jousting competition, as I recall."

He gurgled a laugh. "Jolly tricky that."

"You'll just have to try again," Zoë stated.

"I'm looking forward to visiting your lake," Martha Randall said. She had joined them a few minutes earlier and listened in. "We have a summer place up on the Ottawa River, so I miss the water."

Zoë said, "Thanks for your moral support, but you don't have to risk being up here."

"Perhaps I'm naïve or just terribly arrogant, but right now I'm more angry than anything," Martha said. "So I'd much rather be here with you, hearing about home and imagining some return to normality."

Zoë and Martha had become good friends. Freddie Spencer had been corresponding frequently with Martha, and had recently spent his leave at Cousin Bea's townhouse in London so that he and Martha could be together as much as possible during her free hours in the evenings. Zoë was delighted.

It was over two hours later when the Boy Scouts bugled the "All Clear". Through Zoë's soothing words and images, the patients had fallen asleep.

Exhausted after more than fifteen hours on their feet, Zoë and Martha shuffled back to the VAD residence nearby. Zoë thought it rather silly that they weren't permitted to live at Cousin Bea's, which wasn't much farther, but the VADs were under strict supervision with curfews and other restrictions.

Petrol rationing kept most cars off the roads, and taxis and buses were just beginning to resume their work, so it was strange to walk on the unusually quiet city streets under a full October moon.

"Freddie asked me to marry him," Martha confided. "In his last letter."

"That's terrific news! Will you?"

"It's been a bit of a whirlwind romance, but I do like him. Tremendously. We seem to have so much in common. Do you feel, as I do, that we don't have much time? That we have to grasp at happiness no matter how fleeting it may be?" One of Martha's brothers had been killed during the Hill 70 offensive in August.

"Yes. And I resent every moment that I'm separated from Blake. He said he's going to be transferred back to a base hospital at the end of this upcoming leave. I can't tell you how relieved I'll be. And how terrified I am right now that he won't survive until then."

Zoë had only a couple of weeks left in London. Then she would visit Max at the Granville Special Hospital in Ramsgate, spend a few days at Bovington Abbey, and some time with Ria at Priory Manor before heading over to France. She and Blake would have two precious weeks at Cousin Bea's villa on the Riviera before she began work at the Duchess of Axminster's hospital. She could hardly wait to be reunited with him.

Martha said, "I think I will accept his offer. We'll be very modern and get to know one another properly after we're married. Despite my swagger, I'm really so scared about everything that I just want someone to cling to."

"Freddie is a truly decent and wonderful person," Zoë stated emphatically, and added with a grin, "And worth clinging to."

They linked arms and walked jauntily back to their lodgings, their fatigue momentarily forgotten in the exuberance of youth.

The next morning they discovered that bombs had fallen near Victoria Station, on fashionable Belgravia, and on Hyde Park, where a large missile had summarily dispatched all the fish in the Serpentine. That really had been uncomfortably close, not only to the hospital, but also to Beatrice's place at Lancaster Gate. There had been several hundred more casualties last night, reaffirming that England wasn't beyond Germany's grasp.

·   ·   ·

The letter fluttered from Ria's hand and settled on the counterpane. She reached for a handkerchief to wipe away her tears. Sybil had written,

Cinders must have picked up the bug from one of her patients. All she said was that her head ached and she was feeling a bit giddy, so she refused dinner and went to bed. We couldn't rouse her the next morning, so we rushed her to the Casino. They suspected meningitis. She died without regaining consciousness.

Ria recalled how thrilled Lucinda Ashby-Grey had been to return to the WATS in the spring, and how cheerfully and eagerly she had done her work.

With my former tent-mates all gone, I'm feeling dreadfully bereft. And I haven't been top-hole since the trench fever. Can barely drag myself through the days, and my legs still ache something fierce at times. With this latest offensive, we have a flood of casualties, so there's rarely time to rest in any case. We had an incredible storm a few weeks ago that nearly took off our roof, but virtually leveled the 32nd, 54th, and 55th hospitals, so we had to scramble to transfer the patients to other hospitals that weren't too badly damaged. To top it all off, the bloody Gotha bombers are terrorizing us and either have appalling aim or are targeting the hospitals. I don't like to think that the Hun has stooped that low. Tuppy says that they're really after the military camps and depots that are too close to the hospitals, which is, apparently, against the Geneva Convention. Hard to think that there are actually "rules" in this war. And does that make it our own fault that hospitals are hit?

I can't imagine going through another beastly frigid winter like last year! Maybe I'm in a funk. Tuppy says I should have convalesced longer and should go home for a few months. So I might very well show up on your doorstep one day. Carly tells me she's coming to stay with you at Priory Manor for a few weeks. You'll be running a convalescent home before you know it. Just don't think about coming back here.

Ria wasn't. She had no more to give in that capacity. Like Sybil, she had become disillusioned with the endless appetite of the war machine that demanded so much sacrifice. Undoubtedly Sybil would soon return to England, since it was foolish to keep jeopardizing her health. Without the camaraderie of her closest friends, Sybil had little incentive for staying in France. And Ria had none for returning. Chas had reiterated that her being safely in England was the best way she could support him.

She and Sophie wrote to him daily, and Chas confessed that it was disappointing when the mail was held up, because their chatty letters cheered him immensely.

Ria was overjoyed to be with Sophie and back at Priory Manor, which felt like home. The proud staff had been delighted at their return, and Ria had been impressed with how well they had looked after everything, including the children's farm. She had already contacted the owner and agreed to take the house for an additional year. There was little chance the war would be over by Christmas.

There was a gentle knock on the door, and Sophie peeked her head around to see if Ria was awake. "Bonjour, Mummy Ria!" She scuttled over to the bed and plunked herself on the edge. Ria was propped against the bolsters that Tilda had solicitously arranged, and was sipping her morning tea – a herbal concoction that Branwyn prepared to help Ria regain her strength.

"You look so sad," Sophie said with concern.

"I had some bad news about a WATS friend. But we also have some good things happening today, don't we?" Ria pulled back the covers and allowed Sophie to climb into bed with her, which the child did eagerly.

"Cousin Bea and Uncle Justin are coming!"

Justin had been discharged from hospital, and was to have three months to convalesce before his medical board. As soon as he was upgraded to at least a medical category "C" rating, he would be given a desk job. Grayson had offered to drive Justin and Bea to Priory Manor, as he was planning to make a visit in any case. Since Beatrice hardly drove her car, she still had plenty of her petrol allowance.

Ria and Sophie had been back at Priory Manor for over a month. Chas had moved them from Bovington Abbey during his two weeks of leave at the end of September.

He and Beatrice had accompanied Ria to Buckingham Palace to receive her medal. Seeing Chas's medals, the King had said, "The pair of you should be on a poster. You've done the Empire proud." Ria told Zoë, when they met for dinner afterwards, that it was surely better than being presented at court as a debutante.

"And Cousin Jack's coming tomorrow," Ria said. Jack and Sidonie were stopping in for a night on their way to spend the weekend at Max Beaverbrook's Cherkley Court.

"I will show him my paintings!"

"I'm sure he'd be happy to have one. Daddy Chas says he has the picture you gave him pinned up in his office." And had laughingly told Ria that the chaps were amused, since they had provocative photos of scantily clad women on their walls. "Now help me choose something to wear, and we'll join Lady Meredith and Miss Prescott for breakfast," Ria said. Meredith and Theadora had been staying at Priory Manor for the past two weeks because of the air raids in London, but as those seemed to have stopped, they would be returning to the city today.

"But Mummy Ria, you are supposed to stay in bed!" Sophie said excitedly in French.

Ria had been ordered not to exert herself, so she'd been spending a good part of every morning in bed, with breakfast being delivered and shared with Sophie. But she was too restless and impatient to continue this lethargic routine. Besides, she thought that not getting enough exercise during the day was part of the reason that sleep often eluded her between the nightmares.

"I'm growing stronger every day, and it's time to get back to normal."

The four of them and Johanna had a leisurely breakfast in the sunroom. It promised to be a sunny and mild autumn day.

"I'm afraid we may need sanctuary again when the next full moon approaches at the end of the month," Meredith said. She was still paralyzingly anxious about air raids – her legacy from the *Lusitania* sinking.

"You know that you are most welcome at any time and at short notice," Ria reassured her.

"I must say that this place suits you, Ria," Theadora said. "I'm already curious to know what you'll do when you've recovered," she added with a twinkle in her eyes.

"One of my WATS friends suggested a convalescent home. Considering all the family and friends I have who already do or may need it, it's probably going to become that anyway. One of my cousin Max's friends from school is in Zoë's hospital. He spent quite a few weeks at the cottage, so I know him well. I've told Zoë to let him know that he's invited to stay as soon as he's discharged."

Thea laughed. "You can pick him up from the station by WATS ambulance."

"The Stratton. I'm leaving the Rolls in Calais until the end of the war, and the ambulance was my donation to the cause."

"Can you drive yet?"

"The shifting is still rather painful. Zoë gave me exercises to do, and Sophie is making sure I do them." She smiled affectionately at the child. "What I'm really looking forward to is riding Calypso again."

After Meredith and Thea had gone, Ria, Sophie, and Johanna went to the stables. Calypso nudged Ria's good shoulder when she hugged him. "I promise I'll take you out soon, pet," she said to him.

She was glad to see that the stable boy, Clive, was thriving. He had shot up and filled out from the undersized, scarecrow-thin boy, and was well groomed. She expected that Branwyn had a hand in that, making sure that extra food was sent along to his family so that he could eat his meals here without a guilty conscience. The bullies wouldn't be knocking him down so easily next time. He was also cheerful, whistling while he did his chores.

Ria was humbled to think how little it took to help some people and improve their lives immeasurably.

When Johanna took Sophie inside for morning lessons, Ria wandered about the ruins garden, delighting in the roses that rambled over the centuries old tumble of stones and snipping some of the bountiful perennials for a bouquet. She was momentarily alarmed by the sound of an aeroplane very low overhead, thinking that these days it might as easily be the enemy as the RFC from the aerodrome at Farnborough. And then curious when she spotted an S.E.5 descending towards the meadow. She wandered over, expecting the pilot had had engine trouble, but then she noticed the dragon and dragonfly insignia. She dropped the flowers and ran over. "Chas!" She threw her arms about him, sending a shooting pain through her shoulder, which she did her best to ignore. "What are you doing here?"

"I was chasing rainbows," he said with a mischievous grin, referring to the popular new tune. "And lo and behold, I've found the pot of gold at the end." He pulled her into a warm embrace. "Mmm, I've missed you, my darling," he said as he kissed her.

"Will you be shot for desertion?" she teased.

"The King would never allow it." He whirled her about the field and began singing,

I'm always chasing rainbows,

Watching clouds drifting by,
My schemes are just like all my dreams,
Ending in the sky.

She was instantly transported to the prewar days when life was gay and carefree and filled with music and laughter. This would become one of those punctuated moments suspended in time. One that would give her strength and hope.

"How long can you play hooky?"

"I'm staying overnight," he said as he drew her suggestively closer. "I flew to Boulogne to visit McPherson. He's caught a bullet through his arm – a Blighty. And while I was there I realized that it's really only fifteen minutes across the Channel and a few more to Priory Manor. So I informed the chap I'd designated as OC that I would be back tomorrow, and Hal Goodwin will swear I was with him at Marquise."

"You are devious, Major Thornton."

"That's because you're irresistible, Mrs. Thornton."

It was a wonderful day.

.   .   .

"How bad am I, Dad? Am I going to make it?" the youngster asked frantically, seizing Paul Godfrey's hand in an astonishingly strong grip. The victim was riddled with shrapnel.

The former priest stroked the boy's head and said reassuringly, "You're a fighter, Ogilvie. Just remember that. We'll get you back to Toronto."

But first they had to haul him out of this bog they called a battlefield and to the Dressing Station. The stretcher-bearers struggled to carry the wounded out of the treacherous, cratered mud of Passchendaele. They plodded carefully along duckboards, which were like wooden rafts floating atop the liquid muck.

There was nowhere to run or hide as a shell screamed towards them. Instantly they lowered the stretcher and crouched down, Paul hovering protectively over Ogilvie. The shell dropped only yards away, but buried itself in the mud, thankfully splattering them with slime rather than shrapnel. But one of the bearers was knocked off the narrow walkway by the blast and floundered in the sucking mud. Weighed down by over fifty pounds of sodden greatcoat from the never-ending rain, as well as his gear, he slipped away before a rescue could even be attempted.

It wasn't the first time Paul had seen men drown on this hellish battlefield. As the oldest and the one the others relied upon, Paul said, "God bless McEvoy," because that's what the men liked to hear. "He was truly heroic. Come along, lads. We have to save the living. There'll be plenty of time to remember the dead." Paul took on the added burden of McEvoy's absence.

. . .

Dearest Toni,

Being out of hospital and comfortably ensconced here at Priory Manor has aided my recovery. I am once again walking the lanes that you and I enjoyed last spring. So there are only two things that disturb my equanimity now. One is knowing that you are still in France and in danger from increased raids. The other is that I long for you constantly. I've come to realize how attuned we are, and often think about what you would say if you were here, or want to share a thought or ask your opinion. I miss your strength of mind and character, your wit, courage, determination, enthusiasm, generosity, and innate joy. And so I realize that I'm in love with you. Deeply, blissfully in love.

You would not only put my mind at ease, but also fulfill my dreams if you were to accept my proposal of marriage.

It may be presumptuous of me to think that a beautiful, high-born lady destined for more than a sedate life in Canada would even consider it. Yet I can imagine that the woman I have come to cherish would relish the challenge, and not regret leaving the "old world" behind. But I love you too much to require that of you, Toni, and would surely be able to make a living in England as a solicitor, if you would prefer that we made a home here.

You would make me the happiest man if you would become my wife. We could be married at Christmas, snatch some joy out of these dire and uncertain times, and begin to make a lifetime of happy memories. Now that I have overcome the difficulty of spilling my heart onto this paper, I am impatient to be with you!

I know that you will give this fair consideration, but if there is any other way that I can persuade you of my love and devotion, please let me know. I would do anything to be worthy of your love.

Anxiously awaiting your decision and lovingly yours, Justin

The mail service between Britain and France was impressively quick. A telegram arrived only a few days after Justin had posted the letter.

Decidedly yes! Home at end of month. Love, most definitely,
Toni

. . .

Rosemullion, Toronto

My Darling Zoë,

I expect I needn't tell you how worried we've been about the reports of nightly bombings in London and along the coast where Max is supposed to be recuperating. I would have thought that a hospital for shell-shock victims would be set deep into the quiet countryside where the men could have peace from even the thought of war, not close to military encampments and therefore targets! Papa says that the problem with running the war is that women aren't allowed to take a larger part, for surely we would have arranged things otherwise.

I'm glad you've been able to visit Max, for he has always relied upon you, his "older" sister if only by ten minutes. I gather from your letters that he is worse than he lets on. Do you think that there is any chance he might be invalided home? I expect he would hate that, because I can tell by his self-deprecating manner that he already considers himself a coward, and by coming home, he would be a complete failure. Do try to persuade him that there are many ways he can contribute to the war effort without being in the thick of battle. As far as we are concerned, his wound is as real an any physical one, and earned as honourably. Blake tells me that he tried to persuade Max of that as well. Have I raised you both to be too conscientious, putting duty and honour ahead of your own safety?

Will you be safer in France? I can hardly credit it. Yes, Ria had written quite a glowing description of the Duchess and her hospital. We have a large map pinned on the morning room wall, and the children – Rupert in particular – follow the progress of the war by sticking coloured pins into the places where battles have been reported. So we can see that you are quite a distance from the great mass of pins. And yet not far from where Ria was wounded, so I'm not that reassured. We have very large blue pins marking where you, Max, Ria, and Beatrice are. We know that the others are somewhere in or near the action.

I'm delighted that you and Blake will have a truly relaxing time at Beatrice's villa in Antibes. Surely the war is far away from there. (No pins!)

One is always hopeful that the war might end as quickly as it began, but all this political uncertainty in Russia since the Tsar's abdication doesn't bode well. I shudder to think what might happen if Germany no longer had to fight on two fronts.

Helena had her baby – a boy. She had a long and difficult labour, as the baby was breech. He was quite blue, but the doctor managed to revive him. He's a healthy looking infant now, but rather too quiet. Ellie wonders if he suffered from lack of oxygen for too long and may be somewhat brain damaged. What a pity that would be! The doctor has told Helena that she shouldn't risk any more pregnancies, as the next one might kill her. She and James have taken that rather hard, although James is delighted to finally have a son, whom they've named James Reginald Parker. The children are already calling him "Jimmy". I will write and tell Ria, as I expect that James hasn't bothered to inform her that she has a half-brother.

The Redmonds have lost another son, Michael. Now there is only David left and they have, through some familial connection in the War Office, wrangled an HQ job for him to remove him from the front lines. I don't blame them a bit, and would do the same to safeguard Max. Despite the propaganda, I see nothing patriotic in sacrificing one's children to this war! Almost daily I read familiar names on the casualty lists, and weep to think of all the bright young men whose promising lives were cut short and who will leave no legacy other than a name on a cross.

Rupert says to tell you that Prospect House at Port Sandfield was destroyed by fire, but fortunately it had just closed for the season so no guests were imperiled.

Goodness! I see that I have written nothing but gloomy thoughts and news!

Mrs. O'Rourke is sending some Christmas cake in the next parcel, which she baked earlier this year so that it will arrive in good time to you and Max. She's put lots of rum in to preserve it. Anticipating Prohibition, she managed to squirrel away quite a store of spirits, as she says that she can't be a proper cook without the necessary ingredients. Rupert is a little too fond of her sherry trifle! Did you receive the last shipment in which she included half a dozen jars of Wyndwood blueberry jam?

I'm thankful that this naval convoy system has drastically reduced the number of merchant ships sunk. Papa laughingly said that surely some Admiral's wife thought of it!

Phoebe has quite taken to her nurse, Irene Partridge, whom I find a thoroughly sensible and compassionate woman. Irene takes Phoebe on outings, like shopping at Eaton's and visiting the Museum and the Riverdale Zoo, which delight Phoebe. Her hands have healed, but Albert intends to keep Irene on as a "companion" for her, which I think is an excellent idea. Phoebe particularly likes the fact that Irene is named after a bird, just like she is!

Daphne is quite large already, and Eleanor has determined that she is carrying twins! Edgar is ecstatic and worried, but I have reassured him that Daphne is in no greater danger or distress because of the two babies. What fun it will be to have little ones around again.

Lydia keeps busy with all the usual war work, but is terribly anxious about Max. She stayed with us for a couple of weeks, and Papa told her to scout out a house that would be suitable for them when they are married. She and Esme found a charming one nearby, so Papa has bought it and will rent it out until Max has returned. It has cheered Lydia somewhat to plan a future with Max. She writes to him daily, and I do think that her chatty letters give him some sense of normality.

Simon Carrington has finished OTC, and tried to enlist, as he was tired of being considered a shirker, only to discover that he has a heart murmur and has been rejected. He was also told that the army doesn't want more officers, as they have quite a pool of them in England and it is more efficient to promote experienced men from the ranks anyway. So he wondered if they would consider taking him as a private, but Grace and his parents dissuaded him. I think that the stress of his job and other war work that he does are taking a toll on his health. It's unfortunate that those young men who are contributing so much to the war effort but who are not in uniform earn such disdain from people.

Emma Spencer came to Sunday dinner last week and talked eagerly about her law studies. I'd say she has definitely found her niche! Arthur came as well, of course, and is also in his element, although obviously anxious about his approaching eighteenth birthday. I told him that he must at least finish his year before enlisting. But, of course, with conscription, he may not have that choice.

Felicity has recruited Esme and Claire to help her with another fund-raising concert at Massey Hall. This time it's for the IODE. Tickets can be "purchased" by donating popular records, mouth organs, gramophones, chess sets, games, or money – all to be sent to the hospitals. Hugo Garrick has given them permission to use songs from "Under the Moon" and the girls are, indeed, "over the moon". I do hope that you have a chance to see the musical when it opens in London soon. We have all been caught humming or whistling the

*signature tune, which is most captivating. I trust that you and Ria
will also have a chance to visit with Emily.*
   *Papa and Esme are writing to you as well, so I shall close now.
How I wish I could take you into my arms, my chick! Enjoy your
holiday, and stay safe. Give my love to Blake.*
   Your loving and proud mother

                    .   .   .

   Although Zoë felt guilty for leaving her post in London for the
country club atmosphere of the Duchess of Axminster's hospital,
she was reminded that helping the experienced officers here
return to duty as soon as possible was also important work.
   Once she had settled into very comfortable surroundings, she
quickly repacked for the Riviera and awaited Blake's arrival. The
first thing that struck her, before he took her gratefully into his
arms, was how tired and strained he looked.
   "I've booked us into a little hotel nearby in Wimereux for a few
days," he said. "That's as far as I can manage to go at the
moment."
   Ria's friend, Zachary, the orderly, drove them to the Hotel
Beau Rivage, which overlooked the river a few hundred yards from
the sea. Their room also had a commanding view of the main
street and picturesque railway viaduct.
   They spent two days doing little more than sleeping, strolling
along the beach and seaside promenade, and making love.
   "I was at the Somme, Vimy, Hill 70, but I've never seen
anything like it, Zoë," Blake confessed as they sipped their wine
after dinner. "I couldn't believe they were sending men into that
sea of mud to fight!" He was tense with frustration.
   She gripped his hand across the table. The candlelight
flickered gently between them.
   "I'm sorry. I hadn't meant to burden you with this," he said.
   "Why not? I want to share everything with you, Blake. The
psychiatrist needs to talk as well," she added lightly.
   He guffawed. "You're right, much as I'd like to pretend that
I'm strong and able to take it all in stride." His eyes regarded her
moistly as he squeezed her hand. "I'm so lucky to have you."
   "Tell me about Passchendaele."
   He did, haltingly at first. "I'd heard the stories from the
wounded, but I had to see it for myself.... It was unbelievable.
Heartbreaking. Men disappearing into bottomless mud. The dead
left where they had fallen, since the bearers could hardly manage

to evacuate the wounded. It could easily take them six hours just to carry one man to the Dressing Station. Too many died in agony and unnecessarily because we couldn't bring them out quickly enough." He rubbed his forehead in exasperation. "Our troops not only endured this hell, but triumphed. If you can call gaining a few miles of devastated wasteland a victory."

She stroked his hand.

"Do you know the only thing that gave me any hope for mankind at that moment? I came across Edelina's friend, Paul. He's a stretcher-bearer, and struck me as a Christ-like character – compassionate beyond anything I've seen, revered by his comrades and the men of his battalion, selfless, undaunted, and focused upon his mission to save, not the souls, but the bodies of the men. He infused those around him with strength and a will to survive. He may not believe in God anymore, but he epitomizes the Christian virtues more than many of the padres I've seen. And ironically, he inspires faith."

Blake took Zoë to visit the nearby Canadian #3 General Hospital where he had worked, and introduced her to Lieutenant-Colonel John McCrae. She was thrilled to meet the famous poet-doctor, whom she found most charming.

Because Zoë was, theoretically, a nurse working in France, she was able to procure a pass for leave to the Riviera. The Colonials, especially, had taken eagerly to this new opportunity, the British government having realized that most of them had no family and therefore little reason to take their leaves in England.

By the time they arrived at Cousin Bea's villa on Cap d'Antibes, they were rested enough to enjoy the spectacular setting and put the war behind them for a few days.

Not as grand as its palatial neighbours, Bea's two-storey villa was nonetheless substantial and classically beautiful, with bright, airy rooms flowing onto balconies and terraces. Lush gardens and grounds filled with exotic vegetation echoed summer at a time when there could already be a blanket of snow in Toronto.

But as it was still delightfully warm here, they swam in the small, secluded cove with its rugged, bleached limestone cliffs that bubbled up dramatically from the azure water and were crested by artistically twisted pines with umbrella-like canopies. They strolled along the beaches of Juan-les-Pins, and through the ancient village of Antibes, but had no desire to wander far from home. From short coastal perambulations they could see the spectacular snow-tipped Maritime Alps beyond the rich turquoise and ever-changing blues of the sea. Twice they dined at the opulent Hotel du Cap's Eden Roc pavilion, which perched on the cliff's edge next to a fanciful pool carved out of the rocks. Blake confessed that he was enjoying this indulgent lifestyle.

They savoured being alone together, luxuriating in bed well into the morning, dining by candlelight on the terrace, examining the stars from atop the cliff.

"I feel guilty saying this," Zoë confessed on their last night. "But I dread going back. I know it's terribly selfish to want to wait out the war, but I'm secretly hoping that we'll be stranded here."

"And miss out on the first ever vote that women have in a Federal election?" he teased." That was to be held in mid-December. Only Canadian women with husbands, sons, or brothers in the services would be allowed to vote on this historic occasion. It had been arranged that the overseas troops and nurses could also vote.

"I will vote," Zoë said emphatically.

"For conscription?" It had become a huge and divisive issue in Canada.

She frowned. "I don't know. I'm against compelling men to fight when they have no inclination to. But I also know that our forces need to be replenished. Too many men have died to give up now. I can't help thinking about John McCrae's latest poem, *The Anxious Dead*."

"Yes indeed. Ellie says that there's a conviction among the populace that the shirkers are out making their fortunes as war profiteers, so there's a lot of contempt for able-bodied men who haven't signed on. I know that Simon and Edgar both feel that."

Too soon they were back in the forbidding and chilly grey north. Zoë was frustrated that Blake wouldn't be at the nearby Canadian #3 General Hospital, but at the #1, which was at Etaples, some miles along the coast to the south.

"We'll coordinate days off and meet in Wimereux," Blake said.

Zoë clung to him, unable to utter her hopes or fears.

Chapter 16

Ellie had already heard about the devastating explosion in Halifax when Edgar reached her by telephone at the hospital that afternoon.

"I've hired a Pullman coach, I'm collecting medical supplies, food, blankets, clothes, and such, Irene and Lorna Partridge are coming with me, and I want you along as well, Ellie. It's a bloody disaster out there!"

"When did you become a champion of the broken and dispossessed?" Ellie teased. "It must be Daphne's influence. I'm impressed!"

"We all have to do our bit," he retorted. "I hope to leave tonight. That doesn't give us much time, but I'm sure that they're in dire need. We can't delay."

Ellie could sense his enthusiasm to be helpful in this emergency, for he chafed at not being able to go to war. "You can count on me, Edgar."

With Felicity's help, Edgar amassed an impressive quantity of supplies. Fliss pestered to go along, but her father said there would be enough confusion in Halifax, and that unskilled people would just be a nuisance.

Edgar was frustrated at the delay in getting rail clearance, impressing upon the authorities that he was bringing medical help and needed to be attached to a relief train, not a passenger one, as those had been stopped.

"Look at these headlines," Edgar told Ellie, flourishing a late Thursday edition of the *Toronto Star*. "'Several Miles Area in Utter Ruin as Result of Another Vessel Ramming American Munition Ship. Dead Thick, Fire Rages, Quarter City Lies Flat. Hospitals are Filled to Overflowing, Many Wounded Walk About Untreated.' It's incredible!"

It was Friday morning before they managed to leave Toronto. Fortunately the Pullman provided cozy berths for sleeping, and there was plenty of food aboard. They delayed by a tremendous blizzard, which hit the decimated city particularly hard, dumping a foot and a half of snow and blocking rail lines into Halifax. At various stops en route, the news from Halifax grew increasingly grim. By Saturday, there were estimates of 2000 dead, 9000 injured, 20,000 homeless. The explosion of TNT was eight times what the British had used at the Messines Ridge in the summer, and was felt and heard over two hundred miles away in Cape Breton. There was even some speculation that the blast had been engineered by the Germans.

"Looks like we're well and truly part of the war now," Edgar said. "I never thought that we'd suffer civilian casualties in Canada!"

By the time they pulled into Halifax early Sunday morning, the snowstorm had given way to a deluge of rain and spring-like warmth that was melting the snow and flooding the streets.

"Dear God!" Irene Partridge said as they skirted the hardest hit area.

"Bloody hell!" Ellie echoed.

The north part of the city had been completely flattened, with only a few charred and twisted trees rising out of the mangled wreckage of what had once been homes, shops, factories. Soldiers were digging among the ruins, looking less for survivors now, after the bitterly cold nights, than for bodies.

Further south, buildings stood, some haphazardly, but not one was undamaged.

They registered at City Hall and the three women were sent to Camp Hill Hospital, just west of the Citadel, where exhausted staff were desperate for relief. Edgar would be occupied with helping to distribute the supplies.

They noticed that the windows of the hospital were new, so even it had suffered damage. With patients lying on every available inch of floor, including under occupied beds, Ellie felt they could surely have been in a war zone. Most had had some cursory treatment, but burn victims had been hastily bandaged, and a large number had been blinded by flying glass. Dr. Cox, an eye specialist, was dropping from fatigue, as he'd been operating for days. Ellie was horrified to hear that people had had damaged eyes removed without anesthetics or morphine, because the hospital had run out of both long ago.

She and the Partridges worked through long days and nights. Ellie's first job was to assist a surgeon to reconstruct a man's face, his nose and a side of his face having been almost completely severed. So many of the wounds were horrific. Muscles sliced away from arms or legs, right down to the bones. Gashes in skulls, exposing brains. Shards of glass embedded throughout faces and chests, arms and feet. Multiple broken bones, terrible burns.

Ellie heard incredible stories of survival, and how random it seemed to be – people standing next to family or neighbours and being the only one left alive while the others had been decapitated or crushed. Some had had their clothes blown off and suddenly found themselves sitting naked on the ground a mile from where they had stood only an instant before. Some, having survived the blast, were then swept up in the enormous frigid tidal wave and battered by deadly debris. Others had lost almost their entire families – children, spouses, parents, siblings. No one wanted to dwell on the fact that if it hadn't been for the fires and then the freezing snowstorm, many more survivors would have been pulled from the wreckage of their homes.

When Ellie and the Partridges left the hospital to snatch a few hours sleep, people outside in rags and bandages asked anxiously after loved ones. Their volunteer driver said, in an eerie, matter-of-fact way, "My wife and all four of my kids are dead. Found my sister and one of her brood at Camp Hill, though. Where to, ladies?"

Ellie had noticed that many of the wounded and bereaved were so thoroughly shocked that they didn't seem able to grasp the reality or enormity of their losses. Nor had their numbed senses begun to feel the pain of their injuries.

By mid-week, a somewhat normal hospital routine had been established. Ellie had heard that Boston had sent numerous medical personnel and supplies, and had set up two makeshift hospitals, which had eased the strain considerably. Harvard University had sent an entire hospital unit that was destined for France.

So she was only slightly surprised when Troy suddenly appeared. "Edgar told me you were here," he said. "We ran into each other in a restaurant that's catering to relief workers."

Ellie went unabashedly into his arms. "I should have known you'd come," she said.

"Because I've had front-line experience, my offer was readily accepted when Dr. Ladd was looking for recruits. We've set up a hospital in a boys' school not half a mile from here."

They kissed briefly. "I've missed you," Ellie admitted.

"I'd take you somewhere intimate if I could," he whispered before releasing her.

"Instead we'll have to settle for a cup of tea," she said ruefully.

"This is as bad as what I've seen at the Front, Ellie. Worse really, since it involves women and children," he told her when they sat down with a lukewarm cup of strong tea. "The force of this blast was unprecedented. Apparently there wasn't a single pane of glass undamaged in the entire city or surrounding area. You've seen the injuries – splinters of glass, bits of wood, chunks of metal driven deep into flesh. It's like shrapnel."

"How can you stand to see these gruesome injuries day after day?"

"I suppose we become inured. Almost. It's really hard to deal with the wounded children we've had here, a lot with burns."

She nodded. "I can better appreciate shell-shock. Not only because I can see the effect of the trauma on the victims, but I'm so horrified by what I've seen that I'll never get those grisly images out of my mind. I wouldn't have been much good at the Front after all," she admitted.

"I wouldn't say that, but would you think me terribly old-fashioned if I said I had wanted to protect you from that? Who would have imagined that the full horror of war would come to our shores like this?"

They snatched whatever few moments they could find to be together, Ellie taking comfort from his presence, Troy certain they had forged a deeper bond.

They managed to dine together on Ellie's last evening. "You're going back to France soon," she said sadly.

"Yes, in January." He looked at her regretfully. "Now I won't have time to come to Toronto. The offer still stands, you know." He put his hand over hers.

"I do know." She was terribly tempted, but Jack was still hovering on the sidelines, holding her back.

.   .   .

Ellie and Edgar were back in Toronto in plenty of time for the birth of his twins on Christmas Day. They named the identical boys Matthew and Nathaniel. Daphne was in her element.

Looking at her healthy nephews, Ellie wondered fleetingly why she was resisting Troy's offer of marriage. And why she felt that her work was no longer enough.

Chapter 17

It was a fairytale wedding, with Antonia a princess in her mother's elaborate ivory satin and lace wedding gown. Using the excuse that she couldn't choose among her sisters for the Maid of Honour, Toni asked Ria. Appropriately, Chas was Best Man. Because the weather wasn't good for flying and there was a lull in the hostilities, he and his squadron were on a month's leave.

The vicar performed the ceremony in the baronial great hall at Quincy Castle, and the reception was held afterwards in the oak-paneled banquet hall. As it was two days after Christmas, the rooms were still decorated with garlands, holly, and mistletoe, red ribbons and sparkling balls. A majestic fifteen-foot tall fir tree trimmed with delicate glass ornaments, gingerbread men, and modern electric fairy lights glowed in the great hall. Elsewhere firelight and hundreds of candles warmed the ancient walls, enhancing the medieval atmosphere.

Carly was there with support, both physical and moral, from Jonathan and Eddie, who were still in England on Home Defence duty. She'd had two more operations to deal with her nerve problem, and this time she felt her stump might actually heal properly. She and Jonathan would be married as soon as she could walk up the aisle, which she hoped would be next summer. For now she was confined to a wheelchair.

Sybil, who was on convalescent leave, was delighted to be reunited with her friends. Ria was concerned about her paleness and obvious fatigue, but Sybil said, "It's the best disguise for obtaining sick leave. And I'm in no hurry to return. Adam needs me more than Boss." Adam Bentley's hip had been fractured by a bullet, so he would be in hospital for at least four months. "I've told him that you're running a convalescent home, and that he absolutely must stay with you when he's released from hospital. As will I," she added with a sly grin.

"You have the poor chap at your mercy now, do you?" Eddie teased.

"Dashed right!"

Henrietta Maltby was on regular leave, and enjoying an animated conversation with Henry.

Beatrice was discussing mutual acquaintances with Antonia's mother, while Jack and Sidonie were talking with the Earl, who sat in the House of Lords with her father.

Emily and Hugo had been invited, but *Under the Moon* was now playing, so they had no time to get away. Emily was already becoming the toast of London – with good reason, Ria thought, as she and Chas had just seen the musical and found it utterly delightful, and Emily, astonishingly talented. They had been instantly transported to Muskoka, and Ria insisted that she needed to take all her friends and family to see the show.

Starting with Max, who was staying with her for the holidays. She was terribly concerned by his uncharacteristic silence and moroseness, although he tried to hide that with forced gaiety. She sometimes heard him screaming in the night, and he still suffered from excruciating headaches as well as a lassitude that left him weak and trembling, and often embarrassed by tears. She thought him in no condition to ever be sent back to France, and hoped he wouldn't pass his Medical Board in January.

Max was now striving to control his shaking hands, and spent enormous energy concentrating on polite conversations that left him with sweaty palms and pounding heart.

Alice, who was with awestruck Sophie and Johanna, was struggling with mixed emotions. She had a crush on Justin, and was heartbroken that he was no longer available. She had woven romantic stories in her head about how he would fall madly in love with her when she was older, realizing that she had been the woman he had been waiting for his entire life. But she also admired Antonia, and couldn't help thinking what a lovely couple she and Justin made.

Ria, who had shrewdly interpreted Alice's disconsolate glances, confided to her, "I had a pash for Justin when I was fifteen and he was eighteen. I did everything I could to be near him. He was very kind and indulgent. I suppose that's one of the reasons I love him so dearly, and know that I can always rely on him as a friend."

"Am I so transparent?" Alice asked, equally shrewdly.

Ria laughed. "Only to someone who's been through the same thing!" She gave Alice a quick hug. "Wait until you meet some of our other island friends. Blake, Freddie, and Troy all have younger brothers."

Alice clung to Ria for a jealous moment and said, "I do so want to be in Canada with you."

"You will be, my dearest friend. I shall make certain of that."

Justin had encountered some resistance in his bid to marry Antonia. It wasn't until he had proven his financial worth and insisted that no dowry was necessary that the Earl had relented. But Justin was a bit daunted by his aristocratic in-laws, who drifted in a privileged haze.

They would be appalled and scandalized to know that his maternal grandmother had been a starving Irish orphan rescued from the mean slums of Toronto by his grandfather, a bastard, who had, nonetheless, become a respected businessman and local politician in Launston Mills. Justin had written to inform them of his marriage, and could anticipate his grandfather, Keir, saying that it illustrated once again that Canada was a land of opportunity where proven merit was more important than family lineage.

Justin was reassured when Antonia caught his eye and smiled knowingly. He could almost read her thoughts, and knew she was as eager to get away on their own as he. They would spend a week at a converted castle hotel in St. Ives, Cornwall, which an English acquaintance had recommended. Then they would take up residence in the Netherton's London townhouse in Belgravia – theirs exclusively until they moved to Canada. It had been mostly shut up during the war, the Earl staying at his club whenever he needed to be in the city. Toni's sister, Veronica, had been using it since the summer because she was running a canteen for soldiers at Victoria Station. She had moved reluctantly into a flat with a friend, and was noticeably bitter.

From a few things that Toni had let slip, Justin suspected that there was a fair bit of rivalry between the four sisters, who were close in age. Perhaps that was partly why Toni was eager to move to Canada with him, away from petty jealousies and one-upmanship.

He was somewhat reticent about living in London with Antonia because of the frequent bombings, which were now being carried out even on moonless nights. In the latest one, just over a week ago, an enormous high explosive bomb had fallen near Eaton Square, not far from the Netherton townhouse, damaging scores of buildings. Fires had raged all over London and had been visible as far away as Priory Manor.

Toni had assured him that London was probably safer than Calais. She had resigned from the WATS and been taken on as an ambulance driver by the Red Cross in London to ferry the wounded from the train stations to the hospitals. She would start working when Justin began his job at the War Office in a month's time.

"None of us thought that Toni would be the first one to get married," Veronica said dismissively as she and her sisters joined Justin, edging out the elderly guests who moved on. "She's hardly had any beaux."

"That will leave the field clear for the rest of you then," Justin couldn't resist saying.

Ronni harrumphed. "I doubt that many chaps are keen on girls who prefer tinkering with engines to partying."

"My luck then, isn't it?" he riposted. Although the Upton sisters were renowned in society for their beauty, he thought that Veronica's appeal was decidedly spoiled by her haughty demeanor. "As well as Major Thornton's, and Captain Telford's. The WATS are admired not only for their skill and bravery, but also for their hospitality."

"You mean sipping tea and chatting with hairy old Generals. Ho hum."

Georgina, who seemed unable to drag her eyes away from Chas, said, "I understand that Major Thornton has a younger brother."

"Yes, but he's a POW at the moment," Justin replied, grateful for a change of topic.

"Pity. I expect we'll meet him when we visit you in Canada after the war," Georgie said.

"Yes indeed."

"I couldn't possibly live in Canada," Alexandra, the youngest, opined. "Toni told me that you don't even have indoor *conveniences* at your summer homes!"

Justin hid his amusement. "Some of us now do. The Thorntons and Wyndhams most certainly."

"Captain Wyndham and Lady Sidonie aren't engaged, are they?" Veronica asked. "He's quite a cracker." Jack and Sid were now talking with Eddie, Sybil, Carly, and Jonathan.

"Behave yourself, Ronni," Georgie chided.

"Why? I don't expect *she* does."

"As your solicitor brother-in-law, I'd advise you to keep comments like that to yourself," Justin admonished.

Ronni rolled her eyes, and said, "I'll just maneuver him under some mistletoe to see if he's worth pursuing."

When she had walked away, Georgie said, "She likes being outrageous. We can only hope that she'll grow out of that."

Justin chuckled, as Georgina was barely two years older than nineteen-year-old Veronica.

"I don't see the point in being outrageous," seventeen-year-old Alexandra declared. "It just puts people's backs up."

Antonia slipped her arm through Justin's as she joined them, saying, "Talking about Ronni, are you?"

"Who else?" Alex asked.

"So you see that Ronni gets precisely what she wants. Lots of attention," Toni said.

"She's chatting up either Captain Wyndham or Captain Stratton," Georgie said.

"Likely both," Alex observed.

"Oh Lord!" Toni said.

"I do think that I met Captain Stratton's brother at a party recently. Excuse me," Georgina said as she walked off to join him.

"Georgie can't stand to see Ronni landing one of those peachy chaps," Alex reflected. Antonia, the eldest at twenty-three, was closest to Alexandra, whom she'd often had to champion. "You're lucky that you snagged Justin before either one of them could get their claws into him."

The newlyweds laughed. "Oh, I don't think there was any danger of that," Toni replied with a loving glance at her husband.

"You're absolutely right," he said, raising her hand to his lips.

·   ·   ·

Freddie Spencer and Martha Randall were married with much less pomp and ceremony a month later. Ria, Max, Henry, Beatrice, Justin, and Toni attended the civil wedding in London, along with a couple of nurses who worked with Martha, and one of her brothers, who had managed to obtain leave. They all had lunch at the Savoy afterwards, and then Freddie and Martha set out on an architectural tour of the countryside. Ria was pleased to see Freddie so happy.

Max returned to Priory Manor with Ria. He was to be shipped back to Canada soon, and discharged from the army. His latest medical exam revealed that he had asthma, and because he was still experiencing episodes of dizziness and heart palpitations, the doctors considered him unfit for any kind of service.

Ria was thankful, and thought that this should appease his conscience, although he said, "I feel I've let everyone down."

"Don't be silly!" she admonished. "How could you possibly expect to go back to the smoke and stench of the battlefield when you're struggling for breath? You need to get up to Muskoka and breathe the clean air there. It's why the tuberculosis sanitarium is in Gravenhurst."

"One of the doctors suggested that these attacks are psychological. My way of trying to get out of doing my duty," he replied disconsolately.

"Then he's an ass! Blake says that there's no precedent for the kind of trauma that is sustained on the battlefields, so doctors have no real idea of all the effects of constant shell bursts, gas, and the like on the body. Your injuries are internal, and just as real as a bullet wound. And I do understand the toll it takes on you mentally. I still have nightmares of the *Lusitania* sinking. At first, I was afraid of going to sleep, where I would be plunged back into the breath-snatching, blood-soaked Irish sea watching mutilated bodies floating past, some tugging me under, others staring at me with piteous eyes, crying for help, although I knew they were all dead."

"Dear God, Ria!"

"It does get better – the more I confront it, make some sort of peace with memories I can never completely erase. Now I have other gruesome images that compete for attention," she added wryly.

"The nights are the worst," Max admitted. "Especially in the hospital. The corridors echo with screams as we each wrestle with our demons, and the abject terror in the others' voices frightens us even more. Makes me feel that I *should* be scared, but not so much by what I've seen and experienced as by what it symbolizes. The very nature of this war threatens our humanity and our concept of what it means to be civilized. The military doesn't see it that way, of course. They expect decent men to become merciless butchers without any qualms." Max snorted. "The doctor also told me that shell-shock is a 'manifestation of childishness and femininity'."

Ria fumed. "The bastard! People like him need to be sent to the front lines to experience reality, not sit on their comfortable asses in England making idiotic pronouncements!"

Max smiled.

Branwyn plied him with herbal teas made with nettles, lungwort, eyebright, thyme, and fennel, which eased his breathing, and a soothing bedtime concoction of valerian, lavender, and peppermint. He was looking more rested and comfortable when he had to leave, but Ria was concerned that he was still so morose.

Zoë wrote:

I can't tell you how relieved I am that Max is going home! Blake says that asthma can be dangerous enough without the added physical stress of war. You'll have heard, of course, that Lt. Col. John McCrae died a few days ago. He had asthma all his life, and Blake thinks that the damp cold here contributed to the Colonel's pneumonia and therefore untimely death. We attended his poignant funeral in Wimereux along with so many others, including lots of brass hats, which speaks of the esteem in which the Col. was held. What was almost hardest to bear was to see the Colonel's horse, Bonfire, following the flag-draped coffin, with the Colonel's riding boots reversed in the stirrups. I've never seen a sadder animal, for surely he must have known that his beloved master was gone. I cried hardest then.

Blake told me that the Col. had once offered to let him ride Bonfire, which Blake had politely refused. But it was just one example of the Colonel's generous nature. Blake certainly admired John McCrae as a doctor and humanist, and was terribly saddened by his sudden death.

The cemetery is close to the little hotel where Blake and I occasionally stay. I expect you probably passed it many times. That day was unusually warm, the hills a misty purple while the Channel shimmered in the sunshine. It was ethereally beautiful, and I was once again frustrated that we are not allowed to have cameras in France. The official photographer was there, so I expect photos have already appeared in the press.

Among the many flowers was a wreath of artificial poppies that the officers from the Colonel's hospital had managed to procure from Paris. It was all so poignant. I do think that the Colonel's most famous poem resonates with everyone, for it seems as if a veil of sorrow has descended on all the staff and patients here, although no one except the Duchess had met him. His words will live on and touch many more lives – children yet unborn. That is a noble legacy, is it not?

After a foggy and thus quiet January, air raids began again.

Ria had a phone call from Jonathan Telford one morning in mid-February. Dread gripped her at the sombre tone of his voice as he said, "Carly asked me to ring you." He hesitated as if trying to gather courage or check emotion. "Eddie's been killed in a crash."

"Oh no! Dear God!" She choked back tears as she asked, "What happened?"

"Some sort of equipment failure, we suspect. The plane was too much of a wreck to tell. But you know he was a damn good pilot!"

Ria had seen numerous military funerals, but this was the first where family had been present. Eddie was buried in the churchyard near his home in Surrey, not far from Priory Manor. It was heartbreaking to think that she and his friends would never again see his cheerful face or hear his easy banter. Silent tears were shed. Jonathan never left Carly's side. Ria was grateful for Toni and Justin's presence as they all tried to support Carly. Sybil had already returned to Calais.

Ria was surprised and pleased to see Lance, who said, after the ceremony, "I just arrived home on leave, and Adam Bentley told me what happened." Adam was still in hospital and immobile. "We're losing too many decent chaps."

Ria thought he seemed weary. "It must be hard to keep going. I expect you need a good rest."

He smiled. "I look that bad, do I? I'm glad to see *you* so much better."

"I'm pretty well healed, and spending lazy days at Priory Manor. I can't seem to get up the energy or enthusiasm to do more than look after my household and provide a sanctuary for friends." Damn! She hadn't meant to make that sound like an invitation for him to stay. "I've turned the library into a guest room so that Carly can come for a few weeks. My footman is an amputee and he'll be able to give her lots of help and encouragement."

"Then I'd say you're providing a valuable service and shouldn't feel at all like you need to drive ambulances or join the new Women's Air Force, which I rather suspected you might do."

"Chas was afraid I would as well. As soon as they allow women to fly, I still might. There's no reason why I couldn't ferry planes from the factories to the airfields. And I have connections, since General Sir Hugh Trenchard has dined at Priory Manor," she added with a grin.

"So may I take you up on your offer to meet Calypso?"

She smiled, reminded of their conversation on the beach at Cap Griz-Nez. "Yes, of course. Just let me know what fits into your schedule. Bring your wife, if you'd like."

"She's occupied with other things. I'm going to visit the boys at their prep school near Oxford for a few days."

He came to Priory Manor a week later, arriving just before tea and staying to dinner. Sophie was delighted with the beautifully illustrated copy of *Black Beauty* that he brought her. She and Ria took him for a tour of the grounds and the stable.

"Calypso is splendid," Lance said approvingly, running his hand down the horse's flank. "And Sophie, your Buttercup is charming. I've been thinking more about what I somewhat flippantly said I wanted to do with my life after the war, Ria. I realize I like nothing better than being around horses, so I will breed them. God, it's almost hard to imagine such a genteel life, isn't it? And this is an impressive estate. Do you suppose it might be for sale?"

"I expect so, if the price is right. The Widow Prendergast is getting on, and may not care to live here alone anymore. Isn't your place suitable?"

"No, we have just a couple of acres on the edge of my family's estate in the Cotswolds."

"What fun it would be if you owned it, Lance! Then we could perhaps visit sometimes. I do love this place."

He felt absurdly happy, as if he would be buying it for her. "Can we ring the Widow Prendergast right now and see what she says?"

"Yes, let's!"

Mrs. Prendergast said that she hadn't considered selling Priory Manor, but would talk to her children about it and let Lance know. "At least she didn't say 'no' outright," Ria stated.

They had a lighthearted evening, discussing where Lance would put the paddocks and what else he would need to do to make Priory Manor a suitable location for his new venture.

"The first thing you need is central heating," Ria said.

He chuckled. "You Colonials are too soft."

"No, just practical and not prepared to shun creature comforts for some antiquated idea that suffering builds character."

"Ouch!" Lance laughed fulsomely.

"Bring your wife to have a look at it. I expect she'll want a say in her future home."

But Lance wanted to keep Ria's world untainted by his wife's presence for as long as possible. "I'm certain she'll like it, especially the proximity to London. The boys are quite horse mad, so they'll be delighted to have a stud farm."

When Johanna had taken Sophie up to bed, Ria and Lance sat in the sunroom and smoked cigarettes as they finished the wine. The moon cast an eerie glow on the monks' garden.

"This truly is a beautiful place, Ria," Lance said. And extremely seductive. "I wish I didn't have to go back to the war now that I've found something that excites me. It's as if I *can* envision something *après la guerre.*"

"You certainly look more cheerful."

"Thanks to you."

Ria looked away from his intense gaze. He really did have mesmerizing eyes.

"I expect that this place works magic on all your guests and convalescents," Lance added lightly. The last thing he wanted just now was to overstep the boundaries of their friendship.

"I do believe the monks left a healing atmosphere," she replied with a grin.

"Tell me that there are ghosts and the boys will be particularly keen."

"Surely we all leave an impression of ourselves in places we love."

"Absolutely." It was what Lance was counting on. He was certain he'd feel close to Ria here. And perhaps one day she would share it with him. Life was full of possibilities.

Ria had a note from Lance a few days later.

The Widow Prendergast is prepared to sell me Priory Manor at the end of the war. I thought it prudent to wait, in case I don't make it back. My eldest brother, the heir apparent, was killed yesterday. Who knows where we will all be next week or next year?

Enjoy your sojourn there. I promise not to evict you as soon as the war ends!

Fondly, Lance

.   .   .

Ria was restless and worried about Chas. Having thought Eddie safe in England and one of the skilled and lucky ones who would surely survive the war, she realized how much more dangerous Chas's position was.

It didn't help her state of mind when the new Communist Russia, which had already signed an armistice with Germany three months earlier, ratified a peace treaty with the Central Powers. That meant that the Germans were probably massing all their troops on the Western Front. Thank God the Americans were now arriving in large numbers, and with the ebullience of the popular tune *Over There.*

Over there, over there,

Send the word, send the word, over there,
That the Yanks are coming, the Yanks are coming,
The drums rum-tumming ev'ry where.
So prepare, say a pray'r
Send the word, send the word to beware,
We'll be over, we're coming over,
And we won't come back till it's over over there.

Among them were some of Ria's summer friends, who came to visit her at Priory Manor, grateful to see a familiar face and discuss mutual acquaintances. Marshal Fremont, Randolph and Stanford Vandemeer, Lyle Delacourt, and Stuart Roland all came at various times throughout March.

"I suppose you're sort of a step-sister now," Stuart jested when he had draped himself over the sofa.

Ria chuckled. "I expect I am."

"Swell place you have here. But I was expecting you'd have an aeroplane in the back field and would take me for a flip."

"*Après la guerre.*"

"Yeah, I've heard that a lot already. Hey, Troy told me you'd adopted a little kiddie, so I brought these," he said, pulling out several Cadbury's Dairy Milk Chocolate bars.

He offered them to Sophie, who took them eagerly and said, "Thank you, Lieutenant Roland."

He chuckled. "I can't get used to you Brits calling us Leftenant instead of Lootenant. But it's really cute coming from a kid."

"We Canadians, you mean," Ria corrected with a grin.

"Yeah, OK. Hey, I saw your cousin Emily in *Under The Moon*. Man, she's good! The guys I was with couldn't believe I knew her. They've all fallen for her, but I told them she's married, so they could only admire her from afar. Some of those showgirls aren't averse to a little male company, if you catch my drift."

Ria laughed.

"Say, Victoria, I don't mean to be rude, but I'm feeling a bit pie-eyed and I haven't had more than this cup of tea. Would it be alright if I went to lie down?"

It turned out that Stuart had influenza, and ended up staying with them for over a week. Ria and Sophie both came down with it, as well as Tilda, Patrick, and Gareth. Ria spent a week in bed, a couple of days with high fevers, and was grateful for Branwyn's teas and ministrations. Grayson came to help out, assuring Ria that the Club was in good hands. A former Sergeant who had been declared medically unfit for active service, and who had become engaged to Miss Robertson, had volunteered his services and was most competent.

There was plenty of coughing in Priory Manor, but fortunately no one came down with pneumonia.

Once the local doctor declared Stuart fit enough to return to his regiment, he left reluctantly.

For all his bravado, Stuart seemed to be a scared boy underneath. Ria said, "The best thing you can do for Kurt is to survive. The more of us who remember and talk about him, the longer he'll live in our hearts."

Silenced by emotion, he hugged her tightly. "OK, Sis."

.   .   .

"Follow my leader," Chas said to the two eager boys. The last thing he needed right now was to train new recruits, for the Germans had launched a second massive spring offensive. With the British army in retreat, General Haig had declared that the Allies had their backs to the wall and must fight to the bitter end. But several of Chas's experienced pilots were down with influenza, so he had to make his new pilots combat-ready as quickly as possible. Already they'd had to move their airfield back twice as the German front line forged through the Allied defences.

They were now officially members of the newly created Royal Air Force, independent of the Army and Navy. Chas had been amused to hear his men preening about their smart blue uniforms, which they were sure would draw *birds* even more than the ubiquitous khaki. There was still talk of forming a Wing of Canadian squadrons to support the Canadian troops, but that hadn't happened yet. Chas was now impatient to be in England, or perhaps even in Canada, organizing this, as Beaverbrook had promised him.

He was training the boys to fly in combat formation. As aggressive now in the air as on the ground, the Germans were flying well behind the front lines, machine-gunning troops, harassing the artillery, bombing airfields and other strategic locations. To counteract this, the RAF had up to sixty planes in patrols, so Chas's pilots had to be well versed on the tactics.

Before they went up, he took them verbally through the different maneuvers, ensuring they knew how to respond while staying fifty yards from his wing tips. "If we encounter any Huns, you split-arse back here," he ordered. "No hesitation. No heroics. Understood?" He never allowed the novices to engage in action until they'd had a couple of weeks of intense training and practice under his guidance. It was one of the reasons that his squadron lost so few pilots.

Once they were aloft, he kept a wary eye out. When a dozen Fokker Triplanes suddenly dropped out of the clouds, Chas waved the boys off and tackled the swarm to give his pilots time to escape. There was nothing like aggressive offence to scatter them.

Nonetheless, a few enemy planes took after the fleeing S.E.5as while the others made sport with Chas. Intensely alert, he didn't lose his concentration or forget all the edicts that he had been trying to instill into his squadron. So he constantly turned and attacked. By flying fearlessly head-on at one plane, he caused it to bank away at the last second and into the path of another, one bursting into flames, both spinning to their deaths.

He made it hard for the Huns to shoot at him without fear of hitting each other, but a bullet ripped through the fuselage and shattered his left knee, causing him to black out for a few seconds from the pain. When he regained his senses, he found himself plummeting earthward and yanked out of the dive. But the Jasta was still hard on his heels, so he looped up and dove down on them, machine-gunning another one into a fatal spin.

The next bullet ripped through his left arm and another, into his right shoulder. Although lightheaded from pain, he had no option but to keep attacking.

During the battle, they had come down within reach of British machine gun fire, but as it was too difficult to isolate the enemy in the melee, there was only sporadic assistance from the ground troops.

Chas got one more deadly round of machine gun fire in before spiraling towards the earth. Somehow he managed to flatten out, but his badly shot-up plane crashed heavily into a field and burst into flames. As Chas attempted to scramble out of the cockpit, his last thought was for Ria. *I'm sorry, my darling.*

·   ·   ·

Rafe had tried to keep his nose clean. After the initial decent treatment he'd received from his captors, he'd had a rough journey to the camp in the Black Forest. He'd spent his first night in a local jail in France, in a bitterly cold, dark cell stinking nauseatingly from the unemptied pisspot, the thin mattress greasy with dirt and crawling with lice and God knows what other vermin. He'd spent a week in an overcrowded camp in Mainz where ragged prisoners who had been there since 1914 told stories of cruelty and hardship, of back-breaking labour for the ranks, of beatings and solitary confinement, especially for those trying to escape.

The food had been almost nonexistent – coffee made from burnt barley and a tiny loaf of sour black bread, some thin vegetable soup that was more like dishwater.

So when Rafe had arrived at the officers' camp set up in a new building in Vohrenbach, he had been pleasantly surprised. With potato salads and the occasional scraps of meat, the food had been a big improvement, although the British, in particular, relied on the rations sent from home. There had been an uproar when the British government had recently banned those personal parcels because of the difficulty in monitoring them, and had instead arranged for the Red Cross to send standard packages.

The camp commandant was an easygoing fellow with an English wife, so he had been particularly decent to the British prisoners, allowing them, with a gentleman's promise of not trying to escape, to go for walks outside the camp.

Rafe had quickly realized how lucky he had been to land here, and wouldn't jeopardize his good fortune by attempting to escape. He had envisioned it, of course – an heroic gesture – but what chance had he to get to the Swiss border when he had to negotiate his way through unknown and hostile territory with no food, maps, language, or even proper clothes?

Booze at the canteen had been dirt cheap. With his pay and extra money sent from home if he needed it, Rafe had decided he could spend the rest of the war in a pleasant alcoholic haze.

But his holiday hadn't lasted long. Vohrenbach was turned into a reprisal camp for French prisoners only, so he had been sent to Landshut camp in Bavaria, where all the officers were from the RFC. He'd met up with a couple of chaps from his squadron, including his Flight Commander, and one of Chas's men. While the food there wasn't as good, they had sometimes been able to buy sardines and bottled beer, which was fortunate, since it had taken a while for Rafe's parcels to catch up with him at the new camp. He'd realized that their jailers, like those at Vohrenbach, were decent and respectful.

But after only two months, he and two dozen others had been sent to Holzminden in Prussia, and Rafe had seriously considered trying to escape en route, having heard about that notorious prison. But they had been closely guarded on the three-day train journey, and it had been with trepidation that he'd entered the fiefdom of the brutal commandant, Hauptmann Karl Niemeyer. Here there were a dozen of them crowded into each dormitory. There were only two stoves for over 500 men – they, doing their own cooking of the tinned and packaged food from their Red Cross parcels, since the prison rations consisted only of the odious black bread and dishwater soup.

The recreation yard was too small for baseball, but they managed to play football and some of the chaps had laid out two tennis courts, with racquets and such sent from England. There was quite a decent library with thousands of books that had been sent to the prisoners, and the men had organized classes for the study of languages, engineering, bookkeeping, and such. Rafe decided it was time to improve his French and German. There were even debating and dramatic societies, which proved entertaining.

The camp would have been tolerable if it hadn't been for the sadistic Hauptmann Karl Niemeyer, better known to the men as "Milwaukee Bill" since he had lived in the United States before the war and spoke with a noticeable American twang. But his English was sometimes laughable, and Rafe had made his first mistake by smirking when Niemeyer had said, at roll call, or *Appelle*, "You new men will learn that I don't beat the bushes. I talk like a turkey to you. And I tell you that you gentlemen are a miserable bunch of fockers."

"You!" he'd bellowed, pointing his stick at Rafe. "Schweinehund! Pig dog, stick of shit, focking Limey bastard! What amuses you? Eh? Eh?" He'd poked Rafe with his stick.

When Rafe hadn't responded, Niemeyer had poked him harder in the chest, and said, "I'm talking to you, focker!"

"It's fucker, Sir," Rafe couldn't resist sneering.

Niemeyer had roared. "Don't give me any of your lips, you big stick of focking shit! Throw him in a cell!" he'd ordered his men.

Rafe had been shocked when he'd been hauled off to the punishment cells, and even more upset when he was given only the daily starvation rations and kept locked in solitary confinement for a week without any of his things. The six foot wide cell was in the cellar, cold and damp now that winter was setting in. The window was boarded up so that there was no light from outside. Rafe had shivered under the one thin blanket.

Because of his insubordination, the others had had to stand at attention in the yard for two hours, so he wasn't popular with his roommates when he had returned to his dorm.

And he wasn't so cocky the next time he'd faced Niemeyer at *Appelle*, which was done three times daily to ensure that no one had escaped. Corpulent, arrogant, Niemeyer strutted in front of them, spurs jingling, cape flying, as he harangued them.

"England is a focking oppressor and she will be stamped on! You stupid Canadians have no reason to be here. What has Germany done to make you fight with us? Ach, you are all mercenaries! You care only for money. Big bucks! You have no honour, gentlemen. Or is it that you cannot think for yourself and do only what Mother England tells you? You are stupid barbarians! Dreck! Scheissdreck! We hear how you kill German wounded and prisoners on the battlefield! I know damn all, see!" By now he was shouting and red in the face. "You will be sorry you did not mind your business when Germany crushes the focking British Empire. We killed many in London with our Gotha bombers again. Have you friends in London, gentlemen? Family? Perhaps no more! You must admit that Germany is much superior to Britain. We build better and bigger and faster aeroplanes. Germany will be the top dogs, and we will be generous to our friends. Think about that, gentlemen."

Rafe had learned that Holzminden was where the persistent escapers were incarcerated, and those considered troublemakers.

"So how the hell did I end up here?" he'd asked one of his friends. There were over a hundred Canadians in the camp, and one chap was an acquaintance from Toronto, while another had been at Oxford with Rafe.

One of the men had responded, "Pilots and Canadians have a reputation for being shit disturbers. That's why most of us are here. Rayburn is here because he escaped eight times from other camps."

"Nine's my lucky number," Rayburn had replied with a grin.

Rafe had soon discovered that there was a tunnel being dug, but had refused when he'd been asked if he wanted to help out. He'd thought it a waste of time and effort, and had no interest in being punished when it was discovered, as it was bound to be.

One night he had been in his room just before lights out, and saying to the others, in imitation of Niemeyer, "So, you focking gentlemen think you are going to win the war! I know damned all, see?"

His roommates had suddenly sprung to attention and saluted, but Rafe had realized it was already too late for him. *Shit!* Niemeyer had approached him, saying, "You mock me, Lootenant."

"No, Sir."

"Are you saying that I am stupid? That I cannot believe my ears?"

"No, Sir."

Niemeyer had stood intimidatingly close to Rafe, his big belly almost touching him. "You stick of shit! You are not fit to lick my ass! Do you understand? Say it, Lootenant! SAY IT!" he had screamed, his spit spraying Rafe, who knew better than to wipe it away.

"SAY IT!"

Rafe had swallowed his pride as he'd said obediently, "I'm not fit to lick your ass."

"SIR!"

"Sir."

"AGAIN!"

"I'm not fit to lick your ass, Sir."

"You are a useless stick of shit! SAY IT!"

"I'm a useless stick of shit, Sir."

Niemeyer had grunted. "Damned right. Two weeks in a cell will make you less of a hot dog. The rest of you take everything out of your cupboards, strip your beds and yourselves naked. I've heard that some of you fockers are planning to escape. You will not, WILL NOT I tell you, make me a fool!"

Rafe had frozen, starved, and, been severely depressed during his isolation. And Niemeyer had found himself a whipping boy, especially after he'd discovered that Rafe's brother was the famous Ace who had shot down thirty German planes. No matter how careful Rafe was, Niemeyer found ways to needle and punish him. Rafe had become nervous, and sleep often eluded him.

So when he wrote to his family, he wasn't exaggerating, as so many did to try to get out of Germany.

Dear Mumsy, Pater, and Fliss,

We've heard that some prisoners are being released from German camps into the care of the Swiss or Dutch for the duration. Imagine the freedom! You can't know how bad my nerves have become here. I rarely sleep. My hands are quite shaky, like an old man's. I'm not sure I can take much more.

Surely Pater could put in a word for me with his government cronies. I'm absolutely certain that mountain or sea air would be just the ticket....

At *Appelle* that evening, Niemeyer looked particularly pleased with himself as he said, "So you gentlemen have lost another big Ace. You see that our pilots are much superior. Lootenant Thornton, your brother went down in flames, roasted alive. It's no more than the Schweinehund deserved."

Shocked, Rafe could hardly take in the words. But the smug sneer on Niemeyer's face as he kept taunting him unleashed a bitter rage. "You fucking Hun bastard!" Rafe screamed as he went for him. Although his friends standing beside him pulled Rafe up short, Niemeyer had already motioned to his men.

"Two weeks!" Niemeyer ordered. "You never learn, you stupid Scheissdreck."

Rafe struggled against the guards as they hauled him off, shouting at Niemeyer, "You bloody fucking lunatic son of a bitch!"

"Three weeks, you stinking stick of shit!"

The guards handled him roughly this time. Prisoners who resisted were allowed to be treated with reasonable force, even according to the Hague rules. They punched him, threw him onto the stone floor of the isolation cell, and kicked him a few times for good measure. He lay there bleeding and retching. And weeping for Chas.

·   ·   ·

Ria was frantic, wishing she could fly across the Channel rather than endure what seemed an excruciatingly slow voyage on the ship. She had hardly slept since the telegram had arrived informing her that Chas had been seriously wounded, and that she should make arrangements to go to his bedside as soon as possible.

She knew that that meant the doctors didn't think he would survive. Too often she had seen distraught wives and mothers arrive in France only to find their loved ones already gone.

She felt sure that once she was with him, her own life force could be shared and give him the strength and will to survive.

Please don't die, Chas, she said over and over in her head. *Please don't die.*

He was in a private room at the Casino outside Calais. The CO, whom she knew, greeted her solemnly. Rigid with fear, she said, "Please don't say anything yet. I need to see him."

"As you wish."

Swathed in bandages, Chas was unrecognizable. She dropped down beside him, tears streaming down her face as she looked for somewhere to touch and hold him. His right forearm was free from bandages, but chillingly cold. She kissed it and said, "I'm here, Chas. You can't leave me. Please. I love you, Chas. Remember those two chairs waiting for us on the dock." She stroked his arm gently and kissed it again.

She looked up at the Colonel and said, "Tell me."

"We've extracted the bullets and operated on his knee, and we're confident that we won't have to amputate. But I'm afraid he probably won't regain full use of it. The wounds in his arm and shoulder will heal eventually. But his plane caught on fire when it crashed. Ground troops rushed over and managed to pull him from the wreck, but not before he had sustained some serious burns to the left side of his face and arm and both hands, which complicates his wound. We have to hope that infection doesn't set in. The Major is strong, Mrs. Thornton, and with you here, I'm hopeful that we can pull him through.

"Troops on the ground, including a general, witnessed the dogfight. He was truly heroic. It was why some of them risked their own lives to save him. We can't afford to lose our heroes. We'll do everything we can for him, Mrs. Thornton." He patted her shoulder reassuringly. "I'll leave you with him. Let us know when he regains consciousness."

Ria lost track of time. She sipped the cups of tea left for her only when thirsty, and ignored the trays of food that mocked her knotted innards. She concentrated on his breathing, afraid that if she stopped watching the slight heaving of his chest he would slip away from her. She talked constantly – of the old days, of their plans for the future, of how much she loved and needed him.

A cot was brought in for her, but she usually drifted off for short naps on the chair beside his bed. She didn't want to break the physical contact, sure that it was a lifeline for him. She left him only when his bandages were being changed and she was forced to step out of the room.

At one point she suddenly found herself in Blake's and then Zoë's arms. They had come in response to Bea's telegram, both having been able to take a day's leave. They urged Ria to get some rest while they held vigil. She wept with fatigue and fear, but couldn't sleep. There was little they could do to reassure her.

It was four days before Chas regained consciousness. His pain was unbearable, so he was kept doped up on morphine. But Ria managed to speak with him for short periods when he was lucid.

"You can't leave me, Chas," she stated emphatically. "You have to stay strong. I need you. Sophie needs you. I'll take you home as soon as I can, and you'll heal. Then we can really be a family."

"Ria..." he said on a gasp.

"Shh, don't try to talk. I'll be right here. You need to sleep."

"And you." His one unbandaged eye looked blearily at her.

"I will, my love." She kissed him gently.

When the CO told her that Chas was out of immediate danger, she finally fell into exhausted sleep.

It was hard to watch Chas suffer as he spent more time awake and alert. She tried to distract and reassure him. The visitors helped.

Troy Roland and Hal Goodwin were among the first. The Duchess of Axminster and several of her staff came. Jack stayed for a couple of days. HQ had moved from St. Omer because the Germans had threatened to overrun it, but he was heading back to London in any case. He was shocked and saddened by the extent of Chas's injuries.

With Chas no longer in critical condition, Ria had taken a room at the Hotel Maritime in Calais, within an easy walk along the beach and waterfront from the Casino. Jack, too, stayed at the hotel, and he and Ria once again found themselves in the cellar during the almost nightly air raids.

"I'm so afraid for him," Ria confessed. "I think he'll survive physically, but how will he adjust to being crippled and scarred? Not that I care in the least. I only want him to be free from pain and happy again."

"Chas is a fighter, and I can't see this getting the better of him. He likes to win. He'll just have to establish different goals for himself. But I expect it will take time. You're the one who's going to have to stay strong, Ria." He held her tenderly, and once again thought how easy it was to love her.

Boom Trenchard sent Chas a telegram. *You're well out of it. Go home. Will visit when able.* Trenchard had been unhappy with the new RAF, which reported to a politician rather than General Haig, so he had resigned as Chief of Air Staff.

Chas learned that both of his novice pilots had returned safely to the aerodrome. They accompanied the newly appointed CO of the Flying Dragons, Bruce McPherson, to visit Chas. McPherson's wound had only kept him in England for the winter.

He was visibly moved by Chas's ordeal, and said, "You're a hard act to follow, Sir. I'll do what I can to make you proud of our squadron."

"You can start by calling me Chas, *Major* McPherson."

Ria was thankful to hear the small chuckle that accompanied that remark.

Chas continued. "I couldn't wish for a better man to take over, Bruce. You will keep me informed?"

"Of course! And these youngsters probably owe you their lives." McPherson was all of twenty-one himself.

"Then make good use of them, lads," Chas said in his best fatherly, CO voice, which amused Ria.

"Yes, Sir! We'll napoo lots of Huns for you."

"Use your brains, not just your daring."

"We are all your disciples, Chas," McPherson said. "By the way, Snoopy sends his regards. He refuses to be dislodged from your office and has accepted me, although he keeps one eye cocked to make sure I'm doing things correctly."

"He's a good judge of character," Chas said.

The French awarded Chas the *Légion d'honneur*, their most prestigious decoration. Not to be outdone, the British awarded him their highest military medal, the Victoria Cross. There were congratulatory telegrams from the King and the Prince of Wales, from Prime Minister Borden, Max Beaverbrook, the Astors, colleagues, and friends.

Chas was informed that Baron Manfred von Richthofen, who had downed eighty Allied aircraft, had been killed behind British lines and buried with full military honours.

That the seemingly invincible Red Baron hadn't survived made Chas realize how lucky he was. He clung to Ria during those weeks as he suffered through painful treatments that were supposed to promote healing without scarring. His burned flesh was painted with hot wax, which was then layered with cotton wool and more wax. His left eye was seeping with conjunctivitis, and his vision was blurry, though the doctor assured him that would soon clear up. His wounds would take much longer to heal.

Ria spent most of every day with him, and he hated those nightmare-plagued nights when he was alone and sometimes delirious with pain, wanting only to have her reassuring him that they would soon be able to go home. He was also concerned for her safety, since German bombers were constantly pounding Calais and Boulogne. There was even a fear that the base hospitals would have to be evacuated if the German advance made it as far as the French coast. But Ria refused to go home.

It was three weeks before Chas was stable enough to be shipped to England, where he was sent to the RFC officer's hospital in Eaton Square.

Ria made a quick trip to Bovington Abbey to see Sophie, but refused to take her to London because of the bombings. Toni and Justin insisted that Ria stay with them, since the Netherton townhouse was only a few blocks from the hospital. After long days spent at Chas's bedside, she was grateful for a relaxing chat with supportive friends before collapsing into bed.

Ria hadn't seen Chas without bandages, but having seen and smelled the scorched flesh of others, she was prepared, if apprehensive. Chas noticed the pity and compassion in her eyes when she finally saw the fragile new pink skin.

She kissed the unaffected side of his face, grateful to be able to see and touch more of him, but he drew away from her.

"I expect I look like a gargoyle," he snapped.

"Not to me. I love you more than ever, Chas." She stroked his unblemished cheek. "I'm so thankful that you're out of this war. We've broken the jinx of Monty's book. We've survived."

He cursed the weakness that threatened to unman him with tears.

The largest and last Gotha bomber raid of the war over London occurred on the night of May 19th, but didn't directly affect Ria or any of her friends there.

The devastating one on the French coast most definitely did.

.   .   .

Zoë heard the drone of aeroplanes overhead. As the Duchess's hospital wasn't close to any military installations, no one was concerned, or bothered to shelter in the basement.

It had been an exceptionally warm Whit-Sunday, and Zoë looked out at the luminous night silvered by a full moon. She felt too restless to go to bed. She was sure now that she was pregnant, and could hardly wait to tell Blake. She had thought of sending him a telegram, but wanted to see the joy on his face when she told him. They would meet at Wimereux as soon as this latest German push let up. But she was so impatient to share her excitement that she considered, yet again, writing him a note.

Previous to visiting Chas at the hospital last month, she and Blake had met in the middle of a quiet February, which meant that the baby was due in November. She had been so busy that she hadn't even noticed the lack of her courses at first. But now she was feeling definite changes in her body.

She hoped no one would suspect before she had a chance to see Blake, because she wouldn't be allowed to keep working. Once in England, she would stay with Ria and help Chas to rehabilitate. She knew that massage therapy was critical to burn victims to keep the new skin from contracting. Blake would surely have a fortnight's leave soon, and perhaps he could co-ordinate another with the birth of their child.

If the war was still on. There was a real fear now that the Germans would win.

With sudden resolve, Zoë sat down at her small desk and began to write.

Dearest Blake,

I have some wonderful and exciting news that I can no longer keep to myself. In fact I want to tell the world, so of course you must be the first to know! How I wish you were with me so that we could share this blissful moment....

Thirty miles south at the Canadian #1 General Hospital in Etaples, the air raid warning sounded, and staff scrambled to extinguish the lights and take up their stations. Each medical officer had an assigned ward, and was to remain with the patients until all danger was past. Patients who were mobile took shelter under their beds, but over three hundred with fractured femurs were tethered to their beds by an immovable apparatus.

The doctors and nurses did what they could to keep the men's spirits up as bombs began dropping around them. Blake had never been much of a singer, but he joined in lustily as Nursing Sister Jarvis warbled *The Maple Leaf Forever.*

Defiantly the men added their voices, the non-Canadians humming along.

Our brave fathers, side by side,
For freedom, homes, and loved ones dear,
Firmly stood and nobly died;
And those dear rights which they maintained,
We swear to yield them never!
Our watchword evermore shall be,
The Maple Leaf forever!

Blake wasn't surprised that German bombers were overhead. The hospital was situated next to a strategic bridge over which more than a hundred military trains passed every day. The Germans had driven the British back and compressed the supply lines, so it was obvious for them to now target these critical areas. Blake wondered which War Office idiot had seen fit to place dozens of hospitals in such a vulnerable area, and then allow military camps to rub shoulders with them as well.

The whine and shuddering impact of bombs created islands of fearful silence in their wake. They could see the brightness of flames too close, and knew that part of the vast hospital complex had been hit.

The sound of bombing became more distant, and one of the young patients said in agitation, "Have they gone, Captain Carlyle? Only I don't think I can stand them coming back. It's one thing when I have my rifle and Mills bombs and can face Jerry in a fair fight, but what chance have we got against the bloody bombers?"

One of the other men said, "Put your faith in God."

"Oh yeah?" another challenged. "Where's He been these last four years? Holidaying on another planet?"

"It doesn't hurt to pray," Sister Jarvis stated emphatically. Allowing no further discussion, she began to sing the hymn *Abide With Me.*

When the planes returned there was a direct hit on the end of Blake's ward. He and three of the patients died instantly.

.   .   .

Zoë was numb. She watched the funeral at the graveside as if it were a foreign ceremony that had nothing to do with her. Blake should have been at her side. He wasn't in that flag-draped coffin. That was inconceivable. He was too young, too brilliant, too alive to have been extinguished so easily from this earth. Too much a part of her. She couldn't fathom that she would never see him again.

Troy Roland stood sadly, helplessly at her side. Ria had sent him a frantic telegram, so he had immediately arranged to accompany Zoë to the funeral.

Over sixty staff and patients at the Canadian #1 General had been killed in the raid, and another eighty had been wounded. Nine other hospitals in the district had been hit, resulting in an additional two hundred and fifty casualties.

When the survivors began cleaning up, they were surprised, because of the extent of the damage, that more hadn't been killed. The men's quarters, right next to the railway line, had been incinerated by an incendiary bomb, catching many of the men fast asleep. The officers' huts had been wrecked or obliterated, so it was fortunate that almost all had been on duty in the wards. Part of the Nursing Sisters' quarters had been destroyed, killing three and wounding five. Only a few wards had been somewhat damaged, which was reassuring as there were nearly 1200 patients.

The Etaples cemetery was enormous. Blake would be just another cross in the endless field of crosses.

The Last Post was almost too much to bear, even for Troy. He held Zoë tightly as she sagged against him. He bled for Ellie as well, knowing how close she had been to her elder brother, how she had admired and emulated him. How could he find the words to describe this to her?

After all the mourners had gone, Zoë dropped down beside the flower-strewn mound of earth, and said angrily, "You can't leave me like this, Blake! You can't!"

Troy pulled her up, into his arms. "Zoë..."

"I'm going to have a baby," she wailed. "I didn't even have a chance to tell him!"

"He knows," Troy said with quiet conviction. He held her as she was overwhelmed with grief.

When he suggested it was time to return, she gazed at him blankly and said, "How can I leave my beloved?"

"You have to think of the child now," Troy said gently. "And Blake would want you to go home." There was such anguish in her eyes that he felt his own heart would break.

"How will I get through the days without him? We barely had a chance." She doubled over in pain.

Through Justin, Ria managed to obtain the necessary documents to get to Calais. She took an overnight boat and arrived the following morning. She had cabled Boss that she needed her Rolls, so Sybil fetched her from the harbour in Dragonfly.

"It's bloody depressing, all our friends being killed or maimed," Sybil said. "I've had enough. Been here three years and I can't take it any longer. I've resigned. I'm coming home with you as well, Windy."

"You should never have come back after your fever," Ria said, taking a moment from her profound grief to offer her support.

"Yes well, I'm packing while you fetch your cousin. God, I can't tell you how sorry I am. Blake was the most decent chap!"

The Duchess and her staff were delighted to see Ria, despite the tragic circumstances of her visit.

"You've had too much to contend with, my dear," the Duchess said to Ria. "We'll miss Mrs. Carlyle. Too too sad!"

It was a tearful reunion between the cousins. They spoke little because they understood each other without words. And because it was almost impossible to put voice to their volcanic emotions.

Ria could appreciate only too well that Zoë now felt her own life had ended. "You'll have his baby," she said. "Blake's legacy."

She drove Zoë to the cemetery where they laid fresh flowers on his grave. Zoë had wept so much that she could only stare at the fresh mound of earth with reddened eyes.

"He's not really here, is he?" Ria said. "Not for me. He's at Ouhu and Wyndwood and on the tennis court at Thorncliff." Not behind a sand dune on the French coast. "You need to go there to be with him, Zoë."

Ria and Zoë shared the guest room in the Duchess's villa that night. Ria lay tensely in bed, almost unable to bear Zoë's heart-wrenching weeping. Neither of them slept much.

Ria took her and Sybil back to England the following day. There she enlisted the help of Nancy Astor to have Zoë returned safely to Canada, as civilian women were no longer allowed to cross the Atlantic until after the cessation of hostilities. Because of her contribution to the Canadian Army Medical Corps, Mrs. Astor's request could hardly be ignored. So Zoë would be allowed to bunk in with the Nursing Sisters on a hospital ship that was setting sail from Liverpool in a couple of weeks. Ria cabled her Uncle Richard, *Zoë arriving Halifax aboard Llandovery Castle June 17.*

In the meantime, Ria took Zoë to London with her, to Bea's townhouse, afraid to leave her, recalling only too well Tilda's fall and subsequent miscarriage. But she also needed to be with Chas, whose incipient depression was exacerbated by the news about his friend. He and Zoë had a tearful reunion, which made them both more disconsolate. For a fleeting moment Ria thought of consulting Blake, and then realized with a fresh stab of pain that he was gone. Justin and Toni were supportive, of course, as was Beatrice. Martha Spencer spent her free time with Zoë. Henry and a tearful Alice came for a weekend in London.

Zoë was unable to eat, which worried Ria, as she grew noticeably thinner. Ria urged her to think about feeding the baby if not herself, but Zoë felt as if her insides had shriveled, leaving no room for anything but pain. Ria cabled Ellie, *Zoë inconsolable and pregnant. Fear for baby as Zoë growing weak.*

Ellie wired to Zoë, *You and Blake have created precious new life. Be strong for baby and Blake. He would expect nothing less of you. We need you, sister-in-law, and baby will be our lifeline to Blake.*

As if suddenly realizing the full implications of her pregnancy, Zoë grew desperately concerned about the child, and finally managed to eat.

Sophie also mourned her friend, and was still terribly worried about Daddy Chas, so Ria brought her to London as well.

Sophie went tentatively to Zoë. Holding the blue velvet ribbon Blake had given her and pointing to the scar on her forehead, she said, "Capitaine Uncle Blake found this ribbon growing in my stitches. It is pretty, n'est ce pas?"

Zoë looked at the teary-eyed child and smiled sadly. "Oh yes, it is very pretty." She hugged Sophie tightly and bit back her own tears. She knew how much sorrow Sophie had already endured, and felt her own resilience and determination returning. Ellie was right – Blake would expect her to be strong.

Here, where they had first consummated their love, where she had promised not to cut her hair, where he had told her to move on with her life if anything happened to him, Zoë felt his presence. She took comfort from talking to him as if he were with her. And she treasured his child growing inside her.

Ria took Sophie to see Chas at the hospital. She had warned Sophie about Chas's injuries, and told her that she mustn't be shocked if Daddy Chas looked different. "He is very sick but will soon be better if we show him how much we love him. And perhaps we can make him laugh."

Ria was apprehensive, afraid that Chas would be even more dejected if Sophie showed revulsion at seeing him. But she somehow trusted that the child would focus less on his scars than on the reassurance that Chas wouldn't leave her as well.

And she was right. Sophie stood warily at the threshold of his room, but seeing him looking little different she rushed up to him, crying, "Daddy Chas!" Ria had told her to be careful about touching him, so she stopped short of throwing herself into his arms. But Chas, moved by her genuine joy in seeing him, drew her close.

Sophie laid her head on his chest and said, "You will be home with us soon, Daddy Chas. I miss you!" She looked at him more closely, but not with fear or disgust. "You must not be sad. Mummy Ria said you will be better because we love you."

Chas met Ria's gaze over the child's head. Ria added, "And we need you to come home."

He raised his right hand as an invitation to her. His new skin was still sensitive to temperature and touch, but she took it gingerly in hers.

"Be patient with me," he said brokenly. "I need to adjust."

Zoë went to see him a few days before she was scheduled to leave, and made sure that Chas would receive adequate massage treatment for his wounds and burns. She also showed Ria how to do it once he was out of hospital.

"I hope you'll be back home in time to be Godparents to our child," Zoë said to Ria and Chas. "I know that Blake would have wanted that as well."

Jack was back in London, and solemnly presented Zoë with a watercolour sketch of Blake's grave, having added some poppies at the base of the cross. Seeing Zoë's emotional response, Jack found it difficult not to be moved.

"Thank you," was all she managed to say.

"It was good of you to go to the cemetery and do this," Ria said when Zoë had excused herself.

"I feel lucky, so if I can help..." He shrugged. "I'm sending one to Ellie as well."

"Do you love her?" Ria suddenly asked, but didn't wait for an answer. "Sid seems to be your latest conquest."

"Ria!"

"I don't care how many women you choose to be involved with, Jack, but don't trifle with my friend's emotions. Ellie deserves better than that."

"We understand each other," he said firmly.

"Do you?" she challenged him. "If you're not serious, let Ellie get on with her life. She has other prospects." Ria could see that he was perturbed. Before he could respond with his own questions, she said, "I have great admiration for you, Jack, but if you hurt Ellie, I'll never forgive you."

"Things aren't always forever, Ria."

"Why not? Are you afraid to make a commitment?"

Jack was thinking quickly. His intention to marry Fliss would have to seem natural, not obviously mercenary. So he would have to let Ellie go. Why did that thought hurt so much?

"I care enormously for Ellie, but I think she was right. We have different paths in life. She's a career woman. I suppose I haven't wanted to admit that we have no future together." It wasn't hard for him to look crestfallen.

Ria relented a little. "Just be honest with her, Jack. It's better for you both in the long run."

He rubbed his brow as if trying to stave off emotion. "You're right, of course." Jack realized that he had to be careful if he wanted to become an acceptable husband for Chas's sister. No more obvious affairs, and it was time to lay some groundwork for the rest of the family, Fliss's affections having already being secured. "After the kind of childhood I had, I just want a devoted and contented wife at my side and a houseful of happy wed-fed children." He thought that would resonate with Ria.

"Doesn't sound a bit like Sid."

He chuckled. "Definitely not. We just enjoy one another's company."

Jack balked at having to sever his relationship with Ellie. But she was just one of the sacrifices he had to make on his journey to achieving his goals. It left a bitter taste.

Ria took Zoë to Liverpool and waved her off. Richard and Olivia met her in Halifax. Once again within their loving embrace, Zoë felt like a needy child rather than a widow and mother-to-be.

Olivia said astutely, "Sometimes we need to be looked after, and to allow others to pamper us. It helps us all to heal."

Everyone was stunned to hear that on its return voyage, the *Llandovery Castle* was torpedoed off the coast of Ireland. Hospital ships, with their markings and special running lights, were supposed to be inviolate, and didn't have a naval escort. There was outrage when it was reported that the German submarine had tried to destroy the lifeboats and survivors as well. Only twenty-four of the two hundred and fifty-eight medical personnel and crew survived. All fourteen of the nurses that Zoë had come to know had perished. For many of the war-weary Allies, this atrocity helped to rekindle their determination to defeat the brutish Hun.

·   ·   ·

Rafe strolled along the magnificent broad sandy beach at Scheveningen on the Dutch coast. Only the Channel separated him from freedom in England. But this wasn't at all bad.

He was still recovering from the three-week starvation diet and the beating that had left him with a fractured rib. Of course he hadn't been allowed any letters or news in solitary confinement, so he hadn't discovered that Chas was still alive until he'd returned to his dormitory. But now he and Chas were both well out of the war and healing.

Rafe wasn't allowed to leave the country, and there was no point, since Britain was obliged to return him if he did escape. But why would he want to when his father had set him up in the posh Kurhaus Hotel right on the beach? With his pockets full of money wired from home, he was on his way to the Canadian Officers' Club on the seafront where he could undoubtedly entice some chaps into a poker game.

He'd just chatted up a very pretty girl who worked in a nearby shop. He'd at least learned some French and German at Holzminden, while the girl knew a bit of both. Having come to realize how scarce food was even for the Dutch, he'd invited her to dine at his opulent hotel, and was cheerfully certain his enforced celibacy would soon come to an end.

No, life wasn't at all bad.

Chapter 18

The canoe hissed as Zoë beached it on the sandy shore. She clambered out a bit awkwardly now that she was six months pregnant. Wrapping the blanket around her shoulders against the early morning chill, she went to sit on a granite outcropping at the edge of the beach.

She had been coming here most mornings since returning to the cottage on the Dominion Day weekend. Now it was almost the end of August, and autumn was creeping in. A cool night had dispelled the heat of the past weeks. The morning mist hadn't yet lifted in the grey dawn, so she was encased in a soft cloud, seeing nothing but vague patches of darkness to indicate Ouhu. She had come through this blindly, almost by instinct.

She had always known that Blake, as well as Ellie, felt a special connection to Picnic Island. How many delightful outings and swimming parties had they all had here over the years?

"Your child is kicking hard these days," she said to Blake.

A loon called its hauntingly lonely song, and Zoë was reminded of the "Spirit of the Lake" pantomime she had written the summer of 1914, which had so impressed Blake.

Surrounded by an otherwise silent white shroud that separated her from any visible signs of life, she felt immensely alone. Zoë hugged herself tightly and sobbed with grief. If only she could feel the touch of Blake's hand or hear his voice!

But then she felt a gentle calm descending upon her, as if Blake *were* there, his breath sighing softly against her cheek. "I miss you so much, my love," she said. "So very very much."

The mist thinned and undulated and skittered across the mirror-still water, glowing in the burgeoning dawn. By the time Ellie canoed over to join her, there were only tatters remaining.

"Are you always up so early?" Ellie asked. She was spending this last week of August at the cottage again.

"Yes. I seem to have taken on the rhythm of the sun, falling asleep as soon as it gets dark."

"I noticed you here so I've brought coffee," Ellie said, flourishing a thermos and a couple of cups. "Weak coffee, so that Baby doesn't get too excited."

Zoë smiled. "Thanks."

"Do you feel close to Blake here? I know I do."

"Yes. But I have memories of him everywhere on the lake. Sometimes I can convince myself that he's just around the point or the next island and about to join me. Will it ever stop hurting so much?"

"So they say. Hard to believe, isn't it?" Ellie herself was grappling with the finality of Blake's death. Heroes weren't supposed to die.

Max suddenly appeared around the west end of Ouhu and paddled towards them. "Are chaps allowed to come ashore?" he asked.

"Only certain ones," Ellie said with a grin. "Permission granted. But I didn't bring three cups."

"I can drink from the thermos if there's any coffee left."

Ellie was glad to see that Max didn't shake noticeably as he drained the last of the coffee. When he had returned in the spring, she had been unhappy to see him grey-skinned and hollow-eyed, tense and trembling and startling violently at the slightest unexpected noise. At Blake's urging, she had spent hours encouraging Max to talk about his nightmares that kept sleep at bay.

She had been especially distressed to see how Max had initially pushed Lydia away, claiming she had got herself a bad bargain with him, and so he would release her from her promise. Ellie had intervened, assuring a hurt and despondent Lydia that Max needed her support more than ever. And Lydia had come through like a champion. She had ignored his rebuffs, his moodiness, his silence, and had talked about their shared past and plans for their future, or had just sat quietly with him, holding his hand. When he had finally collapsed into her arms weeping, she knew she could help him heal.

But Ellie wondered if he would ever again be the easy-going character who was forever cheerful and mischievous. He still suffered crushing headaches, although Zoë's massage treatments were helping. He became easily frustrated, and impatient with himself. At times he was vague and distant, his smiles old and sad. At least he breathed more easily at the cottage, so he had been here all summer with his family. Feeling the need to be with her children, Olivia was coordinating her administrative work from the cottage, with able assistants at the convalescent hospital in Toronto carrying out the tasks. Max took her daily to the Grand to make her telephone calls.

Lydia had also been at her family cottage on Red Rock with her mother all summer, and spent most of every day with Max. They were getting married on the upcoming Labour Day weekend. At Max's request it was to be a relatively quiet affair at the cottage, but Lydia no longer cared about an elaborate wedding. Zoë was reassured not only by how deeply Lydia loved Max, but also by how innately strong and sensible she was. Despite everything, she retained her fun-loving nature, and managed to coax some joy out of Max.

He rubbed both hands agitatedly through his hair, as if he were shampooing it, and said, "I don't feel ready. For the wedding."

Zoë and Ellie exchanged glances. Ellie took the lead. "You have your suit and the ring so it can't be that," she said lightly. "What's bothering you?"

Again he rubbed his head and didn't look at either of the women as he finally blurted out, "Intimacy."

Almost with relief, Ellie said, "Neurasthenia often causes a reduced sex drive, but that's temporary and nothing to worry about. When you're relaxed and enjoying emotional intimacy, the other will happen naturally."

"I'm not being fair to Lydia."

"Bullshit! If I hear that one more time, I'll swat you, Max Wyndham!" Ellie declared. "You're not being fair to her if you treat her love and devotion so lightly. She would be devastated without you!" More gently she added, "Open your heart to her, Max. Don't keep things bottled up inside. Despite the fact that you sustained a brain injury and God-knows what other subtle internal damage, you have this absurd idea that you are less a man because you 'cracked' under impossible and unnatural pressures. Do you know that one of the doctors I worked with after the Halifax explosion went back to his rural community and killed himself because he couldn't live with all the horror he had witnessed? We're all damaged by this war, Max. We have only each other to cling to, to make us feel that life can go on. You're so lucky that you and Lydia have a chance at happiness."

Zoë was already weeping, and tears began to trickle down Max's face. The twins hugged each other, and Ellie brusquely wiped her own eyes.

The three of them sat side by side in silence watching the sun infuse the horizon with a brilliant new day.

.   .   .

"Grandmother's angry with you, Helena," Phoebe said.

"Don't be silly," Helena replied dismissively. "Your grandmother is dead."

"And whose fault is that, she says?"

Helena was momentarily startled. "Her own, of course. She was a doddery, obstinate old lady who should have been more careful."

"Oh dear, she didn't like that, Helena. Now she's *really* miffed."

"I'm not interested in your fanciful nonsense, Phoebe."

Phoebe shrugged. "Well, if I were you, I wouldn't sit in her chair. Not unless you want her glaring at you all evening." Phoebe wrinkled her brow. "I don't think she likes you very much anyway."

As Phoebe walked cheerfully away, Helena felt a shiver creep down her spine, almost as if that old battleaxe, Augusta Wyndham, really were standing at her shoulder. She was grateful for the excuse to get up when Olivia and her family walked into the sitting room of the Big cottage, along with Lydia, Claire, and Lizzie.

"I'm always delighted to attend a family gathering, but do you know what this sudden, 'important' meeting is all about?" Helena asked Olivia. Edgar had come by that morning with an invitation for cocktails.

"I don't. Perhaps Daphne's with child again. Edgar is quite the doting father."

As Daphne helped the maid pass around glasses of champagne, Helena whispered to Olivia, "I do think one of us should take Daphne aside and inform her that it's really not apropos for her to interfere with the servants' jobs."

"I think the war has taught us to be a bit more self-sufficient, which I think is a good thing, don't you? Especially considering that Daphne has only one maid."

"I think that running a household successfully requires a somewhat military hierarchy and discipline where everyone knows their job and place. You lose the servants' respect if you don't rise above their level. I've certainly heard my staff bragging about the family's accomplishments."

"You mean Chas and Ria's," Olivia said astutely, with suppressed amusement. "Especially as there are few women who've ever received a medal for heroism from the King."

Helena had no chance to respond as Daphne offered them each a glass. Olivia was right, of course, though Helena hated to admit it.

When Daphne had moved on, Helena said, "Now there's a perfect example of people not knowing their place. Surely Phoebe's nurse doesn't need to attend a family dinner."

Olivia liked Irene Partridge, and enjoyed her company, for she was thoughtful, caring, and astute. She had been an enormous help to Phoebe this past year, surely responsible for Phoebe having had fewer psychotic episodes and seeming generally happier and more relaxed.

Edgar called for attention. "Thank you for coming at such short notice. Welcome to the family, Lydia, although that won't be official for three more days. I'm also delighted to welcome someone else into our family. Irene Partridge has agreed to become my step-mother. That is to say, father has convinced her to marry him."

Helena gasped, but Olivia cried in delight, "Oh how wonderful!" She went over to congratulate Irene and Albert, who put his arm about his fiancé with the biggest smile Olivia had ever seen on his usually dour face. She was so glad that Albert had a chance at some joy in his life.

Phoebe clapped her hands jubilantly. Of course they had informed her ahead of time, but she had been bursting with the secret. Irene wasn't taking Mama's place, Edgar had assured her, but would be there to make them and Papa happy. Phoebe was also excited that she would have a sister of sorts, Dr. Lorna Partridge, who was a friend of Eleanor's. *And* she would be a bridesmaid at the wedding, with Lorna as Maid of Honour. The only thing that could be better would be having her own wedding.

When Phoebe had complained that she was desperate to get married, Irene had told her, "It takes time to find someone you're compatible with. You get to know a boy by talking and dancing with him, and just having fun together. Then you can decide if you like him well enough to spend your whole life with him."

"Daphne said that boys don't marry girls who make love with them. But boys want sex, don't they? And that's having fun. So it doesn't make any sense to me at all."

"I'm afraid that some things just don't," Irene had said. Of course she had been informed about Phoebe's baby. "Think of it this way, Phoebe. Boys don't appreciate anything that is too easy to attain. Respect yourself, and think carefully about whom you want to share yourself with. One day you'll find a decent fellow, and he'll be the most special person in the world to you. Then you can get married and have children, but until then, it's wise to refrain from intimacy."

But Phoebe wondered if Irene had ever exploded with ecstasy when she had sex. If she had sex. Phoebe giggled at the bizarre notion of her father and Irene making love.

"Have you set a date for the wedding?" Olivia asked Irene.

"The 14th of September. The vicar managed to fit us in at St. Paul's and we're hosting a dinner afterwards at the King Edward. Of course it will be a small affair with just family and a few friends."

"And the honeymoon?"

"Albert is keen to show me the mountains, so we're going to a hotel in the Rockies for two weeks, before it closes for the winter. Banff Springs I believe it's called. He has business in British Columbia afterwards, so Phoebe and I will have plenty of time to explore Vancouver."

"You're taking Phoebe along?" Olivia asked in surprise.

Irene chuckled. "At my urging. I think the poor child needs to see something of the world. Lorna is coming with us to Banff for ten days of much-needed rest, so the girls will have a chance to become acquainted. Albert and I aren't teenagers in the first flush of love. We'll have plenty of time to be alone together. In fact, we've spent many delightful evenings this past year getting to know each other. We're practically an old married couple already."

"Albert is a very lucky man. And I'm delighted to have you as a sister-in-law."

"Thank you, Olivia. I know that I'm not the usual sort of Wyndham wife."

"Helena was no heiress, either, so don't let that bother you," Olivia advised. Irene also understood the subtle suggestion that Helena had no right to a superior attitude.

While Phoebe was elatedly telling the young people about her impending train trip out west, Zoë was distracted by the news that Emma had given her a short while ago.

A telegram had arrived informing the Spencers that Freddie had been seriously wounded. Zoë knew how inaccurate these initial reports could be, and prayed that his injuries weren't life threatening. She knew he would send a cable as soon as he could, to elaborate, but until then they were all worried about him. She hoped, too, that his brother, Arthur, who had enlisted in the spring, wouldn't be sent over anytime soon.

Lizzie Wyndham, who was staying at Silver Bay for the week and was once again the official photographer for the wedding, was pondering the latest letter she had received from Rafe.

You can't imagine how bloody boring it is here at Scheveningen. It's either grey or raining, and winds continually roar off the North Sea, so you get sandblasted walking on the beach. A calm and sunny day seems like a bloody miracle, but even then it's never really hot, like it probably is in Toronto or Muskoka right now, nor am I inclined to bathe in the frigid sea. Thank God for the Canadian Officers' Club where I can get cheap booze and play cards.

As we're allowed to travel up to fifteen miles without a special pass, I sometimes go into The Hague, which isn't far and there's at least a bit of nightlife. I've also found a place where I can rent a horse and go for a gallop through the woods or along the dunes, which I swear are the highest things in all of Holland. We Canadians have a baseball team and often play against the American legation in The Hague. So I'm not really complaining when I think of what I left behind.

I was vastly amused to hear that twenty-nine chaps managed to escape from that hell-hole Holzminden through the tunnel they had worked so long and hard to dig. Ten of them actually made it safely to Holland, so those lucky beggars are allowed to go back to England now. I'm damn glad I wasn't at the camp when Niemeyer discovered he'd been duped. I expect he was apoplectic with rage.

That fat bastard still haunts me.

It's bizarre to me that there are Germans holidaying at my hotel! They seem as happy as I am to be out of Germany. I tell you, Lizzie, it was pathetic to see starving women and children in Germany begging for food from us prisoners. If we hadn't had our Red Cross parcels, we wouldn't have survived on that foul bread and watery soup diet. I have to admit to being surprised that our care packages arrived at all, and usually intact. The Germans do have some sort of honour. The Dutch don't have great quantities of food either, as the Germans have been sinking the supply boats in the Channel, and the Dutch charge outrageous prices for what they do have – and everything else actually. Bloody war profiteers everywhere! I don't fraternize with the Germans, of course, although at least one cute Fräulein has given me the eye.

I'm envious of the officers whose wives have been able to come and stay with them. Of course, there are any number of pretty girls about, some of them quite amenable. But I'd far rather be with you, Lizzie, and think about you often, daydreaming about how delicious it will be to hold you in my arms again and taste your lips. Fortunately I haven't lost the small photo of you, though it's dog-eared now from all the handling. How fondly I recall those cold November evenings with you in New York! We'll have to do that again, but with a different ending to our nights, don't you think? I torture myself imagining the delectable possibilities.

With the war on, I trust that there aren't any decent chaps left in Toronto who might be trying to win you over.

I want you, Lizzie.

Love, Rafe

She fingered the gold locket he had given her, which had his photo inside. She longed for him as well. He was right to think that there weren't any interesting men about, but she had thrown herself into her work in any case, and had already built up a favourable reputation in society. The fact that she was a Wyndham stood her in good stead, so she played up the talented socialite angle that had been inspired by Anders' comment. By charging – and receiving – high prices for her work, she was seen as a cut above other photographers.

She had just written back to Rafe, asking him if she should plan a wedding. Allowing her mind to drift into blissful speculation, Lizzie could already envision her stunning gown, and the admiring, proud, besotted look on Rafe's face as he took his new bride on his arm. She was trying to decide if it would be preferable to have a wedding at Thornridge in the city, or at Thorncliff on a summer day, but her thoughts were interrupted by a plaintive howling.

"I wonder what's wrong with Shep?" Rupert said. Shep was Toby's dog.

"I saw Toby go by on the veranda a few minutes ago," Phoebe said. "But Shep wasn't with him."

"He must have hurt himself!" Rupert speculated. "I'll go see."
The ancient caretaker lived year-round in a cabin behind the big house. Shep, an old, arthritic dog, didn't venture far from there these days.

"I'm coming, too," Miles said as the boys ran off.

They came back a few minutes later, ashen and shaking. "Toby's sitting in his chair looking really queer. He didn't wake up. I think he's dead."

"Dear God!" Olivia cried, hugging the boys to her.

Richard, Albert, and Irene rushed out.

When Richard returned, he said sadly, "Irene thinks Toby's heart gave out. He went peacefully. But he's been dead for a while."

Everyone looked at Phoebe. "I saw him out of the corner of my eye, but I know it was him," she informed them, not in the least puzzled by that. Only by the somewhat shocked looks of the others.

Helena glanced over at Augusta Wyndham's rocking chair. She swore that it moved ever so slightly.

•   •   •

Dearest Ellie,

It's hard to believe that it's been almost four years since you and I last touched. So much has changed, hasn't it?

I treasure our friendship. Your letters have helped to keep me sane. But I feel I've been selfish in my need of that lifeline to home and memories of those happy summer days we shared. What fun we had!

Of course, I never expected you to wait for me, so I hope that you have found someone to love you as more than a friend.

This is so difficult for me to write, Ellie! How can I tell you without hurting you, that I love you dearly but that I see no future for us? You have always maintained that your career is important to you, which I respect and admire, as you know. I would never expect you to give up doctoring to become just a wife to a struggling entrepreneur.

Ria implied that you have the prospect of happiness with some other chap, so I don't want to hold you back, or give you the impression that there can be more between us than what we've had.

Forgive me if I've hurt you. I sincerely hope we can still be friends. You are a remarkable woman, Ellie. You deserve someone better than me.

With much love and regret, Jack

Dear Jack,

I always knew that we had no future together, although for a time I did hope. We did have fun, didn't we? I certainly have no regrets.

Yes, I have found someone to share my love as well as my passions. I don't know why it's taken me so long to realize that. I think that in some way, I felt I owed you loyalty.

Of course we will still be friends. We'll see each other at the lake. We'll dance at balls, compete in Regattas. Our children and grandchildren will play together.

I wish you well, Jack, and hope that you find love as well as success, although I fear you will sacrifice the one for the other.

Fondly, Ellie

A popular new song kept playing in Ellie's head.
After you've gone, and left me cryin',
After you've gone, there's no denyin',
You'll feel blue, you'll feel sad,
You'll miss the dearest pal that you've ever had.
There'll come a time, now don't forget it,
There'll come a time, when you'll regret it,
Some day, when you grow lonely,
Your heart will break like mine and you'll want me only,
After you've gone, after you've gone away.

Jack might regret it, but she wouldn't. She was finally free to love Troy. It was exhilarating and frightening and joyous to think that they could now take their relationship to a new level. She just wanted to be absolutely sure before she accepted his proposal of marriage.

Ellie had been contemplating her relationships, and realized that she was too easily enthralled by charming men who were needy. After much soul-searching, she was almost convinced that her desire to be with Troy no longer hinged upon anything but the fact that she loved him and felt incomplete without him.

But still she hesitated to commit herself.

She was playing tennis at the Country Club with Emma Spencer at the end of the week when she ran into Felix and Eugene Roland. Felix had been unable to enlist because of his flat feet, and Eugene was only seventeen. They introduced a couple of girls who were with them, Millicent and Ethel Madison.

They were vivacious young women with the supreme self-confidence that spoke of wealth. Felix managed to take Ellie aside for a moment, and said, "Mom invited the Madisons because she wanted them to see how we spend our summers. She has Millicent targeted for Troy, and Ethel for me, God forbid! Just thought you should know." He winked at her.

Instead of being discouraged, Ellie sat down as soon as she returned to the cottage and wrote a letter.

Dearest Troy,

Yes, I will marry you, if you still want me! And I feel deliriously happy being able to say that with all my heart. I can hardly wait to be with you again!

With the Allies now pushing the Germans back, we're all expecting the war will soon be over, so I won't plan to come to England unless it drags on into the spring. Perhaps you'll be home by Christmas!

You may be interested to know that your mother has your wife picked out – Millicent Madison, whom I expect you know – and is acclimatizing her to Muskoka. That's what Felix told me today.

More seriously, I know that it will be difficult if not impossible for your mother to accept me as a daughter-in-law. I want you to be certain that you won't regret marrying me, since it may well cause a rift in your family. I shall, of course, apply all my limited charm and restraint to being a dutiful daughter-in-law.

You could consider finishing your studies in Toronto, where I have a good job and would be able and happy to support you. Stop laughing! You may be cut off without a penny if you marry me.

I'm excited and impatient and, as always, worried about your safety. Nowhere feels completely safe anymore, except in your arms. How glorious to look forward to making a life together!

Love, always, Ellie

Chapter 19

Ria heard the discordant crashing of piano keys and hurried into the sitting room. Chas was frustrated at his attempt to play. His right hand was healing nicely and regaining dexterity, but the fledgling skin on his more seriously burnt left hand had contracted so that he didn't have full range of motion. Ria gave him regular massage treatments and ensured that he kept up the exercise regime that Zoë had demonstrated.

"I'll play the bass," she suggested, nudging him over on the piano bench. He had been attempting the popular *Russian Rag*.

"What's the point, Ria?" he asked bitterly as he struggled to stand up.

After four months in hospital, Chas had come home to Priory Manor a month ago, in mid August. He was still weak and couldn't put much weight on his left leg as yet, nor walk easily with crutches because of the stress that exerted on his injured arm and shoulder.

She jumped up to help him, but he shrugged her off. "I can do this on my own."

He winced as he shuffled awkwardly to the sofa. "Pour me a cognac, would you?"

"It's still morning," Ria pointed out.

"It eases the pain. I can ring for Patrick."

"Don't be silly," she said, decanting a small measure for him from the drinks trolley.

"Don't look so disapproving, Ria. You were getting this in hospital, too."

"I'm not reproaching you, Chas. I'm worried about your attitude." She sat down beside him and put her hand over his. "You're so angry. I don't know how to help you anymore."

His eyes were distant, almost cold, not that reassuring look that always wrapped her in the security of his love. "There's nothing you can do," he replied, drawing his hand away to pick up the snifter of brandy from the side-table.

"It's going to take time for you to heal. The doctor said a year at least for the burns. Don't be so hard on yourself," she added gently. "The Chas that I know isn't going to let lameness or anything else keep him from regaining his life."

"What life, Ria?" he challenged.

"Whatever you make of it, Chas."

"What trite and meaningless drivel!" he accused. "Life as a cripple freak?"

"Stop it, Chas!"

"Face the facts, Ria. I'm not the man you married."

"You certainly aren't! The greatest tragedy will be if your soul becomes as crippled as your body!"

She marched out, holding back her tears until she was well away. She had tried so hard to be patient and understanding, knowing how difficult it must be for him. But he kept pushing her away and inciting arguments.

Because he couldn't negotiate the stairs easily, he slept in the library, which Ria had turned into a guest room, initially for Carly. She had lain down with him, just to hold and comfort him, but he had turned away from her, saying he needed privacy. So she felt constantly rejected by him, regardless of her efforts to assure him of her love.

Chas clenched his fists despite the pain. Or to punish himself. He was furious and annoyed with himself for once again lashing out at Ria. God knows he didn't want to hurt her, but he was frustrated by his uncharacteristic helplessness and bleak future.

His mother had written:

How I wish I were with you, my darling boy, to help ease your suffering, both physical and mental. Not everyone can comprehend what it is to live with pain and the disappointment of one's diminished abilities. Can you believe that I was once quite a formidable tennis player? I do have an inkling of the darkness you are now wading through to find the light – a way to endure, to cope, to discover new paths to happiness and fulfillment. You can and you will, Chas. I know that your courage goes beyond heroic deeds. This will certainly be a test of it. I also know that Ria has experienced her own torments of body and soul and will help you through this. Your father, bless him, has always been most kind and considerate to me during my dire times.

Please, my darling boy, be patient, be stalwart, know that you are loved and needed and still have much to live for....

But even the possibility of forming a Canadian Wing had been taken from him and given to Billy Bishop, now a Lieutenant-Colonel and Britain's top ace with seventy-two victories. Chas realized how fleeting was glory when you could no longer perform. Who wanted to see a maimed survivor when there were handsome young heroes to idolize? Bishop had even written a best-selling book about his life in the RFC. Chas Thornton, VC, DSO & bar,

MC, Légion d'honneur, would become merely a footnote in the history books. And someone who would evoke pity in others.

He had always taken his good looks for granted. Now when he looked in the mirror, all he could see was the puckered skin on the left side of his face. The doctor had assured him that the new skin would improve over time with massage and exercise. But he would never look the same.

Every night he felt the merciless licking of the flames, heard the terrifying crackling, smelled himself burning. Silently screaming in his dreams, he'd awaken sweating and shaking. In the depths of the spectral, torturous nights he thought that he would welcome death. Even Ria would be better off without him.

He hobbled over to the drinks trolley to refill his glass, pondering yet again how he could save his wife and family from the disgrace of his suicide. If he weren't so bloody weak and crippled, he might be able to fly. Wouldn't it be glorious to once more leave the leaden earth behind, ascend into the gossamer, elysian heavens, and fly, like Icarus, toward the sun! He would go higher than any man before him, until there wasn't sufficient oxygen for him or his aeroplane. Only once had he ventured into the breath-snatching cold and starved, thin air above 20,000 feet. His engine had sputtered in protest, the plane becoming as sluggish as he had. It wouldn't take more than ten minutes at that altitude to drift into blessed unconsciousness. What matter then if he plummeted earthward in a final spectacular twirling dance of destruction? Just an accident, they would say.

He gulped his drink and poured another. Only thoughts of Ria kept him anchored to this unforgiving, wretched earth. He could already imagine suave Major Chadwick comforting and eventually seducing the grieving widow. The hell he would!

Ria went for a long ride on Calypso, stopping in the meadow where Chas had landed his aeroplane almost a year ago when he had dropped in from France. She recalled how he had whirled her about the field as he had sung *I'm Always Chasing Rainbows*. That exuberant, warm, and loving Chas was still there, she knew, suppressed beneath the rage and sorrow. She would cling to that, and try not to take his moodiness to heart.

She returned just in time to take a telephone call.

"Adam asked me to tell you that Lance has been wounded," Sybil said. "A bullet creased his skull and he has some bone splinters embedded in his brain, but removing them might cause more damage so they're not going to operate."

"Dear God!"

"They do expect him to make a full recovery, which I can hardly credit."

"Is he back in England?"

"Yes, just arrived in London."

Ria would have liked to visit him, but knew that Chas, in his fragile mental state, might think that she was turning to another man. "I'll send him flowers and a note. I can't get away."

"I say, Windy, would it be alright if Adam and I came to stay for a few days? We're both chafing under the solicitous ministrations of our mothers when what we really need is some time to ourselves." Recently engaged, they planned to marry as soon as they were both recovered. Adam had been in hospital for eight months, having had two operations on his hip. He was walking with a cane now, and threatened to start riding soon. It was as much as Sybil could do to keep him away from her father's horses.

Sybil was still suffering the aftereffects of trench fever, with aching bones, particularly her shins, and debilitating fatigue at times. Doctors had finally established the cause of the illness – a bacterium carried by lice.

"Of course you're welcome to stay! Come for at least a week. It will be good for Chas as well to have company. In fact, I'll invite Toni and Justin for the weekend, and Carly and Jonathan." They had been married a month ago.

"It will be like old times!" Sybil enthused.

"Yes, indeed."

Chas didn't appear for lunch, but had rung for a tray to be sent to his room. Sophie said, "Is Daddy Chas sick again?"

"I think he is very sad. What can we do to cheer him up?"

"We will take him for a walk to collect wildflowers," she announced promptly. "I will push his wheelchair."

"That's an excellent idea, ma petite. Let's make him a formal invitation after lunch. You can draw some flowers on a card and we'll have Patrick deliver it on the silver tray."

Sophie clapped her hands in glee.

Chas could hardly deny such an appeal from his daughter, Ria thought.

Sophie often spent hours drawing flowers. She collected and pressed them, and examined them minutely to recreate them. So Ria was impressed with the beautiful card that she created – an arrangement of a few dried flowers amid her painted ones. With Ria's help she wrote,

Dear Daddy Chas,

Please will you come with me and Mummy Ria to find flowers? They can make you happy, and you will make me happy. Love, Sophie.

Ria was concerned when they didn't have an immediate response to this appeal. "Daddy Chas may be resting," she said. To distract Sophie, who was obviously hurt, Ria played piano with her, amusing her with the *Tiger Rag* and showing her how to make the piano "roar".

She herself was beginning to despair when Patrick came in and offered the silver tray to Sophie. She snatched the letter with a shriek of joy and then, more sedately, said, "Thank you, Patrick." She tore open the letter. "Look what Daddy Chas says!"

My darling Sophie,

That is the nicest invitation I have had for a long time, and certainly the most beautiful. I should be delighted to accept. Shall we meet at the front door at 4:00 o'clock?

Your loving Daddy Chas

Chas, made more maudlin by excessive booze, had wept when he had received the card – a flood of angry, bitter, helpless tears that washed away those destructive emotions. He had realized that he'd been behaving like a miserable bastard to the very people who loved him most. And whom he didn't want to live without. It was time to stop wallowing in self-pity.

Ria and his mother were right. He could and would rise to the challenges that faced him. And he would triumph. But first he needed to sober up.

Ria immediately noticed the change in him when he stood at the door waiting for them. She embraced him, saying, "Thank God you've come back to us!"

He gripped her as tightly as he could and buried his face in her shoulder, fighting tears. "Forgive me, my darling," he whispered.

"I was so afraid I would lose you again, Chas!" she said emotionally, clinging to him. "I couldn't bear that!"

"Look, Daddy Chas, we've brought a basket for a picnic tea!" Sophie said, tugging on the hem of his jacket. "You must let me push your chair. You mustn't tire yourself with too much walking. Let me help you down the front steps."

Chas gave Ria a quick kiss and said, "We'll continue this later."

Gareth had already taken the wheelchair outside, and now Sophie helped Chas into it. He hated using the chair, so one of his first goals would be to get rid of it. But for now, Sophie was right. She delighted in pushing him about, so he made it into a game.

"OK pilot Sophie, more left rudder. Full throttle to get up that slope."

She giggled. Ace barked happily as he raced ahead and back and around them. He particularly enjoyed sending large flocks of starlings and sparrows wheeling in unison up out of the meadow grass, only to settle back down moments later.

Chas was the first to spot the harebells and red dead nettles, but Sophie beat him to the little blue blossoms of the field speedwell and the pretty pink campion. They collected chestnuts and hazelnuts, and crab apples and elderberries for Mrs. Skitch to make into jam, as well as blackberries, which they munched on. Shrubs and trees and trailing briars wore colourful fruits like proud jewels. Sophie pointed out bittersweet and bryony berries and said, "You can't eat those. Gareth says they're poisonous."

"You can talk with Gareth?" Chas said in surprise.

"Oh yes. He showed me these and did this." She put her hands around her neck, stuck out her tongue, and bulged her eyes, and then burst into delighted giggles as Ria and Chas laughed. She threw her arms around Chas's neck and put her cheek gently next to his scarred one, saying, "You are happy now, Daddy Chas."

"Yes, poppet. Very happy."

Sophie danced in front of them with Ace at her heels as Ria insisted on pushing the chair over the bumpy sections to the summerhouse beside the lake. They helped Chas into the large room where wicker chairs were set about, and a low table provided a spot to lay out the goodies.

"Next summer we'll be doing this in Muskoka," Ria said, as she poured them each a cup of tea from the thermos." They had agreed that they would stay in England for the winter to give Chas time to heal before undertaking the journey, and with the hope that the war would be over by spring so that the Atlantic crossing wouldn't be dangerous.

"I hope so, my darling, but I called Lord Hugh Cecil and told him I'll be fit to do some teaching in a month or so," Chas said. "Bob Smith-Barry is crippled, and doing terrific work at Gosport. He's halved the fatality rate of trainees. I told Cecil I could run a similar school at Farnborough. I might even be able to fly again in a few months."

Ria was surprised and tremendously pleased. Lord Cecil was in charge of recruiting for the RFC and was not only a friend of Winston Churchill, but also of Cousin Bea. "That's wonderful, Chas! How did Lord Cecil react?"

"He was delighted, but added that he might not need my services. He thinks the war will soon be over."

"That's even better news! Is that really possible?"

"We've got the Germans on the run, Ria. So I may have to rethink my next career."

"Could we be home by Christmas?"

"Like I thought I would be four years ago? I can hardly believe I've been gone that long. Let's try, shall we?"

"We'll have to stay at Thornridge until Wyndholme isn't needed as a hospital any longer."

"Mumsy and Fliss would love that. Then they can really fuss over Sophie."

"But we will take Alice and Johanna?" Sophie asked anxiously.

"Alice will be in school, but perhaps she can visit us during the summer holidays," Ria replied, feeling as sad about leaving Alice behind as forlorn Sophie. "We'll certainly take Johanna if she wants to come."

"And Ace and Buttercup?"

"Of course! And Calypso. And, I daresay, some more of the staff," Ria added with a chuckle. Only yesterday Patrick and Tilda had asked permission to get married. Patrick had said, "We have every wish to stay in your employ, Mrs. Thornton."

"I'm delighted to hear that. And we will all look forward to your wedding," she had replied. "You must consider having the reception here. Will the sitting and dining rooms be adequate?"

"Oh, Ma'am, we couldn't! Could we?" Tilda had said with excitement.

"You certainly may. You've helped to make this a welcome home for us. We even have some champagne to contribute."

Tilda had practically been in tears.

Ria had wanted to find the right time to tell Chas, so she did now.

With a smile he said, "I'm not surprised that everyone falls in love with you, Ria."

"Applesauce! I've discovered that a little kindness can sometimes make a world of difference in people's lives."

"Let me reiterate that sentiment. And I'm you're biggest fan."

"That's as it should be."

Chas moved back into their bedroom that night.

.   .   .

Their guests had just left when Ria had a phone call from Beatrice's butler to inform her that Bea was down with influenza. Ria immediately arranged for Grayson to drive her to Priory Manor.

"Such a fuss," Bea said when she arrived. "I would have been perfectly content in my own bed."

"Nonsense, Cousin Bea! You're burning up and can barely talk. You know that there's been an outbreak that seems to be turning into an epidemic. We're going to tuck you into bed and look after you. It's the least we can do!" Ria assured her.

Bea was too weak and achy to protest. Branwyn prepared teas and poultices to help loosen Bea's tight chest, and Ria prayed Bea wouldn't develop pneumonia. The local doctor had nothing to offer or suggest other than aspirins or narcotics. There were already reports of numerous deaths from the flu and its complications.

At Priory Manor, Grayson, Mrs. Skitch, and Beryl also fell ill.

Ria was desperately worried that Chas, in his weakened state, would succumb, so she allowed no one near him who wasn't wearing a gauze mask. He was quarantined in the library.

"There's no need for this, Ria," he protested. "Nearly a third of my men were down with influenza in the spring and I didn't catch it then."

"But you may not avoid this one. It's so much worse than what we had in the spring."

Ria had a tearful call from Alice who said, "We've been told to go home if we can. A lot of the girls are sick. My friend Dorothy died yesterday." Ria could hear her struggling to speak. "It's terribly sad, since her family is in Rhodesia."

"I'm so sorry, Alice. Of course you must come to us!"

"I'm not feeling well, Ria. I don't want to infect all of you."

"Nonsense! We already have it here. I'll come to fetch you."

Alice was burning up and admitted to having a crushing headache when Ria arrived at the school. "I'm scared, Ria," she said fighting back tears. "It was so horrible to watch Dorothy die. Blood was gushing from her nose like a waterfall. And she was coughing up blood. It was like she'd burst inside. There was blood everywhere."

Ria hugged her tightly. "We'll look after you. I think Branwyn's potions have been more effective than what the doctor has to offer."

"My grandparents were happy that you could take me in. They didn't think they could cope with a sick child."

"We would have been unhappy not to have you with us."

Alice coughed almost incessantly during their two-hour journey, and didn't have the strength to walk upstairs when they arrived at Priory Manor. Gareth carried her easily to one of the guest rooms. Ria was terribly concerned by her lethargy and high fever, and began administering Branwyn's potions.

Beatrice, fortunately, seemed to have only a mild case of flu, and was resting comfortably now that her fever had broken.

Beryl turned an alarming blue – heliotrope cyanosis the doctor declared, shaking his head – and was dead within hours. Hers was just one of several funerals that day. Ria began to hate the sound of the church bell tolling.

The doctor fell ill. Mrs. Skitch was recuperating, but melancholy. Alice and Grayson struggled to stay alive. Ria and the staff spelled each other, although none of them slept much. Sophie was frightened for Alice, but Ria wouldn't allow her to keep vigil at her bedside.

Ria heard from Meredith that Theadora was quite ill. Toni had to go home to look after Georgie, Ronni, and Bunny, while Justin was required to take on extra duties in the War Office to cover for the many absentees.

Jack called to tell them that Sidonie's brother, Quentin, had died. "He seemed perfectly fine when she saw him two days ago. She's absolutely devastated."

Ria could well imagine. Sid had now lost her husband and both her brothers.

"She's gone home to Blackthorn, and won't even talk to me. I don't know what I can do to help her."

"I don't expect there's much any of us can do. We can't even get away from here to attend Quentin's funeral. You'll represent the family, won't you, Jack?"

"Yes, of course."

"This is like some sort of nightmare. It doesn't even seem like flu. It's so... violent in some cases. And sometimes so quick."

"Do you need any help there? I had the three-day fever in May, like so many others, which some speculate gives us immunity to this bout of flu."

"No, thanks, Jack. We're managing." Although the village children weren't coming to tend to the animals during this epidemic, Gareth and Enoch were able to cope.

Chas was particularly saddened by Quentin's death. "Sid was so thankful that he was out of battle, so certain that he was now safe. He was a good friend. We've lost too many of those."

It was ten days before Alice and Grayson seemed to have turned the corner. Bea was already regaining her strength, but Ria wouldn't hear of her attempting to return to Bovington just yet. The officers who had been staying with her had both gone to hospital with flu and one had died.

Ria allowed Sophie to sit with Alice who was very weak, but now breathing easily and sleeping well. So Sophie did most of the talking, and read to "her patient".

When Grayson was beginning to feel stronger, he said to Branwyn, "Would you consider living in Canada?"

"I might. Nothing to keep me here."

"Would you consider becoming my wife? I never thought I would fall in love again, but I have," he said, holding her gaze as he anxiously awaited her response.

Her look was penetrating, as if she were trying to read his thoughts. "I would. So long as my Gareth was treated well."

Grayson relaxed against his soft pillow. "I've always wanted children." He took her hand and raised it to his lips. "I feel truly blessed. When I'm stronger I will be able to sing your praises."

She laughed. "I need nothing more than your assurance of love."

"You have that, and my devotion, Branwyn. You've also given me the best medicine for a speedy recovery."

"Then I'm well pleased," she said, touching her lips to his.

So were Ria and Chas. "Would you be willing to be our housekeeper?" Ria asked Branwyn. "I'm so impressed by your abilities. And I think Gareth would be happily engaged in the gardens and on the island."

Branwyn smiled. "I would indeed. Thank you. I knew it was a lucky day when we came into this house."

Ria had a telephone call from Alice's grandfather informing her that Alice's father had died of influenza in Ottawa. Her grandparents were to become her legal guardians.

"Perhaps you would permit me to take on that responsibility," Ria said immediately. "You're aware that my husband and I can provide a secure future for Alice. I'm quite certain that Alice would be only too happy to come back to Canada with us. I assure you that we cherish her, as does our adopted daughter, Sophie."

"A most generous offer. Allow me to discuss this with the family," Professor Peregrine Milford said.

When Ria told Chas she said, "I didn't think you'd disagree with my decision."

"You did absolutely the right thing, Ria. Alice is like family already. I'll come with you to break the news about her father." Chas had insisted a week ago that he could no longer hide in the library.

When she had finished weeping, Alice said, "I haven't seen Dad for over three years. I was hoping that I would be allowed to go home again when the war's over."

Ria told her about wanting to become her guardians. "I know you're almost grown up, but would you like that?" Alice was sixteen.

"Of course! I can't imagine anything better, if I can't go home again." Alice wept anew, but with happy tears as well.

"Our little family is growing," Chas said to Ria when Alice's grandfather agreed. Sophie was ecstatic that Alice would truly be like her sister, and coming to Canada with them.

It was only a few days later that Chas had a call from his London lawyer. When he hung up he poured himself a stiff cognac. Ria found him sitting pensively in the sunroom. "Who was that?" she asked. "Is anything wrong?"

"Sit down, Ria. That was Mr. Venables. It seems he has something that, as he put it, 'belongs to me'." He ran his hand through his hair. Without looking at her he said, "Madeline died of flu. She had me listed as the father on the birth certificate and as next of kin, so the child was sent to England, to the care of Mr. Venables in my stead."

She turned pale. "I see."

"What am I going to do, Ria?" he looked at her in confusion.

She swallowed hard as she declared, "We'll just have to look after him, won't we?"

"Are you sure?"

"You don't have a choice, Chas. You can't let the child go to an orphanage when we're adopting other people's children. He *is* your son. Excuse me."

She hurried from the room, into the garden. Standing behind one of the crumbling Gothic arches, she hugged herself to contain the pain, but it spilled over into tears.

Chas struggled to her side with a cane. "I can't run after you anymore, Ria." He took her into his arms.

"He should have been Reggie," she said in anguish.

"I know, my darling," he murmured, stroking her to soothe her rigid body. Of course he hadn't had the intimate connection that she'd had with their stillborn son, but he had seen the perfect little body, cold and grey, so he could understand some of her pain. But there was nothing more he could say to comfort her. No more pretending, wishing, hoping that they could have other children. Only that they had each other and their adopted family.

Ria said, "I know he's just a child, and it's not his fault. But I'm afraid that whenever I look at him, I'll envision his mother in your arms."

Chas grimaced. "I won't allow Charles to stand between us, Ria. Never again. If you don't want to take him in, I'll find someone to adopt him."

"You would?"

"Yes. You are more important to me than anyone else, Ria."

She knew he would make the sacrifice for her, but probably not without regret. At least Charles was a part of Chas, if not her. And since she loved Chas, she would surely come to love his child. Was it fair to deny him his offspring because she had lost hers? "No. He must come to us."

"Are you certain?"

"Absolutely."

"Thank you, my darling."

Ria knew she would have to move beyond seeing the child as the embodiment of Chas's betrayal, so it was with great trepidation that she first met him. But he was a frightened little boy, not yet three years old. Blonde-haired and blue-eyed, he looked heartbreakingly like Chas – and like the child they should have had.

And her heart melted. Clutching a much-loved teddy bear, he cowered behind the tall grey legs of Mr. Venables, but she went over to him and crouched down, saying in French, "Bonjour, Charles. Je m'appelle Mummy Ria, and this is Sophie. She will be your big sister. You must be hungry. Sit down and we'll have some milk and cookies."

He accepted her outstretched hand and she led him to the sofa. Sophie, who was eight, had been told that she would have a great responsibility as an older sister, so she already took her role seriously. She plunked herself down beside him and began telling him how much fun he would have with Mummy Ria and Daddy Chas. Ace sat quizzically at their feet.

Of course they hadn't told anyone about the child being Chas's son, but only that they had known his mother and so would be adopting him, since he had no other family.

Bea of course knew, and a few astute people weren't fooled, but would keep their own counsel. To Grayson, it explained much that had puzzled him.

Mr. Venables made a grateful exit after talking privately with Chas.

Ria accompanied the children to the stable, as Sophie was eager to show Charles Buttercup. He walked silently between them, clutching his bear as if he were afraid someone would snatch it from him.

Ria asked, "What's your teddy bear's name?"

"Pierrot," he muttered, hugging the teddy even tighter.

"He's a very handsome bear."

"Papa gave him to me."

Ria was shocked. "You saw your Papa?"

The child shook his head. "He flies aeroplanes." A scout from Farnborough roared overhead at that moment and he looked up eagerly. "That's him! He's looking for me! He will bring Maman!" He started running after the plane and waving.

Sophie, seeing Ria's concern said, "Come and I will let you sit on my pony. May he, Mummy Ria?"

"If he'd like to."

But Charles hung his head and blubbered when the plane disappeared. He barely glanced at the pony.

"I expect he's tired," Ria said. "A light supper in the nursery and early to bed for him, I think."

Ria stayed in the nursery and tried to distract him by showing him the colourful illustrations in the *Peter Rabbit* book and allowing Sophie to tell the tale in French. He hardly touched his eggs and toast.

When Johanna started to prepare him for bed Charles began wailing pitifully, "Where is Maman?" Ria tried to take him onto her lap, but he pushed her away. "I don't want you! I want Maman!"

He was kicking and screaming and flailing as Chas entered the room.

Sophie said gently to Charles, "Your Maman is in heaven with God and my parents. She wanted you to be with Mummy Ria and

Daddy Chas. If you're quiet long enough, you will feel her beside you. Come and I will sit with you."

He followed Sophie slowly, dejectedly to the bedroom. Johanna helped him into bed and cleaned up his snotty face. He curled into a ball and fell asleep from exhaustion, cuddling his teddy bear, sucking his thumb and sobbing.

"Poor little mite," Ria said as she and Chas left the nursery.

"I expect he's grieving, and bewildered by all the new people he's had to deal with. Can you live with him, Ria?" Chas asked tentatively.

"When I see him as a distraught orphan, I don't resent him for not being mine as well as yours. Give me time to adjust to this."

But they all needed time to adjust. Charles was in turns sullen or angry or hysterical. He punched Ria and bit Johanna. Only Sophie seemed to be able to reach him. Chas had to stop himself from becoming stern.

But a few days later, when Charles sat disconsolately at the dinner table once again not eating, Ria said with concern, "Do try some of this lovely fish, Charles."

In a flash he picked up his plate and hurled it at her as he screamed, "Non! Non! Non! I hate you! I want Maman!"

Everyone was momentarily stunned. The plate had missed Ria but had shattered glasses, spraying her with wine and food and bits of glass. Chas rose angrily from his chair, bellowing, "That's quite enough of that!"

Charles threw himself onto the floor in a tantrum of tears. He pummeled it with his fists and feet. Before Johanna could go to him, Ria said, "Leave him. He doesn't understand what's happened to his mother, and needs to express his fear and frustration. We'll talk with him when he's calmed down."

Beatrice said, "I'm sorry, my dears, but I do think that children need to be socialized in the nursery before being expected to live up to adult standards. It's much more comfortable for all. And try him with rice pudding. I still remember it fondly from my nursery days. I shall go and sit with Alice."

"I do apologize, Cousin Bea," Ria said, sensing that Bea was right. It was unrealistic of her to expect Charles to sit obediently at table, especially one that was so high he was perched on a stack of pillows. At the small table in the nursery he could be more in control, and none of them had to worry about his manners. It was an inauspicious beginning to their relationship.

When he had worn off his rage and lay there sobbing, Sophie went and sat on the floor beside him. She stroked his head as she said, "I'll be with you always, Charles."

Ria had cleaned herself up and now sat on the floor beside the children. "You are a wonderful big sister, Sophie. I'm very proud of you." To Charles she said, "What would your Maman make for you to eat?"

"Frites," he replied promptly.

"So you and Sophie and Johanna and I will make frites. D'accord?"

His large brimming eyes were no longer resentful.

She rose and held out her hands to both children. "Come along. Bring Pierrot because he won't want to miss out on his cooking lesson."

"Neither do I," Chas said.

Branwyn was only slightly surprised when they invaded the kitchen. Mrs. Skitch was "still poorly", and not inclined to leave her bed just yet. She had been shocked by Beryl's death, and those of several friends and acquaintances in the village.

"Dinner was delicious, as usual, Branwyn, but I'm afraid we have someone here who craves his mother's chips. You won't mind if we make a small batch?"

"I'll help. I have found, Ma'am, that children have simpler tastes, so if you'll allow me to make nursery meals for him, I'm sure we can tempt him to eat."

"I'll leave that in your capable hands, Branwyn."

Charles knelt on a chair so that he could watch them peel and chop a couple of potatoes. Ria took a raw stick and gave it to him, saying, "This one is for Pierrot. What else would you like to eat?"

"Chocolate."

"One of Sophie's favourite things. Shall you and I make hot cocoa?"

He nodded.

Ria helped him to pour the milk into a mug to measure it, and then into a pan. "Now one for Sophie, and Alice, and Johanna, and Aunt Bea. I know that she loves cocoa. Ask Daddy Chas if he wants one."

The child looked up at Chas somewhat fearfully, but Chas smiled and said, "I would be delighted to have one."

Without prompting, Charles said to Ria, "Vous en voulez?"

"Oui merci, mon petit poussin."

Ria showed him how to measure a tablespoon of Fry's Cocoa and a little precious sugar into each mug and stir up a paste with a dollop of milk.

When she poured the hot milk in and let Charles whip it magically into chocolate, Chas said, "Well, I'm impressed."

Ria flashed him a grin.

Branwyn had finished frying the potatoes, so she put a large plate of them in front of Charles. The others each snatched a few, and Chas said, "Yummy! I shall never forget frites with hot chocolate."

"We'll have to have them at the cottage before bed," Ria quipped. She was pleased to see that Charles ate ravenously, if messily. He was sitting on her lap so that he could easily reach the table. When he had finished, he snuggled up against her.

She hugged him gingerly, careful not to alarm him. How strange and wonderful it was to have a tiny Chas in her arms.

He was deeply asleep within a few minutes, and Gareth was summoned to carry him to the nursery.

Sophie declared she would visit Alice before bed. "I'll join you there in a few minutes," Ria said.

As she helped Chas up to the sitting room, he said, "By God, but it's exhausting being a parent! You're wonderful, Ria, and I don't know how to thank you."

"You don't have to thank me, Chas. He's our son now."

The following day they had a phone call from Arthur Spencer, who was in the segregation camp in Rhyl, in Wales. Nearly every one of the thousand troops aboard the ship he had arrived on the previous week had come down with flu. They'd had thirty-two burials at sea, and more had died in hospital. He had fallen ill just after landing, but was recovering well, he assured Ria.

"We're quarantined here for four weeks regardless," he said. "After that may I come to visit? I talked to Freddie and he said you've invited him to Priory Manor to convalesce." Freddie had sustained a messy leg wound that had been stubborn to heal.

"Of course! It will be wonderful to see you again, Arthur! And with any luck, the war will be over before they can send you to France."

"It does seem rather likely, doesn't it?" he said hopefully. "But as a good journalist, I should be looking forward to experiencing the war."

"Talk to the veterans and record their stories. Most would never think of writing them down."

"You're right there, Ria. Good idea," he said enthusiastically. "And perhaps I'll get just enough of a taste of the environment that I'll be able to describe things myself."

"Just a taste, mind you, Arthur. I've been feeling a lot happier now that most of my friends are no longer in the front lines." But the latest casualty had been Randolph Vandemeer, who had died of his wounds. "I read your article in *Maclean's*, and was most impressed and flattered. Just remember that observant chroniclers and thoughtful philosophers are important and not easy to come by."

He laughed.

Jack came to visit a couple of days later. As it was a warm day, he and Ria played tennis, with the others looking on. Alice was in the wheelchair with plenty of blankets keeping her toasty. Chas, Bea, and the children watched from the sidelines as Jack beat Ria in a close match.

When they had finished, Jack showed an excited Charles how to hold the racquet, and helped him hit a ball, while Ria gave Sophie and Johanna another lesson. When they joined the others, Jack said, "You can be a tennis champion if you practice hard, Charles."

"Maman called me Chas." He pronounced it the French way, "Shas".

Ria, Chas, and Jack were momentarily speechless. Both men looked to her for guidance. "That was your Maman's special name for you," she said. "We'll call you Charlie."

.   .   .

Ellie was anxious to finish her rounds at the hospital, but with the hundreds of seriously ill influenza patients, she had been working extremely long days, especially as dozens of nurses and several doctors were sick, with more dropping daily. Over a thousand people in Toronto had died of the flu and its complications in just the past three weeks. She and the medical staff wondered if this virulent disease really was just flu, or some terrifying new virus. Autopsy results puzzled rather than elucidated, the pathologist describing lungs ripped apart or clogged with blood from uncharacteristic pneumonias that killed within hours. More like pneumonic plague – a form of the Black Death – than influenza.

Schools, cinemas, pool halls, even churches had been closed, as had the medical school at the university so that the students could help with the epidemic. A couple of hotels had been turned into temporary hospitals, but for each hospitalized person there were thousands more ill at home, and sometimes no one well enough to look after them, except kind neighbours and hastily-trained volunteers. But they, too, were collapsing. Horror stories were filtering in from the hard-hit United States, where there were scenes truly reminiscent of medieval plagues – carts coming by to collect the dead, who were stacked like cordwood and buried in mass graves.

Every family that Ellie knew had at least one person ill, so she would visit her friends after work, their own physicians overtaxed or sick themselves. Fortunately, most had the usual mild flu and were back on their feet within a week. But not all.

She hadn't even had time to attend J.D. Thornton's funeral. He had seemed to be recovering well, but then suddenly died of heart failure. Fliss and her mother were devastated. James Wyndham had stepped in to help them with all the legal and complicated financial concerns.

Ellie was terribly worried about Edgar and Richard Wyndham, who both had life-threatening cases. Edgar's fever had spiked to an alarming 105°. She prayed that they wouldn't develop the telltale signs of cyanosis, which was almost always fatal. Half of the pneumonia patients were dying.

She was also concerned about Daphne, who was three months pregnant, as well as Zoë. The doctors had noticed that pregnant women had a particularly high mortality rate, so Ellie had been adamant about keeping both quarantined, which was now impossible. Having had the flu in the spring, along with most of the officers in the Duchess's hospital, Zoë claimed that she was immune, although Ellie wasn't convinced it was the same virus.

Another oddity about this flu was that it was killing an unusually high number of young adults. It was especially tragic to see soldiers who had survived their wounds succumbing to "la grippe", which was what happened to Cecil Rankin, a friend of Max Wyndham whom Zoë had nursed the previous year in London.

Esme helped Zoë look after their parents, and Miles was on the mend, as was Emma Spencer, who Zoë had insisted should stay with her family, since Emma had been too ill to return home to Ottawa. Thankfully, Lydia, Claire, and Ellie's brother, Derek, were responding well to bed-rest, fluids, and aspirin.

Ellie was amused by newspaper reports of long line-ups at pharmacies of people with doctors' prescriptions for medicinal alcohol. There were demands from the public for the relaxation of Prohibition, but rumour to the contrary, neither alcohol, tobacco, quinine, opium, turpentine, cocoa, Dr. Chase's Menthol Bag, nor Vicks VapoRub was going to prevent or cure the Spanish Influenza.

Ellie had a sudden intense wave of dizziness and nausea, and grabbed the end of a bed to prevent herself from falling. Hell and damnation! She couldn't be getting sick. Surely she was just overtired. But a slight headache soon felt like her brain was expanding and trying to burst through her skull with sledgehammer force. When violent pains in her legs and back felt as if her bones were breaking, she decided she needed to go home before she collapsed in the hospital. It was the last place she wanted to be.

She had no recollection of actually getting home. She drifted in and out of terrifying abysses, sometimes plummeting into them or lying prostrate, heavy, breathless in some dark and intensely lonely place. Pain kept her from groping for consciousness. Nothing seemed as desirable as oblivion.

But some part of her fiercely wanted to live, forced her to become sentient, revisiting the dreadful agony of what it meant to be alive. She heard Zoë saying, "You can't give up, Ellie. I need you. The baby needs you. Troy needs you. Please Ellie. You have to come back to us."

"Won't let a girl rest," she mumbled through the liquid pain that was beginning to reassemble itself into recognizable body parts – eyes, ears, head, bones, muscles.

"Oh God, Ellie!" Zoë embraced her.

"You shouldn't be here."

"Don't be silly! How could I not look after you? Papa and Edgar are out of danger now. Your mother has a mild case. The others are on the mend. Ria cabled recipes for teas and poultices, which I think have helped."

"Don't need me then."

"Not until you're much improved. What would I do without you as well?"

"Go home and rest," Ellie said. "I'll be OK."

But it was weeks before she was well enough to get out of bed. Even then it was difficult for her to move. Her feet were numb, with "pins and needles" crawling up to her knees. She struggled to walk, but it was like stepping barefoot on sharp pebbles while trying to negotiate a ship's deck at high seas. Her hands also became tingly and stiff. It was terrifying not to have control of her body. She managed to write to Troy, but her hands were clumsy and weak, and the letters took hours of careful work. She burst into tears for no reason, was frail, fragile, frustrated. Pain was a constant, but subtly retreating companion.

And Zoë was often at her bedside.

"Lorna came to see me. She thinks I have neuritis – an inflammation of the peripheral nerves," Ellie told Zoë. "It could become chronic. How am I going to live like this?"

Zoë comforted her while she wept. "I expect you just need a nice long convalescence." But Zoë was worried about Ellie, and also concerned about her own father, who was still weak and unsteady and uncharacteristically melancholic. At least Edgar seemed to have bounced back to full health.

Zoë said, "The epidemic is abating, so they don't need you right now." She suddenly gasped. "But I think I do! My water just broke."

"Bloody hell!"

.   .   .

It took nearly a month for the letter to reach Paul Godfrey on the steadily advancing front lines. Gil, Edelina's scarred handyman, had written,

I thought we were safe at the cottage, but one of our guests brought the plague with him. Edelina was painting. You know how much she loved the autumn colours. She said she was feeling a bit queer and just needed to rest. But she never woke up.

She went peacefully, in the place she loved best. But what will we do without her?

Paul raised his arms and face to the heavens. He let out an anguished cry. "Noooo! Edelina! You can't leave me!"

But there was no thunderbolt or even a German bullet to put him out of his misery. The guns had fallen silent.

.   .   .

Blake Wyndham Carlyle was born minutes before the armistice on November 11, 1918, perhaps the last Canadian baby born during the Great War.

Chapter 20

"I can't believe they're sending you over," Alice said to Arthur Spencer as they sauntered to the summerhouse in the feeble November sunshine.

Arthur shrugged. He had a week of leave and then was to join the Canadians on their march into Germany. "I'm thrilled actually. It's the best way to see some of the Front and get a taste of the war without worrying about being blown up. Rather cowardly of me, I admit, but seeing how much Chas and Freddie are suffering, I'm not eager to join them." Freddie walked with difficulty, his wound still painful. A large hunk of shrapnel had done considerable damage to his thigh, but he had been lucky that his femur hadn't been shattered. "Or my brother Archie. I sure hope I can see his grave."

"I thought it would feel different when the war was over. More exciting. Happier. But all I can think of is my friends who will never return," Alice said. "Even this influenza epidemic feels like another deadly edge of the war."

While those at Priory Manor celebrated the Armistice with champagne and hugs, none of them was inclined to rejoice in the streets, like Londoners and many of the villagers were doing. Chas and Ria were in mourning for J.D., and Alice, for her father.

"I know what you mean, although you've been so much closer to the horrors than I can even imagine. You should write an account of your experiences on the *Lusitania*, Alice." They had already congratulated each other on their journalistic successes.

"I'm not sure I can revisit that. I know that Blake thought talking about it would help. And it certainly did. But those scenes of carnage are seared into my brain, and mostly I've managed to relegate them to a shadowy corner. They still haunt me in dreams, but not constantly anymore."

Alice didn't see the admiring glance he gave her. She had blossomed from a pretty child into an attractive young woman.

She suddenly looked at him with a smile and said, "I can sense an article or two coming out of your journey to Germany. Will you write to me if you have time and tell me your impressions?"

Arthur grinned. "Sure thing!"

They sat down in the summerhouse, out of the nipping breeze that tugged coppery leaves from the trees. Rusty reeds along the shore of the small lake bowed feathery seed heads towards the steely water. "It's going to be so strange going home to Canada," Alice said. "I can hardly believe we're leaving in a few weeks." Chas had booked passage on the White Star Line's *Megantic*, leaving for New York on December 11th. "I'm really going to miss Cousin Bea and Meredith and Theadora, but they promised they would visit us next summer."

"At the cottage."

"I hope you'll be back by then."

"Me too!"

"It will be weird not going home to Ottawa," Alice said. "I have a half-sister now, but of course, I've never even met her. My step-mother wasn't particularly keen on me, so I wonder if I'll ever get to know my sister."

"You've had a really tough time, Alice. You're a pretty amazing girl."

This time she saw his admiring look and felt a blush creeping into her cheeks. She muttered, "I'm blessed to have Ria and Chas and all their family and friends."

"It's decidedly odd that they are practically your parents. And that you already know so many of the Muskoka crowd," Arthur said. "By the way, Ria told me not to tire you."

Alice giggled. "Very maternal. I expect it will be quite strange when I attend her old school. But for now, I'm gloriously free! And in a year or so I'm hoping to go to university. So tell me about your studies!"

They talked until the anemic light began to fade.

"Gosh, I hope you're not chilled," Arthur said sudden concern.

"Just a bit, but we should get back for tea anyway."

There was only a smudge of light on the horizon when they arrived at the house. They warmed themselves by the fire as they joined the others.

Beatrice was back; Justin and Toni were here for Armistice celebrations, as were Meredith and Theadora, who had been grateful to escape from a London gone mad. Freddie was convalescing, and Martha had managed to come down from London for a couple of days. As she was still needed at the hospital and Freddie had been unwilling to leave her behind in England while he was invalided home, he had offered to give a series of lectures on architecture at the various military camps and hospitals where the Khaki University had been set up. The military hoped to keep convalescent and demobilized soldiers productively occupied while they awaited their repatriation to

Canada. After all, many of the boys had interrupted their high school and university studies to serve. Freddie would spend a few weeks at Bea's London townhouse so that he could at least see Martha during her time off before he began his lecture tour in December.

"I can't believe there's so much to do just to pack up and go home," Ria said. She and Grayson would soon be dismantling the Maple Leaf Club at Thameshill, and turning it back into a home. "Alice will have to have a chance to say goodbye to her relatives and collect her things. Grayson and Branwyn are getting married before we leave, and so are Sybil and Adam because they wanted to be sure we could attend. And I'd really hoped to fly again before we go home, but I don't think that will happen."

"Definitely not," Chas stated. "As a mother you have responsibilities, and one is to stay safely on the ground." He grinned at her. "At least until I can go up with you."

"There should be lots of aeroplanes for sale, don't you think?" she asked. "We can cart one back with us. But a seaplane so that we can use it at the cottage."

The Londoners left two days later, Justin and Toni taking Arthur along so that he would have a chance to see the city before setting off for Belgium.

Freddie was disturbed by his wife's absence. He enjoyed being with her, and they never lacked for things to discuss, especially now that they had decided to use some of Martha's substantial dowry to travel through Europe before heading back to Canada. Eagerly they had talked about visiting Paris, Rome, Venice, Florence, Athens, among others. They should both be finished work in a few months, and Freddie had negotiated that his discharge from the army would be in Britain. Lady Beatrice had invited them to visit her villa on the Riviera, where she was looking forward to spending the winter.

But once Martha had gone, Freddie's thoughts invariably turned to Zoë. He worried about her, dreamt of her, longed to see her, touch her, make her happy. He realized he had made a terrible mistake in getting married, since he had never stopped loving Zoë. He hoped that months alone with Martha, sharing adventures, would deepen his affection for her and eclipse his passion for Zoë.

In any case, he had made a commitment to Martha and would have to live with that.

.   .   .

Sidonie had been silent since they had left Cherkley Court, and Jack was concerned about her despondency. Max Beaverbrook was still recovering from a recurring health problem that had laid him low for a few weeks, but Jack was certain that his answer to Sid's appeal wouldn't have been any different if he were in robust health.

Sid had asked him if he would consider rescuing Blackthorn and helping her to restore it. She thought that the money that Quentin had accumulated – with Beaverbrook's help – and left to her would be enough to get her started, and she would find some way to repay him.

Realizing that the crumbling Edwardian mansion was too much of a drain, both financially and emotionally, her grieving parents had already accepted an offer from a wealthy industrialist. "Bloody war profiteer!" Sid had fumed. "We sent our best and brightest young men to fight and die to preserve what we had, and these obnoxious upstarts stay comfortably at home, not only gouging us with extortionist prices to make their obscene fortunes, but then having the unmitigated gall to steal our birthright! And maintaining that they're doing us a bloody favour with such a generous offer! I'm so furious I could kill someone!"

Beaverbrook had said, "I've seen Blackthorn, Sidonie. It's a bad investment. And much as I admire you, no woman is worth that much to me," he'd added with a meaningful look.

Sid had actually blushed.

As they were nearing Priory Manor, Jack, driving Sid's car, said, "I wish there were something I could do to help you, Sid. Why are you so attached to a house?"

"It's not just a house! It's where I come from, who I am, where my soul dwells! Of course you wouldn't understand what it's like to be surrounded by hundreds of years of family history! Ever since I was a child I've felt a special, almost visceral connection with my ancestors, felt that I and my family were obliged to preserve what they had achieved and pass it on to future generations." Almost incidentally, she added quietly. "It's where I was happy."

"There are lots of places to find happiness, Sid, if you open yourself up to new possibilities. Blackthorn will always be a part of you, wherever you are. As will Quentin and Sebastian."

Her eyes burning with tears, Sid was obviously struggling not to weep. But it would never do for her to show such weakness. After a few minutes she said flippantly, "Perhaps I'll just have to seek adventure in the colonies! I'm beginning to despise Britain. I don't think I'll be able to bear it at all after you and the others leave." Her parents were moving to the south of France, where the weather and prices were more conducive to a genteel lifestyle.

Jack and Chas had both been discharged from the RAF, and Jack had just delivered his last painting to Beaverbrook. He had originally planned to stay in England for a while after the war to try to benefit from an alliance with the great man, but the Thorntons needed him now. So he had picked Beaverbrook's brains on how best to help them. Obviously Jack couldn't take over the business – yet – but he could advise Chas and Rafe. And once he was married to Fliss, there was no reason why he couldn't become an equal partner. So he was going home with Chas and Ria, filled with excitement, eager to get on with his life's work.

Sid was her usual irreverent self by the time they arrived at Priory Manor. Rafe had returned from Holland, and also been discharged from the RAF after a debriefing.

"Your vacation with the enemy seems to have done you some good," she said when she embraced Rafe. "In fact, you've matured rather nicely."

"I've missed you, too," he whispered as he kissed her cheek.

"Don't be cruel, Sid," Ria said. "Rafe had quite an ordeal."

"I'm longing to hear all about it."

"Not in front of the children," Ria cautioned.

"You're becoming alarmingly maternal, Ria!" Sidonie chided. "So let me see the newest addition." She looked hard at Charlie, then at Chas, and said with a smirk, "What a beautiful child! And what a remarkable resemblance to Chas."

"Do you think so?" Ria challenged. "It's the blonde hair and blue eyes. And the good looks, of course," she added with a smile at Chas. Their eyes met in silent communication for a moment.

Alice noticed, and pondered the significance of Sidonie's statement. Charlie would be three in a few weeks, which meant that he had been conceived before Ria had arrived in England. Was he the result of the indiscretion that had torn Ria and Chas apart? Golly!

Admiring Ria even more and feeling protective of her new family, Alice said, "My friends said that Ria looks like my sister, and we don't even have the same hair colour!"

Ria stared curiously at Alice, whose guileless response didn't fool her. Hell! Did everybody realize that Charlie was Chas's son?

"Let's go to the sunroom, Rafe," Sidonie said. "I'm *longing* to hear all about your ordeal at the hands of the brutal Hun. Bring that bottle of champers."

Ria sent the children up to the nursery for their supper. Sophie was happy to eat with Charlie. Alice, of course, would dine with the adults, but she always sat with the children while the others were enjoying cocktails.

When they had gone, Ria said to Jack, "Sid seems rather... edgy."

He told them what had transpired at Cherkley Court. "She keeps things bottled up, and puts on this nonchalant performance. But she's drinking a lot, and taking cocaine, I suspect, and being more than usually outrageous. During the Armistice celebrations she threw a rock through a shop window, declaring that the SOB was just another war profiteer. If we hadn't been in the midst of ten thousand other people, she might well have been arrested. I got her the hell out of there." He didn't tell them that she had then drunkenly accused him of being "a bloody bore, darling".

"I expect she feels as if everyone and everything she has known and loved has been stolen from her," Chas said. "If you'd seen what fun we all had at Blackthorn those few Christmases I was there!"

It was not something Ria cared to dwell upon, but she said magnanimously, "So how can we help her?"

There was no time for them to respond. Sid and Rafe rejoined them, she saying, "Break out more champagne. I've finally accepted Rafe's proposal of marriage. So I'll be coming to Canada with you, darlings!"

.   .   .

"Are you sure about this?" Chas asked Rafe when the others had retired for the night. "Sid is adamant about the legal provisions, giving her enormous funds should you die or the marriage not work." By marrying, Sid would be losing her substantial allowance from her deceased husband's family. Only the Grosvenor Square townhouse was hers.

Rafe sneered. "You just can't believe that she might actually desire me. *ME*. Not you!"

"Don't be insulting! I have no interest in her other than as a friend. She's very vulnerable and volatile right now. Probably grasping at straws..."

"Now who's being insulting?"

"I'm just cautioning you that it may be more of a financial alliance than a romantic one."

Rafe hadn't even asked Sid to marry him this time. She had just announced, "I'm going to take you up on your offer to lay the world at my feet." During his internment he had found himself thinking more about Lizzie than Sid. He enjoyed Sid's body, but Lizzie was a delectable challenge. Lady Sidonie Dunston, however, was a feather in his cap. Lizzie might yet become his mistress, a role he thought suited her better than wife in any case.

He said to Chas, "Who the hell cares? When I'm tired of her, there'll be lots of other women to warm my bed. Do you really think that couples don't look elsewhere for amusement? You're the one who's naïve, Chas," he said dismissively. "You don't think that a desirable woman like Ria will succumb to some dashing young man who doesn't bear the scars of war?"

Chas glared at him. "Don't you dare malign Ria like that! I feel sorry for you, Rafe, because you obviously don't know what love is. Your wife should be more to you than some pedigree broodmare."

But Rafe's words rankled, particularly when Lance Chadwick danced with Ria at Sybil and Adam Bentley's wedding a few days later.

The wedding ceremony in Canterbury Cathedral had been magnificent. The reception was being held in Sybil's substantial family estate in the country nearby.

Not being able to dance himself, Chas was jealous of how cheerful Ria seemed in Lance's arms, how gracefully they moved together, how easily they conversed. And he found it irrationally annoying that Lance was taking over Priory Manor, as if he were insinuating himself even deeper into their lives.

Ria was glad that Lance seemed no different despite his head injury. "How *are* you doing?" she asked him.

"Fine, when the headaches stop. I've been told that they should become less frequent and severe. Sometimes my vision is blurred or double, like a wicked hangover, but hopefully that, too, will improve. How are you managing?"

"Wonderfully well. Excited about going home, but, in some ways, sad to be leaving."

"You must come to Priory Manor whenever you wish. And I hope to visit you in Canada."

"Of course! Carly and Jonathan and Sybil and Adam have all promised to come next summer."

"Count on me as well," he said, staring at her intently.

Ria refused him another dance, rejoining Chas who she knew still needed plenty of reassurance. He was self-conscious about appearing in public, and had initially not wanted to attend the wedding. "They don't need an ugly fellow like me spoiling the festivities," he had said.

"Don't be silly, Chas! You're still better looking than most men."

"Only most?" he had teased.

"To me you are the beautiful person I've always loved," she had replied seriously, gently stroking his scarred cheek.

Most of the WATS were still working in France, evacuating the wounded from the base hospitals, but Henrietta Maltby had come home to convalesce from the flu. She said to Ria, "I'm planning to study at Oxford next year. I've been corresponding with your cousin, Henry, and he's got me jolly excited about medieval history!"

"I'm so glad," Ria said, sensing that there was a romance blossoming there, and wishing her and Henry well.

Ria and Sybil hugged in a tearful farewell since they wouldn't see each other until summer. The bride and groom were going to Paris and then Cannes for their honeymoon. "Revisiting the place where I made him fall in love with me almost two years ago," Sybil said.

"There was no coercion required. I fell willingly," Adam corrected with a grin.

Lance felt bereft as he kissed Ria's hand and bid her farewell. He tried to absorb the essence of her through the brief contact and her smiling eyes. He hoped that he would feel her presence at Priory Manor. He could anticipate walking into the sunroom and imagine her glance up at him with pleasure, or suddenly come upon her among the ruins in the garden. She would fill the spaces of the house and his mind. He resolved that he would definitely visit her next summer in the place she loved so well.

Ria and Chas traveled by train to London with Justin and Toni, staying with them for a night. Justin's work at the War Office would continue until most of the troops had been repatriated, so he hoped that he and Toni would be in Canada by summer.

"If you're starting a law practice, I want to be your first client," Chas told Justin. "Nothing like having someone you absolutely trust on your side. I'm sure I won't understand many of the aspects of Pater's business, legal or otherwise."

"I hadn't really thought that far ahead, but of course it's what I had always planned to do. We'll have to see if Toni prefers to live in Toronto or Guelph or some other place."

"I'm sure that won't matter in the least," Chas said. "I expect we can even conduct business at the cottage."

During Freddie's convalescence at Priory Manor, he had drawn up the blueprints for a cottage for Max and Lydia. Max wanted something smaller than his parents' place, but in the same style, as it would perch at the other end of Silver Bay.

Ria had commissioned Freddie to design a modest two-bedroom cottage to sit between the two bays at the point – essentially in the backyard of her cottage – as a wedding gift for Grayson and Branwyn. She had decided that Wyndholme would be closed for the summers, and all the staff, except the gardeners, would be at the lake. Patrick and Tilda would have Toby's cabin, which would be modified with an addition to provide a separate bedroom.

Ria had been saddened by news of Toby's death, and not surprised that Shep's own heart had given out the same day.

Grayson and the others were thrilled with the plans. He said to Ria, "I do believe that Branwyn and Gareth will be delighted with the setting." Ria knew that his first wife hadn't been fond of the island, and so had been relieved to stay at Wyndholme for most of the summer, only coming to Wyndwood occasionally to check on the staff.

Johanna had struggled with the dilemma of returning to Belgium with her mother and sisters or going to Canada. Ria had told her to spend a week with her family to think about it, and had added, "If you don't like Canada, you can always go home again. For now it will be an adventure for you."

The children had missed her and were delighted when Johanna returned, and Ria was thankful that she decided to accompany them. "We will all visit Belgium some time," Ria promised.

With neither having family nearby, Grayson and Branwyn were married quietly in the local church. Ria insisted that the staff and family mingle at a reception in the drawing room. She hired a chef from London to come and prepare a gourmet meal, and surprised and thrilled everyone when Emily and Hugo made an appearance and entertained with a few songs. They provided the newlyweds with tickets to the following evening's performance of

Under the Moon, as the Graysons would be spending several days in London.

Before they left, Grayson spoke privately to Ria. "Thank you for a most delightful and memorable wedding. You've all been tremendously generous."

"I might pay you for looking after us, Grayson, but I consider you a part of the family. So you won't mind if I do this." She gave him a heartfelt hug.

He held her tightly for a moment, a world of unexpressed love and emotion flowing between them, he, more of a father to her than her own had ever been. His eyes were moist when he released her. "Bless you," he said.

.   .   .

Jack had been surprised by Sidonie's precipitous engagement to Rafe, realizing, to his chagrin, that they had been lovers. He was also upset for Lizzie's sake, because she had been certain she would win Rafe over. She had never mentioned love in her many letters, but had conveyed a burning desire and determination to become Rafe's wife.

But Jack was deeply distressed when he discovered that Troy and Ellie would be getting married.

Troy had shown up at Priory Manor, informing them that he had taken an early discharge so that he could resume his studies at Harvard in January. Not having time to await military transport home, he'd managed to procure passage on the *Megantic* as well.

Nice to have the money, Jack thought bitterly. Chas had paid for Jack's exorbitant first class ticket, since he was anxious for Jack to help him with his father's business. Otherwise, Jack would have waited his turn to board a troop ship home.

"I'm really worried about Ellie," Troy said. "She's suffering aftereffects from the influenza. I've seen plenty of that, even in some of my colleagues who fell ill. I need to be with her, to reassure her and help her regain her equilibrium. I haven't told my parents I'm coming home, so I'm traveling all the way to Toronto with you. I'll see them when I'm sure that Ellie is back on her feet. "

"Have you set a date for the wedding?" Ria asked.

"We'd talked about next summer. But not at *my* cottage. I have to tell you that my mother is very much against our marriage. Not that that will stop me."

"Can you afford to defy your family?" Jack asked.

"I've annoyed and disappointed both my parents, since my father expected me to go into the paint business. But he established trust funds for us kids when we were young, and I can live on mine, at least until I'm earning a living. Besides, Ellie said she'd support me," he added with a disarming smile.

"You're most welcome to have the wedding at Wyndwood," Ria said.

As the others discussed that, Jack was struck by intense longing for Ellie, and deep sadness. He had never exposed his soul so completely to anyone as he had to her. Whenever he idly imagined his future, it was with Thornton money, but Ellie at his side. He had been hurt that she had so readily and generously accepted his rejection of her love.

As he and Chas enjoyed a final cigarette in the sunroom before retiring, Chas examined his drink and said, "With prohibition at home, I'd better bring a few dozen crates of Scotch and cognac back."

"The soldiers counted on their rum rations to keep going, but once the heroes return home, they can't even get a bloody drink."

"At least not legally. It's going to be strange being home again. I don't even know what I'll do with myself. I'll be counting on you to help me negotiate the quagmire of Pater's finances."

"I'll do what I can."

"So, do you have any regrets about Ellie?"

Ruefully, carefully Jack replied, "I love her dearly, as a friend. But I was the one who broke things off last summer. I realized it wasn't fair to either of us to drift along as if we had some future together when we're not really suited. When I marry, I want a wife who'll be happy at home, planning dinner parties and raising our children. Ellie and I had a lot of fun together, so I don't think either of us regrets that interlude. God, I can't believe that was already four and a half years ago!" Just to emphasize that his romance with Ellie was ancient history. "I'm really glad she's found herself a like-minded chap. Troy seems like a good egg."

"Top-hole, I'd say."

"Charlie seems to have settled in well," Jack said as a subtle reminder of Chas's affair.

"Thank God! I had my doubts for a while. But kids seem to fall for Ria as readily as grown-ups. I think he's already quite devoted to her. But still a bit reticent with me."

"Once you start teaching him to play tennis and swim and such, you'll form a bond."

Chas snorted. "I can't see myself doing much of that anymore." He took a long drink.

"You may not win tournaments, but you can certainly teach the skills. Maybe Charlie will be a Wimbledon champion one day."

"You'll have me running a tennis school next."

"Why not? Surely all the kiddies on the lake want to learn, and there's nobody around as talented as you to mentor them. And you can teach the older ones to fly."

Chas laughed. "There's nothing like good friends to bolster one's ego! On that encouraging note, I'm off to bed."

Jack stayed for one more cigarette, sitting in the darkness, gazing at the moon-glow on the monastic ruins beyond the windows of the old manor house thousands of miles from home.

A popular tune kept taunting him, spinning in his head like a never-ending record. *Somebody Stole My Gal.*

Gee, but I'm lonesome, lonesome and blue.
I've found out something I never knew.
I know now what it means to be sad,
For I've lost the best gal I ever had
She only left yesterday, Somebody stole her away.
Somebody stole my gal, Somebody stole my pal.

Only in this reflective moment of solitude would Jack allow remorse and yearning to intrude upon his ambition. *I do love you, Ellie.*

The story continues in Book 3 of "The Muskoka Novels".

See **Bonus Features** exclusively at *ElusiveDawn.info*

Thank you for purchasing ***Elusive Dawn***. If you enjoyed it, you can support the author by recommending it to friends.

Comments are always appreciated at
books@mindshadows.com

Author's Notes

To enhance your **Elusive Dawn** experience, see *ElusiveDawn.info*

Once again, numerous biographies, journals, memoirs, letters, newspapers, scholarly tomes, Internet sites, and other sources were consulted to bring this era to life. The Bibliography can be viewed online at *theMuskokaNovels.com*. The following notes might answer some readers' questions:

- Many of the characters' war experiences are loosely based upon those of real people.
- With modern eyes, it's perhaps difficult to understand the eagerness and sense of duty that compelled young men and women to participate in the war.
- The WATS, although fictional, are heavily based on the FANY (First Aid Nursing Yeomanry), and many incidents are taken from their experiences. There was one Canadian in the Corps. Members earned 135 decorations and medals during WWI. The FANY is still in existence.
- The FANY were referred to and called each other "girls", although most were in their 20s, so my use of that word is not pejorative.
- About 2000 Canadian women became VAD nurses, with over 500 seeing service in England and France with the British Red Cross. Six of them died from disease or enemy action.
- The Duchess of Axminster's Officers' Hospital is very loosely modelled after the Duchess of Westminster's hospital at Le Touquet. The ladies did greet the wounded in evening gowns, at least in the early stages of the war.
- All other hospitals mentioned in the book were real.
- Soldiers spent relatively little time in the deadly front-line trenches, so there were periods when they were well behind the lines, resting, training, and playing games to keep fit and busy. Tennis and polo matches, soccer and baseball games, dances and entertainments were all part of the military experience in France.
- Families were invited to the bedside of fatally injured soldiers in France. Special hostels were set up for them.

- Scenes with Billy Bishop were taken from the biography written by his son, and from his own autobiography. Chas, of course, is a fictional character, so when Albert Ball died, Billy Bishop became and then ended the war as the highest scoring British Ace.
- The scene with a captured German pilot is based upon a similar account from Billy Bishop.
- Only three Canadian pilots received VCs, one of them being Billy Bishop.
- Canadian Max Aitken, later Lord Beaverbrook, hired artists to capture the Canadian war experience on canvas. Among them were four who became members of the Group of Seven. This collection of 1000 works is now in the Canadian War Museum in Ottawa.
- The Halifax explosion was the largest man-made explosion until the atomic bomb was dropped on Hiroshima in 1945. About 2000 were killed and over 9000, injured.
- Sir John Craig Eaton took his private Pullman coach, supplies, and medical personnel to Halifax immediately after the explosion.
- From May 1917 to May 1918, air raids on England by German bombers killed over 800 and wounded 2,000. Ironically, of those numbers, 24 were killed by anti-aircraft fire, which also injured 200.
- Nearly 4000 Canadians of all ranks became Prisoners of War. The names and reputations of the camps are real. Of the 40,000 eventually interned in neutral Holland, 53 were Canadian officers. Officers' wives were allowed to live with them in Holland and Switzerland.
- The Great Influenza Pandemic of 1918 is thought to have killed from 30 to 100 million people worldwide. About 50,000 Canadians died and millions more were sick. Many of those who survived had life-long health problems.
- A French aviatrix and nurse disguised herself and flew combat missions for several weeks before being discovered. A young British woman "of good family" also disguised herself as a French pilot but was soon sent back to England.
- In Robert Graves' autobiography, *Goodbye To All That*, he mentions that his German cousin was killed in an air battle by one of Graves' former schoolmates.

- A woman smoking was considered "fast" by the older generation, but modern and liberating by the young.
- Muskoka was ragweed-free until later in the 20th century. Cars were blamed for bringing in into the area.
- Cecil Lewis in his fascinating autobiography, *Sagittarius Rising*, mentions flying secretly from France to England for a weekend rendezvous in London.
- One officer had weekly hampers of goodies delivered to him in France from the famous Fortnum & Mason in London. Apparently they also supplied some POWs.
- The Khaki University instructed over 50,000 Canadian soldiers. Many more attended casual lectures.
- The BBC TV series, "The Duchess of Duke Street", was based upon Rosa Lewis's life. A favourite of King Edward VII, she owned the Cavendish Hotel in London.
- 600,000 Canadians enlisted, 68,000 died and over 170,000 were wounded. Canada's population at that time was less than 8 million. Altogether, 13 million soldiers were killed and at least 20 million more were wounded and maimed in "the war to end all wars". There is no record of the mental and emotional toll that the war took on the participants.
- Some families, like a friend of Nancy Astor, lost all their sons in the war. Vera Brittain, a British VAD nurse who wrote the classic autobiography, *Testament of Youth*, lost her fiancé, only brother, and her two closest male friends.
- Those who fought and died and had the responsibilities of leadership were incredibly young. It's immensely moving to walk through the WWI cemeteries in Belgium and France and witness the enormity of the sacrifices this generation made. Photos can be seen on *ElusiveDawn.info*
- Slang was verified through *The Oxford Dictionary of Slang* and other sources. Words like "necking" and "boyfriend" may seem modern, but were already in use in that era.

We all have soundtracks for our lives – the music we listened to at different times and stages and places, which instantly transports us back whenever we hear it again. Many thanks to ragtime historian and award-winning performer, Bill Edwards, for creating soundtracks for the books – companion CDs that add a dynamic musical dimension to the enjoyment of "The Muskoka Novels". For more info, visit *theMuskokaNovels.com*

About the Author

Gabriele Wills

Born in Germany, Gabriele emigrated to Canada as a young child. She is a graduate of the University of Toronto, with an honours B.Sc. and a B.Ed. in the social sciences and English. As an educator, she has taught in secondary, elementary, and private schools, and worked as a literacy coordinator for two newspapers. For ten years she operated a part-time website design business.

Writing, however, is Gabriele's real love. Her mission is to weave compelling stories around meticulously researched historical context in order to bring the past to life.

She grew up in Lindsay, Ontario, enjoyed several years in Ottawa, and currently resides in Guelph. Although she has relished many visits to Muskoka, she also finds inspiration at the family cottage in the Kawartha Lakes.

Gabriele is always delighted to hear from readers – who help to keep her motivated – and can be contacted at books@mindshadows.com

Other Novels by Gabriele Wills:

The Summer Before The Storm

This acclaimed prequel to **Elusive Dawn** begins in 1914 in the legendary lake district of Muskoka, Canada.

It's the Age of Elegance in the summer playground of the affluent and powerful. But their charmed lives begin to unravel with the onset of the Great War, in which many are destined to become part of the "lost generation".

This richly textured tale takes the reader on an unforgettable journey from romantic moonlight cruises to the horrific sinking of the *Lusitania*, genteel Muskoka to wartime Britain, regattas on the water to combat in the skies over France, extravagant mansions to deadly trenches – from innocence to nationhood.

Set during one of the most turbulent times in modern history, this enthralling epic is the first in "The Muskoka Novels" series.

Moon Hall

Two women who live a century apart. Two stories that interweave to form a rich tapestry of intriguing characters, evocative places, and compelling events.

Escaping from a disintegrating relationship in the city, writer Kit Spencer stumbles upon a quintessential Norman Rockwell village in the Ottawa Valley, where she buys an old stone mansion, "Moon Hall". But her illusions about idyllic country life are soon challenged by reality. In her rural community of farmers, hippies, and yuppies, Kit unwittingly precipitates events that will change them all forever.

Juxtaposed is the tragedy of Violet McAllister, the ghost that reputedly haunts Moon Hall, who comes vividly to life through her long-forgotten diary.

Moon Hall is a gripping tale of relationships in crisis, and touches on the full spectrum of human emotions – from raw violence and dark passions to compassion and love.

Visit *Mindshadows.com* for more information.